THE LOEB CLASSICAL LIBRARY

FOUNDED BY JAMES LOEB 1911

EDITED BY

JEFFREY HENDERSON

EDITOR EMERITUS

G. P. GOOLD

ARISTOPHANES

III

LCL 179

ARISTOPHANES

BIRDS • LYSISTRATA
WOMEN AT THE THESMOPHORIA

EDITED AND TRANSLATED BY

JEFFREY HENDERSON

HARVARD UNIVERSITY PRESS
CAMBRIDGE, MASSACHUSETTS
LONDON, ENGLAND
2000

Library of Congress Catalog Card Number 97-24063
CIP data available from the Library of Congress

ISBN 0-674-99587-2

CONTENTS

BIRDS 1

LYSISTRATA 253

WOMEN AT THE THESMOPHORIA 443

INDEX 616

PREFACE

For advice and criticism as this edition goes forward I wish to express my gratitude to George Goold, Editor Emeritus of the Library; Philippa Goold, Associate Editor; Zeph Stewart, Executive Trustee; and Professor S. Douglas Olson. For sabbatical support I am grateful to the John Simon Guggenheim Memorial Foundation and the College of Arts and Sciences at Boston University.

Jeffrey Henderson

BIRDS

INTRODUCTORY NOTE

Birds was produced by Callistratus[1] at the Dionysia of 414 and placed second; Ameipsias placed first with *Revellers* and Phrynichus third with *The Loner*.[2] *Birds* has the distinction of being the longest surviving comedy from antiquity (largely due to the multiplication of exemplificatory scenes after the parabasis), with the most adult speaking roles (22). Although the plot follows a pattern familiar from Aristophanes' other "heroic" plays—a complaint, a fantastic idea, its implementation following a contest, episodes exemplifying the consequences, and the hero's utopian triumph—it shows greater structural unity than in earlier plays, maintaining suspense by postponing the dénouement until the end, and momentum by having the Chorus Leader deliver the parabasis wholly in character; the plays of 411 show a similar concern for plot unity. *Birds* also has a spectacular chorus, each of whose twenty-four dancers seems to have represented a different bird;[3] the

[1] He had already produced at least three plays for Aristophanes (*Banqueters*, *Babylonians*, and *Acharnians*), and would later produce *Lysistrata*.

[2] It is possible that Phrynichus was also the author of *Revellers* and Ameipsias only its producer.

[3] Although a contemporary vase (Malibu, the J. Paul Getty

lyrics are among Aristophanes' most elaborate and lovely; and the fantasy is truly aetherial.

Information about Aristophanes' career is scanty for the years between *Peace* (D 421) and *Birds*, the period of the Peace of Nicias. There is no sign of the partisan political engagement that had animated his earlier plays, and the datable fragments indicate a turn to mythological and other relatively apolitical subjects. Certainly the political environment had changed. Though the Peace of Nicias was not a true peace (the signatories remained mutually suspicious, and not all of Sparta's allies subscribed), Athens and its empire were quiet enough so that demagogic politics, Aristophanes' favorite theme in the 420s, had fallen into relative abeyance; he would not stoop to attack Hyperbolus, Cleon's successor, a target he declared fit only for lesser poets (*Clouds* 549–59). The political arena was instead dominated by the dashing young aristocrat Alcibiades, now making his first bid for ascendancy, and the wealthy Nicias, a veteran general and conservative stalwart. Their backgrounds, rival policies, and contrasting styles offered great comic potential, but since both were rightists hostile to demagogues (in 416 they colluded in Hyperbolus' ostracism), neither was much bothered by the comic poets.[4]

Birds fits this trend, differing from all of Aristophanes' other extant fifth-century plays in taking no topical issue, political or otherwise, as a theme, either expressly or, like

Museum 82.AE.83), which may illustrate our play, shows two identically costumed bird-dancers.

[4] For the political biases of Aristophanes and his rivals see vol. 1, pp. 12-23.

Knights and *Wasps*, allegorically. To be sure, there is plenty of topical satire, but all of it is incidental to a fantasy that soars above the world's particulars to a conjured realm, where the most familiar hierarchies of empirical reality—earth and sky, nature and culture, polis and wilds, humans, animals, and gods—are blurred, reordered, or even abolished, and whose hero attains power surpassing even that of the gods.

Two old Athenians, Euelpides ("Confident") and Peisetaerus ("Persuader of His Comrade(s)"),[5] have abandoned Athens in order to escape their debts. Led by a jackdaw and a crow, they visit Tereus, once human but now a bird,[6] to learn if on his flights he has ever seen a carefree polis where they could settle. But none of Tereus' suggestions proves satisfactory, for no polis is carefree. Peisetaerus[7] then asks about the life of the birds, which is carefree but lacks a polis. Suddenly he has an astonishing idea: to turn the scattered bird world into a mighty bird polis. Tereus summons the birds, represented by the Chorus. Being inveterate enemies of humankind, the birds are initially hostile, but Peisetaerus wins them over by pointing out that they were the original kings of the universe long before the Olympians took over, and by proposing a

[5] The MSS' "Peisthetaerus" is a grammatically impossible conflation of two original variants, Peithetaerus and (with the more usual formant) Peisetaerus.

[6] Only this element of the myth of Tereus and Procne is relevant; its violent elements (15 n.) are ignored.

[7] Or possibly Euelpides, for editors differ in assigning lines in the prologue; for discussion of the issues see H.-G. Nesselrath in *Museum Helveticum* 53 (1996) 91-99.

plan: the birds will build an aerial city that completely occupies the sky; demand that the Olympians return power to them or face a blockade; and instruct humankind to sacrifice henceforth to the birds, for birds have the power to harm humans if they refuse, but also to give them every blessing if they accept. The birds are delighted with this plan and appoint Peisetaerus their leader; a magical root will give him wings. In the parabasis the Chorus Leader offers a cosmogony justifying the birds' claim to cosmic primogeniture.

Peisetaerus reappears newly winged, and names his new polis Cloudcuckooland. Scarcely has he begun the founding sacrifice when a parade of pests and profiteers, most of them satirizing familiar Athenian types, arrive seeking admission to the new polis; but none is admitted. Meanwhile Iris (Rainbow), messenger of the gods, is intercepted on her way to humankind to announce Zeus' command for a resumption of sacrifices; Peisetaerus contemptuously turns her away. Finally an embassy from the Olympian gods arrives to negotiate a settlement. But Peisetaerus, secretly aided by Prometheus (a traditional defender of humankind against Zeus, and a god held in great affection at Athens), talks them into complete surrender: Zeus will return his scepter to the birds, and to Peisetaerus hand over his thunderbolt and his regal power, personified by a maiden, Princess (*Basileia*, "Sovereignty"). In the finale, the Chorus praise and congratulate Peisetaerus as he weds Princess and becomes the new king of the universe.

The fantasy of *Birds*, though it is set far from Athens and lacks a political theme, nevertheless fits the utopian mold of *Acharnians* and *Peace*: a hero expels, excludes, or renders harmless those forces human, natural, or divine that frustrate personal happiness or impede the common welfare. In this respect Cloudcuckooland is a cosmic avatar of Dicaeopolis' marketplace, a utopian counter-Athens. Peisetaerus too remains very much a contemporary Athenian in his restlessness, his enterprising cleverness, his visionary ideas, his persuasive skill (displaying distinct sophistic elements), and his expansive dreams of power. Like previous comic heroes he wins the freedom to have things his own way and to enjoy untrammeled feasting and sex; it is also made clear that everyone else—birds, humans, and even the gods—are better off under his new regime than they had been under the old (cf. especially 610, 1271–1307, 1605–15, 1726–30).

Peisetaerus' new regime has nevertheless been seen as a sinister affair, along the lines of Orwell's *Animal Farm*. This reading requires that we view the play as fundamentally ironic. But that is a technique unparalleled in ancient comedy, and on any straightforward reading we are always encouraged to identify with Peisetaerus, and therefore to approve of what he does. There is no sign of a coming fall (as in *Clouds*), no qualms or disapproval from the Chorus or any sympathetic character. Nor is there anything that would strike the average spectator as self-evidently sinister. Burlesque treatments of the gods, for example, and expressions of dissatisfaction with their rule are hardly rare in Attic drama, and Peisetaerus' remark that he is roasting "some birds who have been convicted of attempted rebellion against the bird democracy" (1583–85) is merely an incidental joke about the previous year's tyranny-scare and spate of prosecutions in Athens,[8] and is of no importance to the plot of the play.

Still, the grandiosity of Peisetaerus' ambition, his subversion of the natural order of things, and his crowning apotheosis may fairly be thought hubristic even for a comic hero. Perhaps some spectators saw it that way, but probably not most of them, for Peisetaerus' ambition echoes the Athenians' own mood in the spring of 414. The previous summer they had dispatched, on the advice of Alcibiades, a great armada to conquer Sicily. According to Thucydides, who remarks on the expedition's "astonishing audacity" (6.31), the great majority of Athenians were stricken with "lust" for the power and wealth that this conquest would bring, were absolutely confident (*euelpides*) of success, and were so excessively enthusiastic as to view opponents of the expedition as disloyal to the city (6.24). Nor were Athenian spirits dampened even after a year of limited success in Sicily, the recall of Alcibiades from the command on a charge of impiety, and his subsequent defection to Sparta. On the contrary, the Athenians dispatched a second expedition to reinforce the first, and a few months after the performance of *Birds* even sent troops into Laconia in support of Argos (6.105), finally ending the Peace of Nicias.

The allusions to current events in *Birds* reflect this pop-

[8] Cf. Thucydides 6.53-61. The absence of any reference by name to any of the some 65 men denounced or convicted in these scandals in comedies written between 415 and 410 (the period of Alcibiades' first exile) may be the result of the Decree of Syracosius, which somehow limited comic freedom (Schol. *Birds* 1297, Phrynichus fr. 26).

ular optimism: Nicias is praised for his strategic skill at Syracuse (363) and chided for delays (639); a would-be father beater is sent to the Thracian front (1360–71); and the reduction of Melos in 416, one of the most ominous episodes in Thucydides (5.84–111) and remembered after the war as an example of imperial excess, is the subject of a casual joke (186), as is the outlawry of Alcibiades (145–47). The Athenians were now at the peak of their power and confidence, with no inkling that within two years their great armada was to be utterly destroyed and their very survival cast into doubt.

Text

Four papyri preserve fragments of *Birds*; two of them are not cited in the notes: *PBerol. 13231 + 21201(2)* (V/VI), partially preserving lines 819–29, 859–64, and *POxy.* ined. (II), partially preserving lines 1661–76 (cf. Dunbar's edition, p. 733).

There are twelve independent medieval MSS and one leaf of a palimpsest codex (F). Among the pre-triclinian witnesses there has been much horizontal contamination, with only RS, VE (in the first few hundred lines), and AM/ΓU showing consistent affinity as groups; M9, copied from E before E was damaged, can be used to reconstruct E's lost text. Triclinius' text (q) was based on a MS or MSS closely related to ΓU; the MSS descending from its hyparchetypes t and p reflect at least two levels of Triclinian recension as well as later editorial activity.

Sigla

Π1	*PLouvre* ed. H. Weil, *RPh* 6 (1882) 179–85 (VI), lines 1057–85, 1101–27
Π2	*POxy*. 1401 (V), lines 382–4, 460–61
F	Laurentianus 60.9 (X^{ex}), lines 1393–1454
R	Ravennas 429 (*c.* 950)
S	readings found in the Suda
V	Venetus Marcianus 474 (XI/XII)
E	Estensis a.U.5.10 (XIV/XV^{in}), om. lines 222–601
M9	Ambrosianus L41 sup. (XIV), representing E in lines 222–601
A	Parisinus gr. 2712 (XIV^{in})
M	Ambrosianus L 39 sup. (*c.* 1320)
Γ	Laurentianus 31.15 (*c.* 1325)
U	Vaticanus Urbinas 141 (XIV)
a	the consensus of the MSS above
Vp2	Vaticanus Palatinus 67 (XV)
H	Hauniensis 1980 (XV)
C	Parisinus gr. 2717 (XV/XVI)
L	Holkhamensis 88 (XV^{in})
Vv17	Vaticanus gr. 2181 (XIV^{ex})
B	Parisinus gr. 2715 (XIV^{ex})
t	the hyparchetype of LVv17B
p	the hyparchetype of Vp2HC
q	the consensus of pt

ΤΑ ΤΟΥ ΔΡΑΜΑΤΟΣ ΠΡΟΣΩΠΑ

ΕΥΕΛΠΙΔΗΣ, *Ἀθηναῖος*
ΠΕΙΣΕΤΑΙΡΟΣ, *Ἀθηναῖος*
ΘΕΡΑΠΩΝ *Τηρέως*
ΤΗΡΕΥΣ, *ἔποψ γεγενημένος*
ΙΕΡΕΥΣ
ΠΟΙΗΤΗΣ
ΧΡΗΣΜΟΛΟΓΟΣ
ΜΕΤΩΝ
ΕΠΙΣΚΟΠΟΣ *Ἀθηναίων*
ΨΗΦΙΣΜΑΤΟΠΩΛΗΣ
ΑΓΓΕΛΟΣ Α´
ΑΓΓΕΛΟΣ Β´
ΙΡΙΣ
ΚΗΡΥΞ Α´
ΠΑΤΡΑΛΟΙΑΣ
ΚΙΝΗΣΙΑΣ *διθυραμβοποιός*
ΣΥΚΟΦΑΝΤΗΣ
ΠΡΟΜΗΘΕΥΣ
ΠΟΣΕΙΔΩΝ
ΗΡΑΚΛΗΣ
ΤΡΙΒΑΛΛΟΣ *θεός*
ΚΗΡΥΞ Β´

ΧΟΡΟΣ *ὀρνίθων*

ΚΩΦΑ ΠΡΟΣΩΠΑ

ΞΑΝΘΙΑΣ *καὶ* ΜΑΝΟΔΩΡΟΣ/ΜΑΝΗΣ, *οἰκέται Εὐελπίδου καὶ Πεισεταίρου*
ΟΙΚΕΤΑΙ *Τηρέως, δύο*
ΦΟΙΝΙΚΟΠΤΕΡΟΣ *ὄρνις*
ΜΗΔΟΣ *ὄρνις*
ΕΠΟΨ *ὄρνις*
ΚΑΤΩΦΑΓΑΣ *ὄρνις*
ΠΡΟΚΝΗ, *ἀηδὼν γεγενημένη*
ΑΥΛΗΤΗΣ, *κόραξ ἐσκευασμένος*
ΟΙΚΕΤΑΙ, *τοξόται καὶ σφενδονῆται*
ΒΑΣΙΛΕΙΑ

DRAMATIS PERSONAE

EUELPIDES, an Athenian
PEISETAERUS, an Athenian
SLAVE of Tereus
TEREUS, turned hoopoe
PRIEST
POET
ORACLE COLLECTOR
METON
INSPECTOR from Athens
DECREE SELLER
FIRST MESSENGER
SECOND MESSENGER
IRIS
FIRST HERALD
FATHER BEATER
CINESIAS, a dithyrambic poet
INFORMER
PROMETHEUS
POSEIDON
HERACLES
TRIBALLIAN God
SECOND HERALD

CHORUS of Birds

SILENT CHARACTERS

XANTHIAS and MANODORUS (also called MANES), Slaves of Euelpides and Peisetaerus
SLAVES of Tereus
FLAMINGO, a bird
MEDE, a bird
HOOPOE, a bird
GOBBLER, a bird
PROCNE, turned nightingale
PIPER, costumed as a raven
SLAVES, archers and slingers
PRINCESS

ΟΡΝΙΘΕΣ

ΕΥΕΛΠΙΔΗΣ

ὀρθὴν κελεύεις, ᾗ τὸ δένδρον φαίνεται;

ΠΕΙΣΕΤΑΙΡΟΣ

διαρραγείης. ἥδε δ᾽ αὖ κρώζει πάλιν.

ΕΥΕΛΠΙΔΗΣ

τί, ὦ πόνηρ᾽, ἄνω κάτω πλανύττομεν;
ἀπολούμεθ᾽ ἄλλως τὴν ὁδὸν προφορουμένω.

ΠΕΙΣΕΤΑΙΡΟΣ

τὸ δ᾽ ἐμὲ κορώνῃ πειθόμενον τὸν ἄθλιον
ὁδοῦ περιελθεῖν στάδια πλεῖν ἢ χίλια.

ΕΥΕΛΠΙΔΗΣ

τὸ δ᾽ ἐμὲ κολοιῷ πειθόμενον τὸν δύσμορον
ἀποσποδῆσαι τοὺς ὄνυχας τῶν δακτύλων.

2–1761 Πεισ- Dobree: Πεισθ- a

---

1 The name (unattested for a real person) means "Confident."

2 The name (unattested for a real person) means "Persuader of His Comrade(s)."

BIRDS

The stage is arrayed as a wooded, rocky landscape, and the scene building represents first the Hoopoe's nest and later Peisetaerus' house; before it is a thicket. PEISETAERUS, *carrying a crow, and* EUELPIDES, *carrying a jackdaw, enter by a side passage; behind them are their two Slaves, Xanthias and Manodorus, who carry the baggage.*

EUELPIDES[1]

(to his jackdaw) Is it straight ahead you're pointing us, toward that tree over there?

PEISETAERUS[2]

(to his crow) Blast you! *(to Euelpides)* This one keeps croaking "go back!"

EUELPIDES

Look, you wiseacre, what's the point of our trekking back and forth? We're goners if we keep rambling aimlessly every which way.

PEISETAERUS

I'm pitiful, letting a crow convince me to hike more than a hundred miles!

EUELPIDES

And I'm hapless, letting a jackdaw convince me to pound the nails off my toes!

ΠΕΙΣΕΤΑΙΡΟΣ

ἀλλ᾽ οὐδ᾽ ὅποι γῆς ἐσμὲν οἶδ᾽ ἔγωγ᾽ ἔτι.
ἐντευθενὶ τὴν πατρίδ᾽ ἂν ἐξεύροις σύ που;

ΕΥΕΛΠΙΔΗΣ

οὐδ᾽ ἂν μὰ Δία γ᾽ ἐντεῦθεν Ἐξηκεστίδης.

ΠΕΙΣΕΤΑΙΡΟΣ

οἴμοι.

ΕΥΕΛΠΙΔΗΣ

σὺ μέν, ὦ τᾶν, τὴν ὁδὸν ταύτην ἴθι.

ΠΕΙΣΕΤΑΙΡΟΣ

ἦ δεινὰ νὼ δέδρακεν οὐκ τῶν ὀρνέων,
ὁ πινακοπώλης Φιλοκράτης μελαγχολῶν,
ὃς τώδ᾽ ἔφασκε νῷν φράσειν τὸν Τηρέα,
τὸν ἔποφ᾽, ὃς ὄρνις ἐγένετ᾽ <ἄνθρωπός ποτ᾽ ὤν>·
κἀπέδοτο τὸν μὲν Θαρρελείδου τουτονὶ
κολοιὸν ὀβολοῦ, τηνδεδὶ τριωβόλου.
τὼ δ᾽ οὐκ ἄρ᾽ ᾔστην οὐδὲν ἄλλο πλὴν δάκνειν.

16 <ἄνθρωπός ποτ᾽ ὤν> Köchly: ἐκ τῶν ὀρνέων a

---

3 Execestides was evidently vulnerable to the charge of having Carian ancestry (cf. 764) and thus of falsely claiming Athenian citizenship; he was ridiculed also in Phrynichus' *Loner* (fr. 20), produced at this same festival.

4 To judge from 1076–83, Philocrates (otherwise unknown) was a prominent wholesaler of birds.

5 In this myth, as dramatized by Sophocles (cf. *POxy.* 3013), probably in the late 430s, Tereus, King of Thrace, wed the Athe-

PEISETAERUS

I've even lost track of where in the world we are; you, I suppose, could find our native land from here?

EUELPIDES

God no, from here not even Execestides could![3]

PEISETAERUS

(stumbling) Damn!

EUELPIDES

Travel your own path, friend.

PEISETAERUS

He's really done us dirty, that man from the bird market who sells by the tray, that crazy Philocrates.[4] He told us that these two birds would show us the way to Tereus,[5] the hoopoe who once was human and turned into a bird; and he sold us that Son of Tharreleides[6] there, the jackdaw, for an obol, and this crow for three obols. But they turn out to know nothing but nipping. *(to the jackdaw)* What are you

nian princess Procne, but on a later visit to Athens raped her sister Philomela, whose tongue he cut out to prevent her from telling anyone. But she depicted the crime on an embroidery she sent to Procne. The sisters avenged themselves by killing Itys, Procne's only child by Tereus, and serving him to his father for dinner. When Tereus chased the sisters with a sword, the gods changed him into a hoopoe, Procne into a nightingale, and Philomela into a swallow. The nightingale's song was regarded as a lament for Itys.

6 Evidently a man resembling a jackdaw, which is small and noisy, like the diminutive Asopodorus (Eupolis fr. 255), whom the comic poet Teleclides compared to a jackdaw (fr. 46) and who was perhaps the man referred to here.

καὶ νῦν τί κέχηνας; ἔσθ᾽ ὅποι κατὰ τῶν πετρῶν
ἡμᾶς ἔτ᾽ ἄξεις; οὐ γάρ ἐστ᾽ ἐνταῦθά τις
ὁδός.

ΕΥΕΛΠΙΔΗΣ

οὐδὲ μὰ Δί᾽ ἐνταῦθά γ᾽ ἀτραπὸς οὐδαμοῦ.

ΠΕΙΣΕΤΑΙΡΟΣ

ἥδ᾽ ἡ κορώνη τῆς ὁδοῦ τι λέγει πέρι.
οὐ ταὐτὰ κρώζει μὰ Δία νῦν τε καὶ τότε.

ΕΥΕΛΠΙΔΗΣ

τί δὴ λέγει περὶ τῆς ὁδοῦ;

ΠΕΙΣΕΤΑΙΡΟΣ

τί δ᾽ ἄλλο γ᾽ ἢ
βρύκουσ᾽ ἀπέδεσθαί φησί μου τοὺς δακτύλους;

ΕΥΕΛΠΙΔΗΣ

οὐ δεινὸν οὖν δῆτ᾽ ἐστὶν ἡμᾶς δεομένους
ἐς κόρακας ἐλθεῖν καὶ παρεσκευασμένους
ἔπειτα μὴ ᾽ξευρεῖν δύνασθαι τὴν ὁδόν;
ἡμεῖς γάρ, ὦνδρες οἱ παρόντες ἐν λόγῳ,
νόσον νοσοῦμεν τὴν ἐναντίαν Σάκᾳ·
ὁ μὲν γὰρ ὢν οὐκ ἀστὸς εἰσβιάζεται,
ἡμεῖς δὲ φυλῇ καὶ γένει τιμώμενοι,
ἀστοὶ μετ᾽ ἀστῶν, οὐ σοβοῦντος οὐδενὸς
ἀνεπτόμεθ᾽ ἐκ τῆς πατρίδος ἀμφοῖν τοῖν ποδοῖν,
αὐτὴν μὲν οὐ μισοῦντ᾽ ἐκείνην τὴν πόλιν
τὸ μὴ οὐ μεγάλην εἶναι φύσει κεὐδαίμονα
καὶ πᾶσι κοινὴν ἐναποτεῖσαι χρήματα.

gaping at this time? Do you mean to take us into these cliffs somewhere? I tell you, there's no passage here.

EUELPIDES

There isn't even a path around here, anywhere at all.

PEISETAERUS

Here's the crow saying something about the passage; yes indeed, it's croaking differently now.

EUELPIDES

What's it say about the passage, then?

PEISETAERUS

Nothing, only that it's going to chomp off my fingers!

EUELPIDES

(to the spectators) Isn't it terrible that just when we're ready and eager to go to the buzzards, we can't find the way? You see, gentlemen of the audience, we're sick with the opposite of Sacas'[7] sickness: he's a non-citizen trying to force his way in, while we, being of good standing in tribe and clan, solid citizens, with no one trying to shoo us away, have up and left our country with both feet flying. Not that we hate that city *per se*, as if it weren't essentially great and blest and open to everybody to come and watch their wealth fly away in fines. No, it's that the cicadas chirp on

7 Sacas, "the Sacasian" (an Asian Scythian), was a nickname for the tragic dramatist Acestor (cf. *Wasps* 1221), who had evidently had trouble certifying his Athenian citizenship (cf. Metagenes fr. 14).

οἱ μὲν γὰρ οὖν τέττιγες ἕνα μῆν᾿ ἢ δύο
ἐπὶ τῶν κραδῶν ᾄδουσ᾿, Ἀθηναῖοι δ᾿ ἀεὶ
ἐπὶ τῶν δικῶν ᾄδουσι πάντα τὸν βίον.
διὰ ταῦτα τόνδε τὸν βάδον βαδίζομεν,
κανοῦν δ᾿ ἔχοντε καὶ χύτραν καὶ μυρρίνας
πλανώμεθα ζητοῦντε τόπον ἀπράγμονα,
ὅποι καθιδρυθέντε διαγενοίμεθ᾿ ἄν.
ὁ δὲ στόλος νῷν ἐστι παρὰ τὸν Τηρέα,
τὸν ἔποπα, παρ᾿ ἐκείνου πυθέσθαι δεομένω,
εἴ που τοιαύτην εἶδε πόλιν ᾗ ᾿πέπτατο.

ΠΕΙΣΕΤΑΙΡΟΣ

οὗτος.

ΕΥΕΛΠΙΔΗΣ

τί ἐστιν;

ΠΕΙΣΕΤΑΙΡΟΣ

ἡ κορώνη μοι πάλαι
ἄνω τι φράζει.

ΕΥΕΛΠΙΔΗΣ

χὠ κολοιὸς οὑτοσὶ
ἄνω κέχηνεν ὡσπερεὶ δεικνύς τί μοι,
κοὐκ ἔσθ᾿ ὅπως οὐκ ἔστιν ἐνταῦθ᾿ ὄρνεα.
εἰσόμεθα δ᾿ αὐτίκ᾿, ἢν ποιήσωμεν ψόφον.

ΠΕΙΣΕΤΑΙΡΟΣ

ἀλλ᾿ οἶσθ᾿ ὃ δρᾶσον; τῷ σκέλει θένε τὴν πέτραν.

ΕΥΕΛΠΙΔΗΣ

σὺ δὲ τῇ κεφαλῇ γ᾿, ἵν᾿ ᾖ διπλάσιος ὁ ψόφος.

their boughs for only a month or two, whereas the Athenians harp on their lawsuits their whole lives long. That's why we're trekking this trek, and wandering with basket, kettle, and myrtle boughs[8] in search of a peaceable place, where we can settle down and pass our lives. Our mission now is to visit Tereus the Hoopoe; we need to learn from him if anywhere on his flights he's seen that sort of city.

PEISETAERUS

Hey!

EUELPIDES

What is it?

PEISETAERUS

This crow's been trying for quite a while to show me something up there.

EUELPIDES

This jackdaw's been gaping upwards too, as if to point something out to me. There must be birds around here. *(they approach the scene building)* We'll soon find out, if we make some noise.

PEISETAERUS

Know what you should do? Thump that rock with your leg.

EUELPIDES

You thump it with your head, it'll make twice the noise.

[8] Implements used ceremonially in founding a settlement.

ΠΕΙΣΕΤΑΙΡΟΣ

σὺ δ᾽ οὖν λίθῳ κόψον λαβών.

ΕΥΕΛΠΙΔΗΣ

πάνυ γ᾽, εἰ δοκεῖ.

παῖ παῖ.

ΠΕΙΣΕΤΑΙΡΟΣ

τί λέγεις, οὗτος; τὸν ἔποπα παῖ καλεῖς;
οὐκ ἀντὶ τοῦ παιδός σ᾽ ἐχρῆν ἐποποῖ καλεῖν;

ΕΥΕΛΠΙΔΗΣ

ἐποποῖ. ποιήσεις τοί με κόπτειν αὖθις αὖ.
ἐποποῖ.

ΘΕΡΑΠΩΝ ΕΠΟΠΟΣ

τίνες οὗτοι; τίς ὁ βοῶν τὸν δεσπότην;

ΠΕΙΣΕΤΑΙΡΟΣ

Ἄπολλον ἀποτρόπαιε, τοῦ χασμήματος.

ΘΕΡΑΠΩΝ ΕΠΟΠΟΣ

οἴμοι τάλας, ὀρνιθοθήρα τουτωί.

ΠΕΙΣΕΤΑΙΡΟΣ

οὕτως τι δεινὸν οὐδὲ κάλλιον λέγεις.

ΘΕΡΑΠΩΝ ΕΠΟΠΟΣ

ἀπολεῖσθον.

ΠΕΙΣΕΤΑΙΡΟΣ

ἀλλ᾽ οὐκ ἐσμὲν ἀνθρώπω.

ΘΕΡΑΠΩΝ ΕΠΟΠΟΣ

τί δαί;

PEISETAERUS
Well then, get a stone and knock.

EUELPIDES
If you like, I will. *(knocking with a stone)* Boy! Boy!

PEISETAERUS
Hey, what are you saying? Are you calling the Hoopoe "boy"? You should say "oh, Hoopoe," not "hey boy."

EUELPIDES
Oh, Hoopoe! You'll only make me keep knocking, you know. Oh, Hoopoe!

Enter from the stage door Tereus' SLAVE, *a bird with a large beak; Xanthias and Manodorus drop the baggage and retreat to the side; the crow and jackdaw fly away.*

SLAVE
Who's there? Who's shouting for the master?

PEISETAERUS
God save us, what a beak!

SLAVE
Heavens me, here's a pair of birdnappers!

PEISETAERUS
Imagine speaking so harshly, and not more politely!

SLAVE
You two are dead!

PEISETAERUS
But we're not mortals!

SLAVE
Well, what are you?

ΠΕΙΣΕΤΑΙΡΟΣ

ὑποδεδιὼς ἔγωγε, Λιβυκὸν ὄρνεον.

ΘΕΡΑΠΩΝ ΕΠΟΠΟΣ

οὐδὲν λέγεις.

ΠΕΙΣΕΤΑΙΡΟΣ

καὶ μὴν ἐροῦ τὰ πρὸς ποδῶν.

ΘΕΡΑΠΩΝ ΕΠΟΠΟΣ

ὁδὶ δὲ δὴ τίς ἐστιν ὄρνις; οὐκ ἐρεῖς;

ΕΥΕΛΠΙΔΗΣ

ἐπικεχοδὼς ἔγωγε Φασιανικός.

ΠΕΙΣΕΤΑΙΡΟΣ

ἀτὰρ σὺ τί θηρίον ποτ᾽ εἶ, πρὸς τῶν θεῶν;

ΘΕΡΑΠΩΝ ΕΠΟΠΟΣ

ὄρνις ἔγωγε δοῦλος.

ΕΥΕΛΠΙΔΗΣ

ἡττήθης τινὸς
ἀλεκτρυόνος;

ΘΕΡΑΠΩΝ ΕΠΟΠΟΣ

οὔκ, ἀλλ᾽ ὅτε περ ὁ δεσπότης
ἔποψ ἐγένετο, τότε γενέσθαι μ᾽ ηὔξατο
ὄρνιν, ἵν᾽ ἀκόλουθον διάκονόν τ᾽ ἔχῃ.

ΠΕΙΣΕΤΑΙΡΟΣ

δεῖται γὰρ ὄρνις καὶ διακόνου τινός;

ΘΕΡΑΠΩΝ ΕΠΟΠΟΣ

οὗτός γ᾽, ἅτ᾽, οἶμαι, πρότερον ἄνθρωπός ποτ᾽ ὤν.

PEISETAERUS

Me? I'm a yellowbelly, a Libyan bird.

SLAVE

What nonsense!

PEISETAERUS

Really? Then check what's on the back of my legs.

SLAVE

And this other one, what kind of bird is he? Speak up.

EUELPIDES

I'm a brownbottom, from the Pheasance.

PEISETAERUS

(to the Slave) Say, what kind of creature might you be, in heaven's name?

SLAVE

Me, I'm a slavebird.

EUELPIDES

Vanquished by some fighting cock, eh?

SLAVE

No, it's just that when master turned into a hoopoe, he prayed that I become a bird too, so that he could still have an attendant and butler.

PEISETAERUS

Does a bird actually need a butler?

SLAVE

This one does. I guess it's because he once was human.

τοτὲ μὲν ἐρᾷ φαγεῖν ἀφύας Φαληρικάς,
τρέχω 'π' ἀφύας ἐγὼ λαβὼν τὸ τρύβλιον·
ἔτνους δ' ἐπιθυμεῖ, δεῖ τορύνης καὶ χύτρας,
τρέχω 'πὶ τορύνην.

ΠΕΙΣΕΤΑΙΡΟΣ

τροχίλος ὄρνις οὑτοσί.
οἶσθ' οὖν ὃ δρᾶσον, ὦ τροχίλε; τὸν δεσπότην
ἡμῖν κάλεσον.

ΘΕΡΑΠΩΝ ΕΠΟΠΟΣ

ἀλλ' ἀρτίως νὴ τὸν Δία
εὕδει καταφαγὼν μύρτα καὶ σέρφους τινάς.

ΠΕΙΣΕΤΑΙΡΟΣ

ὅμως ἐπέγειρον αὐτόν.

ΘΕΡΑΠΩΝ ΕΠΟΠΟΣ

οἶδα μὲν σαφῶς
ὅτι ἀχθέσεται, σφῷν δ' αὐτὸν εἵνεκ' ἐπεγερῶ.

ΠΕΙΣΕΤΑΙΡΟΣ

κακῶς σύ γ' ἀπόλοι'. ὥς μ' ἀπέκτεινας δέει.

ΕΥΕΛΠΙΔΗΣ

οἴμοι κακοδαίμων, χὠ κολοιός μοἴχεται
ὑπὸ τοῦ δέους.

ΠΕΙΣΕΤΑΙΡΟΣ

ὦ δειλότατον σὺ θηρίον,
δείσας ἀφῆκας τὸν κολοιόν.

He'll get a craving for fish fry from Phalerum, and I grab the pan and run out for the fish. Or he'll want lentil soup, we need a ladle and tureen, so I run for the tureen.

PEISETAERUS

This one's a roadrunner. So, roadrunner, you know what you should do? Call your master for us.

SLAVE

Oh no; he's just started his nap, after a lunch of myrtle berries and gnats.

PEISETAERUS

Wake him anyway.

SLAVE

Well, I'm quite sure he'll be annoyed, but as a favor to you I'll wake him up.

Exit SLAVE.

PEISETAERUS

(calling after him) And to hell with you, for scaring me to death!

EUELPIDES

I'll be damned, my jackdaw flew away from me in terror!

PEISETAERUS

You utter scaredy cat, so frightened that you let him go!

ΕΥΕΛΠΙΔΗΣ

εἰπέ μοι,
σὺ δὲ τὴν κορώνην οὐκ ἀφῆκας καταπεσών;

ΠΕΙΣΕΤΑΙΡΟΣ

μὰ Δί᾿ οὐκ ἔγωγε.

ΕΥΕΛΠΙΔΗΣ

ποῦ γάρ ἐστ᾿;

ΠΕΙΣΕΤΑΙΡΟΣ

ἀπέπτατο.

ΕΥΕΛΠΙΔΗΣ

οὐκ ἆρ᾿ ἀφῆκας; ὦγάθ᾿, ὡς ἀνδρεῖος εἶ.

ΤΗΡΕΥΣ

ἄνοιγε τὴν ὕλην, ἵν᾿ ἐξέλθω ποτέ.

ΠΕΙΣΕΤΑΙΡΟΣ

ὦ Ἡράκλεις, τουτὶ τί ποτ᾿ ἐστὶ θηρίον;
τίς ἡ πτέρωσις; τίς ὁ τρόπος τῆς τριλοφίας;

ΤΗΡΕΥΣ

τίνες εἰσί μ᾿ οἱ ζητοῦντες;

ΕΥΕΛΠΙΔΗΣ

οἱ δώδεκα θεοὶ
εἴξασιν ἐπιτρῖψαί σε.

ΤΗΡΕΥΣ

μῶν με σκώπτετον
ὁρῶντε τὴν πτέρωσιν; ἦ γάρ, ὦ ξένοι,
ἄνθρωπος.

EUELPIDES

Say, didn't you fall down and let your crow loose?

PEISETAERUS

I certainly did not.

EUELPIDES

Then where is it?

PEISETAERUS

It flew off.

EUELPIDES

So, my good man, you didn't let it go, brave fellow that you are?

TEREUS

(within, to his Slave) Unbar the woods, that I may at last come forth.

Enter TEREUS *from the stage door, with a hoopoe's head and wings, but few feathers; two Slaves accompany him.*

PEISETAERUS

Heracles, what kind of beast is this? What plumage? What manner of triple crest?

TEREUS

Who be those that seek me?

EUELPIDES

The Twelve Gods seem to have made a mess of you.

TEREUS

You two aren't making fun of me, are you, for the look of my plumage? Because I'll have you know, friends, I was once human.

ΠΕΙΣΕΤΑΙΡΟΣ

οὐ σοῦ καταγελῶμεν.

ΤΗΡΕΥΣ

ἀλλὰ τοῦ;

ΕΥΕΛΠΙΔΗΣ

τὸ ῥάμφος ἥμιν σου γέλοιον φαίνεται.

ΤΗΡΕΥΣ

τοιαῦτα μέντοι Σοφοκλέης λυμαίνεται
ἐν ταῖς τραγῳδίαισιν ἐμέ, τὸν Τηρέα.

ΠΕΙΣΕΤΑΙΡΟΣ

Τηρεὺς γὰρ εἶ σύ; πότερον ὄρνις ἢ ταῶς;

ΤΗΡΕΥΣ

ὄρνις ἔγωγε.

ΕΥΕΛΠΙΔΗΣ

κᾆτά σοι ποῦ τὰ πτερά;

ΤΗΡΕΥΣ

ἐξερρύηκε.

ΕΥΕΛΠΙΔΗΣ

πότερον ὑπὸ νόσου τινός;

ΤΗΡΕΥΣ

οὔκ, ἀλλὰ τὸν χειμῶνα πάντα τὤρνεα
πτερορρυεῖ τε κaὖθις ἕτερα φύομεν.
ἀλλ᾽ εἴπατόν μοι σφὼ τίν᾽ ἐστόν;

ΠΕΙΣΕΤΑΙΡΟΣ

νώ; βροτώ.

PEISETAERUS

It's not you we're laughing at.

TEREUS

What, then?

EUELPIDES

It's your beak that strikes us funny.

TEREUS

That's how shabbily Sophocles treats me—Tereus!—in his tragedies.

PEISETAERUS

So you're Tereus! Bird or peacock?

TEREUS

Me, I'm a bird.

EUELPIDES

Then where are your feathers?

TEREUS

They've fallen out.

EUELPIDES

From some disease?

TEREUS

No; in winter all birds shed their feathers, and then we grow new ones. But tell me who you two are.

PEISETAERUS

We two? Humans.

ΤΗΡΕΥΣ

ποδαπὼ τὸ γένος;

ΠΕΙΣΕΤΑΙΡΟΣ

ὅθεν αἱ τριήρεις αἱ καλαί.

ΤΗΡΕΥΣ

μῶν ἠλιαστά;

ΕΥΕΛΠΙΔΗΣ

μἀλλὰ θἀτέρου τρόπου,
ἀπηλιαστά.

ΤΗΡΕΥΣ

σπείρεται γὰρ τοῦτ᾽ ἐκεῖ
τὸ σπέρμ᾽;

ΕΥΕΛΠΙΔΗΣ

ὀλίγον ζητῶν ἂν ἐξ ἀγροῦ λάβοις.

ΤΗΡΕΥΣ

πράγους δὲ δὴ τοῦ δεομένω δεῦρ᾽ ἤλθετον;

ΠΕΙΣΕΤΑΙΡΟΣ

σοὶ ξυγγενέσθαι βουλομένω.

ΤΗΡΕΥΣ

τίνος πέρι;

ΠΕΙΣΕΤΑΙΡΟΣ

ὅτι πρῶτα μὲν ἦσθ᾽ ἄνθρωπος ὥσπερ νώ ποτε,
κἀργύριον ὠφείλησας ὥσπερ νώ ποτε,
κοὐκ ἀποδιδοὺς ἔχαιρες ὥσπερ νώ ποτε·
εἶτ᾽ αὖθις ὀρνίθων μεταλλάξας φύσιν

TEREUS

What nationality?

PEISETAERUS

Where the fine triremes come from.

TEREUS

Not a couple of jurors, I hope!

EUELPIDES

Oh no, the other kind: a couple of jurophobes.

TEREUS

Does that seed sprout there?

EUELPIDES

You'll find a little in the country, if you look hard.

TEREUS

Now then, on what business have you two come here?

PEISETAERUS

We want to confer with you.

TEREUS

About what?

PEISETAERUS

Well, originally you were human, like us, and once owed money, like us, and once enjoyed not repaying it, like us; then trading all that for the guise of birds, you've flown the

καὶ γῆν ἐπέπτου καὶ θάλατταν ἐν κύκλῳ,
καὶ πάνθ᾽ ὅσαπερ ἄνθρωπος ὅσα τ᾽ ὄρνις φρονεῖς.
ταῦτ᾽ οὖν ἱκέται νὼ πρὸς σὲ δεῦρ᾽ ἀφίγμεθα,
εἴ τινα πόλιν φράσειας ἡμῖν εὔερον
ὥσπερ σισύραν ἐγκατακλινῆναι μαλθακήν.

ΤΗΡΕΥΣ

ἔπειτα μείζω τῶν Κραναῶν ζητεῖς πόλιν;

ΠΕΙΣΕΤΑΙΡΟΣ

μείζω μὲν οὐδέν, προσφορωτέραν δὲ νῷν.

ΤΗΡΕΥΣ

ἀριστοκρατεῖσθαι δῆλος εἶ ζητῶν.

ΠΕΙΣΕΤΑΙΡΟΣ

ἐγώ;
ἥκιστα· καὶ τὸν Σκελλίου βδελύττομαι.

ΤΗΡΕΥΣ

ποίαν τιν᾽ οὖν ἥδιστ᾽ ἂν οἰκοῖτ᾽ ἂν πόλιν;

ΠΕΙΣΕΤΑΙΡΟΣ

ὅπου τὰ μέγιστα πράγματ᾽ εἴη τοιάδε·
ἐπὶ τὴν θύραν μου πρῴ τις ἐλθὼν τῶν φίλων
λέγοι ταδί· "πρὸς τοῦ Διὸς τοὐλυμπίου
ὅπως παρέσει μοι καὶ σὺ καὶ τὰ παιδία
λουσάμενα πρῴ· μέλλω γὰρ ἑστιᾶν γάμους·
καὶ μηδαμῶς ἄλλως ποιήσῃς· εἰ δὲ μή,
μή μοι τότ᾽ ἔλθῃς, ὅταν ἐγὼ πράττω κακῶς."

circuit of land and sea, and your mind contains everything a human's does, and everything a bird's does too. That's why we've come to visit, hoping you know of a nice cushy city, soft as a woolen blanket, where we could curl up.

TEREUS

Could you be looking for a city greater than the Cranaans'?[9]

PEISETAERUS

Not greater, no, just better suited to us.

TEREUS

You're obviously looking for an aristocracy.

PEISETAERUS

Who me? Not at all. Even Scellias' son makes me sick.[10]

TEREUS

Well then, what kind of city would you most like to live in?

PEISETAERUS

One where my worst troubles would be like this: a friend appears at my door one morning and says, "In the name of Zeus on Olympus, make sure that you and your kids wash up and be at my place bright and early; I'm giving a wedding feast. Now don't let me down, otherwise you needn't visit me when I'm in trouble!"

[9] Cranaus was a mythical king of Athens.

[10] Aristocrates, a signer of the Peace of Nicias in 421, a general in 413/12, and a moderate oligarch in 411 (Thucydides 5.19, 8.9, 89, 92); here his name alone is the joke.

ΤΗΡΕΥΣ

νὴ Δία ταλαιπώρων γε πραγμάτων ἐρᾷς.
τί δαὶ σύ;

ΕΥΕΛΠΙΔΗΣ

τοιούτων ἐρῶ κἀγώ.

ΤΗΡΕΥΣ

τίνων;

ΕΥΕΛΠΙΔΗΣ

ὅπου ξυναντῶν μοι ταδί τις μέμψεται
ὥσπερ ἀδικηθεὶς παιδὸς ὡραίου πατήρ·
"καλῶς γέ μου τὸν υἱόν, ὦ στιλβωνίδη,
εὑρὼν ἀπιόντ᾽ ἀπὸ γυμνασίου λελουμένον
οὐκ ἔκυσας, οὐ προσεῖπας, οὐ προσηγάγου,
οὐκ ὠρχιπέδισας, ὢν ἐμοὶ πατρικὸς φίλος."

ΤΗΡΕΥΣ

ὦ δειλακρίων σύ, τῶν κακῶν οἵων ἐρᾷς.
ἀτὰρ ἔστι γ᾽ ὁποίαν λέγετον εὐδαίμων πόλις
παρὰ τὴν ἐρυθρὰν θάλατταν.

ΕΥΕΛΠΙΔΗΣ

οἴμοι, μηδαμῶς
ἡμῖν γε παρὰ θάλατταν, ἵν᾽ ἀνακύψεται
κλητῆρ᾽ ἄγουσ᾽ ἕωθεν ἡ Σαλαμινία.
Ἑλληνικὴν δὲ πόλιν ἔχεις ἡμῖν φράσαι;

ΤΗΡΕΥΣ

τί οὐ τὸν Ἠλεῖον Λέπρεον οἰκίζετον
ἐλθόνθ᾽;

TEREUS

My word, it's miserable troubles you long for! *(to Euelpides)* And what about you?

EUELPIDES

I long for much the same.

TEREUS

Namely?

EUELPIDES

A city where a blooming boy's father would bump into me and complain in this fashion, as if wronged: "A fine way you treat my son, Mr. Smoothy! You met him leaving the gymnasium after his bath, and you didn't kiss him, didn't chat him up, didn't hug him, didn't fondle his balls—and you my old family friend!"

TEREUS

Poor thing, what troubles you long for! Well, there actually is a happy city of the sort you two are talking about, on the shores of the Red Sea.

EUELPIDES

Oh no, no seaside for us! Not where the *Salaminia* will pop up one morning with a summonser on board.[11] Can't you tell us of a Greek city?

TEREUS

Why not go and settle at Lepreus, in Elis?

[11] One of two sacred galleys in the Athenian navy (the other was the *Paralus*) used for official dispatches and transport.

ΕΥΕΛΠΙΔΗΣ

ὁτιὴ νὴ τοὺς θεοὺς ὅσ᾿ οὐκ ἰδὼν
βδελύττομαι τὸν Λέπρεον ἀπὸ Μελανθίου.

ΤΗΡΕΥΣ

ἀλλ᾿ εἰσὶν ἕτεροι τῆς Λοκρίδος Ὀπούντιοι,
ἵνα χρὴ κατοικεῖν.

ΕΥΕΛΠΙΔΗΣ

ἀλλ᾿ ἔγωγ᾿ Ὀπούντιος
οὐκ ἂν γενοίμην ἐπὶ ταλάντῳ χρυσίου.

ΠΕΙΣΕΤΑΙΡΟΣ

οὗτος δὲ δὴ τίς ἐσθ᾿ ὁ μετ᾿ ὀρνίθων βίος;
σὺ γὰρ οἶσθ᾿ ἀκριβῶς.

ΤΗΡΕΥΣ

οὐκ ἄχαρις εἰς τὴν τριβήν·
οὗ πρῶτα μὲν δεῖ ζῆν ἄνευ βαλλαντίου.

ΕΥΕΛΠΙΔΗΣ

πολλήν γ᾿ ἀφεῖλες τοῦ βίου κιβδηλίαν.

ΤΗΡΕΥΣ

νεμόμεσθα δ᾿ ἐν κήποις τὰ λευκὰ σήσαμα
καὶ μύρτα καὶ μήκωνα καὶ σισύμβρια.

ΕΥΕΛΠΙΔΗΣ

ὑμεῖς μὲν ἆρα ζῆτε νυμφίων βίον.

ΠΕΙΣΕΤΑΙΡΟΣ

φεῦ φεῦ·
ἦ μέγ᾿ ἐνορῶ βούλευμ᾿ ἐν ὀρνίθων γένει

EUELPIDES

For heaven's sake, Lepreus makes me sick, even though I've never seen it, because of Melanthius.[12]

TEREUS

Well, there are the Opuntii in Locris; you should settle there.

EUELPIDES

Not me; I wouldn't become an Opuntius[13] for a talent of gold.

PEISETAERUS

But what about this life with the birds? Tell me about it; you know every detail.

TEREUS

It wears quite nicely. To begin with, you must get by without a purse.

EUELPIDES

You've removed much of life's fraudulence right there.

TEREUS

And in the gardens we feed on white sesame seeds, myrtle berries, poppies, and watermint.[14]

EUELPIDES

Why, you're all living the life of honeymooners!

PEISETAERUS

Aha, aha! Oh what a grand scheme I see in the race of

[12] A tragic poet, who apparently suffered from the skin disease *lepra.*

[13] A man by this name is mentioned as one-eyed at 1294 and beak-nosed in Callias fr. 4 and Eupolis fr. 283.

[14] Items associated in Athenian life with festive occasions.

καὶ δύναμιν ἣ γένοιτ᾽ ἄν, εἰ πίθοισθέ μοι.

ΤΗΡΕΥΣ

τί σοι πιθώμεσθ᾽;

ΠΕΙΣΕΤΑΙΡΟΣ

ὅ τι πίθησθε; πρῶτα μὲν
μὴ περιπέτεσθε πανταχῇ κεχηνότες·
ὡς τοῦτ᾽ ἄτιμον τοὔργον ἐστίν. αὐτίκα
ἐκεῖ παρ᾽ ἡμῖν τοὺς πετομένους ἢν ἔρῃ
"τίς ἐστιν οὗτος;" ὁ Τελέας ἐρεῖ ταδί·
"ἄνθρωπος ὄρνις, ἀστάθμητος, πετόμενος,
ἀτέκμαρτος, οὐδὲν οὐδέποτ᾽ ἐν ταὐτῷ μένων."

ΤΗΡΕΥΣ

νὴ τὸν Διόνυσον εὖ γε μωμᾷ ταυταγί.
τί ἂν οὖν ποιοῖμεν;

ΠΕΙΣΕΤΑΙΡΟΣ

οἰκίσατε μίαν πόλιν.

ΤΗΡΕΥΣ

ποίαν δ᾽ ἂν οἰκίσαιμεν ὄρνιθες πόλιν;

ΠΕΙΣΕΤΑΙΡΟΣ

ἄληθες, ὦ σκαιότατον εἰρηκὼς ἔπος;
βλέψον κάτω.

ΤΗΡΕΥΣ

καὶ δὴ βλέπω.

168 ἐστιν οὗτος Hermann: ὄρνις οὗτος vel οὗτος ὄρνις a

birds, and power that could be yours, if you take my advice!

TEREUS

What advice would you have us take?

PEISETAERUS

What advice should you take? For a start, don't fly around in all directions with your beaks agape; that's discreditable behavior. For example, back where we come from, if among the flighty crowd you ask, "Who's that guy?" Teleas[15] will reply, "The man's a bird, unstable, flighty, unverifiable, never ever staying in the same spot."

TEREUS

By Dionysus, that's a fair criticism. But what can we do about it?

PEISETAERUS

Found a single city.

TEREUS

But what kind of city could mere birds found?

PEISETAERUS

Really, what an utterly doltish remark! Look down.

TEREUS

Very well.

[15] Probably the son of Telenicus, of the deme Pergase, currently serving as a Treasurer of Athena; a wealthy politician (cf. 1024–25) ridiculed elsewhere for gluttony, political trickery, and shiftiness, cf. *Peace* 1008–09, Phrynichus fr. 21, Plato com. fr. 176. Here both the text and the point of the joke are uncertain.

ΠΕΙΣΕΤΑΙΡΟΣ

βλέπε νυν ἄνω.

ΤΗΡΕΥΣ

βλέπω.

ΠΕΙΣΕΤΑΙΡΟΣ

περίαγε τὸν τράχηλον.

ΤΗΡΕΥΣ

νὴ Δία
ἀπολαύσομαί <τί> γ᾽, εἰ διαστραφήσομαι.

ΠΕΙΣΕΤΑΙΡΟΣ

εἶδές τι;

ΤΗΡΕΥΣ

τὰς νεφέλας γε καὶ τὸν οὐρανόν.

ΠΕΙΣΕΤΑΙΡΟΣ

οὐχ οὗτος οὖν δήπου ᾽στὶν ὀρνίθων πόλος;

ΤΗΡΕΥΣ

πόλος; τίνα τρόπον;

ΠΕΙΣΕΤΑΙΡΟΣ

ὥσπερ <ἂν> εἴποι τις, τόπος.
ὅτι δὲ πολεῖται τοῦτο καὶ διέρχεται
ἅπαντα διὰ τούτου, καλεῖται νῦν πόλος.
ἢν δ᾽ οἰκίσητε τοῦτο καὶ φράξηθ᾽ ἅπαξ,
ἐκ τοῦ πόλου τούτου κεκλήσεται πόλις.
ὥστ᾽ ἄρξετ᾽ ἀνθρώπων μὲν ὥσπερ παρνόπων,
τοὺς δ᾽ αὖ θεοὺς ἀπολεῖτε λιμῷ Μηλίῳ.

PEISETAERUS

Now look up.

TEREUS

I'm looking.

PEISETAERUS

Turn your head around.

TEREUS

Yes, it would really do me good to sprain my neck!

PEISETAERUS

Did you see anything?

TEREUS

I saw the clouds and sky.

PEISETAERUS

Well then, surely that's the birds' site?

TEREUS

Site? In what sense?

PEISETAERUS

Their place, you might say. It's a place to *visit*, and where everything makes *transit*, so it's now called merely a *site*. But as soon as you settle and fortify it, this *site* will instead be called a *city*. And then you'll rule over humans as you do over locusts; and as for the gods, you'll destroy them by Melian famine.[16]

[16] In summer 416 the Athenians had besieged the small island of Melos, and upon its surrender exterminated the adult males and enslaved the women and children, for refusing to join the empire (Thucydides 5.84–116).

ΤΗΡΕΥΣ

πῶς;

ΠΕΙΣΕΤΑΙΡΟΣ

ἐν μέσῳ δήπουθεν ἀήρ ἐστι γῆς.
εἶθ', ὥσπερ ἡμεῖς, ἢν ἰέναι βουλώμεθα
Πυθώδε, Βοιωτοὺς δίοδον αἰτούμεθα,
οὕτως, ὅταν θύσωσιν ἄνθρωποι θεοῖς,
191 ἢν μὴ φόρον φέρωσιν ὑμῖν οἱ θεοί,
193 τῶν μηρίων τὴν κνῖσαν οὐ διαφρήσετε.

ΤΗΡΕΥΣ

ἰοὺ ἰού· μὰ γῆν, μὰ παγίδας, μὰ νεφέλας, μὰ
δίκτυα,
μὴ 'γὼ νόημα κομψότερον ἤκουσά πω·
ὥστ' ἂν κατοικίζοιμι μετὰ σοῦ τὴν πόλιν,
εἰ ξυνδοκοίη τοῖσιν ἄλλοις ὀρνέοις.

ΠΕΙΣΕΤΑΙΡΟΣ

τίς ἂν οὖν τὸ πρᾶγμ' αὐτοῖς διηγήσαιτο;

ΤΗΡΕΥΣ

σύ.
ἐγὼ γὰρ αὐτοὺς βαρβάρους ὄντας πρὸ τοῦ
ἐδίδαξα τὴν φωνὴν ξυνὼν πολὺν χρόνον.

ΠΕΙΣΕΤΑΙΡΟΣ

πῶς δῆτ' ἂν αὐτοὺς ξυγκαλέσειας;

ΤΗΡΕΥΣ

ῥᾳδίως.
δευρὶ γὰρ ἐμβὰς αὐτίκα μάλ' εἰς τὴν λόχμην,

TEREUS

How?

PEISETAERUS

Between them and the earth is air, no? So look: just as we must ask the Boeotians for a visa whenever we want to visit Delphi, in the same way, whenever humans sacrifice to the gods, you won't let the aroma of the thigh bones pass through unless the gods pay you tribute.

TEREUS

Oho! So help me earth, snares, gins, and nets, I've never heard a more elegant idea! I'd like to join you in founding this city, if the other birds concur.

PEISETAERUS

And who's going to explain the plan to them?

TEREUS

You are. Look, I've lived with them a long time, and they're not the barbarians they were before I taught them language.

PEISETAERUS

Then how will you call them together?

TEREUS

Easily. I'll just step right into my thicket here and wake up

---

192 [= 1218] del. Beck

ἔπειτ᾽ ἀνεγείρας τὴν ἐμὴν ἀηδόνα,
καλοῦμεν αὐτούς· οἱ δὲ νῷν τοῦ φθέγματος
ἐάνπερ ἐπακούσωσι θεύσονται δρόμῳ.

ΠΕΙΣΕΤΑΙΡΟΣ

ὦ φίλτατ᾽ ὀρνίθων σύ, μή νυν ἕσταθι·
ἀλλ᾽ ἀντιβολῶ σ᾽, ἄγ᾽, ὡς τάχιστ᾽ εἰς τὴν λόχμην
εἴσβαινε κἀνέγειρε τὴν ἀηδόνα.

ΤΗΡΕΥΣ

ἄγε σύννομέ μοι, παῦσαι μὲν ὕπνου,
λῦσον δὲ νόμους ἱερῶν ὕμνων,
οὓς διὰ θείου στόματος θρηνεῖς
τὸν ἐμὸν καὶ σὸν πολύδακρυν Ἴτυν,
ἐλελιζομένη διεροῖς μέλεσιν
γένυος ξουθῆς. καθαρὰ χωρεῖ
διὰ φυλλοκόμου μίλακος ἠχὼ
πρὸς Διὸς ἕδρας, ἵν᾽ ὁ χρυσοκόμας
Φοῖβος ἀκούων τοῖς σοῖς ἐλέγοις
ἀντιψάλλων ἐλεφαντόδετον
φόρμιγγα θεῶν ἵστησι χορούς·
διὰ δ᾽ ἀθανάτων στομάτων χωρεῖ
ξύμφωνος ὁμοῦ
θεία μακάρων ὀλολυγή.

---

[17] Procne, cf. 15 n.

[18] Euripides appears to have borrowed this description of the nightingale in *Helen* 1111–13, produced in 412.

[19] Apollo.

my nightingale,[17] and together we'll call them. If they hear our voices they'll come running.

PEISETAERUS

Dearest of birds, don't just stand there; please, I implore you, step into the thicket as quick as you can and wake up the nightingale!

TEREUS steps behind the thicket

TEREUS

Come, my songmate, leave your sleep,
and loosen the strains of sacred songs,
that from your divine lips bewail
deeply mourned Itys, your child and mine,
trilling forth fluid melodies
from your vibrant throat.[18]

(*emerging on the roof as the piper begins to play the nightingale's song*)

Pure the sound
that ascends through green-tressed bryony
to Zeus' abode, where gold-tressed
Phoebus[19] listens to your songs of grief
and, strumming in response his ivoried
lyre, stirs the gods to their dance;
and from deathless lips arises
in harmonious accord
the divine refrain of the Blest.

ΕΥΕΛΠΙΔΗΣ

ὦ Ζεῦ βασιλεῦ, τοῦ φθέγματος τοὐρνιθίου·
οἷον κατεμελίτωσε τὴν λόχμην ὅλην.

ΠΕΙΣΕΤΑΙΡΟΣ

οὗτος.

ΕΥΕΛΠΙΔΗΣ

τί ἔστιν;

ΠΕΙΣΕΤΑΙΡΟΣ

οὐ σιωπήσει;

ΕΥΕΛΠΙΔΗΣ

τί δαί;

ΠΕΙΣΕΤΑΙΡΟΣ

οὔποψ μελῳδεῖν αὖ παρασκευάζεται.

ΤΗΡΕΥΣ

ἐποποποῖ ποποποποῖ ποποῖ,
ἰὼ ἰὼ ἰτὼ ἰτὼ ἰτὼ ἰτὼ
ἴτω τις ὧδε τῶν ἐμῶν ὁμοπτέρων·

ὅσοι τ᾽ εὐσπόρους ἀγροίκων γύας
νέμεσθε, φῦλα μυρία κριθοτράγων
σπερμολόγων τε γένη
ταχὺ πετόμενα, μαλθακὴν ἱέντα γῆρυν·
ὅσα τ᾽ ἐν ἄλοκι θαμὰ
βῶλον ἀμφιτιττυβίζεθ᾽ ὧδε λεπτὸν
ἡδομένᾳ φωνᾷ·
τιὸ τιὸ τιὸ τιὸ τιὸ τιὸ τιὸ τιό·

EUELPIDES

Lord Zeus, that birdy's voice! How it turned the whole thicket to honey!

PEISETAERUS

Hey there.

EUELPIDES

Yes?

PEISETAERUS

Be quiet!

EUELPIDES

What for?

PEISETAERUS

The Hoopoe's getting ready to sing again.

TEREUS

Epopopoi popopopoi popoi,
ye ye co co co co
come ye hither every bird of fellow feather,

all who range over country acres
richly sown, the myriad tribes who feed on
  barleycorn,
and the races of seed pickers
that swiftly fly, casting a cozy cry;
and all who oft round the clod
in the furrow twitter delicately
this happy sound,
tio tio tio tio tio tio tio tio!

ὅσα θ᾽ ὑμῶν κατὰ κήπους ἐπὶ κισσοῦ
  κλάδεσι νομὸν ἔχει,
  τά τε κατ᾽ ὄρεα τὰ κοτινοτράγα τὰ
    κομαροφάγα,
  ἀνύσατε πετόμενα πρὸς ἐμὰν αὐδάν·
  τριοτὸ τριοτὸ τοτοβρίξ·

οἵ θ᾽ ἑλείας παρ᾽ αὐλῶνας ὀξυστόμους
  ἐμπίδας κάπτεθ᾽, ὅσα τ᾽ εὐδρόσους γῆς τόπους
  ἔχετε λειμῶνά τ᾽ ἐρόεντα Μαραθῶνος
  ὄρνις τε πτεροποίκιλος
  ἀτταγᾶς ἀτταγᾶς·

ὧν τ᾽ ἐπὶ πόντιον οἶδμα θαλάσσης
  φῦλα μετ᾽ ἀλκυόνεσσι ποτῆται,
  δεῦρ᾽ ἴτε πευσόμενοι τὰ νεώτερα·
  πάντα γὰρ ἐνθάδε φῦλ᾽ ἁθροΐζομεν
  οἰωνῶν ταναοδείρων.
ἥκει γάρ τις δριμὺς πρέσβυς
  καινὸς γνώμην
  καινῶν ἔργων τ᾽ ἐγχειρητής.

ἀλλ᾽ ἴτ᾽ εἰς λόγους ἅπαντα,
  δεῦρο δεῦρο δεῦρο δεῦρο·
τοροτοροτοροτοροτίξ,
κικκαβαῦ κικκαβαῦ,
τοροτοροτορολιλιλίξ.

And all of you who pasture on ivy boughs
in the gardens,
and you eaters of oleaster and arbutus
in the hills,
come flying at once to my call:
trioto trioto totobrix!

And you who in marshy vales snap up
keen-mouthed gnats, and all who inhabit
the earth's drizzly places and Marathon's lovely
  meadow,
and the bird with dappled plumage,
francolin, francolin!

And all whose tribes fly with the halcyons
over the deep swell of the sea,
come hither to learn the latest!
Yes, here we're gathering all the tribes
of neck-stretching birds,
for an acute old man has appeared,
novel in ideas
and a doer of novel deeds.

Now all attend the conference,
hither hither hither hither!
Torotorotorotorotix,
kikkabau kikkabau,
torotorotorolililix!

TEREUS disappears from the roof

ΠΕΙΣΕΤΑΙΡΟΣ

ὁρᾷς τιν᾽ ὄρνιν;

ΕΥΕΛΠΙΔΗΣ

μὰ τὸν Ἀπόλλω ᾽γὼ μὲν οὔ.
καίτοι κέχηνά γ᾽ εἰς τὸν οὐρανὸν βλέπων.

ΠΕΙΣΕΤΑΙΡΟΣ

ἄλλως ἄρ᾽ οὔποψ, ὡς ἔοικ᾽, εἰς τὴν λόχμην
ἐμβὰς ἐπόπωζε χαραδριὸν μιμούμενος.

ΤΗΡΕΥΣ

τοροτὶξ τοροτίξ.

ΕΥΕΛΠΙΔΗΣ

ὦγάθ᾽, ἀλλ᾽ <οὖν> οὑτοσὶ καὶ δή τις ὄρνις ἔρχεται.

ΠΕΙΣΕΤΑΙΡΟΣ

νὴ Δί᾽ ὄρνις δῆτα. τίς ποτ᾽ ἐστίν; οὐ δήπου ταῶς;

ΕΥΕΛΠΙΔΗΣ

οὗτος αὐτὸς νῷν φράσει. τίς ἐστιν ὄρνις οὑτοσί;

ΤΗΡΕΥΣ

οὗτος οὐ τῶν ἠθάδων τῶνδ᾽ ὧν ὁρᾶθ᾽ ὑμεῖς ἀεί,
ἀλλὰ λιμναῖος.

ΕΥΕΛΠΙΔΗΣ

βαβαί, καλός γε καὶ φοινικιοῦς.

ΤΗΡΕΥΣ

εἰκότως <γε>· καὶ γὰρ ὄνομ᾽ αὐτῷ ᾽στὶ
φοινικόπτερος.

PEISETAERUS

Do you see any birds?

EUELPIDES

I certainly don't, though I'm all agape from watching the sky.

PEISETAERUS

Then it seems the Hoopoe copied the curlew, going into the thicket and crying hoo-poo for nothing.

TEREUS

(emerging from the thicket in panoply) Torotix torotix!

Flamingo appears on the roof.

EUELPIDES

Maybe so, my friend, but over here, look, a bird is coming!

PEISETAERUS

That's a bird all right! Whatever can it be? Surely not a peacock?

EUELPIDES

Our host here will tell us. *(to Tereus)* What kind of bird is that?

TEREUS

None of those commonplace birds you humans are used to seeing; he's a marsh bird.

EUELPIDES

My, how flamboyantly crimson he is!

TEREUS

Naturally, because his name is Flamingo.

Mede appears on the roof.

ΕΥΕΛΠΙΔΗΣ

οὗτος, ὦ—σέ τοι.

ΠΕΙΣΕΤΑΙΡΟΣ

τί βωστρεῖς;

ΕΥΕΛΠΙΔΗΣ

ἕτερος ὄρνις οὑτοσί.

ΠΕΙΣΕΤΑΙΡΟΣ

νὴ Δί' ἕτερος δῆτα χοὖτος ἔξεδρον χροιὰν ἔχων.
τίς ποτ' ἔσθ' ὁ μουσόμαντις, ἄτοπος ὄρνις ὀριβάτης;

ΤΗΡΕΥΣ

ὄνομα τούτῳ μῆδός ἐστι.

ΕΥΕΛΠΙΔΗΣ

Μῆδος; ὦναξ Ἡράκλεις.
εἶτα πῶς ἄνευ καμήλου Μῆδος ὢν εἰσέπτετο;

ΠΕΙΣΕΤΑΙΡΟΣ

ἕτερος αὖ λόφον καθειληφώς τις ὄρνις οὑτοσί.

ΕΥΕΛΠΙΔΗΣ

τί τὸ τέρας τουτί ποτ' ἐστίν; οὐ σὺ μόνος ἄρ' ἦσθ' ἔποψ,
ἀλλὰ χοὖτος ἕτερος;

275 χροιὰν Zonaras 759 Σ S: χώραν a

EUELPIDES

Ho there, psst—yes, you!

PEISETAERUS

What do you want?

EUELPIDES

Here's another bird!

PEISETAERUS

Oh yes, that's another one all right, and he's also garbed in eccentric color.[20] *(To Tereus)* Who in the world is this vatic songster,[21] this outlandish mountain-ranging bird?

TEREUS

His name is mede.

EUELPIDES

Mede? Lord Heracles! But if he's a Mede, how did he fly here without a camel?

Hoopoe appears on the roof.

PEISETAERUS

Here's still another bird who's secured a crest.

EUELPIDES

What kind of apparition is this? *(to Tereus)* Then you're not the only hoopoe, but he's one too?

[20] Adapting a line from Sophocles' *Tyro* (fr. 654), "What is this bird occupying an eccentric position?"

[21] From Aeschylus' *Edonians* (fr. 60), referring to Orpheus or Dionysus.

ΤΗΡΕΥΣ

οὑτοσὶ μέν ἐστι Φιλοκλέους
ἐξ ἔποπος, ἐγὼ δὲ τούτου πάππος, ὥσπερ εἰ λέγοις
"Ἱππόνικος Καλλίου κἀξ Ἱππονίκου Καλλίας."

ΠΕΙΣΕΤΑΙΡΟΣ

Καλλίας ἄρ' οὗτος οὕρνις ἐστίν. ὡς πτερορρυεῖ.

ΤΗΡΕΥΣ

ἅτε γὰρ ὢν γενναῖος ὑπό <τε> συκοφαντῶν τίλλεται,
αἵ τε θήλειαι πρὸς ἐκτίλλουσιν αὐτοῦ τὰ πτερά.

ΕΥΕΛΠΙΔΗΣ

ὦ Πόσειδον, ἕτερος αὖ τις βαπτὸς ὄρνις οὑτοσί.
τίς ὀνομάζεταί ποθ' οὗτος;

ΤΗΡΕΥΣ

οὑτοσὶ κατωφαγᾶς.

ΠΕΙΣΕΤΑΙΡΟΣ

ἔστι γὰρ κατωφαγᾶς τις ἄλλος ἢ Κλεώνυμος;

ΕΥΕΛΠΙΔΗΣ

πῶς ἂν οὖν Κλεώνυμός γ' ὢν οὐκ ἀπέβαλε τὸν
λόφον;

TEREUS

This one here's the son of Philocles' hoopoe,[22] and I'm his grandfather, just as you might say Hipponicus son of Callias and Callias son of Hipponicus.[23]

PEISETAERUS

So this bird is Callias. He's shed a lot of feathers.

TEREUS

He's pedigreed, you see, so he gets plucked by shysters, and the females too keep plucking away at his plumage.

Gobbler appears on the roof.

EUELPIDES

Poseidon! Here's still another brightly tinted bird. *(to Tereus)* What's this one called, I wonder?

TEREUS

That one? Gobbler.

PEISETAERUS

You mean there's another gobbler besides Cleonymus?[24]

EUELPIDES

If that were really Cleonymus, he'd surely have tossed his crest.

22 Philocles, nephew of Aeschylus and nicknamed "The Lark" (?476, 1295), wrote a tragic tetralogy *Pandionis*, which included Tereus' metamorphosis.

23 For five generations the heads of one wealthy and distinguished family of the Ceryces clan had alternated these names; the current Callias was often ridiculed as a flagrant wastrel.

24 A politician often ridiculed for obesity, gluttony, and effeminacy, and (uniquely in Attic comedy) for having thrown away his shield in battle (see 1470–81).

ΠΕΙΣΕΤΑΙΡΟΣ

ἀλλὰ μέντοι τίς ποθ' ἡ λόφωσις ἡ τῶν ὀρνέων;
ἦ 'πὶ τὸν δίαυλον ἦλθον;

ΤΗΡΕΥΣ

ὥσπερ οἱ Κᾶρες μὲν οὖν
ἐπὶ λόφων οἰκοῦσιν, ὦγαθ', ἀσφαλείας οὕνεκα.

ΠΕΙΣΕΤΑΙΡΟΣ

ὦ Πόσειδον, οὐχ ὁρᾷς ὅσον συνείλεκται κακὸν
ὀρνέων;

ΕΥΕΛΠΙΔΗΣ

ὦναξ Ἄπολλον, τοῦ νέφους. ἰοὺ ἰού·
οὐδ' ἰδεῖν ἔτ' ἔσθ' ὑπ' αὐτῶν πετομένων τὴν
εἴσοδον.

ΠΕΙΣΕΤΑΙΡΟΣ

οὑτοσὶ πέρδιξ.

ΕΥΕΛΠΙΔΗΣ

ἐκεινοσὶ δὲ νὴ Δί' ἀτταγᾶς.

ΠΕΙΣΕΤΑΙΡΟΣ

οὑτοσὶ δὲ πηνέλοψ.

ΕΥΕΛΠΙΔΗΣ

ἐκεινηὶ δέ γ' ἀλκυών.

ΠΕΙΣΕΤΑΙΡΟΣ

τίς γάρ ἐσθ' οὔπισθεν αὐτῆς;

ΕΥΕΛΠΙΔΗΣ

ὅστις ἐστί; κηρύλος.

PEISETAERUS

(to Tereus) But tell me, what's the point of the birds' cresting? Perhaps they've come to march in review?

TEREUS

On the contrary, my friend, they're like the Carians: they nest on crests for safety's sake.

PEISETAERUS

(looking toward the wings) Poseidon, will you look at that! What a hell of a mob of birds has gathered!

EUELPIDES

Lord Apollo, what a cloud of them! Whooee! They're so many you can't see into the wings anymore!

Enter the CHORUS, *each member costumed as a different bird.*

PEISETAERUS

That one's a partridge.

EUELPIDES

And that one's surely a francolin.

PEISETAERUS

And that one's a wigeon.

EUELPIDES

And that one's a halcyon.

PEISETAERUS

So what's that one behind her?

EUELPIDES

That one? A snippet.

ΠΕΙΣΕΤΑΙΡΟΣ

κειρύλος γάρ ἐστιν ὄρνις;

ΕΥΕΛΠΙΔΗΣ

οὐ γάρ ἐστι Σποργίλος;
χαὐτηί γε γλαῦξ.

ΠΕΙΣΕΤΑΙΡΟΣ

τί φῄς; τίς γλαῦκ᾿ Ἀθήναζ᾿ ἤγαγεν;

ΕΥΕΛΠΙΔΗΣ

κίττα, τρυγών, κορυδός, ἐλεᾶς, ὑποθυμίς, περιστερά,
νέρτος, ἱέραξ, φάττα, κόκκυξ, ἐρυθρόπους, κεβλήπυρις,
πορφυρίς, κερχνῄς, κολυμβίς, ἀμπελίς, φήνη, δρύοψ.

ΠΕΙΣΕΤΑΙΡΟΣ

ἰοὺ ἰού, τῶν ὀρνέων.
ἰοὺ ἰού, τῶν κοψίχων.
οἷα πιπίζουσι καὶ τρέχουσι διακεκραγότες.
ἆρ᾿ ἀπειλοῦσίν γε νῷν; οἴμοι, κεχήνασίν γέ τοι
καὶ βλέπουσιν εἰς σὲ κἀμέ.

ΕΥΕΛΠΙΔΗΣ

τοῦτο μὲν κἀμοὶ δοκεῖ.

ΧΟΡΟΣ

ποποποποποπο ποῦ μ᾿ ὃς ἐκάλεσε; τίνα τόπον ἄρα νέμεται;

PEISETAERUS

You mean there's a snip-it bird?

EUELPIDES

Isn't Sporgilus one?[25] And there's an owl.

PEISETAERUS

What? Who's brought an owl to Athens?[26]

EUELPIDES

Jay. Turtledove. Lark. Reed Warbler. Thyme finch. Rock Dove. Vulture. Hawk. Ring Dove. Cuckoo. Redshank. Red-head Shrike. Porphyrion. Kestrel. Dabchick. Bunting. Lammergeier. Woodpecker.

PEISETAERUS

Whooee, all the birds! Whooee, all the peckers! How they peep and run around, outscreeching one another! Say, can they be threatening us? Oh dear, they've certainly got their beaks open, and they're staring at you and me!

EUELPIDES

I think so too!

CHORUS

Whe-whe-whe-whe-whe-whe-where's the one who
called me? What
spot is he settled on?

[25] Sporgilus ("Sparrow") was a barber.
[26] Proverbial, like "coals to Newcastle."

ΤΗΡΕΥΣ

οὑτοσὶ πάλαι πάρειμι κοὐκ ἀποστατῶ φίλων.

ΧΟΡΟΣ

τιτιτιτιτιτι τίνα λόγον ἄρα ποτὲ
  πρὸς ἐμὲ φίλον ἔχων;

ΤΗΡΕΥΣ

κοινόν, ἀσφαλῆ, δίκαιον, ἡδύν, ὠφελήσιμον.
ἄνδρε γὰρ λεπτὼ λογιστὰ δεῦρ᾽ ἀφῖχθον ὡς ἐμέ.

ΧΟΡΟΣ

ποῦ; πᾷ; πῶς φῄς;

ΤΗΡΕΥΣ

φήμ᾽ ἀπ᾽ ἀνθρώπων ἀφῖχθαι δεῦρο πρεσβύτα δύο·
ἥκετον δ᾽ ἔχοντε πρέμνον πράγματος πελωρίου.

ΚΟΡΥΦΑΙΟΣ

ὦ μέγιστον ἐξαμαρτὼν ἐξ ὅτου ᾽τράφην ἐγώ,
πῶς λέγεις;

ΤΗΡΕΥΣ

μήπω φοβηθῇς τὸν λόγον.

ΚΟΡΥΦΑΙΟΣ

τί μ᾽ ἠργάσω;

ΤΗΡΕΥΣ

ἄνδρ᾽ ἐδεξάμην ἐραστὰ τῆσδε τῆς ξυνουσίας.

ΚΟΡΥΦΑΙΟΣ

καὶ δέδρακας τοῦτο τοὔργον;

TEREUS

Here I am ready and waiting, and not aloof from friends.

CHORUS

Wha-wha-wha-wha-wha-wha-what message then
have you got for your friends?

TEREUS

One that concerns our whole community, promotes our security, and is right, gratifying, and advantageous. You see, two men are here to visit me, a pair of subtle thinkers.

CHORUS

Where? How? What do you mean?

TEREUS

I'm telling you, a pair of old men are here from the human world, and they've come bearing the prop of a prodigious plan.

CHORUS LEADER

Ah, you've made the worst blunder since I was fledged! What are you telling us?

TEREUS

Don't be flustered about my news just yet.

CHORUS LEADER

What have you done to me?

TEREUS

I've received two men passionately enamored of our society.

CHORUS LEADER

You've actually done this?

ΤΗΡΕΥΣ

καὶ δεδρακώς γ' ἥδομαι.

ΚΟΡΥΦΑΙΟΣ

κἀστὸν ἤδη που παρ' ἡμῖν;

ΤΗΡΕΥΣ

εἰ παρ' ὑμῖν εἴμ' ἐγώ.

ΧΟΡΟΣ

(στρ) ἔα ἔα·
προδεδόμεθ' ἀνόσιά τ' ἐπάθομεν·
ὃς γὰρ φίλος ἦν ὁμότροφά θ' ἡμῖν
ἐνέμετο πεδία παρ' ἡμῖν,
παρέβη μὲν θεσμοὺς ἀρχαίους,
παρέβη δ' ὅρκους ὀρνίθων.
εἰς δὲ δόλον ἐκάλεσε,
παρέβαλέ τ' ἐμὲ παρὰ
γένος ἀνόσιον, ὅπερ
ἐξότ' ἐγένετ' ἐμοὶ
πολέμιον ἐτράφη.

ΚΟΡΥΦΑΙΟΣ

ἀλλὰ πρὸς μὲν τοῦτον ἡμῖν ἐστιν ὕστερος λόγος·
τὼ δὲ πρεσβύτα δοκεῖ μοι τώδε δοῦναι τὴν δίκην
διαφορηθῆναί θ' ὑφ' ἡμῶν.

ΠΕΙΣΕΤΑΙΡΟΣ

ὡς ἀπωλόμεσθ' ἄρα.

ΕΥΕΛΠΙΔΗΣ

αἴτιος μέντοι σὺ νῷν εἶ τῶν κακῶν τούτων μόνος.
ἐπὶ τί γάρ μ' ἐκεῖθεν ἦγες;

TEREUS

Yes, and I'm glad I did.

CHORUS LEADER

And they're already somewhere among us?

TEREUS

As sure as I'm among you.

CHORUS

Oo, oo!
We are betrayed, we are impiously defiled!
Yes, our former friend, who browsed with us
in the fields that feed us all,
has broken our ancient ordinances,
has broken our avian oaths.
He's lured me into a trap,
he's cast me out among
an unholy race, that
since its very creation
has been groomed to be my foe.

CHORUS LEADER

Well, him we'll settle accounts with later; as for these two codgers, I think they should give us satisfaction on the spot, by being dismembered.

PEISETAERUS

So we're goners.

EUELPIDES

This damned mess we're in is all your fault, you know! *(gesturing toward the spectators)* Why did you bring me here from back there?

ΠΕΙΣΕΤΑΙΡΟΣ

ἵν᾿ ἀκολουθοίης ἐμοί.

ΕΥΕΛΠΙΔΗΣ

ἵνα μὲν οὖν κλάοιμι μεγάλα.

ΠΕΙΣΕΤΑΙΡΟΣ

τοῦτο μὲν ληρεῖς ἔχων
κάρτα· πῶς κλαύσει γάρ, ἢν ἅπαξ γε τὠφθαλμὼ
᾿κκοπῇς;

ΧΟΡΟΣ

(ἀντ) ἰὼ ἰώ·
ἔπαγ᾿ ἔπιθ᾿ ἐπίφερε πολέμιον
ὁρμὰν φονίαν, πτέρυγά τε παντᾷ
ἐπίβαλε περί τε κύκλωσαι·
ὡς δεῖ τώδ᾿ οἰμώζειν ἄμφω
καὶ δοῦναι ῥύγχει φορβάν.
οὔτε γὰρ ὄρος σκιερὸν
οὔτε νέφος αἰθέριον
οὔτε πολιὸν πέλαγος
ἔστιν ὅ τι δέξεται
τώδ᾿ ἀποφυγόντε με.

ΚΟΡΥΦΑΙΟΣ

ἀλλὰ μὴ μέλλωμεν ἤδη τώδε τίλλειν καὶ δάκνειν.
ποῦ ᾿σθ᾿ ὁ ταξίαρχος; ἐπαγέτω τὸ δεξιὸν κέρας.

ΕΥΕΛΠΙΔΗΣ

τοῦτ᾿ ἐκεῖνο. ποῖ φύγω δύστηνος;

346 ἐπίβαλε] περίβαλε Reisig

PEISETAERUS

To keep me company.

EUELPIDES

To make me cry bitter tears is more like it.

PEISETAERUS

Now you're making no sense at all; how do you expect to cry once you've had your eyes pecked out?

CHORUS

Hi ho!
Forward march, launch a hostile
bloody charge, from all sides
put wings to them and surround them!
For both these two must howl
and furnish fodder for my beak.
For there's no dusky mountain,
no lofty cloud,
no leaden sea
to receive this pair
in flight from me.

CHORUS LEADER

Now without further ado let's pluck and peck these two. Where's the lieutenant? Have him bring up the right wing.

EUELPIDES

This is it! Poor goner, where can I hide?

ΠΕΙΣΕΤΑΙΡΟΣ

οὗτος, οὐ μενεῖς;

ΕΥΕΛΠΙΔΗΣ

ἵν' ὑπὸ τούτων διαφορηθῶ;

ΠΕΙΣΕΤΑΙΡΟΣ

πῶς γὰρ ἂν τούτους δοκεῖς
ἐκφυγεῖν;

ΕΥΕΛΠΙΔΗΣ

οὐκ οἶδ' ὅπως ἄν.

ΠΕΙΣΕΤΑΙΡΟΣ

ἀλλ' ἐγώ τοί σοι λέγω,
ὅτι μένοντε δεῖ μάχεσθαι λαμβάνειν τε τῶν χυτρῶν.

ΕΥΕΛΠΙΔΗΣ

τί δὲ χύτρα νώ γ' ὠφελήσει;

ΠΕΙΣΕΤΑΙΡΟΣ

γλαῦξ μὲν οὐ πρόσεισι νῷν.

ΕΥΕΛΠΙΔΗΣ

τοῖς δὲ γαμψώνυξι τοισδί;

ΠΕΙΣΕΤΑΙΡΟΣ

τὸν ὀβελίσκον ἁρπάσας
εἶτα κατάπηξον πρὸ σαυτοῦ.

ΕΥΕΛΠΙΔΗΣ

τοῖσι δ' ὀφθαλμοῖσι τί;

ΠΕΙΣΕΤΑΙΡΟΣ

ὀξύβαφον ἐντευθενὶ προθοῦ λαβὼν ἢ τρύβλιον.

PEISETAERUS

Hold your ground there!

EUELPIDES

And let them dismember me?

PEISETAERUS

But how do you expect to get away?

EUELPIDES

I've no idea.

PEISETAERUS

Well, I'll tell you what we should do: stand and fight, *(indicating the luggage)* and take up some of those kettles!

EUELPIDES

What good will a kettle do us?

PEISETAERUS

It'll keep the owls off us.

EUELPIDES

But what about those with the hooked talons there?

PEISETAERUS

Grab a skewer and plant it in front of you.

EUELPIDES

What about our eyes?

PEISETAERUS

Take out a saucer and shield them, or a bowl.

ΕΥΕΛΠΙΔΗΣ

ὦ σοφώτατ᾿, εὖ γ᾿ ἀνηῦρες αὐτὸ καὶ στρατηγικῶς·
ὑπερακοντίζεις σύ γ᾿ ἤδη Νικίαν ταῖς μηχαναῖς.

ΚΟΡΥΦΑΙΟΣ

ἐλελελεῦ· χώρει, κάθες τὸ ῥύγχος· οὐ μέλλειν ἐχρῆν.
ἕλκε, τίλλε, παῖε, δεῖρε· κόπτε πρώτην τὴν χύτραν.

ΤΗΡΕΥΣ

εἰπέ μοι, τί μέλλετ᾿, ὦ πάντων κάκιστα θηρίων,
ἀπολέσαι παθόντες οὐδὲν ἄνδρε καὶ διασπάσαι
τῆς ἐμῆς γυναικὸς ὄντε ξυγγενεῖ καὶ φυλέτα;

ΚΟΡΥΦΑΙΟΣ

φεισόμεσθα γάρ τι τῶνδε μᾶλλον ἡμεῖς ἢ λύκων;
ἢ τίνας τεισαίμεθ᾿ ἄλλους τῶνδ᾿ ἂν ἐχθίους ἔτι;

ΤΗΡΕΥΣ

εἰ δὲ τὴν φύσιν μὲν ἐχθροί, τὸν δὲ νοῦν εἰσιν φίλοι,
καὶ διδάξοντές τι δεῦρ᾿ ἥκουσιν ὑμᾶς χρήσιμον;

ΚΟΡΥΦΑΙΟΣ

πῶς δ᾿ ἂν οἵδ᾿ ἡμᾶς τι χρήσιμον διδάξειάν ποτε
ἢ φράσειαν, ὄντες ἐχθροὶ τοῖσι πάπποις τοῖς ἐμοῖς;

ΤΗΡΕΥΣ

ἀλλ᾿ ἀπ᾿ ἐχθρῶν δῆτα πολλὰ μανθάνουσιν οἱ σοφοί.
ἡ γὰρ εὐλάβεια σῴζει πάντα. παρὰ μὲν οὖν φίλου

EUELPIDES

Brilliant! A fine piece of improvisation and generalship. In clever stratagems you've already outstripped Nicias![27]

CHORUS LEADER

Eleleleu! Move out, level your beaks, no hanging back! Drag them, pluck them, hit them, flay them! First knock out the kettle!

TEREUS

(interposing himself) Say, you scurviest of all creatures, why do you aim to destroy and mutilate two men who've done you no harm, who are my wife's kinsmen and fellow tribesmen?

CHORUS LEADER

You mean we should show these men any more mercy than wolves? What enemies could we take revenge on more hateful than these?

TEREUS

But suppose they're enemies by nature, yet friends by intention, and they've come here to give you some beneficial instruction?

CHORUS LEADER

How could these men ever give us any beneficial instruction or advice? They were enemies of our very forefeathers.

TEREUS

Yet the wise can learn much from enemies. Caution does save the day—a lesson you can't learn from a friend, but

[27] Probably a reference to the victory at Syracuse the previous autumn, Thucydides 6.63–71.

οὐ μάθοις ἂν τοῦθ᾽, ὁ δ᾽ ἐχθρὸς εὐθὺς ἐξηνάγκασεν.
αὐτίχ᾽ αἱ πόλεις παρ᾽ ἀνδρῶν ἔμαθον ἐχθρῶν κοὐ φίλων
ἐκπονεῖν θ᾽ ὑψηλὰ τείχη ναῦς τε κεκτῆσθαι μακράς·
τὸ δὲ μάθημα τοῦτο σῴζει παῖδας, οἶκον, χρήματα.

ΚΟΡΥΦΑΙΟΣ

ἔστι μὲν λόγων ἀκοῦσαι πρῶτον, ὡς ἡμῖν δοκεῖ.
χρήσιμον μάθοι γὰρ ἄν τι κἀπὸ τῶν ἐχθρῶν σοφός.

ΠΕΙΣΕΤΑΙΡΟΣ

οἵδε τῆς ὀργῆς χαλᾶν εἴξασιν. ἄναγ᾽ ἐπὶ σκέλος.

ΤΗΡΕΥΣ

καὶ δίκαιόν γ᾽ ἐστὶ κἀμοὶ δεῖ νέμειν ὑμᾶς χάριν.

ΚΟΡΥΦΑΙΟΣ

ἀλλὰ μὴν οὐδ᾽ ἄλλο σοί πω πρᾶγμ᾽ ἐνηντιώμεθα.

ΕΥΕΛΠΙΔΗΣ

μᾶλλον εἰρήνην ἄγουσιν.

ΠΕΙΣΕΤΑΙΡΟΣ

νὴ Δί᾽, ὥστε τὴν χύτραν
τώ τε τρυβλίω καθίει·
καὶ τὸ δόρυ χρή, τὸν ὀβελίσκον,
περιπατεῖν ἔχοντας ἡμᾶς
τῶν ὅπλων ἐντός, παρ᾽ αὐτὴν
τὴν χύτραν ἄκραν ὁρῶντας
ἐγγύς· ὡς οὐ φευκτέον νῷν.

382 σοφός Hamaker: σοφόν Π2 a

the first lesson an enemy imposes. For instance, it was from enemies, not friends, that cities learned to build lofty walls and master warships, and that lesson safeguards children, household, and property.

CHORUS LEADER

Well, in our opinion it's possible to hear them out first; a wise person can in fact learn something beneficial even from his enemies.

PEISETAERUS

They look to be slackening their anger. Fall back by steps.

TEREUS

(to the Chorus) It's also the right thing to do, and besides, you should cultivate my good graces.

CHORUS LEADER

Well, we've surely never opposed you in any past dealings.

EUELPIDES

They're acting more peaceable.

PEISETAERUS

Indeed they are. So lower the kettle
and the two bowls;
and we should shoulder the spear—
I mean the skewer—and walk patrol
inside our encampment, looking along
the very rim of the kettle,
close in, since we mustn't run away.

ΕΥΕΛΠΙΔΗΣ

ἐτεόν, ἢν δ᾽ ἄρ᾽ ἀποθάνωμεν,
κατορυχησόμεσθα ποῦ γῆς;

ΠΕΙΣΕΤΑΙΡΟΣ

ὁ Κεραμεικὸς δέξεται νώ.
δημοσίᾳ γὰρ ἵνα ταφῶμεν,
φήσομεν πρὸς τοὺς στρατηγοὺς
μαχομένω τοῖς πολεμίοισιν
ἀποθανεῖν ἐν Ὀρνεαῖς.

ΚΟΡΥΦΑΙΟΣ

ἄναγ᾽ εἰς τάξιν πάλιν εἰς ταὐτόν,
καὶ τὸν θυμὸν κατάθου κύψας
παρὰ τὴν ὀργὴν ὥσπερ ὁπλίτης·
κἀναπυθώμεθα τούσδε τίνες ποτὲ
καὶ πόθεν ἔμολον τίνι τ᾽ ἐπινοίᾳ.
ἰώ, ἔποψ, σέ τοι καλῶ.

ΤΗΡΕΥΣ

καλεῖς δὲ τοῦ κλύειν θέλων;

ΚΟΡΥΦΑΙΟΣ

τίνες ποθ᾽ οἵδε καὶ πόθεν;

ΤΗΡΕΥΣ

ξένω σοφῆς ἀφ᾽ Ἑλλάδος.

---

[28] The Cerameicus, the potters' quarter where military funerals were held; cf. Thucydides 2.34.

EUELPIDES

But tell me, if we do get killed,
where on earth will we be buried?

PEISETAERUS

Potter's Field will take us.[28]
You see, we'll get a state funeral
by telling the generals
that we died fighting the enemy
at Finchburg.[29]

CHORUS LEADER

(to the Chorus)

Re-form ranks as before,
lean over and ground your temper
alongside your anger, like infantrymen;
and let's find out who these men may be,
where they've come from,
and with what in mind.
Hey there, Hoopoe, I'm calling on you!

TEREUS

And what is your wish in calling?

CHORUS LEADER

Who may these men be, and whence?

TEREUS

Two strangers from clever Greece.

[29] In the previous year an Athenian contingent had assisted in the siege of Orneae (~ *orneon* "bird"), a town in the Argolid, but its defenders slipped away and there was no battle; cf. Thucydides 6.7.

ΚΟΡΥΦΑΙΟΣ

τύχη δὲ ποία κομί-
ζει ποτ᾽ αὐτὼ πρὸς ὄρ-
νιθας ἐλθεῖν;

ΤΗΡΕΥΣ

ἔρως
βίου διαίτης τέ σου
καὶ ξυνοικεῖν τέ σοι
καὶ ξυνεῖναι τὸ πᾶν.

ΚΟΡΥΦΑΙΟΣ

τί φῄς;
λέγει δὲ δὴ τίνας λόγους;

ΤΗΡΕΥΣ

ἄπιστα καὶ πέρα κλύειν.

ΚΟΡΥΦΑΙΟΣ

ὁρᾷ τι κέρδος ἐνθάδ᾽ ἄξιον μονῆς,
ὅτῳ πέποιθ᾽ ἐμοὶ ξυνὼν
κρατεῖν ἂν ἢ τὸν ἐχθρὸν ἢ
φίλοισιν ὠφελεῖν ἔχειν;

ΤΗΡΕΥΣ

λέγει μέγαν τιν᾽ ὄλβον, οὔτε λεκτὸν οὔ-
τε πιστόν· ὡς σὰ πάντα καὶ
τὸ τῇδε καὶ τὸ κεῖσε καὶ
τὸ δεῦρο προσβιβᾷ λέγων.

ΚΟΡΥΦΑΙΟΣ

πότερα μαινόμενος;

CHORUS LEADER

And what chance
can have brought them
on a journey to the birds?

TEREUS

A passionate desire
for your way of life,
to share your home
and be with you completely!

CHORUS LEADER

What do you mean?
And what tales is he telling?

TEREUS

Incredible and beyond belief.

CHORUS LEADER

Does he see a way to cash in on his visit,
convinced that being with me
he'll overpower his enemy
or be able to help his friends?

TEREUS

He promises great prosperity, ineffable
and incredible, for he makes a convincing case
that you can have it all, what's here,
and there, and everywhere.

CHORUS LEADER

Is he insane?

---

415 λέγει Dindorf: λέγουσι a

ΤΗΡΕΥΣ

ἄφατον ὡς φρόνιμος.

ΚΟΡΥΦΑΙΟΣ

ἔνι σοφόν τι φρενί;

ΤΗΡΕΥΣ

πυκνότατον κίναδος,
σόφισμα, κύρμα, τρῖμμα, παιπάλημ᾽ ὅλον.

ΚΟΡΥΦΑΙΟΣ

λέγειν λέγειν κέλευέ μοι.
κλύων γὰρ ὧν σύ μοι λέγεις
λόγων ἀνεπτέρωμαι.

ΤΗΡΕΥΣ

ἄγε δὴ σὺ καὶ σὺ τὴν πανοπλίαν μὲν πάλιν
ταύτην λαβόντε κρεμάσατον τὐγἀγαθῇ
εἰς τὸν ἱπνὸν εἴσω πλησίον τοὐπιστάτου·
σὺ δὲ τούσδ᾽ ἐφ᾽ οἷσπερ τοῖς λόγοις ξυνέλεξ᾽ ἐγὼ
φράσον, δίδαξον.

ΠΕΙΣΕΤΑΙΡΟΣ

μὰ τὸν Ἀπόλλω ᾽γὼ μὲν οὔ,
ἢν μὴ διάθωνταί γ᾽ οἵδε διαθήκην ἐμοὶ
ἥνπερ ὁ πίθηκος τῇ γυναικὶ διέθετο,
ὁ μαχαιροποιός, μήτε δάκνειν τούτους ἐμὲ
μήτ᾽ ὀρχίπεδ᾽ ἕλκειν μήτ᾽ ὀρύττειν—

ΕΥΕΛΠΙΔΗΣ

οὔ τί που
τὸν—

TEREUS

Oh, how unutterably sane!

CHORUS LEADER

There's wisdom in his heart?

TEREUS

He's the craftiest fox,
all cleverness, a go-getter, a smoothie, the crème de la craft!

CHORUS LEADER

Tell him to speak, to speak!
For as I listen to the tale you tell
I'm all aflutter.

TEREUS

(to his Slaves) All right then, you and you take my panoply back inside and hang it in the kitchen—knock on wood—by the trivet. *(to Peisetaerus)* And you inform and brief these birds about the proposals I summoned them to hear.

PEISETAERUS

I'll do nothing of the kind, not unless they promise me the same deal as the monkey made with his woman, you know, the knifemaker:[30] that they're not to bite me or yank my balls or poke me in the—

EUELPIDES

You can't mean the—

[30] The various guesses in the scholia show that not even ancient scholars could explain this allusion.

ΠΕΙΣΕΤΑΙΡΟΣ

οὐδαμῶς. οὔκ, ἀλλὰ τὠφθαλμὼ λέγω.

ΚΟΡΥΦΑΙΟΣ

διατίθεμαι 'γώ.

ΠΕΙΣΕΤΑΙΡΟΣ

κατόμοσόν νυν ταῦτά μοι.

ΚΟΡΥΦΑΙΟΣ

ὄμνυμ' ἐπὶ τούτοις, πᾶσι νικᾶν τοῖς κριταῖς
καὶ τοῖς θεαταῖς πᾶσιν,

ΠΕΙΣΕΤΑΙΡΟΣ

ἔσται ταυταγί.

ΚΟΡΥΦΑΙΟΣ

εἰ δὲ παραβαίην, ἑνὶ κριτῇ νικᾶν μόνον.

ΠΕΙΣΕΤΑΙΡΟΣ

ἀκούετε λεῴ· τοὺς ὁπλίτας νυνμενὶ
ἀνελομένους θὤπλ' ἀπιέναι πάλιν οἴκαδε,
σκοπεῖν δ' ὅ τι ἂν προγράφωμεν ἐν τοῖς πινακίοις.

ΧΟΡΟΣ

(στρ) δολερὸν μὲν ἀεὶ κατὰ πάντα δὴ τρόπον
πέφυκεν ἄνθρωπος· σὺ δ' ὅμως λέγε μοι. τάχα γὰρ
τύχοις ἂν χρηστὸν ἐξειπὼν ὅ τι μοι παρορᾷς
ἢ δύναμίν τινα μείζω
παραλειπομένην ὑπ' ἐμῆς φρενὸς ἀξυνέτου·
σὺ δὲ τοῦθ' οὑρᾷς λέγ' εἰς κοινόν.
ὃ γὰρ ἂν σὺ τύχῃς μοι
ἀγαθὸν πορίσας, τοῦτο κοινὸν ἔσται.

PEISETAERUS

No, not at all; the eyes, I was going to say.

CHORUS LEADER

I promise.

PEISETAERUS

Then swear to it.

CHORUS LEADER

Here's my oath: to be victorious by unanimous vote of the judges and the spectators—

PEISETAERUS

That you shall be!

CHORUS LEADER

but if I break my oath, to win by only one vote.

PEISETAERUS

Now hear this: the infantry may retrieve their arms and go back home, but should keep an eye on the boards for any notices we may post.

They give their "armor" to Xanthias and Manodorus, who take it inside, then return.

CHORUS

A treacherous thing always in every way
is human nature. But do make your case, for perhaps
you may divulge a good quality that you see in me
or some greater potential
overlooked by my witless mind.
Explain to us all this perception of yours,
for whatever advantage you may provide me
will be an advantage for us all.

ΚΟΡΥΦΑΙΟΣ

ἀλλ' ἐφ' ὅτῳπερ πράγματι τὴν σὴν ἥκεις γνώμην ἀναπείσων,
λέγε θαρρήσας· ὡς τὰς σπονδὰς οὐ μὴ πρότερον παραβῶμεν.

ΠΕΙΣΕΤΑΙΡΟΣ

καὶ μὴν ὀργῶ νὴ τὸν Δία καὶ προπεφύραται λόγος εἷς μοι,
ὃν διαμάττειν κωλύει οὐδέν. φέρε, παῖ, στέφανον· καταχεῖσθαι
κατὰ χειρὸς ὕδωρ φερέτω ταχύ τις.

ΕΥΕΛΠΙΔΗΣ

δειπνήσειν μέλλομεν; ἢ τί;

ΠΕΙΣΕΤΑΙΡΟΣ

μὰ Δί' ἀλλὰ λέγειν ζητῶ τι πάλαι, μέγα καὶ λαρινὸν ἔπος τι,
ὅ τι τὴν τούτων θραύσει ψυχήν. οὕτως ὑμῶν ὑπεραλγῶ,
οἵτινες ὄντες πρότερον βασιλῆς—

ΚΟΡΥΦΑΙΟΣ

ἡμεῖς βασιλῆς; τίνος;

ΠΕΙΣΕΤΑΙΡΟΣ

ὑμεῖς
πάντων ὁπόσ' ἔστιν, ἐμοῦ πρῶτον, τουδί, καὶ τοῦ Διὸς αὐτοῦ,

CHORUS LEADER

Now then, about this idea of yours that you've come to sell us: explain what kind of business it is, and never fear, we won't break the truce before you've had your say.

PEISETAERUS

Well, I'm positively bursting to tell you, and I've got a special speech all whipped up, so nothing's stopping me from kneading it right into cake. *(to the Slaves)* Bring me a garland, boy, and one of you fetch water to pour over my hands, right away.

EUELPIDES

Are we getting ready for dinner, or what?

PEISETAERUS

No no, it's just that for quite some time I've been trying to put something into words, a big juicy utterance that will shatter these birds to the very soul. *(to the birds)* So sorrowful am I on your account, who once were kings—

CHORUS LEADER

Us kings? Of what?

PEISETAERUS

Yes you, kings of all that exists—starting with yours truly and including Zeus himself—and born a long time before

---

461 πρότερον Π2 a: πρότεροι Hermann

ἀρχαιότεροι πρότεροί τε Κρόνου καὶ Τιτάνων ἐγένεσθε
καὶ Γῆς.

ΚΟΡΥΦΑΙΟΣ

καὶ Γῆς;

ΠΕΙΣΕΤΑΙΡΟΣ

νὴ τὸν Ἀπόλλω.

ΚΟΡΥΦΑΙΟΣ

τουτὶ μὰ Δί᾽ οὐκ ἐπεπύσμην.

ΠΕΙΣΕΤΑΙΡΟΣ

ἀμαθὴς γὰρ ἔφυς κοὐ πολυπράγμων, οὐδ᾽ Αἴσωπον πεπάτηκας,
ὃς ἔφασκε λέγων κορυδὸν πάντων πρώτην ὄρνιθα γενέσθαι,
προτέραν τῆς γῆς, κἄπειτα νόσῳ τὸν πατέρ᾽ αὐτῆς ἀποθνῄσκειν·
γῆν δ᾽ οὐκ εἶναι, τὸν δὲ προκεῖσθαι πεμπταῖον· τὴν δ᾽ ἀποροῦσαν
ὑπ᾽ ἀμηχανίας τὸν πατέρ᾽ αὐτῆς ἐν τῇ κεφαλῇ κατορύξαι.

ΕΥΕΛΠΙΔΗΣ

ὁ πατὴρ ἄρα τῆς κορυδοῦ νυνὶ κεῖται τεθνεὼς Κεφαλῆσιν.

ΠΕΙΣΕΤΑΙΡΟΣ

οὔκουν δῆτ᾽ εἰ πρότεροι μὲν γῆς, πρότεροι δὲ θεῶν ἐγένοντο,

Cronus, and the Titans, and even Earth.[31]

CHORUS LEADER

Even Earth?

PEISETAERUS

I swear by Apollo.

CHORUS LEADER

I certainly never heard that.

PEISETAERUS

That's because you're naturally ignorant and uninquisitive, and you haven't thumbed your Aesop.[32] He says in his fable that the Lark was the first of all birds to be born, before Earth; and then her father died of a disease, but there being no earth, he'd lain out for four days[33] and she was at a loss what to do, until in desperation she buried her father in her own head.

EUELPIDES

So that's why to this day the Lark's father lies dead in the Head.[34]

PEISETAERUS

So if they were born before Earth and before the gods,

[31] For the standard divine succession myth see Hesiod, *Theogony* 133–210.

[32] The legendary animal fabulist, thought to have lived in early sixth-century Samos.

[33] In Athens the "laying out" was held the day after death, and burial followed the next morning.

[34] The deme Cephale ("Head") was the site of a large cemetery. There is perhaps another reference to Philocles the Lark (281 n.), since a Philocles of Cephale is attested in the fourth century (*PA* 14546).

ὡς πρεσβυτάτων ὄντων αὐτῶν ὀρθῶς ἐσθ' ἡ βασιλεία;

ΚΟΡΥΦΑΙΟΣ

νὴ τὸν Ἀπόλλω.

ΕΥΕΛΠΙΔΗΣ

πάνυ τοίνυν χρὴ ῥύγχος βόσκειν σε τὸ λοιπόν·
οὐκ ἀποδώσει ταχέως ὁ Ζεὺς τὸ σκῆπτρον τῷ δρυκολάπτῃ.

ΠΕΙΣΕΤΑΙΡΟΣ

ὡς δ' οὐχὶ θεοὶ τοίνυν ἦρχον τῶν ἀνθρώπων τὸ παλαιόν,
ἀλλ' ὄρνιθες, κἀβασίλευον, πόλλ' ἐστὶ τεκμήρια τούτων.
αὐτίκα δ' ὑμῖν πρῶτ' ἐπιδείξω τὸν ἀλεκτρυόν', ὡς ἐτυράννει
ἦρχέ τε Περσῶν πρῶτος πάντων, Δαρείων καὶ Μεγαβάζων,
ὥστε καλεῖται Περσικὸς ὄρνις ἀπὸ τῆς ἀρχῆς ἔτ' ἐκείνης.

ΕΥΕΛΠΙΔΗΣ

διὰ ταῦτ' ἄρ' ἔχων καὶ νῦν ὥσπερ βασιλεὺς ὁ μέγας διαβάσκει
ἐπὶ τῆς κεφαλῆς τὴν κυρβασίαν τῶν ὀρνίθων μόνος ὀρθήν.

ΠΕΙΣΕΤΑΙΡΟΣ

οὕτω δ' ἴσχυέ τε καὶ μέγας ἦν τότε καὶ πολύς, ὥστ' ἔτι καὶ νῦν

doesn't it follow that the kingship is rightfully theirs by primogeniture?

CHORUS LEADER

I swear by Apollo.

EUELPIDES

Then from now on you should make a point of growing a beak—Zeus won't be quick to return his sceptre to the woodpecker!

PEISETAERUS

Now then, in olden days it wasn't gods who ruled mankind and were kings, but birds, and I can prove this with arguments galore. For example, I'll start by showing you that the cock first ruled and reigned over the Persians, before all those Dariuses and Megabazuses,[35] and that's why he's still called the Persian Bird, in memory of that reign.

EUELPIDES

So that's why to this day he struts about like the Great King, the only bird who gets to wear his hat cocked!

PEISETAERUS

Such was his authority, so great and mighty was he then,

[35] Darius I reigned 522–486 and was repulsed by the Athenians at Marathon in 490; Megabazus (in Greek the name suggests "big-talker") was a commander during his reign.

---

480 οὐκ] ὡς Bentley

ὑπὸ τῆς ῥώμης τῆς τότ᾽ ἐκείνης, ὁπόταν μόνον ὄρθριον ᾄσῃ,
ἀναπηδῶσιν πάντες ἐπ᾽ ἔργον, χαλκῆς, κεραμῆς, σκυλοδέψαι,
σκυτῆς, βαλανῆς, ἀλφιταμοιβοί, τορνευτολυρασπιδοπηγοί·
οἱ δὲ βαδίζουσ᾽ ὑποδησάμενοι νύκτωρ—

ΕΥΕΛΠΙΔΗΣ

ἐμὲ τοῦτό γ᾽ ἐρώτα.
χλαῖναν γὰρ ἀπώλεσ᾽ ὁ μοχθηρὸς Φρυγίων ἐρίων διὰ τοῦτον.
εἰς δεκάτην γάρ ποτε παιδαρίου κληθεὶς ὑπέπινον ἐν ἄστει,
κἄρτι καθηῦδον· καὶ πρὶν δειπνεῖν τοὺς ἄλλους οὗτος ἄρ᾽ ᾖσεν·
κἀγὼ νομίσας ὄρθρον ἐχώρουν Ἁλιμουντάδε, κἄρτι προκύπτω
ἔξω τείχους, καὶ λωποδύτης παίει ῥοπάλῳ με τὸ νῶτον·
κἀγὼ πίπτω μέλλω τε βοᾶν, ὁ δ᾽ ἀπέβλισε θοἰμάτιόν μου.

ΠΕΙΣΕΤΑΙΡΟΣ

ἰκτῖνος δ᾽ οὖν τῶν Ἑλλήνων ἦρχεν τότε κἀβασίλευεν.

ΚΟΡΥΦΑΙΟΣ

τῶν Ἑλλήνων;

that even to this day, as a result of that long-ago power, he has only to sing reveille and everyone jumps up to work, smiths, potters, tanners, cobblers, bathmen, grain traders, the whole carpentering, lyre-pegging, shield-fastening lot. In the dark men put on their shoes and set forth—

EUELPIDES

I'll vouch for that! I, poor bastard, lost a cloak of Phrygian wool, thanks to him. I'd been invited to the city for a child's naming day, and had a bit to drink, and had just fallen asleep when right before dinner that bird up and crowed. I thought it was morning and set off for Halimus. And no sooner do I pop outside the city walls than a mugger clouts me from behind with a club. I fall down, and I'm getting ready to shout for help, but he's already extracted my coat!

PEISETAERUS

To resume: back then the kite was the ruler and king over the Greeks.

CHORUS LEADER

Over the Greeks?

ΠΕΙΣΕΤΑΙΡΟΣ

καὶ κατέδειξέν γ' οὗτος πρῶτος βασιλεύων
προκυλινδεῖσθαι τοῖς ἰκτίνοις.

ΕΥΕΛΠΙΔΗΣ

νὴ τὸν Διόνυσον, ἐγὼ γοῦν
ἐκυλινδούμην ἰκτῖνον ἰδών· κᾆθ' ὕπτιος ὢν ἀναχάσκων
ὀβολὸν κατεβρόχθισα· κᾆτα κενὸν τὸν θύλακον οἴκαδ' ἀφεῖλκον.

ΠΕΙΣΕΤΑΙΡΟΣ

Αἰγύπτου δ' αὖ καὶ Φοινίκης πάσης κόκκυξ βασιλεὺς ἦν·
χὠπόθ' ὁ κόκκυξ εἴποι κόκκυ, τότ' ἂν οἱ Φοίνικες ἅπαντες
τοὺς πυροὺς ἂν καὶ τὰς κριθὰς ἐν τοῖς πεδίοις ἐθέριζον.

ΕΥΕΛΠΙΔΗΣ

τοῦτ' ἄρ' ἐκεῖν' ἦν τοὔπος ἀληθῶς· κόκκυ, ψωλοὶ πεδίονδε.

ΠΕΙΣΕΤΑΙΡΟΣ

ἦρχον δ' οὕτω σφόδρα τὴν ἀρχήν, ὥστ' εἴ τις καὶ βασιλεύοι
ἐν ταῖς πόλεσιν τῶν Ἑλλήνων Ἀγαμέμνων ἢ Μενέλαος,
ἐπὶ τῶν σκήπτρων ἐκάθητ' ὄρνις μετέχων ὅ τι δωροδοκοίη.

PEISETAERUS

That's right, and as king he instituted the custom of rolling on the ground before kites.[36]

EUELPIDES

So help me Dionysus, I rolled when I saw a kite, and when I was on my back with my mouth open I swallowed an obol,[37] so I had to lug my sack home empty.

PEISETAERUS

And furthermore, the cuckoo was king of all Egypt and Phoenicia; and whenever the cuckoo said "cuckoo," all the Phoenicians would start reaping the wheat and barley in their fields.

EUELPIDES

So that's the real meaning of the saying, "Cuckoo! Knobs out and up country!"[38]

PEISETAERUS

And so dominant was their dominion that in the Greek cities if some Agamemnon or Menelaus ever *was* king, a bird would be perched on his sceptre, getting a share of any presents he received.

36 At their first appearance each year, as being harbingers of spring.

37 Lacking pockets, Athenians carried small coins in their mouths.

38 Perhaps a reveille call meaning "arise and prepare to march"; "knobs" translates *psoloi*, a word referring to men with *glandes penis* ("knobs") exposed: in the case of Greeks, by erection, of barbarians, by circumcision.

ΕΥΕΛΠΙΔΗΣ

τουτὶ τοίνυν οὐκ ᾔδη ᾿γώ· καὶ δῆτά μ᾽ ἐλάμβανε θαῦμα,
ὁπότ᾽ ἐξέλθοι Πρίαμός τις ἔχων ὄρνιν ἐν τοῖσι τραγῳδοῖς,
ὁ δ᾽ ἄρ᾽ εἱστήκει τὸν Λυσικράτη τηρῶν ὅ τι δωροδοκοίη.

ΠΕΙΣΕΤΑΙΡΟΣ

ὃ δὲ δεινότατόν <γ᾽> ἐστὶν ἁπάντων, ὁ Ζεὺς γὰρ ὁ νῦν βασιλεύων
αἰετὸν ὄρνιν ἕστηκεν ἔχων ἐπὶ τῆς κεφαλῆς βασιλεὺς ὤν,
ἡ δ᾽ αὖ θυγάτηρ γλαῦχ᾽, ὁ δ᾽ Ἀπόλλων ὡς θεράπων ὢν ἱέρακα.

ΚΟΡΥΦΑΙΟΣ

νὴ τὴν Δήμητρ᾽ εὖ ταῦτα λέγεις. τίνος οὕνεκα ταῦτ᾽ ἄρ᾽ ἔχουσιν;

ΠΕΙΣΕΤΑΙΡΟΣ

ἵν᾽ ὅταν θύων τις ἔπειτ᾽ αὐτοῖς εἰς τὴν χεῖρ᾽, ὡς νόμος ἐστίν,
τὰ σπλάγχνα διδῷ, τοῦ Διὸς αὐτοὶ πρότεροι τὰ σπλάγχνα λάβωσιν.
ὤμνυ τ᾽ οὐδεὶς τότ᾽ <ἂν> ἀνθρώπων θεόν, ἀλλ᾽ ὄρνιθας ἅπαντες.
Λάμπων δ᾽ ὄμνυσ᾽ ἔτι καὶ νυνὶ τὸν χῆν᾽, ὅταν ἐξαπατᾷ τι.

EUELPIDES

You know, that's something I never realized. I was always bewildered when in the tragedies someone like Priam came on with a bird, but of course it was perched there to take note of whatever presents Lysicrates[39] pocketed.

PEISETAERUS

But the most impressive proof of all is that Zeus, the current king, stands there with an eagle on his head as an emblem of his royalty, as does his daughter[40] with an owl, and Apollo, being a servant, with a hawk.

CHORUS LEADER

By Demeter, that's right—but why have they got them?

PEISETAERUS

So that when someone makes a sacrifice and puts the innards into the god's hand, as the custom goes, the birds themselves can grab the innards before Zeus can! And in those days not a soul would swear by a god; they all swore by birds. Even today Lampon[41] swears "by Goose" when

[39] Evidently an office holder or politician; the name is not uncommon.

[40] Athena.

[41] A distinguished authority on oracles and religious protocol, and prominent in public life since the 440s; ridiculed elsewhere in comedy for high living.

οὕτως ὑμᾶς πάντες πρότερον μεγάλους ἁγίους τʼ
  ἐνόμιζον,
  νῦν δʼ ἀνδράποδʼ, ἠλιθίους, Μανᾶς.
  ὥσπερ δʼ ἤδη τοὺς μαινομένους
  βάλλουσʼ ὑμᾶς· κἀν τοῖς ἱεροῖς
  πᾶς τις ἐφʼ ὑμῖν ὀρνιθευτὴς
  ἵστησι βρόχους, παγίδας, ῥάβδους,
  ἕρκη, νεφέλας, δίκτυα, πηκτάς·
  εἶτα λαβόντες πωλοῦσʼ ἁθρόους·
  οἱ δʼ ὠνοῦνται βλιμάζοντες·
  κοὐ μόνον, εἴπερ ταῦτα δοκεῖ δρᾶν,
  ὀπτησάμενοι παρέθενθʼ ὑμᾶς,
  ἀλλʼ ἐπικνῶσιν τυρόν, ἔλαιον,
  σίλφιον, ὄξος, καὶ τρίψαντες
  κατάχυσμʼ ἕτερον γλυκὺ καὶ λιπαρόν,
  κἄπειτα κατεσκέδασαν θερμὸν
  θερμῶν ὑμῶν
  αὐτῶν, ὥσπερ κενεβρείων.

ΧΟΡΟΣ

(ἀντ) πολὺ δὴ πολὺ δὴ χαλεπωτάτους λόγους
ἤνεγκας, ἄνθρωφʼ· ὡς ἐδάκρυσά γʼ ἐμῶν πατέρων
κάκην, οἳ τάσδε τὰς τιμὰς προγόνων παραδόν-
  των ἐπʼ ἐμοῦ κατέλυσαν.
σὺ δέ μοι κατὰ δαίμονα καί <τινα> συντυχίαν
ἀγαθὴν ἥκεις ἐμοὶ σωτήρ.
ἀναθεὶς γὰρ ἐγώ σοι
  τὰ νεόττια κἀμαυτὸν οἰκετεύσω.

he's up to something crooked. That's how high and holy everyone deemed you then; but now you're mere knaves, simpletons, tomfools! These days they pelt you like lunatics; and even in the temples every bird hunter's out to get you, setting nooses, snares, limed twigs, toils, meshes, nets, decoys in traps. And when they've caught you they sell you wholesale, and the customers feel you up. And if they do buy you, they're not content to have you roasted and served up; no, they grate on cheese, oil, silphium, vinegar, and they whip up a second sauce, sweet and shiny, and baste it on hot, when you're hot yourselves, like meat from carcasses!

CHORUS

Very harrowing, yes very, is the tale
you've brought us, human. It made me weep at my fathers'
baseness, who in my own time have wrecked these privileges of mine
that my forebears bequeathed to them.
But now you're here, by the grace of god or some happy chance,
to be my savior.
So shall I live, entrusting to you
my nestlings and myself.

---

523 δ' ἀνδράποδ', ἠλιθίους] δ' αὖ (cf. v. 611) Anon. in *Jenaische Allgem. Lit.-Zeitung* 1823 #30, col. 237

531 κοὐ μόνον Dunbar: κοὐδ' οὖν a

537 θερμῶν ὑμῶν Henderson: τοῦτο καθ' a

547 οἰκετεύσω Hermann: οἰκήσω (vel -κίσω) a: οἰκήσω δή t

ΚΟΡΥΦΑΙΟΣ

ἀλλ᾽ ὅ τι χρὴ δρᾶν, σὺ δίδασκε παρών· ὡς ζῆν οὐκ ἄξιον ἡμῖν,
εἰ μὴ κομιούμεθα παντὶ τρόπῳ τὴν ἡμετέραν βασιλείαν.

ΠΕΙΣΕΤΑΙΡΟΣ

καὶ δὴ τοίνυν πρῶτα διδάσκω μίαν ὀρνίθων πόλιν εἶναι,
κἄπειτα τὸν ἀέρα πάντα κύκλῳ καὶ πᾶν τουτὶ τὸ μεταξὺ
περιτειχίζειν μεγάλαις πλίνθοις ὀπταῖς ὥσπερ Βαβυλῶνα.

ΚΟΡΥΦΑΙΟΣ

ὦ Κεβριόνη καὶ Πορφυρίων, ὡς σμερδαλέον τὸ πόλισμα.

ΠΕΙΣΕΤΑΙΡΟΣ

κἀπειδὰν τοῦτ᾽ ἐπανεστήκῃ, τὴν ἀρχὴν τὸν Δί᾽ ἀπαιτεῖν·
κἂν μὲν μὴ φῇ μηδ᾽ ἐθελήσῃ μηδ᾽ εὐθὺς γνωσιμαχήσῃ,
ἱερὸν πόλεμον πρωυδᾶν αὐτῷ, καὶ τοῖσι θεοῖσιν ἀπειπεῖν
διὰ τῆς χώρας τῆς ὑμετέρας ἐστυκόσι μὴ διαφοιτᾶν,
ὥσπερ πρότερον μοιχεύσοντες τὰς Ἀλκμήνας κατέβαινον
καὶ τὰς Ἀλόπας καὶ τὰς Σεμέλας· ἤνπερ δ᾽ ἐπίωσ᾽, ἐπιβάλλειν

CHORUS LEADER

Now it's up to you to instruct us what we should do, because our life won't be worth living unless at all costs we recover our sovereignty.

PEISETAERUS

Very well then, my first instruction is this: make a single city of birds; then encircle the whole atmosphere, all the area between earth and sky, with a wall of big baked bricks, like Babylon.

CHORUS LEADER

Cebriones and Porphyrion,[42] what a redoubtable citadel!

PEISETAERUS

And when that's up and ready, reclaim your rulership from Zeus; and if he refuses, and isn't willing, and doesn't give up at once, declare a holy war against him, and deny the gods the right to travel through your territory with erections, the way they used to descend for adultery with their Alcmenes[43] and Alopes[44] and Semeles.[45] And if they do

[42] Two of the Giants, whose rebellion against the Olympian gods was crushed in the Plain of Phlegra (cf. 824–25); *porphyrion* was also the name of a bird.

[43] Alcmene, Amphitryon's wife, was mother by Zeus of Heracles.

[44] Alope, Cercyon's daughter, was mother by Poseidon of Hippothoon.

[45] Semele, Cadmus' daughter, was mother by Zeus of Dionysus.

---

553 Κεβριόνη Brunck: Κεβριόνα a

σφραγῖδ᾽ αὐτοῖς ἐπὶ τὴν ψωλήν, ἵνα μὴ βινῶσ᾽ ἔτ᾽ ἐκείνας.
τοῖς δ᾽ ἀνθρώποις ὄρνιν ἕτερον πέμψαι κήρυκα κελεύω,
ὡς ὀρνίθων βασιλευόντων θύειν ὄρνισι τὸ λοιπόν,
κἄπειτα θεοῖς ὕστερον αὖθις· προσνείμασθαι δὲ πρεπόντως
τοῖσι θεοῖσιν τῶν ὀρνίθων ὃς ἂν ἁρμόττῃ καθ᾽ ἕκαστον·
ἢν Ἀφροδίτῃ θύῃ, κριθὰς ὄρνιθι φαληρίδι θύειν·
ἢν δὲ Ποσειδῶνί τις οἶν θύῃ, νήττῃ πυροὺς καθαγίζειν·
ἢν δ᾽ Ἡρακλέει θύῃ τι, λάρῳ ναστοὺς θύειν μελιτοῦντας·
κἂν Διὶ θύῃ βασιλεῖ κριόν, βασιλεύς ἐστ᾽ ὀρχίλος ὄρνις,
ᾧ προτέρῳ δεῖ τοῦ Διὸς αὐτοῦ σέρφον ἐνόρχην σφαγιάζειν.

ΕΥΕΛΠΙΔΗΣ

ἥσθην σέρφῳ σφαγιαζομένῳ. βροντάτω νῦν ὁ μέγας Ζάν.

ΚΟΡΥΦΑΙΟΣ

καὶ πῶς ἡμᾶς νομιοῦσι θεοὺς ἄνθρωποι κοὐχὶ κολοιούς,
οἳ πετόμεσθα πτέρυγάς τ᾽ ἔχομεν;

ΠΕΙΣΕΤΑΙΡΟΣ

λῃρεῖς. καὶ νὴ Δί᾽ ὅ γ᾽ Ἑρμῆς

trespass, then clap a seal on their boners, so they can't fuck those women anymore. And I urge you to despatch another bird as a herald to mankind, announcing that, the birds being sovereign, they must henceforth sacrifice to the birds, and only afterwards to the gods; and that they must aptly assign to each of the gods the bird who's a fitting counterpart: if the sacrifice is to Aphrodite, sacrifice nuts to the phall-arope bird; if the sacrifice is a sheep to Poseidon, consecrate granola to the duck; if something's to be sacrificed to Heracles, sacrifice honeypies to the cormorant; and if it's a ram sacrifice to Zeus the King, the nuthatch is a king bird,[46] and it's to him, ahead of Zeus himself, that a gnat with intact nuts must be slaughtered.

EUELPIDES

I like that, slaughtering a gnat! So let the great Zan[47] thunder away!

CHORUS LEADER

But how are humans supposed to believe we're gods and not daws? We fly around and wear wings.

PEISETAERUS

That's nonsense! Why, Hermes certainly flies around and

[46] It is unclear what bird *orchilos* refers to (perhaps the wren), and why it was a "king" bird (perhaps a reference to the wren's gold crown or to Aesop's fable [Perry 434]); the translation preserves the pun on *orcheis* "testicles."

[47] A cultic form of Zeus' name.

πέτεται θεὸς ὢν πτέρυγάς τε φορεῖ, κἄλλοι γε θεοὶ πάνυ πολλοί.
αὐτίκα Νίκη πέτεται πτερύγοιν χρυσαῖν καὶ νὴ Δί᾽ Ἔρως γε·
Ἶριν δέ γ᾽ Ὅμηρος ἔφασκ᾽ ἰκέλην εἶναι τρήρωνι πελείῃ.

ΕΥΕΛΠΙΔΗΣ

ὁ Ζεὺς δ᾽ ἡμῖν οὐ βροντήσας πέμψει πτερόεντα κεραυνόν;

ΠΕΙΣΕΤΑΙΡΟΣ

ἢν δ᾽ οὖν ὑμᾶς μὲν ὑπ᾽ ἀγνοίας εἶναι νομίσωσι τὸ μηδέν,
τούτους δὲ θεοὺς τοὺς ἐν Ὀλύμπῳ; τότε χρὴ στρούθων νέφος ἀρθὲν
καὶ σπερμολόγων ἐκ τῶν ἀγρῶν τὸ σπέρμ᾽ αὐτῶν ἀνακάψαι·
κἄπειτ᾽ αὐτοῖς ἡ Δημήτηρ πυροὺς πεινῶσι μετρείτω.

ΕΥΕΛΠΙΔΗΣ

οὐκ ἐθελήσει μὰ Δί᾽, ἀλλ᾽ ὄψει προφάσεις αὐτὴν παρέχουσαν.

ΠΕΙΣΕΤΑΙΡΟΣ

οἱ δ᾽ αὖ κόρακες τῶν ζευγαρίων, οἷσιν τὴν γῆν καταροῦσιν,
καὶ τῶν προβάτων τοὺς ὀφθαλμοὺς ἐκκοψάντων ἐπὶ πείρᾳ·
εἶθ᾽ Ἀπόλλων ἰατρός <γ᾽> ὢν ἰάσθω· μισθοφορεῖ δέ.

sports wings, and he's a god, and so do a great many other gods; Victory, for example, flies on golden wings, and so does Cupid, and Homer pronounced Iris to be "like to a trembling dove."[48]

EUELPIDES

And won't Zeus thunder at us and hurl his "wingéd lightning bolt"?

PEISETAERUS

But if out of ignorance they still think that you're nothing and the Olympians are gods, then a cloud of sparrows and seed pickers must arise and gobble up their seed in the fields. When they're famished, let Demeter dole out grain to them!

EUELPIDES

She'll certainly renege; mark my words, she'll just make excuses.[49]

PEISETAERUS

And let the ravens peck out the eyes of the oxen harnessed to plough their land, and of their sheep, as a challenge. Then let Apollo the Healer heal them—and earn his fee!

48 *Homeric Hymn to Apollo* 114.

49 Like populist politicians, cf. *Knights* 1100–06, *Wasps* 715–18.

---

576 ΕΥ. Bentley: ΠΕΙΣ. PC: ʼΕΠ. cett. πέμψει] πέμπει Anon. Parisinus saec. MDII (v. ed. Dunbar, p. 51) et Tyrwhitt

ΕΥΕΛΠΙΔΗΣ

μή, πρίν γ᾽ ἂν ἐγὼ τὼ βοιδαρίω τὠμὼ πρώτιστ᾽ ἀποδῶμαι.

ΠΕΙΣΕΤΑΙΡΟΣ

ἢν δ᾽ ἡγῶνται σὲ θεόν, σὲ Ζῆνα, σὲ Γῆν, σὲ Κρόνον, σὲ Ποσειδῶ,
ἀγάθ᾽ αὐτοῖσιν πάντα παρέσται.

ΚΟΡΥΦΑΙΟΣ

λέγε δή μοι τῶν ἀγαθῶν ἕν.

ΠΕΙΣΕΤΑΙΡΟΣ

πρῶτα μὲν αὐτῶν τὰς οἰνάνθας οἱ πάρνοπες οὐ κατέδονται,
ἀλλὰ γλαυκῶν λόχος εἷς αὐτοὺς καὶ κερχνῄδων ἐπιτρίψει.
εἶθ᾽ οἱ κνῖπες καὶ ψῆνες ἀεὶ τὰς συκᾶς οὐ κατέδονται,
ἀλλ᾽ ἀναλέξει πάντας καθαρῶς αὐτοὺς ἀγέλη μία κιχλῶν.

ΚΟΡΥΦΑΙΟΣ

πλουτεῖν δὲ πόθεν δώσομεν αὐτοῖς; καὶ γὰρ τούτου σφόδρ᾽ ἐρῶσιν.

ΠΕΙΣΕΤΑΙΡΟΣ

τὰ μέταλλ᾽ αὐτοῖς μαντευομένοις οὗτοι δώσουσι τὰ χρηστά,
τάς τ᾽ ἐμπορίας τὰς κερδαλέας πρὸς τὸν μάντιν κατεροῦσιν,
ὥστ᾽ ἀπολεῖται τῶν ναυκλήρων οὐδείς.

EUELPIDES

No—at least not until I've sold my own little pair of oxen!

PEISETAERUS

But if they accept you as their god, you as their Zeus, you as their Earth, you as their Cronus, you as their Poseidon, then all good things will be theirs.

CHORUS LEADER

Give me an example of these good things.

PEISETAERUS

For starters, the locusts won't devour their vine blooms; a single contingent of owls and kestrels will wipe them out. Then again, the mites and the gallflies won't always be devouring their fig trees; a single flock of thrushes will eat them clean up.

CHORUS LEADER

But how will we give them wealth? Because that's a strong passion of theirs.

PEISETAERUS

When they practice augury these birds will give them the motherlodes, and to the diviner they'll reveal the profitable voyages, so that no shipowner will be lost.

---

586 *σε Ζῆνα* Sommerstein in *CQ* 48 (1998) 9–10 praeeuntibus Blaydes et Dunbar: *σε βίον* a

ΚΟΡΥΦΑΙΟΣ

πῶς οὐκ ἀπολεῖται;

ΠΕΙΣΕΤΑΙΡΟΣ

προερεῖ τις ἀεὶ τῶν ὀρνίθων μαντευομένῳ περὶ τοῦ πλοῦ·
"νυνὶ μὴ πλεῖ, χειμὼν ἔσται." "νυνὶ πλεῖ, κέρδος ἐπέσται."

ΕΥΕΛΠΙΔΗΣ

γαῦλον κτῶμαι καὶ ναυκληρῶ, κοὐκ ἂν μείναιμι παρ' ὑμῖν.

ΠΕΙΣΕΤΑΙΡΟΣ

τοὺς θησαυρούς τ' αὐτοῖς δείξουσ' οὓς οἱ πρότερον κατέθεντο
τῶν ἀργυρίων· οὗτοι γὰρ ἴσασι· λέγουσι δέ τοι τάδε πάντες·
"οὐδεὶς οἶδεν τὸν θησαυρὸν τὸν ἐμὸν πλὴν εἴ τις ἄρ' ὄρνις."

ΕΥΕΛΠΙΔΗΣ

πωλῶ γαῦλον, κτῶμαι σμινύην, καὶ τὰς ὑδρίας ἀνορύττω.

ΚΟΡΥΦΑΙΟΣ

πῶς δ' ὑγίειαν δώσουσ' αὐτοῖς, οὖσαν παρὰ τοῖσι θεοῖσιν;

ΠΕΙΣΕΤΑΙΡΟΣ

ἢν εὖ πράττωσ', οὐχ ὑγιεία μεγάλη τοῦτ' ἐστί;

CHORUS LEADER

They won't be lost? How so?

PEISETAERUS

When he asks the diviner about his voyage, one of the birds will always tip him off: "Don't sail just now, a storm's on its way"; "Sail now, there's a profit in store."

EUELPIDES

I'm buying a merchantman and becoming a shipowner—not staying here with you guys!

PEISETAERUS

And they'll show them the hoards of silver that the old-timers buried; these birds know where they are. You do hear everyone say, "None but some bird knows where *my* treasure lies."

EUELPIDES

I'm selling that merchantman, getting a shovel, and digging up pots!

CHORUS LEADER

But how will the birds give them health? That rests with the gods.

PEISETAERUS

If they're wealthy, they're plenty healthy, no?

---

599 *πρότερον*] *πρότεροι* Vpc M A t

ΕΥΕΛΠΙΔΗΣ

σάφ᾽ ἴσθι,
ὡς ἄνθρωπός γε κακῶς πράττων ἀτεχνῶς οὐδεὶς ὑγιαίνει.

ΚΟΡΥΦΑΙΟΣ

πῶς δ᾽ εἰς γῆράς ποτ᾽ ἀφίξονται; καὶ γὰρ τοῦτ᾽ ἔστ᾽ ἐν Ὀλύμπῳ.
ἢ παιδάρι᾽ ὄντ᾽ ἀποθνῄσκειν δεῖ;

ΠΕΙΣΕΤΑΙΡΟΣ

μὰ Δί᾽ ἀλλὰ τριακόσι᾽ αὐτοῖς
ἔτι προσθήσουσ᾽ ὄρνιθες ἔτη.

ΚΟΡΥΦΑΙΟΣ

παρὰ τοῦ;

ΠΕΙΣΕΤΑΙΡΟΣ

παρὰ τοῦ; παρ᾽ ἑαυτῶν.
οὐκ οἶσθ᾽ ὅτι πέντ᾽ ἀνδρῶν γενεὰς ζώει λακέρυζα κορώνη;

ΕΥΕΛΠΙΔΗΣ

αἰβοῖ, πολλῷ κρείττους οὗτοι τοῦ Διὸς ἡμῖν βασιλεύειν.

ΠΕΙΣΕΤΑΙΡΟΣ

οὐ γὰρ πολλῷ;
πρῶτον μέν <γ᾽> οὐχὶ νεὼς ἡμᾶς
οἰκοδομεῖν δεῖ λιθίνους αὐτοῖς,
οὐδὲ θυρῶσαι χρυσαῖσι θύραις,
ἀλλ᾽ ὑπὸ θάμνοις καὶ πρινιδίοις

EUELPIDES

You know it! No human's healthy at all if he's doing poorly.

CHORUS LEADER

But how will they reach old age? That's also up to Olympus. Or are they to die when they're tykes?

PEISETAERUS

Heavens no, the birds will add an extra three hundred years to their lives.

CHORUS LEADER

Where from?

PEISETAERUS

Where? From themselves: don't you know that "five ages of man lives the croaking crow"?[50]

EUELPIDES

Dammit, these birds are far better kings for us than Zeus!

PEISETAERUS

Far better for sure! To begin with, we needn't build them marble temples and gild the gates with gold; they'll make their homes in copses and woods, while for the bird VIPs

[50] Cf. Hesiod, fr. 304.

---

611 lacunam unius metri suspiceres (cf. v. 523), suppl. e.g. <κρείττους, πολλῷ> Blaydes

οἰκήσουσιν. τοῖς δ᾽ αὖ σεμνοῖς
τῶν ὀρνίθων δένδρον ἐλαίας
ὁ νεὼς ἔσται. κοὐκ εἰς Δελφοὺς
οὐδ᾽ εἰς Ἄμμων᾽ ἐλθόντες ἐκεῖ
θύσομεν, ἀλλ᾽ ἐν ταῖσιν κομάροις
καὶ τοῖς κοτίνοις στάντες, ἔχοντες
κριθάς, πυροὺς εὐξόμεθ᾽ αὐτοῖς
ἀνατείνοντες τὼ χεῖρ᾽ ἀγαθῶν
διδόναι τὸ μέρος· καὶ ταῦθ᾽ ἡμῖν
παραχρῆμ᾽ ἔσται
πυροὺς ὀλίγους προβαλοῦσιν.

ΚΟΡΥΦΑΙΟΣ

ὦ φίλτατ᾽ ἐμοὶ πολὺ πρεσβυτῶν ἐξ ἐχθίστου μεταπίπτων,
οὐκ ἔστιν ὅπως ἂν ἐγώ ποθ᾽ ἑκὼν τῆς σῆς γνώμης ἔτ᾽ ἀφείμην.

ΧΟΡΟΣ

ἐπαυχήσας δὲ τοῖσι σοῖς λόγοις
ἐπηπείλησα καὶ κατώμοσα,
ἐὰν σὺ παρ᾽ ἐμὲ θέμενος ὁμόφρονας λόγους
δίκαιος ἄδολος ὅσιος ἐπὶ θεοὺς ἴῃς,
ἐμοὶ φρονῶν ξυνῳδά, μὴ πολὺν χρόνον
θεοὺς ἔτι σκῆπτρα τἀμὰ τρίψειν.

ΚΟΡΥΦΑΙΟΣ

ἀλλ᾽ ὅσα μὲν δεῖ ῥώμῃ πράττειν, ἐπὶ ταῦτα τεταξόμεθ᾽ ἡμεῖς·

an olive tree will be their temple. And we'll not be going to Delphi or Ammon[51] and sacrificing there; instead we'll stand among strawberries and wild olives holding grains of barley and wheat in our outstretched hands, and pray to the birds to give us a share of blessings; and we'll get these blessings right away, just for tossing them a few grains of wheat!

CHORUS LEADER

Old man, my worst enemy changed into my very best friend, it's impossible that I could ever choose to discard this idea of yours!

CHORUS

Emboldened by your words,
I give notice and solemnly swear:
if you bring to my cause congenial proposals,
and fairly, squarely, righteously attack the gods,
tuning your thoughts to mine, then not much longer
will the gods be abusing my sceptre!

CHORUS LEADER

So in the tasks that call for brawn, we're ready for duty; in

[51] A ram-headed Egyptian god, identified by the Greeks with Zeus, who had an oracular shrine at the Siwa oasis in Libya.

---

632 δίκαιος ἄδολος ὅσιος Bergk: δικαίους ἀδόλους ὁσίους a

ὅσα δὲ γνώμῃ δεῖ βουλεύειν, ἐπὶ σοὶ τάδε πάντ'
ἀνάκειται.

ΠΕΙΣΕΤΑΙΡΟΣ

καὶ μὴν μὰ τὸν Δί' οὐχὶ νυστάζειν ἔτι
ὥρα 'στὶν ἡμῖν οὐδὲ μελλονικιᾶν,
ἀλλ' ὡς τάχιστα δεῖ τι δρᾶν.

ΤΗΡΕΥΣ

πρῶτον δέ γε
εἰσέλθετ' εἰς νεοττιάν τε τὴν ἐμὴν
καὶ τἀμὰ κάρφη καὶ τὰ παρόντα φρύγανα,
καὶ τοὔνομ' ἡμῖν φράσατον.

ΠΕΙΣΕΤΑΙΡΟΣ

ἀλλὰ ῥᾴδιον.
ἐμοὶ μὲν ὄνομα Πεισέταιρος, τῳδεδὶ
Εὐελπίδης Κριῶθεν.

ΤΗΡΕΥΣ

ἀλλὰ χαίρετον
ἄμφω.

ΠΕΙΣΕΤΑΙΡΟΣ

δεχόμεθα.

ΤΗΡΕΥΣ

δεῦρο τοίνυν εἴσιτον.

ΠΕΙΣΕΤΑΙΡΟΣ

ἴωμεν· εἰσηγοῦ σὺ λαβὼν ἡμᾶς.

ΤΗΡΕΥΣ

ἴθι.

the plans that call for brains, you're in charge of all that.

PEISETAERUS

Well then, there's absolutely no time left for napping or a spell of Nicias' Paralysis;[52] no, we've got to accomplish something, and fast!

TEREUS

Yes, but first come inside, into my nest, my sticks and such twigs as I have, and both of you tell us your names.

PEISETAERUS

That's easy enough: my name is Peisetaerus, and this one here is Euelpides of Crioa.[53]

TEREUS

A hearty welcome to you both.

PEISETAERUS

Thank you.

TEREUS

Well then, do come in, right this way.

PEISETAERUS

(*to Euelpides*) Let's go in. (*to Tereus*) Please, show us in.

TEREUS

Come on!

52 Nicias had urged caution in sending the armada against Sicily (Thucydides 6.8, 25) and then had failed to follow up his victory before Syracuse (6.71, cf. Plutarch, *Life of Nicias* 16.8–9).

53 For the significance of the names see 1–2 nn. Crioa and the variant Thria were actual Attic demes, but the comic point is unclear.

---

645 Θριῆθεν M A U t

ΠΕΙΣΕΤΑΙΡΟΣ

ἀτάρ, τὸ δεῖνα, δεῦρ᾿ ἐπανάκρουσαι πάλιν.
φέρ᾿ ἴδω, φράσον νῷν, πῶς ἐγώ τε χοὐτοσὶ
ξυνεσόμεθ᾿ ὑμῖν πετομένοις οὐ πετομένω;

ΤΗΡΕΥΣ

καλῶς.

ΠΕΙΣΕΤΑΙΡΟΣ

ὅρα νυν, ὡς ἐν Αἰσώπου λόγοις
ἐστὶν λεγόμενον δή τι, τὴν ἀλώπεχ᾿, ὡς
φλαύρως ἐκοινώνησεν αἰετῷ ποτε.

ΤΗΡΕΥΣ

μηδὲν φοβηθῇς· ἔστι γάρ τι ῥιζίον,
ὃ διατραγόντ᾿ ἔσεσθον ἐπτερωμένω.

ΠΕΙΣΕΤΑΙΡΟΣ

οὕτω μὲν εἰσίωμεν. ἄγε δή, Ξανθία
καὶ Μανόδωρε, λαμβάνετε τὰ στρώματα.

ΚΟΡΥΦΑΙΟΣ

οὗτος, σὲ καλῶ, σὲ λέγω.

ΤΗΡΕΥΣ

τί καλεῖς;

ΚΟΡΥΦΑΙΟΣ

τούτους μὲν ἄγων μετὰ σαυτοῦ
ἀρίστισον εὖ· τὴν δ᾿ ἡδυμελῆ ξύμφωνον ἀηδόνα Μούσαις
κατάλειφ᾿ ἡμῖν δεῦρ᾿ ἐκβιβάσας, ἵνα παίσωμεν μετ᾿ ἐκείνης.

PEISETAERUS

But, um, hold on, reverse oars, back this way! Look here, tell us, how can I and my pal here be your partners when you all can fly and we can't?

TEREUS

Just fine.

PEISETAERUS

Mind you now, there's a story in Aesop's fables about the fox, how once upon a time she fared poorly in partnership with an eagle.[54]

TEREUS

Never fear, there's a certain little root; chew it and you'll have wings.

PEISETAERUS

It's a deal; let's go inside. (*to the Slaves*) Come on then, Xanthias and Manodorus, pick up the baggage.

CHORUS LEADER

(*to Tereus*) Yoo hoo! Yes you. A word, please.

TEREUS

What is it?

CHORUS LEADER

Do take these men with you and give them a good lunch; but that mellifluous nightingale, singer in the Muses' choir, bring her out here and leave her with us; we'd like to play with her.

[54] Aesop 1 Perry, first attested in Archilochus, frags. 172–81 West. The eagle had betrayed the fox by feeding her cubs to its eaglets, and the flightless fox could only curse the eagle; but when the eagle took hot goat-meat from an altar she set her nest afire, and the fox ate the eaglets as they fell.

ΠΕΙΣΕΤΑΙΡΟΣ

ὢ τοῦτο μέντοι νὴ Δί᾽ αὐτοῖσιν πιθοῦ.
ἐκβίβασον ἐκ τοῦ βουτόμου τοὐρνίθιον·

ΕΥΕΛΠΙΔΗΣ

ἐκβίβασον αὐτοῦ, πρὸς θεῶν, αὐτήν, ἵνα
καὶ νὼ θεασώμεσθα τὴν ἀηδόνα.

ΤΗΡΕΥΣ

ἀλλ᾽ εἰ δοκεῖ σφῷν, ταῦτα χρὴ δρᾶν. ἡ Πρόκνη,
ἔκβαινε καὶ σαυτὴν ἐπιδείκνυ τοῖς ξένοις.

ΠΕΙΣΕΤΑΙΡΟΣ

ὦ Ζεῦ πολυτίμηθ᾽, ὡς καλὸν τοὐρνίθιον·
ὡς δ᾽ ἁπαλόν, ὡς δὲ λευκόν.

ΕΥΕΛΠΙΔΗΣ

ἆρά γ᾽ οἶσθ᾽ ὅτι
ἐγὼ διαμηρίζοιμ᾽ ἂν αὐτὴν ἡδέως;

ΠΕΙΣΕΤΑΙΡΟΣ

ὅσον δ᾽ ἔχει τὸν χρυσόν, ὥσπερ παρθένος.

ΕΥΕΛΠΙΔΗΣ

ἐγὼ μὲν αὐτὴν κἂν φιλῆσαί μοι δοκῶ.

ΠΕΙΣΕΤΑΙΡΟΣ

ἀλλ᾽, ὦ κακόδαιμον, ῥύγχος ὀβελίσκοιν ἔχει.

ΕΥΕΛΠΙΔΗΣ

ἀλλ᾽ ὥσπερ ᾠὸν νὴ Δί᾽ ἀπολέψαντα χρὴ
ἀπὸ τῆς κεφαλῆς τὸ λέμμα κᾆθ᾽ οὕτω φιλεῖν.

ΤΗΡΕΥΣ

ἴωμεν.

PEISETAERUS

Oh yes, by all means do as they ask! Bring the chick out of the tickle grass.

EUELPIDES

Heavens yes, do bring her out; we want to have a look at the nightingale too.

TEREUS

Well, if that's what you both want, I must oblige. Oh, Procne! Come outside and present yourself to our guests.

Enter Procne, costumed as a girl piper with wings and a bird's head.

PEISETAERUS

God almighty, what a beautiful chick! So tender and fair!

EUELPIDES

Know what? I'd be glad to spread those drumsticks!

PEISETAERUS

She's got quite a choker, like a debutante!

EUELPIDES

Me, I think I'd also like to give her a kiss.

PEISETAERUS

Look, you screw-up, she's got a couple of skewers for a beak!

EUELPIDES

OK, it's like an egg: we'll just have to peel that shell off her head and kiss her that way!

TEREUS

Let's go inside!

ΠΕΙΣΕΤΑΙΡΟΣ

ἡγοῦ δὴ σὺ νῷν τὐχἀγαθῇ.

ΧΟΡΟΣ

ὦ φίλη, ὦ ξουθή,
ὦ φίλτατον ὀρνέων,
πάντων ξύννομε τῶν ἐμῶν
ὕμνων, ξύντροφ᾽ ἀηδοῖ,
ἦλθες ἦλθες ὤφθης,
ἡδὺν φθόγγον ἐμοὶ φέρουσ᾽.
ἀλλ᾽, ὦ καλλιβόαν κρέκουσ᾽
αὐλὸν φθέγμασιν ἠρινοῖς,
ἄρχου τῶν ἀναπαίστων.

ΚΟΡΥΦΑΙΟΣ

ἄγε δὴ φύσιν ἄνδρες ἀμαυρόβιοι, φύλλων γενεᾷ προσόμοιοι,
ὀλιγοδρανέες, πλάσματα πηλοῦ, σκιοειδέα φῦλ᾽ ἀμενηνά,
ἀπτῆνες ἐφημέριοι, ταλαοὶ βροτοί, ἀνέρες εἰκελόνειροι,
προσέχετε τὸν νοῦν τοῖς ἀθανάτοις ἡμῖν, τοῖς αἰὲν ἐοῦσιν,
τοῖς αἰθερίοις, τοῖσιν ἀγήρῳς, τοῖς ἄφθιτα μηδομένοισιν,
ἵν᾽ ἀκούσαντες πάντα παρ᾽ ἡμῶν ὀρθῶς περὶ τῶν μετεώρων,
φύσιν οἰωνῶν γένεσίν τε θεῶν ποταμῶν τ᾽ Ἐρέβους τε Χάους τε

PEISETAERUS

After you, then, and good luck to us!

All except Procne and the Chorus exit into Tereus' nest.

CHORUS

Ah darling warbler,
ah, dearest of birds,
songmate of all my hymns,
my nightingale companion,
you're here, you're here, you're manifest,
bringing sweet sound to me.
Now, weaver of springtime tunes
on the fair-toned pipes,
lead off our anapests.

CHORUS LEADER

Now then, ye men by nature just faintly alive, like to the race of leaves, do-littles, artefacts of clay, tribes shadowy and feeble, wingless ephemerals, suffering mortals, dreamlike people: pay attention to us, the immortals, the everlasting, the etherial, the ageless, whose counsels are imperishable; once you hear from us an accurate account of all celestial phenomena, and know correctly the nature of birds and the genesis of gods, rivers, Erebus, and Chaos,

εἰδότες ὀρθῶς, Προδίκῳ παρ᾽ ἐμοῦ κλάειν εἴπητε τὸ λοιπόν.
Χάος ἦν καὶ Νὺξ Ἔρεβός τε μέλαν πρῶτον καὶ Τάρταρος εὐρύς·
Γῆ δ᾽ οὐδ᾽ Ἀὴρ οὐδ᾽ Οὐρανὸς ἦν· Ἐρέβους δ᾽ ἐν ἀπείροσι κόλποις
τίκτει πρώτιστον ὑπηνέμιον Νὺξ ἡ μελανόπτερος ᾠόν,
ἐξ οὗ περιτελλομέναις ὥραις ἔβλαστεν Ἔρως ὁ ποθεινός,
στίλβων νῶτον πτερύγοιν χρυσαῖν, εἰκὼς ἀνεμώκεσι δίναις.
οὗτος δὲ Χάει πτερόεντι μιγεὶς νύχιος κατὰ Τάρταρον εὐρὺν
ἐνεόττευσεν γένος ἡμέτερον, καὶ πρῶτον ἀνήγαγεν εἰς φῶς.
πρότερον δ᾽ οὐκ ἦν γένος ἀθανάτων, πρὶν Ἔρως ξυνέμειξεν ἅπαντα·
ξυμμειγνυμένων δ᾽ ἑτέρων ἑτέροις γένετ᾽ Οὐρανὸς Ὠκεανός τε
καὶ Γῆ πάντων τε θεῶν μακάρων γένος ἄφθιτον. ὧδε μέν ἐσμεν
πολὺ πρεσβύτατοι πάντων μακάρων ἡμεῖς. ὡς δ᾽ ἐσμὲν Ἔρωτος
πολλοῖς δῆλον· πετόμεσθά <τε> γὰρ καὶ τοῖσιν ἐρῶσι σύνεσμεν·
πολλοὺς δὲ καλοὺς ἀπομωμοκότας παῖδας πρὸς τέρμασιν ὥρας

thenceforth you'll be able to tell Prodicus from me to go to hell![55]

In the beginning were Chaos and Night and black Erebus and broad Tartarus, and no Earth, Air, or Sky. And in the boundless bosom of Erebus did black-winged Night at the very start bring forth a wind egg, from which as the seasons revolved came forth Eros the seductive, like to swift whirlwinds, his back aglitter with wings of gold. And mating by night with winged Chaos in broad Tartarus, he hatched our own race and first brought it up to daylight. There was no race of immortal gods before Eros commingled everything; then as this commingled with that, Sky came to be, and Ocean and Earth, and the whole imperishable race of blessed gods. Thus we're far older than all the blessed gods, and it's abundantly clear that we're the offspring of Eros: we fly, and we keep company with lovers. Many are the fair boys who swore they wouldn't, and al-

[55] Prodicus of Ceos, a contemporary of Socrates with broad scientific and philosophical interests, traced the origin of gods to primitive nature- and hero-worship.

---

698 νύχιος Halbertsma: νυχίῳ vel νυχίων a S: μύχιος West

διὰ τὴν ἰσχὺν τὴν ἡμετέραν διεμήρισαν ἄνδρες ἐρασταί,
ὁ μὲν ὄρτυγα δούς, ὁ δὲ πορφυρίων', ὁ δὲ χῆν', ὁ δὲ Περσικὸν ὄρνιν.
πάντα δὲ θνητοῖς ἐστιν ἀφ' ἡμῶν τῶν ὀρνίθων τὰ μέγιστα.
πρῶτα μὲν ὥρας φαίνομεν ἡμεῖς ἦρος, χειμῶνος, ὀπώρας·
σπείρειν μέν, ὅταν γέρανος κρώζουσ' εἰς τὴν Λιβύην μεταχωρῇ·
καὶ πηδάλιον τότε ναυκλήρῳ φράζει κρεμάσαντι καθεύδειν,
εἶτα δ' Ὀρέστῃ χλαῖναν ὑφαίνειν, ἵνα μὴ ῥιγῶν ἀποδύῃ.
ἰκτῖνος δ' αὖ μετὰ ταῦτα φανεὶς ἑτέραν ὥραν ἀποφαίνει,
ἡνίκα πεκτεῖν ὥρα προβάτων πόκον ἠρινόν· εἶτα χελιδών,
ὅτε χρὴ χλαῖναν πωλεῖν ἤδη καὶ ληδάριόν τι πρίασθαι.
ἐσμὲν δ' ὑμῖν Ἄμμων, Δελφοί, Δωδώνη, Φοῖβος Ἀπόλλων.
ἐλθόντες γὰρ πρῶτον ἐπ' ὄρνις οὕτω πρὸς ἅπαντα τρέπεσθε,
πρός τ' ἐμπορίαν, καὶ πρὸς βιότου κτῆσιν, καὶ πρὸς γάμον ἀνδρός.
ὄρνιν τε νομίζετε πάνθ' ὅσαπερ περὶ μαντείας διακρίνει·

most made it to the end of their eligible bloom, but thanks to our power men in love did get between their thighs, one with the gift of a quail, another with a porphyrion, a goose, or a Persian bird. And mortals get all their greatest blessings from us birds. To start with, we reveal the seasons of spring, winter, and autumn. It's time to sow when the crane whoops off to Africa; that's when it tells the shipowner to hang up his rudder and go to sleep, and Orestes[56] to weave a cloak so he won't be cold when he's out mugging people. And then it's the kite's turn to appear and reveal another season, when it's time to shear the sheep's spring wool. And then there's the swallow when you should be selling your coat and buying a jacket. And we're your Ammon,[57] your Delphi, your Dodona,[58] your Phoebus Apollo, for you don't embark on any course without first consulting the birds—about business, about acquiring a livelihood, about a man's getting married. Whatever's decisive in prophecy you deem a bird: to you, an ominous utterance is a bird, a

[56] The nickname of the son of one Timocrates (schol. *Birds* 1487), after the mythical hero who wandered insane to Athens after killing his own mother.

[57] See 619 n.

[58] In Epirus, in NW Greece, where Zeus had an oracle.

φήμη γ᾽ ὑμῖν ὄρνις ἐστί, πταρμόν τ᾽ ὄρνιθα καλεῖτε,
ξύμβολον ὄρνιν, φωνὴν ὄρνιν, θεράποντ᾽ ὄρνιν, ὄνον ὄρνιν.
ἆρ᾽ οὐ φανερῶς ἡμεῖς ὑμῖν ἐσμὲν μαντεῖος Ἀπόλλων;
ἢν οὖν ἡμᾶς νομίσητε θεούς,
ἕξετε χρῆσθαι μάντεσι, μούσαις,
αὔραις, ὥραις, χειμῶνι, θέρει
μετρίῳ, πνίγει· κοὐκ ἀποδράντες
καθεδούμεθ᾽ ἄνω σεμνυνόμενοι
παρὰ ταῖς νεφέλαις ὥσπερ χὠ Ζεύς·
ἀλλὰ παρόντες δώσομεν ὑμῖν
αὐτοῖς, παισίν, παίδων παισίν,
πλουθυγίειαν, βίον, εἰρήνην,
νεότητα, γέλωτα, χορούς, θαλίας
γάλα τ᾽ ὀρνίθων. ὥστε παρέσται
κοπιᾶν ὑμῖν ὑπὸ τῶν ἀγαθῶν·
οὕτω πλουτήσετε πάντες.

ΧΟΡΟΣ

(*στρ*) Μοῦσα λοχμαία,
τιοτιοτιοτιοτίγξ,
ποικίλη, μεθ᾽ ἧς ἐγὼ νά-
παισί <*τε καὶ*> *κορυφαῖς ἐν ὀρείαις,*
τιοτιοτιοτιοτίγξ,
ἱζόμενος μελίας ἔπι φυλλοκόμου,
τιοτιοτιοτιοτίγξ,

sneeze you call a bird, a chance meeting's a bird, a sound's a bird, a good-luck servant's a bird, a braying donkey's a bird. So aren't we obviously your prophetic Apollo? Well then, if you treat us as gods you'll have the benefit of prophets, muses, breezes, seasons—winter, mild summer, stifling heat. And we won't run off and sit up there preening among the clouds, like Zeus, but ever at hand we'll bestow on you, your children, and your children's children healthy wealthiness, happiness, prosperity, peace, youth, hilarity, dances, festivities, and birds' milk. Why, you're liable to knock yourself out from good living, that's how rich you'll all be!

CHORUS

Bosky Muse—
tio tio tio tio tinx!—
of intricate tone, joining you
mid the vales and mountain peaks—
tio tio tio tio tinx!—
perched on a leaf-tressed ash—
tio tio tio tio tinx!—

δι᾽ ἐμῆς γέννος ξουθῆς μελέων
Πανὶ νόμους ἱεροὺς ἀναφαίνω
σεμνά τε Μητρὶ χορεύματ᾽ Ὀρείᾳ,
τοτοτοτοτοτοτοτοτοτίγξ,
ἔνθεν ὡσπερεὶ μέλιττα
Φρύνιχος ἀμβροσίων μελέων ἀπε-
βόσκετο καρπὸν ἀεὶ
φέρων γλυκεῖαν ᾠδάν,
τιοτιοτιοτιοτίγξ.

ΚΟΡΥΦΑΙΟΣ

εἰ μετ᾽ ὀρνίθων τις ὑμῶν, ὦ θεαταί, βούλεται
διαπλέκειν ζῶν ἡδέως τὸ λοιπόν, ὡς ἡμᾶς ἴτω.
ὅσα γὰρ ἐνθάδ᾽ ἐστὶν αἰσχρὰ τοῖς νόμῳ κρατουμένοις,
ταῦτα πάντ᾽ ἐστὶν παρ᾽ ἡμῖν τοῖσιν ὄρνισιν καλά.
εἰ γὰρ ἐνθάδ᾽ ἐστὶν αἰσχρὸν τὸν πατέρα τύπτειν νόμῳ,
τοῦτ᾽ ἐκεῖ καλὸν παρ᾽ ἡμῖν ἐστιν, ἤν τις τῷ πατρὶ
προσδραμὼν εἴπῃ πατάξας· "αἶρε πλῆκτρον, εἰ μαχεῖ."
εἰ δὲ τυγχάνει τις ὑμῶν δραπέτης ἐστιγμένος,
ἀτταγᾶς οὗτος παρ᾽ ἡμῖν ποικίλος κεκλήσεται.
εἰ δὲ τυγχάνει τις ὢν Φρὺξ μηδὲν ἧττον Σπινθάρου,
φρυγίλος ὄρνις ἐνθάδ᾽ ἔσται τοῦ Φιλήμονος γένους.
εἰ δὲ δοῦλός ἐστι καὶ Κὰρ ὥσπερ Ἐξηκεστίδης,

755 τοῖς νόμῳ κρατουμένοις Henderson praeeunte van Leeuwen: τῷ νόμῳ κρατούμενα a

from my vibrant throat I pour forth
sacred strains of song for Pan
and holy dance tunes for the Mountain Mother[59]—
to to to to to to to to to tinx!—
whence like a bee
Phrynichus[60] ever sipped the nectar
of ambrosial music
to bring forth his sweet song—
tio tio tio tio tinx!

CHORUS LEADER

Spectators, if any of you wants to sew up the rest of his life pleasantly with the birds, come to us. Because all things shameful here, for people controlled by custom, are admirable among us birds. Say by custom it's shameful here to hit your father; up there it's admirable for someone to rush his father, hit him, and say "Put up your spur if you mean to fight!" And if you happen to be a runaway slave with a branded forehead, with us you'll be called a dappled francolin; if you happen to be no less a Phrygian than Spintharus,[61] up there you'll be a pigeon of Philemon's[62] breed; if you're a slave and a Carian like Execestides, join

59 Cybele, the Anatolian mother goddess; both she and Pan were worshipped at Athens.

60 The songs of this tragic poet, an older contemporary of Aeschylus, were still popular among the older generation, cf. *Wasps* 220, 268–69, 1490.

61 Phrygians at Athens would be slaves; the Spintharus teased here for foreign ancestry may be the father of the fourth-century statesman Eubulus.

62 Unknown.

φυσάτω πάππους παρ' ἡμῖν, καὶ φανοῦνται φράτερες.
εἰ δ' ὁ Πεισίου προδοῦναι τοῖς ἀτίμοις τὰς πύλας
βούλεται, πέρδιξ γενέσθω, τοῦ πατρὸς νεόττιον·
ὡς παρ' ἡμῖν οὐδὲν αἰσχρόν ἐστιν ἐκπερδικίσαι.

ΧΟΡΟΣ

(ἀντ.) τοιάδε κύκνοι,
τιοτιοτιοτιοτίγξ,
συμμιγῆ βοὴν ὁμοῦ πτε-
ροῖσι κρέκοντες ἴαχον Ἀπόλλω,
τιοτιοτιοτιοτίγξ,
ὄχθῳ ἐφεζόμενοι παρ' Ἕβρον ποταμόν,
τιοτιοτιοτιοτίγξ,
διὰ δ' αἰθέριον νέφος ἦλθε βοά·
πτῆξε δὲ φῦλά τε ποικίλα θηρῶν,
κύματά τ' ἔσβεσε νήνεμος αἴθρη,
τοτοτοτοτοτοτοτοτοτοτίγξ·
πᾶς δ' ἐπεκτύπησ' Ὄλυμπος·
εἷλε δὲ θάμβος ἄνακτας· Ὀλυμπιά-
δες δὲ μέλος Χάριτες
Μοῦσαί τ' ἐπωλόλυξαν,
τιοτιοτιοτιοτίγξ.

766 Πεισ- Daubuz: Πισ- a

us and generate some forefeathers, and proper kinfolk will materialize; and if Peisias' son wants to betray the gates to the outlaws, let him become a partridge, a chick of the old cock, since among us there's nothing shameful in playing partridge tricks.[63]

CHORUS[64]

Just so did swans—
tio tio tio tio tinx!—
beating wings in unison
raise a harmonious whoop for Apollo—
tio tio tio tio tinx!—
gathered on the bank by Hebrus River—
tio tio tio tio tinx!
their whooping pierced the cloud of heaven;
the manifold tribes of beasts were cowed,
and the cloudless clear air quenched the waves—
to to to to to to to to to tinx!—
All Olympus reverberated,
amazement seized its lords, and the Olympian
Graces and Muses
replied in cheerful song—
tio tio tio tio tinx!

63 Peisias' son was perhaps the Cleombrotus called "son of Partridge" (cf. 1292–93) in Phrynichus com. fr. 55; "the outlaws" are probably those denounced in the sacrileges of 415 who had fled Athens and were condemned *in absentia*; "tricks" refers to the partridge's skill at evading pursuers.

64 Probably recollecting Apollo's journey from the Hyperboreans to Delphi in a swan-drawn chariot, which Alcaeus had described in a famous paean (fr. 307).

ΚΟΡΥΦΑΙΟΣ

οὐδέν ἐστ᾽ ἄμεινον οὐδ᾽ ἥδιον ἢ φῦσαι πτερά.
αὐτίχ᾽ ὑμῶν τῶν θεατῶν εἴ τις ἦν ὑπόπτερος,
εἶτα πεινῶν τοῖς χοροῖσι τῶν τραγῳδῶν ἤχθετο,
ἐκπτόμενος ἂν οὗτος ἠρίστησεν ἐλθὼν οἴκαδε,
κᾆτ᾽ ἂν ἐμπλησθεὶς ἐφ᾽ ἡμᾶς αὖθις αὖ κατέπτατο.
εἴ τε Πατροκλείδης τις ὑμῶν τυγχάνει χεζητιῶν,
οὐκ ἂν ἐξίδισεν εἰς θοἰμάτιον, ἀλλ᾽ ἀνέπτατο,
κἀποπαρδὼν κἀναπνεύσας αὖθις αὖ κατέπτατο.
εἴ τε μοιχεύων τις ὑμῶν ἐστιν ὅστις τυγχάνει,
κᾆθ᾽ ὁρᾷ τὸν ἄνδρα τῆς γυναικὸς ἐν βουλευτικῷ,
οὗτος ἂν πάλιν παρ᾽ ὑμῶν πτερυγίσας ἀνέπτατο,
εἶτα βινήσας ἐκεῖθεν αὖθις αὖ κατέπτατο.
ἆρ᾽ ὑπόπτερον γενέσθαι παντός ἐστιν ἄξιον;
ὡς Διειτρέφης γε πυτιναῖα μόνον ἔχων πτερὰ
ᾑρέθη φύλαρχος, εἶθ᾽ ἵππαρχος, εἶτ᾽ ἐξ οὐδενὸς
μεγάλα πράττει κἀστὶ νυνὶ ξουθὸς ἱππαλεκτρυών.

ΠΕΙΣΕΤΑΙΡΟΣ

ταυτὶ τοιαυτί. μὰ Δί᾽ ἐγὼ μὲν πρᾶγμά πω
γελοιότερον οὐκ εἶδον οὐδεπώποτε.

796 κατέπτατο S: καθέζετο a

---

65 Two decrees survive whose proposer(s) bore this name: *IG* i³ 63 (420) and Andocides 1.73–80 (405); our man was nicknamed "The Shitter," according to the scholiast.

66 The 500 members of the Council had a block of reserved seats at the front, cf. *Peace* 887, 906.

67 Despite his comic caricature as a distasteful arriviste (cf.

CHORUS LEADER

There's nothing better or merrier than sprouting wings. Say one of you spectators had wings, and got hungry, and grew bored with the tragic performances; then he'd have flown out of here, gone home, had lunch, and when he was full, flown back here to see us. And supposing some Patrocleides[65] in the audience needed to shit, he wouldn't have soaked his cloak; no, he'd have flown off, blown a fart, caught his breath, and flown back here again. And if there's anyone among you who happens to be an adulterer, and sees the lady's husband in the Councillors' seats,[66] he'd have used his wings to launch himself out of the audience, gone and fucked her, and then flown back here again. So isn't getting wings worth any price? Take Dieitrephes:[67] equipped only with the wings from chianti bottles,[68] he was elected tribal commander, then cavalry commander, till now, having started from nothing, he's flying high, an actual zooming horsecock.[69]

Enter PEISETAERUS *and* EUELPIDES, *now winged.*

PEISETAERUS

Ta da, here we are! God, I've never seen a funnier sight.

also Cratinus fr. 251, Plato Com. fr. 31), Dieitrephes' family was in fact distinguished. In his current generalship he would command the Thracians responsible for the massacre at Mycalessus (Thucydides 7.29–30), and later he became an oligarch (8.64).

68 As the wicker handles were called.

69 A mythical winged beast with the front end of a horse and the rear end of a cock, often depicted by Attic painters of the sixth and early fifth centuries and mentioned by Aeschylus in *Myrmidons* fr. 134 (cf. *Frogs* 933); used of strutting officers also in *Peace* 1177.

ΕΥΕΛΠΙΔΗΣ

ἐπὶ τῷ γελᾷς;

ΠΕΙΣΕΤΑΙΡΟΣ

ἐπὶ τοῖσι σοῖς ὠκυπτέροις.
οἶσθ᾽ ᾧ μάλιστ᾽ ἔοικας ἐπτερωμένος;
εἰς εὐτέλειαν χηνὶ συγγεγραμμένῳ.

ΕΥΕΛΠΙΔΗΣ

σὺ δὲ κοψίχῳ γε σκάφιον ἀποτετιλμένῳ.

ΠΕΙΣΕΤΑΙΡΟΣ

ταυτὶ μὲν ᾐκάσμεσθα κατὰ τὸν Αἰσχύλον·
"τάδ᾽ οὐχ ὑπ᾽ ἄλλων, ἀλλὰ τοῖς αὑτῶν πτεροῖς."

ΚΟΡΥΦΑΙΟΣ

ἄγε δὴ τί χρὴ δρᾶν;

ΠΕΙΣΕΤΑΙΡΟΣ

πρῶτον ὄνομα τῇ πόλει
θέσθαι τι μέγα καὶ κλεινόν, εἶτα τοῖς θεοῖς
θῦσαι μετὰ τοῦτο.

ΕΥΕΛΠΙΔΗΣ

ταῦτα κἀμοὶ συνδοκεῖ.

ΚΟΡΥΦΑΙΟΣ

φέρ᾽ ἴδω, τί δ᾽ ἡμῖν ὄνομ᾽ ἄρ᾽ ἔσται τῇ πόλει;

ΠΕΙΣΕΤΑΙΡΟΣ

βούλεσθε τὸ μέγα τοῦτο τοὐκ Λακεδαίμονος
Σπάρτην ὄνομα καλῶμεν αὐτήν;

EUELPIDES

What are you laughing at?

PEISETAERUS

Those wing feathers of yours. Know what you look just like in those wings? A painted goose, done cheaply!

EUELPIDES

And you look like a blackbird with a bowl cut!

PEISETAERUS

To quote Aeschylus, we're stuck with these comparisons "not by others but by our own feathers."[70]

CHORUS LEADER

All right, what's on the agenda?

PEISETAERUS

First, we should give our city a name, something grand and notable; and then sacrifice to the gods.

EUELPIDES

My sentiments exactly.

CHORUS LEADER

Let's see then, what name will our city have?

PEISETAERUS

How about giving it that great Lacedaemonian name—Sparta?

[70] *Myrmidons* fr. 139, where Achilles, blaming himself for Patroclus' death, recalls an eagle shot by an arrow fletched with eagle feathers.

ΕΥΕΛΠΙΔΗΣ

Ἡράκλεις·
Σπάρτην γὰρ ἂν θείμην ἐγὼ τἠμῇ πόλει;
οὐδ' ἂν χαμεύνῃ πάνυ γε κειρίαν γ' ἔχων.

ΠΕΙΣΕΤΑΙΡΟΣ

τί δῆτ' ὄνομ' αὐτῇ θησόμεσθ';

ΚΟΡΥΦΑΙΟΣ

ἐντευθενὶ
ἐκ τῶν νεφελῶν καὶ τῶν μετεώρων χωρίων
χαῦνόν τι πάνυ.

ΠΕΙΣΕΤΑΙΡΟΣ

βούλει Νεφελοκοκκυγίαν;

ΚΟΡΥΦΑΙΟΣ

ἰοὺ ἰού·
καλόν γ' ἀτεχνῶς <σὺ> καὶ μέγ' ηὗρες τοὔνομα.

ΕΥΕΛΠΙΔΗΣ

ἆρ' ἐστὶν αὕτη γ' ἡ Νεφελοκοκκυγία,
ἵνα καὶ τὰ Θεογένους τὰ πολλὰ χρήματα
τά τ' Αἰσχίνου 'σθ' ἅπαντα;

ΠΕΙΣΕΤΑΙΡΟΣ

καὶ λῷον μὲν οὖν·
τὸ Φλέγρας πεδίον, ἵν' οἱ θεοὶ τοὺς γηγενεῖς
ἀλαζονευόμενοι καθυπερηκόντισαν.

822 Θεο- Dindorf: Θεα- a
823 λῷον Bentley cl. Σ: λῷστον a

EUELPIDES

Great Heracles, do you think I'd stick *my* city with the name Sparta? I wouldn't even use esparto twine for a mattress—if I had nice wide slats instead.

PEISETAERUS

Then what name *will* we give it?

CHORUS LEADER

A name suggesting all this, the clouds and the aerial spaces; something very highfalutin.

PEISETAERUS

How about Cloudcuckooland?

CHORUS LEADER

Yes, yes! You've found an absolutely great and wonderful name!

EUELPIDES

Sure, this must be the same Cloudcuckooland where most of Theogenes'[71] assets are, and all of Aeschines'.[72]

PEISETAERUS

No, even better than that: it's the Plain of Phlegra, where the Gods outshot the Earthborn at bragging![73]

71 A common name, here perhaps the Theogenes ridiculed for imaginary wealth in Eupolis' *Demes* fr. 99.5, 9, cf. fr. 135.

72 Ridiculed as a boaster also in *Wasps* 459, 1243.

73 See 553 n.

ΚΟΡΥΦΑΙΟΣ

λιπαρὸν τὸ χρῆμα τῆς πόλεως. τίς δαὶ θεὸς
πολιοῦχος ἔσται; τῷ ξανοῦμεν τὸν πέπλον;

ΠΕΙΣΕΤΑΙΡΟΣ

τί δ᾽ οὐκ Ἀθηναίαν ἐῶμεν πολιάδα;

ΕΥΕΛΠΙΔΗΣ

καὶ πῶς ἂν ἔτι γένοιτ᾽ ἂν εὔτακτος πόλις,
ὅπου θεὸς γυνὴ γεγονυῖα πανοπλίαν
ἕστηκ᾽ ἔχουσα, Κλεισθένης δὲ κερκίδα;

ΚΟΡΥΦΑΙΟΣ

τίς δαὶ καθέξει τῆς πόλεως τὸ Πελαργικόν;

ΠΕΙΣΕΤΑΙΡΟΣ

ὄρνις ἀφ᾽ ἡμῶν τοῦ γένους τοῦ Περσικοῦ,
ὅσπερ λέγεται δεινότατος εἶναι πανταχοῦ
Ἄρεως νεοττός.

ΕΥΕΛΠΙΔΗΣ

ὦ νεοττὲ δέσποτα.
ὡς δ᾽ ὁ θεὸς ἐπιτήδειος οἰκεῖν ἐπὶ πετρῶν.

ΠΕΙΣΕΤΑΙΡΟΣ

ἄγε νυν σὺ μὲν βάδιζε πρὸς τὸν ἀέρα
καὶ τοῖσι τειχίζουσι παραδιακόνει,
χάλικας παραφόρει, πηλὸν ἀποδὺς ὄργασον,
λεκάνην ἀνένεγκε, κατάπεσ᾽ ἀπὸ τῆς κλίμακος,
φυλακὰς κατάστησαι, τὸ πῦρ ἔγκρυπτ᾽ ἀεί,

833 ἡμῶν] ὑμῶν Kock

CHORUS LEADER

A gleaming[74] great city! Now what god shall be Citadel Guardian? For whom shall we weave the Robe?[75]

PEISETAERUS

Why not let Athena Polias hold that post?

EUELPIDES

And just how can a city remain well disciplined, where a god born a woman stands there wearing full armor, while Cleisthenes[76] plies a spindle?

CHORUS LEADER

Then who *will* be taking charge of the city's Storkade?[77]

PEISETAERUS

One of our birds, of the Persian breed,[78] the one universally known as a very fearsome Chick of Ares.

EUELPIDES

My Lord Chick! And a god so well suited to life on the rocks.

PEISETAERUS

(to Euelpides) Come on now, you take off for the sky and make yourself useful to the wall builders: bring them up gravel, roll up your sleeves and mix mortar, hand up a trough, fall off the ladder, station watchmen, keep the em-

[74] A favorite epithet of Athens, cf. *Acharnians* 637–40, *Knights* 1329, Pindar fr. 76.

[75] Athena Polias, Citadel Guardian of Athens, was presented with a robe at the Panathenaea.

[76] Often ridiculed as a beardless effeminate.

[77] The *Pelargikon*, designating the Mycenaean walls of the Acropolis and an enclosure at its foot.

[78] See 483–84.

κωδωνοφορῶν περίτρεχε καὶ κάθευδ᾽ ἐκεῖ.
κήρυκα δὲ πέμψον τὸν μὲν εἰς θεοὺς ἄνω,
ἕτερον δ᾽ ἄνωθεν αὖ παρ᾽ ἀνθρώπους κάτω,
κἀκεῖθεν αὖθις παρ᾽ ἐμέ.

ΕΥΕΛΠΙΔΗΣ

σὺ δέ γ᾽ αὐτοῦ μένων
οἴμωζε παρ᾽ ἔμ᾽.

ΠΕΙΣΕΤΑΙΡΟΣ

ἴθ᾽, ὦγάθ᾽, οἷ πέμπω σ᾽ ἐγώ.
οὐδὲν γὰρ ἄνευ σοῦ τῶνδ᾽ ἃ λέγω πεπράξεται.
ἐγὼ δ᾽ ἵνα θύσω τοῖσι καινοῖσιν θεοῖς,
τὸν ἱερέα πέμψοντα τὴν πομπὴν καλῶ.
παῖ παῖ, τὸ κανοῦν αἴρεσθε καὶ τὴν χέρνιβα.

ΧΟΡΟΣ

(στρ) ὁμορροθῶ, συνθέλω,
συμπαραινέσας ἔχω
προσόδια μεγάλα σεμνὰ προσιέναι θεοῖ-
σιν, ἅμα δὲ προσέτι χάριτος ἕνε-
κα προβάτιόν τι θύειν.
ἴτω ἴτω ἴτω δὲ Πυθιὰς βοά,
συναυλείτω δὲ Χαῖρις ᾠδᾷ.

858 συναυλείτω . . . ᾠδᾷ Hermann: συνᾳδέτω . . . ᾠδὰν a

79 Modelled on a chorus from Sophocles' *Peleus*, according to the scholia.

bers glowing, run a tour with the bell, and bed down on site. Send one herald up to the gods, and another down to mankind below, and then report back to me.

EUELPIDES

Yes, and you can stay right here and report to me—in hell!

Exit EUELPIDES.

PEISETAERUS

Go where I tell you, there's a good fellow; none of what I've talked about will get done without you. As for me, I'd better sacrifice to the new gods, so I'll invite the priest to organize the procession. *(calling through the stage door)* Boy! Boy! You boys pick up the basket and the holy water.

Enter Xanthias and Manodorus with sacrificial requisites and a Piper costumed as a raven.

CHORUS[79]

I am with you, I concur,
I hereby endorse your advice
to approach the gods with grand and solemn hymns
as we curry their favor as well
by sacrificing a wee sheep.[80]
Up up up with a Pythian cry,
and let Chaeris pipe as we sing.[81]

Enter a PRIEST *leading a goat.*

[80] An anticlimactic victim for so important a ceremony, and the priest's goat even more so.

[81] A lyre player and piper often ridiculed in comedy for poor technique.

ΠΕΙΣΕΤΑΙΡΟΣ

παῦσαι σὺ φυσῶν. Ἡράκλεις, τουτὶ τί ἦν;
τουτὶ μὰ Δί' ἐγὼ πολλὰ δὴ καὶ δείν' ἰδὼν
οὔπω κόρακ' εἶδον ἐμπεφορβειωμένον.
ἱερεῦ, σὸν ἔργον, θῦε τοῖς καινοῖς θεοῖς.

ΙΕΡΕΥΣ

δράσω τάδ'. ἀλλὰ ποῦ 'στιν ὁ τὸ κανοῦν ἔχων;
εὔχεσθε Ἑστίᾳ τῇ ὀρνιθείῳ
καὶ ἰκτίνῳ τῷ ἑστιούχῳ
καὶ ὄρνισιν Ὀλυμπίοις καὶ Ὀλυμπίασι
πᾶσι καὶ πάσῃσιν—

ΠΕΙΣΕΤΑΙΡΟΣ

ὦ Σουνιέρακε, χαῖρ', ἄναξ Πελαργικέ.

ΙΕΡΕΥΣ

καὶ κύκνῳ Πυθίῳ καὶ Δηλίῳ
καὶ Λητοῖ Ὀρτυγομήτρᾳ
καὶ Ἀρτέμιδι Ἀκαλανθίδι—

ΠΕΙΣΕΤΑΙΡΟΣ

οὐκέτι Κολαινίς, ἀλλ' Ἀκαλανθὶς Ἄρτεμις.

ΙΕΡΕΥΣ

καὶ φρυγίλῳ Σαβαζίῳ
καὶ στρούθῳ μεγάλῃ
Μητρὶ θεῶν καὶ ἀνθρώπων—

868 πελάργιε Sommerstein

PEISETAERUS

(to the Piper) Stop your piping! Heracles, what *is* this? I've certainly seen many amazing sights, but this I've never seen, a raven wearing a piper's harness! Priest, you're on; start sacrificing to the new gods.

PRIEST

That I will, but where's the boy with the basket? All pray: to Hestia of the Birds, to Kite their Hearthkeeper, to the Olympian birds and birdesses each and all—

PEISETAERUS

Hail, Hawk of Sunium,[82] Lord of the Seastork!

PRIEST

and the Swan of Pytho and Delos,[83] and Leto the Quail Mother,[84] and Artemis the Curlew—

PEISETAERUS

No more Colaenis,[85] now it's Artemis Curlew!

PRIEST

and Pigeon Sabazius, and the Great Ostrich Mother of gods and men—

[82] Adapting an epithet of Poseidon.

[83] Apollo.

[84] I.e. the corncrake, alluding to Ortygia (Quail Island), where Leto gave birth to Artemis.

[85] Artemis' cult title in the deme Myrrhinus.

ΠΕΙΣΕΤΑΙΡΟΣ

Δέσποινα Κυβέλη, στροῦθε, μῆτερ Κλεοκρίτου.

ΙΕΡΕΥΣ

διδόναι Νεφελοκοκκυγιεῦσιν
ὑγίειαν καὶ σωτηρίαν
αὐτοῖσι καὶ Χίοισι—

ΠΕΙΣΕΤΑΙΡΟΣ

Χίοισιν ἥσθην πανταχοῦ προσκειμένοις.

ΙΕΡΕΥΣ

καὶ ἥρωσιν ὄρνισι καὶ ἡρώων παισί,
πορφυρίωνι και πελεκᾶντι
καὶ πελεκίνῳ καὶ φλέξιδι
καὶ τέτρακι καὶ ταῶνι
καὶ ἐλεᾷ καὶ βασκᾷ
καὶ ἐλασᾷ καὶ ἐδωλίῳ
καὶ καταρράκτῃ καὶ μελαγκορύφῳ
καὶ αἰγιθάλλῳ—

ΠΕΙΣΕΤΑΙΡΟΣ

παῦ᾽· ἐς κόρακας· παῦσαι καλῶν. ἰοὺ ἰού·
ἐπὶ ποῖον, ὦ κακόδαιμον, ἱερεῖον καλεῖς
ἁλιαιέτους καὶ γῦπας; οὐχ ὁρᾷς ὅτι
ἰκτῖνος εἷς ἂν τοῦτό γ᾽ οἴχοιθ᾽ ἁρπάσας;
ἄπελθ᾽ ἀφ᾽ ἡμῶν καὶ σὺ καὶ τὰ στέμματα·
ἐγὼ γὰρ αὐτὸς τουτογὶ θύσω μόνος.

886 ἐδωλίῳ Sommerstein cl. Σ et Phot.: ἐρῳδίῳ a

PEISETAERUS

Lady Cybele the Ostrich, mother of Cleocritus![86]

PRIEST

grant to the inhabitants of Cloudcuckooland health and security, and for the Chians as well—[87]

PEISETAERUS

It's funny how the Chians get tacked on everywhere!

PRIEST

and the Avian heroes and the Heroes' children, Porphyrion and White Pelican and Grey Pelican and Red Hawk and Grouse and Peacock and Reed Warbler and Teal and Harrier and Heron[88] and Tern and Black Tit and Blue Tit—

PEISETAERUS

Stop, damn you, stop your invitations! Whew! How big do you think this victim is, you jinx, that you're inviting eagles and vultures to share? Don't you realize that a single kite could snatch this away? Get out of here, and take your wreaths with you! I'll perform this sacrifice all by myself.

Exit PRIEST.

86 Perhaps the archon of 413/12 and/or the Herald of the Mysteries who worked to restore democracy in 403 (Xenophon *Hellenica* 2.4.20–22).

87 In the Athenian empire Chios and Methymna enjoyed the special status of autonomous allies.

88 Translating the mss' *erodios*, which displaced the original *edolios*, an unidentified (and therefore untranslatable) bird.

ΧΟΡΟΣ

(ἀντ) εἶτ᾽ αὖθις αὖ τἄρα σοι
δεῖ με δεύτερον μέλος
χέρνιβι θεοσεβὲς ὅσιον ἐπιβοᾶν, καλεῖν
δὲ μάκαρας, ἕνα τινὰ μόνον, εἴ-
περ ἱκανὸν ἕξετ᾽ ὄψον.
τὰ γὰρ παρόντα θύματ᾽ οὐδὲν ἄλλο πλὴν
γένειόν τ᾽ ἐστὶ καὶ κέρατα.

ΠΕΙΣΕΤΑΙΡΟΣ

θύοντες εὐξώμεσθα τοῖς πτερίνοις θεοῖς.

ΠΟΙΗΤΗΣ

Νεφελοκοκκυγίαν
τὰν εὐδαίμονα κλῇσον, ὦ
Μοῦσα, τεαῖς ἐν ὕμνων
ἀοιδαῖς.

ΠΕΙΣΕΤΑΙΡΟΣ

τουτὶ τὸ πρᾶγμα ποδαπόν; εἰπέ μοι, τίς εἶ;

ΠΟΙΗΤΗΣ

ἐγὼ μελιγλώσσων ἐπέων ἱεὶς ἀοιδὰν
Μουσάων θεράπων ὀτρηρός,
κατὰ τὸν Ὅμηρον.

ΠΕΙΣΕΤΑΙΡΟΣ

ἔπειτα δῆτα δοῦλος ὢν κόμην ἔχεις;

ΠΟΙΗΤΗΣ

οὔκ, ἀλλὰ πάντες ἐσμὲν οἱ διδάσκαλοι
Μουσάων θεράποντες ὀτρηροί,
κατὰ τὸν Ὅμηρον.

CHORUS

Then once more in your service
I must raise a second song,
godfearing and pious, for the ablution,
and invite the blessed gods—just one of them,
if you all want to have enough meat,
for the sacrifice you've got there is nothing
but a goatee and horns.

PEISETAERUS

As we sacrifice, let us pray to the feathered gods.

Enter POET.

POET

"Cloudcuckooland
the Blest now celebrate,
O Muse, in your hymns of song!"

PEISETAERUS

Now where did this thing come from? Please identify yourself.

POET

"I am he that launches a song of honey-tongued
verses,
the Muses' eager vassal,"
to quote Homer.

PEISETAERUS

You mean you're a slave, with hair that long?

POET

"No, we master singers all are
the Muses' eager vassals,"
to quote Homer.

ΠΕΙΣΕΤΑΙΡΟΣ

οὐκ ἐτὸς ὀτρηρὸν καὶ τὸ ληδάριον ἔχεις.
ἀτάρ, ὦ ποιητά, κατὰ τί δεῦρ᾽ ἀνεφθάρης;

ΠΟΙΗΤΗΣ

μέλη πεποίηκ᾽ εἰς τὰς Νεφελοκοκκυγίας
τὰς ὑμετέρας κύκλιά τε πολλὰ καὶ καλὰ
καὶ παρθένεια καὶ κατὰ τὰ Σιμωνίδου.

ΠΕΙΣΕΤΑΙΡΟΣ

ταυτὶ σὺ πότ᾽ ἐποίησας; ἀπὸ ποίου χρόνου;

ΠΟΙΗΤΗΣ

πάλαι, πάλαι δὴ τήνδ᾽ ἐγὼ κλῄζω πόλιν.

ΠΕΙΣΕΤΑΙΡΟΣ

οὐκ ἄρτι θύω τὴν δεκάτην ταύτης ἐγώ,
καὶ τοὔνομ᾽ ὥσπερ παιδίῳ νυνδὴ ᾽θέμην;

ΠΟΙΗΤΗΣ

ἀλλά τις ὠκεῖα Μουσάων φάτις
οἷάπερ ἵππων ἀμαρυγά.
σὺ δὲ πάτερ, κτίστορ Αἴτνας,
ζαθέων ἱερῶν ὁμώνυμε,
δὸς ἐμὶν ὅ τι περ τεᾷ κεφαλᾷ θέ-
λεις πρόφρων δόμεν.

ΠΕΙΣΕΤΑΙΡΟΣ

τουτὶ παρέξει τὸ κακὸν ἡμῖν πράγματα,
εἰ μή τι τούτῳ δόντες ἀποφευξούμεθα.

930 δόμεν West praeeunte Blaydes: δόμεν ἐμὶν τείν fere codd.

PEISETAERUS

No wonder you've got a meager jacket to match! Now why the hell did you come up here, poet?

POET

I've composed songs for your Cloudcuckooland, lots of fine dithyrambs, maiden songs, and songs à la Simonides.[89]

PEISETAERUS

When did you compose these songs? Starting when?

POET

I've been celebrating this city for a long, long time.

PEISETAERUS

But I've just begun its tenth-day sacrifice, and named it, like a baby, just moments ago!

POET

"Nay, the Muses' voice is a swift one,
like the twinkle of horses' hooves.
But you, father, founder of Aetna,
namesake of holy rites,
grant me whatever you wish by your nod
graciously to grant."[90]

PEISETAERUS

This pest is going to cause us problems unless we give him something, and thus give him the slip. *(to a Slave)* You

[89] Simonides of Ceos (*c.* 566–468), reputedly the first poet to compose for a fee, had an ancient reputation for avarice, cf. testimonia 22–3 Campbell, *Peace* 697–99.

[90] Adapting a poem by Pindar (fr. 105a) written for the Syracusan ruler Hieron, who founded Aetna in 476/5.

οὗτος, σὺ μέντοι σπολάδα καὶ χιτῶν᾽ ἔχεις,
ἀπόδυθι καὶ δὸς τῷ ποιητῇ τῷ σοφῷ.
ἔχε τὴν σπολάδα· πάντως δέ μοι ῥιγῶν δοκεῖς.

ΠΟΙΗΤΗΣ

τόδε μὲν οὐκ ἀέκουσα φίλα
  Μοῦσα δῶρον δέχεται·
τὺ δὲ τεᾷ φρενὶ μάθε
  Πινδάρειον ἔπος—

ΠΕΙΣΕΤΑΙΡΟΣ

ἄνθρωπος ἡμῶν οὐκ ἀπαλλαχθήσεται

ΠΟΙΗΤΗΣ

νομάδεσσι γὰρ ἐν Σκύθαις ἀλᾶται στρατῶν
  ὃς ὑφαντοδόνητον ἔσθος οὐ πέπαται.
ἀκλεὴς δ᾽ ἔβα
  σπολὰς ἄνευ χιτῶνος.
ξύνες ὅ τοι λέγω.

ΠΕΙΣΕΤΑΙΡΟΣ

ξυνίημ᾽ ὅτι βούλει τὸν χιτωνίσκον λαβεῖν.
ἀπόδυθι· δεῖ γὰρ τὸν ποιητὴν ὠφελεῖν.
ἄπελθε τουτονὶ λαβών.

ΠΟΙΗΤΗΣ

ἀπέρχομαι,
κἀς τὴν πόλιν γ᾽ ἐλθὼν ποιήσω τοιαδί·
"κλῇσον, ὦ χρυσόθρονε, τὰν τρομεράν, κρυεράν·
νιφόβολα πεδία πολύπορά τ᾽ ἤλυθον."
ἀλαλαί.

there, you've got a shirt and vest; take one off and give it to our artful poet. *(to the Poet)* Here, take this vest; you seem to me quite frigid.

POET

"With no reluctance does my dear
Muse accept this gift;
but learn you in your heart
a Pindaric saying—"[91]

PEISETAERUS

The fellow just won't part from us!

POET

"Yea among Scythian nomads does wander apart from
his people
the one who possesses no shuttle-actuated raiment;
and inglorious does go"—a jerkin without a jacket.
Pray understand what I mean.

PEISETAERUS

I understand that you want to snag that short jacket. *(to the other Slave)* Take it off; we've got to help the poet. *(giving the jacket to the Poet)* Take this, and off you go.

POET

I'm off, and when I get back I'm going to compose something like this in honor of your city:
"Celebrate, Muse on golden throne, the shivering,
freezing land;
to the snowblown many-pathed plains have I come."
Hurrah!

Exit POET.

[91] Pindar fr. 105b.

ΠΕΙΣΕΤΑΙΡΟΣ

νὴ τὸν Δί᾽ ἀλλ᾽ ἤδη πέφευγας ταυταγὶ
τὰ κρυερὰ τονδὶ τὸν χιτωνίσκον λαβών.
τουτὶ μὰ Δί᾽ ἐγὼ τὸ κακὸν οὐδέποτ᾽ ἤλπισα,
οὕτω ταχέως τοῦτον πεπύσθαι τὴν πόλιν.
αὖθις σὺ περιχώρει λαβὼν τὴν χέρνιβα.
εὐφημία ᾽στω.

ΧΡΗΣΜΟΛΟΓΟΣ

μὴ κατάρξῃ τοῦ τράγου.

ΠΕΙΣΕΤΑΙΡΟΣ

σὺ δ᾽ εἶ τίς;

ΧΡΗΣΜΟΛΟΓΟΣ

ὅστις; χρησμολόγος.

ΠΕΙΣΕΤΑΙΡΟΣ

οἴμωζέ νυν.

ΧΡΗΣΜΟΛΟΓΟΣ

ὦ δαιμόνιε, τὰ θεῖα μὴ φαύλως φέρε·
ὡς ἔστι Βάκιδος χρησμὸς ἄντικρυς λέγων
εἰς τὰς Νεφελοκοκκυγίας.

ΠΕΙΣΕΤΑΙΡΟΣ

κᾄπειτα πῶς
ταῦτ᾽ οὐκ ἐχρησμολόγεις σὺ πρὶν ἐμὲ τὴν πόλιν
τήνδ᾽ οἰκίσαι;

PEISETAERUS

(calling after him) But surely you've escaped from the freezing cold, now that you've snagged that jacket!—Good god, that was an annoyance I never expected, that he should have heard about our city so soon. *(to a Slave)* Boy, make another circuit with that holy water. Auspicious speech, please.

Enter ORACLE COLLECTOR

ORACLE COLLECTOR

Don't start on that goat!

PEISETAERUS

What? Who are you?

ORACLE COLLECTOR

Why, an oracle collector.

PEISETAERUS

Then to hell with you.

ORACLE COLLECTOR

You daredevil, don't make light of religious matters! There is an oracle of Bacis[92] explicitly referring to Cloudcuckooland.

PEISETAERUS

How come you didn't divulge this oracle *before* I founded the city?

[92] A legendary prophet whose oracles, many of which concerned international relations, were collected and discussed during the Peloponnesian War, cf. *Knights* 123–4, 1003–4, *Peace* 1070.

ΧΡΗΣΜΟΛΟΓΟΣ

τὸ θεῖον ἐνεπόδιζέ με.

ΠΕΙΣΕΤΑΙΡΟΣ

ἀλλ᾽ οὐδὲν οἷον εἰσακοῦσαι τῶν ἐπῶν.

ΧΡΗΣΜΟΛΟΓΟΣ

"ἀλλ᾽ ὅταν οἰκήσωσι λύκοι πολιαί τε κορῶναι
ἐν ταὐτῷ τὸ μεταξὺ Κορίνθου καὶ Σικυῶνος—"

ΠΕΙΣΕΤΑΙΡΟΣ

τί οὖν προσήκει δῆτ᾽ ἐμοὶ Κορινθίων;

ΧΡΗΣΜΟΛΟΓΟΣ

ἠνίξαθ᾽ ὁ Βάκις τοῦτο πρὸς τὸν ἀέρα.
"πρῶτον Πανδώρᾳ θῦσαι λευκότριχα κριόν·
ὃς δέ κ᾽ ἐμῶν ἐπέων ἔλθῃ πρώτιστα προφήτης,
τῷ δόμεν ἱμάτιον καθαρὸν καὶ καινὰ πέδιλα—"

ΠΕΙΣΕΤΑΙΡΟΣ

ἔνεστι καὶ τὰ πέδιλα;

ΧΡΗΣΜΟΛΟΓΟΣ

λαβὲ τὸ βυβλίον.
"καὶ φιάλην δοῦναι καὶ σπλάγχνων χεῖρ᾽
ἐνιπλῆσαι,—"

ΠΕΙΣΕΤΑΙΡΟΣ

καὶ σπλάγχνα διδόν᾽ ἔνεστι;

---

93 Riddling, because these territories were contiguous.
94 Athens and Corinth had long been bitter enemies.

ORACLE COLLECTOR
Religious scruple restrained me.

PEISETAERUS
Well, nothing beats listening to the actual verses.

ORACLE COLLECTOR
"Nay when wolves and grey crows shall together have
their abode
in the place twixt Corinth and Sicyon—"[93]

PEISETAERUS
But what have I got to do with any Corinthians?[94]

ORACLE COLLECTOR
By that enigma Bacis meant the sky.
"first sacrifice to Pandora[95] a ram with white fleece,
and whosoever arrives first as expounder of my
words,
to him give a spotless cloak and fresh sandals—"

PEISETAERUS
Are sandals really in there?

ORACLE COLLECTOR
(showing him) Here's the book.
"and give him the chalice, and fill up his hands with
innards—"

PEISETAERUS
Giving innards is in there too?

[95] Not the allegorical girl with the jar of evils in Hesiod's *Works* 42–105, but the earth goddess whose name means "giver of all gifts," some of which the Oracle Collector now hopes to receive.

ΧΡΗΣΜΟΛΟΓΟΣ

λαβὲ τὸ βυβλίον.
"κἂν μέν, θέσπιε κοῦρε, ποιῇς ταῦθ' ὡς ἐπιτέλλω,
αἰετὸς ἐν νεφέλῃσι γενήσεαι· αἰ δέ κε μὴ δῷς,
οὐκ ἔσει οὐ τρυγών, οὐ λάιος, οὐ δρυκολάπτης."

ΠΕΙΣΕΤΑΙΡΟΣ

καὶ ταῦτ' ἔνεστ' ἐνταῦθα;

ΧΡΗΣΜΟΛΟΓΟΣ

λαβὲ τὸ βυβλίον.

ΠΕΙΣΕΤΑΙΡΟΣ

οὐδὲν ἄρ' ὅμοιός ἐσθ' ὁ χρησμὸς τουτῳί,
ὃν ἐγὼ παρὰ τἀπόλλωνος ἐξεγραψάμην·
"αὐτὰρ ἐπὴν ἄκλητος ἰὼν ἄνθρωπος ἀλαζὼν
λυπῇ θύοντας καὶ σπλαγχνεύειν ἐπιθυμῇ,
δὴ τότε χρὴ τύπτειν αὐτὸν πλευρῶν τὸ μεταξὺ—"

ΧΡΗΣΜΟΛΟΓΟΣ

οὐδὲν λέγειν οἶμαί σε.

ΠΕΙΣΕΤΑΙΡΟΣ

λαβὲ τὸ βυβλίον.
"καὶ φείδου μηδὲν μηδ' αἰετοῦ ἐν νεφέλῃσιν,
μήτ' ἢν Λάμπων ᾖ μήτ' ἢν ὁ μέγας Διοπείθης."

979 οὐ λάιος Meineke: οὐδ' (οὐκ A) αἰετός a

ORACLE COLLECTOR

Here's the book.

"and if, inspired youth, you carry out the orders I give you,
you shall become an eagle midst the clouds; but if you give not,
you shall be not a turtledove, not a rock thrush, not a woodpecker."

PEISETAERUS

That's in there too?

ORACLE COLLECTOR

Here's the book.

PEISETAERUS

(producing a book) Well now, your oracle doesn't match this one at all, an oracle I personally wrote down from Apollo:

"Yea when a charlatan type who arrives uninvited
vexes the sacrificers and desires a share of the innards,
then must you smite him in the place twixt the ribs—"

ORACLE COLLECTOR

You must be kidding.

PEISETAERUS

Here's the book.

"and spare not even an eagle midst the clouds,
not if he be Lampon nor yet the great Diopeithes."[96]

96 An oracular expert and prosecutor of atheists and intellectuals.

ΧΡΗΣΜΟΛΟΓΟΣ

καὶ ταῦτ᾽ ἔνεστ᾽ ἐνταῦθα;

ΠΕΙΣΕΤΑΙΡΟΣ

λαβὲ τὸ βυβλίον.
οὐκ εἶ θύραζ᾽; ἐς κόρακας.

ΧΡΗΣΜΟΛΟΓΟΣ

οἴμοι δείλαιος.

ΠΕΙΣΕΤΑΙΡΟΣ

οὔκουν ἑτέρωσε χρησμολογήσεις ἐκτρέχων;

ΜΕΤΩΝ

ἥκω παρ᾽ ὑμᾶς—

ΠΕΙΣΕΤΑΙΡΟΣ

ἕτερον αὖ τουτὶ κακόν.
τί δ᾽ αὖ σὺ δράσων; τίς ἰδέα βουλεύματος;
τίς ἡπίνοια, τίς ὁ κόθορνος τῆς ὁδοῦ;

ΜΕΤΩΝ

γεωμετρῆσαι βούλομαι τὸν ἀέρα
ὑμῖν διελεῖν τε κατὰ γύας.

ΠΕΙΣΕΤΑΙΡΟΣ

πρὸς τῶν θεῶν,
σὺ δ᾽ εἶ τίς ἀνδρῶν;

994 τίς ὁ κόθορνος τῆς] τίς ποθ᾽ οὔρνις τῆς Blaydes: τῆς κοθορνωτῆς Sommerstein
996 κατὰ γύας Dawes: κατ᾽ ἀγυιάς a

ORACLE COLLECTOR

That's in there too?

PEISETAERUS

(hitting him with the book) Here's the book! Now get the hell out of here!

ORACLE COLLECTOR

Oh mercy me!

Exit ORACLE COLLECTOR

PEISETAERUS

Go on, scat! Do your oracle mongering somewhere else!

Enter METON, *wearing effeminate boots and carrying outsized geometrical instruments.*

METON[97]

I have come here—

PEISETAERUS

(aside) Here's another nuisance. *(to Meton)* And what have *you* come here to do? What form does your plan take? What idea, what buskin, is afoot?

METON

I want to survey the air for you and parcel it into acres.

PEISETAERUS

Good heavens, who on earth are you?

97 The famous geometer and astronomer. His unmanly caricature in this scene may be connected with the rumor that he had resorted to arson just before the expedition to Sicily in order to evade service, cf. Plutarch *Nicias* 13.7–8, *Alcibiades* 17.5–6, Aelian *Varia Historia* 13.12.

ΜΕΤΩΝ

ὅστις εἴμ' ἐγώ; Μέτων,
ὃν οἶδεν Ἑλλὰς χὠ Κολωνός.

ΠΕΙΣΕΤΑΙΡΟΣ

εἰπέ μοι,
ταυτὶ δέ σοι τί ἐστι;

ΜΕΤΩΝ

κανόνες ἀέρος.
αὐτίκα γὰρ ἀήρ ἐστι τὴν ἰδέαν ὅλος
κατὰ πνιγέα μάλιστα. προσθεὶς οὖν ἐγὼ
τὸν κανόν' ἄνωθεν τουτονὶ τὸν καμπύλον,
ἐνθεὶς διαβήτην—μανθάνεις;

ΠΕΙΣΕΤΑΙΡΟΣ

οὐ μανθάνω.

ΜΕΤΩΝ

ὀρθῷ μετρήσω κανόνι προστιθείς, ἵνα
ὁ κύκλος γένηταί σοι τετράγωνος κἀν μέσῳ
ἀγορά, φέρουσαι δ' ὦσιν εἰς αὐτὴν ὁδοὶ
ὀρθαὶ πρὸς αὐτὸ τὸ μέσον, ὥσπερ δ' ἀστέρος
αὐτοῦ κυκλοτεροῦς ὄντος ὀρθαὶ πανταχῇ
ἀκτῖνες ἀπολάμπωσιν.

ΠΕΙΣΕΤΑΙΡΟΣ

ἅνθρωπος Θαλῆς.
Μέτων—

ΜΕΤΩΝ

τί ἐστιν;

METON

Who am I? Meton, renowned in Greece, and in Colonus too.[98]

PEISETAERUS

And pray tell what's all this you've got?

METON

Air rulers. Because for starters, the sky in its entirety is like a casserole cover. Accordingly, by positioning this ruler, which is curved, over its top, inserting a compass—do you follow?

PEISETAERUS

I don't follow.

METON

—and laying a straight ruler alongside it I'll take a measure, so that you will get a circle squared, with a marketplace in the middle, and so there will be straight streets running into it and meeting at the very center, so that just as from a star, itself being round, rays will beam out straight in every direction.

PEISETAERUS

The man's a Thales.[99] Meton—

METON

What is it?

[98] A district of downtown Athens where Meton had set up a sundial, cf. fr. 227, Philochorus FGrH 328 F 122.

[99] The early sixth-century founder of the Milesian school of natural science and philosophy, who had become a byword for genius, cf. *Clouds* 180.

ΠΕΙΣΕΤΑΙΡΟΣ

ἴσθ' ὁτιὴ φιλῶ σ' ἐγώ,
κἀμοὶ πιθόμενος ὑπαποκίνει τῆς ὁδοῦ.

ΜΕΤΩΝ

τί δ' ἐστὶ δεινόν;

ΠΕΙΣΕΤΑΙΡΟΣ

ὥσπερ ἐν Λακεδαίμονι
ξενηλατοῦσι καὶ κεκίνηνταί τινες.
πληγαὶ συχναὶ κατ' ἄστυ.

ΜΕΤΩΝ

μῶν στασιάζετε;

ΠΕΙΣΕΤΑΙΡΟΣ

μὰ τὸν Δί' οὐ δῆτ'.

ΜΕΤΩΝ

ἀλλὰ πῶς;

ΠΕΙΣΕΤΑΙΡΟΣ

ὁμοθυμαδὸν
σποδεῖν ἅπαντας τοὺς ἀλαζόνας δοκεῖ.

ΜΕΤΩΝ

ὑπάγοιμί γ' ἆρ' ἄν.

ΠΕΙΣΕΤΑΙΡΟΣ

νὴ Δί', ὡς οὐκ οἶδ' ἂν εἰ
φθαίης ἄν· ἐπίκεινται γὰρ ἐγγὺς αὑταιί.

ΜΕΤΩΝ

οἴμοι κακοδαίμων.

PEISETAERUS

You know I'm fond of you, so take my advice and hit the road.

METON

What's the problem?

PEISETAERUS

It's like Sparta: they're expelling foreigners, and punches have started flying pretty thick and fast all over town.

METON

You're not having a civil war, are you?

PEISETAERUS

God no, not that!

METON

What then?

PEISETAERUS

There's a unanimous decision to beat up all charlatans.

METON

In that case I *will* be going.

PEISETAERUS

Good idea; I don't know if you can get away in time, because those punches are close at hand. *(punching him)*

METON

Heaven help me!

Exit METON

1013 -τοῦσι Elmsley: -τοῦνται a S: -τοῦντες v.l. Σ

ΠΕΙΣΕΤΑΙΡΟΣ

οὐκ ἔλεγον ἐγὼ πάλαι;
οὐκ ἀναμετρήσει σαυτὸν ἀπιὼν ἀλλαχῇ;

ΕΠΙΣΚΟΠΟΣ

ποῦ πρόξενοι;

ΠΕΙΣΕΤΑΙΡΟΣ

τίς ὁ Σαρδανάπαλλος οὑτοσί;

ΕΠΙΣΚΟΠΟΣ

ἐπίσκοπος ἥκω δεῦρο τῷ κυάμῳ λαχὼν
εἰς τὰς Νεφελοκοκκυγίας.

ΠΕΙΣΕΤΑΙΡΟΣ

ἐπίσκοπος;
ἔπεμψε δὲ τίς σε δεῦρο;

ΕΠΙΣΚΟΠΟΣ

φαῦλον βυβλίον
Τελέου τι.

ΠΕΙΣΕΤΑΙΡΟΣ

βούλει δῆτα τὸν μισθὸν λαβὼν
μὴ πράγματ᾽ ἔχειν ἀλλ᾽ ἀπιέναι;

ΕΠΙΣΚΟΠΟΣ

νὴ τοὺς θεούς.
ἐκκλησιάσαι γοῦν ἐδεόμην οἴκοι μένων·
ἔστιν γὰρ ἃ δι᾽ ἐμοῦ πέπρακται Φαρνάκῃ.

---

100 Exemplifying the travelling inspectors sent by Assembly decree to enforce Athenian policies in the cities of the empire.

PEISETAERUS

Haven't I been trying to warn you? Go somewhere else, and survey yourself!

Enter INSPECTOR, *well dressed and carrying a pair of ballot boxes.*

INSPECTOR[100]

Where can I find consuls?

PEISETAERUS

Who's this Sardanapallus?[101]

INSPECTOR

I'm an Inspector, duly allotted to visit Cloudcuckooland.

PEISETAERUS

Inspector? On whose authority?

INSPECTOR

Some petty bill of Teleas'.

PEISETAERUS

Then would you like to take your pay and just leave, without any fuss?

INSPECTOR

I believe I will. I should be back home anyway, speaking in the Assembly; there's some business I've been handling for Pharnaces.[102]

[101] According to the Greeks, the wealthy and degenerate last king of Assyria before the loss of that empire to the Medes and Babylonians in the late seventh century.

[102] Persian satrap of Dascyleion until *c.* 413, when he was succeeded by his brother Pharnabazus, cf. Thucydides 2.67, 8.6, 58.

ΠΕΙΣΕΤΑΙΡΟΣ

ἄπιθι λαβών· ἔστιν δ' ὁ μισθὸς οὑτοσί.

ΕΠΙΣΚΟΠΟΣ

τουτὶ τί ἦν;

ΠΕΙΣΕΤΑΙΡΟΣ

ἐκκλησία περὶ Φαρνάκου.

ΕΠΙΣΚΟΠΟΣ

μαρτύρομαι τυπτόμενος ὢν ἐπίσκοπος.

ΠΕΙΣΕΤΑΙΡΟΣ

οὐκ ἀποσοβήσεις; οὐκ ἀποίσεις τὼ κάδω;
οὐ δεινά; καὶ πέμπουσιν ἤδη 'πισκόπους
εἰς τὴν πόλιν, πρὶν καὶ τεθύσθαι τοῖς θεοῖς;

ΨΗΦΙΣΜΑΤΟΠΩΛΗΣ

"ἐὰν δ' ὁ Νεφελοκοκκυγιεὺς τὸν Ἀθηναῖον ἀδικῇ—"

ΠΕΙΣΕΤΑΙΡΟΣ

τουτὶ τί ἐστιν αὖ κακόν, τὸ βυβλίον;

ΨΗΦΙΣΜΑΤΟΠΩΛΗΣ

ψηφισματοπώλης εἰμὶ καὶ νόμους νέους
ἥκω παρ' ὑμᾶς δεῦρο πωλήσων.

ΠΕΙΣΕΤΑΙΡΟΣ

τὸ τί;

ΨΗΦΙΣΜΑΤΟΠΩΛΗΣ

"χρῆσθαι Νεφελοκοκκυγιᾶς τοῖς αὐτοῖς μέτροισι

1040 τοῖς αὐτοῖς Boissonade: τοῖσδε τοῖς a

PEISETAERUS

Take your pay and leave; I've got it right here (*punches him*).

INSPECTOR

Hey, what was that?

PEISETAERUS

An assembly about Pharnaces.

INSPECTOR

Witnesses! Inspector under attack!

INSPECTOR runs off.

PEISETAERUS

Shoo, shoo, away with you! And take your ballot boxes too! Amazing—they're already sending inspectors to our city, before we've even held our founding sacrifice!

Enter DECREE SELLER, with a large book.

DECREE SELLER

(*reading*) "And if a Cloudcuckoolander commits an offence against an Athenian—"

PEISETAERUS

What sort of nuisance is this now, this book?

DECREE SELLER

I'm a decree seller, and I'm here to sell you some new laws.

PEISETAERUS

For instance?

DECREE SELLER

"The Cloudcuckoolanders are to use the selfsame mea-

καὶ σταθμοῖσι καὶ ψηφίσμασι καθάπερ Ὀλοφύξιοι.”

ΠΕΙΣΕΤΑΙΡΟΣ

σὺ δέ γ᾽ οἷσπερ Ὠτοτύξιοι χρήσει τάχα.

ΨΗΦΙΣΜΑΤΟΠΩΛΗΣ

οὗτος, τί πάσχεις;

ΠΕΙΣΕΤΑΙΡΟΣ

οὐκ ἀποίσεις τοὺς νόμους;
πικροὺς ἐγώ σοι τήμερον δείξω νόμους.

ΕΠΙΣΚΟΠΟΣ

καλοῦμαι Πεισέταιρον ὕβρεως εἰς τὸν Μουνιχιῶνα μῆνα.

ΠΕΙΣΕΤΑΙΡΟΣ

ἄληθες, οὗτος; ἔτι γὰρ ἐνταῦθ᾽ ἦσθα σύ;

ΨΗΦΙΣΜΑΤΟΠΩΛΗΣ

“ἐὰν δέ τις ἐξελαύνῃ τοὺς ἄρχοντας καὶ μὴ δέχηται
κατὰ τὴν στήλην—”

ΠΕΙΣΕΤΑΙΡΟΣ

οἴμοι κακοδαίμων, καὶ σὺ γὰρ ἐνταῦθ᾽ ἦσθ᾽ ἔτι;

ΕΠΙΣΚΟΠΟΣ

ἀπολῶ σε καὶ γράψω σε μυρίας δραχμάς—

---

103 Parodying the language of the Coinage Decree (*IG* i3 1453 = ML 45, date uncertain), and substituting “decrees” for “coin-

sures, weights, and decrees as the Olophyxians."[103]

PEISETAERUS

And *you'll* soon be getting the same as the Black-and-Bluesians! (*strikes him*)

DECREE SELLER

Hey, what's the matter with you?

PEISETAERUS

Take your laws away from here! In a moment I'll be showing you some laws you won't like!

DECREE SELLER runs off; INSPECTOR reappears.

INSPECTOR

I summon Peisetaerus to appear in the month of Munychion on a charge of assault!

PEISETAERUS

Oh, is that right? What are you still doing here?

DECREE SELLER reappears.

DECREE SELLER

"And should anyone expel the officials and refuse them entry under the terms of the decree—"

PEISETAERUS

Heaven help me, are you still here too?

INSPECTOR

I'll ruin you! I'll write you up for a ten thousand drachma—

age." Olophyxos was a small Athenian ally on the Athos peninsula; Peisetaerus counters with the made-up name "Ototyxians," punning on *ototoi* (a cry of pain).

ΠΕΙΣΕΤΑΙΡΟΣ

ἐγὼ δὲ σοῦ γε τὼ κάδω διασκεδῶ.

ΨΗΦΙΣΜΑΤΟΠΩΛΗΣ

μέμνησ᾽ ὅτε τῆς στήλης κατετίλας ἑσπέρας;

ΠΕΙΣΕΤΑΙΡΟΣ

αἰβοῖ· λαβέτω τις αὐτόν. οὗτος, οὐ μενεῖς;
ἀπίωμεν ἡμεῖς ὡς τάχιστ᾽ ἐντευθενὶ
θύσοντες εἴσω τοῖς θεοῖσι τὸν τράγον.

ΧΟΡΟΣ

(στρ) ἤδη ᾽μοὶ τῷ παντόπτᾳ
καὶ παντάρχᾳ θνητοὶ πάντες
θύσουσ᾽ εὐκταίαις εὐχαῖς.
πᾶσαν μὲν γὰρ γᾶν ὀπτεύω,
σῴζω δ᾽ εὐθαλεῖς καρποὺς
κτείνων παμφύλων γένναν
θηρῶν, ἃ πᾶν τ᾽ ἐν γαίᾳ
ἐκ κάλυκος αὐξανόμενον γένυσι παμφάγοις
δένδρεσί τ᾽ ἐφημένα καρπὸν ἀποβόσκεται.
κτείνω δ᾽ οἳ κήπους εὐώδεις
φθείρουσιν λύμαις ἐχθίσταις·
ἑρπετά τε καὶ δάκετα <πάνθ᾽> ὅσαπερ
ἔστιν, ὑπ᾽ ἐμᾶς πτέρυγος
ἐν φοναῖς ὄλλυται.

1069 suppl. Dissen et Dobree

PEISETAERUS

And I'll smash both of your ballot boxes!

INSPECTOR flees.

DECREE SELLER

Do you recall those evenings when you used to crap on the inscribed decree?

PEISETAERUS

Pew! Somebody grab hold of him!

DECREE SELLER flees.

Hey, why don't you stick around? (*to Slaves*) Let's get away from here as fast as we can, inside, where we can sacrifice the goat to the gods.

PEISETAERUS and Slaves go inside.

CHORUS

To me, the omniscient
and omnipotent, shall all mortals
now sacrifice with pious prayers.
For I keep watch over all the earth,
and keep safe the blooming crops
by slaying the brood of all species
of critters, who with omnivorous jaws
devour all that in soil sprouts from the pod
and the fruit of the trees where they perch;
and I slay those who spoil fragrant gardens
with defilements most offensive;
and upon creepers and biters every one
from the force of my wing
comes murderous destruction.

ΚΟΡΥΦΑΙΟΣ

τῇδε μέντοι θἠμέρᾳ μάλιστ᾽ ἐπαναγορεύεται·
ἢν ἀποκτείνῃ τις ὑμῶν Διαγόραν τὸν Μήλιον,
λαμβάνειν τάλαντον, ἤν τε τῶν τυράννων τίς τινα
τῶν τεθνηκότων ἀποκτείνῃ, τάλαντον λαμβάνειν.
βουλόμεσθ᾽ οὖν νῦν ἀνειπεῖν ταῦτα χἠμεῖς ἐνθάδε·
ἢν ἀποκτείνῃ τις ὑμῶν Φιλοκράτη τὸν Στρούθιον,
λήψεται τάλαντον, ἢν δὲ ζῶντά γ᾽ ἀγάγῃ, τέτταρα,
ὅτι συνείρων τοὺς σπίνους πωλεῖ καθ᾽ ἑπτὰ τοὐβολοῦ,
εἶτα φυσῶν τὰς κίχλας δείκνυσι καὶ λυμαίνεται,
τοῖς τε κοψίχοισιν εἰς τὰς ῥῖνας ἐγχεῖ τὰ πτερά,
τὰς περιστεράς θ᾽ ὁμοίως ξυλλαβὼν εἵρξας ἔχει,
κἀπαναγκάζει παλεύειν δεδεμένας ἐν δικτύῳ.
ταῦτα βουλόμεσθ᾽ ἀνειπεῖν· κεἴ τις ὄρνιθας τρέφει
εἰργμένους ὑμῶν ἐν αὐλῇ, φράζομεν μεθιέναι.
ἢν δὲ μὴ πείθησθε, συλληφθέντες ὑπὸ τῶν ὀρνέων
αὖθις ὑμεῖς αὖ παρ᾽ ἡμῖν δεδεμένοι παλεύσετε.

ΧΟΡΟΣ

(ἀντ) εὔδαιμον φῦλον πτηνῶν
οἰωνῶν, οἳ χειμῶνος μὲν
χλαίνας οὐκ ἀμπισχνοῦνται·

1078 ζῶντά γ᾽ ἀγάγῃ Burges: ζωνταπ̣αγαγη Π1: ζῶντ᾽ ἀγάγῃ a

---

104 Presumably (but not demonstrably) the first day of the Dionysia.

CHORUS LEADER

On this particular day,[104] you know, we hear it again proclaimed that whoever of you kills Diagoras the Melian[105] shall get a talent, and whoever kills any of the long deceased tyrants[106] shall get a talent. So now we want to make our own announcement right here: whoever of you kills Philocrates the Sparrovian shall get a talent, and four for bringing him in alive, on the grounds that he strings finches together and sells them seven an obol; furthermore that he inflates thrushes for degrading display; and crams the noses of blackbirds with their own feathers; and captures pigeons, keeps them caged, and forces them to play decoy, tethered to a net. That's the announcement we want to make. And whoever of you keeps caged birds in the yard, we order you to let them go; if you disobey, you will be captured by the birds, and it will be your turn to play decoy on our turf.

CHORUS

Happy the race of feathered
birds, who in the winter
need wear no woolen cloaks;

[105] Dubbed "Diagoras of Quibbleton" by Hermippus in 430 (fr. 43) and aligned with Socrates in *Clouds* 830; outlawed for writings critical of the Eleusinian Mysteries, cf. Craterus *FGrH* 342 F 16 and Melanthius 326 F 3.

[106] Though the last Athenian tyrant had been expelled in 510 and there had been no real threat of a return to tyranny since the Persian Wars, demagogues kept the threat alive (cf. e.g. *Wasps* 488–507), and the recent scandals surrounding Alcibiades had reawakened popular fears of antidemocratic plots (Thucydides 6.53 ff.).

οὐδ᾽ αὖ θερμὴ πνίγους ἡμᾶς
ἀκτὶς τηλαυγὴς θάλπει·
ἀλλ᾽ ἀνθηρῶν λειμώνων
φύλλ᾽ ἐν κόλποις ἐνναίω,
ἡνίκ᾽ ἂν ὁ θεσπέσιος ὀξὺ μέλος ἀχέτας
θάλπεσι μεσημβρινοῖς ἡλιομανὴς βοᾷ.
χειμάζω δ᾽ ἐν κοίλοις ἄντροις
νύμφαις οὐρείαις ξυμπαίζων·
ἠρινά τε βοσκόμεθα παρθένια
λευκότροφα μύρτα Χαρί-
των τε κηπεύματα.

ΚΟΡΥΦΑΙΟΣ

τοῖς κριταῖς εἰπεῖν τι βουλόμεσθα τῆς νίκης πέρι,
ὅσ᾽ ἀγάθ᾽, ἢν κρίνωσιν ἡμᾶς, πᾶσιν αὐτοῖς
δώσομεν,
ὥστε κρείττω δῶρα πολλῷ τῶν Ἀλεξάνδρου λαβεῖν.
πρῶτα μὲν γάρ, οὗ μάλιστα πᾶς κριτὴς ἐφίεται,
γλαῦκες ὑμᾶς οὔποτ᾽ ἐπιλείψουσι Λαυρειωτικαί·
ἀλλ᾽ ἐνοικήσουσιν ἔνδον, ἔν τε τοῖς βαλλαντίοις
ἐννεοττεύσουσι κἀκλέψουσι μικρὰ κέρματα.
εἶτα πρὸς τούτοισιν ὥσπερ ἐν ἱεροῖς οἰκήσετε·
τὰς γὰρ ὑμῶν οἰκίας ἐρέψομεν πρὸς αἰετόν·
κἂν λαχόντες ἀρχίδιον εἶθ᾽ ἁρπάσαι βούλησθέ τι,
ὀξὺν ἱερακίσκον εἰς τὰς χεῖρας ὑμῖν δώσομεν.
ἢν δέ που δειπνῆτε, πρηγορεῶνας ὑμῖν πέμψομεν.
ἢν δὲ μὴ κρίνητε, χαλκεύεσθε μηνίσκους φορεῖν
ὥσπερ ἀνδριάντες· ὡς ὑμῶν ὃς ἂν μὴ μῆν᾽ ἔχῃ,

nor in summer's stifling heat
do the long rays roast us.
For I dwell among the flora
in the lap of flowery meadows,
when the sun-crazy cicada with voice divine
in the noonday heat intones his keen song;
and I winter in hollow caverns,
frolicking with mountain nymphs;
and in spring we graze on myrtle berries,
maidenly in their white florets,
and the fruits of the Graces' garden.

CHORUS LEADER

We'd like to say a word to the judges about winning the prize, namely all the benefits we'll bestow on them all if they vote for us, so they'll get far better gifts than Paris got.[107] Let's begin with what every judge craves most, those owls from Laureium:[108] they will never run out on you, no, they'll move into your house, and nest in your wallets, and hatch out small change. On top of that, you'll live in houses like temples, because we'll roof them with eagle gables. If you draw a nice little post, then want to do some pilfering, we'll equip you with a sharp crowbar. And if you go out for dinner, we'll send you each off with a gizzard. But if you vote against us, you'd better make some copper lids to wear, like statues, because any of you who doesn't

[107] Priam's son Alexander, better known as Paris, served as the judge of a divine beauty contest and got Helen as a bribe from Aphrodite for picking her over Hera and Athena.

[108] Coins made from silver mined at Laureium and bearing Athena's owl as an emblem.

ὅταν ἔχητε χλανίδα λευκήν, τότε μάλισθ᾽ οὕτω δίκην
δώσεθ᾽ ἡμῖν, πᾶσι τοῖς ὄρνισι κατατιλώμενοι.

ΠΕΙΣΕΤΑΙΡΟΣ

τὰ μὲν ἱέρ᾽ ἡμῖν ἐστιν, ὦρνιθες, καλά.
ἀλλ᾽ ὡς ἀπὸ τοῦ τείχους πάρεστιν ἄγγελος
οὐδείς, ὅτου πευσόμεθα τἀκεῖ πράγματα.
ἀλλ᾽ οὑτοσὶ τρέχει τις Ἀλφειὸν πνέων.

ΑΓΓΕΛΟΣ Α´

ποῦ ποῦ ᾽στι, ποῦ ποῦ ποῦ ᾽στι, ποῦ ποῦ ποῦ ᾽στι, ποῦ,
ποῦ Πεισέταιρός ἐστιν ἄρχων;

ΠΕΙΣΕΤΑΙΡΟΣ

οὑτοσί.

ΑΓΓΕΛΟΣ Α´

ἐξῳκοδόμηταί σοι τὸ τεῖχος.

ΠΕΙΣΕΤΑΙΡΟΣ

εὖ λέγεις.

ΑΓΓΕΛΟΣ Α´

κάλλιστον ἔργον καὶ μεγαλοπρεπέστατον·
ὥστ᾽ ἂν ἐπάνω μὲν Προξενίδης ὁ Κομπασεὺς
καὶ Θεογένης ἐναντίω δύ᾽ ἅρματε,
ἵππων ὑπόντων μέγεθος ὅσον ὁ δούριος,
ὑπὸ τοῦ πλάτους ἂν παρελασαίτην.

have a lid, whenever you're wearing a white suit, that's just when you'll pay the piper, getting crapped on by all of the birds.

Enter PEISETAERUS.

PEISETAERUS

Our sacrifice, dear birds, has been auspicious. But how strange that no messenger is here from the wall, to brief us on how things are going there. Wait, here comes someone on the run, panting like an Olympic sprinter.

Enter FIRST MESSENGER.

FIRST MESSENGER

Whe whe where's, whe whe whe where's, whe whe whe where's, whe whe where's Peisetaerus, the ruler?

PEISETAERUS

Right here.

FIRST MESSENGER

Your wall is all built.

PEISETAERUS

Good news!

FIRST MESSENGER

A very fine and very impressive achievement; it's so wide on top, Proxenides of Braggarton[109] and Theogenes could hitch two chariots to horses the size of the wooden one,[110] and pass each other head-on!

[109] Also called a braggart in *Wasps* 324–25.

[110] In which the Greeks concealed themselves in order to enter Troy.

ΠΕΙΣΕΤΑΙΡΟΣ

Ἡράκλεις.

ΑΓΓΕΛΟΣ Α΄

τὸ δὲ μῆκός ἐστι, καὶ γὰρ ἐμέτρησ᾽ αὔτ᾽ ἐγώ,
ἑκατοντορόγυιον.

ΠΕΙΣΕΤΑΙΡΟΣ

ὦ Πόσειδον, τοῦ μάκρους.
τίνες ᾠκοδόμησαν αὐτὸ τηλικουτονί;

ΑΓΓΕΛΟΣ Α΄

ὄρνιθες, οὐδεὶς ἄλλος, οὐκ Αἰγύπτιος
πλινθοφόρος, οὐ λιθουργός, οὐ τέκτων παρῆν,
ἀλλ᾽ αὐτόχειρες, ὥστε θαυμάζειν ἐμέ.
ἐκ μέν γε Λιβύης ἧκον ὡς τρισμύριαι
γέρανοι θεμελίους καταπεπωκυῖαι λίθους·
τούτους δ᾽ ἐτύκιζον αἱ κρέκες τοῖς ῥύγχεσιν.
ἕτεροι δ᾽ ἐπλινθούργουν πελαργοὶ μύριοι·
ὕδωρ δ᾽ ἐφόρουν κάτωθεν εἰς τὸν ἀέρα
οἱ χαραδριοὶ καὶ τἄλλα ποτάμι᾽ ὄρνεα.

ΠΕΙΣΕΤΑΙΡΟΣ

ἐπηλοφόρουν δ᾽ αὐτοῖσι τίνες;

ΑΓΓΕΛΟΣ Α΄

ἐρῳδιοὶ
λεκάναισι.

ΠΕΙΣΕΤΑΙΡΟΣ

τὸν δὲ πηλὸν ἐνεβάλλοντο πῶς;

1139 -ούργουν Bergk: -οφόρουν a

PEISETAERUS

Heracles!

FIRST MESSENGER

And as for its height—and I measured it myself—it's a hundred fathoms.

PEISETAERUS

Poseidon, that's high! Who built it so tall?

FIRST MESSENGER

Birds and birds alone, with no Egyptian brickbearer in sight, no mason, no carpenter, all with their own hands, an amazing sight to see. From Libya there came some thirty thousand cranes, who'd swallowed stones for the foundations, and these the corncrakes blocked with their bills, while another ten thousand storks made bricks, and the curlews with their fellow river birds brought water up to the sky.

PEISETAERUS

And who brought clay for them?

FIRST MESSENGER

Herons, in hods.

PEISETAERUS

And how did they get the clay into the hods?

ΑΓΓΕΛΟΣ Α΄

τοῦτ᾽, ὦγάθ᾽, ἐξηύρητο καὶ σοφώτατα·
οἱ χῆνες ὑποτύπτοντες ὥσπερ ταῖς ἄμαις
εἰς τὰς λεκάνας ἐνέβαλλον αὐτὸν τοῖν ποδοῖν.

ΠΕΙΣΕΤΑΙΡΟΣ

τί δῆτα πόδες ἂν οὐκ ἂν ἐργασαίατο;

ΑΓΓΕΛΟΣ Α΄

καὶ νὴ Δί᾽ αἱ νῆτταί γε περιεζωσμέναι
ἐπλινθοβόλουν· ἄνω δὲ τὸν ὑπαγωγέα
ἐπέτοντ᾽ ἔχουσαι κατόπιν, ὥσπερ παιδία,
τὸν πηλὸν ἐν τοῖς στόμασιν αἱ χελιδόνες.

ΠΕΙΣΕΤΑΙΡΟΣ

τί δῆτα μισθωτοὺς ἂν ἔτι μισθοῖτό τις;
φέρ᾽ ἴδω, τί δαί; τὰ ξύλινα τοῦ τείχους τίνες
ἀπηργάσαντ᾽;

ΑΓΓΕΛΟΣ Α΄

ὄρνιθες ἦσαν τέκτονες
σοφώτατοι πελεκᾶντες, οἳ τοῖς ῥύγχεσιν
ἀπεπελέκησαν τὰς πύλας· ἦν δ᾽ ὁ κτύπος
αὐτῶν πελεκώντων ὥσπερ ἐν ναυπηγίῳ.
καὶ νῦν ἅπαντ᾽ ἐκεῖνα πεπύλωται πύλαις
καὶ βεβαλάνωται καὶ φυλάττεται κύκλῳ,
ἐφοδεύεται, κωδωνοφορεῖται, πανταχῇ
φυλακαὶ καθεστήκασι καὶ φρυκτωρίαι
ἐν τοῖσι πύργοις. ἀλλ᾽ ἐγὼ μὲν ἀποτρέχων
ἀπονίψομαι· σὺ δ᾽ αὐτὸς ἤδη τἄλλα δρᾶ.

FIRST MESSENGER

That, my friend, was sheer genius: the geese dug their feet into it like shovels, and scooped it right into the herons' hods.

PEISETAERUS

I guess nothing's impossible if you put your feet to it!

FIRST MESSENGER

And by god there were the ducks, wearing belts and laying the bricks; and up flew the swallows with the trowel at their rear, like kiddies,[111] and plaster in their mouths.

PEISETAERUS

Then why go on hiring workmen? Let's see, what else? Who did the woodwork for the wall?

FIRST MESSENGER

The carpenter birds, very skilled, were woodpeckers, who pecked out the gates with their beaks; the din of their pecking was just like a shipyard! And now all those gateways are gated and bolted and surrounded by guards, patrolled by bell ringers; everywhere sentries are in place, with signal fires on the towers. As for me, I'm off to have a bath; see to the rest yourself.

Exit FIRST MESSENGER

[111] The Greek is obscure and possibly corrupt.

1149 -*βόλουν* Higham: -*φόρουν* a S
1151 *καὶ* Lenting: *τὸν* a

ΚΟΡΥΦΑΙΟΣ

οὗτος, τί ποιεῖς; ἆρα θαυμάζεις ὅτι
οὕτω τὸ τεῖχος ἐκτετείχισται ταχύ;

ΠΕΙΣΕΤΑΙΡΟΣ

νὴ τοὺς θεοὺς ἔγωγε· καὶ γὰρ ἄξιον·
ἴσα γὰρ ἀληθῶς φαίνεταί μοι ψεύδεσιν.
ἀλλ᾽ ὅδε φύλαξ γὰρ τῶν ἐκεῖθεν ἄγγελος
εἰσθεῖ πρὸς ἡμᾶς δεῦρο πυρρίχην βλέπων.

ΑΓΓΕΛΟΣ Β´

ἰοὺ ἰού, ἰοὺ ἰού, ἰοὺ ἰού.

ΠΕΙΣΕΤΑΙΡΟΣ

τί τὸ πρᾶγμα τουτί;

ΑΓΓΕΛΟΣ Β´

δεινότατα πεπόνθαμεν.
τῶν γὰρ θεῶν τις ἄρτι τῶν παρὰ τοῦ Διὸς
διὰ τῶν πυλῶν εἰσέπτατ᾽ εἰς τὸν ἀέρα,
λαθὼν κολοιοὺς φύλακας ἡμεροσκόπους.

ΠΕΙΣΕΤΑΙΡΟΣ

ὦ δεινὸν ἔργον καὶ σχέτλιον εἰργασμένος.
τίς τῶν θεῶν;

ΑΓΓΕΛΟΣ Β´

οὐκ ἴσμεν· ὅτι δ᾽ εἶχε πτερά,
τοῦτ᾽ ἴσμεν.

ΠΕΙΣΕΤΑΙΡΟΣ

οὔκουν δῆτα περιπόλους ἐχρῆν
πέμψαι κατ᾽ αὐτὸν εὐθύς;

CHORUS LEADER

Hey there, what's the matter? Amazed that the wall's been walled up so quickly?

PEISETAERUS

Heavens above, I certainly am; and rightly so. To tell the truth, it sounds like a mighty tall tale! But look, here's a guard coming on the run to report on events over there, looking like a war dancer.

Enter SECOND MESSENGER

SECOND MESSENGER

S.O.S! S.O.S! S.O.S!

PEISETAERUS

What's all this fuss?

SECOND MESSENGER

We've got terrible problems! One of the gods, Zeus' gods, has just now flown through the gates into our airspace, dodging the jackdaws, our daytime sentries.

PEISETAERUS

A dire deed defiantly done! Which one of the gods?

SECOND MESSENGER

We don't know; he had wings, we know that much.

PEISETAERUS

Then shouldn't you have sent a border patrol after him at once?

ΑΓΓΕΛΟΣ Β´

ἀλλ᾽ ἐπέμψαμεν
τρισμυρίους ἱέρακας ἱπποτοξότας·
χωρεῖ δὲ πᾶς τις ὄνυχας ἠγκυλωμένος,
κερχνῄς, τριόρχης, γύψ, κύμινδις, αἰετός·
ῥύμῃ τε καὶ πτεροῖσι καὶ ῥοιζήμασιν
αἰθὴρ δονεῖται τοῦ θεοῦ ζητουμένου·
κἄστ᾽ οὐ μακρὰν ἄπωθεν, ἀλλ᾽ ἐνταῦθά που
ἤδη ᾽στίν.

ΠΕΙΣΕΤΑΙΡΟΣ

οὐκοῦν σφενδόνας δεῖ λαμβάνειν
καὶ τόξα. χώρει δεῦρο πᾶς ὑπηρέτης·
τόξευε, παῖε· σφενδόνην τίς μοι δότω.

ΧΟΡΟΣ

(στρ) πόλεμος αἴρεται, πόλεμος οὐ φατός,
πρὸς ἐμὲ καὶ θεούς. ἀλλὰ φύλαττε πᾶς
ἀέρα περινέφελον, ὃν Ἔρεβος ἐτέκετο,
μή σε λάθῃ θεῶν τις ταύτῃ περῶν.

ΚΟΡΥΦΑΙΟΣ

ἄθρει δὲ πᾶς κύκλῳ σκοπῶν·
ὡς ἐγγὺς ἤδη δαίμονος πεδαρσίου
δίνης πτερωτὸς φθόγγος ἐξακούεται.

ΠΕΙΣΕΤΑΙΡΟΣ

αὕτη σύ, ποῖ ποῖ ποῖ πέτει; μέν᾽ ἥσυχος,
ἔχ᾽ ἀτρέμας αὐτοῦ· στῆθ᾽· ἐπίσχες τοῦ δρόμου.
τίς εἶ; ποδαπή; λέγειν ἐχρῆν ὁπόθεν ποτ᾽ εἶ.

SECOND MESSENGER

We've done that, thirty thousand mounted archer hawks, and every bird with hooked talons is going along, kestrel, buzzard, vulture, great owl, eagle, and the sky's awhirl with the whirring of wings as the god's hunted down. And he's not far off; no, he's already somewhere nearby.

Exit SECOND MESSENGER

PEISETAERUS

Then shouldn't we be taking up slings and arrows? All support personnel fall in! Shoot and sling! Somebody give me a sling!

Enter Xanthias and Manes with the weapons.

CHORUS

War's broken out, war beyond words,
between me and the gods! Now everyone stand guard
on the cloud-girt air, scion of Erebus,
in case some god sneaks past you here unseen.

CHORUS LEADER

And everyone be alert on every side; the sound of an airborne god's whirring wings is already audible nearby.

IRIS *appears aloft on the stage crane.*

PEISETAERUS

You there! Where where where are you flying? Be still! Stay right where you are! Halt! Stop moving! Who are you? Where from? You'd better start explaining just where you're from!

ΙΡΙΣ

παρὰ τῶν θεῶν ἔγωγε τῶν Ὀλυμπίων.

ΠΕΙΣΕΤΑΙΡΟΣ

ὄνομα δέ σοι τί; Πάραλος ἢ Σαλαμινία;

ΙΡΙΣ

Ἶρις ταχεῖα.

ΠΕΙΣΕΤΑΙΡΟΣ

<πότερα> πλοῖον ἢ κύων;

ΙΡΙΣ

τί δὲ τοῦτο;

ΠΕΙΣΕΤΑΙΡΟΣ

ταυτηνί τις οὐ ξυλλήψεται
ἀναπτόμενος τρίορχος;

ΙΡΙΣ

ἐμὲ ξυλλήψεται;
τί ποτ᾽ ἐστὶ τουτὶ τὸ κακόν;

ΠΕΙΣΕΤΑΙΡΟΣ

οἰμώξει μακρά.

ΙΡΙΣ

ἄτοπόν γε τουτὶ πρᾶγμα.

ΠΕΙΣΕΤΑΙΡΟΣ

κατὰ ποίας πύλας
εἰσῆλθες εἰς τὸ τεῖχος, ὦ μιαρωτάτη;

1203 τί; Πάραλος ἢ Σαλαμινία; Robert: τί ἐστι; πλοῖον ἢ κυνῆ a S

IRIS[112]

From the gods I hail, the Olympian gods.

PEISETAERUS

And what's your name? Paralus or Salaminia?[113]

IRIS

Iris the Speedy.

PEISETAERUS

Boat or bitch?

IRIS

What *is* this?

PEISETAERUS

One of you cockerels, fly up and grab her!

IRIS

Grab me? What the hell is that supposed to mean?

PEISETAERUS

You're going to be awfully sorry!

IRIS

This is quite extraordinary.

PEISETAERUS

By what gate did you pass through the wall, you slut?

[112] Goddess of the rainbow and messenger of Zeus in epic and tragedy, but often rudely treated in satyr drama.

[113] See 146 n.

1204 ‹πότερα› πλοῖον ἢ κύων; Robert: Πάραλος ἢ Σαλαμινία a

ΙΡΙΣ

οὐκ οἶδα μὰ Δί᾽ ἔγωγε, κατὰ ποίας πύλας.

ΠΕΙΣΕΤΑΙΡΟΣ

ἤκουσας αὐτῆς οἷον εἰρωνεύεται;
πρὸς τοὺς κολοιάρχους προσῆλθες;

ΙΡΙΣ

πῶς λέγεις;

ΠΕΙΣΕΤΑΙΡΟΣ

σφραγῖδ᾽ ἔχεις παρὰ τῶν πελαργῶν;

ΙΡΙΣ

τί τὸ κακόν;

ΠΕΙΣΕΤΑΙΡΟΣ

οὐκ ἔλαβες;

ΙΡΙΣ

ὑγιαίνεις μέν;

ΠΕΙΣΕΤΑΙΡΟΣ

οὐδὲ σύμβολον
ἐπέβαλεν ὀρνίθαρχος οὐδείς σοι παρών;

ΙΡΙΣ

μὰ Δί᾽ οὐκ ἔμοιγ᾽ ἐπέβαλεν οὐδείς, ὦ μέλε.

ΠΕΙΣΕΤΑΙΡΟΣ

κᾄπειτα δῆθ᾽ οὕτω σιωπῇ διαπέτει
διὰ τῆς πόλεως τῆς ἀλλοτρίας καὶ τοῦ χάους;

ΙΡΙΣ

ποίᾳ γὰρ ἄλλῃ χρὴ πέτεσθαι τοὺς θεούς;

IRIS

I have absolutely no idea what gate.

PEISETAERUS

Just listen to Miss Innocent! Did you accost the Duty Daws?

IRIS

I beg your pardon?

PEISETAERUS

Did the Storks punch your ticket?

IRIS

How dare you!

PEISETAERUS

You didn't accept a pass?

IRIS

You are sane, I trust?

PEISETAERUS

And no Top Cock was around to enter your passage?

IRIS

Listen, mister, nobody's entered me at all!

PEISETAERUS

And so you just fly in this stealthy way through a city that's not yours, and through the void?

IRIS

But where else are the gods supposed to fly?

1212 προσῆλθες; : πῶς Bachmann: πῶς (del. t) προσῆλθες; οὐ a

ΠΕΙΣΕΤΑΙΡΟΣ

οὐκ οἶδα μὰ Δί' ἔγωγε· τῇδε μὲν γὰρ οὔ.
ἀδικεῖς δὲ καὶ νῦν. ἆρά γ' οἶσθα τοῦθ' ὅτι
δικαιότατ' ἂν ληφθεῖσα πασῶν Ἰρίδων
ἀπέθανες, εἰ τῆς ἀξίας ἐτύγχανες;

ΙΡΙΣ

ἀλλ' ἀθάνατός εἰμ'.

ΠΕΙΣΕΤΑΙΡΟΣ

ἀλλ' ὅμως ἂν ἀπέθανες.
δεινότατα γάρ τοι πεισόμεσθ', ἐμοὶ δοκεῖ,
εἰ τῶν μὲν ἄλλων ἄρχομεν, ὑμεῖς δ' οἱ θεοὶ
ἀκολαστανεῖτε, κοὐδέπω γνώσεσθ' ὅτι
ἀκροατέον ὑμῖν ἐν μέρει τῶν κρειττόνων.
φράσον δέ μοι νῦν τὼ πτέρυγε ποῖ ναυστολεῖς;

ΙΡΙΣ

ἐγὼ πρὸς ἀνθρώπους πέτομαι παρὰ τοῦ πατρὸς
φράσουσα θύειν τοῖς Ὀλυμπίοις θεοῖς
μηλοσφαγεῖν τε βουθύτοις ἐπ' ἐσχάραις
κνισᾶν τ' ἀγυιάς.

ΠΕΙΣΕΤΑΙΡΟΣ

τί σὺ λέγεις; ποίοις θεοῖς;

ΙΡΙΣ

ποίοισιν; ἡμῖν, τοῖς ἐν οὐρανῷ θεοῖς.

ΠΕΙΣΕΤΑΙΡΟΣ

θεοὶ γὰρ ὑμεῖς;

PEISETAERUS

I've absolutely no idea, but not through here. In fact, you're breaking the law right now. Do you realize that if you got what's coming to you, you'd deserve more than all other Irises to be captured and put to death?

IRIS

But I'm deathless!

PEISETAERUS

You'd be put to death anyway. Look here, we'll be in a terrible fix, the way I see it, if we're to be the rulers but you gods intend to misbehave and ignore the fact that it's now your turn to obey your superiors. So tell me right now where you're navigating those wings.

IRIS

I'll have you know I'm flying from the Father to mankind to deliver this message: give sacrifice to the Olympian gods; slaughter sheep on sacrificial altars; and fill the boulevards with their aromas.

PEISETAERUS

What do you mean? What gods?

IRIS

I mean us, the gods in heaven.

PEISETAERUS

So you're gods, eh?

1229 *μοι νῦν* Henderson: *τοί μοι* a

ΙΡΙΣ

τίς γάρ ἐστ᾽ ἄλλος θεός;

ΠΕΙΣΕΤΑΙΡΟΣ

ὄρνιθες ἀνθρώποισι νῦν εἰσιν θεοί,
οἷς θυτέον αὐτούς, ἀλλὰ μὰ Δί᾽ οὐ τῷ Διί.

ΙΡΙΣ

ὦ μῶρε, μῶρε, μὴ θεῶν κίνει φρένας
δεινάς, ὅπως μή σου γένος πανώλεθρον
Διὸς μακέλλῃ πᾶν ἀναστρέψει Δίκη,
λιγνὺς δὲ σῶμα καὶ δόμων περιπτυχὰς
καταιθαλώσει σου Λικυμνίοις βολαῖς.

ΠΕΙΣΕΤΑΙΡΟΣ

ἄκουσον, αὕτη· παῦε τῶν παφλασμάτων·
ἔχ᾽ ἀτρέμα. φέρ᾽ ἴδω, πότερα Λυδὸν ἢ Φρύγα
ταυτὶ λέγουσα μορμολύττεσθαι δοκεῖς;
ἆρ᾽ οἶσθ᾽ ὅτι Ζεὺς εἴ με λυπήσει πέρα,
μέλαθρα μὲν αὐτοῦ καὶ δόμους Ἀμφίονος
καταιθαλώσω πυρφόροισιν αἰετοῖς,
πέμψω δὲ πορφυρίωνας εἰς τὸν οὐρανὸν
ὄρνις ἐπ᾽ αὐτὸν παρδαλᾶς ἐνημμένους
πλεῖν ἑξακοσίους τὸν ἀριθμόν; καὶ δή ποτε
εἷς Πορφυρίων αὐτῷ παρέσχε πράγματα.
σὺ δ᾽ εἴ με λυπήσεις τι, τῆς διακόνου
πρώτης ἀνατείνας τὼ σκέλει διαμηριῶ
τὴν Ἶριν αὐτήν, ὥστε θαυμάζειν ὅπως
οὕτω γέρων ὢν στύομαι τριέμβολον.

IRIS

Who else do you consider a god?

PEISETAERUS

Birds are gods to humans now, and to them must humans sacrifice, not, by Zeus, to Zeus!

IRIS

Ah fool, fool! Provoke not the terrible spleen of the gods, lest Justice wielding the Spade of Zeus utterly eradicate all your race; lest fiery fumes inflame your body and the enfolding embrace of your palace with thunderbolts Licymnian![114]

PEISETAERUS

Hey listen, stop your spluttering! Whoa there! Say, do you think it's a Lydian or a Phrygian you're trying to spook with that kind of talk? Do you realize that if Zeus annoys me any further, I shall inflame his manse and the halls of Amphion with flame-throwing eagles,[115] and I shall send into the sky against him porphyrion birds clad in leopard skins,[116] more than six hundred strong? And there was a time when just one Porphyrion caused him some trouble! And as for you, if you annoy me one bit, I'll deal with the servant girl first, Iris herself, spread her legs and screw her, and she'll be amazed how an old hulk like me can stay aloft for three rammings!

114 According to scholia "a character in Euripides' *Licymnius* was thunderstruck," but no further details are known.

115 Adapted, according to scholia, from Aeschylus' *Niobe* (fr. 160); cf. also Sophocles *Antigone* 2 and 1155.

116 553 n.; some painters thus depicted the Giants.

ΙΡΙΣ

διαρραγείης, ὦ μέλ᾽, αὐτοῖς ῥήμασιν.

ΠΕΙΣΕΤΑΙΡΟΣ

οὐκ ἀποσοβήσεις; οὐ ταχέως; εὐρὰξ, πατάξ.

ΙΡΙΣ

ἦ μήν σε παύσει τῆς ὕβρεως οὑμὸς πατήρ.

ΠΕΙΣΕΤΑΙΡΟΣ

οἴμοι τάλας. οὔκουν ἑτέρωσε πετομένη
καταιθαλώσεις τῶν νεωτέρων τινά;

ΧΟΡΟΣ

(ἀντ) ἀποκεκλῄκαμεν διογενεῖς θεοὺς
μηκέτι τὴν ἐμὴν διαπερᾶν πόλιν,
μηδέ τιν᾽ ἱερόθυτον ἀνὰ δάπεδον <ἓν> ἔτι
τῇδε βροτῶν θεοῖσι πέμπειν καπνόν.

ΠΕΙΣΕΤΑΙΡΟΣ

δεινόν γε τὸν κήρυκα τὸν παρὰ τοὺς βροτοὺς
οἰχόμενον, εἰ μηδέποτε νοστήσει πάλιν.

ΚΗΡΥΞ Α´

ὦ Πεισέταιρ᾽, ὦ μακάρι᾽, ὦ σοφώτατε,
ὦ κλεινότατ᾽, ὦ σοφώτατ᾽, ὦ γλαφυρώτατε,
ὦ τρισμακάρι᾽, ὦ—κατακέλευσον.

ΠΕΙΣΕΤΑΙΡΟΣ

τί σὺ λέγεις;

1266 <ἓν> Dunbar praeeunte Stahl

IRIS

Blast you, mister, you and your foul language!

PEISETAERUS

Buzz off now, and make it quick! Shoo, shoo!

IRIS

I swear my father will put a stop to your insolence!

PEISETAERUS

Good grief, fly somewhere else why don't you, and inflame some younger man.

IRIS flies off.

CHORUS

We have barred the gods sprung from Zeus
from any further passage through my city,
and no more shall any mortal on a single killing floor
send savory smoke to the gods by this route.

PEISETAERUS

It's terribly worrisome, the herald who went to mankind, if he never comes back again.

Enter FIRST HERALD, holding a golden crown.

FIRST HERALD

Hail Peisetaerus, Hail the Blest One, Hail the Most Wise, Hail the Most Illustrious, Hail the Most Wise, Hail the Most Slick, Hail the Triple Blest, Hail the—just give me my cue!

PEISETAERUS

What's your message?

ΚΗΡΥΞ Α´

στεφάνῳ σε χρυσῷ τῷδε σοφίας οὕνεκα
στεφανοῦσι καὶ τιμῶσιν οἱ πάντες λεῴ.

ΠΕΙΣΕΤΑΙΡΟΣ

δέχομαι. τί δ' οὕτως οἱ λεῴ τιμῶσί με;

ΚΗΡΥΞ Α´

ὦ κλεινοτάτην αἰθέριον οἰκίσας πόλιν,
οὐκ οἶσθ' ὅσην τιμὴν παρ' ἀνθρώποις φέρει
ὅσους τ' ἐραστὰς τῆσδε τῆς χώρας ἔχεις;
πρὶν μὲν γὰρ οἰκίσαι σε τήνδε τὴν πόλιν,
ἐλακωνομάνουν ἅπαντες ἄνθρωποι τότε,
ἐκόμων, ἐπείνων, ἐρρύπων, ἐσωκράτων,
ἐσκυταλιοφόρουν· νῦν δ' ὑποστρέψαντες αὖ
ὀρνιθομανοῦσι, πάντα δ' ὑπὸ τῆς ἡδονῆς
ποιοῦσιν ἅπερ ὄρνιθες ἐκμιμούμενοι.
πρῶτον μὲν εὐθὺς πάντες ἐξ εὐνῆς ἅμα
ἐπέτονθ' ἕωθεν ὥσπερ ἡμεῖς ἐπὶ νομόν·
κἆπειτ' ἂν ἅμα κατῆραν εἰς τὰ βιβλία,
εἶτ' ἂν ἐνέμοντ' ἐνταῦθα τὰ ψηφίσματα.
ὠρνιθομάνουν δ' οὕτω περιφανῶς ὥστε καὶ
πολλοῖσιν ὀρνίθων ὀνόματ' ἦν κείμενα.
Πέρδιξ μὲν εἷς κάπηλος ὠνομάζετο
χωλός, Μενίππῳ δ' ἦν Χελιδὼν τοὔνομα,
Ὀπουντίῳ δ' ὀφθαλμὸν οὐκ ἔχων Κόραξ,
Κορυδὸς Φιλοκλέει, Χηναλώπηξ Θεογένει,
Ἶβις Λυκούργῳ, Χαιρεφῶντι Νυκτερίς,
Συρακοσίῳ δὲ Κίττα· Μειδίας δ' ἐκεῖ

FIRST HERALD

With this crown of gold all the people recognize and reward you for your wisdom.

PEISETAERUS

I accept it. But why do the people honor me this way?

FIRST HERALD

O founder of the most glorious aetherial city, don't you realize how greatly you're esteemed among mankind, and how many of them you can count as lovers of this land? Why, before you built this city all men were crazy about the Spartans: they wore their hair long, went hungry, never bathed, acted like Socrates, brandished batons. But now they've about-faced and gone bird-crazy, and they're having a wonderful time imitating birds in everything they do. For starters, at the crack of dawn they all fly the coop together, just like us, to root for writs; then they flock to the archives and there sharpen their bills. They're so blatantly bird-crazy that many even had bird names added to their own. There's one lame barkeep called Partridge;[117] Menippus took the name Swallow;[118] Opuntius is the One-Eyed Raven; Philocles the Lark; Theogenes the Sheldrake;[119] Lycurgus the Ibis;[120] Chaerephon the Bat;[121] Syracosius the Jay;[122] and Meidias is called Quail, and you

117 766–68 n. 118 Unidentifiable. 119 Unidentifiable.

120 Son of Lycomedes and grandfather of the homonymous fourth-century statesman; the nickname implies some connection with Egypt, cf. Cratinus fr. 32, Pherecrates fr. 11.

121 The associate of Socrates, often satirized as sallow, thin, and umbratile.

122 A politician ridiculed for his "barking" oratory (Eupolis fr. 220) and for legislating against comic poets (Phrynichus fr. 27).

Ὄρτυξ ἐκαλεῖτο· καὶ γὰρ ἥκειν ὄρτυγι
ὑπὸ στυφοκόπου τὴν κεφαλὴν πεπληγμένῳ.
ᾖδον δ᾿ ὑπὸ φιλορνιθίας πάντες μέλη,
ὅπου χελιδὼν ἦν τις ἐμπεποιημένη
ἢ πηνέλοψ ἢ χήν τις ἢ περιστερὰ
ἢ πτέρυγες, ἢ πτεροῦ τι καὶ σμικρὸν προσῆν.
τοιαῦτα μὲν τἀκεῖθεν. ἓν δέ σοι λέγω·
ἥξουσ᾿ ἐκεῖθεν δεῦρο πλεῖν ἢ μυρίοι
πτερῶν δεόμενοι καὶ τρόπων γαμψωνύχων,
ὥστε πτερῶν σοι τοῖς ἐποίκοις δεῖ ποθέν.

ΠΕΙΣΕΤΑΙΡΟΣ

οὐκ ἆρα μὰ Δί᾿ ἡμῖν ἔτ᾿ ἔργον ἑστάναι.
ἀλλ᾿ ὡς τάχιστα σὺ μὲν ἰὼν τὰς ἀρρίχους
καὶ τοὺς κοφίνους ἅπαντας ἐμπίμπλη πτερῶν·
Μανῆς δὲ φερέτω μοι θύραζε τὰ πτερά·
ἐγὼ δ᾿ ἐκείνων τοὺς προσιόντας δέξομαι.

ΧΟΡΟΣ

(στρ) ταχὺ δὴ πολυάνορα τάνδε πόλιν
καλεῖ τις ἀνθρώπων·

ΠΕΙΣΕΤΑΙΡΟΣ

τύχη μόνον προσείη.

ΧΟΡΟΣ

κατέχουσι δ᾿ ἔρωτες ἐμᾶς πόλεως.

---

123 A public official (Metagenes fr. 12) and avid bird fighter (Phrynichus fr. 43, Plato com. fr. 116); in the game of quail-

know he did look like a quail who'd been knocked on the head by a hard tapper.[123] And from sheer ornithophilia they're all singing songs with a swallow in the lyrics, or a duck, or a goose, or a pigeon, or wings, or just a bit of feather attached. So that's the situation down below. But I'll tell you one thing: more than ten thousand of them will be making the trip up here, wanting wings and a raptor's way of life. So somewhere you'll have to find wings for the new arrivals.

Exit FIRST HERALD.

PEISETAERUS

Then we certainly have no time to stand around. (*to Xanthias*) You go as quick as you can and fill all the hampers and baskets with wings, and have Manes bring the wings out here to me; I'll greet the visitors as they arrive.

Xanthias and Manes go inside; during the following duet Manes brings out basketsfull of wings.

CHORUS

Soon some human will be calling
this city very well-manned.

PEISETAERUS

Just so our luck holds.

CHORUS

Passion for my city grips the world.

tapping the bird's handler bet the tapper that his bird would stay in the ring, cf. Pollux 9.102, 109.

ΠΕΙΣΕΤΑΙΡΟΣ

θᾶττον φέρειν κελεύω.

ΧΟΡΟΣ

τί γὰρ οὐκ ἔνι ταύτῃ
  καλὸν ἀνδρὶ μετοικεῖν;
Σοφία, Πόθος, ἀμβρόσιαι Χάριτες
  τό τε τῆς ἀγανόφρονος Ἡσυχίας
  εὐήμερον πρόσωπον.

ΠΕΙΣΕΤΑΙΡΟΣ

ὡς βλακικῶς διακονεῖς.
οὐ θᾶττον ἐγκονήσεις;

ΧΟΡΟΣ

(ἀντ) φερέτω κάλαθον ταχύ τις πτερύγων.
  σὺ δ᾽ αὖθις ἐξόρμα.

ΠΕΙΣΕΤΑΙΡΟΣ

τύπτων γε τοῦτον ὡδί.

ΧΟΡΟΣ

πάνυ γὰρ βραδύς ἐστί τις ὥσπερ ὄνος.

ΠΕΙΣΕΤΑΙΡΟΣ

Μανῆς γάρ ἐστι δειλός.

ΧΟΡΟΣ

σὺ δὲ τὰ πτερὰ πρῶτον
  διάθες τάδε κόσμῳ·
τά τε μουσίχ᾽ ὁμοῦ τά τε μαντικὰ καὶ
  τὰ θαλάττι᾽. ἔπειτα δ᾽ ὅπως φρονίμως
  πρὸς ἄνδρ᾽ ὁρῶν πτερώσεις.

PEISETAERUS

(to Manes)

Faster with those wings, I say!

CHORUS

For is anything missing here
that's good for a settler to have?
We've Wisdom, Desire, immortal Graces,
and the happy countenance
of kindhearted Tranquillity.

PEISETAERUS

(to Manes)

That's pretty lazy service!
Speed it up there!

CHORUS

Quickly, a basket of wings over here;
tell him again to hurry.

PEISETAERUS

I will, by hitting him like this!

CHORUS

Yes, he's a slowpoke, slow as an ass.

PEISETAERUS

A good-for-nothing Manes!

CHORUS

But first you must arrange
these wings in proper order:
musical wings here, prophetic there,
and maritime, and then be sure you shrewdly
size up the man when you wing him.

ΠΕΙΣΕΤΑΙΡΟΣ

οὔ τοι μὰ τὰς κερχνῇδας ἔτι σου σχήσομαι,
οὕτως ὁρῶν σε δειλὸν ὄντα καὶ βραδύν.

ΠΑΤΡΑΛΟΙΑΣ

<εἰ γὰρ> γενοίμαν αἰετὸς ὑψιπέτας,
ὡς ἀμποταθείην ὑπὲρ ἀτρυγέτου
γλαυκᾶς ἐπ᾽ οἶδμα λίμνας.

ΠΕΙΣΕΤΑΙΡΟΣ

ἔοικεν οὐ ψευδαγγελήσειν ἄγγελος·
ᾄδων γὰρ ὅδε τις αἰετοὺς προσέρχεται.

ΠΑΤΡΑΛΟΙΑΣ

αἰβοῖ.
οὐκ ἔστιν οὐδὲν τοῦ πέτεσθαι γλυκύτερον.
[ἐρῶ δ᾽ ἔγώ τι τῶν ἐν ὄρνισιν νόμων.]
ὀρνιθομανῶ γὰρ καὶ πέτομαι καὶ βούλομαι
οἰκεῖν μεθ᾽ ὑμῶν κἀπιθυμῶ τῶν νόμων.

ΠΕΙΣΕΤΑΙΡΟΣ

ποίων νόμων; πολλοὶ γὰρ ὀρνίθων νόμοι.

ΠΑΤΡΑΛΟΙΑΣ

πάντων· μάλιστα δ᾽ ὅτι καλὸν νομίζεται
τὸν πατέρα τοῖς ὄρνισιν ἄγχειν καὶ δάκνειν.

ΠΕΙΣΕΤΑΙΡΟΣ

καὶ νὴ Δί᾽ ἀνδρεῖόν γε πάνυ νομίζομεν,
ὃς ἂν πεπλήγῃ τὸν πατέρα νεοττὸς ὤν.

1337 <εἰ γὰρ> White 1338 ὑπὲρ] ὕπαρ Bergk
1343 del. Dobree, ab Ar. Byz. ad lacunam explendam

PEISETAERUS

(*to Manes*) By the kestrels I swear you're in for it now; look how uselessly slow you are!

Manes runs into the house.

Enter FATHER BEATER

FATHER BEATER

O to become a high-flying eagle
and soar beyond the barren pale
over the waves of the gray sea![124]

PEISETAERUS

That messenger's message looks to be accurate: here comes someone singing about eagles.

FATHER BEATER

Hi ho! Nothing's as much fun as flying! Yes, I'm bird-crazy, I'm on the wing, I want to live with you, I yearn for your laws.

PEISETAERUS

What laws do you mean? Birds have many laws.

FATHER BEATER

All of them! Especially the one where the birds think it's fine to peck and throttle your father.

PEISETAERUS

We do in fact consider a bird very manly who's beaten up his father while still a chick.

124 From Sophocles' *Oenomaus* (fr. 476).

---

compositum indicare videtur ΣVEΓ: versum Pisitaeri excidisse putat Kakridis, e.g. *πτερῶν ἄρ' ἥκεις δεόμενος; φέρε νυν φράσον* Dunbar

ΠΑΤΡΑΛΟΙΑΣ

διὰ ταῦτα μέντοι δεῦρ᾽ ἀνοικισθεὶς ἐγὼ
ἄγχειν ἐπιθυμῶ τὸν πατέρα καὶ πάντ᾽ ἔχειν.

ΠΕΙΣΕΤΑΙΡΟΣ

ἀλλ᾽ ἔστιν ἡμῖν τοῖσιν ὄρνισιν νόμος
παλαιὸς ἐν ταῖς τῶν πελαργῶν κύρβεσιν·
"ἐπὴν ὁ πατὴρ ὁ πελαργὸς ἐκπετησίμους
πάντας ποιήσῃ τοὺς πελαργιδέας τρέφων,
δεῖ τοὺς νεοττοὺς τὸν πατέρα πάλιν τρέφειν."

ΠΑΤΡΑΛΟΙΑΣ

ἀπέλαυσά γ᾽ ἆρα νὴ Δί᾽ ἐλθὼν ἐνθαδί,
εἴπερ γέ μοι καὶ τὸν πατέρα βοσκητέον.

ΠΕΙΣΕΤΑΙΡΟΣ

οὐδέν γ᾽· ἐπειδήπερ γὰρ ἦλθες, ὦ μέλε,
εὔνους, πτερώσω σ᾽ ὥσπερ ὄρνιν ὀρφανόν.
σοὶ δ᾽, ὦ νεανίσκ᾽, οὐ κακῶς ὑποθήσομαι,
ἀλλ᾽ οἷάπερ αὐτὸς ἔμαθον ὅτε παῖς ἦ. σὺ γὰρ
τὸν μὲν πατέρα μὴ τύπτε, ταυτηνδὶ λαβὼν
τὴν πτέρυγα καὶ τουτὶ τὸ πλῆκτρον θἀτέρᾳ,
νομίσας ἀλεκτρυόνος ἔχειν τονδὶ λόφον,
φρούρει, στρατεύου, μισθοφορῶν σαυτὸν τρέφε.
τὸν πατέρ᾽ ἔα ζῆν. ἀλλ᾽ ἐπειδὴ μάχιμος εἶ,
εἰς τἀπὶ Θρᾴκης ἀποπέτου κἀκεῖ μάχου.

ΠΑΤΡΑΛΟΙΑΣ

νὴ τὸν Διόνυσον εὖ γέ μοι δοκεῖς λέγειν,
καὶ πείσομαί σοι.

FATHER BEATER

That's exactly why I yearn to immigrate here, to throttle my father and take all he has.

PEISETAERUS

But we birds have a law, an ancient one on the Storks' Tablets:[125] "When the father stork has provided for all his storklings and got them fully fledged, then the chicks must in their turn provide for their father."

FATHER BEATER

A fat lot of good it's done me coming here, if I'll even have to feed my father now!

PEISETAERUS

No, you won't. Seeing that you came here well disposed, my lad, I'm going to fit you with wings like an orphan bird. And young man, let me give you some pretty good advice, the sort of thing I myself was taught as a boy: don't beat your father. Instead, take this wing, and this spur in your other hand, and consider this crest your cockscomb. Now stand guard! Go on campaign! Work for a living! Let your father live his life! Since you want to fight, fly off to the Thracian front and fight there![126]

FATHER BEATER

By Dionysus, that does sound like good advice, and I'll follow it.

[125] Recalling the tablets in the Athenian agora on which were inscribed the laws of Draco and Solon; one of these concerned mistreatment of parents, cf. [Aristotle] *Constitution of the Athenians* 56.6.

[126] See Thucydides 7.9.

ΠΕΙΣΕΤΑΙΡΟΣ

νοῦν ἄρ᾽ ἕξεις νὴ Δία.

ΚΙΝΗΣΙΑΣ

ἀναπέτομαι δὴ πρὸς Ὄλυμπον πτερύγεσσι κούφαις·
πέτομαι δ᾽ ὁδὸν ἄλλοτ᾽ ἐπ᾽ ἄλλαν μελέων—

ΠΕΙΣΕΤΑΙΡΟΣ

τουτὶ τὸ πρᾶγμα φορτίου δεῖται πτερῶν.

ΚΙΝΗΣΙΑΣ

ἀφόβῳ φρενὶ σώματί τε νέαν ἐφέπων.

ΠΕΙΣΕΤΑΙΡΟΣ

ἀσπαζόμεσθα φιλύρινον Κινησίαν.
τί δεῦρο πόδα σὺ κυλλὸν ἀνὰ κύκλον κυκλεῖς;

ΚΙΝΗΣΙΑΣ

ὄρνις γενέσθαι βούλομαι
λιγύφθογγος ἀηδών.

ΠΕΙΣΕΤΑΙΡΟΣ

παῦσαι μελῳδῶν, ἀλλ᾽ ὅ τι λέγεις εἰπέ μοι.

ΚΙΝΗΣΙΑΣ

ὑπὸ σοῦ πτερωθεὶς βούλομαι μετάρσιος
ἀναπτόμενος ἐκ τῶν νεφελῶν καινὰς λαβεῖν
ἀεροδονήτους καὶ νιφοβόλους ἀναβολάς.

ΠΕΙΣΕΤΑΙΡΟΣ

ἐκ τῶν νεφελῶν γὰρ ἄν τις ἀναβολὰς λάβοι;

PEISETAERUS

That's certainly the smart thing to do.

Exit FATHER BEATER

Enter CINESIAS.

CINESIAS[127]

See, I soar up to Olympus on weightless wings,[128]
I soar now on this path of song, and now on that—

PEISETAERUS

This here's going to take a whole load of wings!

CINESIAS

with fearless mind and body in quest of a new path.

PEISETAERUS

Our greetings to twiggy Cinesias! Why do you whirl your bandy foot hither in a pirouette?

CINESIAS

I wish to become a bird,
a clear-voiced nightingale.

PEISETAERUS

Stop that vocalizing, and tell me what you're saying.

CINESIAS

I want wings from you, to fly on high and snatch from the clouds fresh preludes air-propelled and snowswept.

PEISETAERUS

You're saying you can snatch preludes from the clouds?

[127] A tall, thin composer of dithyrambs in the avant-garde style noted for astrophic "preludes," musical complexity, elaborate language, and high emotionalism.

[128] From Anacreon fr. 378.

ΚΙΝΗΣΙΑΣ

κρέμαται μὲν οὖν ἐντεῦθεν ἡμῶν ἡ τέχνη.
τῶν διθυράμβων γὰρ τὰ λαμπρὰ γίγνεται
ἀέρια καὶ σκοτεινὰ καὶ κυαναυγέα
καὶ πτεροδόνητα· σὺ δὲ κλύων εἴσει τάχα.

ΠΕΙΣΕΤΑΙΡΟΣ

οὐ δῆτ᾽ ἔγωγε.

ΚΙΝΗΣΙΑΣ

νὴ τὸν Ἡρακλέα σύ γε.
ἅπαντα γὰρ δίειμί σοι τὸν ἀέρα.
εἴδωλα πετηνῶν
αἰθεροδρόμων
οἰωνῶν ταναοδείρων—

ΠΕΙΣΕΤΑΙΡΟΣ

ὠόπ.

ΚΙΝΗΣΙΑΣ

ἀνάδρομος ἁλάμενος
ἅμ᾽ ἀνέμων πνοαῖσι βαίην—

ΠΕΙΣΕΤΑΙΡΟΣ

νὴ τὸν Δί᾽ ἦ ᾽γώ σου καταπαύσω τὰς πνοάς.

ΚΙΝΗΣΙΑΣ

τοτὲ μὲν νοτίαν στείχων πρὸς ὁδόν,
τοτὲ δ᾽ αὖ βορέᾳ σῶμα πελάζων
ἀλίμενον αἰθέρος αὔλακα τέμνων—
χαρίεντά γ᾽, ὦ πρεσβῦτ᾽, ἐσοφίσω καὶ σοφά.

CINESIAS

Why, our whole art depends on them! In dithyrambs the dazzling bits are airy, dusky, darkly flashing, wing-propelled. Just listen, and you'll soon understand.

PEISETAERUS

I'd just as soon not.

CINESIAS

You absolutely must! Here, I'll run through the whole air for you:

> Ah visions of wingéd
> sky-coursing
> long-necked birds—

PEISETAERUS

Whoa!

CINESIAS

> oh to shoot up with a leap
> and run with the breaths of the winds—

PEISETAERUS

So help me god, I'll put a stop to *your* breaths! (*chases Cinesias with a pair of wings*)

CINESIAS

(dodging)

> first travelling a southerly course,
> then swinging my body northwards,
> cleaving a harborless furrow of sky—

(*stops, struck*) That's a very witty trick, old man, and tricky!

1395 ἀνάδρομος Henderson: τὸν ἀλάδρομον *vel sim.* a

ΠΕΙΣΕΤΑΙΡΟΣ

οὐ γὰρ σὺ χαίρεις πτεροδόνητος γενόμενος;

ΚΙΝΗΣΙΑΣ

ταυτὶ πεποίηκας τὸν κυκλιοδιδάσκαλον,
ὃς ταῖσι φυλαῖς περιμάχητός εἰμ᾽ ἀεί;

ΠΕΙΣΕΤΑΙΡΟΣ

βούλει διδάσκειν καὶ παρ᾽ ἡμῖν οὖν μένων
Λεωτροφίδῃ χορὸν πετομένων ὀρνέων
Κρεκοπίδα φυλήν;

ΚΙΝΗΣΙΑΣ

καταγελᾷς μου, δῆλος εἶ.
ἀλλ᾽ οὖν ἔγωγ᾽ οὐ παύσομαι, τοῦτ᾽ ἴσθ᾽ ὅτι,
πρὶν ἂν πτερωθεὶς διαδράμω τὸν ἀέρα.

ΣΥΚΟΦΑΝΤΗΣ

ὄρνιθες τίνες οἵδ᾽ οὐδὲν ἔχοντες πτεροποίκιλοι,
τανυσίπτερε ποικίλα χελιδοῖ;

ΠΕΙΣΕΤΑΙΡΟΣ

τουτὶ τὸ κακὸν οὐ φαῦλον ἐξεγρήγορεν.
ὅδ᾽ αὖ μινυρίζων δεῦρό τις προσέρχεται.

ΣΥΚΟΦΑΝΤΗΣ

τανυσίπτερε ποικίλα μάλ᾽ αὖθις.

1407 Κρεκ- Kock: Κερκ- a

129 For dithyrambic contests each of the ten Athenian tribes produced its own choruses.

PEISETAERUS

I thought you enjoy being wing-propelled!

CINESIAS

Is this how you treat me, the director of cyclic choruses whose services the tribes always fight for?[129]

PEISETAERUS

Then would you like to stay here with us and serve as director for Leotrophides,[130] with a chorus of flying birds, of the Corncrake Tribe?[131]

CINESIAS

Obviously you're making fun of me. But I'll have you know I don't intend to stop, not until I get my wings and scamper through the air!

Exit CINESIAS.

Enter INFORMER, *wearing a threadbare cloak.*

INFORMER

Who are these birds, these have-nots with dappled
wings?
O long-winged iridescent swallow![132]

PEISETAERUS

This is no small nuisance that's reared its head. Here comes another one warbling away.

INFORMER

I repeat, O long-winged iridescent!

[130] Ridiculed elsewhere as being very thin, like Cinesias.
[131] Punning on the Athenian tribe name Cecropis.
[132] Adapted from Alcaeus fr. 345.

ΠΕΙΣΕΤΑΙΡΟΣ

εἰς θοἰμάτιον τὸ σκόλιον ᾄδειν μοι δοκεῖ,
δεῖσθαι δ᾽ ἔοικεν οὐκ ὀλίγων χελιδόνων.

ΣΥΚΟΦΑΝΤΗΣ

τίς ὁ πτερῶν δεῦρ᾽ ἐστὶ τοὺς ἀφικνουμένους;

ΠΕΙΣΕΤΑΙΡΟΣ

ὁδὶ πάρεστιν· ἀλλ᾽ ὅτου δεῖ χρὴ λέγειν.

ΣΥΚΟΦΑΝΤΗΣ

πτερῶν, πτερῶν δεῖ· μὴ πύθῃ τὸ δεύτερον.

ΠΕΙΣΕΤΑΙΡΟΣ

μῶν εὐθὺ Πελλήνης πέτεσθαι διανοεῖ;

ΣΥΚΟΦΑΝΤΗΣ

μὰ Δί᾽, ἀλλὰ κλητήρ εἰμι νησιωτικὸς
καὶ συκοφάντης—

ΠΕΙΣΕΤΑΙΡΟΣ

ὦ μακάριε τῆς τέχνης.

ΣΥΚΟΦΑΝΤΗΣ

καὶ πραγματοδίφης. εἶτα δέομαι πτερὰ λαβὼν
κύκλῳ περισοβεῖν τὰς πόλεις καλούμενος.

ΠΕΙΣΕΤΑΙΡΟΣ

ὑπαὶ πτερύγων τι προσκαλεῖ σοφώτερον;

ΣΥΚΟΦΑΝΤΗΣ

μὰ Δί᾽, ἀλλ᾽ ἵν᾽ οἱ λῃσταί τε μὴ λυπῶσί με,

---

133 Alluding to the proverb "one swallow does not a summer make."

PEISETAERUS

I think he's singing that song about his cloak; he's likely to need more than a few swallows![133]

INFORMER

Who is it that gives wings to newcomers?

PEISETAERUS

That's me. But you must tell me what you need.

INFORMER

Its wings I want, wings! Do not ask me twice.[134]

PEISETAERUS

You don't intend to fly straight to Pellene, do you?[135]

INFORMER

God no; I'm a subpoena server working the islands, and an informer—

PEISETAERUS

What a glorious profession!

INFORMER

—and a lawsuit snoop. So I want to get wings and buzz around the islands serving subpoenas.

PEISETAERUS

Will you subpoena them any more efficiently with wingpower?

INFORMER

God no, it's so the bandits don't jump me, and so I can

134 From Aeschylus' *Myrmidons* (fr. 140), substituting "wings" for "weapons."

135 A Peloponnesian city where warm cloaks were awarded as prizes in chariot races; currently on hostile terms with Athens.

μετὰ τῶν γεράνων τ᾽ ἐκεῖθεν ἀναχωρῶ πάλιν,
ἀνθ᾽ ἕρματος πολλὰς καταπεπωκὼς δίκας.

ΠΕΙΣΕΤΑΙΡΟΣ

τουτὶ γὰρ ἐργάζει σὺ τοὔργον; εἰπέ μοι,
νεανίας ὢν συκοφαντεῖς τοὺς ξένους;

ΣΥΚΟΦΑΝΤΗΣ

τί γὰρ πάθω; σκάπτειν γὰρ οὐκ ἐπίσταμαι.

ΠΕΙΣΕΤΑΙΡΟΣ

ἀλλ᾽ ἔστιν ἕτερα νὴ Δί᾽ ἔργα σώφρονα,
ἀφ᾽ ὧν διαζῆν ἄνδρα χρῆν τοσουτονὶ
ἐκ τοῦ δικαίου μᾶλλον ἢ δικορραφεῖν.

ΣΥΚΟΦΑΝΤΗΣ

ὦ δαιμόνιε, μὴ νουθέτει μ᾽, ἀλλὰ πτέρου.

ΠΕΙΣΕΤΑΙΡΟΣ

νῦν τοι λέγων πτερῶ σε.

ΣΥΚΟΦΑΝΤΗΣ

καὶ πῶς ἂν λόγοις
ἄνδρα πτερώσειας σύ;

ΠΕΙΣΕΤΑΙΡΟΣ

πάντες τοι λόγοις
ἀναπτεροῦνται.

ΣΥΚΟΦΑΝΤΗΣ

πάντες;

ΠΕΙΣΕΤΑΙΡΟΣ

οὐκ ἀκήκοας,

make the return trip with the cranes, once I've filled up on lots of lawsuits for ballast.

PEISETAERUS

So that's your line of work, is it? An able-bodied young man like yourself informing on foreigners for a living?

INFORMER

But what am I supposed to do? I don't know how to use a shovel.

PEISETAERUS

But surely there are other respectable occupations, where a man your size should be making an honest living instead of cobbling up lawsuits.

INFORMER

Listen, mister, don't lecture me, just wing me.

PEISETAERUS

Know what? I'm winging you now, just by talking.

INFORMER

And just how can you wing a man with mere words?

PEISETAERUS

Words, you see, set everyone aflutter.

INFORMER

Everyone?

PEISETAERUS

Haven't you been in the barber shops and heard boys'

ὅταν λέγωσιν οἱ πατέρες ἑκάστοτε
τῶν μειρακίων ἐν τοῖσι κουρείοις ταδί·
"δεινῶς γέ μου τὸ μειράκιον Διειτρέφης
λέγων ἀνεπτέρωκεν ὥσθ' ἱππηλατεῖν";
ὁ δέ τις τὸν αὑτοῦ φησιν ἐπὶ τραγῳδίᾳ
ἀνεπτερῶσθαι καὶ πεποτῆσθαι τὰς φρένας.

ΣΥΚΟΦΑΝΤΗΣ

λόγοισί γ' ἆρα καὶ πτεροῦνται;

ΠΕΙΣΕΤΑΙΡΟΣ

φήμ' ἐγώ.
ὑπὸ γὰρ λόγων ὁ νοῦς τε μετεωρίζεται
ἐπαίρεταί τ' ἄνθρωπος. οὕτω καὶ σ' ἐγὼ
ἀναπτερώσας βούλομαι χρηστοῖς λόγοις
τρέψαι πρὸς ἔργον νόμιμον.

ΣΥΚΟΦΑΝΤΗΣ

ἀλλ' οὐ βούλομαι.

ΠΕΙΣΕΤΑΙΡΟΣ

τί δαὶ ποιήσεις;

ΣΥΚΟΦΑΝΤΗΣ

τὸ γένος οὐ καταισχυνῶ·
παππῷος ὁ βίος συκοφαντεῖν ἐστί μοι.
ἀλλὰ πτέρου με ταχέσι καὶ κούφοις πτεροῖς
ἱέρακος ἢ κερχνῇδος, ὡς ἂν τοὺς ξένους
καλεσάμενος κᾆτ' ἐγκεκληκὼς ἐνθαδὶ
κατ' αὖ πέτωμαι πάλιν ἐκεῖσε.

fathers say, "It's terrible how Dieitrephes has been talking to my boy and setting him all aflutter for horse racing!" And someone else says that his boy's mind has gone all aflutter for tragedy and flown the coop.

INFORMER

So they actually get wings from words?

PEISETAERUS

That's right: by words is the mind uplifted and a person transported. That's just how I want to set you aflutter too: with worthwhile words to convert you to legitimate work.

INFORMER

But that's not what I want.

PEISETAERUS

Then what do you intend to do?

INFORMER

I'll not disgrace my family: informing has been our livelihood since my grandfather's day. Just rig me with the light, fast wings of a hawk or a kestrel, so I can subpoena the foreigners, get a judgment here, then fly back there again.

ΠΕΙΣΕΤΑΙΡΟΣ

μανθάνω.
ὡδὶ λέγεις· ὅπως ἂν ὠφλήκῃ δίκην
ἐνθάδε πρὶν ἥκειν ὁ ξένος.

ΣΥΚΟΦΑΝΤΗΣ

πάνυ μανθάνεις.

ΠΕΙΣΕΤΑΙΡΟΣ

κᾄπειθ᾽ ὁ μὲν πλεῖ δεῦρο, σὺ δ᾽ ἐκεῖσ᾽ αὖ πέτει
ἁρπασόμενος τὰ χρήματ᾽ αὐτοῦ.

ΣΥΚΟΦΑΝΤΗΣ

πάντ᾽ ἔχεις.
βέμβικος οὐδὲν διαφέρειν δεῖ.

ΠΕΙΣΕΤΑΙΡΟΣ

μανθάνω
βέμβικα. καὶ μὴν ἔστι μοι, νὴ τὸν Δία,
κάλλιστα Κορκυραῖα τοιαυτὶ πτερά.

ΣΥΚΟΦΑΝΤΗΣ

οἴμοι τάλας, μάστιγ᾽ ἔχεις.

ΠΕΙΣΕΤΑΙΡΟΣ

πτερὼ μὲν οὖν,
οἷσί σε ποιήσω τήμερον βεμβικιᾶν.

ΣΥΚΟΦΑΝΤΗΣ

οἴμοι τάλας.

ΠΕΙΣΕΤΑΙΡΟΣ

οὐ πτερυγιεῖς ἐντευθενί;
οὐκ ἀπολιβάξεις, ὦ κάκιστ᾽ ἀπολούμενος;

PEISETAERUS

I get it: you mean the foreigner's case will be lost by default before he gets here.

INFORMER

Quite right.

PEISETAERUS

And then while he's sailing here, you're flying back there to snatch his property.

INFORMER

That's the whole story. It means whizzing around just like a top.

PEISETAERUS

A top—I know what you mean. (*rummaging*) And by god I've actually got some wings here that'll do just perfectly; they're from Corcyra.[136]

INFORMER

Good grief, that's a whip!

PEISETAERUS

No, a pair of wings; I'll use them this very day to make you whizz around like a top!

INFORMER

Good grief!

Exit INFORMER *on the run.*

PEISETAERUS

Now flutter away from here! Clear off! Goddamned pest!

136 Well known for the manufacture of double-thonged whips.

πικρὰν τάχ᾿ ὄψει στρεψοδικοπανουργίαν.
ἀπίωμεν ἡμεῖς ξυλλαβόντες τὰ πτερά.

ΧΟΡΟΣ

(στρ) πολλὰ δὴ καὶ καινὰ καὶ θαυ-
μάστ᾿ ἐπεπτόμεσθα καὶ
δεινὰ πράγματ᾿ εἴδομεν.
ἔστι γὰρ δένδρον πεφυκὸς
ἔκτοπόν τι Καρδίας ἀ-
πωτέρω Κλεώνυμος,
χρήσιμον μὲν οὐδέν, ἄλ-
λως δὲ δειλὸν καὶ μέγα.
τοῦτο τοῦ μὲν ἦρος ἀεὶ
βλαστάνει καὶ συκοφαντεῖ,
τοῦ δὲ χειμῶνος πάλιν τὰς
ἀσπίδας φυλλορροεῖ.

(ἀντ) ἔστι δ᾿ αὖ χώρα πρὸς αὐτῷ
τῷ σκότῳ πόρρω τις ἐν
τῇ λύχνων ἐρημίᾳ,
ἔνθα τοῖς ἥρωσιν ἄνθρω-
ποι ξυναριστῶσι καὶ ξύν-
εισι πλὴν τῆς ἑσπέρας.
τηνικαῦτα δ᾿ οὐκέτ᾿ ἦν
ἀσφαλὲς ξυντυγχάνειν.
εἰ γὰρ ἐντύχοι τις ἥρῳ
τῶν βροτῶν νύκτωρ Ὀρέστῃ,
γυμνὸς ἦν πληγεὶς ὑπ᾿ αὐτοῦ
πάντα τἀπιδέξια.

You'll soon get a bitter dose of sleazy shysterism! (*to Slaves*) Come on, let's gather up these wings and go.

PEISETAERUS and Slaves go inside.

CHORUS

Many wondrous novelties
have we overflown, and
many amazements have we seen.
There's a tree, quite exotic,
that grows beyond Wimpdom,
and it's called Cleonymus,
good for nothing, but otherwise
voluminous and yellow.
Each and every springtime
it sprouts denunciations,
while in wintertime, by contrast,
its shields drop off like leaves.

Then there's a far-off country,
at the very edge of darkness
in the lampless steppes,
where people meet the heroes
for lunch and conversation,
except in the evening:
that's when it's no longer
safe to meet them.
For if any mortal happened
to run into the hero Orestes,
he'd get stripped and paralyzed
all down his right-hand side.

Enter PROMETHEUS, muffled and carrying a parasol.

ΠΡΟΜΗΘΕΥΣ

οἴμοι τάλας, ὁ Ζεὺς ὅπως μή μ᾽ ὄψεται.
ποῦ Πεισέταιρος ἔστ᾽;

ΠΕΙΣΕΤΑΙΡΟΣ

ἔα, τουτὶ τί ἦν;
τίς ὁ συγκαλυμμός;

ΠΡΟΜΗΘΕΥΣ

τῶν θεῶν ὁρᾷς τινα
ἐμοῦ κατόπιν ἐνταῦθα;

ΠΕΙΣΕΤΑΙΡΟΣ

μὰ Δί᾽ ἐγὼ μὲν οὔ.
τίς δ᾽ εἶ σύ;

ΠΡΟΜΗΘΕΥΣ

πηνίκ᾽ ἐστὶν ἄρα τῆς ἡμέρας;

ΠΕΙΣΕΤΑΙΡΟΣ

ὁπηνίκα; σμικρόν τι μετὰ μεσημβρίας.
ἀλλὰ σὺ τίς εἶ;

ΠΡΟΜΗΘΕΥΣ

βουλυτός, ἢ περαιτέρω;

ΠΕΙΣΕΤΑΙΡΟΣ

οἴμ᾽, ὡς βδελύττομαί σε.

ΠΡΟΜΗΘΕΥΣ

τί γὰρ ὁ Ζεὺς ποιεῖ;
ἀπαιθριάζει τὰς νεφέλας ἢ ξυννέφει;

PROMETHEUS

Oh what a fix! Zeus mustn't see me! Where's Peisetaerus?

PEISETAERUS emerges, carrying a potty.

PEISETAERUS

Yipes, what is this? What's this mufflement?

PROMETHEUS

Do you see any of the gods back there behind me?

PEISETAERUS

I certainly can't see any. But who are you?

PROMETHEUS

Then what's the time of day?

PEISETAERUS

The time? A little after midday. But who are you?

PROMETHEUS

Quitting time, or later?

PEISETAERUS

Damn it, I'm getting sick of this!

PROMETHEUS

And what's Zeus doing? Is he clearing the clouds away, or gathering them?

ΠΕΙΣΕΤΑΙΡΟΣ

οἴμωζε μεγάλ᾽.

ΠΡΟΜΗΘΕΥΣ

οὕτω μὲν ἐκκεκαλύψομαι.

ΠΕΙΣΕΤΑΙΡΟΣ

ὦ φίλε Προμηθεῦ.

ΠΡΟΜΗΘΕΥΣ

παῦε παῦε, μὴ βόα.

ΠΕΙΣΕΤΑΙΡΟΣ

τί γάρ ἐστι;

ΠΡΟΜΗΘΕΥΣ

σίγα, μὴ κάλει μου τοὔνομα·
ἀπὸ γάρ μ᾽ ὀλεῖς, εἴ μ᾽ ἐνθάδ᾽ ὁ Ζεὺς ὄψεται.
ἀλλ᾽ ἵνα φράσω σοι πάντα τἄνω πράγματα,
τουτὶ λαβών μου τὸ σκιάδειον ὑπέρεχε,
ἄνωθεν ὡς ἂν μή μ᾽ ὁρῶσιν οἱ θεοί.

ΠΕΙΣΕΤΑΙΡΟΣ

ἰοὺ ἰού·
εὖ γ᾽ ἐπενόησας αὐτὸ καὶ προμηθικῶς.
ὑπόδυθι ταχὺ δὴ κᾆτα θαρρήσας λέγε.

ΠΡΟΜΗΘΕΥΣ

ἄκουε δή νυν.

ΠΕΙΣΕΤΑΙΡΟΣ

ὡς ἀκούοντος λέγε.

ΠΡΟΜΗΘΕΥΣ

ἀπόλωλεν ὁ Ζεύς.

PEISETAERUS

Go straight to hell!

PROMETHEUS

In that case, I'll get unmuffled.

PEISETAERUS

Prometheus, old friend![137]

PROMETHEUS

Shh, shh! Don't shout!

PEISETAERUS

Why, what's up?

PROMETHEUS

Be quiet, don't mention my name. You'll be the death of me, if Zeus sees me here. Look, I'm going to tell you everything that's going on up there, so take this parasol and hold it over me, so the gods above won't see me.

PEISETAERUS

Aha! That was good thinking, positively Promethean. Quick, get under here, and speak freely.

PROMETHEUS

Then listen to this.

PEISETAERUS

Go on, I'm listening.

PROMETHEUS

Zeus is finished!

137 Prometheus was worshipped at Athens as a fire god and patron of craftsmen.

ΠΕΙΣΕΤΑΙΡΟΣ

πηνίκ᾽ ἄττ᾽ ἀπώλετο;

ΠΡΟΜΗΘΕΥΣ

ἐξ οὗπερ ὑμεῖς ᾠκίσατε τὸν ἀέρα.
θύει γὰρ οὐδεὶς οὐδὲν ἀνθρώπων ἔτι
θεοῖσιν, οὐδὲ κνῖσα μηρίων ἄπο
ἀνῆλθεν ὡς ἡμᾶς ἀπ᾽ ἐκείνου τοῦ χρόνου,
ἀλλ᾽ ὡσπερεὶ Θεσμοφορίοις νηστεύομεν
ἄνευ θυηλῶν· οἱ δὲ βάρβαροι θεοὶ
πεινῶντες ὥσπερ Ἰλλυριοὶ κεκριγότες
ἐπιστρατεύσειν φάσ᾽ ἄνωθεν τῷ Διί,
εἰ μὴ παρέξει τἀμπόρι᾽ ἀνεῳγμένα,
ἵν᾽ εἰσάγοιτο σπλάγχνα κατατετμημένα.

ΠΕΙΣΕΤΑΙΡΟΣ

εἰσὶν γὰρ ἕτεροι βάρβαροι θεοί τινες
ἄνωθεν ὑμῶν;

ΠΡΟΜΗΘΕΥΣ

οὐ γάρ εἰσι βάρβαροι,
ὅθεν ὁ πατρῷός ἐστιν Ἐξηκεστίδῃ;

ΠΕΙΣΕΤΑΙΡΟΣ

ὄνομα δὲ τούτοις τοῖς θεοῖς τοῖς βαρβάροις
τί ἐστιν;

ΠΡΟΜΗΘΕΥΣ

ὅ τι ἐστίν; Τριβαλλοί.

1527 -*ίδῃ* Brunck: -*ίδης* a

PEISETAERUS

And approximately when was he finished?

PROMETHEUS

From the very moment you colonized the air. Now not a single human sacrifices to the gods any more, and since then not a whiff of thigh bones has wafted up to us; no, without burnt offerings we're as good as fasting at the Thesmophoria.[138] And the barbarian gods are so hungry they're shrieking like Illyrians and threatening to march down against Zeus[139] unless he gets the trading posts reopened so they can import their ration of innards.

PEISETAERUS

So there are some other gods, barbarians, up-country from you?

PROMETHEUS

How could we have no barbarians? That's where Execestides gets his ancestral god.

PEISETAERUS

And what's the name of these barbarian gods?

PROMETHEUS

Their name? Triballians.[140]

[138] For this festival see *Women at the Thesmophoria*, Introductory Note.

[139] Like an indigenous populace against colonists on the coast.

[140] A Thracian tribe allied with Athens and noted for their savagery.

ΠΕΙΣΕΤΑΙΡΟΣ

μανθάνω.
ἐντεῦθεν ἆρα τοὐπιτριβείης ἐγένετο.

ΠΡΟΜΗΘΕΥΣ

μάλιστα πάντων. ἓν δέ σοι λέγω σαφές·
ἥξουσι πρέσβεις δεῦρο περὶ διαλλαγῶν
παρὰ τοῦ Διὸς καὶ τῶν Τριβαλλῶν τῶν ἄνω·
ὑμεῖς δὲ μὴ σπένδεσθ', ἐὰν μὴ παραδιδῷ
τὸ σκῆπτρον ὁ Ζεὺς τοῖσιν ὄρνισιν πάλιν,
καὶ τὴν Βασίλειαν σοὶ γυναῖκ' ἔχειν διδῷ.

ΠΕΙΣΕΤΑΙΡΟΣ

τίς ἐστιν ἡ Βασίλεια;

ΠΡΟΜΗΘΕΥΣ

καλλίστη κόρη,
ἥπερ ταμιεύει τὸν κεραυνὸν τοῦ Διὸς
καὶ τἄλλ' ἁπαξάπαντα, τὴν εὐβουλίαν,
τὴν εὐνομίαν, τὴν σωφροσύνην, τὰ νεώρια,
τὴν λοιδορίαν, τὸν κωλακρέτην, τὰ τριώβολα.

ΠΕΙΣΕΤΑΙΡΟΣ

ἅπαντά γ' ἆρ' αὐτῷ ταμιεύει;

ΠΡΟΜΗΘΕΥΣ

φήμ' ἐγώ.
ἥ γ' ἢν σὺ παρ' ἐκείνου παραλάβῃς, πάντ' ἔχεις.
τούτων ἕνεκα δεῦρ' ἦλθον, ἵνα φράσαιμί σοι·
ἀεί ποτ' ἀνθρώποις γὰρ εὔνους εἴμ' ἐγώ.

PEISETAERUS

I get it; that must be where "balls to you" comes from.

PROMETHEUS

Altogether likely. But I'll tell you one thing for sure: ambassadors will be coming here about a settlement, from Zeus and the Triballians up-country. But don't you ratify a treaty unless Zeus returns his scepter to the birds and gives you Princess for your bride.

PEISETAERUS

Who's this Princess?

PROMETHEUS

A most beautiful maiden, who looks after Zeus' thunderbolt and everything else too: good counsel, law and order, decency, shipyards, mudslinging, paymasters, three-obol fees.

PEISETAERUS

You mean she looks after everything for him?

PROMETHEUS

That's right: win her from him and you'll have it all. That's why I came here, to let you in on this. I've always been a friend to humanity.

ΠΕΙΣΕΤΑΙΡΟΣ

μόνον θεῶν γὰρ διὰ σ᾽ ἀπανθρακίζομεν.

ΠΡΟΜΗΘΕΥΣ

μισῶ δ᾽ ἅπαντας τοὺς θεούς, ὡς οἶσθα σύ—

ΠΕΙΣΕΤΑΙΡΟΣ

νὴ τὸν Δί᾽ ἀεὶ δῆτα θεομισὴς ἔφυς,
Τίμων καθαρός.

ΠΡΟΜΗΘΕΥΣ

ἀλλ᾽ ὡς ἂν ἀποτρέχω πάλιν
φέρε τὸ σκιάδειον, ἵνα με κἂν ὁ Ζεὺς ἴδῃ
ἄνωθεν, ἀκολουθεῖν δοκῶ κανηφόρῳ.

ΠΕΙΣΕΤΑΙΡΟΣ

καὶ τὸν δίφρον γε διφροφόρει τονδὶ λαβών.

ΧΟΡΟΣ

(στρ) πρὸς δὲ τοῖς Σκιάποσιν λί-
μνη τις ἔστ᾽, ἄλουτος οὗ
ψυχαγωγεῖ Σωκράτης.
ἔνθα καὶ Πείσανδρος ἦλθε
δεόμενος ψυχὴν ἰδεῖν ἣ
ζῶντ᾽ ἐκεῖνον προὔλιπε,
σφάγι᾽ ἔχων κάμηλον ἀ-

141 The proverbial Athenian misanthrope.

142 A maiden chosen for this honor in a religious procession might be accompanied by assistants bearing a parasol and a stool.

143 Recalling Odysseus' visit to the underworld as described

PEISETAERUS

Yes, if it weren't for you we wouldn't have barbecues.

PROMETHEUS

And I hate all the gods, as you know.

PEISETAERUS

Yes, you've always been on hateful terms with the gods, an absolute Timon.[141]

PROMETHEUS

But now I've got to run back again, so give me my parasol; this way, even if Zeus does see me from up there, he'll think I'm attending a basket bearer.[142]

PEISETAERUS

(*handing him the potty*) You may as well carry her stool too; here it is.

Exit PROMETHEUS; PEISETAERUS *goes inside*.

CHORUS[143]

Far away by the Shadefoots
lies a swamp, where all unwashed
Socrates conjures spirits.
Pisander[144] paid a visit there,
asking to see the spirit
that deserted him in life.
For sacrifice he brought a baby

in *Odyssey* 11 and dramatized in Aeschylus' *Spirit Conjurers* (*Psychagogoi*), cf. its fr. 273a.

144 A general and democratic politician, later turned oligarch (see *Lysistrata*, Introductory Note); ridiculed elsewhere for cowardice (Eupolis fr. 35, Xenophon *Symposium* 2.14).

μνόν τιν', ἧς λαιμοὺς τεμὼν
ὥσπερ οὑδυσσεὺς ἀπῆλθε,
κᾆτ' ἀνῆλθ' αὐτῷ κάτωθεν
πρὸς τὸ λαῖμα τῆς καμήλου
Χαιρεφῶν ἡ νυκτερίς.

ΠΟΣΕΙΔΩΝ

τὸ μὲν πόλισμα τῆς Νεφελοκοκκυγίας
ὁρᾶν τοδὶ πάρεστιν, οἷ πρεσβεύομεν.
οὗτος, τί δρᾷς; ἐπαρίστερ' οὕτως ἀμπέχει;
οὐ μεταβαλεῖς θοἰμάτιον ὧδ' ἐπιδέξια;
τί, ὦ κακόδαιμον; Λαισποδίας εἶ τὴν φύσιν;
ὦ δημοκρατία, ποῖ προβιβᾷς ἡμᾶς ποτε,
εἰ τουτονγί γ' ἐχειροτόνησαν οἱ θεοί;
ἕξεις ἀτρέμας; οἴμωζε· πολὺ γὰρ δή σ' ἐγὼ
ἑόρακα πάντων βαρβαρώτατον θεῶν.
ἄγε δή, τί δρῶμεν, Ἡράκλεις;

ΗΡΑΚΛΗΣ

ἀκήκοας
ἐμοῦ γ', ὅτι τὸν ἄνθρωπον ἄγχειν βούλομαι,
ὅστις ποτ' ἔσθ' ὁ τοὺς θεοὺς ἀποτειχίσας.

ΠΟΣΕΙΔΩΝ

ἀλλ', ὦγάθ', ᾑρήμεσθα περὶ διαλλαγῶν
πρέσβεις.

1563 πρὸς τὸ λαῖμα cett. S^{rel} Σ^{rel}, cf. S λ 185 λαῖμα· τὸ αἷμα: πρὸς τὸ λαῖτμα V S^{A} $^{\lambda}\Sigma^{R}$: πρὸς τὸ δέρμα $^{\gamma\rho}\Sigma^{REM\Gamma}$: πρός τε θαῖμα Henderson

camel and cut its throat,
like Odysseus, then backed off;
and up from below arose to him,
drawn by the camel's gore,
Chaerephon the bat.

Enter POSEIDON, HERACLES, and TRIBALLIAN GOD.

POSEIDON

This municipality now present to our view is Cloud-cuckooland, the goal of our embassy. (*to Triballian*) Here, what do you think you're doing, draping your cloak like that, from right to left? Please reverse it, this way, from left to right. Oh, you sorry bungler! Are you built like Laespodias?[145] Ah democracy, what will you bring us to in the end, if the gods can elect this person ambassador? (*adjusting Triballian's cloak*) Please hold still! To hell with you! You're the most barbaric god I've ever laid eyes on. Well now, Heracles, what should we do?

HERACLES

You've heard *my* opinion: I want to strangle the guy, whoever he is, that's blockaded the gods.

POSEIDON

Listen, colleague, our charge is to discuss a settlement.

[145] A politician, probably elected general shortly before *Birds*, who presumably tried to hide misshapen calves by draping his cloak very low.

ΗΡΑΚΛΗΣ

διπλασίως μᾶλλον ἄγχειν μοι δοκεῖ.

ΠΕΙΣΕΤΑΙΡΟΣ

τὴν τυρόκνηστίν τις δότω· φέρε σίλφιον·
τυρὸν φερέτω τις· πυρπόλει τοὺς ἄνθρακας.

ΠΟΣΕΙΔΩΝ

τὸν ἄνδρα χαίρειν οἱ θεοὶ κελεύομεν
τρεῖς ὄντες ἡμεῖς.

ΠΕΙΣΕΤΑΙΡΟΣ

ἀλλ' ἐπικνῶ τὸ σίλφιον.

ΗΡΑΚΛΗΣ

τὰ δὲ κρέα τοῦ ταῦτ' ἐστίν;

ΠΕΙΣΕΤΑΙΡΟΣ

ὄρνιθές τινες
ἐπανιστάμενοι τοῖς δημοτικοῖσιν ὀρνέοις
ἔδοξαν ἀδικεῖν.

ΗΡΑΚΛΗΣ

εἶτα δῆτα σίλφιον
ἐπικνῇς πρότερον αὐτοῖσιν;

ΠΕΙΣΕΤΑΙΡΟΣ

ὦ χαῖρ', Ἡράκλεις.
τί ἐστι;

ΠΟΣΕΙΔΩΝ

πρεσβεύοντες ἡμεῖς ἥκομεν
παρὰ τῶν θεῶν περὶ πολέμου καταλλαγῆς.

HERACLES

All the more reason to strangle him, if you ask me.

Enter PEISETAERUS *and Slaves, with brazier, table, and cooking utensils.*

PEISETAERUS

Someone hand me the cheese grater. Pass the silphium. Someone get the cheese. Poke up these coals.

POSEIDON

We bid the gentleman greetings, a committee of three gods.

PEISETAERUS

Wait, I'm grating silphium on this.

HERACLES

And what sort of meat is that?[146]

PEISETAERUS

Some birds who've been convicted of attempted rebellion against the bird democracy.

HERACLES

So that's why you're grating silphium on them first?

PEISETAERUS

Oh, hello, Heracles. What's up?

POSEIDON

We have come as ambassadors from the gods to discuss an end to the war.

146 Heracles traditionally had an insatiable appetite.

ΠΕΙΣΕΤΑΙΡΟΣ

ἔλαιον οὐκ ἔνεστιν ἐν τῇ ληκύθῳ.

ΗΡΑΚΛΗΣ

καὶ μὴν τά γ᾽ ὀρνίθεια λιπάρ᾽ εἶναι πρέπει.

ΠΟΣΕΙΔΩΝ

ἡμεῖς τε γὰρ πολεμοῦντες οὐ κερδαίνομεν,
ὑμεῖς τ᾽ ἂν ἡμῖν τοῖς θεοῖς ὄντες φίλοι
ὄμβριον ὕδωρ ἂν εἴχετ᾽ ἐν τοῖς τέλμασιν,
ἀλκυονίδας τ᾽ ἂν ἤγεθ᾽ ἡμέρας ἀεί.
τούτων πέρι πάντων αὐτοκράτορες ἥκομεν.

ΠΕΙΣΕΤΑΙΡΟΣ

ἀλλ᾽ οὔτε πρότερον πώποθ᾽ ἡμεῖς ἤρξαμεν
πολέμου πρὸς ὑμᾶς, νῦν τ᾽ ἐθέλομεν, εἰ δοκεῖ,
ἐὰν τὸ δίκαιον ἀλλὰ νῦν ἐθέλητε δρᾶν,
σπονδὰς ποιεῖσθαι. τὰ δὲ δίκαι᾽ ἐστὶν ταδί·
τὸ σκῆπτρον ἡμῖν τοῖσιν ὄρνισιν πάλιν
τὸν Δί᾽ ἀποδοῦναι· κἂν διαλλαττώμεθα
ἐπὶ τοῖσδε, τοὺς πρέσβεις ἐπ᾽ ἄριστον καλῶ.

ΗΡΑΚΛΗΣ

ἐμοὶ μὲν ἀποχρῇ ταῦτα, καὶ ψηφίζομαι.

ΠΟΣΕΙΔΩΝ

τί, ὦ κακόδαιμον; ἠλίθιος καὶ γάστρις εἶ.
ἀποστερεῖς τὸν πατέρα τῆς τυραννίδος;

ΠΕΙΣΕΤΑΙΡΟΣ

ἄληθες; οὐ γὰρ μεῖζον ὑμεῖς οἱ θεοὶ
ἰσχύσετ᾽, ἢν ὄρνιθες ἄρξωσιν κάτω;

PEISETAERUS

There's no oil in the bottle.

HERACLES

And bird meat should be glistening with it.

POSEIDON

For we gods are gaining nothing by the war; while for your part, friendly relations with the gods would win you rainwater for your puddles and halcyon days to enjoy year round. On all these issues we are authorized to ratify an agreement.

PEISETAERUS

But it was never our side that initiated hostilities against you, and we are now ready to ratify a treaty, if you like, as long as you're ready even at this late hour to do what's right. And what's right amounts to this: Zeus returns the sceptre back to us birds. If we can reach an agreement on these terms, I invite the embassy to lunch.

HERACLES

That's good enough for me; I vote aye.

POSEIDON

You what, you damned fool? You're an idiotic greedy-guts. Would you rob your father of his rule?

PEISETAERUS

How can you say that? Won't you gods actually have greater power if birds are sovereign down below? At pres-

---

1598 τὸ Elmsley cl. Σ: τι a

νῦν μέν γ᾽ ὑπὸ ταῖς νεφέλαισιν ἐγκεκρυμμένοι
κύψαντες ἐπιορκοῦσιν ὑμᾶς οἱ βροτοί·
ἐὰν δὲ τοὺς ὄρνις ἔχητε συμμάχους,
ὅταν ὀμνύῃ τις τὸν κόρακα καὶ τὸν Δία,
ὁ κόραξ παρελθὼν τοὐπιορκοῦντος λάθρᾳ
προσπτάμενος ἐκκόψει τὸν ὀφθαλμὸν θενών.

ΠΟΣΕΙΔΩΝ

νὴ τὸν Ποσειδῶ ταῦτά γέ τοι καλῶς λέγεις.

ΗΡΑΚΛΗΣ

κἀμοὶ δοκεῖ.

ΠΕΙΣΕΤΑΙΡΟΣ

τί δαὶ σὺ φῄς;

ΤΡΙΒΑΛΛΟΣ

νὰ Βαισατρεῦ.

ΗΡΑΚΛΗΣ

ὁρᾷς, ἐπαινεῖ χοὖτος.

ΠΕΙΣΕΤΑΙΡΟΣ

ἕτερόν νυν ἔτι
ἀκούσαθ᾽ ὅσον ὑμᾶς ἀγαθὸν ποιήσομεν.
ἐάν τις ἀνθρώπων ἱερεῖόν τῳ θεῶν
εὐξάμενος εἶτα διασοφίζηται λέγων·
"μενετοὶ θεοί", καὶ μἀποδιδῷ μισητίᾳ,
ἀναπράξομεν καὶ ταῦτα.

ΠΟΣΕΙΔΩΝ

φέρ᾽ ἴδω τῷ τρόπῳ;

ent, mortals can hide beneath the clouds, and with bowed heads swear false oaths in your names; but if you have the birds for allies, whenever anyone swears "by the Raven and by Zeus," the Raven will happen by and swoop down on that perjurer before he knows it, and peck out his eye like a shot.

POSEIDON

By Poseidon, that's a very good point.

HERACLES

I agree.

PEISETAERUS

And what do you say?

TRIBALLIAN GOD

Yeah Bubba.

HERACLES

See? He's in favor too.

PEISETAERUS

Now listen to what else we'll do for your benefit. If a human vows an offering to a god and then tries to squirm out of it with a sophism like "the gods are patient,"[147] and out of avarice doesn't fulfill it, we'll make him pay up.

POSEIDON

I'd like to know how.

147 The full proverb was "the gods are patient, but keep their promises."

ΠΕΙΣΕΤΑΙΡΟΣ

ὅταν διαριθμῶν ἀργυρίδιον τύχῃ
ἄνθρωπος οὗτος, ἣ καθῆται λούμενος,
καταπτάμενος ἰκτῖνος ἁρπάσας λάθρᾳ
προβάτοιν δυοῖν τιμὴν ἀνοίσει τῷ θεῷ.

ΗΡΑΚΛΗΣ

τὸ σκῆπτρον ἀποδοῦναι πάλιν ψηφίζομαι
τούτοις ἐγώ.

ΠΟΣΕΙΔΩΝ

καὶ τὸν Τριβαλλόν νυν ἐροῦ.

ΗΡΑΚΛΗΣ

ὁ Τριβαλλός, οἰμώζειν δοκεῖ σοι;

ΤΡΙΒΑΛΛΟΣ

σαὺ νάκα
βακτάρι κροῦσα.

ΗΡΑΚΛΗΣ

φησί μ' εὖ λέγειν πάνυ.

ΠΟΣΕΙΔΩΝ

εἴ τοι δοκεῖ σφῷν ταῦτα, κἀμοὶ συνδοκεῖ.

ΗΡΑΚΛΗΣ

οὗτος, δοκεῖ δρᾶν ταῦτα τοῦ σκήπτρου πέρι.

ΠΕΙΣΕΤΑΙΡΟΣ

καὶ νὴ Δί' ἕτερόν γ' ἐστὶν οὗ 'μνήσθην ἐγώ.
τὴν μὲν γὰρ Ἥραν παραδίδωμι τῷ Διί,
τὴν δὲ Βασίλειαν τὴν κόρην γυναῖκ' ἐμοὶ
ἐκδοτέον ἐστίν.

PEISETAERUS

When this guy happens to be counting his pennies or sitting in the bath, a kite will swoop down, filch a two-sheep penalty, and deliver it to the god.

The three gods withdraw for a conference.

HERACLES

I vote aye again, to give them back the sceptre.

POSEIDON

Then ask the Triballian too.

HERACLES

(*waving his club*) Hey Triballian, how would you like some real pain?

TRIBALLIAN GOD

No hittum hide wit bat.

HERACLES

He says I'm quite right.

POSEIDON

Well, if that's how you both vote, I'll go along with you.

HERACLES

(*to Peisetaerus*) You there: we've voted to accept your terms regarding the sceptre.

PEISETAERUS

And there's another request that I definitely recall making: Hera I concede to Zeus, but the girl Princess must be given to me as my wife.

ΠΟΣΕΙΔΩΝ

οὐ διαλλαγῶν ἐρᾷς.
ἀπίωμεν οἴκαδ᾽ αὖθις.

ΠΕΙΣΕΤΑΙΡΟΣ

ὀλίγον μοι μέλει.
μάγειρε, τὸ κατάχυσμα χρὴ ποιεῖν γλυκύ.

ΗΡΑΚΛΗΣ

ὦ δαιμόνι᾽ ἀνθρώπων Πόσειδον, ποῖ φέρει;
ἡμεῖς περὶ γυναικὸς μιᾶς πολεμήσομεν;

ΠΟΣΕΙΔΩΝ

τί δαὶ ποιῶμεν;

ΗΡΑΚΛΗΣ

ὅ τι; διαλλαττώμεθα.

ΠΟΣΕΙΔΩΝ

τί ᾦζύρ᾽; οὐκ οἶσθ᾽ ἐξαπατώμενος πάλαι;
βλάπτεις δέ τοι σὺ σαυτόν. ἢν γὰρ ἀποθάνῃ
ὁ Ζεὺς παραδοὺς τούτοισι τὴν τυραννίδα,
πένης ἔσει σύ· σοῦ γὰρ ἅπαντα γίγνεται
τὰ χρήμαθ᾽, ὅσ᾽ ἂν ὁ Ζεὺς ἀποθνῄσκων καταλίπῃ.

ΠΕΙΣΕΤΑΙΡΟΣ

οἴμοι τάλας, οἷόν σε περισοφίζεται.
δεῦρ᾽ ὡς ἔμ᾽ ἀποχώρησον, ἵνα τί σοι φράσω.
διαβάλλεταί σ᾽ ὁ θεῖος, ὦ πόνηρε σύ.
τῶν γὰρ πατρῴων οὐδ᾽ ἀκαρῆ μέτεστί σοι
κατὰ τοὺς νόμους· νόθος γὰρ εἶ κοὐ γνήσιος.

POSEIDON

It's not a settlement you're hot for. (*to his colleagues*) Let's go back home.

PEISETAERUS

That's of little concern to me. Cook, be sure you make the sauce sweet.

HERACLES

Man alive, Poseidon, what's your rush? Over a single woman we're out to fight a war?

POSEIDON

Well, what can we do?

HERACLES

Why, we settle.

POSEIDON

What, you chump? Don't you realize that you've been getting duped all along? What's more, you're harming yourself. Look, if Zeus surrenders his rule to these birds, you'll be left a pauper when he dies, because you now stand to get the whole estate that he leaves behind at his death.

PEISETAERUS

Good grief, how he's trying to fast-talk you! Come aside here, I want a word with you. Your uncle's out to cheat you, poor fellow. Of your father's estate you don't get a single penny; that's the law.[148] You see, you're a bastard, illegitimate.

[148] Throughout this passage, Athenian laws are assumed to apply to the gods; Heracles' mother was the mortal Alcmene, wife of Amphitryon.

ΗΡΑΚΛΗΣ

ἐγὼ νόθος; τί λέγεις;

ΠΕΙΣΕΤΑΙΡΟΣ

σὺ μέντοι νὴ Δία
ὤν γε ξένης γυναικός. ἢ πῶς ἄν ποτε
ἐπίκληρον εἶναι τὴν Ἀθηναίαν δοκεῖς,
οὖσαν θυγατέρ', ὄντων ἀδελφῶν γνησίων;

ΗΡΑΚΛΗΣ

τί δ' ἢν ὁ πατὴρ ἐμοὶ διδῷ τὰ χρήματα
νοθεῖ' ἀποθνῄσκων;

ΠΕΙΣΕΤΑΙΡΟΣ

ὁ νόμος αὐτὸν οὐκ ἐᾷ.
οὗτος ὁ Ποσειδῶν πρῶτος, ὃς ἐπαίρει σε νῦν,
ἀνθέξεταί σοι τῶν πατρῴων χρημάτων
φάσκων ἀδελφὸς αὐτὸς εἶναι γνήσιος.
ἐρῶ δὲ δὴ καὶ τὸν Σόλωνός σοι νόμον·
"νόθῳ δὲ μὴ εἶναι ἀγχιστείαν παίδων ὄντων
γνησίων·
ἐὰν δὲ παῖδες μὴ ὦσι γνήσιοι, τοῖς ἐγγυτάτω
γένους
μετεῖναι τῶν χρημάτων."

ΗΡΑΚΛΗΣ

ἐμοὶ δ' ἄρ' οὐδὲν τῶν πατρῴων χρημάτων
μέτεστιν;

ΠΕΙΣΕΤΑΙΡΟΣ

οὐ μέντοι μὰ Δία. λέξον δέ μοι,

HERACLES

Me, a bastard? What are you talking about?

PEISETAERUS

That's exactly what you are, your mother being an alien. Why else do you think that Athena as a daughter could be called The Heiress, if she had legitimate brothers?

HERACLES

But couldn't my father at his death still leave me his property as a bastard's portion?

PEISETAERUS

The law won't let him. Poseidon here, who's now getting your hopes up, will be the first to dispute your claim to your father's property, declaring himself the legitimate brother. I'll even quote you the law of Solon:[149] "A bastard shall not qualify as next of kin, if there are legitimate children; if there are no legitimate children, the next of kin shall share the property."

HERACLES

You mean I have no share in my father's property?

PEISETAERUS

Absolutely none. Tell me, has your father inducted you

[149] Solon's codification (early sixth century), to which Athenians tended to attribute their oldest laws; for the law on intestacy cf. Demosthenes 43.51, Isaeus 6.47.

1656 *νοθεῖ᾽ ἀπο-* Daubuz, cf. γρΣ^VEΓ S Harpocr. Pollux: *νόθῳ ᾽ξαπο- vel sim.* a

ἤδη σ᾽ ὁ πατὴρ εἰσήγαγ᾽ εἰς τοὺς φράτερας;

ΗΡΑΚΛΗΣ

οὐ δῆτ᾽ ἐμέ γε. καὶ τοῦτ᾽ ἐθαύμαζον πάλαι.

ΠΕΙΣΕΤΑΙΡΟΣ

τί δῆτ᾽ ἄνω κέχηνας αἴκειαν βλέπων;
ἀλλ᾽ ἢν μεθ᾽ ἡμῶν ᾖς, καταστήσας σ᾽ ἐγὼ
τύραννον ὀρνίθων παρέξω σοι γάλα.

ΗΡΑΚΛΗΣ

δίκαι᾽ ἔμοιγε καὶ πάλαι δοκεῖς λέγειν
περὶ τῆς κόρης, κἄγωγε παραδίδωμί σοι.

ΠΕΙΣΕΤΑΙΡΟΣ

τί δαὶ σὺ φῄς;

ΠΟΣΕΙΔΩΝ

τἀναντία ψηφίζομαι.

ΠΕΙΣΕΤΑΙΡΟΣ

ἐν τῷ Τριβαλλῷ πᾶν τὸ πρᾶγμα. τί σὺ λέγεις;

ΤΡΙΒΑΛΛΟΣ

καλανι κοραυνα καὶ μεγαλα βασιλιναυ
ὀρνιτο παραδίδωμι.

ΗΡΑΚΛΗΣ

παραδοῦναι λέγει.

ΠΟΣΕΙΔΩΝ

μὰ τὸν Δί᾽ οὐχ οὗτός γε παραδοῦναι λέγει,
εἰ μὴ βαβάζει γ᾽ ὥσπερ αἱ χελιδόνες.

1681 βαβάζει γ᾽ Bentley: βαδίζειν a

into his phratry yet?[150]

HERACLES

Not me he hasn't, and that's always made me wonder.

PEISETAERUS

So why gape at the sky with an assaultive glare, when you could side with us? I'll appoint you ruler, and supply you with birds' milk.

HERACLES

Your claim to the girl sounds fair to me, as ever; I'm for handing her over to you.

PEISETAERUS

(*to Poseidon*) And what about you?

POSEIDON

I vote against.

PEISETAERUS

The whole business depends on the Triballian. (*to Triballian*) What do you say?

TRIBALLIAN GOD

Lovey tall missy Princessy I hand over birdie.

HERACLES

He says, hand her over.

POSEIDON

No, by Zeus, he's not saying hand her over; he's just twittering like the swallows.

[150] A religious guild whose members traced descent from a common ancestor; membership was a standard proof of citizenship, and the induction of young men as new members included lavish feasting.

ΗΡΑΚΛΗΣ

οὐκοῦν παραδοῦναι ταῖς χελιδόσιν λέγει.

ΠΟΣΕΙΔΩΝ

σφώ νυν διαλλάττεσθε καὶ ξυμβαίνετε·
ἐγὼ δ', ἐπειδὴ σφῷν δοκεῖ, σιγήσομαι.

ΗΡΑΚΛΗΣ

ἡμῖν ἃ λέγεις σὺ πάντα συγχωρεῖν δοκεῖ.
ἀλλ' ἴθι μεθ' ἡμῶν αὐτὸς εἰς τὸν οὐρανόν,
ἵνα τὴν Βασίλειαν καὶ τὰ πάντ' ἐκεῖ λάβῃς.

ΠΕΙΣΕΤΑΙΡΟΣ

εἰς καιρὸν ἆρα κατεκόπησαν οὑτοιὶ
εἰς τοὺς γάμους.

ΗΡΑΚΛΗΣ

βούλεσθε δῆτ' ἐγὼ τέως
ὀπτῶ τὰ κρέα ταυτὶ μένων; ὑμεῖς δ' ἴτε.

ΠΟΣΕΙΔΩΝ

ὀπτᾷς σὺ κρέα; πολλήν γε τενθείαν λέγεις.
οὐκ εἶ μεθ' ἡμῶν;

ΗΡΑΚΛΗΣ

εὖ γε μένταν διετέθην.

ΠΕΙΣΕΤΑΙΡΟΣ

ἀλλὰ γαμικὴν χλανίδα δότω τις δεῦρό μοι.

ΧΟΡΟΣ

(ἀντ) ἔστι δ' ἐν Φαναῖσι πρὸς τῇ
κλεψύδρᾳ πανοῦργον Ἐγ-

HERACLES

All right, he's saying hand her over to the swallows.

POSEIDON

Very well, you two negotiate the terms of a settlement; if that's your decision, I'll keep quiet.

HERACLES

(*to Peisetaerus*) We've decided to agree to all your proposals. Now come with us to heaven yourself, and there get Princess and everything else.

PEISETAERUS

Then these birds have been cut up just in time for my wedding!

HERACLES

And if you like, I'll stay behind here in the meantime, and roast the meat; you go on ahead.

POSEIDON

You? Roast meat? An orgy of gobbling, you mean. Better come with us.

HERACLES

My, I would have liked that job.

PEISETAERUS

Now someone fetch me a wedding jacket!

All exit.

CHORUS

Over in the land of Extortia, near
the Water Cache,[151] dwells the wicked

151 Of fountain houses and also of the device used to time speeches in Athenian lawcourts.

γλωττογαστόρων γένος,
οἳ θερίζουσίν τε καὶ σπεί-
ρουσι καὶ τρυγῶσι ταῖς γλώτ-
ταισι συκάζουσί τε·
βάρβαροι δ' εἰσὶν γένους,
Γοργίαι τε καὶ Φίλιπποι.
κἀπὸ τῶν ἐγγλωττογαστό-
ρων ἐκείνων τῶν φιλίππων
πανταχοῦ τῆς Ἀττικῆς ἡ
γλῶττα χωρὶς τέμνεται.

ΚΗΡΥΞ Β΄

ὦ πάντ' ἀγαθὰ πράττοντες, ὦ μείζω λόγου,
ὦ τρισμακάριον πτηνὸν ὀρνίθων γένος,
δέχεσθε τὸν τύραννον ὀλβίοις δόμοις.
προσέρχεται γὰρ οἷος οὔτε παμφαὴς
ἀστὴρ ἰδεῖν ἔλαμψε χρυσαυγεῖ δρόμῳ,
οὔθ' ἡλίου τηλαυγὲς ἀκτίνων σέλας
τοιοῦτον ἐξέλαμψεν οἷος ἔρχεται
ἔχων γυναικὸς κάλλος οὐ φατὸν λέγειν,
πάλλων κεραυνόν, πτεροφόρον Διὸς βέλος.
ὀσμὴ δ' ἀνωνόμαστος εἰς βάθος κύκλου
χωρεῖ, καλὸν θέαμα, θυμιαμάτων δ'
αὖραι διαψαίρουσι πλεκτάνην καπνοῦ.

1710 δρόμῳ E p: δόμῳ cett.
1712 οἷος Dindorf: οἷον a

race of Thrive-by-Tongues,
who do their harvesting and sowing
and vintaging by tongue,
and also their culling.
They're a race of barbarians,
Gorgiases and Philippuses.[152]
It's from these philippic
Thrive-by-Tongues
that all over Attica
the tongue is specially excised.[153]

Enter SECOND HERALD.

SECOND HERALD

Attention, you achievers of complete success, greater than words can say, you triple-blessed winged race of birds: welcome your ruler to his prosperous palace! Yea he draws near, more dazzling to behold than any meteor flaring on its path of golden beams, more than even the flare of the sun's far-beaming splendor of rays, as he comes bringing a lady of beauty surpassing description, and brandishing the thunderbolt, winged missile of Zeus. A fragrance unnamable ascends to the welkin's very depths, a fair spectacle, and breezes puff asunder the wreaths of smoke from the incense.

Enter PEISETAERUS, *wielding the thunderbolt, with Princess, as royal couple.*

[152] Gorgias, a Sicilian, taught rhetoric at Athens, and Philippus (a common name) was either his son (cf. *Wasps* 421) or a disciple.

[153] In sacrifices, cf. *Peace* 1109, Homer, *Odyssey* 3.332–41.

ὁδὶ δὲ καὐτός ἐστιν. ἀλλὰ χρὴ θεᾶς
μούσης ἀνοίγειν ἱερὸν εὔφημον στόμα.

ΧΟΡΟΣ

ἄναγε δίεχε πάραγε πάρεχε,
περιπέτεσθε μάκαρα μάκαρι σὺν τύχᾳ.
ὦ φεῦ φεῦ τῆς ὥρας, τοῦ κάλλους.
ὦ μακαριστὸν σὺ γάμον τῇδε πόλει γήμας.

ΚΟΡΥΦΑΙΟΣ

μεγάλαι μεγάλαι κατέχουσι τύχαι
γένος ὀρνίθων
διὰ τόνδε τὸν ἄνδρ᾽. ἀλλ᾽ ὑμεναίοις
καὶ νυμφιδίοισι δέχεσθ᾽ ᾠδαῖς
αὐτὸν καὶ τὴν Βασίλειαν.

ΧΟΡΟΣ

(στρ) Ἥρᾳ ποτ᾽ Ὀλυμπίᾳ
τὸν ἠλιβάτων θρόνων
ἄρχοντα θεοῖς μέγαν
Μοῖραι ξυνεκο<ί>μισαν
ἐν τοιῷδ᾽ ὑμεναίῳ.
Ὑμὴν ὤ, Ὑμέναι᾽ ὤ.
<Ὑμὴν ὤ, Ὑμέναι᾽ ὤ.>
(ἀντ) ὁ δ᾽ ἀμφιθαλὴς Ἔρως
χρυσόπτερος ἡνίας
ηὔθυνε παλιντόνους,
Ζηνὸς πάροχος γάμων

1734 suppl. Bentley 1736b suppl. Dindorf

And here he is himself! Now let the divine Muse open her holy lips in auspicious song!

Exit SECOND HERALD.

CHORUS

Get back! Divide! Form up! Make room!
Fly by the man blest with blest luck!
My oh my, her youth, her beauty!
What a blessing for this city is the marriage you have made!

CHORUS LEADER

Great, great is the luck that embraces
the race of birds
thanks to this man; now with wedding
and bridal songs please welcome
Himself and His Princess!

CHORUS

Once were Olympian Hera
and the mighty lord of the lofty
throne of the gods
united by the Fates
with such a wedding song.
Hymen Hymenaeus!
Hymen Hymenaeus!

And blooming Eros
of the golden wings guided
the straining reins
as best man at the wedding

τῆς τ᾽ εὐδαίμονος Ἥρας.
Ὑμὴν ὦ, Ὑμέναι᾽ ὦ.
Ὑμὴν ὦ, Ὑμέναι᾽ ὦ.

ΠΕΙΣΕΤΑΙΡΟΣ

ἐχάρην ὕμνοις, ἐχάρην ᾠδαῖς·
ἄγαμαι δὲ λόγων.

ΚΟΡΥΦΑΙΟΣ

ἄγε νυν αὐτοῦ καὶ τὰς χθονίας
κλῄσατε βροντὰς
τάς τε πυρώδεις Διὸς ἀστεροπὰς
δεινόν τ᾽ ἀργῆτα κεραυνόν.

ΧΟΡΟΣ

ὦ μέγα χρύσεον ἀστεροπῆς φάος
ὦ Διὸς ἄμβροτον ἔγχος
πυρφόρον, ὦ χθόνιαι βαρυαχέες
ὀμβροφόροι θ᾽ ἅμα βρονταί,
αἷς ὅδε νῦν χθόνα σείει,
Δῖα δὲ πάντα κρατήσας
καὶ πάρεδρον Βασίλειαν ἔχει Διός.
Ὑμὴν ὦ, Ὑμέναι᾽ ὦ.

ΚΟΡΥΦΑΙΟΣ

ἕπεσθέ νυν γάμοισιν, ὦ
φῦλα πάντα συννόμων
πτεροφόρ᾽, ἐπὶ <δά>πεδον Διὸς
καὶ λέχος γαμήλιον.

of Zeus and thriving Hera.
Hymen Hymenaeus!
Hymen Hymenaeus!

PEISETAERUS

I'm pleased by your chants, pleased by your songs,
and bowled over by your words.

CHORUS LEADER

Come then, celebrate too
his earth-shaking thunders
and the fiery lightnings of Zeus
and the awesome fulgent thunderbolt.

CHORUS

Great golden glare of lightning!
Zeus' immortal fire-bearing
shaft! Thunders rumbling heavily
in the ground and also bringing rain!
With you this man now shakes the earth,
new master of Zeus' estate
and of Princess, attendant of Zeus' throne.
Hymen Hymenaeus!

CHORUS LEADER

Follow now the wedding party,
all you winged tribes
of fellow songsters, to Zeus' yard
and to the bridal bower.

1752 Δῖα δὲ Haupt: διὰ σὲ τὰ a
1757 suppl. Meineke

ΠΕΙΣΕΤΑΙΡΟΣ

ὄρεξον, ὦ μάκαιρα, σὴν
χεῖρα καὶ πτερῶν ἐμῶν
λαβοῦσα συγχόρευσον· αἴ-
ρων δὲ κουφιῶ σ᾽ ἐγώ.

ΧΟΡΟΣ

ἀλαλαλαί, ἰὴ παιών·
τήνελλα καλλίνικος, ὦ
δαιμόνων ὑπέρτατε.

PEISETAERUS

Hold out your hand, my happy one,
and holding to my wings
join me for a dance; I'll
lift you up and swing you!

PEISETAERUS and Princess, dancing, lead the way off; the Chorus follow.

CHORUS

Hip hip hooray! Hail Paeon!
Hail your success, you
highest of divinities!

LYSISTRATA

INTRODUCTORY NOTE

Lysistrata was produced by Callistratus[1] in 411; we lack information about the festival, the competitors, and the prize, but internal evidence strongly favors the Lenaea.[2]

With the war once again threatening Athenian territory and destabilizing the democratic regime, Aristophanes returned in *Lysistrata* to the politically engaged style of comedy so prominent in his plays of the 420s, renewing his call for a negotiated settlement of the war, attacking the motives of its proponents, and appealing for panhellenic unity abroad and for both social and political unity at home. *Lysistrata* is notable too for its complex and ingenious plot, which continues a trend toward greater structural unity already apparent in *Birds*; for its sparkling depictions of a broad array of characters; for its remarkable blend of gaiety and earnestness; and for its apparent introduction of the first comic heroine.

The war began to go decisively against the Athenians in 413, when their great armada against Sicily was wiped out at Syracuse, with crippling losses of men, material, and wealth. Now a Spartan army of occupation once again sur-

[1] For this man see *Birds*, Introductory Note.

[2] On the dating see further *Women at the Thesmophoria*, Introductory Note.

rounded Athens; important territory fell out of Athenian control; and several major allies quickly defected from the empire, with others threatening to follow. Many believed that the Athenians would soon be helpless, but by the end of 412 they had managed to refurbish their navy and win back some strategically important territory. The political and fiscal discipline required to stave off defeat was facilitated by the Assembly's willingness to accept restraints on its own autonomy, in particular the appointment of a board of ten elderly statesmen (including the tragic poet Sophocles) called Probouloi ("executive councillors"), who could expedite the war effort by bypassing the Assembly. An unnamed member of this board is the heroine's antagonist in *Lysistrata*.

Nevertheless, as the winter of 412/11 set in, Athens was still straitened financially and increasingly volatile politically. Thucydides provides a rough, and much debated, chronology (8.1–60).[3] Spartan negotiations with the Persian satrap Tissaphernes, which began in December and would produce an accord by late March, threatened to tip the balance of war decisively against Athens. Meanwhile, officers of the main Athenian naval base at Samos had also made secret contact with Tissaphernes, using as their intermediary the exiled Alcibiades, who promised to bring Persia into alliance with Athens if the Athenians would recall him and agree to "a more moderate constitution with a rather smaller number eligible for offices" (8.53). In mid-December the general Pisander was deputized to go to

[3] For recent discussion see H. Avery, "The Chronology of Peisander's Mission to Athens," *Classical Philology* 94 (1999) 127-46.

Athens to engineer the acceptance of Alcibiades' demands. After meeting privately with political sympathizers, Pisander put his proposals before the Assembly, which authorized him to lead an embassy to Alcibiades and Tissaphernes. Although Alcibiades proved unable to deliver Persian support, the officers proceeded with their conspiracy; over the following months they launched a campaign of propaganda, intimidation, and assassination that by summer had succeeded in installing an oligarchic government.

The topical references and plot assumptions in *Lysistrata* suit the period after Pisander had returned to Athens but before the Assembly had heard his proposals: he is the only politician singled out by name for abuse, but is portrayed as being the same democratic extremist as he had "always" been (489–92). The play contains no hint of possible constitutional changes (cf. 577–78, which condemn factions of all stripes); no awareness of antidemocratic sentiment at Samos (cf. 313); no allusion to Alcibiades; no thought of money from the Persians (the plot assumes the availability only of the Acropolis funds, cf. 170–79, 486–97); and makes emphatic calls for panhellenic cooperation against Persia that would be pointless after the Assembly had authorized Pisander's embassy. Since this cannot have happened as late as the Dionysia, *Lysistrata* must have been produced at the Lenaea, which in 411 probably fell in early to mid-February.[4]

[4] The resulting delay of some two months between the deputizing of Pisander and his proposals to the Assembly remains mysterious; Pisander may have needed the time to test the political waters, or he may not have gone to Athens immediately, perhaps

In the play, an Athenian woman named Lysistrata organizes and successfully prosecutes a panhellenic women's conspiracy that forces the men of Athens and Sparta to negotiate a settlement of the war and promise never to fight one another again. Her name, though borne by actual women, is dramatically apt: it means "Disbander of Armies," with the first element (*Lysi-*) also connoting the power of sexual desire to "loosen" a man's limbs. Her conspiracy consists of two separate initiatives. One is a conjugal strike (supported by the goddess Aphrodite) whereby the young wives from all the warring states will refuse to perform their domestic (especially sexual) duties until their husbands lay down their arms and come home to stay. The other is the occupation of the Acropolis (supported by the goddess Athena), whereby the older women of Athens will deny access to the funds needed to continue the war. When the older women have secured the Acropolis the young wives join them there.

The strike plot, described in the prologue and illustrated later in the play by Cinesias and Myrrhine, succeeds virtually unopposed: after only six days the young warriors are sexually desperate enough to agree to whatever terms Lysistrata demands. The occupation plot contains the agonistic component of the play: strife between semichoruses of old men who storm the Acropolis, and old women who repulse them; and a debate between Lysistrata and an elderly Magistrate who has come to arrest her. When the occupation plot has eliminated official

because the officers thought it prudent to wait until the Peloponnesians had beached their fleet for the winter (late January, cf. Thucydides 8.44.4).

opposition, and the strike plot has made the young husbands capitulate to their wives, Athenian and Spartan ambassadors negotiate their differences and promise eternal friendship. Reconciliation of the semichoruses prefigures reconciliation between the warring cities and symbolizes the end of bitter divisiveness between sexes and citizens generally.

The comic fantasy of *Lysistrata* lies in its projection of women's characteristic roles outside the domestic sphere. Aristophanes assimilates the polis (Athens) to the individual household, and the aggregate of poleis (Greece) to a neighborhood. For, in effect, Lysistrata converts the Acropolis into a household for all citizen women. Its exclusivity turns the tables on the men, who have neglected their wives and excluded them from the process of policy making. And just as a wife might protect the household money from a spendthrift husband, so Lysistrata bars the Magistrate's access to the state treasuries. Fantastic, too, is the strength, independence, and discipline displayed by the women versus the weakness, dependency, and rapid capitulation of the men: a reversal of prevailing gender stereotypes and one that in Athenian terms could only reflect badly on the men.

The characterizations are also socially and politically pointed. The old men of the chorus are rank-and-file veterans of the democracy's wars against tyrants and barbarians, but now live on state pay, dissipate Athens' inherited wealth by their unreasoning support of the war, and have forgotten the panhellenic solidarity that once made Greece prosperous and secure. The old politicians, represented by the Magistrate, prosecute the war solely to make a profit at the expense of ordinary citizens and soldiers.

The old women of the chorus boast of lifelong service in the city's most venerable religious institutions and belong to the upper stratum of Athenian society. The young husbands and wives, both Athenian and foreign, wish only for the restoration of sexual and domestic normality. The caricature of Spartans is amusing but benign.

Putting not a hero but a heroine in charge of the plot was apparently a novelty, perhaps prompted at least in part by the ticklishness of an appeal for peace in 411, for despite their hardships most Athenians were determined to persevere in the war; even during the summer, when the oligarchs repeatedly sought a treaty with Sparta (Thucydides 8.70–71, 90), both the military (8.77–78) and the people (8.97) steadfastly opposed negotiation. By contrast, Aristophanes' earlier peace plays were produced at times when a negotiated settlement was supported by a significant minority (*Acharnians* in 425) or actually imminent (*Peace* in 421). A heroine provided a respectable citizen who could make plausible arguments for reconciliation at home and abroad while at the same time standing outside and above the prevailing political turmoil and military uncertainty. Furthermore, women as a united class modeled the important theme of solidarity: their concerted action in a just cause contrasts sharply with the factional and chaotic actions of the men, just as the old notion of a "race of women" exemplified Aristophanes' wished-for "race of Greeks" once again united against barbarians (cf. especially 1128–34). At the same time, the intrinsic humor in the spectacle of women turning the tables on and besting the men provided constant comic relief, and so defused potential spectator indignation.

Though Lysistrata may have been partially inspired by

such traditional figures as Homer's Andromache (cf. lines 519–20) and the virtuous heroines of Euripides' recent tragedies, she remains an extraordinary invention. Identified neither as a young housewife nor as an older woman, she is the master strategist, commander, and spokesman, while the other women are her agents. She understands and uses her helpers' talents but does not herself share in them; in fact she pointedly differentiates herself from the other women, especially the ludicrous young wives. She champions not only the interests of her own sex but also the traditional values of all Greeks male and female, and she possesses a degree of intelligence, will, and eloquence that would have been considered extraordinary in a citizen of either sex. In her possession of the most admired attributes of power, wisdom, and statesmanship, in her dual role as defender of home and of polis, in her acquaintance with both domestic and martial arts, in her panhellenic outlook, in her advocacy of internal solidarity, in her self-discipline and immunity to sexual temptation, in her appeal to young and old, and in her close connection with the Acropolis, Lysistrata finds her closest analogue in Athena herself.

Perhaps also in Athena's chief priestess. The Acropolis cult of Athena Polias was the city's oldest and most revered religious institution. Its priestess, who served for life, came always from the ancient family of the Eteobutadae and had an official residence on the Acropolis, where she managed the cult and its female personnel, and where she discharged many ritual functions on behalf of the polis, including the guardianship of Athena's treasuries. Since Athena's temple symbolized the ideal Athenian household, and her priestly personnel epitomized every household's female managers, the Polias priestess—the highest public position a woman could hold—was in effect the First Lady of Athens. She had a public visibility and authority unavailable to any other woman.

In 411 the Polias priestess was Lysimache, who held office for sixty-four years and who appears to have been known, or thought, to be opposed to the war (*Peace* 991–92). Since her name is very close to our heroine's[5] and may be specifically alluded to in the play itself (554), it is not unlikely that Aristophanes intended to assimilate Lysistrata to Lysimache in order to invest his heroine with some of the priestess' authority and further strengthen her association with the goddess. Close portraiture, however, is unlikely: the priestess, like the goddess, was but one associative element of a unique heroine, who in the course of the play resorts to tactics arguably unbecoming a priestess, and achieves a stature that no woman, Lysimache included, could ever actually attain.

Still other elements from the world of cult and myth inform the plot of *Lysistrata*: the Amazons (678–79), the Lemnian women (299–300), and the many festivals in which women ritually exclude, defy, or even replace men; the Magistrate, forcibly dressed as a woman and symbolically killed (530–38, 599–607), recalls the mythical kings (e.g. Lycurgus and Pentheus) whom Dionysus' maenads overpower. Nor can the prominence of Athena behind the heroine, and of the Acropolis in the plot, fail to have reminded the spectators of the foundation myth of Athens it-

[5] The name Lysistrata was in fact borne by more than one Polias priestess in later times, and perhaps in earlier times too, since Lysimache is the first identifiable incumbent.

self: Athena had challenged Poseidon for the city and won, only to support, in her uniquely inclusive way, the primacy of male institutions in the polis.[6] In 411 Aristophanes used such traditional myths and rituals as symbolic ingredients in a comedy intended in no small part to remind males of the crucial role women played in the maintenance and success of those institutions.

Text

Three papyri preserve fragments of *Lysistrata*; one of these is not cited in the notes, *PAnt*. 75+211 (V/VI), partially preserving lines 307–13, 318–20, 342–46, 353–62. There are five independent medieval MSS, which divide into two groups: (1) R, which alone preserves the complete text, and Mu2 (XV), which, though copied directly from R, incorporates the work of an early editor who made simple emendations and supplied many line attributions; and (2) ΓBVp2H, which descend from a lost MS lacking lines 62–131, 200–67, 820–89, 1098–1236. Γ is the main ancestor of B and Vp2H, which descend from a hyparchetype p. But Γ subsequently lost lines 1035-end as well, so that for lines 1035–97 and 1237-end this group is represented only by Bp. Two 15th-c. MSS, which contain only scholia to *Lysistrata* and which were copied from Γ before its mutilation (Neapolitanus II D 49 and Oxoniensis Bodleianus Baroccianus 38B), provide some additional information about the lost text of Γ. In two sections of the play (roughly 280–590 and 900–50) both B and (to a lesser extent) p con-

[6] The central text for this role of Athena is Aeschylus' *Eumenides*.

tain significant readings from an otherwise lost source independent of R and Γ. The Suda's quotations derive from texts similar to R and include the sections missing in ΓBp.

Sigla

Π1	*PColon.* 14 (IV), lines 145–53, 182–87, 197–99, 188
Π2	*PBodl.gr. class. e 87(P)* (IV/V), lines 433–47, 469–84
R	Ravennas 429 (*c.* 950)
S	readings found in the Suda
	all the following MSS lack lines 62–131, 200–67, 820–89, 1098–1236
Γ	Leidensis Vossianus gr. F52 (*c.* 1325), also lacking lines 1035-end
B	Parisinus gr. 2715 (XIV^{ex})
Vp2	Vaticanus Palatinus 67 (XV)
H	Hauniensis 1980 (XV)
a	the consensus of RΓBp (1–1034) or RBp (1035-end)
p	the hyparchetype of Vp2H

Annotated Editions

F. H. M. Blaydes (Halle 1880)
J. van Leeuwen (Leiden 1903)
B. B. Rogers (London 1911), with English translation
U. von Wilamowitz-Moellendorff (Berlin 1927)
J. J. Henderson (Oxford 1987)
A. H. Sommerstein (Warminster 1990), with English translation

ΤΑ ΤΟΥ ΔΡΑΜΑΤΟΣ ΠΡΟΣΩΠΑ

ΛΥΣΙΣΤΡΑΤΗ
ΚΑΛΟΝΙΚΗ
ΜΥΡΡΙΝΗ
ΛΑΜΠΙΤΩ *γυνὴ Λακωνική*
ΠΡΟΒΟΥΛΟΣ
ΓΡΑΥΣ Α
ΓΡΑΥΣ Β
ΓΡΑΥΣ Γ
ΓΥΝΗ Α
ΓΥΝΗ Β
ΓΥΝΗ Γ
ΓΥΝΗ Δ
ΚΙΝΗΣΙΑΣ *ἀνὴρ Μυρρίνης*
ΠΑΙΔΙΟΝ *Κινησίου καὶ Μυρρίνης*
ΚΗΡΥΞ *Λακεδαιμονίων*
ΛΑΚΕΔΑΙΜΟΝΙΩΝ ΠΡΕΣΒΕΥΤΗΣ
ΑΘΗΝΑΙΩΝ ΠΡΕΣΒΕΥΤΗΣ Α
ΑΘΗΝΑΙΩΝ ΠΡΕΣΒΕΥΤΗΣ Β

ΧΟΡΟΣ *γερόντων*
ΧΟΡΟΣ *γυναικῶν*

ΚΩΦΑ ΠΡΟΣΩΠΑ

ΓΥΝΑΙΚΕΣ ΑΤΤΙΚΑΙ
ΙΣΜΗΝΙΑ *γυνὴ Θηβαία*
ΓΥΝΗ ΚΟΡΙΝΘΙΑ
ΓΥΝΑΙΚΕΣ ΛΑΚΩΝΙΚΑΙ
ΣΚΥΘΑΙΝΑ *θεράπαινα Λυσιστράτης*
ΘΕΡΑΠΟΝΤΕΣ *τοῦ Προβούλου δύο*
ΤΟΞΟΤΑΙ *τέτταρες*
ΓΡΑΕΣ
ΜΑΝΗΣ, *οἰκέτης Κινησίου*
ΛΑΚΕΔΑΙΜΟΝΙΩΝ ΠΡΕΣΒΕΥΤΑΙ
ΘΕΡΑΠΟΝΤΕΣ *τῶν πρεσβευτῶν τῶν Λακεδαιμονίων*
ΑΘΗΝΑΙΩΝ ΠΡΕΣΒΕΥΤΑΙ
ΔΙΑΛΛΑΓΗ
ΘΥΡΩΡΟΣ

DRAMATIS PERSONAE

LYSISTRATA
CALONICE
MYRRHINE
LAMPITO, a Spartan wife
MAGISTRATE
FIRST OLD WOMAN
SECOND OLD WOMAN
THIRD OLD WOMAN
FIRST WIFE
SECOND WIFE
THIRD WIFE
FOURTH WIFE
CINESIAS, Myrrhine's husband
BABY of Cinesias and Myrrhine
HERALD from Sparta
SPARTAN DELEGATE
FIRST ATHENIAN DELEGATE
SECOND ATHENIAN DELEGATE

CHORUS of Old Men
CHORUS of Old Women

SILENT CHARACTERS

ATHENIAN WIVES
ISMENIA, a Theban wife
CORINTHIAN WIFE
SPARTAN WIVES
SCYTHIAN GIRL, Lysistrata's slave
SLAVES of the Magistrate
SCYTHIAN POLICEMEN, four
OLD WOMEN
MANES, Cinesias' slave
SPARTAN DELEGATES
SLAVES of the Spartan Delegates
ATHENIAN DELEGATES
RECONCILIATION
DOORKEEPER

ΛΥΣΙΣΤΡΑΤΗ

ΛΥΣΙΣΤΡΑΤΗ

ἀλλ᾽ εἴ τις εἰς Βακχεῖον αὐτὰς ἐκάλεσεν,
ἢ ᾽ς Πανὸς ἢ ᾽πὶ Κωλιάδ᾽ εἰς Γενετυλλίδος,
οὐδ᾽ ἂν διελθεῖν ἦν ἂν ὑπὸ τῶν τυμπάνων.
νῦν δ᾽ οὐδεμία πάρεστιν ἐνταυθοῖ γυνή·
πλὴν ἥ γ᾽ ἐμὴ κωμῆτις ἥδ᾽ ἐξέρχεται.
χαῖρ᾽, ὦ Καλονίκη.

ΚΑΛΟΝΙΚΗ

καὶ σύ γ᾽, ὦ Λυσιστράτη.
τί συντετάραξαι; μὴ σκυθρώπαζ᾽, ὦ τέκνον·
οὐ γὰρ πρέπει σοι τοξοποιεῖν τὰς ὀφρῦς.

ΛΥΣΙΣΤΡΑΤΗ

ἀλλ᾽, ὦ Καλονίκη, κάομαι τὴν καρδίαν,
καὶ πόλλ᾽ ὑπὲρ ἡμῶν τῶν γυναικῶν ἄχθομαι,
ὁτιὴ παρὰ μὲν τοῖς ἀνδράσιν νενομίσμεθα
εἶναι πανοῦργοι—

ΚΑΛΟΝΙΚΗ

καὶ γάρ ἐσμεν νὴ Δία.

---

[1] Bacchus (Dionysus), Pan, and the Genetyllides (goddesses of procreation) all had erotic associations.

LYSISTRATA

A neighborhood in Athens, after dawn. The scene building has a large central door and two smaller, flanking doors. From one of these LYSISTRATA *emerges and looks expectantly up and down the street.*

LYSISTRATA

Now if someone had invited them to a revel for Bacchus, or to Pan's shrine, or to Genetyllis' at Colias,[1] the streets would be impassible, what with their tambourines. But as it is, there's not a single woman here. *(the far door opens)* Except that my neighbor here's coming out. Good morning, Calonice.[2]

CALONICE

And you, Lysistrata.[3] What's bothering you? Don't frown, child. Knitted brows don't become you.

LYSISTRATA

But my heart's on fire, Calonice, and I'm terribly annoyed about us women. You know, according to the men we're capable of any sort of mischief—

CALONICE

And so we surely are!

[2] The name means "Fair Victory."
[3] The name means "Disbander of Armies."

ΛΥΣΙΣΤΡΑΤΗ

εἰρημένον δ' αὐταῖς ἀπαντᾶν ἐνθάδε
βουλευσομέναισιν οὐ περὶ φαύλου πράγματος,
εὕδουσι κοὐχ ἥκουσιν.

ΚΑΛΟΝΙΚΗ

ἀλλ', ὦ φιλτάτη,
ἥξουσι· χαλεπή τοι γυναικῶν ἔξοδος.
ἡ μὲν γὰρ ἡμῶν περὶ τὸν ἄνδρ' ἐκύπτασεν,
ἡ δ' οἰκέτην ἤγειρεν, ἡ δὲ παιδίον
κατέκλινεν, ἡ δ' ἔλουσεν, ἡ δ' ἐψώμισεν.

ΛΥΣΙΣΤΡΑΤΗ

ἀλλ' ἦν γὰρ ἕτερα τῶνδε προὐργιαίτερα
αὐταῖς.

ΚΑΛΟΝΙΚΗ

τί δ' ἐστίν, ὦ φίλη Λυσιστράτη,
ἐφ' ὅ τι ποθ' ἡμᾶς τὰς γυναῖκας ξυγκαλεῖς;
τί τὸ πρᾶγμα; πηλίκον τι;

ΛΥΣΙΣΤΡΑΤΗ

μέγα.

ΚΑΛΟΝΙΚΗ

μῶν καὶ παχύ;

ΛΥΣΙΣΤΡΑΤΗ

νὴ τὸν Δία καὶ παχύ.

ΚΑΛΟΝΙΚΗ

κᾆτα πῶς οὐχ ἥκομεν;

LYSISTRATA

but when they're told to meet here to discuss a matter of no trifling importance, they sleep in and don't show up.

CALONICE

Honey, they'll be along. You know, it's a lot of trouble for wives to get out of the house: we're giving hubby a hand, or waking up a slave, or putting the baby to bed, or bathing it, or feeding it a snack.

LYSISTRATA

Nonetheless, there was other business that should matter more than all of that.

CALONICE

Well, Lysistrata dear, what exactly is this business you're calling us women together for? What's the deal? Is it a big one?

LYSISTRATA

It's big.

CALONICE

Not juicy as well?

LYSISTRATA

Oh yes, it's big *and* juicy.

CALONICE

Then how come we're not all here?

ΛΥΣΙΣΤΡΑΤΗ

οὐχ οὗτος ὁ τρόπος· ταχὺ γὰρ ἂν ξυνήλθομεν.
ἀλλ' ἔστιν ὑπ' ἐμοῦ πρᾶγμ' ἀνεζητημένον
πολλαῖσί τ' ἀγρυπνίαισιν ἐρριπτασμένον.

ΚΑΛΟΝΙΚΗ

ἦ πού τι λεπτόν ἐστι τοὐρριπτασμένον;

ΛΥΣΙΣΤΡΑΤΗ

οὕτω γε λεπτὸν ὥσθ' ὅλης τῆς Ἑλλάδος
ἐν ταῖς γυναιξίν ἐστιν ἡ σωτηρία.

ΚΑΛΟΝΙΚΗ

ἐν ταῖς γυναιξίν; ἐπ' ὀλίγου γ' ἄρ' εἴχετο.

ΛΥΣΙΣΤΡΑΤΗ

ὡς ἔστ' ἐν ἡμῖν τῆς πόλεως τὰ πράγματα,
ἢ μηκέτ' εἶναι μήτε Πελοποννησίους—

ΚΑΛΟΝΙΚΗ

βέλτιστα τοίνυν μηκέτ' εἶναι νὴ Δία.

ΛΥΣΙΣΤΡΑΤΗ

Βοιωτίους τε πάντας ἐξολωλέναι.

ΚΑΛΟΝΙΚΗ

μὴ δῆτα πάντας γ', ἀλλ' ἄφελε τὰς ἐγχέλεις.

ΛΥΣΙΣΤΡΑΤΗ

περὶ τῶν Ἀθηνῶν δ' οὐκ ἐπιγλωττήσομαι
τοιοῦτον οὐδέν, ἀλλ' ὑπονόησον σύ μοι.
ἢν δὲ ξυνέλθωσ' αἱ γυναῖκες ἐνθάδε,
αἵ τ' ἐκ Βοιωτῶν αἵ τε Πελοποννησίων
ἡμεῖς τε, κοινῇ σώσομεν τὴν Ἑλλάδα.

LYSISTRATA

That's not what I meant! If it were, we'd all have shown up quickly enough. No, it's something I've been thinking hard about, tossing it around night after sleepless night.

CALONICE

After all that tossing it must be limp by now.

LYSISTRATA

So limp that the salvation of all Greece lies in the women's hands!

CALONICE

In the women's hands? A precarious place to be!

LYSISTRATA

Yes, our country's future depends on us: whether the Peloponnesians become extinct—

CALONICE

Well, that would be all right with me!

LYSISTRATA

and all the Boeotians are annihilated—

CALONICE

Not all of them, please—do spare the eels![4]

LYSISTRATA

I won't say anything like that about the Athenians; you get the point. But if the women gather together here—the Boeotian women, the Peloponnesian women, and ourselves—together we'll be able to rescue Greece!

[4] Eels from Lake Copais were a great delicacy, but contraband during the war.

ΚΑΛΟΝΙΚΗ

τί δ' ἂν γυναῖκες φρόνιμον ἐργασαίατο
ἢ λαμπρόν, αἳ καθήμεθ' ἐξηνθισμέναι,
κροκωτοφοροῦσαι καὶ κεκαλλωπισμέναι
καὶ Κιμβερίκ' ὀρθοστάδια καὶ περιβαρίδας;

ΛΥΣΙΣΤΡΑΤΗ

ταῦτ' αὐτὰ γάρ τοι κἄσθ' ἃ σώσειν προσδοκῶ,
τὰ κροκωτίδια καὶ τὰ μύρα χαἰ περιβαρίδες
χἤγχουσα καὶ τὰ διαφανῆ χιτώνια.

ΚΑΛΟΝΙΚΗ

τίνα δὴ τρόπον ποθ';

ΛΥΣΙΣΤΡΑΤΗ

ὥστε τῶν νῦν μηδένα
ἀνδρῶν ἐπ' ἀλλήλοισιν αἴρεσθαι δόρυ—

ΚΑΛΟΝΙΚΗ

κροκωτὸν ἄρα νὴ τὼ θεὼ 'γὼ βάψομαι.

ΛΥΣΙΣΤΡΑΤΗ

μηδ' ἀσπίδα λαβεῖν—

ΚΑΛΟΝΙΚΗ

Κιμβερικὸν ἐνδύσομαι.

ΛΥΣΙΣΤΡΑΤΗ

μηδὲ ξιφίδιον.

ΚΑΛΟΝΙΚΗ

κτήσομαι περιβαρίδας.

ΛΥΣΙΣΤΡΑΤΗ

ἆρ' οὐ παρεῖναι τὰς γυναῖκας δῆτ' ἐχρῆν;

CALONICE

But what can mere women do that's intelligent or illustrious? We sit around the house looking pretty, wearing saffron dresses, and make-up, and Cimberic gowns, and pleasure-boat slippers.

LYSISTRATA

Exactly! That's exactly what I think will rescue Greece: our fancy little dresses, our perfumes and our slippers, our rouge and our see-through underwear!

CALONICE

Just how do you mean?

LYSISTRATA

They'll guarantee that not one of the men who are still alive will raise his spear against another—

CALONICE

In that case, by the Two Goddesses,[5] I'll have a dress dyed saffron!

LYSISTRATA

nor hoist his shield—

CALONICE

I'll wear a Cimberic gown!

LYSISTRATA

nor even pull a knife!

CALONICE

I'll go shopping for slippers!

LYSISTRATA

So shouldn't the women have arrived by now?

[5] Demeter and Kore (Persephone).

ΚΑΛΟΝΙΚΗ

οὐ γὰρ μὰ Δί' ἀλλὰ πετομένας ἥκειν πάλαι.

ΛΥΣΙΣΤΡΑΤΗ

ἀλλ', ὦ μέλ', ὄψει τοι σφόδρ' αὐτὰς Ἀττικάς,
ἅπαντα δρώσας τοῦ δέοντος ὕστερον.
ἀλλ' οὐδὲ Παράλων οὐδεμία γυνὴ πάρα,
οὐδ' ἐκ Σαλαμῖνος.

ΚΑΛΟΝΙΚΗ

ἀλλ' ἐκεῖναί γ' οἶδ' ὅτι
ἐπὶ τῶν κελήτων διαβεβήκασ' ὄρθριαι.

ΛΥΣΙΣΤΡΑΤΗ

οὐδ' ἃς προσεδόκων κἀλογιζόμην ἐγὼ
πρώτας παρέσεσθαι δεῦρο τὰς Ἀχαρνέων
γυναῖκας, οὐχ ἥκουσιν.

ΚΑΛΟΝΙΚΗ

ἡ γοῦν Θεογένους
ὡς δεῦρ' ἰοῦσα τἀκάτειον ἤρετο.
ἀτὰρ αἵδε καὶ δή σοι προσέρχονταί τινες.

ΛΥΣΙΣΤΡΑΤΗ

αἵδ' αὖθ' ἕτεραι χωροῦσί τινες.

63 Θεο- Σ[R]: Θεα- R S
64 *θοὐκάτειον ἤρετο* Bentley et Daubuz cl. Σ[RS]

CALONICE

By now? My god, they should have taken wing and flown here ages ago!

LYSISTRATA

Well, my friend, you'll find they're typically Athenian: everything they do, they do too late. There isn't even a single woman here from the Paralia, nor from Salamis.[6]

CALONICE

Don't worry, I just know they've been astride their pinnaces since dawn.

LYSISTRATA

And the women I reckoned would be here first, and counted on, the women from Acharnae, they're not here either.

CALONICE

Well, Theogenes'[7] wife, for one, was rigging her jib[8] to come here.

Groups of women begin to enter from both sides, among them MYRRHINE.

But look, here come some of your women now!

LYSISTRATA

And there come some others, over there!

[6] Two regions of Attica that evoke the names of Athens' two fastest ships, the *Paralus* and the *Salaminia.*

[7] Perhaps the shipowner, Theogenes of Acharnae, ridiculed elsewhere as greedy, boastful, and boorish.

[8] Or, with the scholiasts' variant, "was consulting a shrine of Hecate" (a goddess popular with women).

ΚΑΛΟΝΙΚΗ

ἰοὺ ἰού,

πόθεν εἰσίν;

ΛΥΣΙΣΤΡΑΤΗ

Ἀναγυρουντόθεν.

ΚΑΛΟΝΙΚΗ

νὴ τὸν Δία·

ὁ γοῦν Ἀνάγυρός μοι κεκινῆσθαι δοκεῖ.

ΜΥΡΡΙΝΗ

μῶν ὕστεραι πάρεσμεν, ὦ Λυσιστράτη;
τί φῄς; τί σιγᾷς;

ΛΥΣΙΣΤΡΑΤΗ

οὐκ ἐπαινῶ, Μυρρίνη,
ἥκουσαν ἄρτι περὶ τοιούτου πράγματος.

ΜΥΡΡΙΝΗ

μόλις γὰρ ηὗρον ἐν σκότῳ τὸ ζώνιον.
ἀλλ' εἴ τι πάνυ δεῖ, ταῖς παρούσαισιν λέγε.

ΛΥΣΙΣΤΡΑΤΗ

μὰ Δί' ἀλλ' ἐπαναμείνωμεν ὀλίγου γ' οὕνεκα
τάς τ' ἐκ Βοιωτῶν τάς τε Πελοποννησίων
γυναῖκας ἐλθεῖν.

ΜΥΡΡΙΝΗ

πολὺ σὺ κάλλιον λέγεις.
ἡδὶ δὲ καὶ δὴ Λαμπιτὼ προσέρχεται.

---

9 Anagyrus, a deme named after the malodorous plant *Anagyris foetida*.

CALONICE

Phew! Where are *they* from?

LYSISTRATA

From Stinkton.[9]

CALONICE

Of course; I knew someone was raising a stink.

MYRRHINE[10]

I hope we're not too late, Lysistrata. What do you say? Why don't you say something?

LYSISTRATA

Myrrhine, I don't applaud anyone who shows up late for important business.

MYRRHINE

Well, I couldn't find my girdle; it was dark. But now that we're here, tell us what's so important.

LYSISTRATA

No, let's wait a little while, until the women from Boeotia and the Peloponnese get here.

MYRRHINE

That's a much better plan. And look, here's Lampito[11] coming now!

Enter LAMPITO, *accompanied by other Spartan Wives; Ismenia, a Theban Wife; and a Corinthian Wife.*

[10] Myrrhine ("Myrtle"), a very common name in life and in comedy, was particularly apt for this play, being associated with Aphrodite, used in bridal garlands, and slang for vulva.

[11] Lampito was an actual royal name in Sparta, but no contemporary of that name is known.

ΛΥΣΙΣΤΡΑΤΗ

ὦ φιλτάτη Λάκαινα, χαῖρε, Λαμπιτοῖ.
οἷον τὸ κάλλος, ὦ γλυκυτάτη, φαίνεται.
ὡς δ' εὐχροεῖς, ὡς δὲ σφριγᾷ τὸ σῶμά σου.
κἂν ταῦρον ἄγχοις.

ΛΑΜΠΙΤΩ

μάλα γ', οἰῶ, ναὶ τὼ σιώ·
γυμνάδδομαί γα καὶ ποτὶ πυγὰν ἅλλομαι.

ΚΑΛΟΝΙΚΗ

ὡς δὴ καλὸν τὸ χρῆμα τῶν τιτθῶν ἔχεις.

ΛΑΜΠΙΤΩ

ᾇπερ ἱερεῖόν τοί μ' ὑποψαλάσσετε.

ΛΥΣΙΣΤΡΑΤΗ

ἡδὶ δὲ ποδαπή 'σθ' ἡ νεᾶνις ἡτέρα;

ΛΑΜΠΙΤΩ

πρέσβειρά τοι ναὶ τὼ σιὼ Βοιωτία
ἵκει ποθ' ὑμέ.

ΜΥΡΡΙΝΗ

νὴ Δί' ὡς Βοιωτία
καλόν γ' ἔχουσα τὸ πεδίον.

ΚΑΛΟΝΙΚΗ

καὶ νὴ Δία
κομψότατα τὴν βληχώ γε παρατετιλμένη.

84 ἱαρεῖόν van Herwerden

LYSISTRATA

Greetings, Lampito, my very dear Spartan friend! My darling, how vivid your beauty! What rosy cheeks, what firmness of physique! You could throttle a bull!

LAMPITO[12]

It's true, I think, by the Twin Gods.[13] I do take exercise, and I jump-kick my butt.

CALONICE

And what a fine set of tits you've got!

LAMPITO

Hey, you're feeling me up like a beast for sacrifice!

LYSISTRATA

And this other young lady here, where's she from?

LAMPITO

By the Twin Gods, she's here as the representative of Boeotia.

MYRRHINE

She certainly looks like Boeotia, with all her lush bottomland.

CALONICE

Indeed, and with her bush most elegantly pruned.

[12] In *Lysistrata* all the Spartans speak a caricatured version of Laconian, their local dialect.

[13] The Dioscuri, Castor and Pollux, brothers of Helen and special patrons of the Spartans.

ΛΥΣΙΣΤΡΑΤΗ

τίς δ' ἡτέρα παῖς;

ΛΑΜΠΙΤΩ

χαΐα ναὶ τὼ σιώ,
Κορινθία δ' αὖ.

ΚΑΛΟΝΙΚΗ

χαΐα νὴ τὸν Δία
δήλη 'στὶν οὖσα ταυταγὶ κἀντευθενί.

ΛΑΜΠΙΤΩ

τίς δ' αὖ συναλίαξε τόνδε τὸν στόλον
τὸν τᾶν γυναικῶν;

ΛΥΣΙΣΤΡΑΤΗ

ἥδ' ἐγώ.

ΛΑΜΠΙΤΩ

μύσιδδέ τυ
ὅ τι λῇς ποθ' ἁμέ.

ΚΑΛΟΝΙΚΗ

νὴ Δί', ὦ φίλη γύναι,
λέγε δῆτα τὸ σπουδαῖον ὅ τι τοῦτ' ἐστί σοι.

ΛΥΣΙΣΤΡΑΤΗ

λέγοιμ' ἂν ἤδη. πρὶν <δὲ> λέγειν, ὑμᾶς τοδὶ
ἐπερήσομαί, τι μικρόν.

ΚΑΛΟΝΙΚΗ

ὅ τι βούλει γε σύ.

94 *μύσιδδέ τυ* Valckenaer: *μυσιδδέτω* a

LYSISTRATA
And who's this other girl?

LAMPITO
A lady of substance, by the Twin Gods, from Corinth.

CALONICE
She's substantial all right, both frontside and backside.

LAMPITO
Now who's convened this assembly of women?

LYSISTRATA
Right here; I'm the one.

LAMPITO
Then do explain what you want of us.

CALONICE
Yes, dear lady, do speak up. What's this important business of yours?

LYSISTRATA
I'm ready to tell you. But before I tell you, I want to ask you a small question; it won't take long.

CALONICE
Ask away.

ΛΥΣΙΣΤΡΑΤΗ

τοὺς πατέρας οὐ ποθεῖτε τοὺς τῶν παιδίων
ἐπὶ στρατιᾶς ἀπόντας; εὖ γὰρ οἶδ᾿ ὅτι
πάσαισιν ὑμῖν ἐστιν ἀποδημῶν ἀνήρ.

ΚΑΛΟΝΙΚΗ

ὁ γοῦν ἐμὸς ἀνὴρ πέντε μῆνας, ὦ τάλαν,
ἄπεστιν ἐπὶ Θρᾴκης φυλάττων Εὐκράτη.

ΜΥΡΡΙΝΗ

ὁ δ᾿ ἐμός γε τελέους ἑπτὰ μῆνας ἐν Πύλῳ.

ΛΑΜΠΙΤΩ

ὁ δ᾿ ἐμός γα, καἴ κ᾿ ἐκ τᾶς ταγᾶς ἔλσῃ ποκά,
πορπακισάμενος φροῦδος ἀμπτάμενος ἔβα.

ΚΑΛΟΝΙΚΗ

ἀλλ᾿ οὐδὲ μοιχοῦ καταλέλειπται φεψάλυξ.
ἐξ οὗ γὰρ ἡμᾶς προὔδοσαν Μιλήσιοι,
οὐκ εἶδον οὐδ᾿ ὄλισβον ὀκτωδάκτυλον,
ὃς ἦν ἂν ἡμῖν σκυτίνη ᾿πικουρία.

ΛΥΣΙΣΤΡΑΤΗ

ἐθέλοιτ᾿ ἂν οὖν, εἰ μηχανὴν εὕροιμ᾿ ἐγώ,
μετ᾿ ἐμοῦ καταλῦσαι τὸν πόλεμον;

ΚΑΛΟΝΙΚΗ

νὴ τὼ θεὼ
ἐγὼ μὲν ἄν, κἂν εἴ με χρείη τοὔγκυκλον
τουτὶ καταθεῖσαν ἐκπιεῖν αὐθημερόν.

LYSISTRATA

Don't you all pine for your children's fathers when they're off at war? I'm sure that every one of you has a husband away from home.

CALONICE

My husband's been away five months, my dear, at the Thracian front; he's guarding Eucrates.[14]

MYRRHINE

And mine's been at Pylos seven whole months.

LAMPITO

And mine, whenever he does come home from the regiment, is soon strapping on his shield and flying off again.

CALONICE

Even lovers have vanished without a trace. Ever since the Milesians revolted from us, I haven't even seen a six-inch dildo, which might have been a consolation, however small.[15]

LYSISTRATA

Well, if I could devise a plan to end the war, would you be ready to join me?

CALONICE

By the Two Goddesses, I would, even if I had to pawn this dress and, on the very same day, drink up the proceeds!

[14] Substituting the name of an Athenian commander, not certainly identifiable, for the name of a city that the Athenians were besieging.

[15] Miletus, a notable exporter of dildoes (cf. fr. 592.16–28), had defected the previous summer (Thucydides 8.17).

ΜΥΡΡΙΝΗ

ἐγὼ δέ γ' ἄν, κἂν ὡσπερεὶ ψῆτταν δοκῶ
δοῦναι ἂν ἐμαυτῆς παρατεμοῦσα θἤμισυ.

ΛΑΜΠΙΤΩ

ἐγὼν δὲ καί κα ποττὸ Ταΰγετόν γ' ἄνω
ἔλσοιμ' ὅπᾳ μέλλοιμί γ' εἰράναν ἰδῆν.

ΛΥΣΙΣΤΡΑΤΗ

λέγοιμ' ἄν· οὐ δεῖ γὰρ κεκρύφθαι τὸν λόγον.
ἡμῖν γάρ, ὦ γυναῖκες, εἴπερ μέλλομεν
ἀναγκάσειν τοὺς ἄνδρας εἰρήνην ἄγειν,
ἀφεκτέ' ἐστι—

ΚΑΛΟΝΙΚΗ

τοῦ; φράσον.

ΛΥΣΙΣΤΡΑΤΗ

ποιήσετ' οὖν;

ΚΑΛΟΝΙΚΗ

ποιήσομεν, κἂν ἀποθανεῖν ἡμᾶς δέῃ.

ΛΥΣΙΣΤΡΑΤΗ

ἀφεκτέα τοίνυν ἐστὶν ἡμῖν τοῦ πέους.
τί μοι μεταστρέφεσθε; ποῖ βαδίζετε;
αὗται, τί μοιμυᾶτε κἀνανεύετε;
τί χρὼς τέτραπται; τί δάκρυον κατείβεται;
ποιήσετ' ἢ οὐ ποιήσετ'; ἢ τί μέλλετε;

ΚΑΛΟΝΙΚΗ

οὐκ ἂν ποιήσαιμ', ἀλλ' ὁ πόλεμος ἑρπέτω.

MYRRHINE

As for me, I'd even cut myself in two like a flounder and donate half to the cause!

LAMPITO

And I would climb to the summit of Taygetus,[16] if I could catch sight of peace from there.

LYSISTRATA

Here goes, then; no need to beat around the bush. Ladies, if we're going to force the men to make peace, we're going to have to give up—

CALONICE

Give up what? Tell us.

LYSISTRATA

You'll do it, then?

CALONICE

We'll do it, even if it means our death!

LYSISTRATA

All right. We're going to have to give up—the prick. Why are you turning away from me? Where are you going? Why are you all pursing your lips and shaking your heads? What means your altered color and tearful droppings? Will you do it or not? What are you waiting for?

CALONICE

Count me out; let the war drag on.

[16] The tallest peak in Laconia.

ΜΥΡΡΙΝΗ

μὰ Δί' οὐδ' ἔγὼ γάρ, ἀλλ' ὁ πόλεμος ἑρπέτω.

ΛΥΣΙΣΤΡΑΤΗ

ταυτὶ σὺ λέγεις, ὦ ψῆττα; καὶ μὴν ἄρτι γε
ἔφησθα σαυτῆς κἂν παρατεμεῖν θἤμισυ.

ΚΑΛΟΝΙΚΗ

ἄλλ', ἄλλ' ὅ τι βούλει. κἄν με χρῇ, διὰ τοῦ πυρὸς
ἐθέλω βαδίζειν. τοῦτο μᾶλλον τοῦ πέους·
οὐδὲν γὰρ οἷον, ὦ φίλη Λυσιστράτη,

ΛΥΣΙΣΤΡΑΤΗ

τί δαὶ σύ;

ΓΥΝΗ Α´

κἀγὼ βούλομαι διὰ τοῦ πυρός.

ΛΥΣΙΣΤΡΑΤΗ

ὦ παγκατάπυγον θἠμέτερον ἅπαν γένος.
οὐκ ἐτὸς ἀφ' ἡμῶν εἰσιν αἱ τραγῳδίαι·
οὐδὲν γάρ ἐσμεν πλὴν Ποσειδῶν καὶ σκάφη.
ἀλλ', ὦ φίλη Λάκαινα,—σὺ γὰρ ἐὰν γένῃ
μόνη μετ' ἐμοῦ, τὸ πρᾶγμ' ἀνασωσαίμεσθ' ἔτ'
<ἄν>—
ξυμψήφισαί μοι.

ΛΑΜΠΙΤΩ

χαλεπὰ μὲν ναὶ τὼ σιὼ
γυναῖκας ὑπνῶν ἐστ' ἄνευ ψωλᾶς μόνας.
ὅμως γα μάν· δεῖ τᾶς γὰρ εἰράνας μάλ' αὖ.

MYRRHINE

Me too, by Zeus; let the war drag on.

LYSISTRATA

This from you, Ms. Flounder? Weren't you saying just a moment ago that you'd cut yourself in half?

CALONICE

Anything else you want, anything at all! I'm even ready to walk through fire; rather that than the prick. There's nothing like it, my dear Lysistrata.

LYSISTRATA

And what about you?

ATHENIAN WIFE

I'm ready to walk through fire too.

LYSISTRATA

Oh what a low and horny race are we! No wonder tragedies get written about us: we're nothing but Poseidon and a tub.[17] But my dear Spartan, if you alone would side with me, we might still salvage the plan; give me your vote!

LAMPITO

By the Twin Gods, it's difficult for females to sleep alone without the hard-on. But no matter, I assent; we need peace.

[17] In a myth twice dramatized by Sophocles, Tyro was seduced by the god Poseidon disguised as her lover, and exposed the resulting twin boys in a tub by the river.

ΛΥΣΙΣΤΡΑΤΗ

ὦ φιλτάτη σὺ καὶ μόνη τούτων γυνή.

ΚΑΛΟΝΙΚΗ

εἰ δ' ὡς μάλιστ' ἀπεχοίμεθ' οὗ σὺ δὴ λέγεις,—
ὃ μὴ γένοιτο,—μᾶλλον ἂν διὰ τουτογὶ
γένοιτ' ἂν εἰρήνη;

ΛΥΣΙΣΤΡΑΤΗ

πολύ γε νὴ τὼ θεώ.
εἰ γὰρ καθήμεθ' ἔνδον ἐντετριμμέναι,
κἀν τοῖς χιτωνίοισι τοῖς ἀμοργίνοις
γυμναὶ παρίοιμεν δέλτα παρατετιλμέναι,
στύοιντο δ' ἄνδρες κἀπιθυμοῖεν σπλεκοῦν,
ἡμεῖς δὲ μὴ προσίοιμεν, ἀλλ' ἀπεχοίμεθα,
σπονδὰς ποιήσαιντ' ἂν ταχέως, εὖ οἶδ' ὅτι.

ΛΑΜΠΙΤΩ

ὁ γῶν Μενέλαος τᾶς Ἑλένας τὰ μᾶλά πᾳ
γυμνᾶς παραυιδὼν ἐξέβαλ', οἰῶ, τὸ ξίφος.

ΚΑΛΟΝΙΚΗ

τί δ', ἢν ἀφιῶσ' ἄνδρες ἡμᾶς, ὦ μέλε;

ΛΥΣΙΣΤΡΑΤΗ

τὸ τοῦ Φερεκράτους, κύνα δέρειν δεδαρμένην.

ΚΑΛΟΝΙΚΗ

φλυαρία ταῦτ' ἐστὶ τὰ μεμιμημένα.
ἐὰν λαβόντες δ' εἰς τὸ δωμάτιον βίᾳ
ἕλκωσιν ἡμᾶς;

153 προσϊδο[ιμεν] Π1

LYSISTRATA

You're an absolute dear, and the only real woman here!

CALONICE

Well, what if we did abstain from, uh, what you say, which heaven forbid: would peace be likelier to come on that account?

LYSISTRATA

Absolutely, by the Two Goddesses. If we sat around at home all made up, and walked past them wearing only our diaphanous underwear, with our pubes plucked in a neat triangle, and our husbands got hard and hankered to ball us, but we didn't go near them and kept away, they'd sue for peace, and pretty quick, you can count on that!

LAMPITO

Like Menelaus! As soon as he peeked at bare Helen's melons, he threw his sword away, I reckon.[18]

CALONICE

But what if our husbands pay us no attention?

LYSISTRATA

As Pherecrates said, skin the skinned dog.[19]

CALONICE

Facsimiles are nothing but poppycock. And what if they grab us and drag us into the bedroom by force?

[18] Menelaus, King of Sparta, bent on killing his unfaithful wife Helen after the fall of Troy, dropped his sword at the sight of her; Euripides had apparently added the detail about her breasts in *Andromache* 627–31.

[19] I.e., "use a dildo." The comic poet Pherecrates was an older contemporary of Aristophanes; ancient scholars could not locate this quotation.

ΛΥΣΙΣΤΡΑΤΗ

ἀντέχου σὺ τῶν θυρῶν.

ΚΑΛΟΝΙΚΗ

ἐὰν δὲ τύπτωσιν;

ΛΥΣΙΣΤΡΑΤΗ

παρέχειν χρὴ κακὰ κακῶς·
οὐ γὰρ ἔνι τούτοις ἡδονὴ τοῖς πρὸς βίαν.
κἄλλως ὀδυνᾶν χρή· κἀμέλει ταχέως πάνυ
ἀπεροῦσιν. οὐ γὰρ οὐδέποτ᾽ εὐφρανθήσεται
ἀνήρ, ἐὰν μὴ τῇ γυναικὶ ξυμφέρῃ.

ΚΑΛΟΝΙΚΗ

εἴ τοι δοκεῖ σφῷν ταῦτα, χἠμῖν ξυνδοκεῖ.

ΛΑΜΠΙΤΩ

καὶ τὼς μὲν ἁμῶν ἄνδρας ἁμὲς πείσομες
παντᾷ δικαίως ἄδολον εἰράναν ἄγην·
τὸν τῶν Ἀσαναίων γα μὰν ῥυάχετον
πᾷ κά τις ἀμπείσειεν αὖ μὴ πλαδδιῆν;

ΛΥΣΙΣΤΡΑΤΗ

ἡμεῖς ἀμέλει σοι τά γε παρ᾽ ἡμῖν πείσομεν.

ΛΑΜΠΙΤΩ

οὔχ, ᾇς πόδας κ᾽ ἔχωντι ταὶ τριήρεες
καὶ τὠργύριον τὤβυσσον ᾖ πὰρ τᾷ σιῷ.

ΛΥΣΙΣΤΡΑΤΗ

ἀλλ᾽ ἔστι καὶ τοῦτ᾽ εὖ παρεσκευασμένον·
καταληψόμεθα γὰρ τὴν ἀκρόπολιν τήμερον.
ταῖς πρεσβυτάταις γὰρ προστέτακται τοῦτο δρᾶν,

LYSISTRATA

Hold onto the door.

CALONICE

And what if they beat us?

LYSISTRATA

Then submit, but disagreeably: men get no pleasure in sex when they have to force you. And make them suffer in other ways as well. Don't worry, they'll soon give in. No husband can have a happy life if his wife doesn't want him to.

CALONICE

Well, if the two of you agree to this, then we agree too.

LAMPITO

And we will convince *our* menfolk to keep a completely fair and honest peace. But how can anyone keep your Athenian rabble from acting like lunatics?

LYSISTRATA

Don't worry, we'll handle the persuasion on our side.

LAMPITO

Not so, as long as your battleships are under canvas and your Goddess' temple[20] has a bottomless fund of money.

LYSISTRATA

No, that's also been well provided for: we're going to occupy the Acropolis this very day. The older women are assigned that part: while we're working out our agreement

[20] The treasury of Athena on the Acropolis.

ἕως ἂν ἡμεῖς ταῦτα συντιθώμεθα,
θύειν δοκούσαις καταλαβεῖν τὴν ἀκρόπολιν.

ΛΑΜΠΙΤΩ

παντᾷ κ' ἔχοι· καὶ τᾷδε γὰρ λέγεις καλῶς.

ΛΥΣΙΣΤΡΑΤΗ

τί δῆτα ταῦτ' οὐχ ὡς τάχιστα, Λαμπιτοῖ,
ξυνωμόσαμεν, ὅπως ἂν ἀρρήκτως ἔχῃ;

ΛΑΜΠΙΤΩ

πάρφαινε μὰν τὸν ὅρκον, ὡς ὀμιώμεθα.

ΛΥΣΙΣΤΡΑΤΗ

καλῶς λέγεις. ποῦ 'σθ' ἡ Σκύθαινα; ποῖ βλέπεις;
θὲς εἰς τὸ πρόσθεν ὑπτίαν τὴν ἀσπίδα,
καί μοι δότω τὰ τόμιά τις.

ΚΑΛΟΝΙΚΗ

Λυσιστράτη,
τίν' ὅρκον ὁρκώσεις ποθ' ἡμᾶς;

ΛΥΣΙΣΤΡΑΤΗ

ὅντινα;
εἰς ἀσπίδ', ὥσπερ, φασίν, Αἰσχύλος ποτέ,
μηλοσφαγούσας.

ΚΑΛΟΝΙΚΗ

μὴ σύ γ', ὦ Λυσιστράτη,
εἰς ἀσπίδ' ὀμόσῃς μηδὲν εἰρήνης πέρι.

down here, they'll occupy the Acropolis, pretending to be up there for a sacrifice.

LAMPITO

Sounds perfect, like the rest of your proposals.

LYSISTRATA

Then why not ratify them immediately, Lampito, by taking an oath, so that the terms will be unbreakable?

LAMPITO

Unveil the oath, then, and we'll all swear to it.

LYSISTRATA

Well said. Where's the Scythian girl?

A Scythian Girl comes out of the scene building with a shield.

What are you gawking at? Put that shield down in front of us—no, the other way—and someone give me the severings.

CALONICE

Lysistrata, what kind of oath are you planning to make us swear?

LYSISTRATA

What kind? The kind they say Aeschylus once had people swear, slaughtering an animal over a shield.[21]

CALONICE

Lysistrata, please don't take any oath about peace over a shield!

[21] In *Seven Against Thebes* 42–48, where the Seven vow to take Thebes or die in the attempt.

ΛΥΣΙΣΤΡΑΤΗ

τίς ἂν οὖν γένοιτ᾽ ἂν ὅρκος;

ΚΑΛΟΝΙΚΗ

εἰ λευκόν ποθεν

ἵππον λαβοῦσαι τόμιον ἐντεμοίμεθα;

ΛΥΣΙΣΤΡΑΤΗ

ποῖ λευκὸν ἵππον;

ΚΑΛΟΝΙΚΗ

ἀλλὰ πῶς ὀμούμεθα

ἡμεῖς;

ΛΥΣΙΣΤΡΑΤΗ

ἐγώ σοι νὴ Δί᾽, ἢν βούλῃ, φράσω.
θεῖσαι μέλαιναν κύλικα μεγάλην ὑπτίαν,
μηλοσφαγοῦσαι Θάσιον οἴνου σταμνίον
ὀμόσωμεν εἰς τὴν κύλικα μὴ ᾽πιχεῖν ὕδωρ.

ΛΑΜΠΙΤΩ

φεῦ δᾶ, τὸν ὅρκον ἄφατον ὡς ἐπαινίω.

ΛΥΣΙΣΤΡΑΤΗ

φερέτω κύλικά τις ἔνδοθεν καὶ σταμνίον.

ΜΥΡΡΙΝΗ

ὦ φίλταται γυναῖκες, ‹ὁ› κεραμὼν ὅσος.

ΚΑΛΟΝΙΚΗ

ταύτην μὲν ἄν τις εὐθὺς ἥσθείη λαβών.

LYSISTRATA

Then what kind of oath will it be?

CALONICE

What if we got a white stallion[22] somewhere and cut a piece off him?

LYSISTRATA

White stallion? Get serious.

CALONICE

Well, how *are* we going to swear?

LYSISTRATA

If you'd like to know, I can certainly tell you. We put a big black wine cup hollow up, right here; we slaughter a magnum of Thasian wine into it; and we swear not to pour any water into the cup!

LAMPITO

Oh da, I can't find words to praise that oath!

LYSISTRATA

Somebody go inside and fetch a cup and a magnum.

The Scythian Girl takes the shield inside and returns with a huge wine bottle and cup.

MYRRHINE

Dearest ladies, what a jumbo jug!

CALONICE

Just touching this could make a person merry!

[22] A costly and exotic sacrifice, perhaps recalling the oath taken by Helen's suitors, cf. Pausanias 3.20.9.

ΛΥΣΙΣΤΡΑΤΗ

καταθεῖσα ταύτην προσλαβοῦ μοι τοῦ κάπρου.
δέσποινα Πειθοῖ καὶ κύλιξ φιλοτησία,
τὰ σφάγια δέξαι ταῖς γυναιξὶν εὐμενής.

ΚΑΛΟΝΙΚΗ

εὔχρων γε θαῖμα κἀποπυτίζει καλῶς.

ΛΑΜΠΙΤΩ

καὶ μὰν ποτόδδει γ' ἁδὺ ναὶ τὸν Κάστορα.

ΜΥΡΡΙΝΗ

ἐᾶτε πρώτην μ', ὦ γυναῖκες, ὀμνύναι.

ΚΑΛΟΝΙΚΗ

μὰ τὴν Ἀφροδίτην οὔκ, ἐάν γε μὴ λάχῃς.

ΛΥΣΙΣΤΡΑΤΗ

λάζυσθε πᾶσαι τῆς κύλικος, ὦ Λαμπιτοῖ·
λεγέτω δ' ὑπὲρ ὑμῶν μί' ἅπερ ἂν κἀγὼ λέγω·
ὑμεῖς δ' ἐπομεῖσθε ταῦτα κἀμπεδώσετε.
οὐκ ἔστιν οὐδεὶς οὔτε μοιχὸς οὔτ' ἀνήρ—

ΚΑΛΟΝΙΚΗ

οὐκ ἔστιν οὐδεὶς οὔτε μοιχὸς οὔτ' ἀνήρ—

ΛΥΣΙΣΤΡΑΤΗ

ὅστις πρὸς ἐμὲ πρόσεισιν ἐστυκώς. λέγε.

ΚΑΛΟΝΙΚΗ

ὅστις πρὸς ἐμὲ πρόσεισιν ἐστυκώς. παπαῖ,
ὑπολύεταί μου τὰ γόνατ', ὦ Λυσιστράτη.

LYSISTRATA

Hands off! Now all join me in laying hands upon this boar. Mistress Persuasion and Cup of Fellowship, graciously receive this sacrifice from the women. *(She opens the bottle and pours wine into the cup)*

CALONICE

The blood's a good color and spurts out nicely.

LAMPITO

It smells good too, by Castor!

MYRRHINE

Ladies, let me be the first to take the oath!

CALONICE

Hold on, by Aphrodite! Not unless you draw the first lot!

LYSISTRATA

All of you lay your hands upon the cup; you too Lampito. Now one of you, on behalf of you all, must repeat after me the terms of the oath, and the rest of you will then swear to abide by them. No man of any kind, lover or husband—

CALONICE

No man of any kind, lover or husband—

LYSISTRATA

shall approach me with a hard-on. Speak up!

CALONICE

Shall approach me with a hard-on. Oh god, my knees are buckling, Lysistrata!

ΛΥΣΙΣΤΡΑΤΗ

οἴκοι δ' ἀταυρώτη διάξω τὸν βίον—

ΚΑΛΟΝΙΚΗ

οἴκοι δ' ἀταυρώτη διάξω τὸν βίον—

ΛΥΣΙΣΤΡΑΤΗ

κροκωτοφοροῦσα καὶ κεκαλλωπισμένη—

ΚΑΛΟΝΙΚΗ

κροκωτοφοροῦσα καὶ κεκαλλωπισμένη—

ΛΥΣΙΣΤΡΑΤΗ

ὅπως ἂν ἁνὴρ ἐπιτυφῇ μάλιστά μου·

ΚΑΛΟΝΙΚΗ

ὅπως ἂν ἁνὴρ ἐπιτυφῇ μάλιστά μου·

ΛΥΣΙΣΤΡΑΤΗ

κοὐδέποθ' ἑκοῦσα τἀνδρὶ τὠμῷ πείσομαι.

ΚΑΛΟΝΙΚΗ

κοὐδέποθ' ἑκοῦσα τἀνδρὶ τὠμῷ πείσομαι.

ΛΥΣΙΣΤΡΑΤΗ

ἐὰν δέ μ' ἄκουσαν βιάζηται βίᾳ—

ΚΑΛΟΝΙΚΗ

ἐὰν δέ μ' ἄκουσαν βιάζηται βίᾳ—

ΛΥΣΙΣΤΡΑΤΗ

κακῶς παρέξω κοὐχὶ προσκινήσομαι.

ΚΑΛΟΝΙΚΗ

κακῶς παρέξω κοὐχὶ προσκινήσομαι.

LYSISTRATA
At home in celibacy shall I pass my life—

CALONICE
At home in celibacy shall I pass my life—

LYSISTRATA
wearing a saffron dress and all dolled up—

CALONICE
wearing a saffron dress and all dolled up—

LYSISTRATA
so that my husband will get as hot as a volcano for me—

CALONICE
so that my husband will get as hot as a volcano for me—

LYSISTRATA
but never willingly shall I surrender to my husband.

CALONICE
but never willingly shall I surrender to my husband.

LYSISTRATA
If he should use force to force me against my will—

CALONICE
If he should use force to force me against my will—

LYSISTRATA
I will submit coldly and not move my hips.

CALONICE
I will submit coldly and not move my hips.

ΛΥΣΙΣΤΡΑΤΗ

οὐ πρὸς τὸν ὄροφον ἀνατενῶ τὼ Περσικά.

ΚΑΛΟΝΙΚΗ

οὐ πρὸς τὸν ὄροφον ἀνατενῶ τὼ Περσικά.

ΛΥΣΙΣΤΡΑΤΗ

οὐ στήσομαι λέαιν᾿ ἐπὶ τυροκνήστιδος.

ΚΑΛΟΝΙΚΗ

οὐ στήσομαι λέαιν᾿ ἐπὶ τυροκνήστιδος.

ΛΥΣΙΣΤΡΑΤΗ

ταῦτ᾿ ἐμπεδοῦσα μὲν πίοιμ᾿ ἐντευθενί—

ΚΑΛΟΝΙΚΗ

ταῦτ᾿ ἐμπεδοῦσα μὲν πίοιμ᾿ ἐντευθενί—

ΛΥΣΙΣΤΡΑΤΗ

εἰ δὲ παραβαίην, ὕδατος ἐμπλῇθ᾿ ἡ κύλιξ.

ΚΑΛΟΝΙΚΗ

εἰ δὲ παραβαίην, ὕδατος ἐμπλῇθ᾿ ἡ κύλιξ.

ΛΥΣΙΣΤΡΑΤΗ

συνεπόμνυθ᾿ ὑμεῖς ταῦτα πᾶσαι;

ΠΑΣΑΙ

νὴ Δία.

ΛΥΣΙΣΤΡΑΤΗ

φέρ᾿ ἐγὼ καθαγίσω τήνδε.

ΚΑΛΟΝΙΚΗ

τὸ μέρος γ᾿, ὦ φίλη,

ὅπως ἂν ὦμεν εὐθὺς ἀλλήλων φίλαι.

LYSISTRATA
I will not raise my Persian slippers toward the ceiling.

CALONICE
I will not raise my Persian slippers toward the ceiling.

LYSISTRATA
I won't crouch down like the lioness on a cheesegrater.

CALONICE
I won't crouch down like the lioness on a cheesegrater.

LYSISTRATA
If I live up to these vows, may I drink from this cup.

CALONICE
If I live up to these vows, may I drink from this cup.

LYSISTRATA
But if I break them, may the cup be full of water.

CALONICE
But if I break them, may the cup be full of water.

LYSISTRATA
So swear you one and all?

ALL
So swear we all!

LYSISTRATA
All right, then, I'll consecrate the cup. *(She takes a long drink)*

CALONICE
Only your share, my friend; lets make sure we're all on friendly terms from the very start.

After they drink, a joyful cry of women is heard offstage.

ΛΑΜΠΙΤΩ

τίς ὠλολυγά;

ΛΥΣΙΣΤΡΑΤΗ

τοῦτ᾽ ἐκεῖν᾽ οὑγὼ ᾽λεγον·
αἱ γὰρ γυναῖκες τὴν ἀκρόπολιν τῆς θεοῦ
ἤδη καθειλήφασιν. ἀλλ᾽, ὦ Λαμπιτοῖ,
σὺ μὲν βάδιζε καὶ τὰ παρ᾽ ὑμῖν εὖ τίθει,
τασδὶ δ᾽ ὁμήρους κατάλιφ᾽ ἡμῖν ἐνθάδε.
ἡμεῖς δὲ ταῖς ἄλλαισι ταῖσιν ἐν πόλει
ξυνεμβάλωμεν εἰσιοῦσαι τοὺς μοχλούς.

ΚΑΛΟΝΙΚΗ

οὔκουν ἐφ᾽ ἡμᾶς ξυμβοηθήσειν οἴει
τοὺς ἄνδρας εὐθύς;

ΛΥΣΙΣΤΡΑΤΗ

ὀλίγον αὐτῶν μοι μέλει.
οὐ γὰρ τοσαύτας οὔτ᾽ ἀπειλὰς οὔτε πῦρ
ἥξουσ᾽ ἔχοντες ὥστ᾽ ἀνοῖξαι τὰς πύλας
ταύτας, ἐὰν μὴ ᾽φ᾽ οἷσιν ἡμεῖς εἴπομεν.

ΚΑΛΟΝΙΚΗ

μὰ τὴν Ἀφροδίτην οὐδέποτέ γ᾽· ἄλλως γὰρ ἂν
ἄμαχοι γυναῖκες καὶ μιαραὶ κεκλῄμεθ᾽ ἄν.

LAMPITO

What's that hurrah?

LYSISTRATA

It's just as I was telling you before: the women have occupied the Acropolis and the Goddess' temple. Now, Lampito: you be off and see to your end of the bargain, but leave these women here with us as hostages.

Exit LAMPITO.

Meanwhile, let's go inside with the other women on the Acropolis and help bar the gates.

CALONICE

But don't you think the men will quickly launch a concerted counterattack on us?

LYSISTRATA

I'm not worried about them. They can't come against us with enough threats or fire to get these gates open, except on the terms we've agreed on.

CALONICE

No they can't, so help me Aphrodite! Otherwise we women wouldn't deserve to be called rascals you can't win a fight with!

All exit into the central door of the scene building, which henceforth represents the Acropolis gates.

Enter MEN'S CHORUS, *elderly and poorly dressed; each dancer carries a pair of logs, an unlit torch, and a bucket of live coals.*

ΚΟΡΥΦΑΙΟΣ

χώρει, Δράκης, ἡγοῦ βάδην, εἰ καὶ τὸν ὦμον ἀλγεῖς
κορμοῦ τοσουτονὶ βάρος χλωρᾶς φέρων ἐλαίας.

ΧΟΡΟΣ ΓΕΡΟΝΤΩΝ

(στρ) ἦ πόλλ᾽ ἄελπτ᾽ ἔνεστιν ἐν τῷ μακρῷ βίῳ, φεῦ,
ἐπεὶ τίς ἄν ποτ᾽ ἤλπισ᾽, ὦ Στρυμόδωρ᾽, ἀκοῦσαι
γυναῖκας, ἃς ἐβόσκομεν κατ᾽ οἶκον ἐμφανὲς κακόν,
κατὰ μὲν ἅγιον ἔχειν βρέτας,
κατά τ᾽ ἀκρόπολιν ἐμὰν λαβεῖν
κλῄθροισί τ᾽ αὖ καὶ μοχλοῖ-
σι τὰ προπύλαια πακτοῦν;

ΚΟΡΥΦΑΙΟΣ

ἀλλ᾽ ὡς τάχιστα πρὸς πόλιν σπεύσωμεν, ὦ Φιλοῦργε,
ὅπως ἂν αὐταῖς ἐν κύκλῳ θέντες τὰ πρέμνα ταυτί,
ὅσαι τὸ πρᾶγμα τοῦτ᾽ ἐνεστήσαντο καὶ μετῆλθον,
μίαν πυρὰν νήσαντες ἐμπρήσωμεν αὐτόχειρες
πάσας, ἀπὸ ψήφου μιᾶς, πρώτην δὲ τὴν Λύκωνος.

ΧΟΡΟΣ ΓΕΡΟΝΤΩΝ

(ἀντ) οὐ γὰρ μὰ τὴν Δήμητρ᾽ ἐμοῦ ζῶντος ἐγχανοῦνται·
ἐπεὶ οὐδὲ Κλεομένης, ὃς αὐτὴν κατέσχε πρῶτος,

---

23 The names given to members of this semichorus are generic for old men.

24 The ancient olivewood image of Athena Polias.

25 Because Lycon's wife had a reputation for promiscuity (Eupolis 232), the men imagine (wrongly) that she must be the

MEN'S LEADER

Onward, Draces,[23] lead the way, even if your shoulder does ache from toting such a heavy load of green olivewood.

MEN'S CHORUS

If you live long enough you'll get many surprises, yes sir!
Well, Strymodorus, who in the world ever thought we'd hear
that women, the blatant nuisance we've reared in our homes,
now control the Sacred Image[24]
and occupy my Acropolis,
And to top it all, with bolts and bars
close off the citadel gates?

MEN'S LEADER

Let's hurry to the Acropolis, Philurgus, full speed ahead, so we can lay these logs in a circle around all the women who have instigated or abetted this business. Let's erect a single pyre and incinerate them with our own hands, all of them on a single vote, starting with Lycon's wife![25]

MEN'S CHORUS

By Demeter, they'll not laugh at me while I'm alive!
Not even Cleomenes,[26] the first to occupy this place,

ringleader; her husband and their son Autolycus (characters in Xenophon's *Symposium*) were also notorious for high living, cf. *Wasps* 1301, Cratinus 214, Eupolis 61.

[26] A Spartan king (*c.* 520–490) who in 508 had occupied the Acropolis for two days on the invitation of Athenian oligarchs, and was allowed to leave under truce, paving the way for the restoration of the democratic leader Cleisthenes.

ἀπῆλθεν ἀψάλακτος, ἀλλ᾽ ὅμως Λακωνικὸν πνέων
ᾤχετο θὤπλα παραδοὺς ἐμοί,
σμικρὸν ἔχων πάνυ τριβώνιον,
πεινῶν ῥυπῶν ἀπαράτιλ-
τος, ἓξ ἐτῶν ἄλουτος.

ΚΟΡΥΦΑΙΟΣ

οὕτως ἐπολιόρκησ᾽ ἐγὼ τὸν ἄνδρ᾽ ἐκεῖνον ὠμῶς
ἐφ᾽ ἑπτακαίδεκ᾽ ἀσπίδων πρὸς ταῖς πύλαις
καθεύδων.
τασδὶ δὲ τὰς Εὐριπίδῃ θεοῖς τε πᾶσιν ἐχθρὰς
ἐγὼ οὐκ ἄρα σχήσω παρὼν τολμήματος τοσούτου;
μή νυν ἔτ᾽ ἐν <τῇ> τετραπόλει τοὐμὸν τροπαῖον εἴη.

ΧΟΡΟΣ ΓΕΡΟΝΤΩΝ

(στρ) ἀλλ᾽ αὐτὸ γάρ μοι τῆς ὁδοῦ
λοιπόν ἐστι χωρίον
τὸ πρὸς πόλιν τὸ σιμόν, οἷ σπουδὴν ἔχω.
πῶς <δή> ποτ᾽ ἐξαμπρεύσομεν
τοῦτ᾽ ἄνευ κανθηλίου;
ὡς ἐμοῦ γε τὼ ξύλω τὸν ὦμον ἐξιπώκατον.
ἀλλ᾽ ὅμως βαδιστέον,
καὶ τὸ πῦρ φυσητέον,
μή μ᾽ ἀποσβεσθὲν λάθῃ
πρὸς τῇ τελευτῇ τῆς ὁδοῦ.
φῦ φῦ.
ἰοὺ ἰοὺ τοῦ καπνοῦ.

(ἀντ) ὡς δεινόν, ὦναξ Ἡράκλεις,

left here intact. No, for all he breathed the Spartan spirit,
he left without his weapons—surrendering to me!—
with only a little bitty jacket on his back,
starving, filthy, unshaven,
unwashed for six whole years.

MEN'S LEADER

That's the way I laid siege to that fellow—savagely! We camped before the gates in ranks seventeen deep. And now shall I stand by and do nothing to put down the effrontery of these women, enemies of all the gods and of Euripides?[27] Then my trophy in the Tetrapolis may as well disappear![28]

MEN'S CHORUS

My trek is nearly done;
all that remains is the steep stretch
up to the Acropolis, where I can't wait to be!
How in the world are we going to haul
these loads up there without a donkey?
This pair of logs is utterly crushing my shoulder!
But I've got to soldier on,
and keep my fire alight.
It mustn't go out on me before I've reached my goal.
Ouch, ugh! The smoke!

How terribly, Lord Heracles, this smoke

[27] Euripides' reputation as a misogynist, first attested here, underlies the plot of *Women at the Thesmophoria*.

[28] The stone monument at Marathon, one of the four associated towns of the Tetrapolis, that commemorated the great Athenian victory over the Persians in 490.

προσπεσόν μ᾿ ἐκ τῆς χύτρας
ὥσπερ κύων λυττῶσα τὠφθαλμὼ δάκνει.
κἄστιν γε Λήμνιον τὸ πῦρ
τοῦτο πάσῃ μηχανῇ·
οὐ γὰρ <ἄν> ποθ᾿ ὧδ᾿ ὀδὰξ ἔβρυκε τὰς λήμας ἐμοῦ.
σπεῦδε πρόσθεν εἰς πόλιν
καὶ βοήθει τῇ θεῷ.
ἢ πότ᾿ αὐτῇ μᾶλλον ἢ
νῦν, ὦ Λάχης, ἀρήξομεν;
φῦ φῦ.
ἰοὺ ἰοὺ τοῦ καπνοῦ.

ΚΟΡΥΦΑΙΟΣ

τουτὶ τὸ πῦρ ἐγρήγορεν θεῶν ἕκατι καὶ ζῇ.
οὔκουν ἄν, εἰ τὼ μὲν ξύλω θείμεσθα πρῶτον αὐτοῦ,
τῆς ἀμπέλου δ᾿ εἰς τὴν χύτραν τὸν φανὸν ἐγκαθέντες
ἅψαντες εἶτ᾿ εἰς τὴν θύραν κριηδὸν ἐμπέσοιμεν,
κἂν μὴ καλούντων τοὺς μοχλοὺς χαλῶσιν αἱ γυναῖκες,
ἐμπιμπράναι χρὴ τὰς θύρας καὶ τῷ καπνῷ πιέζειν.
θώμεσθα δὴ τὸ φορτίον. φεῦ τοῦ καπνοῦ, βαβαιάξ.
τίς ξυλλάβοιτ᾿ ἂν τοῦ ξύλου τῶν ἐν Σάμῳ στρατηγῶν;
ταυτὶ μὲν ἤδη τὴν ῥάχιν θλίβοντά μου πέπαυται.
σὸν δ᾿ ἔργον ἐστίν, ὦ χύτρα, τὸν ἄνθρακ᾿ ἐξεγείρειν,
τὴν λαμπάδ᾿ ἡμμένην ὅπως πρώτιστ᾿ ἐμοὶ προσοίσει.

jumped from the bucket and attacked me!
It bit both my eyes like a rabid bitch!
And as for this fire, it's Lemnian
in every possible way; [29] otherwise
it wouldn't have bitten into my bloodshot eyes that way!
Hurry forth to the citadel,
run to the Goddess' rescue!
When would be a better time than now to help her, Laches?
Ouch, ugh! The smoke!

MEN'S LEADER

This fire's awake, by the grace of the gods, and plenty lively too. Let's place our logs right here, then dip our torches into the buckets, and when they're lighted we'll charge the gates like rams. If the women don't unbolt the gates when we invite their surrender, we'll set the portals afire and smoke them into submission. Very well, let's put the logs down. Phew, that smoke! Damn! Would any of the generals at Samos care to help us with this wood?[30] (*laying down the logs*) These have finally stopped crushing my back! Now it's your job, bucket, to rouse your coals to flame and thus supply me—step one!—with a lighted torch. Lady

[29] The island, then an Athenian colony, was volcanic; its name puns on *lemai* "bloodshot eyes"; and according to legend, its women had once murdered their husbands.

[30] Since the end of summer 412 Samos had been the headquarters of the Athenians' Aegean fleet.

δέσποινα Νίκη, ξυγγενοῦ τῶν τ᾽ ἐν πόλει γυναικῶν
τοῦ νῦν παρεστῶτος θράσους θέσθαι τροπαῖον
ἡμᾶς.

ΚΟΡΥΦΑΙΑ

λιγνὺν δοκῶ μοι καθορᾶν καὶ καπνόν, ὦ γυναῖκες,
ὥσπερ πυρὸς καομένου· σπευστέον ἐστὶ θᾶττον.

ΧΟΡΟΣ ΓΥΝΑΙΚΩΝ

(στρ) πέτου πέτου, Νικοδίκη,
πρὶν ἐμπεπρῆσθαι Καλύκην
τε καὶ Κρίτυλλαν περιφυσήτω
ὑπό τ᾽ ἀνέμων ἀργαλέων
ὑπό τε γερόντων ὀλέθρων.
ἀλλὰ φοβοῦμαι τόδε· μῶν ὑστερόπους βοηθῶ;
νῦν δὴ γὰρ ἐμπλησαμένη τὴν ὑδρίαν κνεφαία
μόλις ἀπὸ κρήνης ὑπ᾽ ὄχλου καὶ θορύβου
καὶ πατάγου χυτρείου,
δούλαισιν ὠστιζομένη
στιγματίαις θ᾽, ἁρπαλέως
ἀραμένη, ταῖσιν ἐμαῖς
δημότισιν καομέναις
φέρουσ᾽ ὕδωρ βοηθῶ.

(ἀντ) ἤκουσα γὰρ τυφογέρον-
τας ἄνδρας ἔρρειν, στελέχη
φέροντας ὥσπερ βαλανεύσοντας

324 τ᾽ ἀνέμων Oeri: τε νόμων a

Victory,[31] be our ally, help us win a trophy over the women on the Acropolis and their present audacity!

Enter the WOMEN'S CHORUS *on the run; its members are nicely dressed and carry water pitchers on their heads.*

WOMEN'S LEADER

I think I can see sparks and smoke, fellow women, as if a fire were ablaze. We must hurry all the faster!

WOMEN'S CHORUS

Fly, fly, Nicodice,[32]
before Calyce and Critylla go up
in flames, fanned all around
by nasty winds
and old men who mean death!
I'm filled with dread: am I too late to help?
I've just come from the well with my pitcher;
I could hardly fill it in the dim light of dawn,
in the throng and crash and clatter of pots,
fighting the elbows of housemaids
and branded slaves; zealously
I hoisted it onto my head, and to aid the women,
my fellow citizens faced with fire,
here I am with water!

I've heard that some frantic old men
are on the loose, toting logs
up to the Acropolis, about three talents' worth,[33]

[31] I.e., Athena Nike, whose temple stands on the right as one faces the Propylaea, the main entrance to the Acropolis.
[32] The women's names, like the men's, are apparently generic.
[33] Around 175 pounds, a comic exaggeration.

εἰς πόλιν ὡς τριτάλαντα βάρος,
δεινότατ᾽ ἀπειλοῦντας ἐπῶν
ὡς πυρὶ χρὴ τὰς μυσαρὰς γυναῖκας ἀνθρακεύειν.
ἅς, ὦ θεά, μή ποτ᾽ ἐγὼ πιμπραμένας ἴδοιμι,
ἀλλὰ πολέμου καὶ μανιῶν ῥυσαμένας
Ἑλλάδα καὶ πολίτας·
ἐφ᾽ οἷσπερ, ὦ χρυσολόφα
  πολιοῦχε, σὰς ἔσχον ἕδρας.
καί σε καλῶ ξύμμαχον, ὦ
  Τριτογένει᾽, ἤν τις ἐκεί-
  νας ὑποπιμπρῇσιν ἀνήρ,
φέρειν ὕδωρ μεθ᾽ ἡμῶν.

ΚΟΡΥΦΑΙΑ

ἔασον, ὤ, τουτὶ τί ἦν; ἄνδρες πονωπονηροί·
οὐ γάρ ποτ᾽ ἂν χρηστοί γ᾽ ἔδρων οὐδ᾽ εὐσεβεῖς τάδ᾽
  ἄνδρες.

ΚΟΡΥΦΑΙΟΣ

τουτὶ τὸ πρᾶγμ᾽ ἡμῖν ἰδεῖν ἀπροσδόκητον ἥκει·
ἑσμὸς γυναικῶν οὑτοσὶ θύρασιν αὖ βοηθεῖ.

ΚΟΡΥΦΑΙΑ

τί βδύλλεθ᾽ ἡμᾶς; οὔ τί που πολλαὶ δοκοῦμεν εἶναι;
καὶ μὴν μέρος γ᾽ ἡμῶν ὁρᾶτ᾽ οὔπω τὸ μυριοστόν.

ΚΟΡΥΦΑΙΟΣ

ὦ Φαιδρία, ταύτας λαλεῖν ἐάσομεν τοσαυτί;
οὐ περικατᾶξαι τὸ ξύλον τύπτοντ᾽ ἐχρῆν τιν᾽ αὐταῖς;

---

[34] An ancient epithet of Athena thought to recall her birth near a mythical river or lake.

like stokers at the public bathhouse,
screaming the direst threats, that
"we've got to burn these horrible women to
charcoal."
Goddess, may I never see these women aflame,
but rather see them rescue from war and madness
Greece and their fellow countrymen!
For to that end, Golden Crested
Guardian of the Citadel, have they seized your
shrine.
And I invite you to be our ally,
Tritogeneia,[34] and if any
man among them sets it afire,
to be there with water!

WOMEN'S LEADER

Hold on! Hey! What's this? Men! Awful, nasty men! No gentlemen, no god-fearing men would ever be caught doing this!

MEN'S LEADER

This here's a complication we didn't count on facing: this swarm of women outside the gates is here to help the others!

WOMEN'S LEADER

Fear and trembling, eh? Don't tell me we seem a lot to handle, because you haven't even seen the tiniest fraction of our forces yet!

MEN'S LEADER

Phaedrias, are we going to let these women jabber on? Why hasn't somebody busted a log over their heads?

ΚΟΡΥΦΑΙΑ

θώμεσθα δὴ τὰς κάλπιδας χἠμεῖς χαμᾶζ', ὅπως ἄν,
ἢν προσφέρῃ τὴν χεῖρά τις, μὴ τοῦτό μ' ἐμποδίζῃ.

ΚΟΡΥΦΑΙΟΣ

εἰ νὴ Δί' ἤδη τὰς γνάθους τούτων τις ἢ δὶς ἢ τρὶς
ἔκοψεν ὥσπερ Βουπάλου, φωνὴν ἂν οὐκ ἂν εἶχον.

ΚΟΡΥΦΑΙΑ

καὶ μὴν ἰδού· παταξάτω τις· στᾶσ' ἐγὼ παρέξω,
κοὐ μή ποτ' ἄλλη σου κύων τῶν ὄρχεων λάβηται.

ΚΟΡΥΦΑΙΟΣ

εἰ μὴ σιωπήσει, θενών σου 'κκοκκιῶ τὸ γῆρας.

ΚΟΡΥΦΑΙΑ

ἅψαι μόνον Στρατυλλίδος τῷ δακτύλῳ προσελθών—

ΚΟΡΥΦΑΙΟΣ

τί δ', ἢν σποδῶ τοῖς κονδύλοις; τί μ' ἐργάσει τὸ δεινόν;

ΚΟΡΥΦΑΙΑ

βρύκουσά σου τοὺς πλεύμονας καὶ τἄντερ' ἐξαμήσω.

ΚΟΡΥΦΑΙΟΣ

οὐκ ἔστ' ἀνὴρ Εὐριπίδου σοφώτερος ποιητής·
οὐδὲν γὰρ ὧδε θρέμμ' ἀναιδές ἐστιν ὡς γυναῖκες.

ΚΟΡΥΦΑΙΑ

αἰρώμεθ' ἡμεῖς θοὔδατος τὴν κάλπιν, ὦ Ῥοδίππη.

WOMEN'S LEADER

We too should ground our pitchers, so they won't be in our way if anyone lays a hand on us.

MEN'S LEADER

By god, if someone had socked them in the mouth a couple of times, like Bupalus,[35] they wouldn't be making any noise!

WOMEN'S LEADER

OK, here's my mouth; someone take a sock at it; I'll stand here and take it. But then I'm the last bitch that ever grabs you by the balls!

MEN'S LEADER

If you don't shut up, I'll knock you right out of your old hide!

WOMEN'S LEADER

Come over here and just touch Stratyllis with the tip of your finger.

MEN'S LEADER

What if I give you the one-two punch? Got anything scary to counter with?

WOMEN'S LEADER

I'll rip out your lungs and your guts with my fangs.

MEN'S LEADER

No poet's wiser than Euripides: as he says, no beast exists so shameless as womankind!

WOMEN'S LEADER

Let's pick up our water pitchers, Rhodippe.

[35] A Chian sculptor vilified by the sixth-century iambic poet Hipponax (fr. 120).

ΚΟΡΥΦΑΙΟΣ

τί δ', ὦ θεοῖς ἐχθρά, σὺ δεῦρ' ὕδωρ ἔχουσ' ἀφίκου;

ΚΟΡΥΦΑΙΑ

τί δ' αὖ σὺ πῦρ, ὦ τύμβ', ἔχων; ὡς σαυτὸν ἐμπυρεύσων;

ΚΟΡΥΦΑΙΟΣ

ἐγὼ μὲν ἵνα νήσας πυρὰν τὰς σὰς φίλας ὑφάψω.

ΚΟΡΥΦΑΙΑ

ἐγὼ δέ γ', ἵνα τὴν σὴν πυρὰν τούτῳ κατασβέσαιμι.

ΚΟΡΥΦΑΙΟΣ

τοὐμὸν σὺ πῦρ κατασβέσεις;

ΚΟΡΥΦΑΙΑ

τοὔργον τάχ' αὐτὸ δείξει.

ΚΟΡΥΦΑΙΟΣ

οὐκ οἶδά σ' εἰ τῇδ' ὡς ἔχω τῇ λαμπάδι σταθεύσω.

ΚΟΡΥΦΑΙΑ

εἰ ῥύμμα τυγχάνεις ἔχων, λουτρόν <γέ σοι> παρέξω.

ΚΟΡΥΦΑΙΟΣ

ἐμοὶ σὺ λουτρόν, ὦ σαπρά;

ΚΟΡΥΦΑΙΑ

καὶ ταῦτα νυμφικόν γε.

ΚΟΡΥΦΑΙΟΣ

ἤκουσας αὐτῆς τοῦ θράσους;

MEN'S LEADER

Why are you here with water, you witch?

WOMEN'S LEADER

And why are you here with fire, you tomb? To burn yourself up?

MEN'S LEADER

Me, I'm here to build a pyre and burn up your friends.

WOMEN'S LEADER

And I've come to put it out with this.

MEN'S LEADER

You put out my fire?

WOMEN'S LEADER

That's what you soon will see.

MEN'S LEADER

I think I might barbecue you on the spot with this torch of mine.

WOMEN'S LEADER

Got any soap with you? I'll give you a bath.

MEN'S LEADER

You give me a bath, you rotten crone?

WOMEN'S LEADER

A bath fit for a bridegroom!

MEN'S LEADER

Listen to her insolence!

---

377 suppl. Reisig

ΚΟΡΥΦΑΙΑ

ἐλευθέρα γάρ εἰμι.

ΚΟΡΥΦΑΙΟΣ

σχήσω σ᾽ ἐγὼ τῆς νῦν βοῆς.

ΚΟΡΥΦΑΙΑ

ἀλλ᾽ οὐκέτ᾽ ἠλιάζει.

ΚΟΡΥΦΑΙΟΣ

ἔμπρησον αὐτῆς τὰς κόμας.

ΚΟΡΥΦΑΙΑ

σὸν ἔργον, ὦχελῷε.

ΚΟΡΥΦΑΙΟΣ

οἴμοι τάλας.

ΚΟΡΥΦΑΙΑ

μῶν θερμὸν ἦν;

ΚΟΡΥΦΑΙΟΣ

ποῖ θερμόν; οὐ παύσει; τί δρᾷς;

ΚΟΡΥΦΑΙΑ

ἄρδω σ᾽, ὅπως ἀναβλαστανεῖς.

ΚΟΡΥΦΑΙΟΣ

ἀλλ᾽ αὖός εἰμ᾽ ἤδη τρέμων.

ΚΟΡΥΦΑΙΑ

οὐκοῦν, ἐπειδὴ πῦρ ἔχεις, σὺ χλιανεῖς σεαυτόν.

---

36 Jury service, for which a small stipend was paid by the polis, was popular with impecunious old men.

WOMEN'S LEADER

I'll have you know I'm a free woman!

MEN'S LEADER

I'll put a stop to your bellowing.

WOMEN'S LEADER

You're not on a jury now, you know.[36]

MEN'S LEADER

Torch her hair!

WOMEN'S LEADER

(*dousing them*) Achelous, you're on![37]

MEN'S LEADER

Wooh! Damn!

WOMEN'S LEADER

I hope it wasn't too hot?

MEN'S LEADER

Hot? Stop it! What do you think you're doing?

WOMEN'S LEADER

I'm watering you, so you'll bloom again.

MEN'S LEADER

But I'm already dried out from shivering!

WOMEN'S LEADER

You've got fire there; why not sit by it and get warm?

Enter MAGISTRATE, *with two Slaves carrying crowbars, and four Scythian Policemen.*

[37] Achelous, a river in NW Greece, was metonymic for "water," especially in ritual contexts.

ΠΡΟΒΟΥΛΟΣ

ἆρ᾽ ἐξέλαμψε τῶν γυναικῶν ἡ τρυφὴ
χὠ τυμπανισμὸς χοἰ πυκνοὶ Σαβάζιοι,
ὅ τ᾽ Ἀδωνιασμὸς οὗτος οὑπὶ τῶν τεγῶν,
οὗ ᾽γώ ποτ᾽ ὢν ἤκουον ἐν τἠκκλησίᾳ;
ἔλεγεν ὁ μὴ ὥρασι μὲν Δημόστρατος
πλεῖν εἰς Σικελίαν, ἡ γυνὴ δ᾽ ὀρχουμένη
"αἰαῖ Ἄδωνιν" φησίν. ὁ δὲ Δημόστρατος
ἔλεγεν ὁπλίτας καταλέγειν Ζακυνθίων,
ἡ δ᾽ ὑποπεπωκυῖ᾽ ἡ γυνὴ ᾽πὶ τοῦ τέγους
"κόπτεσθ᾽ Ἄδωνιν" φησίν. ὁ δ᾽ ἐβιάζετο,
ὁ θεοῖσιν ἐχθρὸς καὶ μιαρὸς Χολοζύγης.
τοιαῦτ᾽ ἀπ᾽ αὐτῶν ἐστιν ἀκολαστάσματα.

ΚΟΡΥΦΑΙΟΣ

τί δῆτ᾽ ἄν, εἰ πύθοιο καὶ τὴν τῶνδ᾽ ὕβριν;
αἳ τἄλλα θ᾽ ὑβρίκασι κἀκ τῶν καλπίδων
ἔλουσαν ἡμᾶς, ὥστε θαἰματίδια
σείειν πάρεστιν ὥσπερ ἐνεουρηκότας.

ΠΡΟΒΟΥΛΟΣ

νὴ τὸν Ποσειδῶ τὸν ἁλυκὸν δίκαιά γε.
ὅταν γὰρ αὐτοὶ ξυμπονηρευώμεθα
ταῖσιν γυναιξὶ καὶ διδάσκωμεν τρυφᾶν,
τοιαῦτ᾽ ἀπ᾽ αὐτῶν βλαστάνει βουλεύματα.
οἳ λέγομεν ἐν τῶν δημιουργῶν τοιαδί·

---

[38] A Phrygian god similar to Dionysus, whose worship had recently become popular at Athens, especially among women and slaves.

MAGISTRATE

So the women's profligacy has flared up again, has it, the tomtoms, the steady chants of "Sabazios,"[38] this worship of Adonis on the rooftops?[39] I heard it all once before while sitting in Assembly. Demostratus[40] (bad luck to him!) was moving that we send an armada to Sicily,[41] while his wife was dancing and yelling "Poor young Adonis!" Then Demostratus moved that we sign up some Zakynthian infantry, but his wife up on the roof was getting drunk and crying "Beat your breast for Adonis!" But he just went on making his motions, that godforsaken, disgusting Baron Bluster! From women, I say, you get this kind of riotous extravagance!

MEN'S LEADER

(*indicating the Women's Chorus*) Save your breath till you hear about *their* atrocities! They've committed every outrage, even doused us with those pitchers. So now we get to shake water out of our clothes as if we'd peed in them!

MAGISTRATE

By Poseidon the Salty, it serves us right! When we ourselves abet our wives' misbehavior and teach them profligacy, these are the sort of schemes they bring to flower! Aren't we the ones who go to the shops and say this kind of

39 Adonis (in myth, the mortal youth whom Aphrodite loved) was a Semitic import not recognized by the city. His cult was celebrated in mid-summer on rooftops by women, who planted quickly withering gardens and lamented the death of the young god. 40 A democratic politician evidently still prominent.

41 For the assemblies leading up to the departure of the armada for Sicily in summer 415, see Thucydides 6.1–32, with Plutarch *Nicias* 12–13 and *Alcibiades* 18.

"ὦ χρυσοχόε, τὸν ὅρμον ὃν ἐπεσκεύασας,
ὀρχουμένης μου τῆς γυναικὸς ἑσπέρας
ἡ βάλανος ἐκπέπτωκεν ἐκ τοῦ τρήματος.
ἐμοὶ μὲν οὖν ἔστ' εἰς Σαλαμῖνα πλευστέα·
σὺ δ' ἢν σχολάσῃς, πάσῃ τέχνῃ πρὸς ἑσπέραν
ἐλθὼν ἐκείνῃ τὴν βάλανον ἐνάρμοσον."
ἕτερος δέ τις πρὸς σκυτοτόμον ταδὶ λέγει
νεανίαν καὶ πέος ἔχοντ' οὐ παιδικόν·
"ὦ σκυτοτόμε, τῆς μου γυναικὸς τοῦ ποδὸς
τὸ δακτυλίδιον πιέζει τὸ ζυγόν,
ἅθ' ἁπαλὸν ὄν· τοῦτ' οὖν σὺ τῆς μεσημβρίας
ἐλθὼν χάλασον, ὅπως ἂν εὐρυτέρως ἔχῃ."
τοιαῦτ' ἀπήντηκ' εἰς τοιαυτὶ πράγματα,
ὅτε γ' ὢν ἐγὼ πρόβουλος, ἐκπορίσας ὅπως
κωπῆς ἔσονται, τἀργυρίου νυνὶ δέον,
ὑπὸ τῶν γυναικῶν ἀποκέκλῃμαι τῶν πυλῶν.
ἀλλ' οὐδὲν ἔργον ἑστάναι. φέρε τοὺς μοχλούς,
ὅπως ἂν αὐτὰς τῆς ὕβρεως ἐγὼ σχέθω.
τί κέχηνας, ὦ δύστηνε; ποῖ δ' αὖ σὺ βλέπεις,
οὐδὲν ποιῶν ἀλλ' ἢ καπηλεῖον σκοπῶν;
οὐχ ὑποβαλόντες τοὺς μοχλοὺς ὑπὸ τὰς πύλας
ἐντεῦθεν ἐκμοχλεύσετ'; ἐνθενδὶ δ' ἐγὼ
ξυνεκμοχλεύσω.

ΛΥΣΙΣΤΡΑΤΗ

μηδὲν ἐκμοχλεύετε·
ἐξέρχομαι γὰρ αὐτομάτη. τί δεῖ μοχλῶν;
οὐ γὰρ μοχλῶν δεῖ μᾶλλον ἢ νοῦ καὶ φρενῶν.

thing: "Goldsmith, about that choker you made me: my wife was having a ball the other night, and now the prong's slipped out of the hole. Me, I've got to cruise over to Salamis,[42] so if you've got time, by all means visit her in the evening and fit a prong in her hole." Another husband says this to a shoemaker, a teenager sporting no boyish cock: "Shoemaker, about my wife's tootsy: the thong is squeezing her pinky winky, where she's tender. So why don't you drop in on her some lunchtime and loosen it up so there's more play down there?" That's the sort of thing that's led to all this, when I, a Magistrate, have lined up timber for oars and now come to get the necessary funds, and find myself standing at the gates, locked out by women! But it's no use just standing here. (*to the two Slaves*) Bring the crowbars; I'll put a stop to their arrogance. What are you gaping at, you sorry fool? And where are you staring? I said crowbar, not winebar![43] Come on, put those crowbars under the gates and start jimmying on that side; I'll do the jimmying over here.

LYSISTRATA

(*emerging from the gates*): Don't be doing any jimmying; I'm coming out on my very own. Why do you need crowbars? It's not crowbars you need, but rather brains and sense.

42 An overnight voyage.

43 Like women, slaves were stereotypically bibulous.

ΠΡΟΒΟΥΛΟΣ

ἄληθες, ὦ μιαρὰ σύ; ποῦ ʼστὶ τοξότης;
ξυλλάμβαν᾽ αὐτὴν κὠπίσω τὼ χεῖρε δεῖ.

ΛΥΣΙΣΤΡΑΤΗ

εἰ τἄρα νὴ τὴν Ἄρτεμιν τὴν χεῖρά μοι
ἄκραν προσοίσει δημόσιος ὤν, κλαύσεται.

ΠΡΟΒΟΥΛΟΣ

ἔδεισας, οὗτος; οὐ ξυναρπάσει μέσην
καὶ σὺ μετὰ τούτου χἀνύσαντε δήσετον;

ΓΡΑΥΣ Α

εἰ τἄρα νὴ τὴν Πάνδροσον ταύτῃ μόνον
τὴν χεῖρ᾽ ἐπιβαλεῖς, ἐπιχεσεῖ πατούμενος.

ΠΡΟΒΟΥΛΟΣ

ἰδού γ᾽ ἐπιχεσεῖ. ποῦ ʼστιν ἕτερος τοξότης;
ταύτην προτέραν ξύνδησον, ὁτιὴ καὶ λαλεῖ.

ΓΡΑΥΣ Β

εἰ τἄρα νὴ τὴν Φωσφόρον τὴν χεῖρ᾽ ἄκραν
ταύτῃ προσοίσεις, κύαθον αἰτήσεις τάχα.

ΠΡΟΒΟΥΛΟΣ

τουτὶ τί ἦν; ποῦ τοξότης; ταύτης ἔχου.
παύσω τιν᾽ ὑμῶν τῆσδ᾽ ἐγὼ τῆς ἐξόδου.

---

[44] One of the daughters of the mythical King Cecrops, and worshipped as a heroine on the Acropolis.

[45] A title of Hecate, a popular women's goddess associated with the moon and with the birth and rearing of children; her epithet here puns on "eye" or "eye salve."

MAGISTRATE

Really, you witch! Where's a policeman? (*to First Policeman*) Grab her and tie both hands behind her back.

LYSISTRATA

If he so much as touches me with his fingertip, mere public servant that he is, so help me Artemis he'll go home crying!

MAGISTRATE

What, are you scared? (*to Second Policeman*) You there, help him out; grab her around the waist and tie her up, on the double!

Enter First Old Woman from the gates.

FIRST OLD WOMAN

If you so much as lay a hand on her, so help me Pandrosos,[44] I'll beat the shit out of you!

MAGISTRATE

Beat the shit out of me? Where's another policeman? (*to Third Policeman*) Tie her up first, the one with the dirty mouth!

Enter Second Old Woman from the gates.

SECOND OLD WOMAN

If you raise your fingertip to her, so help me our Lady of Light,[45] you'll be begging for an eye cup!

MAGISTRATE

What's going on? Where's a policeman? (*to Fourth Policeman*) Arrest her. I'll foil at least one of these sallies of yours!

Enter Third Old Woman from the gates.

ΓΡΑΥΣ Γ

εἰ τἄρα νὴ τὴν Ταυροπόλον ταύτῃ πρόσει,
ἐκκοκκιῶ σου τὰς στενοκωκύτους τρίχας.

ΠΡΟΒΟΥΛΟΣ

οἴμοι κακοδαίμων· ἐπιλέλοιφ᾽ ὁ τοξότης.
ἀτὰρ οὐ γυναικῶν οὐδέποτ᾽ ἔσθ᾽ ἡττητέα
ἡμῖν· ὁμόσε χωρῶμεν αὐταῖς, ὦ Σκύθαι,
ξυνταξάμενοι.

ΛΥΣΙΣΤΡΑΤΗ

νὴ τὼ θεὼ γνώσεσθ᾽ ἄρα
ὅτι καὶ παρ᾽ ἡμῖν εἰσι τέτταρες λόχοι
μαχίμων γυναικῶν ἔνδον ἐξωπλισμένων.

ΠΡΟΒΟΥΛΟΣ

ἀποστρέφετε τὰς χεῖρας αὐτῶν, ὦ Σκύθαι.

ΛΥΣΙΣΤΡΑΤΗ

ὦ ξύμμαχοι γυναῖκες, ἐκθεῖτ᾽ ἔνδοθεν,
ὦ σπερμαγοραιολεκιθολαχανοπώλιδες,
ὦ σκοροδοπανδοκευτριαρτοπώλιδες,
οὐχ ἕλξετ᾽, οὐ παιήσετ᾽, οὐκ ἀράξετε,
οὐ λοιδορήσετ᾽, οὐκ ἀναισχυντήσετε;
παύσασθ᾽, ἐπαναχωρεῖτε, μὴ σκυλεύετε.

ΠΡΟΒΟΥΛΟΣ

οἴμ᾽ ὡς κακῶς πέπραγέ μου τὸ τοξικόν.

THIRD OLD WOMAN

If you come near her, so help me Tauropolus,[46] I'll rip out your hair till you scream!

MAGISTRATE

Damn my luck, I'm out of policemen. But men must never, ever be worsted by women! Form up ranks, Scythians, and let's charge them!

LYSISTRATA

By the Two Goddesses, you'll soon discover that we also have four squadrons of fully armed combat women, waiting inside!

MAGISTRATE

Scythians, twist their arms behind their backs!

LYSISTRATA

Women of the reserve, come out double-time!

Enter Old Women.

Forward, you spawn of the marketplace, you soup and vegetable mongers! Forward, you landladies, you hawkers of garlic and bread! Tackle them! Hit them! Smash them! Call them names, the nastier the better! That's enough! Withdraw! Don't strip the bodies!

Policemen run away howling; Old Women reenter the Acropolis.

MAGISTRATE

How awful! What a rout of my archer troops!

46 Under this title Artemis had an east-Attic cult that featured all-night ceremonies.

ΛΥΣΙΣΤΡΑΤΗ

ἀλλὰ τί γὰρ ᾤου; πότερον ἐπὶ δούλας τινὰς
ἥκειν ἐνόμισας, ἢ γυναιξὶν οὐκ οἴει
χολὴν ἐνεῖναι;

ΠΡΟΒΟΥΛΟΣ

νὴ τὸν Ἀπόλλω καὶ μάλα
πολλήν γ', ἐάνπερ πλησίον κάπηλος ᾖ.

ΚΟΡΥΦΑΙΟΣ

ὦ πόλλ' ἀναλώσας ἔπη πρόβουλε τῆσδε <τῆς> γῆς,
τί τοῖσδε σαυτὸν εἰς λόγον τοῖς θηρίοις ξυνάπτεις;
οὐκ οἶσθα λουτρὸν οἷον αἵδ' ἡμᾶς ἔλουσαν ἄρτι
ἐν τοῖσιν ἱματιδίοις, καὶ ταῦτ' ἄνευ κονίας;

ΚΟΡΥΦΑΙΑ

ἀλλ', ὦ μέλ', οὐ χρὴ προσφέρειν τοῖς πλησίοισιν εἰκῇ
τὴν χεῖρ'· ἐὰν δὲ τοῦτο δρᾷς, κυλοιδιᾶν ἀνάγκη.
ἐπεὶ 'θέλω 'γὼ σωφρόνως ὥσπερ κόρη καθῆσθαι,
λυποῦσα μηδέν' ἐνθαδί, κινοῦσα μηδὲ κάρφος,
ἢν μή τις ὥσπερ σφηκιὰν βλίττῃ με κἀρεθίζῃ.

ΧΟΡΟΣ ΓΕΡΟΝΤΩΝ

(στρ) ὦ Ζεῦ, τί ποτε χρησόμεθα τοῖσδε τοῖς κνωδάλοις;
οὐ γὰρ ἔτ' ἀνεκτὰ τάδε γ', ἀλλὰ βασανιστέον
τόδε σοι τὸ πάθος μετ' ἐμοῦ,
ὅ τι βουλόμεναί ποτε τὴν
Κραναὰν κατέλαβον, ἐφ' ὅ τι τε
μεγαλόπετρον ἄβατον ἀκρόπολιν,
ἱερὸν τέμενος.

LYSISTRATA

Well, what did you expect? Did you think you were going up against a bunch of slave girls? Or did you think women lack gall?

MAGISTRATE

Oh yes, they've got plenty of that, provided there's a wine bar nearby.

MEN'S LEADER

You've little to show for all your talk, Magistrate of this country! What's the point of fighting a battle of words with beasts like these? Don't you comprehend the kind of bath they've given us just now—when we were still in our clothes, and without soap to boot?

WOMEN'S LEADER

Well, sir, you shouldn't lift your hand against your neighbors just anytime you feel like it. If you do, you're going to end up with a black eye. You see, I'd rather be sitting modestly at home like a maiden, bothering no one here, stirring not a single blade of grass. But if anyone annoys me and rifles my nest, they'll find a wasp inside.

MEN'S CHORUS

Zeus, how on earth shall we deal with these
monsters?
This is past what I can bear; now's time to investigate
this incident along with me,
what they thought they were doing
when they occupied Cranaus'[47] citadel
and the great crag of the Acropolis,
a restricted, holy place.

[47] A mythical king of Athens.

ΚΟΡΥΦΑΙΟΣ

ἀλλ᾿ ἀνερώτα καὶ μὴ πείθου καὶ πρόσφερε πάντας ἐλέγχους·
ὡς αἰσχρὸν ἀκωδώνιστον ἐᾶν τὸ τοιοῦτον πρᾶγμα μεθέντας.

ΠΡΟΒΟΥΛΟΣ

καὶ μὴν αὐτῶν τοῦτ᾿ ἐπιθυμῶ νὴ τὸν Δία πρῶτα πυθέσθαι,
ὅ τι βουλόμεναι τὴν πόλιν ἡμῶν ἀπεκλῄσατε τοῖσι μοχλοῖσιν.

ΛΥΣΙΣΤΡΑΤΗ

ἵνα τἀργύριον σῶν κατέχοιμεν καὶ μὴ πολεμοῖτε δι᾿ αὐτό.

ΠΡΟΒΟΥΛΟΣ

διὰ τἀργύριον πολεμοῦμεν γάρ;

ΛΥΣΙΣΤΡΑΤΗ

καὶ τἄλλα γε πάντ᾿ ἐκυκήθη.
ἵνα γὰρ Πείσανδρος ἔχοι κλέπτειν χοἰ ταῖς ἀρχαῖς ἐπέχοντες
ἀεί τινα κορκορυγὴν ἐκύκων. οἱ δ᾿ οὖν τοῦδ᾿ οὕνεκα δρώντων
ὅ τι βούλονται· τὸ γὰρ ἀργύριον τοῦτ᾿ οὐκέτι μὴ καθέλωσιν.

ΠΡΟΒΟΥΛΟΣ

ἀλλὰ τί δράσεις;

MEN'S LEADER

Now question her and don't give in; cross-examine everything she says. It's scandalous to let this sort of behavior go unchallenged.

MAGISTRATE

Here's the first thing I'd really like to find out from them: what did you hope to gain by putting our Acropolis under lock and key?

LYSISTRATA

To keep the money safe, and to keep you from using it to finance the war.

MAGISTRATE

We're at war on account of the money, is that it?

LYSISTRATA

Yes, and that's why everything else got messed up too. It was for opportunities to steal that Pisander and the others who aimed to hold office were always fomenting some kind of commotion. So let them keep fomenting to their hearts' content: they'll be withdrawing no more money from this place.

MAGISTRATE

But what do you plan to do?

ΛΥΣΙΣΤΡΑΤΗ

τοῦτό μ' ἐρωτᾷς; ἡμεῖς ταμιεύσομεν αὐτό.

ΠΡΟΒΟΥΛΟΣ

ὑμεῖς ταμιεύσετε τἀργύριον;

ΛΥΣΙΣΤΡΑΤΗ

τί <δὲ> δεινὸν τοῦτο νομίζεις;

οὐ καὶ τἄνδον χρήματα πάντως ἡμεῖς ταμιεύομεν ὑμῖν;

ΠΡΟΒΟΥΛΟΣ

ἀλλ' οὐ ταὐτόν.

ΛΥΣΙΣΤΡΑΤΗ

πῶς οὐ ταὐτόν;

ΠΡΟΒΟΥΛΟΣ

πολεμητέον ἔστ' ἀπὸ τούτου.

ΛΥΣΙΣΤΡΑΤΗ

ἀλλ' οὐδὲν δεῖ πρῶτον πολεμεῖν.

ΠΡΟΒΟΥΛΟΣ

πῶς γὰρ σωθησόμεθ' ἄλλως;

ΛΥΣΙΣΤΡΑΤΗ

ἡμεῖς ὑμᾶς σώσομεν.

ΠΡΟΒΟΥΛΟΣ

ὑμεῖς;

ΛΥΣΙΣΤΡΑΤΗ

ἡμεῖς μέντοι.

LYSISTRATA

You're asking me that? We'll manage it for you.

MAGISTRATE

You'll manage the money?

LYSISTRATA

What's so strange about that? Don't we manage the household finances for you already?

MAGISTRATE

That's different.

LYSISTRATA

How so?

MAGISTRATE

These are war funds!

LYSISTRATA

But there shouldn't even be a war.

MAGISTRATE

How else are we to protect ourselves?

LYSISTRATA

We'll protect you.

MAGISTRATE

You?

LYSISTRATA

Yes, us.

ΠΡΟΒΟΥΛΟΣ

σχέτλιόν γε.

ΛΥΣΙΣΤΡΑΤΗ

ὡς σωθήσει, κἂν μὴ βούλῃ.

ΠΡΟΒΟΥΛΟΣ

δεινόν <γε> λέγεις.

ΛΥΣΙΣΤΡΑΤΗ

ἀγανακτεῖς,

ἀλλὰ ποιητέα ταῦτ᾽ ἐστὶν ὅμως.

ΠΡΟΒΟΥΛΟΣ

νὴ τὴν Δήμητρ᾽ ἄδικόν γε.

ΛΥΣΙΣΤΡΑΤΗ

σωστέον, ὦ τᾶν.

ΠΡΟΒΟΥΛΟΣ

κεἰ μὴ δέομαι;

ΛΥΣΙΣΤΡΑΤΗ

τοῦδ᾽ οὕνεκα καὶ πολὺ μᾶλλον.

ΠΡΟΒΟΥΛΟΣ

ὑμῖν δὲ πόθεν περὶ τοῦ πολέμου τῆς τ᾽ εἰρήνης
ἐμέλησεν;

ΛΥΣΙΣΤΡΑΤΗ

ἡμεῖς φράσομεν.

ΠΡΟΒΟΥΛΟΣ

λέγε δὴ ταχέως, ἵνα μὴ κλάῃς.

LYSISTRATA

MAGISTRATE

What brass!

LYSISTRATA

You'll be protected whether you like it or not.

MAGISTRATE

You're going too far!

LYSISTRATA

Angry, are you? It still must be done.

MAGISTRATE

By Demeter, you've got no right!

LYSISTRATA

You must be saved, dear fellow.

MAGISTRATE

Even if I don't ask to be?

LYSISTRATA

All the more so!

MAGISTRATE

How come you're concerned with war and peace anyway?

LYSISTRATA

We'll tell you.

MAGISTRATE

Well, make it snappy, unless you want to get hurt.

ΛΥΣΙΣΤΡΑΤΗ

ἀκροῶ δή,
καὶ τὰς χεῖρας πειρῶ κατέχειν.

ΠΡΟΒΟΥΛΟΣ

ἀλλ᾽ οὐ δύναμαι· χαλεπὸν γὰρ
ὑπὸ τῆς ὀργῆς αὐτὰς ἴσχειν.

ΓΡΑΥΣ Α

κλαύσει τοίνυν πολὺ μᾶλλον.

ΠΡΟΒΟΥΛΟΣ

τοῦτο μέν, ὦ γραῦ, σαυτῇ κρώξαις. σὺ δέ μοι λέγε.

ΛΥΣΙΣΤΡΑΤΗ

ταῦτα ποιήσω.
ἡμεῖς τὸν μὲν πρότερόν γε χρόνον <σιγῇ γ᾽> ἠνειχόμεθ᾽ <ὑμῶν>
ὑπὸ σωφροσύνης τῆς ἡμετέρας τῶν ἀνδρῶν ἅττ᾽ ἐποιεῖτε·
οὐ γὰρ γρύζειν εἰᾶθ᾽ ἡμᾶς· καίτοὐκ ἠρέσκετέ γ᾽ ἡμᾶς.
ἀλλ᾽ ᾐσθανόμεσθα καλῶς ὑμῶν, καὶ πολλάκις ἔνδον ἂν οὖσαι
ἠκούσαμεν ἄν τι κακῶς ὑμᾶς βουλευσαμένους μέγα πρᾶγμα·
εἶτ᾽ ἀλγοῦσαι τἄνδοθεν ὑμᾶς ἐπανηρόμεθ᾽ ἂν γελάσασαι
"τί βεβούλευται περὶ τῶν σπονδῶν ἐν τῇ στήλῃ παραγράψαι
ἐν τῷ δήμῳ τήμερον ὑμῖν;" "τί δὲ σοὶ τοῦτ᾽;" ἦ δ᾽ ὃς ἂν ἀνήρ·

LYSISTRATA

Listen then, and try to control your fists.

MAGISTRATE

I can't; I'm so angry I can't keep my hands to myself.

FIRST OLD WOMAN

Then you're the one who'll get hurt!

MAGISTRATE

Croak those curses at yourself, old bag! (*to Lysistrata*) You, start talking.

LYSISTRATA

Gladly.[48] Before now, and for quite some time, we maintained our decorum and suffered <in silence> whatever you men did, because you wouldn't let us make a sound. But you weren't exactly all we could ask for. No, we knew only too well what you were up to, and many a time we'd hear in our homes about a bad decision you'd made on some great issue of state. Then, masking the pain in our hearts, we'd put on a smile and ask you, "How did the Assembly go today? Any decision about a rider to the peace treaty?"[49] And my husband would say, "What's that to you?

[48] The following account recalls the conversation between Hector and Andromache in *Iliad* 6.

[49] In 419/18 the Athenians appended to the text of the Peace of 421 "the Spartans have violated their oaths," cf. Thucydides 5.56.

"οὐ σιγήσει;" κἀγὼ 'σίγων.

ΓΡΑΥΣ Α

ἀλλ' οὐκ ἂν ἐγώ ποτ' ἐσίγων.

ΠΡΟΒΟΥΛΟΣ

κἂν ᾤμωζές γ', εἰ μὴ 'σίγας.

ΛΥΣΙΣΤΡΑΤΗ

τοιγὰρ <ἐγὼ> μὲν τότ' ἐσίγων.
<αὖθις δ'> ἕτερόν τι πονηρότερον βούλευμ' ἐπεπύσμεθ' ἂν ὑμῶν·
εἶτ' ἠρόμεθ' ἄν· "πῶς ταῦτ', ὦνερ, διαπράττεσθ' ὧδ' ἀνοήτως;"
ὁ δέ μ' εὐθὺς ὑποβλέψας <ἂν> ἔφασκ', εἰ μὴ τὸν στήμονα νήσω,
ὀτοτύξεσθαι μακρὰ τὴν κεφαλήν· "πόλεμος δ' ἄνδρεσσι μελήσει."

ΠΡΟΒΟΥΛΟΣ

ὀρθῶς γε λέγων νὴ Δί' ἐκεῖνος.

ΛΥΣΙΣΤΡΑΤΗ

πῶς ὀρθῶς, ὦ κακόδαιμον,
εἰ μηδὲ κακῶς βουλευομένοις ἐξῆν ὑμῖν ὑποθέσθαι;
ὅτε δὴ δ' ὑμῶν ἐν ταῖσιν ὁδοῖς φανερῶς ἠκούομεν ἤδη·
"οὐκ ἔστιν ἀνὴρ ἐν τῇ χώρᾳ."—"μὰ Δί' οὐ δῆτ' <ἔσθ'>," ἕτερός τις,—
μετὰ ταῦθ' ἡμῖν εὐθὺς ἔδοξεν σῶσαι τὴν Ἑλλάδα κοινῇ

Shut up!" And I'd shut up.

FIRST OLD WOMAN

I wouldn't have shut up!

MAGISTRATE

If you hadn't shut up you'd have got a beating!

LYSISTRATA

Well, that's why I did shut up—then. But later on we began to hear about even worse decisions you'd made, and then we would ask, "Husband, how come you're handling this so stupidly?" And right away he'd glare at me and tell me to get back to my sewing if I didn't want major damage to my head: "War shall be the business of menfolk," unquote.[50]

MAGISTRATE

He was right on the mark, I say.

LYSISTRATA

How could he be right, you sorry fool, when we were forbidden to offer advice even when your policy was wrong? But then, when we began to hear you in the streets openly crying, "There isn't a man left in the land," and someone else saying, "God knows, there isn't, not a one," after that we women decided to lose no more time, and to band to-

[50] Hector at *Iliad* 6.492.

ταῖσι γυναιξὶν συλλεχθείσαις. ποῖ γὰρ καὶ χρῆν ἀναμεῖναι;
ἢν οὖν ἡμῶν χρηστὰ λεγουσῶν ἐθελήσητ' ἀντακροᾶσθαι
κἀντισιωπᾶν ὥσπερ χἠμεῖς, ἐπανορθώσαιμεν ἂν ὑμᾶς.

ΠΡΟΒΟΥΛΟΣ

ὑμεῖς ἡμᾶς; δεινόν γε λέγεις κοὐ τλητὸν ἔμοιγε.

ΛΥΣΙΣΤΡΑΤΗ

σιώπα.

ΠΡΟΒΟΥΛΟΣ

σοί γ', ὦ κατάρατε, σιωπῶ 'γώ, καὶ ταῦτα κάλυμμα φορούσῃ
περὶ τὴν κεφαλήν; μή νυν ζῴην.

ΛΥΣΙΣΤΡΑΤΗ

ἀλλ' εἰ τοῦτ' ἐμπόδιόν σοι,
παρ' ἐμοῦ τουτὶ τὸ κάλυμμα λαβὼν
ἔχε καὶ περίθου περὶ τὴν κεφαλήν,
κᾆτα σιώπα.

ΓΡΑΥΣ Α

καὶ τουτογὶ τὸν καλαθίσκον.

ΛΥΣΙΣΤΡΑΤΗ

κᾆτα ξαίνειν ξυζωσάμενος
κυάμους τρώγων·
πόλεμος δὲ γυναιξὶ μελήσει.

gether to save Greece. What was the point of waiting any longer? So, if you're ready to listen in your turn as we give you good advice, and to shut up as we had to, we can put you back on the right track.

MAGISTRATE

You put us? Outrageous! I won't stand for it!

LYSISTRATA

Shut up!

MAGISTRATE

Me shut up for you? A damned woman, with a veil on your face no less? I'd rather die!

LYSISTRATA

If the veil is a problem for you, here, take mine, it's yours, put it on your head, and then shut up!

FIRST OLD WOMAN

And take this sewing basket too.

LYSISTRATA

Now hitch up your clothes and start sewing; chew some beans while you work. War shall be the business of womenfolk!

ΚΟΡΥΦΑΙΑ

αἴρεσθ᾽ ἄνω, γυναῖκες, ἀπὸ τῶν καλπίδων, ὅπως ἂν
ἐν τῷ μέρει χἠμεῖς τι ταῖς φίλαισι συλλάβωμεν.

ΧΟΡΟΣ ΓΥΝΑΙΚΩΝ

(ἀντ) ἔγω<γε> γὰρ <ἂν> οὔποτε κάμοιμ᾽ ἂν ὀρχουμένη,
οὐδὲ καματηρὸς ἂν ἕλοι γόνατά μου κόπος.
ἐθέλω δ᾽ ἐπὶ πᾶν ἰέναι
μετὰ τῶνδ᾽ ἀρετῆς ἕνεχ᾽, αἷς
ἔνι φύσις, ἔνι χάρις, ἔνι θράσος,
ἔνι <δὲ> τὸ σοφόν, ἔνι φιλόπολις
ἀρετὴ φρόνιμος.

ΚΟΡΥΦΑΙΑ

ἀλλ᾽, ὦ τηθῶν ἀνδρειοτάτη καὶ μητριδίων ἀκαληφῶν,
χωρεῖτ᾽ ὀργῇ καὶ μὴ τέγγεσθ᾽· ἔτι γὰρ νῦν οὔρια θεῖτε.

ΛΥΣΙΣΤΡΑΤΗ

ἀλλ᾽ ἤνπερ ὅ <τε> γλυκύθυμος Ἔρως χἠ Κυπρογένει᾽ Ἀφροδίτη
ἵμερον ἡμῶν κατὰ τῶν κόλπων καὶ τῶν μηρῶν καταπνεύσῃ,
κᾆτ᾽ ἐντέξῃ τέτανον τερπνὸν τοῖς ἀνδράσι καὶ ῥοπαλισμούς,
οἶμαί ποτε Λυσιμάχας ἡμᾶς ἐν τοῖς Ἕλλησι καλεῖσθαι.

ΠΡΟΒΟΥΛΟΣ

τί ποιησάσας;

WOMEN'S LEADER

Rouse yourselves, women, away from those pitchers, it's our turn to pitch in with a little help for our friends!

WOMEN'S CHORUS

Oh yes! I'll dance with unflagging energy;
no toilsome effort will weary my knees.
I'm ready to face anything
with women as courageous as these:
they've got character, charm, and guts,
they've got intelligence and heart
that's both patriotic and smart!

WOMEN'S LEADER

Now, most valiant of prickly mommies and spikey grannies, attack furiously and don't go mushy: you're still running with the wind!

LYSISTRATA

If Eros of the sweet soul and Cyprian Aphrodite imbue our thighs and breasts with desire, and infect the men with sensuous rigidity and bouts of truncheonitis, then I believe all Greece will one day call us Disbanders of Battles.[51]

MAGISTRATE

For what achievement?

[51] *Lysimachai*, possibly alluding to the priestess Lysimache; see Introductory Note.

---

541 suppl. Enger

ΛΥΣΙΣΤΡΑΤΗ

ἢν παύσωμεν πρώτιστον μὲν ξὺν ὅπλοισιν
ἀγοράζοντας καὶ μαινομένους.

ΓΡΑΥΣ Α

νὴ τὴν Παφίαν Ἀφροδίτην.

ΛΥΣΙΣΤΡΑΤΗ

νῦν μὲν γὰρ δὴ κἀν ταῖσι χύτραις καὶ τοῖς λαχάνοισιν ὁμοίως
περιέρχονται κατὰ τὴν ἀγορὰν ξὺν ὅπλοις ὥσπερ Κορύβαντες.

ΠΡΟΒΟΥΛΟΣ

νὴ Δία· χρὴ γὰρ τοὺς ἀνδρείους.

ΛΥΣΙΣΤΡΑΤΗ

καὶ μὴν τό γε πρᾶγμα γέλοιον,
ὅταν ἀσπίδ᾽ ἔχων καὶ Γοργόνα τις κᾆτ᾽ ὠνῆται κορακίνους.

ΓΡΑΥΣ Α

νὴ Δί᾽ ἐγὼ γοῦν ἄνδρα κομήτην φυλαρχοῦντ᾽ εἶδον ἐφ᾽ ἵππου
εἰς τὸν χαλκοῦν ἐμβαλλόμενον πῖλον λέκιθον παρὰ γραός·
ἕτερος δ᾽ αὖ Θρᾷξ πέλτην σείων κἀκόντιον ὥσπερ ὁ Τηρεὺς
ἐδεδίσκετο τὴν ἰσχαδόπωλιν καὶ τὰς δρυπεπεῖς κατέπινεν.

LYSISTRATA

If to begin with we can stop people from going to the market fully armed and acting crazy.

FIRST OLD WOMAN

Paphian Aphrodite be praised!

LYSISTRATA

At this very moment, all around the market, in the pottery shops and the grocery stalls, they're walking around in arms like Corybants![52]

MAGISTRATE

I say a man's got to act like a man!

LYSISTRATA

But it's totally ridiculous when a man with a Gorgon-blazoned shield goes shopping for sardines!

FIRST OLD WOMAN

Amen! I saw a long-haired fellow, a cavalry captain, on horseback, buying porridge from an old woman and packing it into his brass hat. Another one, a Thracian, was shaking his shield and spear like Tereus;[53] he scared the fig lady out of her wits and gulped down all the ripe ones!

[52] Eastern divinities associated with ecstatic dancing, and a popular way to refer to lunatics.

[53] Thracian mercenaries struck Athenians as wild and uncivilized; for the myth of Tereus see *Birds* 15 n.

ΠΡΟΒΟΥΛΟΣ

πῶς οὖν ὑμεῖς δυναταὶ παῦσαι τεταραγμένα πράγματα πολλὰ
ἐν ταῖς χώραις καὶ διαλῦσαι;

ΛΥΣΙΣΤΡΑΤΗ

φαύλως πάνυ.

ΠΡΟΒΟΥΛΟΣ

πῶς; ἀπόδειξον.

ΛΥΣΙΣΤΡΑΤΗ

ὥσπερ κλωστῆρ᾽, ὅταν ἡμῖν ᾖ τεταραγμένος, ὧδε λαβοῦσαι,
ὑπενεγκοῦσαι τοῖσιν ἀτράκτοις τὸ μὲν ἐνταυθοῖ, τὸ δ᾽ ἐκεῖσε,
οὕτως καὶ τὸν πόλεμον τοῦτον διαλύσομεν, ἤν τις ἐάσῃ,
διενεγκοῦσαι διὰ πρεσβειῶν τὸ μὲν ἐνταυθοῖ, τὸ δ᾽ ἐκεῖσε.

ΠΡΟΒΟΥΛΟΣ

ἐξ ἐρίων δὴ καὶ κλωστήρων καὶ ἀτράκτων πράγματα δεινὰ
παύσειν οἴεσθ᾽; ὡς ἀνόητοι.

ΛΥΣΙΣΤΡΑΤΗ

κἂν ὑμῖν γ᾽ εἴ τις ἐνῆν νοῦς,
ἐκ τῶν ἐρίων τῶν ἡμετέρων ἐπολιτεύεσθ᾽ ἂν ἅπαντα.

ΠΡΟΒΟΥΛΟΣ

πῶς δή; φέρ᾽ ἴδω.

LYSISTRATA

MAGISTRATE

So how will you women be able to put a stop to such a complicated international mess, and sort it all out?

LYSISTRATA

Very easily.

MAGISTRATE

How? Show me.

LYSISTRATA

(taking the sewing basket from the Magistrate and using its contents to illustrate) It's rather like a ball of yarn when it gets tangled up. We hold it this way, and carefully wind out the strands on our spindles, now this way, now that way. That's how we'll wind up this war, if we're allowed: unsnarling it by sending embassies, now this way, now that way.

MAGISTRATE

You really think your way with wool and yarnballs and spindles can stop a terrible crisis? How brainless!

LYSISTRATA

I do think so, and if *you* had any brains you'd handle all the polis' business the way we handle our wool!

MAGISTRATE

How then? I'm all ears.

ΛΥΣΙΣΤΡΑΤΗ

πρῶτον μὲν ἐχρῆν, ὥσπερ πόκον, ἐν βαλανείῳ
ἐκπλύναντας τὴν οἰσπώτην ἐκ τῆς πόλεως, ἐπὶ κλίνης
ἐκραβδίζειν τοὺς μοχθηροὺς καὶ τοὺς τριβόλους ἀπολέξαι,
καὶ τούς γε συνισταμένους τούτους καὶ τοὺς πιλοῦντας ἑαυτοὺς
ἐπὶ ταῖς ἀρχαῖσι διαξῆναι καὶ τὰς κεφαλὰς ἀποτῖλαι·
εἶτα ξαίνειν εἰς καλαθίσκον κοινὴν εὔνοιαν ἅπαντας
καταμειγνύντας· τούς τε μετοίκους κεἴ τις ξένος ἢ φίλος ὑμῖν,
κεἴ τις ὀφείλῃ τῷ δημοσίῳ, καὶ τούτους ἐγκαταμεῖξαι·
καὶ νὴ Δία τάς γε πόλεις, ὁπόσαι τῆς γῆς τῆσδ᾽ εἰσὶν ἄποικοι,
διαγιγνώσκειν ὅτι ταῦθ᾽ ὑμῖν ὥσπερ τὰ κατάγματα κεῖται
χωρὶς ἕκαστον· κᾆτ᾽ ἀπὸ τούτων πάντων τὸ κάταγμα λαβόντας
δεῦρο ξυνάγειν καὶ ξυναθροίζειν εἰς ἕν, κἄπειτα ποιῆσαι
τολύπην μεγάλην κᾆτ᾽ ἐκ ταύτης τῷ δήμῳ χλαῖναν ὑφῆναι.

ΠΡΟΒΟΥΛΟΣ

οὔκουν δεινὸν ταυτὶ ταύτας ῥαβδίζειν καὶ τολυπεύειν,

LYSISTRATA

Imagine the polis as a fleece just shorn. First, put it in a bath and wash out all the sheep dung; spread it on a bed and beat out the riff-raff with a stick, and pluck out the thorns; as for those who clump and knot themselves together to snag government positions, card them out and pluck off their heads. Next, card the wool into a sewing basket of unity and goodwill, mixing in everyone. The resident aliens and any other foreigner who's your friend, and anyone who owes money to the people's treasury, mix them in there too. And oh yes, the cities that are colonies of this land: imagine them as flocks of your fleece, each one lying apart from the others. So take all these flocks and bring them together here, joining them all and making one big bobbin. And from this weave a fine new cloak for the people.

MAGISTRATE

Isn't it awful how these women go like this with their sticks,

---

583 ὑμῖν B: ἡμῖν R Γ p

αἷς οὐδὲ μετῆν πάνυ τοῦ πολέμου;

ΛΥΣΙΣΤΡΑΤΗ

καὶ μήν, ὦ παγκατάρατε,
πλεῖν ἢ διπλοῦν γ᾽ αὐτοῦ φέρομεν. πρώτιστον μέν γε τεκοῦσαι
κἀκπέμψασαι παῖδας ὁπλίτας—

ΠΡΟΒΟΥΛΟΣ

σίγα, μὴ μνησικακήσῃς.

ΛΥΣΙΣΤΡΑΤΗ

εἶθ᾽ ἡνίκα χρῆν εὐφρανθῆναι καὶ τῆς ἥβης ἀπολαῦσαι,
μονοκοιτοῦμεν διὰ τὰς στρατιάς. καὶ θἠμέτερον μὲν ἐάσω,
περὶ τῶν δὲ κορῶν ἐν τοῖς θαλάμοις γηρασκουσῶν ἀνιῶμαι.

ΠΡΟΒΟΥΛΟΣ

οὔκουν κἄνδρες γηράσκουσιν;

ΛΥΣΙΣΤΡΑΤΗ

μὰ Δί᾽ ἀλλ᾽ οὐκ εἶπας ὅμοιον.
ὁ μὲν ἥκων γάρ, κἂν ᾖ πολιός, ταχὺ παῖδα κόρην γεγάμηκεν·
τῆς δὲ γυναικὸς μικρὸς ὁ καιρός, κἂν τούτου μὴ ᾽πιλάβηται,
οὐδεὶς ἐθέλει γῆμαι ταύτην, ὀττευομένη δὲ κάθηται.

ΠΡΟΒΟΥΛΟΣ

ἀλλ᾽ ὅστις ἔτι στῦσαι δυνατὸς—

and like that with their bobbins, when they share none of the war's burdens?

LYSISTRATA

None? You monster! We bear more than our fair share, in the first place by giving birth to sons and sending them off to the army—

MAGISTRATE

Enough of that! Don't open old wounds.

LYSISTRATA

Then, when we ought to be having fun and enjoying our bloom of youth, we sleep alone because of the campaigns. And to say no more about our own case, it pains me to think of the maidens growing old in their rooms.

MAGISTRATE

Men grow old too, don't they?

LYSISTRATA

That's quite a different story. When a man comes home he can quickly find a girl to marry, even if he's a greybeard. But a woman's prime is brief; if she doesn't seize it, no one wants to marry her, and she sits at home looking for good omens.[54]

MAGISTRATE

But any man who can still get a hard-on—

54 That is, omens foretelling marriage.

ΛΥΣΙΣΤΡΑΤΗ

σὺ δὲ δὴ τί μαθὼν οὐκ ἀποθνῄσκεις;
χωρίον ἐστίν· σορὸν ὠνήσει·
μελιτοῦτταν ἐγὼ καὶ δὴ μάξω.
λαβὲ ταυτὶ καὶ στεφάνωσαι.

ΓΡΑΥΣ Α

καὶ ταυτασὶ δέξαι παρ᾽ ἐμοῦ.

ΓΡΑΥΣ Β

καὶ τουτονγὶ λαβὲ τὸν στέφανον.

ΛΥΣΙΣΤΡΑΤΗ

τοῦ δεῖ; τί ποθεῖς; χώρει ᾽ς τὴν ναῦν·
ὁ Χάρων σε καλεῖ,
σὺ δὲ κωλύεις ἀνάγεσθαι.

ΠΡΟΒΟΥΛΟΣ

εἶτ᾽ οὐχὶ δεινὰ ταῦτα πάσχειν ἔστ᾽ ἐμέ;
νὴ τὸν Δί᾽ ἀλλὰ τοῖς προβούλοις ἄντικρυς
ἐμαυτὸν ἐπιδείξω βαδίζων ὡς ἔχω.

ΛΥΣΙΣΤΡΑΤΗ

μῶν ἐγκαλεῖς ὅτι οὐχὶ προὐθέμεσθά σε;
ἀλλ᾽ εἰς τρίτην γοῦν ἡμέραν σοι πρῴ πάνυ
ἥξει παρ᾽ ἡμῶν τὰ τρίτ᾽ ἐπεσκευασμένα.

ΚΟΡΥΦΑΙΟΣ

οὐκέτ᾽ ἔργον ἐγκαθεύδειν ὅστις ἔστ᾽ ἐλεύθερος.
ἀλλ᾽ ἐπαποδυώμεθ᾽, ὦνδρες, τουτῳὶ τῷ πράγματι.

LYSISTRATA

Why don't you just drop dead? Here's a grave site; buy a coffin; I'll start kneading you a honeycake.[55] (*removing her garland*) Use these for a wreath.

FIRST OLD WOMAN

(*handing him ribbons*) You can have these from me.

SECOND OLD WOMAN

And this crown from me.

LYSISTRATA

All set? Need anything else? Get on the boat, then; Charon is calling your name and you're holding him up![56]

MAGISTRATE

Isn't it shocking that I'm being treated like this? So help me god, I'm going straight to the other magistrates to display myself just as I am!

MAGISTRATE exits with his slaves.

LYSISTRATA

I hope you won't complain about the funeral we gave you. I tell you what: the day after tomorrow, first thing in the morning, we'll perform the third-day offerings at your grave!

LYSISTRATA and OLD WOMEN exit into the Acropolis.

MEN'S LEADER

No free man should be asleep now! Let's strip for action, men, and meet this emergency! (*they remove their jackets*)

55 Among women's traditional duties was managing funerals.

56 Charon ferried dead souls across the river Styx into the underworld.

ΧΟΡΟΣ ΓΕΡΟΝΤΩΝ

(στρ) ἤδη γὰρ ὄζειν ταδὶ πλειόνων
καὶ μειζόνων πραγμάτων μοι δοκεῖ,
καὶ μάλιστ᾽ ὀσφραίνομαι τῆς Ἱππίου τυραννίδος·
καὶ πάνυ δέδοικα μὴ τῶν Λακώνων τινὲς
δεῦρο συνεληλυθότες ἄνδρες εἰς Κλεισθένους
τὰς θεοῖς ἐχθρὰς γυναῖκας ἐξεπαίρουσιν δόλῳ
καταλαβεῖν τὰ χρήμαθ᾽ ἡμῶν τόν τε μισθόν,
ἔνθεν ἔζων ἐγώ.

ΚΟΡΥΦΑΙΟΣ

δεινὰ γάρ τοι τάσδε γ᾽ ἤδη τοὺς πολίτας νουθετεῖν,
καὶ λαλεῖν γυναῖκας οὔσας ἀσπίδος χαλκῆς πέρι,
καὶ διαλλάττειν πρὸς ἡμᾶς ἀνδράσιν Λακωνικοῖς,
οἷσι πιστὸν οὐδὲν εἰ μή περ λύκῳ κεχηνότι.
ἀλλὰ ταῦθ᾽ ὕφηναν ἡμῖν, ὦνδρες, ἐπὶ τυραννίδι.
ἀλλ᾽ ἐμοῦ μὲν οὐ τυραννεύσουσ᾽, ἐπεὶ φυλάξομαι
καὶ "φορήσω τὸ ξίφος" τὸ λοιπὸν "ἐν μύρτου κλαδί,"
ἀγοράσω τ᾽ ἐν τοῖς ὅπλοις ἑξῆς Ἀριστογείτονι,
ὧδέ θ᾽ ἑστήξω παρ᾽ αὐτόν· αὐτὸ γάρ μοι γίγνεται
τῆς θεοῖς ἐχθρᾶς πατάξαι τῆσδε γραὸς τὴν γνάθον.

MEN'S CHORUS

I think I smell much bigger trouble in this,
a definite whiff of Hippias' tyranny![57]
I'm terrified that certain men from Sparta
have gathered at the house of Cleisthenes
and scheme to stir up our godforsaken women
to seize the Treasury and my jury pay,
my very livelihood.

MEN'S LEADER

It's shocking, you know, that they're lecturing the citizens now, and running their mouths—mere women!—about brazen shields. And to top it off they're trying to make peace between us and the men of Sparta, who are no more trustworthy than a starving wolf. Actually, this plot they weave against us, gentlemen, aims at tyranny! Well, they'll never tyrannize over *me*: from now on I'll be on my guard, I'll "carry my sword in a myrtle branch"[58] and go to market fully armed right up beside Aristogiton.[59] I'll stand beside him like this (*posing like Aristogiton's statue*): that way I'll be ready to smack this godforsaken old hag right in the jaw! (*advances on the Women's Leader*)

[57] The last Athenian tyrant, expelled in 510; his name (based on *hippos* "horse") suggests the equestrian position in sexual intercourse (woman on top).

[58] Quoting from a patriotic drinking song (*PMG* 893–96) about the tyrant-slayers (next note); the phrase might also connote the sexual penetration of women.

[59] In the marketplace stood bronze statues of Harmodius and Aristogiton, the young men who killed Hipparchus, the brother of the tyrant Hippias, in 514; they and their descendants were subsequently revered as tyrant-slayers and freedom fighters.

ΚΟΡΥΦΑΙΑ

οὐκ ἄρ᾽ εἰσιόντα σ᾽ οἴκαδ᾽ ἡ τεκοῦσα γνώσεται.
ἀλλὰ θώμεσθ᾽, ὦ φίλαι γρᾶες, ταδὶ πρῶτον χαμαί.

ΧΟΡΟΣ ΓΥΝΑΙΚΩΝ

(ἀντ) ἡμεῖς γάρ, ὦ πάντες ἀστοί, λόγων
  κατάρχομεν τῇ πόλει χρησίμων·
εἰκότως, ἐπεὶ χλιδῶσαν ἀγλαῶς ἔθρεψέ με·
ἑπτὰ μὲν ἔτη γεγῶσ᾽ εὐθὺς ἠρρηφόρουν·
εἶτ᾽ ἀλετρὶς ἦ δεκέτις οὖσα τἀρχηγέτι,
καὶ χέουσα τὸν κροκωτὸν ἄρκτος ἦ Βραυρωνίοις·
κἀκανηφόρουν ποτ᾽ οὖσα παῖς καλὴ ᾽χουσ᾽
  ἰσχάδων ὁρμαθόν.

ΚΟΡΥΦΑΙΑ

ἆρα προὐφείλω τι χρηστὸν τῇ πόλει παραινέσαι;
εἰ δ᾽ ἐγὼ γυνὴ πέφυκα, τοῦτο μὴ φθονεῖτέ μοι,
ἢν ἀμείνω γ᾽ εἰσενέγκω τῶν παρόντων πραγμάτων.
τοὐράνου γάρ μοι μέτεστι· καὶ γὰρ ἄνδρας
  εἰσφέρω.

644–5 τἀρχηγέτι et Βραυρωνίοις transp. Sommerstein
645 καὶ χέουσα Stinton: καταχέουσα R: κατέχουσα Γ Β p

---

60 The Arrhephoroi were two girls who spent a year living on the Acropolis serving Athena Polias, principally by weaving her robe and carrying it in the Panathenaic procession, the most prestigious of all processions. The girls, selected by the Assembly and the King Archon, were between seven and eleven years old and came only from the noblest Athenian families.

WOMEN'S LEADER

Just try it, and your own mommy won't recognize you when you get home! Come on, fellow hags, let's start by putting these jackets on the ground. (*they remove their jackets*)

WOMEN'S CHORUS

Citizens of Athens, we begin
by offering the city valuable advice,
and fittingly, for she raised me in splendid luxury.
As soon as I turned seven I was an Arrephoros;[60]
then when I was ten I was a Grinder[61] for the
Foundress;[62]
and shedding my saffron robe I was a Bear at the
Brauronia;[63]
and once, when I was a fair girl, I carried the Basket,
wearing a necklace of dried figs.[64]

WOMEN'S LEADER

Thus I owe it to the polis to offer some good advice. And even if I *was* born a woman, don't hold it against me if I manage to suggest something better than what we've got now. I have a stake in our community: my contribution is

61 Wellborn girls who served a goddess—probably Demeter at Eleusis—by grinding ritual cakes.

62 That is, Artemis, the patron deity of the Brauronia.

63 The Brauronia, open to select girls five to ten years old, culminated in the Ritual of the Bears (*Arcteia*), in which at some point the girls removed a saffron-dyed robe and performed (as vase paintings show) naked.

64 Maiden basket-bearers were a feature of many processions, the figs symbolizing fertility; the climactic placement here suggests the Panathenaea.

τοῖς δὲ δυστήνοις γέρουσιν οὐ μέτεσθ᾽ ὑμῖν, ἐπεὶ
τὸν ἔρανον τὸν γενόμενον παππῷον ἐκ τῶν Μηδικῶν
εἶτ᾽ ἀναλώσαντες οὐκ ἀντεισφέρετε τὰς εἰσφοράς,
ἀλλ᾽ ὑφ᾽ ὑμῶν διαλυθῆναι προσέτι κινδυνεύομεν.
ἆρα γρυκτόν ἐστιν ὑμῖν; εἰ δὲ λυπήσεις τί με,
τῷδέ σ᾽ ἀψήκτῳ πατάξω τῷ κοθόρνῳ τὴν γνάθον.

ΧΟΡΟΣ ΓΕΡΟΝΤΩΝ

(στρ) ταῦτ᾽ οὖν οὐχ ὕβρις τὰ πράγματ᾽ ἐστὶ πολλή;
κἀπιδώσειν μοι δοκεῖ τὸ χρῆμα μᾶλλον.
ἀλλ᾽ ἀμυντέον τὸ πρᾶγμ᾽ ὅστις γ᾽ ἐνόρχης ἔστ᾽ ἀνήρ.

ΚΟΡΥΦΑΙΟΣ

ἀλλὰ τὴν ἐξωμίδ᾽ ἐκδυώμεθ᾽, ὡς τὸν ἄνδρα δεῖ
ἀνδρὸς ὄζειν εὐθύς, ἀλλ᾽ οὐκ ἐντεθριῶσθαι πρέπει.

ΧΟΡΟΣ ΓΕΡΟΝΤΩΝ

ἀλλ᾽ ἄγετε λευκόποδες,
οἵπερ ἐπὶ Λειψύδριον
ἤλθομεν ὅτ᾽ ἦμεν ἔτι,
νῦν δεῖ, νῦν ἀνηβῆσαι πάλιν κἀναπτερῶσαι
πᾶν τὸ σῶμα κἀποσείσασθαι τὸ γῆρας τόδε.

ΚΟΡΥΦΑΙΟΣ

εἰ γὰρ ἐνδώσει τις ἡμῶν ταῖσδε κἂν σμικρὰν λαβήν,
οὐδὲν ἐλλείψουσιν αὗται λιπαροῦς χειρουργίας,

653 *γενόμενον* Geel: *λεγόμενον* a S
664 *λευκ-* Hermann cl. Hesych. λ 1392: *λυκ-* a S Photius

men. You miserable geezers have no stake, since you've squandered your paternal inheritance, won in the Persian Wars, and now pay no taxes in return. On the contrary, we're all headed for bankruptcy on account of you! Have you anything to grunt in rebuttal? Any more trouble from you and I'll clobber you with this rawhide boot right in the jaw! (*raises her foot at the Men's Leader*)

MEN'S CHORUS

Now doesn't this behavior of theirs amount to
 extreme hubris?
And I do believe the situation will only get worse.
Every man with any balls must stand up to this
 threat!

MEN'S LEADER

Let's doff our shirts, because a man's got to smell like a man from the word go, and shouldn't be all wrapped up like souvlaki. (*they remove their shirts*)

MEN'S CHORUS

Come on, Whitefeet![65]
We went against Leipsydrium[66]
when we still were something;
now we've got to rejuvenate, and give wing
to our whole bodies, and slough off this old skin!

MEN'S LEADER

If any man among us gives these women even the tiniest handhold, there's no limit to what their nimble hands will

[65] A military nickname of disputed, but evidently patriotic, significance.

[66] In the hills of northern Attica, where rebels battled the tyrant Hippias after his brother's assassination.

ἀλλὰ καὶ ναῦς τεκτανοῦνται, κἀπιχειρήσουσ᾽ ἔτι
ναυμαχεῖν καὶ πλεῖν ἐφ᾽ ἡμᾶς, ὥσπερ Ἀρτεμισία.
ἢν δ᾽ ἐφ᾽ ἱππικὴν τράπωνται, διαγράφω τοὺς ἱππέας·
ἱππικώτατον γάρ ἐστι χρῆμα κἄποχον γυνή,
κοὐκ ἂν ἀπολίσθοι τρέχοντος. τὰς Ἀμαζόνας σκόπει,
ἃς Μίκων ἔγραψ᾽ ἐφ᾽ ἵππων μαχομένας τοῖς ἀνδράσιν.
ἀλλὰ τούτων χρῆν ἁπασῶν εἰς τετρημένον ξύλον
ἐγκαθαρμόσαι λαβόντας τουτονὶ τὸν αὐχένα.

ΧΟΡΟΣ ΓΥΝΑΙΚΩΝ

(ἀντ) εἰ νὴ τὼ θεώ με ζωπυρήσεις, λύσω
τὴν ἐμαυτῆς ὗν ἐγὼ δή, καὶ ποιήσω
τήμερον τοὺς δημότας βωστρεῖν σ᾽ ἐγὼ πεκτούμενον.

ΚΟΡΥΦΑΙΑ

ἀλλὰ χἠμεῖς, ὦ γυναῖκες, θᾶττον ἐκδυώμεθα,
ὡς ἂν ὄζωμεν γυναικῶν αὐτοδὰξ ὠργισμένων.

ΧΟΡΟΣ ΓΥΝΑΙΚΩΝ

νῦν πρὸς ἔμ᾽ ἴτω τις, ἵνα
μήποτε φάγῃ σκόροδα
μηδὲ κυάμους μέλανας.
ὡς εἰ καὶ μόνον κακῶς ἐρεῖς, ὑπερχολῶ γάρ,

---

[67] A queen of Halicarnassus who commanded naval actions against the Greeks during the Persian invasion of 480, cf. Herodotus 7.99, 8.68–69, 87–88.

do. Why, they'll even be building frigates and launching naval attacks, cruising against us like Artemisia.[67] And if they turn to horsemanship, you can scratch our cavalry: there's nothing like a woman when it comes to mounting and riding; even riding hard she won't slip off. Just look at the Amazons in Mikon's paintings,[68] riding chargers in battle against men.[69] Our duty is clear: grab each woman's neck and lock it in the wooden stocks! (*advances on the Women's Leader.*)

WOMEN'S CHORUS

By the Two Goddesses, if you fire me up
I'll come at you like a wild sow and clip you bare,
and this very day you'll go bleating to your friends for help!

WOMEN'S LEADER

Quickly, women, let's take off our shirts too, because we've got to smell like women mad enough to bite! (*remove their shirts*)

WOMEN'S CHORUS

All right now, someone attack me:
he'll eat no more garlic
and chew no more beans.
If you so much as curse at me, I'll boil over with such rage,

68 These paintings, commissioned in mid-century, adorned the Stoa Poikile and the Theseum, cf. Pausanias 1.15, 17.

69 Legend had it that the Amazons (like the Persians) once invaded Attica and occupied the Acropolis, and were routed by the Athenians in battle.

αἰετὸν τίκτοντα κάνθαρός σε μαιεύσομαι.

ΚΟΡΥΦΑΙΑ

οὐ γὰρ ὑμῶν φροντίσαιμ᾽ ἄν, ἣν ἐμοὶ ζῇ Λαμπιτὼ
ἥ τε Θηβαία φίλη παῖς εὐγενὴς Ἰσμηνία.
οὐ γὰρ ἔσται δύναμις, οὐδ᾽ ἢν ἑπτάκις σὺ ψηφίσῃ,
ὅστις, ὦ δύστην᾽, ἀπήχθου πᾶσι καὶ τοῖς γείτοσιν.
ὥστε κἀχθὲς θἠκάτῃ ποιοῦσα παιγνίαν ἐγὼ
ταῖσι παισὶ τὴν ἑταίραν ἐκάλεσ᾽ ἐκ τῶν γειτόνων,
παῖδα χρηστὴν κἀγαπητὴν ἐκ Βοιωτῶν ἔγχελυν,
οἱ δὲ πέμψειν οὐκ ἔφασκον διὰ τὰ σὰ ψηφίσματα.
κοὐχὶ μὴ παύσησθε τῶν ψηφισμάτων τούτων, πρὶν ἂν
τοῦ σκέλους ὑμᾶς λαβών τις ἐκτραχηλίσῃ φέρων.
ἄνασσα πράγους τοῦδε καὶ βουλεύματος,
τί μοι σκυθρωπὸς ἐξελήλυθας δόμων;

ΛΥΣΙΣΤΡΑΤΗ

κακῶν γυναικῶν ἔργα καὶ θήλεια φρὴν
ποιεῖ μ᾽ ἀθυμεῖν περιπατεῖν τ᾽ ἄνω κάτω.

ΚΟΡΥΦΑΙΑ

τί φῄς; τί φῄς;

ΛΥΣΙΣΤΡΑΤΗ

ἀληθῆ, ἀληθῆ.

---

[70] In Aesop's Fable 3, the beetle avenges a wrong done it by an eagle by breaking the eagle's eggs; these had been placed in Zeus' lap for safekeeping, but when the beetle dropped dung into Zeus' lap, he unthinkingly jumped up and spilled the eggs. Here there is an implied threat to the men's testicles.

I'll be the beetle midwife to your eagle's eggs.[70]

WOMEN'S LEADER

You men don't worry me a bit, not while my Lampito lives and my Ismenia, the noble Theban girl. You'll have no power to do anything about us, not even if you pass a decree seven times: that's how much everyone hates you, you sad sack, and especially our neighbors. Why, just yesterday I threw a party for the girls in honor of Hecate,[71] and I invited my friend from next door, a fine girl who's very special to me: an eel from Boeotia.[72] But they said they wouldn't let her come because of your decrees. And you'll never, ever stop passing these decrees until someone grabs you by the leg, throws you away, and breaks your neck! (*She makes a grab for the Men's Leader's leg.*)

Enter LYSISTRATA *from the Acropolis.*

O mistress of this venture and stratagem,
why come you from the palace so dour of mien?[73]

LYSISTRATA

The deeds of ignoble women and the female heart
do make me pace dispirited to and fro.

WOMEN'S LEADER

What say you? What say you?

LYSISTRATA

'Tis true, too true!

[71] See 64 n.

[72] See 36 n.

[73] Lines 706–17 (except 715) are tragic pastiche.

ΚΟΡΥΦΑΙΑ

τί δ᾽ ἐστὶ δεινόν; φράζε ταῖς σαυτῆς φίλαις.

ΛΥΣΙΣΤΡΑΤΗ

ἀλλ᾽ αἰσχρὸν εἰπεῖν καὶ σιωπῆσαι βαρύ.

ΚΟΡΥΦΑΙΑ

μή νύν με κρύψῃς ὅ τι πεπόνθαμεν κακόν.

ΛΥΣΙΣΤΡΑΤΗ

βινητιῶμεν, ᾗ βράχιστον τοῦ λόγου.

ΚΟΡΥΦΑΙΑ

ἰὼ Ζεῦ.

ΛΥΣΙΣΤΡΑΤΗ

τί Ζῆν᾽ ἀυτεῖς; ταῦτα δ᾽ οὖν οὕτως ἔχει.
ἐγὼ μὲν οὖν αὐτὰς ἀποσχεῖν οὐκέτι
οἵα τ᾽ ἀπὸ τῶν ἀνδρῶν· διαδιδράσκουσι γάρ.
τὴν μέν γε πρώτην διαλέγουσαν τὴν ὀπὴν
κατέλαβον ᾗ τοῦ Πανός ἐστι ταὐλίον,
τὴν δ᾽ ἐκ τροχιλείας αὖ κατειλυσπωμένην,
τὴν δ᾽ αὐτομολοῦσαν· τὴν δ᾽ ἐπὶ στρούθου μίαν
ἤδη πέτεσθαι διανοουμένην κάτω
εἰς Ὀρσιλόχου χθὲς τῶν τριχῶν κατέσπασα.
πάσας τε προφάσεις ὥστ᾽ ἀπελθεῖν οἴκαδε
ἕλκουσιν. ἡδὶ γοῦν τις αὐτῶν ἔρχεται.
αὕτη σύ, ποῖ θεῖς;

---

[74] For Pan see 2 n. This grotto, on the northern slope of the Acropolis, was where Apollo raped the Athenian princess Creusa;

WOMEN'S LEADER

What dire thing? Pray tell it to your friends.

LYSISTRATA

'Tis shame to say and grief to leave unsaid.

WOMEN'S LEADER

Hide not from me the damage we have taken.

LYSISTRATA

The story in briefest compass: we need a fuck!

WOMEN'S LEADER

Ah, Zeus!

LYSISTRATA

Why rend the air for Zeus? Anyway, that's the way it is. The truth is, I can't keep them away from their husbands any longer; they're running off in all directions. The first one I caught was over there by Pan's Grotto,[74] excavating the hole; yet another was trying to escape by clambering down a pulley cable. And yesterday another one mounted a sparrow[75] and was about to fly off to Orsilochus' house[76] when I pulled her off by her hair. They're coming up with every kind of excuse to go home.

FIRST WIFE rushes from the Acropolis.

Hey you! What's your hurry?

the resulting child, Ion, became the ancestor of the Ionian peoples.

75 Sparrows were emblematic of sexual appetite and eaten as aphrodisiacs, and "sparrow" was a slang term for both penis and vagina.

76 Evidently a ladies' man, otherwise unknown.

ΓΥΝΗ Α

οἴκαδ᾽ ἐλθεῖν βούλομαι.
οἴκοι γάρ ἐστιν ἔριά μοι Μιλήσια
ὑπὸ τῶν σέων κατακοπτόμενα.

ΛΥΣΙΣΤΡΑΤΗ

ποίων σέων;
οὐκ εἶ πάλιν;

ΓΥΝΗ Α

ἀλλ᾽ ἥξω ταχέως νὴ τὼ θεώ,
ὅσον διαπετάσασ᾽ ἐπὶ τῆς κλίνης μόνον.

ΛΥΣΙΣΤΡΑΤΗ

μὴ διαπετάννυ, μηδ᾽ ἀπέλθῃς μηδαμῇ.

ΓΥΝΗ Α

ἀλλ᾽ ἐῶ ᾽πολέσθαι τἄρι᾽;

ΛΥΣΙΣΤΡΑΤΗ

ἢν τούτου δέῃ.

ΓΥΝΗ Β

τάλαιν᾽ ἐγώ, τάλαινα τῆς ἀμόργιδος,
ἣν ἄλοπον οἴκοι καταλέλοιφ᾽.

ΛΥΣΙΣΤΡΑΤΗ

αὕτη ᾽τέρα
ἐπὶ τὴν ἄμοργιν τὴν ἄλοπον ἐξέρχεται.
χώρει πάλιν δεῦρ᾽.

ΓΥΝΗ Β

ἀλλὰ νὴ τὴν Φωσφόρον
ἔγωγ᾽ ἀποδείρασ᾽ αὐτίκα μάλ᾽ ἀνέρχομαι.

LYSISTRATA

FIRST WIFE

I want to go home. I've got some Milesian woolens in the house, and the moths are chomping them all up.

LYSISTRATA

Moths indeed! Get back inside.

FIRST WIFE

By the Two Goddesses, I'll be right back; just let me spread them on the bed!

LYSISTRATA

Don't you spread anything, or go anywhere.

FIRST WIFE

So I'm supposed to let my woolens be wasted?

LYSISTRATA

If that's what it takes.

SECOND WIFE rushes from the Acropolis.

SECOND WIFE

Oh my god, my god, my flax! I forgot to shuck it when I left the house!

LYSISTRATA

Here's another one off to shuck her flax. March right back here.

SECOND WIFE

By our Lady of Light, I'll be back in a flash; just let me do a little shucking.

ΛΥΣΙΣΤΡΑΤΗ

μή, μὴ 'ποδείρῃς· ἢν γὰρ ἄρξῃς τουτουί,
ἑτέρα γυνὴ ταὐτὸν ποιεῖν βουλήσεται.

ΓΥΝΗ Γ

ὦ πότνι' Ἰλείθυ', ἐπίσχες τοῦ τόκου
ἕως ἂν εἰς ὅσιον μόλω 'γὼ χωρίον.

ΛΥΣΙΣΤΡΑΤΗ

τί ταῦτα ληρεῖς;

ΓΥΝΗ Γ

αὐτίκα μάλα τέξομαι.

ΛΥΣΙΣΤΡΑΤΗ

ἀλλ' οὐκ ἐκύεις σύ γ' ἐχθές.

ΓΥΝΗ Γ

ἀλλὰ τήμερον.
ἀλλ' οἴκαδέ μ' ὡς τὴν μαῖαν, ὦ Λυσιστράτη,
ἀπόπεμψον ὡς τάχιστα.

ΛΥΣΙΣΤΡΑΤΗ

τίνα λόγον λέγεις;
τί τοῦτ' ἔχεις τὸ σκληρόν;

ΓΥΝΗ Γ

ἄρρεν παιδίον.

ΛΥΣΙΣΤΡΑΤΗ

μὰ τὴν Ἀφροδίτην οὐ σύ γ' ἀλλ' ἢ χαλκίον

742 Ἰλείθυ' Coulon cl. titulis: Εἰλείθυ(ι)α vel Εἰλήθυ(ι)α a testt.

LYSISTRATA

No! No shucking! If *you* start doing it, some other wife will want to do the same.

THIRD WIFE rushes from the Acropolis.

THIRD WIFE

O Lady Hileithya, hold back the baby till I can get to a more profane spot![77]

LYSISTRATA

What are you raving about?

THIRD WIFE

I'm about to deliver a child!

LYSISTRATA

But you weren't pregnant yesterday.

THIRD WIFE

But today I am. Please, Lysistrata, send me home to the midwife, right away!

LYSISTRATA

What's the story? What's this thing you've got under there? It's hard.

THIRD WIFE

It's a boy.

LYSISTRATA

By Aphrodite, it's obvious you've got something metallic

[77] Childbirth, of which Hileithya (variously spelled) was the goddess, was forbidden in sanctuaries like the Acropolis.

ἔχειν τι φαίνει κοῖλον· εἴσομαι δ᾽ ἐγώ.
ὦ καταγέλαστ᾽, ἔχουσα τὴν ἱερὰν κυνῆν
κυεῖν ἔφασκες;

ΓΥΝΗ Γ

καὶ κυῶ γε νὴ Δία.

ΛΥΣΙΣΤΡΑΤΗ

τί δῆτα ταύτην εἶχες;

ΓΥΝΗ Γ

ἵνα μ᾽ εἰ καταλάβοι
ὁ τόκος ἔτ᾽ ἐν πόλει, τέκοιμ᾽ εἰς τὴν κυνῆν
εἰσβᾶσα ταύτην, ὥσπερ αἱ περιστεραί.

ΛΥΣΙΣΤΡΑΤΗ

τί λέγεις; προφασίζει· περιφανῆ τὰ πράγματα.
οὐ τἀμφιδρόμια τῆς κυνῆς αὐτοῦ μενεῖς;

ΓΥΝΗ Γ

ἀλλ᾽ οὐ δύναμαι ᾽γωγ᾽ οὐδὲ κοιμᾶσθ᾽ ἐν πόλει,
ἐξ οὗ τὸν ὄφιν εἶδον τὸν οἰκουρόν ποτε.

ΓΥΝΗ Δ

ἐγὼ δ᾽ ὑπὸ τῶν γλαυκῶν γε τάλαιν᾽ ἀπόλλυμαι
ταῖς ἀγρυπνίαισι κικκαβαζουσῶν ἀεί.

ΛΥΣΙΣΤΡΑΤΗ

ὦ δαιμόνιαι, παύσασθε τῶν τερατευμάτων.
ποθεῖτ᾽ ἴσως τοὺς ἄνδρας· ὑμᾶς δ᾽ οὐκ οἴει
ποθεῖν ἐκείνους; ἀργαλέας γ᾽ εὖ οἶδ᾽ ὅτι

763 ὑμᾶς Sommerstein: ἡμᾶς a

and hollow under there. Let's have a look. Ridiculous girl! You're big with the sacred helmet, not with child![78]

THIRD WIFE

But I *am* with child, I swear!

LYSISTRATA

Then what were you doing with this?

THIRD WIFE

Well, if I began to deliver here in the citadel, I could get into the helmet and have my baby there, like a pigeon.

LYSISTRATA

What kind of story is that? Excuses! It's quite obvious what's going on. You'll have to stay here till your—helmet has its naming day.

THIRD WIFE

But I can't even *sleep* on the Acropolis, ever since I saw the snake that guards the temple.

FOURTH WIFE rushes from the Acropolis.

FOURTH WIFE

And what about poor me—listening to the owls go *woo woo* all night is killing me!

LYSISTRATA

You nutty girls, enough of your horror stories! I guess you do miss your husbands; but do you think they don't miss you? They're spending some very rough nights, I assure

[78] That is, the helmet from the great bronze statue of Athena Promachus on the Acropolis.

ἄγουσι νύκτας. ἀλλ᾽ ἀνάσχεσθ᾽, ὦγαθαί,
καὶ προσταλαιπωρήσατ᾽ ἔτ᾽ ὀλίγον χρόνον·
ὡς χρησμὸς ἡμῖν ἐστιν ἐπικρατεῖν, ἐὰν
μὴ στασιάσωμεν. ἔστι δ᾽ ὁ χρησμὸς οὑτοσί.

ΓΥΝΗ Γ

λέγ᾽ αὐτὸν ἡμῖν ὅ τι λέγει.

ΛΥΣΙΣΤΡΑΤΗ

σιγᾶτε δή.
ἀλλ᾽ ὁπόταν πτήξωσι χελιδόνες εἰς ἕνα χῶρον,
τοὺς ἔποπας φεύγουσαι, ἀπόσχωνταί τε φαλήτων,
παῦλα κακῶν ἔσται, τὰ δ᾽ ὑπέρτερα νέρτερα θήσει
Ζεὺς ὑψιβρεμέτης—

ΓΥΝΗ Γ

ἐπάνω κατακεισόμεθ᾽ ἡμεῖς;

ΛΥΣΙΣΤΡΑΤΗ

ἢν δὲ διαστῶσιν καὶ ἀνάπτωνται πτερύγεσσιν
ἐξ ἱεροῦ ναοῖο χελιδόνες, οὐκέτι δόξει
ὄρνεον οὐδ᾽ ὁτιοῦν καταπυγωνέστερον εἶναι.

ΓΥΝΗ Γ

σαφής γ᾽ ὁ χρησμὸς νὴ Δί᾽. ὦ πάντες θεοί.

ΛΥΣΙΣΤΡΑΤΗ

μή νυν ἀπείπωμεν ταλαιπωρούμεναι,
ἀλλ᾽ εἰσίωμεν. καὶ γὰρ αἰσχρὸν τουτογί,
ὦ φίλταται, τὸν χρησμὸν εἰ προδώσομεν.

you. Just be patient, good ladies, and put up with this only a little bit longer. There's an oracle predicting victory for us, but only if we stick together. (*produces a scroll*) Here's the oracle right here.

THIRD WIFE

Tell us what it says.

LYSISTRATA

Be quiet, then.

> Yea, when the swallows hole up in a single home,
> fleeing the hoopoes[79] and leaving the phallus alone,
> then are their problems solved, and high-thundering
> Zeus
> shall reverse what's up and what's down—

THIRD WIFE

You mean *we'll* be lying on top?

LYSISTRATA

But:

> if the swallows begin to argue and fly away
> down from the citadel holy, all will say,
> no bird more disgustingly horny lives today!

THIRD WIFE

A pretty explicit oracle. Ye gods!

LYSISTRATA

Then let's not quit when the going is tough, but let's go back inside. Dear comrades, it would be a real shame if we betray the oracle.

All exit into the Acropolis.

[79] See *Birds* 15 n.

ΧΟΡΟΣ ΓΕΡΟΝΤΩΝ

(στρ) *μῦθον βούλομαι λέξαι τιν᾽ ὑμῖν, ὅν ποτ᾽ ἤκουσ᾽*
783 *αὐτὸς ἔτι παῖς ὤν.*
784/5 *οὕτως ἦν νεανίσκος Μελανίων τις,*
786/7 *ὃς φεύγων γάμον ἀφίκετ᾽ ἐς ἐρημίαν, κἀν*
788 *τοῖς ὄρεσιν ᾤκει·*
791 *καὶ κύνα τιν᾽ εἶχεν,*
789 *κᾆτ᾽ ἐλαγοθήρει*
790 *πλεξάμενος ἄρκυς,*
792 *κοὐκέτι κατῆλθε πάλιν οἴκαδ᾽ ὑπὸ μίσους.*
793/4 *οὕτω τὰς γυναῖκας ἐβδελύχθη*
795 *᾽κεῖνος, ἡμεῖς τ᾽ οὐδὲν ἧττον*
τοῦ Μελανίωνος, οἱ σώφρονες.

ΚΟΡΥΦΑΙΟΣ

βούλομαί σε, γραῦ, κύσαι—

ΚΟΡΥΦΑΙΑ

κρομμύων γ᾽ ἄρ᾽ οὐκ ἔδει.

ΚΟΡΥΦΑΙΟΣ

κἀνατείνας λακτίσαι.

ΚΟΡΥΦΑΙΑ

800 *τὴν λόχμην πολλὴν φορεῖς.*

ΚΟΡΥΦΑΙΟΣ

καὶ Μυρωνίδης γὰρ ἦν
τραχὺς ἐντεῦθεν μελάμπυ-
γός τε τοῖς ἐχθροῖς ἅπασιν·

791 ante 789 (om. 790) S: del. Weise

MEN'S CHORUS

I want to tell you all a tale that once I heard
when but a lad.
In olden times lived a young man named Melanion.[80]
In flight from marriage he went off to the wilderness
and lived in the mountains
and kept a dog
and wove traps
and hunted rabbits;
but he never went home again because of his hatred.
That's how much he loathed women.
And, being wise, we loathe them just
as much as Melanion did.

MEN'S LEADER

I'd like to kiss you, old thing—

WOMEN'S LEADER

Then you'll lay off the onions!

MEN'S LEADER

and lift a leg to kick you!

WOMEN'S LEADER

That's a lot of bush you're sporting!

MEN'S LEADER

Well, Myronides too was bristly down there,
and hairy-arsed to all his enemies;

80 Melanion is best known for using the trick of the golden apples to win a footrace against the huntress-maiden Atalante and thus her hand in marriage; here the old men may refer to a version of the myth in which Melanion was celibate and Atalante his divine companion, like Hippolytus and Artemis in Euripides' play *Hippolytus*.

ὧς δὲ καὶ Φορμίων.

ΧΟΡΟΣ ΓΥΝΑΙΚΩΝ

(ἀντ) κἀγὼ βούλομαι μῦθόν τιν' ὑμῖν ἀντιλέξαι
807 τῷ Μελανίωνι.
808/9 Τίμων ἦν τις ἀίδρυτος ἀβάτοισιν
810/1 ἐν σκώλοισι τὰ πρόσωπα περιειργμένος, Ἐ-
ρινύων ἀπορρώξ.
οὗτος οὖν ὁ Τίμων
814a ᾤχεθ' ὑπὸ μίσους
814b <εἰς τόπον ἔρημον>
πολλὰ καταρασάμενος ἀνδράσι πονηροῖς.
οὕτω 'κεῖνος ἡμῖν ἀντεμίσει
τοὺς πονηροὺς ἄνδρας ἀεί,
819/0 ταῖσι δὲ γυναιξὶν ἦν φίλτατος.

ΚΟΡΥΦΑΙΑ

τὴν γνάθον βούλει θένω;

ΚΟΡΥΦΑΙΟΣ

μηδαμῶς· ἔδεισά γε.

ΚΟΡΥΦΑΙΑ

ἀλλὰ κρούσω τῷ σκέλει;

ΚΟΡΥΦΑΙΟΣ

τὸν σάκανδρον ἐκφανεῖς.

ΚΟΡΥΦΑΙΑ

ἀλλ' ὅμως ἂν οὐκ ἴδοις

814 lacunam posuit Biset, suppl. Blaydes
817 ἡμῖν Bergk cl. Σ^R: ὑμῶν a

so too was Phormion.[81]

WOMEN'S CHORUS

I too want to tell you all a tale in reply
to your Melanion.
There once was a drifter named Timon,[82]
his visage girded by impregnable thorns,
an offshoot of the Furies.
So this Timon
wandered off because of his hatred
‹into a desolate place,›
constantly cursing the wickedness of men.
That's how much he joined us in loathing
wicked men, ever and always.
But he was a dear friend to women.

WOMEN'S LEADER

How would you like a punch in the mouth?

MEN'S LEADER

No no! You're really scaring me!

WOMEN'S LEADER

Then how about a good swift kick?

MEN'S LEADER

If you do you'll be flashing your twat!

WOMEN'S LEADER

Even so, old lady though I am,

[81] Two Athenian generals of the past, who were remembered for hardiness and courage.

[82] A legendary misanthrope, and a main character in several Greek comedies, who (despite the women's claim) is elsewhere said to have hated men and women alike.

καίπερ οὔσης γραὸς ὄντ᾽ αὐ-
τὸν κομήτην, ἀλλ᾽ ἀπεψι-
λωμένον τῷ λύχνῳ.

ΛΥΣΙΣΤΡΑΤΗ

ἰοὺ ἰού, γυναῖκες, ἴτε δεῦρ᾽ ὡς ἐμὲ
ταχέως.

ΓΥΝΗ

τί δ᾽ ἐστίν; εἰπέ μοι, τίς ἡ βοή;

ΛΥΣΙΣΤΡΑΤΗ

ἄνδρ᾽, <ἄνδρ᾽> ὁρῶ προσιόντα παραπεπληγμένον,
τοῖς τῆς Ἀφροδίτης ὀργίοις εἰλημμένον.
ὦ πότνια, Κύπρου καὶ Κυθήρων καὶ Πάφου
μεδέουσ᾽, ἴθ᾽ ὀρθὴν ἥνπερ ἔρχει τὴν ὁδόν.

ΓΥΝΗ

ποῦ δ᾽ ἐστίν, ὅστις ἐστί;

ΛΥΣΙΣΤΡΑΤΗ

παρὰ τὸ τῆς Χλόης.

ΓΥΝΗ

ὢ νὴ Δί᾽ ἐστὶ δῆτα. τίς κἄστίν ποτε;

ΛΥΣΙΣΤΡΑΤΗ

ὁρᾶτε. γιγνώσκει τις ὑμῶν;

ΜΥΡΡΙΝΗ

νὴ Δία
ἔγωγε· κἄστιν οὑμὸς ἀνὴρ Κινησίας.

you'll never see it
long-haired, but depilated
with the lamp.

LYSISTRATA appears on the roof.

LYSISTRATA

Hurray! Ladies, come here, quickly!

MYRRHINE and several other Wives join Lysistrata.

WIFE

What is it? What's all the shouting?

LYSISTRATA

A man! I see a man coming this way, stricken, in the grip of Aphrodite's mysterious powers. Lady Aphrodite, mistress of Cyprus and Cythera and Paphos, let the path that you've embarked on be upright!

WIFE

Where is he, whoever he is?

LYSISTRATA

He's by Chloe's shrine.

WIFE

Oh yes, now I see him! But who is he?

LYSISTRATA

Take a good look. Anyone recognize him?

MYRRHINE

Oh God, I do. And it's my own husband, Cinesias!

ΛΥΣΙΣΤΡΑΤΗ

σὸν ἔργον ἤδη τοῦτον ὀπτᾶν καὶ στρέφειν
κἀξηπεροπεύειν καὶ φιλεῖν καὶ μὴ φιλεῖν,
καὶ πάνθ᾽ ὑπέχειν πλὴν ὧν σύνοιδεν ἡ κύλιξ.

ΜΥΡΡΙΝΗ

ἀμέλει, ποιήσω ταῦτ᾽ ἐγώ.

ΛΥΣΙΣΤΡΑΤΗ

καὶ μὴν ἐγὼ
ξυνηπεροπεύσω <σοὶ> παραμένουσ᾽ ἐνθαδί,
καὶ ξυσταθεύσω τοῦτον. ἀλλ᾽ ἀπέλθετε.

ΚΙΝΗΣΙΑΣ

οἴμοι κακοδαίμων, οἷος ὁ σπασμός μ᾽ ἔχει
χὠ τέτανος ὥσπερ ἐπὶ τροχοῦ στρεβλούμενον.

ΛΥΣΙΣΤΡΑΤΗ

τίς οὗτος οὑντὸς τῶν φυλάκων ἑστώς;

ΚΙΝΗΣΙΑΣ

ἐγώ.

ΛΥΣΙΣΤΡΑΤΗ

ἀνήρ;

ΚΙΝΗΣΙΑΣ

ἀνὴρ δῆτ᾽.

ΛΥΣΙΣΤΡΑΤΗ

οὐκ ἄπει δῆτ᾽ ἐκποδών;

ΚΙΝΗΣΙΑΣ

σὺ δ᾽ εἶ τίς ἡκβάλλουσά μ᾽;

LYSISTRATA

Then it's your job to roast him, to torture him, to bamboozle him, to love him and not to love him, and to give him anything he wants, except what you and our wine cup know about.

MYRRHINE

Don't you worry, I'll do it!

LYSISTRATA

And I'll stick around to help you bamboozle and roast him. Now everyone get out of sight!

Exit Wives, enter CINESIAS *with Manes, who holds a baby.*

CINESIAS

Oh, oh, evil fate! I've got terrible spasms and cramps. It's like I'm being broken on the rack!

LYSISTRATA

Who goes there, poking up within our defense perimeter?

CINESIAS

Me.

LYSISTRATA

A man?

CINESIAS

(*brandishing his phallus*): Of course a man!

LYSISTRATA

In that case clear out of here!

CINESIAS

And who are you to throw me out?

ΛΥΣΙΣΤΡΑΤΗ

ἡμεροσκόπος.

ΚΙΝΗΣΙΑΣ

πρὸς τῶν θεῶν νυν ἐκκάλεσόν μοι Μυρρίνην.

ΛΥΣΙΣΤΡΑΤΗ

ἰδοὺ καλέσω ᾽γὼ Μυρρίνην σοι; σὺ δὲ τίς εἶ;

ΚΙΝΗΣΙΑΣ

ἀνὴρ ἐκείνης, Παιονίδης Κινησίας.

ΛΥΣΙΣΤΡΑΤΗ

ὦ χαῖρε φίλτατ᾽· οὐ γὰρ ἀκλεὲς τοὔνομα
τὸ σὸν παρ᾽ ἡμῖν ἐστιν οὐδ᾽ ἀνώνυμον.
ἀεὶ γὰρ ἡ γυνή σ᾽ ἔχει διὰ στόμα.
κἂν ᾠὸν ἢ μῆλον λάβῃ, "Κινησίᾳ
τουτὶ γένοιτο," φησίν.

ΚΙΝΗΣΙΑΣ

ὦ πρὸς τῶν θεῶν—

ΛΥΣΙΣΤΡΑΤΗ

νὴ τὴν Ἀφροδίτην· κἂν περὶ ἀνδρῶν γ᾽ ἐμπέσῃ
λόγος τις, εἴρηκ᾽ εὐθέως ἡ σὴ γυνὴ
ὅτι λῆρός ἐστι τἄλλα πρὸς Κινησίαν.

ΚΙΝΗΣΙΑΣ

ἴθι νυν κάλεσον αὐτήν.

ΛΥΣΙΣΤΡΑΤΗ

τί οὖν; δώσεις τί μοι;

LYSISTRATA

The daytime sentry.

CINESIAS

Then in the gods' name call Myrrhine out here to me.

LYSISTRATA

Listen to him, "call Myrrhine"! And who might you be?

CINESIAS

Her husband, Cinesias, from Paeonidae.[83]

LYSISTRATA

Well hello, darling! Among us *your* name is hardly unknown or unmentioned. Your wife always has you on her lips; she'll be eating an egg or an apple and she'll say, "This one's for Cinesias."

CINESIAS

Oh gods!

LYSISTRATA

Aphrodite be my witness! And whenever the conversation turns to men, your wife speaks right up and says, "Compared with Cinesias, all the rest are trash!"

CINESIAS

Come on now, call her out!

LYSISTRATA

Ahem. Got anything for me?

83 Possibly the poet Cinesias (an uncommon name) caricatured in *Birds*, but the name was more likely chosen for the pun on *kinein* "screw," just as the deme name Paeonidae reminds us of *paiein* "bang."

ΚΙΝΗΣΙΑΣ

ἔγωγέ <σοι> νὴ τὸν Δί', ἤν βούλῃ γε σύ.
ἔχω δὲ τοῦθ᾽· ὅπερ οὖν ἔχω, δίδωμί σοι.

ΛΥΣΙΣΤΡΑΤΗ

φέρε νυν καλέσω καταβᾶσά σοι.

ΚΙΝΗΣΙΑΣ

ταχύ νυν πάνυ·
ὡς οὐδεμίαν ἔχω γε τῷ βίῳ χάριν,
ἐξ οὗπερ αὕτη 'ξῆλθεν ἐκ τῆς οἰκίας,
ἀλλ᾽ ἄχθομαι μὲν εἰσιών, ἔρημα δὲ
εἶναι δοκεῖ μοι πάντα, τοῖς δὲ σιτίοις
χάριν οὐδεμίαν οἶδ᾽ ἐσθίων. ἔστυκα γάρ.

ΜΥΡΡΙΝΗ

φιλῶ φιλῶ 'γὼ τοῦτον· ἀλλ᾽ οὐ βούλεται
ὑπ᾽ ἐμοῦ φιλεῖσθαι. σὺ δέ με τούτῳ μὴ κάλει.

ΚΙΝΗΣΙΑΣ

ὦ γλυκύτατον Μυρρινίδιον, τί ταῦτα δρᾷς;
κατάβηθι δεῦρο.

ΜΥΡΡΙΝΗ

μὰ Δί' ἐγὼ μὲν αὐτόσ᾽ οὔ.

ΚΙΝΗΣΙΑΣ

ἐμοῦ καλοῦντος οὐ καταβήσει Μυρρίνη;

ΜΥΡΡΙΝΗ

οὐ γὰρ δεόμενος οὐδὲν ἐκκαλεῖς ἐμέ.

ΚΙΝΗΣΙΑΣ

ἐγὼ οὐ δεόμενος; ἐπιτετριμμένος μὲν οὖν.

CINESIAS

(*Indicating his phallus*): Indeed I do, if you want it. Then what about this? (*tossing her a purse*) It's all I've got, and you're welcome to it.

LYSISTRATA

All right, I'll go down and call her for you.

LYSISTRATA leaves the ramparts.

CINESIAS

Make it quick, now! (*alone*) I've had no joy or pleasure in my life since the day she left my home. I go into the house and feel agony; everything looks empty to me; I get no pleasure from the food I eat. Because I'm horny!

MYRRHINE appears on the ramparts.

MYRRHINE

I love that man, I love him! But he doesn't want my love. Please don't make me go out to him!

CINESIAS

Myrrhinikins, dearest, why are you doing this? Come down here!

MYRRHINE

I'm positively not going down there!

CINESIAS

You won't come down when I ask you, Myrrhine?

MYRRHINE

You're asking me, but you don't really want me.

CINESIAS

Me not want you? Why, I'm in agony without you!

ΜΥΡΡΙΝΗ

ἄπειμι.

ΚΙΝΗΣΙΑΣ

μὴ δῆτ᾽, ἀλλὰ τῷ γοῦν παιδίῳ
ὑπάκουσον. οὗτος, οὐ καλεῖς τὴν μαμμίαν;

ΠΑΙΔΙΟΝ

μαμμία, μαμμία, μαμμία.

ΚΙΝΗΣΙΑΣ

αὕτη, τί πάσχεις; οὐδ᾽ ἐλεεῖς τὸ παιδίον
ἄλουτον ὂν κἄθηλον ἕκτην ἡμέραν;

ΜΥΡΡΙΝΗ

ἔγωγ᾽ ἐλεῶ δῆτ᾽· ἀλλ᾽ ἀμελὴς αὐτῷ πατήρ
ἐστιν.

ΚΙΝΗΣΙΑΣ

κατάβηθ᾽, ὦ δαιμονία, τῷ παιδίῳ.

ΜΥΡΡΙΝΗ

οἷον τὸ τεκεῖν. καταβατέον.

ΚΙΝΗΣΙΑΣ

τί γὰρ πάθω;
ἐμοὶ γὰρ αὕτη καὶ νεωτέρα δοκεῖ
πολλῷ γεγενῆσθαι κἀγανώτερον βλέπειν·
χἃ δυσκολαίνει πρὸς ἐμὲ καὶ βρενθύεται,
ταῦτ᾽ αὐτὰ δή ᾽σθ᾽ ἃ καί μ᾽ ἐπιτρίβει τῷ πόθῳ.

MYRRHINE

Goodbye.

CINESIAS

No, wait! At least listen to the baby. Come on you, yell for mommy!

BABY

Mommy! Mommy! Mommy!

CINESIAS

Hey, what's wrong with you? Don't you feel sorry for the baby, unwashed and unsuckled for six days already?

MYRRHINE

Him I feel sorry for; too bad his father doesn't care about him.

CINESIAS

Come down here, you screwy woman, and see to your child!

MYRRHINE

How momentous is motherhood! I have to go down there.

MYRRHINE disappears from the roof.

CINESIAS

(*to the spectators*) What choice do I have? Yes, she seems much younger than I remember, and has a sexier look in her eyes. And the way she acted prickly to me and very stuck-up, that's exactly what makes me want her even more!

Enter MYRRHINE from the Acropolis gates.

ΜΥΡΡΙΝΗ

ὦ γλυκύτατον σὺ τεκνίδιον κακοῦ πατρός,
φέρε σε φιλήσω, γλυκύτατον τῇ μαμμίᾳ.

ΚΙΝΗΣΙΑΣ

τί, ὦ πονήρα, ταῦτα ποιεῖς χἀτέραις
πείθει γυναιξί; κἀμέ τ' ἄχθεσθαι ποιεῖς
αὐτή τε λυπεῖ.

ΜΥΡΡΙΝΗ

μὴ πρόσαγε τὴν χεῖρά μοι.

ΚΙΝΗΣΙΑΣ

τὰ δ' ἔνδον ὄντα τἀμὰ καὶ σὰ χρήματα
χεῖρον διατίθης.

ΜΥΡΡΙΝΗ

ὀλίγον αὐτῶν μοι μέλει.

ΚΙΝΗΣΙΑΣ

ὀλίγον μέλει σοι τῆς κρόκης φορουμένης
ὑπὸ τῶν ἀλεκτρυόνων;

ΜΥΡΡΙΝΗ

ἔμοιγε νὴ Δία.

ΚΙΝΗΣΙΑΣ

τὰ τῆς Ἀφροδίτης ἱέρ' ἀνοργίαστά σοι
χρόνον τοσοῦτόν ἐστιν. οὐ βαδιεῖ πάλιν;

ΜΥΡΡΙΝΗ

μὰ Δί' οὐκ ἔγωγ', ἢν μὴ διαλλαχθῆτέ γε
καὶ τοῦ πολέμου παύσησθε.

MYRRHINE

My sweetie, my bitty baby, that's got such a bad father, let me give you a kiss, mommy's little dearest!

CINESIAS

What do you think you're doing, you naughty girl, listening to those other women and giving me a hard time and hurting yourself as well?

MYRRHINE

Don't you lay your hands on me!

CINESIAS

You know you've let our house, your things and mine, become an utter mess?

MYRRHINE

It doesn't bother me.

CINESIAS

It doesn't bother you that the hens are pulling your woolens apart?

MYRRHINE

Not a bit.

CINESIAS

And what a long time it's been since you've celebrated Aphrodite's holy mysteries. Won't you come home?

MYRRHINE

I certainly will not, not until you men agree to a settlement and stop the war.

ΚΙΝΗΣΙΑΣ

τοιγάρ, ἢν δοκῇ,
ποιήσομεν καὶ ταῦτα.

ΜΥΡΡΙΝΗ

τοιγάρ, ἢν δοκῇ,
κἄγωγ᾽ ἄπειμ᾽ ἐκεῖσε· νῦν δ᾽ ἀπομώμοκα.

ΚΙΝΗΣΙΑΣ

σὺ δ᾽ ἀλλὰ κατακλίνηθι μετ᾽ ἐμοῦ διὰ χρόνου.

ΜΥΡΡΙΝΗ

οὐ δῆτα· καίτοι σ᾽ οὐκ ἐρῶ γ᾽ ὡς οὐ φιλῶ.

ΚΙΝΗΣΙΑΣ

φιλεῖς; τί οὖν οὐ κατεκλίνης, ὦ Μύρριον;

ΜΥΡΡΙΝΗ

ὦ καταγέλαστ᾽, ἐναντίον τοῦ παιδίου;

ΚΙΝΗΣΙΑΣ

μὰ Δί᾽ ἀλλὰ τοῦτό γ᾽ οἴκαδ᾽, ὦ Μανῆ, φέρε.
ἰδοὺ τὸ μέν σοι παιδίον καὶ δὴ ᾽κποδών·
σὺ δ᾽ οὐ κατακλινεῖ;

ΜΥΡΡΙΝΗ

ποῦ γὰρ ἄν τις καί, τάλαν,
δράσειε τοῦθ᾽;

ΚΙΝΗΣΙΑΣ

ὅπου; τὸ τοῦ Πανὸς καλόν.

ΜΥΡΡΙΝΗ

καὶ πῶς ἔθ᾽ ἁγνὴ δῆτ᾽ ἀνέλθοιμ᾽ εἰς πόλιν;

CINESIAS
All right, if that's what's decided, then that's what we'll do.

MYRRHINE
All right, if that's what's decided, then I'll be coming home. But meanwhile I've sworn to stay here.

CINESIAS
But at least lie down with me; it's been so long.

MYRRHINE
No, I won't. But I'm not saying I don't love you.

CINESIAS
You love me? Then why not lie down, Myrrie?

MYRRHINE
You must be joking! Right here in front of the baby?

CINESIAS
Of course not! Manes, take it home.

Exit Manes.

There you are, the kid's out of the way. Won't you lie down?

MYRRHINE
But my dear, just where could a person do it?

CINESIAS
Where? Pan's Grotto[84] will do fine.

MYRRHINE
But how could I go back up to the Acropolis no longer pure?

[84] See 721 n.

ΚΙΝΗΣΙΑΣ

κάλλιστα δήπου, λουσαμένη τῇ Κλεψύδρᾳ.

ΜΥΡΡΙΝΗ

ἔπειτ᾽ ὀμόσασα δῆτ᾽ ἐπιορκήσω, τάλαν;

ΚΙΝΗΣΙΑΣ

εἰς ἐμὲ τράποιτο· μηδὲν ὅρκου φροντίσῃς.

ΜΥΡΡΙΝΗ

φέρε νυν ἐνέγκω κλινίδιον νῷν.

ΚΙΝΗΣΙΑΣ

μηδαμῶς·
ἀρκεῖ χαμαὶ νῷν.

ΜΥΡΡΙΝΗ

μὰ τὸν Ἀπόλλω, μή σ᾽ ἐγὼ
καίπερ τοιοῦτον ὄντα κατακλινῶ χαμαί.

ΚΙΝΗΣΙΑΣ

ἥ τοι γυνὴ φιλεῖ με, δήλη ᾽στὶν καλῶς.

ΜΥΡΡΙΝΗ

ἰδού, κατάκεισ᾽ ἀνύσας τι, κἀγὼ ᾽κδύομαι.
καίτοι, τὸ δεῖνα, ψίαθός ἐστ᾽ ἐξοιστέα.

ΚΙΝΗΣΙΑΣ

ποία ψίαθος; μή μοί γε.

ΜΥΡΡΙΝΗ

νὴ τὴν Ἄρτεμιν,
αἰσχρὸν γὰρ ἐπὶ τόνου γε.

CINESIAS

Very easily done: just wash off in the Clepsydra.[85]

MYRRHINE

You're telling me, dear, that I should break the oath I swore?

CINESIAS

Let that be on my head; don't you worry about any oath.

MYRRHINE

All right then, let me fetch us a bed.

CINESIAS

Nothing doing; the ground will serve for us.

MYRRHINE

Apollo no! I wouldn't dream of letting you lie on the ground, no matter what kind of man you are.

Myrrhine goes into Pan's Grotto.

CINESIAS

You know, she really loves me, that's quite obvious!

MYRRHINE

(*returning with a cot*) There we are! Lie right down while I undress. But wait, um, yes, a mattress! Must go get one.

CINESIAS

What do you mean, a mattress? No thanks.

MYRRHINE

By Artemis, it's nasty on cords.

85 A spring on the northwest slope of the Acropolis.

ΚΙΝΗΣΙΑΣ

δός μοί νυν κύσαι.

ΜΥΡΡΙΝΗ

ἰδού.

ΚΙΝΗΣΙΑΣ

παπαιάξ. ἧκέ νυν ταχέως πάνυ.

ΜΥΡΡΙΝΗ

ἰδοὺ ψίαθος. κατάκεισο, καὶ δὴ 'κδύομαι.
καίτοι, τὸ δεῖνα, προσκεφάλαιον οὐκ ἔχεις.

ΚΙΝΗΣΙΑΣ

ἀλλ' οὐδὲ δέομ' ἔγωγε.

ΜΥΡΡΙΝΗ

νὴ Δί' ἀλλ' ἐγώ.

ΚΙΝΗΣΙΑΣ

ἀλλ' ἦ τὸ πέος τόδ' Ἡρακλῆς ξενίζεται;

ΜΥΡΡΙΝΗ

ἀνίστασ', ἀναπήδησον. ἤδη πάντ' ἔχω;

ΚΙΝΗΣΙΑΣ

ἅπαντα δῆτα. δεῦρό νυν, ὦ χρυσίον.

ΜΥΡΡΙΝΗ

τὸ στρόφιον ἤδη λύομαι. μέμνησό νυν·
μή μ' ἐξαπατήσῃς τὰ περὶ τῶν διαλλαγῶν.

CINESIAS

Well then, give me a kiss.

MYRRHINE

There.

CINESIAS

Oh lordy! Get the mattress quick!

MYRRHINE

(*returning with a mattress*) There we are! Lie back down and I'll get my clothes off. But wait, um, a pillow, you haven't got a pillow!

CINESIAS

But I don't need one!

MYRRHINE

But I do!

CINESIAS

Is this cock of mine supposed to be Heracles waiting for his dinner?[86]

MYRRHINE

(*returning with a pillow*) Lift up now, upsy daisy. There, is that everything?

CINESIAS

Everything for sure. Now come here, my little treasure!

MYRRHINE

I'm just getting my breastband off. But remember: don't break your promise about a peace settlement.

86 Heracles was portrayed in myths as having a huge appetite for food and sex.

ΚΙΝΗΣΙΑΣ

νὴ Δί᾽ ἀπολοίμην.

ΜΥΡΡΙΝΗ

ἀλλὰ σισύραν οὐκ ἔχεις.

ΚΙΝΗΣΙΑΣ

μὰ Δί᾽ οὐδὲ δέομαί γ᾽, ἀλλὰ βινεῖν βούλομαι.

ΜΥΡΡΙΝΗ

ἀμέλει, ποιήσεις τοῦτο· ταχὺ γὰρ ἔρχομαι.

ΚΙΝΗΣΙΑΣ

ἄνθρωπος ἐπιτρίψει με διὰ τὰ στρώματα.

ΜΥΡΡΙΝΗ

ἔπαιρε σαυτόν.

ΚΙΝΗΣΙΑΣ

ἀλλ᾽ ἐπῆρται τουτογί.

ΜΥΡΡΙΝΗ

βούλει μυρίσω σε;

ΚΙΝΗΣΙΑΣ

μὰ τὸν Ἀπόλλω μή μέ γε.

ΜΥΡΡΙΝΗ

νὴ τὴν Ἀφροδίτην, ἤν τε βούλῃ γ᾽ ἤν τε μή.

ΚΙΝΗΣΙΑΣ

εἴθ᾽ ἐκχυθείη τὸ μύρον, ὦ Ζεῦ δέσποτα.

ΜΥΡΡΙΝΗ

πρότεινε δὴ τὴν χεῖρα κἀλείφου λαβών.

CINESIAS

So help me Zeus, I hope to die if I do!

MYRRHINE

You don't have a blanket.

CINESIAS

It's not a blanket I want—I want a fuck!

MYRRHINE

Don't worry, that's just what you're going to get. I'll be back in a flash.

CINESIAS

That woman will drive me nuts with all her bedding!

MYRRHINE

(*returning with a blanket*): Get up.

CINESIAS

I've already got it up!

MYRRHINE

Want some scent?

CINESIAS

Apollo no, none for me.

MYRRHINE

But I will, so help me Aphrodite, whether you like it or not.

CINESIAS

Then let the scent flow! Lord Zeus!

MYRRHINE

(*returning with a round bottle of perfume*) Hold out your hand. Take some and rub it in.

ΚΙΝΗΣΙΑΣ

οὐχ ἡδὺ τὸ μύρον μὰ τὸν Ἀπόλλω τουτογί,
εἰ μὴ διατριπτικόν γε κοὐκ ὄζον γάμων.

ΜΥΡΡΙΝΗ

τάλαιν' ἐγώ, τὸ Ῥόδιον ἤνεγκον μύρον.

ΚΙΝΗΣΙΑΣ

ἀγαθόν· ἔα αὔτ', ὦ δαιμονία.

ΜΥΡΡΙΝΗ

λῃρεῖς ἔχων.

ΚΙΝΗΣΙΑΣ

κάκιστ' ἀπόλοιθ' ὁ πρῶτος ἑψήσας μύρον.

ΜΥΡΡΙΝΗ

λαβὲ τόνδε τὸν ἀλάβαστον.

ΚΙΝΗΣΙΑΣ

ἀλλ' ἕτερον ἔχω.
ἀλλ' ᾠζυρά, κατάκεισο καὶ μή μοι φέρε
μηδέν.

ΜΥΡΡΙΝΗ

ποιήσω ταῦτα νὴ τὴν Ἄρτεμιν.
ὑπολύομαι γοῦν. ἀλλ' ὅπως, ὦ φίλτατε,
σπονδὰς ποιεῖσθαι ψηφιεῖ.

ΚΙΝΗΣΙΑΣ

βουλεύσομαι.
ἀπολώλεκέν με κἀπιτέτριφεν ἡ γυνὴ
τά τ' ἄλλα πάντα κἀποδείρασ' οἴχεται.

CINESIAS

I really dislike this scent; it takes a long time warming up and it doesn't smell conjugal.

MYRRHINE

Oh silly me, I brought the Rhodian scent![87]

CINESIAS

It's fine! Let it go, you screwy woman!

MYRRHINE

What are you babbling about?

CINESIAS

Goddamn the man who first decocted scent!

MYRRHINE

(*returning with a long, cylindrical bottle*) Here, try this tube.

CINESIAS

I've got one of my own! Now lie down, you witch, and don't bring me anything more.

MYRRHINE

That's what I'll do, so help me Artemis; I'm just getting my shoes off. But remember, darling, you're going to vote for peace.

MYRRHINE dashes into the Acropolis.

CINESIAS

I'll give it serious consideration. (*finding Myrrhine gone*) The woman's destroyed me, annihilated me! Not only that: she's pumped me up and dropped me flat!

[87] Why this was a mistake is unclear.

οἴμοι τί πάθω; τίνα βινήσω,
τῆς καλλίστης πασῶν ψευσθείς;
πῶς ταυτηνὶ παιδοτροφήσω;
ποῦ Κυναλώπηξ;
μίσθωσόν μοι τὴν τίτθην.

ΚΟΡΥΦΑΙΟΣ

ἐν δεινῷ γ᾽, ὦ δύστηνε, κακῷ
τείρει ψυχὴν ἐξαπατηθείς.
κἄγωγ᾽ οἰκτίρω σ᾽· αἰαῖ.
ποῖος γὰρ νέφρος ἂν ἀντίσχοι,
ποία ψυχή, ποῖοι δ᾽ ὄρχεις,
ποία δ᾽ ὀσφύς, ποῖος δ᾽ ὄρρος
κατατεινόμενος
καὶ μὴ βινῶν τοὺς ὄρθρους;

ΚΙΝΗΣΙΑΣ

ὦ Ζεῦ, δεινῶν ἀντισπασμῶν.

ΚΟΡΥΦΑΙΟΣ

ταυτὶ μέντοι νυνί σ᾽ ἐποίησ᾽
ἡ παμβδελύρα καὶ παμμυσάρα.

ΚΙΝΗΣΙΑΣ

μὰ Δί᾽ ἀλλὰ φίλη καὶ παγγλυκέρα.

ΚΟΡΥΦΑΙΟΣ

ποία γλυκερά; μιαρὰ μιαρά.

ΚΙΝΗΣΙΑΣ

<μιαρὰ μιαρα> δῆτ᾽, ὦ Ζεῦ Ζεῦ.

Ah, what shall I do? Whom shall I screw,
cheated of the loveliest of them all!
How will I raise and rear this orphaned cock?
Is Fox Dog[88] out there anywhere?
Lease me a nursemaid!

MEN'S LEADER

Yes, frightful agony, you wretch,
does rack the soul of one so sore bediddled.
Sure I do feel for you, alas!
What kidney could bear it,
what soul, what balls,
what loins, what crotch,
thus stretched on the rack
and never getting a morning fuck?

CINESIAS

Ah Zeus! The cramps attack anew!

MEN'S LEADER

And this is what she's done to you,
the detestable, revolting shrew!

CINESIAS

No, she's totally sweet and dear!

MEN'S LEADER

Sweet, you say! She's vile, vile!

CINESIAS

Yes, vile, vile! O Zeus, Zeus,

[88] The nickname of the pimp or brothel keeper Philostratus, cf. *Knights* 1069.

---

972 suppl. Beer

εἴθ᾽ αὐτὴν ὥσπερ τοὺς θωμοὺς
μεγάλῳ τυφῷ καὶ πρηστῆρι
ξυστρέψας καὶ ξυγγογγύλας
οἴχοιο φέρων, εἶτα μεθείης,
ἡ δὲ φέροιτ᾽ αὖ πάλιν εἰς τὴν γῆν,
κᾆτ᾽ ἐξαίφνης
περὶ τὴν ψωλὴν περιβαίη.

ΚΗΡΥΞ

πᾷ τᾶν Ἀσανᾶν ἐστιν ἁ γερωχία
ἢ τοὶ πρυτάνιες; λῶ τι μυσίξαι νέον.

ΚΙΝΗΣΙΑΣ

σὺ δ᾽ εἶ τί; πότερ᾽ ἄνθρωπος ἢ Κονίσαλος;

ΚΗΡΥΞ

κᾶρυξ ἐγών, ὦ κυρσάνιε, ναὶ τὼ σιὼ
ἔμολον ἀπὸ Σπάρτας περὶ τᾶν διαλλαγᾶν.

ΚΙΝΗΣΙΑΣ

κἄπειτα δόρυ δῆθ᾽ ὑπὸ μάλης ἥκεις ἔχων;

ΚΗΡΥΞ

οὐ τὸν Δί᾽ οὐκ ἐγώνγα.

ΚΙΝΗΣΙΑΣ

ποῖ μεταστρέφει;
τί δὴ προβάλλει τὴν χλαμύδ᾽; ἦ βουβωνιᾷς
ὑπὸ τῆς ὁδοῦ;

975 ξυγγογγύλας Cobet: ξυγγογγυλίσας a
984 περὶ τᾶν δ.] δ. πέρι van Herwerden

please hit her like a heap of grain
with a great tornado and firestorm,
sweeping her up and twirling her
into the sky, and then let go
and let her fall back down to earth again,
to land smack dab
on the point of my hard-on!

Enter HERALD.

HERALD[89]

Where be the Senate of Athens or the Prytanies? I wish to tell them some news.

CINESIAS

And what might you be? Are you human? Or a Conisalus?[90]

HERALD

By the Twain, I'm a Herald, youngun, come from Sparta about the settlement.

CINESIAS

And that's why you've come hiding a spear in your clothes?

HERALD

I'm not, I swear!

CINESIAS

Why are you twisting away from me? And why hold your coat out in front of you? Got a swollen groin from the long ride, maybe?

[89] On the Spartan Herald's dialect see 81 n.
[90] A demon or divinity associated with ithyphallic dances.

ΚΗΡΥΞ

ἀλεός γα ναὶ τὸν Κάστορα
ὤνθρωπος.

ΚΙΝΗΣΙΑΣ

ἀλλ᾽ ἔστυκας, ὦ μιαρώτατε.

ΚΗΡΥΞ

οὐ τὸν Δί᾽ οὐκ ἐγώνγα· μηδ᾽ αὖ πλαδδίη,

ΚΙΝΗΣΙΑΣ

τί δ᾽ ἐστί σοι τοδί;

ΚΗΡΥΞ

σκυτάλα Λακωνικά.

ΚΙΝΗΣΙΑΣ

εἴπερ γε, χαὔτη ᾽στὶ σκυτάλη Λακωνική.
ἀλλ᾽ ὡς πρὸς εἰδότ᾽ ἐμὲ σὺ τἀληθῆ λέγε.
τί τὰ πράγμαθ᾽ ὑμῖν ἐστι τἀν Λακεδαίμονι;

ΚΗΡΥΞ

ὀρσὰ Λακεδαίμων πᾶἁ καὶ τοὶ σύμμαχοι
ἅπαντες ἐστύκαντι· Πελλάνας δὲ δεῖ.

ΚΙΝΗΣΙΑΣ

ἀπὸ τοῦ δὲ τουτὶ τὸ κακὸν ὑμῖν ἐνέπεσεν;
ἀπὸ Πανός;

ΚΗΡΥΞ

οὔκ, ἀλλ᾽ ἆρχε μέν, οἰῶ, Λαμπιτώ,
ἔπειτα τἄλλαι ταὶ κατὰ Σπάρταν ἁμᾶ
γυναῖκες ᾇπερ ἀπὸ μιᾶς ὑσπλαγίδος
ἀπήλαἁν τὼς ἄνδρας ἀπὸ τῶν ὑσσάκων.

HERALD

By Castor, the man's crazy!

CINESIAS

Why, you've got a hard-on, you dirty rascal!

HERALD

I certainly do not! Don't be talking twaddle.

CINESIAS

Then what do you call *that*?

HERALD

A Spartan walking stick.

CINESIAS

Then *this* is a Spartan walking stick too. Listen, I know what's up; you can be straight with me. How are things going in Sparta?

HERALD

All Sparta rises, and our allies all have hard-ons. We need Pellana.[91]

CINESIAS

Who caused this calamity to befall you? Was it Pan?[92]

HERALD

No, the one who started it, I reckon, was Lampito, and then the other women in Sparta all together, as from a starting gate, excluded the men from their pork pies.

91 Significance obscure: either a place name with a sexual significance now lost, or a pun on an unattested word meaning vagina or anus.

92 Pan (2 n.), frequently portrayed as ithyphallic, could also inflict ithyphallism.

ΚΙΝΗΣΙΑΣ

πῶς οὖν ἔχετε;

ΚΗΡΥΞ

μογίομες· ἂν γὰρ τὰν πόλιν
ἅπερ λυχνοφορίοντες ὑποκεκύφαμες.
ταὶ γὰρ γυναῖκες οὐδὲ τῶ μύρτω σιγῆν
ἐῶντι, πρίν χ᾽ ἅπαντες ἐξ ἑνὸς λόγω
σπονδὰς ποιηὥμεσθα ποττὰν Ἑλλάδα.

ΚΙΝΗΣΙΑΣ

τουτὶ τὸ πρᾶγμα πανταχόθεν ξυνομώμοται
ὑπὸ τῶν γυναικῶν· ἄρτι νυνὶ μανθάνω.
ἀλλ᾽ ὡς τάχιστα φράζε περὶ διαλλαγῶν
πρέσβεις ἀποπέμπειν αὐτοκράτορας ἐνθαδί.
ἐγὼ δ᾽ ἑτέρους ἐνθένδε τῇ βουλῇ φράσω
πρέσβεις ἑλέσθαι τὸ πέος ἐπιδείξας τοδί.

ΚΗΡΥΞ

ποτάομαι· κράτιστα γὰρ παντᾷ λέγεις.

ΚΟΡΥΦΑΙΟΣ

οὐδέν ἐστι θηρίον γυναικὸς ἀμαχώτερον,
οὐδὲ πῦρ, οὐδ᾽ ὧδ᾽ ἀναιδὴς οὐδεμία πάρδαλις.

ΚΟΡΥΦΑΙΑ

ταῦτα μέντοι <σὺ> ξυνιεὶς εἶτα πολεμεῖς ἐμοί,
ἐξόν, ὦ πόνηρέ, σοι βέβαιον ἔμ᾽ ἔχειν φίλην;

ΚΟΡΥΦΑΙΟΣ

ὡς ἐγὼ μισῶν γυναῖκας οὐδέποτε παύσομαι.

CINESIAS

So how are you faring?

HERALD

We're hard up! We walk around town hunched over, like men carrying lamps. The women won't let us even touch their cherries till all of us unanimously agree to make peace with the rest of Greece.

CINESIAS

So this business is a global conspiracy by all the women! Now I get it! Very well, you go back to Sparta as quick as you can and tell them to send delegates here with full powers to negotiate a treaty. And I'll arrange for our Council to choose their own ambassadors; this cock of mine will be Exhibit A.

HERALD

I'll fly. Your advice is absolutely capital.

HERALD and CINESIAS exit in opposite directions.

MEN'S LEADER

No beast, nor even fire, is harder to battle than a woman, and no leopard is so ferocious.

WOMEN'S LEADER

So you understand that, and yet you're still fighting me, when it's possible, you rascal, to have our lasting friendship?

MEN'S LEADER

Because I'll never stop hating women!

ΚΟΡΥΦΑΙΑ

ἀλλ᾽ ὅταν βούλῃ σύ. νῦν δ᾽ οὖν οὔ σε περιόψομαι
γυμνὸν ὄνθ᾽ οὕτως. ὅρα γὰρ ὡς καταγέλαστος εἶ.
ἀλλὰ τὴν ἐξωμίδ᾽ ἐνδύσω σε προσιοῦσ᾽ ἐγώ.

ΚΟΡΥΦΑΙΟΣ

τοῦτο μὲν μὰ τὸν Δί᾽ οὐ πονηρὸν ἐποιήσατε·
ἀλλ᾽ ὑπ᾽ ὀργῆς γὰρ πονηρᾶς καὶ τότ᾽ ἀπέδυν ἐγώ.

ΚΟΡΥΦΑΙΑ

πρῶτα μὲν φαίνει γ᾽ ἀνήρ, εἶτ᾽ οὐ καταγέλαστος εἶ.
κεἴ με μὴ ᾽λύπεις, ἐγώ σου κἂν τόδε τὸ θηρίον
τοὐπὶ τὠφθαλμῷ λαβοῦσ᾽ ἐξεῖλον ἄν, ὃ νῦν ἔνι.

ΚΟΡΥΦΑΙΟΣ

τοῦτ᾽ ἄρ᾽ ἦν με τοὐπιτρῖβον. δακτύλιος οὑτοσί·
ἐκσκάλευσον αὐτό, κᾆτα δεῖξον ἀφελοῦσά μοι·
ὡς τὸν ὀφθαλμόν γέ μου νὴ τὸν Δία πάλαι δάκνει.

ΚΟΡΥΦΑΙΑ

ἀλλὰ δράσω ταῦτα· καίτοι δύσκολος ἔφυς ἀνήρ.
ἦ μέγ᾽, ὦ Ζεῦ, χρῆμ᾽ ἰδεῖν τῆς ἐμπίδος ἔνεστί σοι.
οὐχ ὁρᾷς; οὐκ ἐμπίς ἐστιν ἥδε Τρικορυσία;

ΚΟΡΥΦΑΙΟΣ

νὴ Δί᾽ ὤνησάς γέ μ᾽, ὡς πάλαι γέ μ᾽ ἐφρεωρύχει,
ὥστ᾽, ἐπειδὴ ᾽ξῃρέθη, ῥεῖ μου τὸ δάκρυον πολύ.

ΚΟΡΥΦΑΙΑ

ἀλλ᾽ ἀποψήσω σ᾽ ἐγώ, καίτοι πάνυ πονηρὸς εἶ,
καὶ φιλήσω.

WOMEN'S LEADER

Well, choose your own time. But meanwhile I'm not going to let you go undressed like that. Just look how ridiculous you are! I'm coming over and putting your shirt back on.

MEN'S LEADER

That's certainly no mean thing you've done; in fact, it was mean of me to take it off in anger before.

WOMEN'S LEADER

Now you look like a man again, and not so ridiculous. And if you weren't so nasty to me I'd have grabbed that bug in your eye and taken it out; it's still in there now.

MEN'S LEADER

So that's what's been tormenting me! Here's a scraper; please dig it out of my eye, then show it to me when you've pulled it out, because it's really been biting my eye for quite some time.

WOMEN'S LEADER

All right, I will, though you're a born grouch. My god, what a humongous gnat you've got in there! See this? Isn't it positively Tricorysian?[93]

MEN'S LEADER

You've certainly helped me out, because that thing's been digging wells in me for a long time, and now that it's out, my eyes are streaming copious tears.

WOMEN'S LEADER

Then I'll wipe them away—though you're quite a rascal—and kiss you.

[93] The deme Tricorythus abutted a large marsh on the Bay of Marathon.

ΚΟΡΥΦΑΙΟΣ

μὴ φιλήσῃς.

ΚΟΡΥΦΑΙΑ

ἤν τε βούλῃ γ᾽ ἤν τε μή.

ΚΟΡΥΦΑΙΟΣ

ἀλλὰ μὴ ὥρασ᾽ ἵκοισθ᾽· ὡς ἐστὲ θωπικαὶ φύσει,
κἄστ᾽ ἐκεῖνο τοὔπος ὀρθῶς κοὐ κακῶς εἰρημένον,
οὔτε σὺν πανωλέθροισιν οὔτ᾽ ἄνευ πανωλέθρων.
ἀλλὰ νυνὶ σπένδομαί σοι, καὶ τὸ λοιπὸν οὐκέτι
οὔτε δράσω φλαῦρον οὐδὲν οὔθ᾽ ὑφ᾽ ὑμῶν πείσομαι.
ἀλλὰ κοινῇ συσταλέντες τοῦ μέλους ἀρξώμεθα.

ΧΟΡΟΣ

(στρ) οὐ παρασκευαζόμεσθα
τῶν πολιτῶν οὐδέν᾽, ὦνδρες,
φλαῦρον εἰπεῖν οὐδὲ ἕν,
ἀλλὰ πολὺ τοὔμπαλιν
πάντ᾽ ἀγαθὰ καὶ λέγειν καὶ
δρᾶν· ἱκανὰ γὰρ τὰ κακὰ
καὶ τὰ παρακείμενα.
ἀλλ᾽ ἐπαγγελλέτω πᾶς ἀνὴρ καὶ γυνή,
εἴ τις ἀργυρίδιον
δεῖται λαβεῖν, μνᾶς ἢ δύ᾽ ἢ τρεῖς· ὡς ἔσω
᾽στὶν κἄχομεν βαλλάντια.
κἄν ποτ᾽ εἰρήνη φανῇ,
ὅστις ἂν νυνὶ δανείσηται παρ᾽ ἡμῶν,

MEN'S LEADER

Don't kiss me!

WOMEN'S LEADER

I'll kiss you whether you like it or not!

MEN'S LEADER

The worst of luck to you! You're natural sweet-talkers, and that ancient adage is right on the mark and no mistake: "Can't live with the pests or without the pests either." But now I'll make peace with you, and nevermore mistreat you or suffer mistreatment from you. Now let's come together, and begin our song.

The semichoruses unite into a single chorus.

CHORUS

We don't intend, gentlemen,
to say anything about any citizen
that's slanderous in the slightest,
but quite the opposite:
to say and do only
what's nice, because you've already got
more than enough troubles.
So let every man and woman tell us
if they need to have a little cash,
say two or three minas;[94] we've got it at home,
and we've even got purses to put it in.
And if peace should ever break out,
anyone that borrows from us now

[94] 200–300 drachmas, enough to support an ordinary family for a year.

ἢν λάβῃ, μηκέτ' ἀποδῷ.

(ἀντ) ἑστιᾶν δὲ μέλλομεν ξέ-
νους τινὰς Καρυστίους, ἄν-
δρας καλούς τε κἀγαθούς.
κἄστι <μὲν> ἔτνος τι, καὶ
δελφάκιον ἦν τί μοι, καὶ
τοῦτο τέθυχ', ὥστε γίγ-
νεσθ' ἁπαλὰ καὶ καλά.
ἥκετ' οὖν εἰς ἐμοῦ τήμερον· πρῴ δὲ χρὴ
τοῦτο δρᾶν λελουμένους
αὐτούς τε καὶ τὰ παιδί', εἶτ' εἴσω βαδί-
ζειν, μηδ' ἐρέσθαι μηδένα,
ἀλλὰ χωρεῖν ἄντικρυς
ὥσπερ οἴκαδ' εἰς ἑαυτῶν γεννικῶς, ὡς
ἡ θύρα κεκλῄσεται.

ΚΟΡΥΦΑΙΟΣ

καὶ μὴν ἀπὸ τῆς Σπάρτης οἱδὶ πρέσβεις ἕλκοντες ὑπήνας
χωροῦσ', ὥσπερ χοιροκομεῖον περὶ τοῖς μηροῖσιν ἔχοντες.
ἄνδρες Λάκωνες, πρῶτα μέν μοι χαίρετε,
εἶτ' εἴπαθ' ἡμῖν πῶς ἔχοντες ἥκετε.

ΛΑΚΕΔΑΙΜΟΝΙΩΝ ΠΡΕΣΒΕΥΤΗΣ

τί δεῖ ποθ' ὑμὲ πολλὰ μυσίδδην ἔπη;
ὁρῆν γὰρ ἔξεσθ' ὡς ἔχοντες ἵκομες.

1057 ἢν Willems: ἂν (ἃν Sophianus) a

need no longer repay it—if he's had it!

We're getting set to entertain
some visitors from Carystus today;[95]
they're fine and handsome gentlemen.
There's some soup, and I had
a nice piglet and
sacrificed it, so it's turning
into tasty tenders.
So visit me at home today; and
do get up early and take a bath,
you and the kids, and walk right in.
You needn't ask anyone's permission,
just go straight on inside
as if into your own home,
because the door will be locked!

Enter SPARTAN DELEGATES, *with Slaves.*

CHORUS LEADER

Look, here come delegates from Sparta, trailing long beards and wearing something like a pig pen around their thighs. Gentlemen of Sparta: first, my greetings! Then tell us, how are you faring?

SPARTAN DELEGATE

What's the use of wasting lots of words? It's plain to see how we're faring. (*they open their cloaks*)

[95] Troops from this ally were stationed in Athens.

1062 ὥστε Palmer: ὥστε τὰ κρέα a   1063–4 γίγνεσθ' Sommerstein: γενέσθ' p γρΣ[R]: ἔξεσθ' R: ἔξεσθ' B

ΚΟΡΥΦΑΙΟΣ

βαβαί· νενεύρωται μὲν ἥδε συμφορὰ
δεινῶς τεθερμῶσθαί τε χεῖρον φαίνεται.

ΛΑΚΕΔΑΙΜΟΝΙΩΝ ΠΡΕΣΒΕΥΤΗΣ

ἄφατα. τί κα λέγοι τις; ἀλλ' ὁπᾷ σέλει
παντᾷ τις ἐλσὼν ἁμὶν εἰράναν σέτω.

ΚΟΡΥΦΑΙΟΣ

καὶ μὴν ὁρῶ καὶ τούσδε τοὺς αὐτόχθονας
ὥσπερ παλαιστὰς ἄνδρας ἀπὸ τῶν γαστέρων
θαἰμάτι' ἀποστέλλοντας· ὥστε φαίνεται
ἀσκητικὸν τὸ χρῆμα τοῦ νοσήματος.

ΑΘΗΝΑΙΩΝ ΠΡΕΣΒΕΥΤΗΣ Α

τίς ἂν φράσειε ποῦ 'στιν ἡ Λυσιστράτη;
ὡς ἄνδρες ἡμεῖς οὑτοιὶ τοιουτοί.

ΚΟΡΥΦΑΙΟΣ

χαὔτη ξυνᾴδει θἀτέρᾳ ταύτῃ νόσος.
ἦ που πρὸς ὄρθρον σπασμὸς ὑμᾶς λαμβάνει;

ΑΘΗΝΑΙΩΝ ΠΡΕΣΒΕΥΤΗΣ Α

μὰ Δί' ἀλλὰ ταυτὶ δρῶντες ἐπιτετρίμμεθα.
ὥστ' εἴ τις ἡμᾶς μὴ διαλλάξει ταχύ,
οὐκ ἔσθ' ὅπως οὐ Κλεισθένη βινήσομεν.

ΚΟΡΥΦΑΙΟΣ

εἰ σωφρονεῖτε, θαἰμάτια λήψεσθ', ὅπως
τῶν ἑρμοκοπιδῶν μή τις ὑμᾶς ὄψεται.

---

96 The Greek puns on *asketikon* ("pertaining to athletic training") and *askitikon* ("suffering from abdominal swelling").

CHORUS LEADER

Wow! This condition has grown terribly tense, and looks to be inflamed worse than before.

SPARTAN DELEGATE

Unspeakable! What can one say? Just let someone come and make peace for us on any terms he likes.

Enter ATHENIAN DELEGATES.

CHORUS LEADER

Look, now I see these native sons holding their cloaks away from their bellies too, like men wrestling! Looks like a bad case of prickly heat.[96]

FIRST ATHENIAN DELEGATE

Who can tell us where Lysistrata is? Because we men are present, and palpably so. (*they open their cloaks*)

CHORUS LEADER

Their condition seems to jibe with these others. Now, does this cramping seize you in the wee hours?

FIRST ATHENIAN DELEGATE

Yes, and what's worse, we're worn absolutely raw by being in this condition! I mean, if someone doesn't reconcile us soon, there's no way we won't be fucking Cleisthenes!

CHORUS LEADER

If you've got any sense, you'll cover up there: you don't want one of the Herm-Docker clan to spot you.[97]

[97] In 415, just before the departure of the Sicilian expedition, the faces and phalli of the pillar-images of Hermes, which stood in the streets throughout Athens, were mutilated. Since not all of the perpetrators had been identified, Aristophanes suggests that some were among the spectators, cf. Thucydides 6.27.

ΑΘΗΝΑΙΩΝ ΠΡΕΣΒΕΥΤΗΣ Α

νὴ τὸν Δί᾽ εὖ μέντοι λέγεις.

ΛΑΚΕΔΑΙΜΟΝΙΩΝ ΠΡΕΣΒΕΥΤΗΣ

ναὶ τὼ σιὼ
παντᾷ γα. φέρε τὸ ἔσθος ἀμβαλώμεθα.

ΑΘΗΝΑΙΩΝ ΠΡΕΣΒΕΥΤΗΣ Α

ὦ χαίρεθ᾽, οἱ Λάκωνες· αἰσχρά γ᾽ ἐπάθομεν.

ΛΑΚΕΔΑΙΜΟΝΙΩΝ ΠΡΕΣΒΕΥΤΗΣ

ὦ πολυχαρείδα, δεινά γ᾽ αὖ πεπόνθαμες,
αἰκ εἶδον ἁμὲ τὤνδρες ἀμπεφλασμένως.

ΑΘΗΝΑΙΩΝ ΠΡΕΣΒΕΥΤΗΣ Α

ἄγε δή, Λάκωνες, αὔθ᾽ ἕκαστα χρὴ λέγειν.
ἐπὶ τί πάρεστε δεῦρο;

ΛΑΚΕΔΑΙΜΟΝΙΩΝ ΠΡΕΣΒΕΥΤΗΣ

περὶ διαλλαγᾶν
πρέσβης.

ΑΘΗΝΑΙΩΝ ΠΡΕΣΒΕΥΤΗΣ Α

καλῶς δὴ λέγετε· χἠμεῖς τουτογί.
τί οὐ καλοῦμεν δῆτα τὴν Λυσιστράτην,
ἥπερ διαλλάξειεν ἡμᾶς ἂν μόνη;

ΛΑΚΕΔΑΙΜΟΝΙΩΝ ΠΡΕΣΒΕΥΤΗΣ

ναὶ τὼ σιώ, καἰ λῆτε, τὸν Λυἵστρατον.

ΑΘΗΝΑΙΩΝ ΠΡΕΣΒΕΥΤΗΣ Α

ἀλλ᾽ οὐδὲν ἡμᾶς, ὡς ἔοικε, δεῖ καλεῖν·
αὐτὴ γάρ, ὡς ἤκουσεν, ἥδ᾽ ἐξέρχεται.

FIRST ATHENIAN DELEGATE

That's certainly good advice.

SPARTAN DELEGATE

By the Twain Gods, it is indeed. Come on, let's put our cloaks back on!

FIRST ATHENIAN DELEGATE

Greetings, Spartans! We've had a terrible time.

SPARTAN DELEGATE

Dear colleague, we've had a fearful time, if those men saw us fiddling with ourselves.

FIRST ATHENIAN DELEGATE

Come on, then, Spartans, let's talk details. What is the purpose of your visit?

SPARTAN DELEGATE

As delegates for a settlement.

FIRST ATHENIAN DELEGATE

Very good to hear it; that's what we are too. So why don't we invite Lysistrata, since she's the only one who can reconcile us?

SPARTAN DELEGATE

Sure, by the Twain Gods, and Lysistratus too if you like![98]

Enter LYSISTRATA *from the Acropolis gates.*

FIRST ATHENIAN DELEGATE

Well, it seems we needn't invite her: she must have heard us, for here she comes herself.

[98] Perhaps teasing an effeminate Lysistratus, possibly the son of Macareus of Amphitrope mentioned in Schol. *Wasps* 787.

ΚΟΡΥΦΑΙΟΣ

χαῖρ᾽, ὦ πασῶν ἀνδρειοτάτη· δεῖ δὴ νυνί σε γενέσθαι
δεινὴν <μαλακήν,> ἀγαθὴν φαύλην, σεμνὴν ἀγανήν, πολύπειρον·
ὡς οἱ πρῶτοι τῶν Ἑλλήνων τῇ σῇ ληφθέντες ἴυγγι
συνεχώρησάν σοι καὶ κοινῇ τἀγκλήματα πάντ᾽ ἐπέτρεψαν.

ΛΥΣΙΣΤΡΑΤΗ

ἀλλ᾽ οὐχὶ χαλεπὸν τοὔργον, εἰ λάβοι γέ τις
ὀργῶντας ἀλλήλων τε μὴ ᾽κπειρωμένους.
τάχα δ᾽ εἴσομαι ᾽γώ. ποῦ ᾽στιν ἡ Διαλλαγή;
πρόσαγε λαβοῦσα πρῶτα τοὺς Λακωνικούς,
καὶ μὴ χαλεπῇ τῇ χειρὶ μηδ᾽ αὐθαδικῇ,
μηδ᾽ ὥσπερ ἡμῶν ἄνδρες ἀμαθῶς τοῦτ᾽ ἔδρων,
ἀλλ᾽ ὡς γυναῖκας εἰκός, οἰκείως πάνυ.
ἢν μὴ διδῷ τὴν χεῖρα, τῆς σάθης ἄγε.
ἴθι καὶ σὺ τούτους τοὺς Ἀθηναίους ἄγε·
οὗ δ᾽ ἂν διδῶσι, πρόσαγε τούτου λαβομένη.
ἄνδρες Λάκωνες, στῆτε παρ᾽ ἐμὲ πλησίον,
ἐνθένδε δ᾽ ὑμεῖς, καὶ λόγων ἀκούσατε.
ἐγὼ γυνὴ μέν εἰμι, νοῦς δ᾽ ἔνεστί μοι.
αὐτὴ δ᾽ ἐμαυτῆς οὐ κακῶς γνώμης ἔχω,
τοὺς δ᾽ ἐκ πατρός τε καὶ γεραιτέρων λόγους
πολλοὺς ἀκούσασ᾽ οὐ μεμούσωμαι κακῶς.
λαβοῦσα δ᾽ ὑμᾶς λοιδορῆσαι βούλομαι

1109 suppl. Wilamowitz

CHORUS LEADER

Hail, bravest of all women! Now you must be forceful and flexible, high-class and vulgar, haughty and sweet, a woman for all seasons; because the head men of Greece, caught by your charms, have gathered together and are jointly submitting all their disputes to you for arbitration.

LYSISTRATA

Well, it's not a hard job, if you catch them when they're hot for it and not testing each other for weaknesses. I'll soon find out. Where's Reconciliation?

Enter Reconciliation, costumed as a naked girl, from the Acropolis.

Take hold of the Spartans first and bring them here; don't handle them with a rough or hectoring hand, or ignorantly, the way our husbands used to handle us, but use a wife's touch, like home sweet home. If he won't give you his hand, lead him by his weenie. Now go and fetch those Athenians too; take hold of whatever part they offer and bring them here. Spartans, stand close to me, and you Athenians stand on this side. Now listen to what I have to say. It's true I'm a woman, but still I've got a mind: I'm pretty intelligent in my own right, and because I've listened many a time to the conversations of my father and other elders, I'm pretty well educated too.[99] Now that you're my captive audience I'm ready to give you the

[99] Lines 1124–27 are paratragic and at least partially quote from Euripides' *Wise Melanippe* (1124 = fr. 483).

κοινῇ δικαίως, οἳ μιᾶς γε χέρνιβος
βωμοὺς περιρραίνοντες ὥσπερ ξυγγενεῖς
Ὀλυμπίασιν, ἐν Πύλαις, Πυθοῖ—πόσους
εἴποιμ' ἂν ἄλλους, εἴ με μηκύνειν δέοι;—
ἐχθρῶν παρόντων βαρβάρῳ στρατεύματι
Ἕλληνας ἄνδρας καὶ πόλεις ἀπόλλυτε.
εἷς μὲν λόγος μοι δεῦρ' ἀεὶ περαίνεται.

ΑΘΗΝΑΙΩΝ ΠΡΕΣΒΕΥΤΗΣ Α

ἐγὼ δ' ἀπόλλυμαί γ' ἀπεψωλημένος.

ΛΥΣΙΣΤΡΑΤΗ

εἶτ', ὦ Λάκωνες, πρὸς γὰρ ὑμᾶς τρέψομαι,
οὐκ ἴσθ' ὅτ' ἐλθὼν δεῦρο Περικλείδας ποτὲ
ὁ Λάκων Ἀθηναίων ἱκέτης καθέζετο
ἐπὶ τοῖσι βωμοῖς ὠχρὸς ἐν φοινικίδι
στρατιὰν προσαιτῶν; ἡ δὲ Μεσσήνη τότε
ὑμῖν ἐπέκειτο χὠ θεὸς σείων ἅμα.
ἐλθὼν δὲ σὺν ὁπλίταισι τετρακισχιλίοις
Κίμων ὅλην ἔσωσε τὴν Λακεδαίμονα.
ταυτὶ παθόντες τῶν Ἀθηναίων ὕπο
δῃοῦτε χώραν, ἧς ὕπ' εὖ πεπόνθατε;

ΑΘΗΝΑΙΩΝ ΠΡΕΣΒΕΥΤΗΣ Α

ἀδικοῦσιν οὗτοι νὴ Δί', ὦ Λυσιστράτη.

ΛΑΚΕΔΑΙΜΟΝΙΩΝ ΠΡΕΣΒΕΥΤΗΣ

ἀδικίομες· ἀλλ' ὁ πρωκτὸς ἄφατον ὡς καλός.

tongue-lashing you deserve—both of you. You two sprinkle altars from the same cup like kinsmen, at Olympia, at Thermopylae, at Pytho—how many other places could I mention if I had to extend the list—yet when enemies are available with their barbarian armies, it's Greek men and Greek cities you're determined to destroy. That takes me through one of my arguments.[100]

FIRST ATHENIAN DELEGATE

My cock is bursting out of its skin and killing me!

LYSISTRATA

Next, Spartans, I'm going to turn to you. Don't you remember when Pericleidas the Spartan came here once and sat at the altars as a suppliant of the Athenians, pale in his scarlet uniform, begging for troops? That time when Messenia was up in arms against you and the god was shaking you with an earthquake? And Cimon went with four thousand infantrymen and rescued all Sparta? After being treated that way by the Athenians, you're now out to ravage the country that's treated you well?[101]

FIRST ATHENIAN DELEGATE

They're guilty as can be, Lysistrata!

SPARTAN DELEGATE

We're guilty, but what an unspeakably fine arse!

[100] Line 1135 quotes Euripides' *Erechtheus*, fr. 363.

[101] After the earthquake of 464 Sparta's subject communities revolted, and Athens sent military assistance. Lysistrata omits the sequel: the pro-Spartan Athenian commander Cimon was dismissed by the Spartans, and his subsequent political eclipse paved the way for the first Peloponnesian War.

ΛΥΣΙΣΤΡΑΤΗ

ὑμᾶς δ᾽ ἀφήσειν τοὺς Ἀθηναίους <μ᾽> οἴει;
οὐκ ἴσθ᾽ ὅθ᾽ ὑμᾶς οἱ Λάκωνες αὖθις αὖ
κατωνάκας φοροῦντας ἐλθόντες δορὶ
πολλοὺς μὲν ἄνδρας Θετταλῶν ἀπώλεσαν,
πολλοὺς δ᾽ ἑταίρους Ἱππίου καὶ ξυμμάχους,
ξυνεκβαλόντες τῇ τόθ᾽ ἡμέρᾳ μόνοι
κἠλευθέρωσαν κἀντὶ τῆς κατωνάκης
τὸν δῆμον ὑμῶν χλαῖναν ἠμπέσχον πάλιν;

ΛΑΚΕΔΑΙΜΟΝΙΩΝ ΠΡΕΣΒΕΥΤΗΣ

οὔπα γυναῖκ᾽ ὄπωπα χαἰωτέραν.

ΑΘΗΝΑΙΩΝ ΠΡΕΣΒΕΥΤΗΣ Α

ἐγὼ δὲ κύσθον γ᾽ οὐδέπω καλλίονα.

ΛΥΣΙΣΤΡΑΤΗ

τί δῆθ᾽ ὑπηργμένων γε πολλῶν κἀγαθῶν
μάχεσθε κοὐ παύεσθε τῆς μοχθηρίας;
τί δ᾽ οὐ διηλλάγητε; φέρε, τί τοὐμποδών;

ΛΑΚΕΔΑΙΜΟΝΙΩΝ ΠΡΕΣΒΕΥΤΗΣ

ἁμές γα λῶμες, αἴ τις ἁμὶν τὤγκυκλον
λῇ τοῦτ᾽ ἀποδόμεν.

ΛΥΣΙΣΤΡΑΤΗ

ποῖον, ὦ τᾶν;

1154 ξυνεκβαλόντες van Herwerden: ξυνεκμαχοῦντες R

LYSISTRATA

Do you think I'm going to let you Athenians off? Don't you remember how the Spartans in turn, when you were dressed in slaves' rags, came with their spears and wiped out many Thessalian fighters, many friends and allies of Hippias? That day when they were the only ones helping you to drive him out? And how they liberated you, and replaced your slaves' rags with a warm cloak, as suits a free people?[102]

SPARTAN DELEGATE

I've never seen a classier woman!

FIRST ATHENIAN DELEGATE

And I've never seen a lovelier cunt!

LYSISTRATA

So why, after so many fine favors done, are you fighting instead of calling a halt to your misbehavior? Why not make peace? Come on, what's in the way?

SPARTAN DELEGATE

We're ready, if they're ready to return to us this abutment.[103]

LYSISTRATA

What abutment, sir?

[102] The Spartan king Cleomenes helped expel the Athenian tyrant Hippias in 510. Again Lysistrata omits the sequel: Cleomenes returned three years later in a failed attempt to undermine the Athenians' new democracy, cf. 274–80.

[103] Each of the places specified has a sexual double meaning that could be illustrated by reference to Reconciliation's body.

ΛΑΚΕΔΑΙΜΟΝΙΩΝ ΠΡΕΣΒΕΥΤΗΣ

τὰν Πύλον,
τᾶσπερ πάλαι δεόμεθα καὶ βλιμάδδομες.

ΑΘΗΝΑΙΩΝ ΠΡΕΣΒΕΥΤΗΣ Α

μὰ τὸν Ποσειδῶ τοῦτο μέν γ' οὐ δράσετε.

ΛΥΣΙΣΤΡΑΤΗ

ἄφετ', ὠγάθ', αὐτοῖς.

ΑΘΗΝΑΙΩΝ ΠΡΕΣΒΕΥΤΗΣ Α

κᾆτα τίνα κινήσομεν;

ΛΥΣΙΣΤΡΑΤΗ

ἕτερόν γ' ἀπαιτεῖτ' ἀντὶ τούτου χωρίον.

ΑΘΗΝΑΙΩΝ ΠΡΕΣΒΕΥΤΗΣ Α

τὸ δεῖνα τοίνυν, παράδοθ' ἡμῖν τουτονὶ
πρώτιστα τὸν Ἐχινοῦντα καὶ τὸν Μηλιᾶ
κόλπον τὸν ὄπισθεν καὶ τὰ Μεγαρικὰ σκέλη.

ΛΑΚΕΔΑΙΜΟΝΙΩΝ ΠΡΕΣΒΕΥΤΗΣ

οὐ τὼ σιώ, οὐκὶ πάντα γ', ὦ λισσάνιε.

ΛΥΣΙΣΤΡΑΤΗ

ἐᾶτε, μηδὲν διαφέρου περὶ σκελοῖν.

ΑΘΗΝΑΙΩΝ ΠΡΕΣΒΕΥΤΗΣ Α

ἤδη γεωργεῖν γυμνὸς ἀποδὺς βούλομαι.

SPARTAN DELEGATE

Pylos[104] here, that for a long time we've been coveting and feeling out.

FIRST ATHENIAN DELEGATE

So help me Poseidon, that you won't get!

LYSISTRATA

Give it to them, good sir.

FIRST ATHENIAN DELEGATE

Then who will *we* be able to harrass?

LYSISTRATA

Just ask for some other place in return for that one.

FIRST ATHENIAN DELEGATE

Well, let's see now. First of all give us Echinous here and the Malian Gulf behind it and both Legs.[105]

SPARTAN DELEGATE

By the Twain Gods, we're not handing over *everything*, dear fellow!

LYSISTRATA

Let it go: don't be squabbling about a pair of legs.

FIRST ATHENIAN DELEGATE

Now I'm ready to strip down and start ploughing!

104 Literally "gate," exploiting the stereotype of Spartan predilection for anal intercourse with either sex; the Athenians will opt for the vagina, and so the settlement will be mutually satisfactory.

105 Echinous (literally "sea urchin place" for female pubis); Malian Inlet (*malon* "apple" for buttocks); Legs (for the connecting walls) of Megara.

ΛΑΚΕΔΑΙΜΟΝΙΩΝ ΠΡΕΣΒΕΥΤΗΣ

ἐγὼν δὲ κοπραγωγῆν γα πρῴ ναὶ τὼ σιώ.

ΛΥΣΙΣΤΡΑΤΗ

ἐπὴν διαλλαγῆτε, ταῦτα δράσετε.
ἀλλ᾽ εἰ δοκεῖ δρᾶν ταῦτα, βουλεύσασθε καὶ
τοῖς ξυμμάχοις ἐλθόντες ἀνακοινώσατε.

ΑΘΗΝΑΙΩΝ ΠΡΕΣΒΕΥΤΗΣ Α

ποίοισιν, ὦ τᾶν, ξυμμάχοις; ἐστύκαμεν.
οὐ ταὐτὰ δόξει τοῖσι συμμάχοισι νῷν,
βινεῖν, ἅπασιν;

ΛΑΚΕΔΑΙΜΟΝΙΩΝ ΠΡΕΣΒΕΥΤΗΣ

τοῖσι γῶν ναὶ τὼ σιὼ
ἁμοῖσι.

ΑΘΗΝΑΙΩΝ ΠΡΕΣΒΕΥΤΗΣ Α

καὶ γὰρ ναὶ μὰ Δία Καρυστίοις.

ΛΥΣΙΣΤΡΑΤΗ

καλῶς λέγετε. νῦν οὖν ὅπως ἁγνεύσετε,
ὅπως ἂν αἱ γυναῖκες ὑμᾶς ἐν πόλει
ξενίσωμεν ὧν ἐν ταῖσι κίσταις εἴχομεν.
ὅρκους δ᾽ ἐκεῖ καὶ πίστιν ἀλλήλοις δότε.
κἄπειτα τὴν αὑτοῦ γυναῖχ᾽ ὑμῶν λαβὼν
ἄπεισ᾽ ἕκαστος.

ΑΘΗΝΑΙΩΝ ΠΡΕΣΒΕΥΤΗΣ Α

ἀλλ᾽ ἴωμεν ὡς τάχος.

1174 πρῴ Biset: πρῶτα R

SPARTAN DELEGATE

And bright and early I want to start spreading manure, by the Twain Gods!

LYSISTRATA

You both may do those things after you've ratified the settlement. Now then, if after due deliberation you do decide to settle, go back and confer with your allies.

FIRST ATHENIAN DELEGATE

Allies, dear lady? We're too hard up for that! Won't our allies, all of them, come to the same decision we have, namely, to fuck?

SPARTAN DELEGATE

Ours will, by the Twain Gods!

FIRST ATHENIAN DELEGATE

And so, for sure, will the Carystians![106]

LYSISTRATA

You make a good case. For the time being see to it you remain pure, so that we women can host you on the Acropolis with what we brought in our boxes. There you may exchange pledges of mutual trust, and then each of you may reclaim his own wife and go home.

FIRST ATHENIAN DELEGATE

Well, let's get moving right away.

[106] See 1059 n.

ΛΑΚΕΔΑΙΜΟΝΙΩΝ ΠΡΕΣΒΕΥΤΗΣ

ἄγ᾽ ὀπᾷ τυ λῇς.

ΑΘΗΝΑΙΩΝ ΠΡΕΣΒΕΥΤΗΣ Α

νὴ τὸν Δί᾽ ὡς τάχιστ᾽ ἄγε.

ΧΟΡΟΣ

(στρ) στρωμάτων δὲ ποικίλων καὶ
χλανιδίων καὶ ξυστίδων καὶ
χρυσίων, ὅσ᾽ ἐστί μοι,
οὐ φθόνος ἔνεστί μοι
πᾶσι παρέχειν φέρειν τοῖς
παισίν, ὁπόταν τε θυγά-
τηρ τινὶ κανηφορῇ.
πᾶσιν ὑμῖν λέγω λαμβάνειν τῶν ἐμῶν
χρημάτων νῦν ἔνδοθεν,
καὶ μηδὲν οὕτως εὖ σεσημάνθαι τὸ μὴ οὐ-
χὶ τοὺς ῥύπους ἀνασπάσαι,
χἄττ᾽ <ἂν> ἔνδον ᾖ φορεῖν.
ὄψεται δ᾽ οὐδὲν σκοπῶν, εἰ μή τις ὑμῶν
ὀξύτερον ἐμοῦ βλέπει.

(ἀντ) εἰ δέ τῳ μὴ σῖτος ὑμῶν
ἔστι, βόσκει δ᾽ οἰκέτας καὶ
σμικρὰ πολλὰ παιδία,
ἔστι παρ᾽ ἐμοῦ λαβεῖν
πυρίδια λεπτὰ μέν, ὁ δ᾽
ἄρτος ἀπὸ χοίνικος ἰ-

1193 παισίν Bentley: πᾶσιν a

SPARTAN DELEGATE

Lead on wherever you wish.

FIRST ATHENIAN DELEGATE

God yes, as quick as you can!

Exit LYSISTRATA, *Reconciliation, and the* DELEGATES; *the Slaves sit down outside the Acropolis gates, which are attended by a Doorkeeper.*

CHORUS

Intricate tapestries,
nice clothes and fine gowns,
and gold jewellery—all that I own
I'll ungrudgingly provide
to everyone for their
sons, and whenever a daughter
marches with the basket.[107]
I now invite you all to help yourselves
to the possessions in my house;
nothing is sealed up so tight
that you can't break the seals
and carry away whatever's inside.
But you won't see anything unless
your eyes are sharper than mine.

If anyone's out of bread
but has slaves to feed
and lots of little kids,
you can get flour from my house—
puny grains, true,
but a pound of them grow up to be

[107] See 646 n.

δεῖν μάλα νεανίας.
ὅστις οὖν βούλεται τῶν πενήτων ἴτω
εἰς ἐμοῦ σάκους ἔχων
καὶ κωρύκους· ὡς λήψεται πυρούς. ὁ μα-
νῆς δ' οὑμὸς αὐτοῖς ἐμβαλεῖ.
πρός γε μέντοι τὴν θύραν
προαγορεύω μὴ βαδίζειν τὴν ἐμήν, ἀλλ'
εὐλαβεῖσθαι τὴν κύνα.

ΑΘΗΝΑΙΩΝ ΠΡΕΣΒΕΥΤΗΣ Α

ἄνοιγε τὴν θύραν σύ. παραχωρεῖν ἔδει.
ὑμεῖς, τί κάθησθε; μῶν ἐγὼ τῇ λαμπάδι
ὑμᾶς κατακαύσω; φορτικὸν τὸ χωρίον.
οὐκ ἂν ποιήσαιμ'. εἰ δὲ πάνυ δεῖ τοῦτο δρᾶν,
ὑμῖν χαρίσασθαι προσταλαιπωρήσομεν.

ΑΘΗΝΑΙΩΝ ΠΡΕΣΒΕΥΤΗΣ Β

χἠμεῖς γε μετὰ σοῦ ξυνταλαιπωρήσομεν.
οὐκ ἄπιτε; κωκύσεσθε τὰς τρίχας μακρά.

ΑΘΗΝΑΙΩΝ ΠΡΕΣΒΕΥΤΗΣ Α

οὐκ ἄπιθ', ὅπως ἂν οἱ Λάκωνες ἔνδοθεν
καθ' ἡσυχίαν ἀπίωσιν εὐωχημένοι;

ΑΘΗΝΑΙΩΝ ΠΡΕΣΒΕΥΤΗΣ Β

οὔπω τοιοῦτον συμπόσιον ὄπωπ' ἐγώ.
ἦ καὶ χαρίεντες ἦσαν οἱ Λακωνικοί·
ἡμεῖς δ' ἐν οἴνῳ συμπόται σοφώτατοι.

a loaf that's very hearty to see.
Any of the poor are welcome
to come to my house with sacks
and bags to carry the flour away; my houseboy
will pour it in for them.
A warning though:
don't come to my door—
beware of the watchdog there!

FIRST ATHENIAN DELEGATE

(*within the Acropolis*) Open the door, you! (*bursts through the door, sending the Doorkeeper tumbling*) You should have got out of the way. (*other Athenians emerge*) You there, why are you sitting around? Want me to singe you with this torch? What a stale routine! I refuse to do it. (*to the spectators*) Well, if it's absolutely necessary, we'll go the extra mile, to do you all a favor. (*chases the Slaves with his torch*)

SECOND ATHENIAN DELEGATE

(*joining the First*) And we'll help you go that extra mile! (*to the Slaves*) Scram, you! You'll cry for your hair if you don't!

FIRST ATHENIAN DELEGATE

Yes scram, so the Spartans can come out after their banquet without being bothered.

The Slaves are chased off.

SECOND ATHENIAN DELEGATE

I've never seen such a party! The Spartans were really charming, and we were superb company ourselves over the drinks.

ΑΘΗΝΑΙΩΝ ΠΡΕΣΒΕΥΤΗΣ Α

ὀρθῶς γ', ὁτιὴ νήφοντες οὐχ ὑγιαίνομεν.
ἢν τοὺς Ἀθηναίους ἐγὼ πείσω λέγων,
μεθύοντες ἀεὶ πανταχοῖ πρεσβεύσομεν.
νῦν μὲν γὰρ ὅταν ἔλθωμεν εἰς Λακεδαίμονα
νήφοντες, εὐθὺς βλέπομεν ὅ τι ταράξομεν·
ὥσθ' ὅ τι μὲν ἂν λέγωσιν οὐκ ἀκούομεν,
ἃ δ' οὐ λέγουσι, ταῦθ' ὑπονενοήκαμεν,
ἀγγέλλομεν δ' οὐ ταὐτὰ τῶν αὐτῶν πέρι.
νυνὶ δ' ἅπαντ' ἤρεσκεν· ὥστ' εἰ μέν γέ τις
ᾄδοι Τελαμῶνος, Κλειταγόρας ᾄδειν δέον,
ἐπῃνέσαμεν ἂν καὶ πρὸς ἐπιωρκήσαμεν.
ἀλλ' οὑτοιὶ γὰρ αὖθις ἔρχονται πάλιν
εἰς ταὐτόν. οὐκ ἐρρήσετ', ὦ μαστιγίαι;

ΑΘΗΝΑΙΩΝ ΠΡΕΣΒΕΥΤΗΣ Β

νὴ τὸν Δί'· ὡς ἤδη γε χωροῦσ' ἔνδοθεν.

ΛΑΚΕΔΑΙΜΟΝΙΩΝ ΠΡΕΣΒΕΥΤΗΣ

ὦ πολυχαρείδα, λαβὲ τὰ φυάτήρια,
ἵν' ἐγὼν διποδιάξω τε κἀείσω καλὸν
ἐς τὼς Ἀσαναίως τε χἄμ' ἄεισμ' ἁμᾶ.

1244 χἄμ' ἄεισμ' Meineke: *καὶ ἡμᾶς* R S: *καὶ ἐς ἡμᾶς* B p

---

108 Two popular drinking songs; *Telamon* (cf. *PMG* 898–99) was warlike, while *Cleitagora* began (we have only the opening, cf. *Wasps* 1245–47) by referring to peace and prosperity.

FIRST ATHENIAN DELEGATE

That figures, because when we're sober we get unhinged. If the Athenians will take my advice, from now on we'll go on all our diplomatic missions drunk. As it is, when we go to Sparta sober, we at once start looking for ways to stir up trouble. And so when they say something we don't hear it, and when they don't say anything we read things into that, and we each come away with different reports of the same discussions. But this time everything was agreeable. When somebody sang *Telamon* when he should have been singing *Cleitagora*,[108] we'd applaud him and even swear up and down that—

The Slaves approach.

Hey, those slaves are back again! Get lost, you whip-fodder!

They chase the Slaves away.

SECOND ATHENIAN DELEGATE

Well now, here they come out of the gates.

Enter SPARTAN DELEGATES *from the Acropolis; their leader carries bagpipes.*

SPARTAN DELEGATE

(*to the stage-piper or a piper who accompanies the Spartans*) Grab the pipes, my good man, and I'll dance a two-step and sing a fine song for the Athenians and ourselves.

ΑΘΗΝΑΙΩΝ ΠΡΕΣΒΕΥΤΗΣ Α

λαβὲ δῆτα τὰς φυσαλλίδας πρὸς τῶν θεῶν·
ὡς ἥδομαί γ᾽ ὑμᾶς ὁρῶν ὀρχουμένους.

ΛΑΚΕΔΑΙΜΟΝΙΩΝ ΠΡΕΣΒΕΥΤΗΣ

ὅρμαὸν τῷ κυρσανίῳ,
Μναμόνα, τὰν τεὰν
Μῶάν, ἅτις οἶδεν ἁμὲ τώς τ᾽ Ἀσαναί-
ως, ὅκα τοὶ μὲν ἐπ᾽ Ἀρταμιτίῳ
πρώκροον σιείκελοι
ποττὰ κᾶλα,
τὼς Μήδως τ᾽ ἐνίκων·
ἁμὲ δ᾽ αὖ Λεωνίδας
ἆγεν ᾇπερ τὼς κάπρως
σάγοντας, οἰῶ, τὸν ὀδόντα· πολὺς δ᾽
ἀμφὶ τὰς γένυας ἀφρὸς ἄνσεεν,
πολὺς δ᾽ ἁμᾶ καττῶν σκελῶν ἵετο.
ἦν γὰρ τὦνδρες οὐκ ἐλάσσως
τᾶς ψάμμας τοὶ Πέρσαι.
ἀγροτέρα σηροκτόνε, μόλε
δεῦρο, παρσένε σιά,
ποττὰς σπονδάς,
ὡς συνέχῃς πολὺν ἁμὲ χρόνον. νῦν δ᾽
αὖ φιλία τ᾽ ἀὲς εὔπορος εἴη
ταῖσι συνθήκαισι, καὶ τᾶν αἱμυλᾶν ἀ-

1262 ἀγροτέρα Dindorf: ἀγροτέρ᾽ Ἄρτεμι a

FIRST ATHENIAN DELEGATE

Gods above, do take the pipes: I just love to watch you people dance!

SPARTAN DELEGATE

Memory, speed to this lad
your own Muse, who knows
about us and the Athenians,
about that day at Artemisium[109]
when they spread sail like gods
against the armada
and defeated the Medes;
while we were led by Leonidas,[110]
like wild boars we were, yes,
gnashing our tusks, our jaws running
streams of foam, and our legs too.
The enemy outnumbered
the sands on the shore, those Persians.
Goddess of the Wilds, Beast Killer,[111]
come this way, maiden goddess,
to join in the treaty,
and keep us together for a long time.
Now let friendship in abundance
attend our agreement always, and let us

[109] The naval battle against the Persians in 480, in which 200 of the 333 Greek ships were Athenian, cf. Herodotus 8.1–21.

[110] Leonidas led the defense against the Persians at Thermopylae, in which all 300 Spartans were killed; this action occurred at the same time as Artemisium, cf. Herodotus 7.175–238.

[111] Artemis under this special title (*Agrotera*) was worshipped at both Sparta and Athens, where her annual sacrifice commemorated the battle of Marathon in 490.

λωπέκων παυαἵμεθα.
ὦ, δεῦρ᾽ ἴθι, δεῦρο,
ὦ κυναγὲ παρσένε.

ΑΘΗΝΑΙΩΝ ΠΡΕΣΒΕΥΤΗΣ Α

ἄγε νυν ἐπειδὴ τἄλλα πεποίηται καλῶς,
ἀπάγεσθε ταύτας, ὦ Λάκωνες, τασδεδὶ
ὑμεῖς· ἀνὴρ δὲ παρὰ γυναῖκα καὶ γυνὴ
στήτω παρ᾽ ἄνδρα, κᾆτ᾽ ἐπ᾽ ἀγαθαῖς ξυμφοραῖς
ὀρχησάμενοι θεοῖσιν εὐλαβώμεθα
τὸ λοιπὸν αὖθις μὴ ᾿ξαμαρτάνειν ἔτι.

πρόσαγε χορόν, ἔπαγε <δὲ> Χάριτας,
ἐπὶ δὲ κάλεσον Ἄρτεμιν,
ἐπὶ δὲ δίδυμον εὔφρον᾽ Ἰήιον
ἐπὶ δὲ Νύσιον, ὃς μετὰ μαινάσι
βάκχιος ὄμματα δαίεται,
Δία τε πυρὶ φλεγόμενον, ἐπὶ δὲ
πότνιαν ἄλοχον ὀλβίαν
εἶτα δὲ δαίμονας, οἷς ἐπιμάρτυσι
χρησόμεθ᾽ οὐκ ἐπιλήσμοσιν
Ἡσυχίας πέρι τῆς μεγαλόφρονος,
ἣν ἐποίησε θεὰ Κύπρις.

ΧΟΡΟΣ

ἀλαλαί, ἰὴ παιών.
αἴρεσθ᾽ ἄνω, ἰαί,

1281 δίδυμον Enger: δίδυμον ἄγε (ἄγετε Bp) χορὸν a
1289 ἀγανόφρονος Reisig cl. *Av.* 1321

ever abandon foxy stratagems.
O come this way, this way,
o Virgin Huntress!

Lysistrata escorts the Athenian and Spartan Wives from the Acropolis.

FIRST ATHENIAN DELEGATE

Well! Now that everything else has been wrapped up so nicely, it's time for you Spartans to reclaim these wives of yours, and you Athenians, these here. Let's have husband stand by wife and wife by husband, and then to celebrate our great good fortune let's have a dance for the gods. And let's be sure never again to make the same mistakes!

Bring on the dance, include the Graces,
and invite Artemis,
and her twin brother, the benign Healer,[112]
and the Nysian whose eyes flash
bacchic among his maenads,[113]
and Zeus alight with flame
and the thriving Lady his consort;[114]
and invite the divine powers
we would have as witnesses
to remember always this humane Peace,
which the goddess Cypris[115] has fashioned.

CHORUS

Alalai, yay Paian!
Shake a leg, iai!

112 Apollo.

113 Dionysus was reared on the legendary mountain of Nysa.

114 Hera. 115 Aphrodite.

ὡς ἐπὶ νίκῃ, ἰαί.
εὐοῖ, εὐοῖ, εὐαῖ, εὐαῖ.

ΑΘΗΝΑΙΩΝ ΠΡΕΣΒΕΥΤΗΣ Α

<ὦ> Λάκων, πρόφαινε δὴ σὺ μοῦσαν ἐπὶ νέᾳ νέαν.

ΛΑΚΕΔΑΙΜΟΝΙΩΝ ΠΡΕΣΒΕΥΤΗΣ

Ταΰγετον αὖτ' ἐραννὸν ἐκλιπῶά,
Μῶά μόλε, <μόλε,> Λάκαινα, πρεπτὸν ἁμὶν
κλέωά τὸν Ἀμύκλαις σιὸν
καὶ Χαλκίοικον Ἀσάναν,
Τυνδαρίδας τ' ἀγασώς,
τοὶ δὴ πὰρ Εὐρώταν ψιάδδοντι.
εἶα μάλ' ἔμβη,
ὢ εἶα κοῦφα πᾶλον, ὡς
Σπάρταν ὑμνίωμες,
τᾷ σιῶν χοροὶ μέλοντι
καὶ ποδῶν κτύπος,
χᾆτε πῶλοι ταὶ κόραι
πὰρ τὸν Εὐρώταν
ἀμπάλλοντι πυκνὰ ποδοῖν
ἀγκονίωαί,
ταὶ δὲ κόμαι σείονται
ᾇπερ Βακχᾶν θυρσαδδωᾶν καὶ παιδδωᾶν.
ἁγῆται δ' ἁ Λήδας παῖς
ἁγνὰ χοραγὸς εὐπρεπής.

1298 σιὸν Valckenaer: Ἀπόλλω σιὸν (σεὸν B) a
1299 Ἀσάναν a: ἄνασσαν γρΣ[R]

Dance to victory, iai!
Evoi evoi, evai evai!

FIRST ATHENIAN DELEGATE

Now, my dear Spartan, your turn to give us some music: a novel song to match a novel song!

SPARTAN DELEGATE

Come back again from fair Taygetus,
Spartan Muse, come and distinguish this occasion
with a hymn to the God of Amyclae[116]
and Athena of the Brazen House[117]
and Tyndareos' fine sons,[118]
who gallop beside the Eurotas.
Ho there, hop!
Hey there, jump sprightly!
Let's sing a hymn to Sparta,
home of dances for the gods
and of stomping feet,
where by the Eurotas' banks
young girls frisk like fillies,
raising underfoot
dust clouds,
and tossing their tresses
like maenads waving their wands and playing,
led by Leda's daughter,[119]
their chorus leader pure and pretty.

[116] Apollo's sanctuary in Sparta, on the river Eurotas.
[117] The Spartan equivalent of Athena Polias at Athens.
[118] See 81 n.
[119] I.e., Helen, worshipped at Sparta not as the adulterous wife of epic poetry but as the ideal Spartan maiden and bride.

ἀλλ᾽ ἄγε, κόμαν παραμπύκιδδε χερί, ποδοῖν τε πάδη
ᾇ τις ἔλαφος, κρότον δ᾽ ἁμᾶ ποίη χορωφελήταν,
τὰν δ᾽ αὖ σιὰν τὰν παμμάχον, τὰν Χαλκίοικον ὕμνη.

(*To the chorus*) Come now, band your hair with your hand, with your feet start hopping like a deer, and start making some noise to spur the dance! And sing for the goddess who's won a total victory, Athena of the Brazen House!

All exit dancing, the chorus singing a traditional hymn to Athena.

WOMEN AT THE THESMOPHORIA

INTRODUCTORY NOTE

No production notices for *Women at the Thesmophoria* survive, but the available evidence favors the Dionysia of 411.

For the year there are three firm indicators. (1) A scholium on line 190 puts Euripides' death "in the sixth year" after the production, which by normal inclusive reckoning gives us 411, if the Marmor Parium is correct in dating Euripides' death to 407/6 (*FGrH* 239 A 63). Other sources date it to 406/5, the same year as the death of Sophocles, but this is probably a case of biographical synchronism, for it is incompatible with the plausible report in the *Life of Euripides* (44–47) that Sophocles led his chorus in mourning for him at a dramatic festival, which could be no later than the Dionysia of 406. (2) Lines 1060–61 refer to "last year's" production of Euripides' *Andromeda*, placed by a scholium on *Frogs* 53 "in the eighth year" before that play's production (406/5), i.e. in 412. (3) The reference in line 804 to Charminus' defeat at Syme in winter 412/11 (Thucydides 8.41–42), in a passage belittling Athenian naval performance generally, both rules out an earlier date and would lack point at a later date, since by the following year the Athenian navy had recovered its dominance in the Aegean.

For the festival the evidence, though less straightforward, clearly points to the Dionysia. Since *Lysistrata*, securely attested for 411, can be assigned with confidence to the Lenaea,[1] then *Women at the Thesmophoria* was presumably produced at the later festival, for though a poet could have two comedies produced at the same festival,[2] this was certainly rare. The internal evidence also indicates the Dionysia: whereas *Lysistrata* reflects the political status quo before the Assembly authorized Pisander's embassy to negotiate with Alcibiades and the Persians even at the cost of changing the democratic constitution, *Women at the Thesmophoria* reflects the period during which those negotiations were under way, condemning medizers (336–37, 365–66), subverters of the constitution (361–62), and aspirants to tyranny (338–39, 1143–44) in passages whose detachability from the action suggests that they were inserted not long before the performance.[3] Finally, Aristophanes is likelier to have planned *Lysistrata* for the parochial Lenaea and *Women at the Thesmophoria* for the cosmopolitan Dionysia than vice versa: the former is densely topical and sharply critical of current Athenian policy, while the latter is largely apolitical, is set at a festi-

[1] See *Lysistrata*, Introductory Note.

[2] Aristophanes seems to have done so at the Lenaea of 422 and Phrynichus at the Dionysia of 414 (see the Introductory Notes to *Wasps* and *Birds*), with only one of the plays being produced by its author, as we would expect to be the rule in competition; if this was the case in 411, Aristophanes presumably produced *Women at the Thesmophoria*, since Callistratus produced *Lysistrata*.

[3] See Thucydides 8.56–59, 65.2–66.5. It is highly unlikely that these passages would have been either inserted or left in the play after the failure of the embassy had been announced or the oligarchs' campaign of terror and assassination had already begun.

val widely celebrated in the Greek world, and satirizes an internationally popular poet.[4] Indeed, it seems that *Women at the Thesmophoria* itself soon gained an audience abroad, since we find its parodic hostage scene (688–764) depicted on a bell crater from southern Italy *c.* 370.[5]

Women at the Thesmophoria was never intended to be a politically engaged play, but rather a satire of wives and their portrayal in Euripides' tragedies, using extensive parody and the theme of gender inversion to explore the nature of dramatic mimesis both comic and tragic. The plot takes off from Euripides' reputation (assumed in *Lysistrata* 283–84 and 368–69 but not attested earlier) as a portrayer of wicked wives, and is built around scenes from the dramas of adventure and intrigue with happy endings that Euripides had been composing after the failure of his Trojan trilogy in 415.

Euripides (then about seventy years old) goes with his Kinsman[6] to ask the young tragic poet Agathon for help in a crisis: the matrons of Athens, assembled for the Thesmophoria, plan to decree his death because his scandalous heroines have alerted husbands to their hitherto secret misbehavior. Would Agathon, who claims that his effeminacy enables him to create realistic female charac-

4 For Euripides' contemporary celebrity see Plutarch, *Life of Nicias* 29.2–3.

5 Martin von Wagner Museum, Würzburg, H5697.

6 This character is referred to in the play only as *kedestes*, denoting any close relative by marriage. Ancient commentators identified him with Euripides' father-in-law Mnesilochus, but Euripides' high-handed treatment of him makes this unlikely, and we know of no comic hero who represents an actual person.

ters, be willing to disguise himself as a woman, infiltrate the Thesmophoria, and plead Euripides' case? When Agathon refuses, the Kinsman volunteers to undertake the mission. Shaven and disguised as a woman, the Kinsman attends the festival and contributes a defense speech that outrages rather than mollifies the matrons: Euripides, he argues, has not revealed even the tiniest fraction of the whole truth. The women become suspicious, and with the help of another Athenian effeminate, Cleisthenes, soon expose the Kinsman as a male intruder and sentence him to death. But the Kinsman, in parody of Euripides' *Telephus*, seizes a hostage (a wine skin disguised as a baby girl) and takes refuge at an altar, where he is guarded first by Critylla, a tough old woman, and then by a barbarian Archer. Euripides tries to rescue the Kinsman by reenacting rescue scenes from his own recent plays (*Palamedes*, *Helen*, and *Andromeda*), but these fail to deceive Critylla and the Archer. Finally, Euripides disguises himself as an old bawd, distracts the Archer with a dancing girl, and frees the Kinsman, having promised the women that he will never again portray them unfavorably.

The Thesmophoria was an appropriate dramatic venue both for a women's assembly and a confrontation between the genders. Its principal deities were the archetypal mother Demeter, goddess of cereal crops and human fertility, and her daughter Kore (Attic Pherephatta or Persephone). Their myth told how Hades, god of the underworld, kidnapped Kore and forced her to be his queen, and of Demeter's angry search for Kore, her blighting of the land in retaliation, and her final compromise with Hades: Demeter would provide crops for half the year but withhold them during the other half, when Kore lived with her infernal husband. This myth provided the pattern for, and explanation of the festival's rituals, mysteries, and sexual symbolism; the power, solidarity, and self-sufficiency of its celebrants; and its pervasive atmosphere of hostility toward men.

Aristophanes avoids satirizing the women's ritual activities *per se*, choosing only a few superficial details as the basis for his comic fantasy, whereby the female festive community parodies the male civic polis, and the women's assembly parodies the men's, including the ability to condemn an enemy. The assimilation is enhanced if the Thesmophoria actually met on Pnyx Hill, where the Athenian assembly (composed exclusively of adult citizen men) normally sat. This cannot be verified and may be part of the fantasy, but if so Aristophanes does not exploit it, as he does with the women's fantastic transgressions of male space in *Lysistrata* and *Assemblywomen*: our play takes the festival's location for granted, giving no hint that this was abnormal procedure.

The setting is the second day of Thesmophoria, a gloomy fast in which the women reverted to ancient ways, appropriate to the spirit of vengefulness with which they attack Euripides. The capture of a male spy (the Kinsman) recalls not only Euripides' *Telephus* but also episodes from Thesmophorian legends, much as the fate of the Magistrate in *Lysistrata* recalls the mythical victims of Dionysus' maenads. And Euripides, in his attempts to rescue the Kinsman from death and in his final compromise with the women, lightly suggests Demeter herself.

Euripides' reputation as a misogynist was evidently based not only on the predilection of so many of his female characters for misconduct but also on their unprecedented intensity and vividness. These characters were of course already present in the traditional myths, and other tragic poets had also dramatized them. But Euripides was distinct in having frequently embellished the myths, making wicked characters (male and female) even worse; inviting the audience at least to empathize with them; and making their speech and behavior seem closer to everyday experience than was customary in tragedy. In *Women at the Thesmophoria* the realism of the women created by Agathon and Euripides is a central element of the plot. Thus Euripides' portrayal of women could be thought relevant to the women who inhabited the spectators' own households.

If such realism was traditionally a hallmark not of tragedy but of comedy, then Euripides has transgressed the boundaries not only of gender but also of genre. Aristophanes puts Euripidean realism to the test of real life, or at any rate real life as fabricated by comedy: can the Kinsman bring off his role as a matron at the Thesmophoria, and when that fails, can Euripides rescue him by restaging his escape scenes? In the end, Euripidean tragedy is exposed as being just as artificial as the female costumes worn by Agathon, Euripides, and the Kinsman, and just as inadequate in the face of actual women, past masters of illusion and deception. Meanwhile, comedy reveals its own superiority at depicting the real world: the Kinsman's speech on the misbehavior of women is more realistic (according to the motive stereotypes) than Euripides' plays, and when Euripides' own stratagems have failed he is forced to resort to a comic ruse to rescue himself and the Kinsman.

Thus it seems that the comic poet has exposed and punished Euripides' genre transgression just as effectively as the women have punished his gender transgression. Euripidean realism is effective only when an audience suspends its disbelief and cooperates with the artifice, which Critylla and the Archer refuse to do. By contrast comedy, like its on-stage representative, the earthy and irrepressible Kinsman, can maintain its own generic integrity while incorporating tragedy, and also (at least in the case of Euripides) go tragedy one better. On the dramatic stage as in the women's world, normality is restored: Euripides will continue to write plays, but not about real women, and the rebellious matrons will go back to being (or at least seeming to be) proper wives.

Text

Four papyri preserve fragments of *Women at the Thesmophoria*; two of these are not cited in the notes, *POxy. 3839* (II/III), containing lines 25 (?), 742–66, 941–956, and *POxy. 3840* (IV), containing lines 1185–93. Only one independent medieval MS (R) preserves the text. Mu2 (XV), though copied directly from R, incorporates the work of an early editor who made simple emendations and supplied many line attributions.

Sigla

Π1	*PSI* 1194 + *PSI* xiv p. xv (II), lines 139–46, 237–46, 272–88, 94–96, 804–9
Π2	*POxy*. 1176 fr. 39 col. xii 1–16 (II), lines 335–37, 374–75[7]
R	Ravennas 429 (*c.* 950)

[7] This is a copy of Satyrus' *Life of Euripides*, which quotes these lines.

WOMEN AT THE THESMOPHORIA

Annotated Editions

F. H. M. Blaydes (Halle 1880).
A. von Velsen (Leipzig 1883).
J. van Leeuwen (Leiden 1904).
B. B. Rogers (London 1904), with English translation.
A. H. Sommerstein (Warminster 1994), with English translation.

ΤΑ ΤΟΥ ΔΡΑΜΑΤΟΣ ΠΡΟΣΩΠΑ

ΚΗΔΕΣΤΗΣ
Εὐριπίδου
ΕΥΡΙΠΙΔΗΣ
ΘΕΡΑΠΩΝ
Ἀγάθωνος
ΑΓΑΘΩΝ
ΚΡΙΤΥΛΛΑ
ΜΙΚΑ
ΣΤΕΦΑΝΟΠΩΛΙΣ
ΚΛΕΙΣΘΕΝΗΣ
ΠΡΥΤΑΝΙΣ
ΤΟΞΟΤΗΣ *Σκύθης*
ΗΧΩ

ΧΟΡΟΣ *Θεσμοφοριαζουσῶν*

ΚΩΦΑ ΠΡΟΣΩΠΑ
ΓΥΝΑΙΚΕΣ *Ἀττικαί*
ΜΑΝΙΑ *τίτθη Μίκας*
ΕΛΑΦΙΟΝ
ΤΕΡΗΔΩΝ

DRAMATIS PERSONAE

KINSMAN of Euripides
EURIPIDES
SLAVE of Agathon
AGATHON
CRITYLLA
MICA
GARLAND SELLER
CLEISTHENES
MARSHAL
SCYTHIAN POLICEMAN
ECHO

CHORUS of women celebrating the Thesmophoria

SILENT CHARACTERS
ATHENIAN WOMEN
MANIA, Mica's nurse
ELAPHIUM
TEREDON

ΘΕΣΜΟΦΟΡΙΑΖΟΥΣΑΙ

ΚΗΔΕΣΤΗΣ

ὦ Ζεῦ, χελιδὼν ἆρά ποτε φανήσεται;
ἀπολεῖ μ᾽ ἀλύων ἄνθρωπος ἐξ ἑωθινοῦ.
οἷόν τε, πρὶν τὸν σπλῆνα κομιδῇ μ᾽ ἐκβαλεῖν,
παρὰ σοῦ πυθέσθαι ποῖ μ᾽ ἄγεις, ὦὐριπίδη;

ΕΥΡΙΠΙΔΗΣ

ἀλλ᾽ οὐκ ἀκούειν δεῖ σε πάνθ᾽ ὅσ᾽ αὐτίκα
ὄψει παρεστώς.

ΚΗΔΕΣΤΗΣ

πῶς λέγεις; αὖθις φράσον·
οὐ δεῖ μ᾽ ἀκούειν;

ΕΥΡΙΠΙΔΗΣ

οὐχ ἅ γ᾽ ἂν μέλλῃς ὁρᾶν.

ΚΗΔΕΣΤΗΣ

οὐδ᾽ ἆρ᾽ ὁρᾶν δεῖ μ᾽;

ΕΥΡΙΠΙΔΗΣ

οὐχ ἅ γ᾽ ἂν ἀκούειν δέῃ.

ΚΗΔΕΣΤΗΣ

πῶς μοι παραινεῖς; δεξιῶς μέντοι λέγεις.

WOMEN AT THE THESMOPHORIA

EURIPIDES and KINSMAN walk from a side passage toward the scene building.

KINSMAN

Ah Zeus, will the spring swallow ever show up? This guy will be the death of me, plodding around since daybreak. Might it be possible, before I puke out my guts, to find out from you, Euripides, just where you're taking me?

EURIPIDES

You needn't hear it all, since you're going to see it for yourself.

KINSMAN

What? Say again? I needn't hear?

EURIPIDES

No, not what you're about to see.

KINSMAN

And I needn't see either?

EURIPIDES

No, not what you need to hear.

KINSMAN

What are you telling me? It's pretty subtle. You say that I

οὐ φῂς σὺ χρῆναί μ' οὔτ' ἀκούειν οὔθ' ὁρᾶν;

ΕΥΡΙΠΙΔΗΣ

χωρὶς γὰρ αὐτοῖν ἑκατέρου 'στὶν ἡ φύσις.

[ΚΗΔΕΣΤΗΣ

τοῦ μήτ' ἀκούειν μήθ' ὁρᾶν;

ΕΥΡΙΠΙΔΗΣ

εὖ ἴσθ' ὅτι.]

ΚΗΔΕΣΤΗΣ

πῶς χωρίς;

ΕΥΡΙΠΙΔΗΣ

οὕτω ταῦτα διεκρίθη τότε.
Αἰθὴρ γὰρ ὅτε τὰ πρῶτα διεχωρίζετο
καὶ ζῷ' ἐν αὑτῷ ξυνετέκνου κινούμενα,
ᾧ μὲν βλέπειν χρὴ πρῶτ' ἐμηχανήσατο
ὀφθαλμὸν ἀντίμιμον ἡλίου τροχῷ,
ἀκοῆς δὲ χοάνην ὦτα διετετρήνατο.

ΚΗΔΕΣΤΗΣ

διὰ τὴν χοάνην οὖν μήτ' ἀκούω μήθ' ὁρῶ;
νὴ τὸν Δί' ἥδομαί γε τουτὶ προσμαθών.
οἷόν γέ πού 'στιν αἱ σοφαὶ ξυνουσίαι.

ΕΥΡΙΠΙΔΗΣ

πόλλ' ἂν μάθοις τοιαῦτα παρ' ἐμοῦ.

ΚΗΔΕΣΤΗΣ

πῶς ἂν οὖν
πρὸς τοῖς ἀγαθοῖς τούτοισιν ἐξεύροιμ' ὅπως
ἔτι προσμάθοιμι χωλὸς εἶναι τὼ σκέλει;

should neither hear nor see?

EURIPIDES

I'm saying that these two are by nature mutually distinct.

[KINSMAN

What, not hearing and not seeing?

EURIPIDES

To be sure.]

KINSMAN

How do you mean, distinct?

EURIPIDES

This is how they were separated long ago: Aether, when in primordial time he began to separate from Earth and with her begat within himself living things astir, first fashioned for sight the eye, counter image of the solar disc, and, as a funnel for hearing, drilled the ear.

KINSMAN

So because of this funnel I'm not to hear or see? I'm certainly delighted to have this additional lesson. These deep conversations really are something!

EURIPIDES

You could learn many other such lessons from me.

KINSMAN

As a matter of fact I'd love to figure out how to learn another fine lesson: how to go lame in both legs!

---

[12] del. van Herwerden

ΕΥΡΙΠΙΔΗΣ

βάδιζε δευρὶ καὶ πρόσεχε τὸν νοῦν.

ΚΗΔΕΣΤΗΣ

ἰδού.

ΕΥΡΙΠΙΔΗΣ

ὁρᾷς τὸ θύριον τοῦτο;

ΚΗΔΕΣΤΗΣ

νὴ τὸν Ἡρακλέα

οἶμαί γε.

ΕΥΡΙΠΙΔΗΣ

σίγα νυν.

ΚΗΔΕΣΤΗΣ

σιωπῶ τὸ θύριον.

ΕΥΡΙΠΙΔΗΣ

ἄκου᾽.

ΚΗΔΕΣΤΗΣ

ἀκούω καὶ σιωπῶ τὸ θύριον.

ΕΥΡΙΠΙΔΗΣ

ἐνταῦθ᾽ Ἀγάθων ὁ κλεινὸς οἰκῶν τυγχάνει
ὁ τραγῳδοποιός.

ΚΗΔΕΣΤΗΣ

ποῖος οὗτος Ἀγάθων;

EURIPIDES

Come along here and pay attention.

They mount the stage and move toward the central door of the stage building.

KINSMAN

Now what?

EURIPIDES

Do you see that doorway?

KINSMAN

By Heracles, I believe I do!

EURIPIDES

Be quiet now.

KINSMAN

I'm being quiet about the doorway.

EURIPIDES

Listen.

KINSMAN

I'm listening and being quiet about the doorway.

EURIPIDES

This happens to be the dwelling of the renowned tragic poet Agathon.[1]

KINSMAN

What Agathon do you mean?

[1] Agathon, having won first prize in his debut in 416, was the most innovative tragic poet of the younger generation, and famed for his personal beauty and promiscuous passive homosexuality.

ΕΥΡΙΠΙΔΗΣ

ἔστιν τις Ἀγάθων—

ΚΗΔΕΣΤΗΣ

μῶν ὁ μέλας, ὁ καρτερός;

ΕΥΡΙΠΙΔΗΣ

οὔκ, ἀλλ᾽ ἕτερός τις. οὐχ ἑόρακας πώποτε;

ΚΗΔΕΣΤΗΣ

μῶν ὁ δασυπώγων;

ΕΥΡΙΠΙΔΗΣ

οὐχ ἑόρακας πώποτε;

ΚΗΔΕΣΤΗΣ

μὰ τὸν Δί᾽ οὔπω γ᾽ ὥστε κἀμέ γ᾽ εἰδέναι.

ΕΥΡΙΠΙΔΗΣ

καὶ μὴν βεβίνηκας σύ γ᾽, ἀλλ᾽ οὐκ οἶσθ᾽ ἴσως.
ἀλλ᾽ ἐκποδὼν πτήξωμεν, ὡς ἐξέρχεται
θεράπων τις αὐτοῦ πῦρ ἔχων καὶ μυρρίνας,
προθυσόμενος, ἔοικε, τῆς ποιήσεως.

ΘΕΡΑΠΩΝ

εὔφημος πᾶς ἔστω λαός,
στόμα συγκλῄσας· ἐπιδημεῖ γὰρ
θίασος Μουσῶν ἔνδον μελάθρων
τῶν δεσποσύνων μελοποιῶν.
ἐχέτω δὲ πνοὰς νήνεμος αἰθήρ,
κῦμα δὲ πόντου μὴ κελαδείτω
γλαυκόν—

EURIPIDES

There is an Agathon—

KINSMAN

You don't mean the suntanned, strong one?

EURIPIDES

No, a different one. You've never seen him?

KINSMAN

Not the one with the full beard?

EURIPIDES

You've never seen him?

KINSMAN

Absolutely not, as far as I know.

EURIPIDES

Well, you must have fucked him, though you might not know it. But let's hunker out of the way; one of his slaves is coming outside with brazier and myrtle sprigs, probably to make an offering for his master's success in poetic composition.

Enter Agathon's Slave.

SLAVE

Let the folk keep holy silence,
gating the mouth, for here sojourns
the holy company of Muses within
the suzerain's halls, fashioning song.
Let Aether windless hold his breath,
and the whelming brine its boom,
gray—

---

32 ἑόρακας Bentley: ἑόρακα R

ΚΗΔΕΣΤΗΣ

βομβάξ.

ΕΥΡΙΠΙΔΗΣ

σίγα. τί λέγει;

ΘΕΡΑΠΩΝ

πτηνῶν τε γένη κατακοιμάσθω,
θηρῶν τ' ἀγρίων πόδες ὑλοδρόμων
μὴ λυέσθων—

ΚΗΔΕΣΤΗΣ

βομβαλοβομβάξ.

ΘΕΡΑΠΩΝ

μέλλει γὰρ ὁ καλλιεπὴς Ἀγάθων
πρόμος ἡμέτερος—

ΚΗΔΕΣΤΗΣ

μῶν βινεῖσθαι;

ΘΕΡΑΠΩΝ

τίς ὁ φωνήσας;

ΚΗΔΕΣΤΗΣ

νήνεμος αἰθήρ.

ΘΕΡΑΠΩΝ

δρυόχους τιθέναι δράματος ἀρχάς.
κάμπτει δὲ νέας ἁψῖδας ἐπῶν,
τὰ δὲ τορνεύει, τὰ δὲ κολλομελεῖ,
καὶ γνωμοτυπεῖ κἀντονομάζει
καὶ κηροχυτεῖ καὶ γογγύλλει
καὶ χοανεύει—

KINSMAN

Blah!

EURIPIDES

Shhh! What's he say?

SLAVE

Let the feathered tribes lie down in rest,
and the paws of wild beasts that course the woods
be checked—

KINSMAN

Blah blah blah!

SLAVE

for that mellifluous Agathon,
our champion, prepares—

KINSMAN

to get fucked?

SLAVE

Who uttered that?

KINSMAN

Windless Aether.

SLAVE

— to lay the keel of his inchoate drama.
He's warping fresh strakes of verses;
some he planes down, others he couples,
minting aphorisms, swapping meanings,
channeling wax and rounding the mold
and funneling metal—

ΚΗΔΕΣΤΗΣ

καὶ λαικάζει.

ΘΕΡΑΠΩΝ

τίς ἀγροιώτας πελάθει θριγκοῖς;

ΚΗΔΕΣΤΗΣ

ὃς ἕτοιμος σοῦ τοῦ τε ποιητοῦ
τοῦ καλλιεποῦς <κατὰ> τοῦ θριγκοῦ
συγγογγύλας καὶ συστρέψας
τουτὶ τὸ πέος χοανεῦσαι.

ΘΕΡΑΠΩΝ

ἦ που νέος γ᾽ ὢν ἦσθ᾽ ὑβριστής, ὦ γέρον.

ΕΥΡΙΠΙΔΗΣ

ὦ δαιμόνιε, τοῦτον μὲν ἔα χαίρειν, σὺ δὲ
Ἀγάθωνά μοι δεῦρ᾽ ἐκκάλεσον πάσῃ τέχνῃ.

ΘΕΡΑΠΩΝ

μηδὲν ἱκέτευ᾽· αὐτὸς γὰρ ἔξεισιν τάχα·
καὶ γὰρ μελοποιεῖν ἄρχεται. χειμῶνος οὖν
ὄντος κατακάμπτειν τὰς στροφὰς οὐ ῥᾴδιον,
ἢν μὴ προΐῃ θύρασι πρὸς τὸν ἥλιον.

ΕΥΡΙΠΙΔΗΣ

τί οὖν ἐγὼ δρῶ;

ΘΕΡΑΠΩΝ

περίμεν᾽, ὡς ἐξέρχεται.

60 suppl. Faber

KINSMAN

and sucking cocks.

SLAVE

What yokel draws nigh the ramparts?

KINSMAN

One who's ready to take you and your
mellifluous poet, and spin you around,
and bend you over, and up your rampart
funnel this cock of mine.

SLAVE

Old man, I can't imagine what a rapist you were when you were a boy.

EURIPIDES

(*to Slave*): My good fellow, forget about him! Just summon Agathon here to me; it's urgent.

SLAVE

Supplicate not; the master shall soon emerge. You see, he's beginning to fashion a song, and, it being wintertime,[2] he's hard put to limber his riffs without coming outdoors into the sun.

EURIPIDES

So what should I be doing?

SLAVE

Wait around; he's coming out.

Exit Slave.

[2] In 412/11 the Thesmophoria, which normally fell in October, had fallen in November.

ΕΥΡΙΠΙΔΗΣ

ὦ Ζεῦ, τί δρᾶσαι διανοεῖ με τήμερον;

ΚΗΔΕΣΤΗΣ

νὴ τοὺς θεοὺς ἐγὼ πυθέσθαι βούλομαι
τί τὸ πρᾶγμα τουτί. τί στένεις; τί δυσφορεῖς;
οὐ χρῆν σε κρύπτειν ὄντα κηδεστὴν ἐμόν.

ΕΥΡΙΠΙΔΗΣ

ἔστιν κακόν μοι μέγα τι προπεφυραμένον.

ΚΗΔΕΣΤΗΣ

ποῖόν τι;

ΕΥΡΙΠΙΔΗΣ

τῇδε θἠμέρᾳ κριθήσεται
εἴτ᾽ ἔστ᾽ ἔτι ζῶν εἴτ᾽ ἀπόλωλ᾽ Εὐριπίδης.

ΚΗΔΕΣΤΗΣ

καὶ πῶς; ἐπεὶ νῦν γ᾽ οὔτε τὰ δικαστήρια
μέλλει δικάζειν οὔτε βουλῆς ἐσθ᾽ ἕδρα,
ἐπείπερ ἐστὶ Θεσμοφορίων ἡ μέση.

ΕΥΡΙΠΙΔΗΣ

τοῦτ᾽ αὐτὸ γάρ τοι κἀπολεῖν με προσδοκῶ.
αἱ γὰρ γυναῖκες ἐπιβεβουλεύκασί μοι
κἀν Θεσμοφόροιν μέλλουσι περί μου τήμερον
ἐκκλησιάζειν ἐπ᾽ ὀλέθρῳ.

80 ἐπείπερ ἐστὶ Nauck: ἐπεὶ τρίτη 'στὶ R, cf. Σ

---

[3] Perhaps from Euripides' *Bellerophon*, cf. *Peace* 58, 62.

EURIPIDES

O Zeus, what do you mean to do to me today?[3]

KINSMAN

I'd truly like to be told what's going on here. What's all this groaning? What's the trouble? You shouldn't be hiding it from me: I'm your kinsman.

EURIPIDES

Some rather nasty trouble has been cooked up for me.

KINSMAN

Like what?

EURIPIDES

This very day it will be adjudged: does Euripides live on, or is he a goner?

KINSMAN

How can that be? The courts won't be trying cases today, and the Council isn't in session either, because it's the middle day of the Thesmophoria.[4]

EURIPIDES

Precisely; that's what I expect will make a goner of me. The women, you see, have devised a plot against me, and today in the sanctuary of the Two Thesmophoroi[5] they're going to hold an assembly[6] on the question of my destruction.

[4] The "Fast Day" (*nesteia*), when the celebrants abstained from food and drink.

[5] Demeter Thesmophoros and Pherrephatta (Persephone or Kore, "Maiden") were the principal deities of the Thesmophoria.

[6] As for the Thesmophoria women formed a cultic organization headed by their own elected leaders (*archousai*), here Aristophanes imagines the women turning it into a political assembly, as the men did on the Pnyx.

ΚΗΔΕΣΤΗΣ

τιὴ τί δή;

ΕΥΡΙΠΙΔΗΣ

ὁτιὴ τραγῳδῶ καὶ κακῶς αὐτὰς λέγω.

ΚΗΔΕΣΤΗΣ

νὴ τὸν Ποσειδῶ καὶ δίκαιά <γ᾽> ἂν πάθοις.
ἀτὰρ τίν᾽ εἰς ταύτας σὺ μηχανὴν ἔχεις;

ΕΥΡΙΠΙΔΗΣ

Ἀγάθωνα πεῖσαι τὸν τραγῳδοδιδάσκαλον
εἰς Θεσμοφόροιν ἐλθεῖν.

ΚΗΔΕΣΤΗΣ

τί δράσοντ᾽; εἰπέ μοι.

ΕΥΡΙΠΙΔΗΣ

ἐκκλησιάσοντ᾽ ἐν ταῖς γυναιξὶ χἂν δέῃ
λέξονθ᾽ ὑπὲρ ἐμοῦ.

ΚΗΔΕΣΤΗΣ

πότερα φανερὸν ἢ λάθρᾳ;

ΕΥΡΙΠΙΔΗΣ

λάθρᾳ, στολὴν γυναικὸς ἠμφιεσμένον.

ΚΗΔΕΣΤΗΣ

τὸ πρᾶγμα κομψὸν καὶ σφόδρ᾽ ἐκ τοῦ σοῦ τρόπου·
τοῦ γὰρ τεχνάζειν ἡμέτερος ὁ πυραμοῦς.

ΕΥΡΙΠΙΔΗΣ

σίγα.

KINSMAN

Whatever for?

EURIPIDES

Because I make tragedy of them and slander them.

KINSMAN

Well, it would certainly serve you right. But what's your strategy against these women?

EURIPIDES

To persuade Agathon, the tragic producer, to go to the Thesmophorium.

KINSMAN

And do what? Tell me.

EURIPIDES

To attend the women's assembly and say whatever's necessary on my behalf.

KINSMAN

Openly or in disguise?

EURIPIDES

In disguise, dressed up like a woman.

KINSMAN

A pretty cute bit, and just your style. We take the cake for craftiness!

EURIPIDES

Shh!

---

87 *εἰς ταύτας* Sandbach: *ἐκ ταύτης* R

ΚΗΔΕΣΤΗΣ

τί δ' ἐστίν;

ΕΥΡΙΠΙΔΗΣ

Ἀγάθων ἐξέρχεται.

ΚΗΔΕΣΤΗΣ

καὶ ποῦ <'σθ';

ΕΥΡΙΠΙΔΗΣ

ὅπου> 'στίν; οὗτος οὐκκυκλούμενος.

ΚΗΔΕΣΤΗΣ

ἀλλ' ἦ τυφλὸς μέν εἰμ'; ἐγὼ γὰρ οὐχ ὁρῶ
ἄνδρ' οὐδέν' ἐνθάδ' ὄντα, Κυρήνην δ' ὁρῶ.

ΕΥΡΙΠΙΔΗΣ

σίγα· μελῳδεῖν αὖ παρασκευάζεται.

ΚΗΔΕΣΤΗΣ

μύρμηκος ἀτραπούς, ἢ τί διαμινυρίζεται;

ΑΓΑΘΩΝ

ἱερὰν χθονίαιν
δεξάμεναι λαμπάδα, κοῦραι, ξὺν ἐλευθέρᾳ
πατρίδι χορεύσασθε βοάν.

96 suppl. Meineke
101 χθονίαιν Meineke: χθονίαις R
103 πραπίδι Wecklein

KINSMAN

What?

EURIPIDES

Agathon's coming out.

AGATHON, reclining on a chaise longue and surrounded by feminine paraphernalia, is wheeled out on the eccyclema.

KINSMAN

Where is he?

EURIPIDES

Where is he? Right there, the man who's being rolled out.

KINSMAN

Well, I must be blind, because I can't see any *man* there at all, only Cyrene![7]

EURIPIDES

Shh; he's getting ready to sing his aria.

KINSMAN

What's that he's vocalizing, ant tracks or something?

AGATHON[8]

as leader
Maidens, take up the holy
torch of the Nether Twain,[9] and with country
freed, dance a loud cry!

[7] A celebrated courtesan, cf. *Frogs* 1327–28 with scholia.

[8] Agathon's song imagines the maidens of Troy celebrating after the Greeks had lifted their siege; its rhythms, mainly Ionic, suggest asiatic luxury and effeminacy.

[9] Demeter and Persephone.

τίνι δαιμόνων ὁ κῶμος;
λέγε νυν. εὐπ‹ε›ίστως δὲ τοὐμὸν
δαίμονας ἔχει σεβίσαι.

ἄγε νῦν, ὀλβίζετε, Μοῦσα‹ι›,
χρυσέων ῥύτορα τόξων
Φοῖβον, ὃς ἱδρύσατο χώρας
γύαλα Σιμουντίδι γᾷ.

χαῖρε καλλίσταις ἀοιδαῖς,
Φοῖβ᾿, ἐν εὐμούσοισι τιμαῖς
γέρας ἱερὸν προφέρων.

τάν τ᾿ ἐν ὄρεσι δρυογόνοισι
κόραν ἀείσατ᾿ Ἄρτεμιν ἀγροτέραν.

ἕπομαι κλῄζουσα σεμνὰν
γόνον ὀλβίζουσα Λατοῦς,
Ἄρτεμιν ἀπειρολεχῆ.

Λατώ τε κρούματά τ᾿ Ἀσιάδος ποδὶ
παράρυθμ᾿ εὔρυθμα Φρυγίων
διὰ νεύματα Χαρίτων.

σέβομαι Λατώ τ᾿ ἄνασσαν

as chorus
For which deity hold we our revel?
O say! I'm obediently disposed
when it comes to adoring the gods.
as leader
Come now, Muses, venerate
him who draws golden arrows,
Phoebus, who founded our country's vales
in the land of the Simois.[10]
as chorus
Take joy in our song most fair,
Phoebus, the first to flaunt the holy gift
of our musical tribute.
as leader
Hymn too the maiden born in the oak-birthing
mountains, Artemis of the Wild.
as chorus
I follow you, invoking, praising
the holy spawn of Leto,
Artemis untried in bed!
as leader
Yes Leto, and the chords of the Asian strings
beating nicely against the beat as the Phrygian
Graces nod the tempo.
as chorus
I venerate Lady Leto

[10] Apollo, who with Poseidon built the walls of Troy; the Simois was a river in the Trojan plain.

---

105 suppl. Reiske 107 ὀλβίζετε (ὄλβιζε iam Bentley) Gannon: ὅπλιζε R suppl. Wilamowitz

κίθαρίν τε ματέρ᾽ ὕμνων
ἄρσενι βοᾷ δοκίμων.

τᾷ φάος ἔσσυτο δαιμονίοις
ὄμμασιν, ὑμετέρας τε δι᾽
αἰφνιδίου ὀπός· ὧν χάριν
  ἄνακτ᾽ ἄγαλλε<τε> Φοῖβον.

χαῖρ᾽, ὄλβιε παῖ Λατοῦς.

ΚΗΔΕΣΤΗΣ

ὡς ἡδὺ τὸ μέλος, ὦ πότνιαι Γενετυλλίδες,
καὶ θηλυδριῶδες καὶ κατεγλωττισμένον
καὶ μανδαλωτόν, ὥστ᾽ ἐμοῦ γ᾽ ἀκροωμένου
ὑπὸ τὴν ἕδραν αὐτὴν ὑπῆλθε γάργαλος.
καί σ᾽, ὦ νεανίσχ᾽, εἴ τις εἶ, κατ᾽ Αἰσχύλον
ἐκ τῆς Λυκουργείας ἐρέσθαι βούλομαι.
ποδαπὸς ὁ γύννις; τίς πάτρα; τίς ἡ στολή;
τίς ἡ τάραξις τοῦ βίου; τί βάρβιτος
λαλεῖ κροκωτῷ; τί δὲ λυρὰ κεκρυφάλῳ;
τί λήκυθος καὶ στρόφιον; ὡς οὐ ξύμφορα.
τίς δαὶ κατόπτρου καὶ ξίφους κοινωνία;
σύ τ᾽ αὐτός, ὦ παῖ, πότερον ὡς ἀνὴρ τρέφει;
καὶ ποῦ πέος; ποῦ χλαῖνα; ποῦ Λακωνικαί;
ἀλλ᾽ ὡς γυνὴ δῆτ᾽; εἶτα ποῦ τὰ τιτθία;
τί φῄς; τί σιγᾷς; ἀλλὰ δῆτ᾽ ἐκ τοῦ μέλους
ζητῶ σ᾽, ἐπειδή γ᾽ αὐτὸς οὐ βούλει φράσαι;

125 δοκίμων Schöne: δοκίμῳ R S: δόκιμον Dindorf, cf. Σ[R]

and the cithara, mother of songs
renowned for their masculine clangor.
as leader
Whereby did a sparkle whisk from eyes
divine, as also by virtue of your
startling vociferation; wherefore
all glorify Lord Phoebus!
as chorus
Hail, happy scion of Leto!

KINSMAN

Holy Genetyllides,[11] what a pretty song! How feministic and tongue-gagged and deep-kissed! Just hearing it brought a tingle to my very butt! And you, young lad, I want to ask you, à la Aeschylus' *Lycurgeia*,[12] what kind of female you are. Whence comes this femme? What's its homeland? What's its dress? What confoundment of living is this? What has a lute to chat about with a party dress? Or a lyre with a hairnet? Here's an oil flask and a brassiere: how ill-fitting! And what's this society of mirror and sword? And you yourself, child, are you being raised male? Then where's your dick? Your suit? Your Spartan shoes? All right, say you're a woman: then where are your tits? Well? Why don't you answer? Or must I find you out from your song, since you yourself refuse to speak?

[11] See *Lysistrata*, 2 n.

[12] A tetralogy dramatizing the struggle between the Thracian king Lycurgus and Dionysus, who in the first play, *Edonians* (as in Euripides' *Bacchae*, 453 ff.), is taunted for his effeminate qualities.

---

127 ὑμ- Nietzsche: ἡμ- R   128 suppl. Austin

ΑΓΑΘΩΝ

ὦ πρέσβυ πρέσβυ, τοῦ φθόνου μὲν τὸν ψόγον
ἤκουσα, τὴν δ᾽ ἄλγησιν οὐ παρεσχόμην·
ἐγὼ δὲ τὴν ἐσθῆθ᾽ ἅμα <τῇ> γνώμῃ φορῶ.
χρὴ γὰρ ποιητὴν ἄνδρα πρὸς τὰ δράματα
ἃ δεῖ ποιεῖν, πρὸς ταῦτα τοὺς τρόπους ἔχειν.
αὐτίκα γυναικεῖ᾽ ἢν ποιῇ τις δράματα,
μετουσίαν δεῖ τῶν τρόπων τὸ σῶμ᾽ ἔχειν.

ΚΗΔΕΣΤΗΣ

οὐκοῦν κελητίζεις, ὅταν Φαίδραν ποιῇς;

ΑΓΑΘΩΝ

ἀνδρεῖα δ᾽ ἢν ποιῇ τις, ἐν τῷ σώματι
ἔνεσθ᾽ ὑπάρχον τοῦθ᾽. ἃ δ᾽ οὐ κεκτήμεθα,
μίμησις ἤδη ταῦτα συνθηρεύεται.

ΚΗΔΕΣΤΗΣ

ὅταν σατύρους τοίνυν ποιῇς, καλεῖν ἐμέ,
ἵνα συμποιῶ σοὔπισθεν ἐστυκὼς ἐγώ.

ΑΓΑΘΩΝ

ἄλλως τ᾽ ἄμουσόν ἐστι ποιητὴν ἰδεῖν
ἀγρεῖον ὄντα καὶ δασύν. σκέψαι δ᾽ ὅτι
Ἴβυκος ἐκεῖνος κἀνακρέων ὁ Τήιος
κἀλκαῖος, οἵπερ ἁρμονίαν ἐχύμισαν,
ἐμιτροφόρουν τε καὶ διεκλῶντ᾽ Ἰωνικῶς.
καὶ Φρύνιχος,—τοῦτον γὰρ οὖν ἀκήκοας—
αὐτός τε καλὸς ἦν καὶ καλῶς ἠμπίσχετο·

163 διεκλῶντ᾽ Toup: διεκίνων R: διεκίνουν S

AGATHON

Old man, old man, I heard your envious mockery, yet felt no pain thereat. I coordinate my clothing with my thoughts. To be a poet, a man must suit his behavior to the requirements of his plays. If, say, he's writing plays about women, his body must partake of women's behavior.

KINSMAN

So when you're writing a *Phaedra*, you climb on top?[13]

AGATHON

If one writes about men, that element of the body is at hand. But qualities we do not have must be sought by mimicry.

KINSMAN

Well, let me know when you're writing about satyrs; I'll get behind you with my hard-on and show you how.

AGATHON

Besides, 'tis discordant to see a poet looking loutish and shaggy. Observe that the renowned Ibycus, and Anacreon of Teos, and Alcaeus—poets who put some spice into music—used to wear bonnets and cavort Ionian style.[14] And Phrynichus—you must have heard of *him*—was both beautiful and beautifully dressed.[15] And that's why his

[13] Phaedra's love for her stepson, dramatized by both Sophocles and Euripides, made her a byword for the wanton wife.

[14] These lyric poets of the previous century were known especially for their love songs.

[15] A tragic poet of the Aeschylean period, noted for the sweetness of his poetry.

διὰ τοῦτ᾽ ἄρ᾽ αὐτοῦ καὶ κάλ᾽ ἦν τὰ δράματα.
ὅμοια γὰρ ποιεῖν ἀνάγκη τῇ φύσει.

ΚΗΔΕΣΤΗΣ

ταῦτ᾽ ἄρ᾽ ὁ Φιλοκλέης αἰσχρὸς ὢν αἰσχρῶς ποιεῖ,
ὁ δὲ Ξενοκλέης ὢν κακὸς κακῶς ποιεῖ,
ὁ δ᾽ αὖ Θέογνις ψυχρὸς ὢν ψυχρῶς ποιεῖ.

ΑΓΑΘΩΝ

ἅπασ᾽ ἀνάγκη. ταῦτα γάρ τοι γνοὺς ἐγὼ
ἐμαυτὸν ἐθεράπευσα.

ΚΗΔΕΣΤΗΣ

πῶς, πρὸς τῶν θεῶν;

ΕΥΡΙΠΙΔΗΣ

παῦσαι βαΰζων· καὶ γὰρ ἐγὼ τοιοῦτος ἦν
ὢν τηλικοῦτος, ἡνίκ᾽ ἠρχόμην ποιεῖν.

ΚΗΔΕΣΤΗΣ

μὰ τὸν Δί᾽, οὐ ζηλῶ σε τῆς παιδεύσεως.

ΕΥΡΙΠΙΔΗΣ

ἀλλ᾽ ὧνπερ οὕνεκ᾽ ἦλθον, ἔα μ᾽ εἰπεῖν.

ΚΗΔΕΣΤΗΣ

λέγε.

ΕΥΡΙΠΙΔΗΣ

Ἀγάθων, "σοφοῦ πρὸς ἀνδρός, ὅστις ἐν βραχεῖ
πολλοὺς καλῶς οἷός τε συντέμνειν λόγους."
ἐγὼ δὲ καινῇ ξυμφορᾷ πεπληγμένος
ἱκέτης ἀφῖγμαι πρὸς σέ.

plays were also beautiful. For as we are made, so must we compose.

KINSMAN

That must be why the revolting Philocles writes so revoltingly, and the base Xenocles[16] so basely, or the frigid Theognis[17] so frigidly!

AGATHON

It's an absolute rule, and because I understood that, I doctored myself up.

KINSMAN

How, for heaven's sake?

EURIPIDES

Stop your barking! I was the same way at his age, when I began to write.

KINSMAN

I certainly don't envy you your rearing!

EURIPIDES

All right, let me tell you why I've come.

AGATHON

Do say.

EURIPIDES

Agathon, "'tis the sage man who can say much in a few finely trimmed words."[18] Smitten by novel misfortune, I am come a suppliant to your door.

16 A son of the tragic poet and general Carcinus; he seems to have suffered a recent theatrical or political embarrassment, cf. 440–42.

17 Long noted for the "frigidity" of his style, cf. *Acharnians* 138–40.

18 From Euripides' *Aeolus*, fr. 28.

ΑΓΑΘΩΝ

τοῦ χρείαν ἔχων;

ΕΥΡΙΠΙΔΗΣ

μέλλουσί μ᾽ αἱ γυναῖκες ἀπολεῖν τήμερον
τοῖς Θεσμοφορίοις, ὅτι κακῶς αὐτὰς λέγω.

ΑΓΑΘΩΝ

τίς οὖν παρ᾽ ἡμῶν ἐστιν ὠφέλειά σοι;

ΕΥΡΙΠΙΔΗΣ

ἡ πᾶσ᾽. ἐὰν γὰρ ἐγκαθεζόμενος λάθρᾳ
ἐν ταῖς γυναιξίν, ὡς δοκῶν εἶναι γυνή,
ὑπεραποκρίνῃ μου, σαφῶς σώσεις ἐμέ.
μόνος γὰρ ἂν λέξειας ἀξίως ἐμοῦ.

ΑΓΑΘΩΝ

ἔπειτα πῶς οὐκ αὐτὸς ἀπολογεῖ παρών;

ΕΥΡΙΠΙΔΗΣ

ἐγὼ φράσω σοι. πρῶτα μὲν γιγνώσκομαι·
ἔπειτα πολιός εἰμι καὶ πώγων᾽ ἔχω,
σὺ δ᾽ εὐπρόσωπος, λευκός, ἐξυρημένος,
γυναικόφωνος, ἁπαλός, εὐπρεπὴς ἰδεῖν.

ΑΓΑΘΩΝ

Εὐριπίδη—

ΕΥΡΙΠΙΔΗΣ

τί ἐστιν;

ΑΓΑΘΩΝ

ἐποίησάς ποτε·
"χαίρεις ὁρῶν φῶς, πατέρα δ᾽ οὐ χαίρειν δοκεῖς;"

AGATHON

What is your need?

EURIPIDES

The women at the Thesmophoria are preparing to destroy me this very day, because I slander them.

AGATHON

So what can we contribute to your cause?

EURIPIDES

Everything! If you attend the women's meeting covertly—because you'll pass for a woman—and rebut their accusations against me, you'll surely be my salvation. For you alone could speak in a manner worthy of me.

AGATHON

Then why don't you go and make your own defense?

EURIPIDES

I'll tell you. First, I'm well known. Second, I'm an old graybeard. You, by contrast, are good-looking, pale, clean shaven, soft, presentable, and you sound like a woman.

AGATHON

Euripides—

EURIPIDES

Well?

AGATHON

—did you yourself once write, "You love life, son: do you think your father doesn't?"[19]

19 *Alcestis* 691, where Pheres rejects his son's request to die in his place.

ΕΥΡΙΠΙΔΗΣ

ἔγωγε.

ΑΓΑΘΩΝ

μή νυν ἐλπίσῃς τὸ σὸν κακὸν
ἡμᾶς ὑφέξειν. καὶ γὰρ ἂν μαινοίμεθ᾽ ἄν.
ἀλλ᾽ αὐτὸς ὅ γε σόν ἐστιν οἰκείως φέρε.
τὰς συμφορὰς γὰρ οὐχὶ τοῖς τεχνάσμασιν
φέρειν δίκαιον, ἀλλὰ τοῖς παθήμασιν.

ΚΗΔΕΣΤΗΣ

καὶ μὴν σύ γ᾽, ὦ κατάπυγον, εὐρύπρωκτος εἶ
οὐ τοῖς λόγοισιν, ἀλλὰ τοῖς παθήμασιν.

ΕΥΡΙΠΙΔΗΣ

τί δ᾽ ἐστὶν ὅτι δέδοικας ἐλθεῖν αὐτόσε;

ΑΓΑΘΩΝ

κάκιον ἀπολοίμην ἂν ἢ σύ.

ΕΥΡΙΠΙΔΗΣ

πῶς;

ΑΓΑΘΩΝ

ὅπως;
δοκῶν γυναικῶν ἔργα νυκτερείσια
κλέπτειν ὑφαρπάζειν τε θήλειαν Κύπριν.

ΚΗΔΕΣΤΗΣ

ἰδού γε κλέπτειν· νὴ Δία βινεῖσθαι μὲν οὖν.
ἀτὰρ ἡ πρόφασίς γε νὴ Δί᾽ εἰκότως ἔχει.

ΕΥΡΙΠΙΔΗΣ

τί οὖν; ποιήσεις ταῦτα;

EURIPIDES

I did.

AGATHON

Then don't expect us to shoulder your misfortune. We'd have to be crazy! No, your own burden you must privately shoulder yourself. Misfortune should by rights be confronted not with tricky contrivances but in a spirit of submission.

KINSMAN

You certainly got *your* wide asshole, you faggot, not with words but in the spirit of submission!

EURIPIDES

What is it that makes you afraid to go to that particular place?

AGATHON

I would perish more wretchedly than you!

EURIPIDES

Why?

AGATHON

Why, you ask? I'd appear to be stealing the nocturnal doings of women and absconding with the female Cypris.[20]

KINSMAN

"Stealing" he says! Getting fucked is more like it. Still, his excuse is pretty plausible.

EURIPIDES

What's it to be, then? Will you do it?

[20] I.e., Aphrodite; Agathon fears that he would make a more attractive woman than the women themselves, and so provoke their hatred.

ΑΓΑΘΩΝ

μὴ δόκει γε σύ.

ΕΥΡΙΠΙΔΗΣ

ὢ τρισκακοδαίμων, ὡς ἀπόλωλ᾽.

ΚΗΔΕΣΤΗΣ

Εὐριπίδη,
ὦ φίλτατ᾽, ὦ κηδεστά, μὴ σαυτὸν προδῷς.

ΕΥΡΙΠΙΔΗΣ

πῶς οὖν ποιήσω δῆτα;

ΚΗΔΕΣΤΗΣ

τοῦτον μὲν μακρὰ
κλάειν κέλευ᾽, ἐμοὶ δ᾽ ὅ τι βούλει χρῶ λαβών.

ΕΥΡΙΠΙΔΗΣ

ἄγε νυν, ἐπειδὴ σαυτὸν ἐπιδίδως ἐμοί,
ἀπόδυθι τουτὶ θοἰμάτιον.

ΚΗΔΕΣΤΗΣ

καὶ δὴ χαμαί.
ἀτὰρ τί μέλλεις δρᾶν μ᾽;

ΕΥΡΙΠΙΔΗΣ

ἀποξυρεῖν ταδί,
τὰ κάτω δ᾽ ἀφεύειν.

ΚΗΔΕΣΤΗΣ

ἀλλὰ πρᾶττ᾽, εἴ σοι δοκεῖ·
ἢ μὴ ᾽πιδοῦναι ᾽μαυτὸν ὤφελόν ποτε.

AGATHON

Don't count on it.

EURIPIDES

Triple wretched me, ah thus to perish!

KINSMAN

Euripides! Dearest fellow! Kinsman! Don't give up on yourself!

EURIPIDES

But what will I do?

KINSMAN

Tell this guy to go to hell, and put me to use however you want.

EURIPIDES

Well, now! Since you've signed yourself over to me, take off that cloak.

KINSMAN

There, it's on the ground. But what do you mean to do to me?

EURIPIDES

To shave this clean, and singe you off down there.

KINSMAN

Then go right ahead, if you think it best; otherwise I should never have handed myself over to you.

ΕΥΡΙΠΙΔΗΣ

Ἀγάθων, σὺ μέντοι ξυροφορεῖς ἑκάστοτε,
χρῆσόν τί νυν ἡμῖν ξυρόν.

ΑΓΑΘΩΝ

αὐτὸς λάμβανε
ἐντεῦθεν ἐκ τῆς ξυροδόκης.

ΕΥΡΙΠΙΔΗΣ

γενναῖος εἶ.
κάθιζε· φύσα τὴν γνάθον τὴν δεξιάν.

ΚΗΔΕΣΤΗΣ

οἴμοι.

ΕΥΡΙΠΙΔΗΣ

τί κέκραγας; ἐμβαλῶ σοι πάτταλον,
ἢν μὴ σιωπᾷς.

ΚΗΔΕΣΤΗΣ

ἀτταταῖ ἰατταταῖ.

ΕΥΡΙΠΙΔΗΣ

οὗτος σύ, ποῖ θεῖς;

ΚΗΔΕΣΤΗΣ

εἰς τὸ τῶν σεμνῶν θεῶν·
οὐ γὰρ μὰ τὴν Δήμητρά γ᾽ ἐνταυθοῖ μενῶ
τεμνόμενος.

ΕΥΡΙΠΙΔΗΣ

οὔκουν καταγέλαστος δῆτ᾽ ἔσει
τὴν ἡμίκραιραν τὴν ἑτέραν ψιλὴν ἔχων;

EURIPIDES

Agathon, you've always got razors with you; how about lending us one?

AGATHON

Take one yourself from my razor case.

EURIPIDES

You're a gentleman. (*to Kinsman*) Sit down. Blow out your cheek, the right one.

KINSMAN

Oh no!

EURIPIDES

What's this bellyaching? If you don't quiet down I'll have to stick a peg in your mouth.

KINSMAN

Ayeeee!

EURIPIDES

Hey, where are you running off to?

KINSMAN

To the shrine of the Venerable Goddesses![21] Because, by Demeter, I'm not about to sit here getting cut up!

EURIPIDES

Then won't you look ridiculous, walking around with one side of your face shaved!

[21] A cave near the Areopagus offering asylum from enemies.

ΚΗΔΕΣΤΗΣ

ὀλίγον μέλει μοι.

ΕΥΡΙΠΙΔΗΣ

μηδαμῶς, πρὸς τῶν θεῶν,
προδῷς με. χώρει δεῦρο.

ΚΗΔΕΣΤΗΣ

κακοδαίμων ἐγώ.

ΕΥΡΙΠΙΔΗΣ

ἔχ' ἀτρέμα σαυτὸν κἀνάκυπτε. ποῖ στρέφει;

ΚΗΔΕΣΤΗΣ

μῦ μῦ.

ΕΥΡΙΠΙΔΗΣ

τί μύζεις; πάντα πεποίηται καλῶς.

ΚΗΔΕΣΤΗΣ

οἴμοι κακοδαίμων, ψιλὸς οὖν στρατεύσομαι.

ΕΥΡΙΠΙΔΗΣ

μὴ φροντίσῃς· ὡς εὐπρεπὴς φανεῖ πάνυ.
βούλει θεᾶσθαι σαυτόν;

ΚΗΔΕΣΤΗΣ

εἰ δοκεῖ, φέρε.

ΕΥΡΙΠΙΔΗΣ

ὁρᾷς σεαυτόν;

ΚΗΔΕΣΤΗΣ

οὐ μὰ Δί', ἀλλὰ Κλεισθένη.

KINSMAN

I don't care!

EURIPIDES

In the name of heaven, don't let me down! Come back here.

KINSMAN

What a fix I'm in!

EURIPIDES

Now hold still, and tilt your head back. Quit squirming!

KINSMAN

Mmm mmm.

EURIPIDES

What are you mmm-ing for? It's all done, and you look fine!

KINSMAN

Damn the luck; when I rejoin my regiment I'll literally be a leatherneck!

EURIPIDES

Don't worry about it: you'll be so good-looking. (*holding up a mirror*) Want to see yourself?

KINSMAN

OK, if you like.

EURIPIDES

Do you see yourself?

KINSMAN

God no, I see Cleisthenes!

ΕΥΡΙΠΙΔΗΣ

ἀνίστασ᾽, ἵν᾽ ἀφεύσω σε, κἀγκύψας ἔχε.

ΚΗΔΕΣΤΗΣ

οἴμοι κακοδαίμων, δελφάκιον γενήσομαι.

ΕΥΡΙΠΙΔΗΣ

ἐνεγκάτω τις ἔνδοθεν δᾷδ᾽ ἢ λύχνον.
ἐπίκυπτε· τὴν κέρκον φυλάττου νυν ἄκραν.

ΚΗΔΕΣΤΗΣ

ἐμοὶ μελήσει νὴ Δία, πλήν γ᾽ ὅτι κάομαι.
οἴμοι τάλας. ὕδωρ ὕδωρ, ὦ γείτονες,
πρὶν ἀντιλαβέσθαι πρωκτὸν <ἕτερον> τῆς φλογός.

ΕΥΡΙΠΙΔΗΣ

θάρρει.

ΚΗΔΕΣΤΗΣ

τί θαρρῶ καταπεπυρπολημένος;

ΕΥΡΙΠΙΔΗΣ

ἀλλ᾽ οὐκέτ᾽ οὐδὲν πρᾶγμά σοι· τὰ πλεῖστα γὰρ
ἀποπεπόνηκας.

ΚΗΔΕΣΤΗΣ

φεῦ, ἰοὺ τῆς ἀσβόλου.
αἰθὸς γεγένημαι πάντα τὰ περὶ τὴν τράμιν.

ΕΥΡΙΠΙΔΗΣ

μὴ φροντίσῃς· ἕτερος γὰρ αὐτὰ σπογγιεῖ.

242 suppl. Medaglia ex Π1

EURIPIDES

Get up so I can singe you; bend over and don't move.

KINSMAN

Damn the luck, I'm going to be roast pig!

EURIPIDES

Somebody bring out a torch or a lamp.

Slave brings out a lighted torch and hands it to Euripides.

Bend over. Now watch out for the tip of your dick.

KINSMAN

I'll watch out, all right—only I'm on fire! Oh no, no! (*to the audience*) Water! Water, neighbors, before somebody *else's* arse catches fire!

EURIPIDES

Be brave!

KINSMAN

How am I supposed to be brave when I'm being turbo-vulcanized?

EURIPIDES

You've got nothing more to fret about; you've suffered through the worst part.

KINSMAN

Yuk! Oh, the soot! All around my crotch I'm blackened!

EURIPIDES

Don't worry, someone else will sponge it off.

ΚΗΔΕΣΤΗΣ

οἰμώξετ᾽ ἆρ᾽, εἴ τις τὸν ἐμὸν πρωκτὸν πλυνεῖ.

ΕΥΡΙΠΙΔΗΣ

Ἀγάθων, ἐπειδὴ σαυτὸν ἐπιδοῦναι φθονεῖς,
ἀλλ᾽ ἱμάτιον γοῦν χρῆσον ἡμῖν τουτῳὶ
καὶ στρόφιον· οὐ γὰρ ταῦτά γ᾽ ὡς οὐκ ἔστ᾽ ἐρεῖς.

ΑΓΑΘΩΝ

λαμβάνετε καὶ χρῆσθ᾽· οὐ φθονῶ.

ΚΗΔΕΣΤΗΣ

τί οὖν λάβω;

ΕΥΡΙΠΙΔΗΣ

ὅ τι; τὸν κροκωτὸν πρῶτον ἐνδύου λαβών.

ΚΗΔΕΣΤΗΣ

νὴ τὴν Ἀφροδίτην, ἡδύ γ᾽ ὄζει ποσθίου.
σύζωσον ἀνύσας.

ΕΥΡΙΠΙΔΗΣ

αἶρέ νυν στρόφιον.

ΑΓΑΘΩΝ

ἰδού·

ΚΗΔΕΣΤΗΣ

ἴθι νυν κατάστειλόν με τὰ περὶ τὼ σκέλει.

ΕΥΡΙΠΙΔΗΣ

κεκρυφάλου δεῖ καὶ μίτρας.

ΑΓΑΘΩΝ

ἡδὶ μὲν οὖν
κεφαλὴ περίθετος, ἣν ἐγὼ νύκτωρ φορῶ.

KINSMAN

If anyone tries to wipe *my* arse for me, he'll be sorry!

EURIPIDES

Agathon, since you refuse to offer yourself, at least loan us a dress for this fellow here, and a brassiere; you won't deny you've got them.

AGATHON

Take them and use them; I don't mind.

KINSMAN

Which one should I take?

EURIPIDES

Hmm. This party dress here; try it on first.

KINSMAN

By Aphrodite, it has a nice scent of weenie. Quick, belt it up.

EURIPIDES

Now hand me a brassiere.

AGATHON

Here.

KINSMAN

Come on, arrange the pleats around my legs.

EURIPIDES

We need a hairnet and a hat.

AGATHON

Even better, this wig that I wear after dark.

ΕΥΡΙΠΙΔΗΣ

νὴ τὸν Δί', ἀλλὰ κἀπιτηδεία πάνυ.

ΚΗΔΕΣΤΗΣ

ἆρ' ἁρμόσει μοι;

ΕΥΡΙΠΙΔΗΣ

νὴ Δί', ἀλλ' ἄριστ' ἔχει.
φέρ' ἔγκυκλόν τι.

ΑΓΑΘΩΝ

λάμβαν' ἀπὸ τῆς κλινίδος.

ΕΥΡΙΠΙΔΗΣ

ὑποδημάτων δεῖ.

ΑΓΑΘΩΝ

τἀμὰ ταυτὶ λάμβανε.

ΚΗΔΕΣΤΗΣ

ἆρ' ἁρμόσει μοι; χαλαρὰ γοῦν χαίρεις φορῶν.

ΑΓΑΘΩΝ

σὺ τοῦτο γίγνωσκ'. ἀλλ', ἔχεις γὰρ ὧν δέει,
εἴσω τις ὡς τάχιστά μ' εἰσκυκλησάτω.

ΕΥΡΙΠΙΔΗΣ

ἀνὴρ μὲν ἡμῖν οὑτοσὶ καὶ δὴ γυνὴ
τό γ' εἶδος. ἢν λαλῇς δ', ὅπως τῷ φθέγματι
γυναικιεῖς εὖ καὶ πιθανῶς.

ΚΗΔΕΣΤΗΣ

πειράσομαι.

EURIPIDES

By god, that's just the thing!

KINSMAN

Well, will it fit me?

EURIPIDES

It's simply perfect! (*to Agathon*) Let's have a wrap.

AGATHON

Take it from the couch.

EURIPIDES

We need pumps.

AGATHON

Take mine here.

KINSMAN

Will they fit me? (*putting them on*) You certainly like some wiggle room!

AGATHON

That's your own business; you have what you need. Now someone roll me back inside, on the double!

The eccyclema rolls back inside the house, the door closing behind it.

EURIPIDES

Our gentleman here is a real lady, at least to look at. But when you talk, be sure your voice sounds feminine, and be convincing!

KINSMAN

I'll try.

ΕΥΡΙΠΙΔΗΣ

βάδιζε τοίνυν.

ΚΗΔΕΣΤΗΣ

μὰ τὸν Ἀπόλλω οὔκ, ἤν γε μὴ
ὀμόσῃς ἐμοί—

ΕΥΡΙΠΙΔΗΣ

τί χρῆμα;

ΚΗΔΕΣΤΗΣ

συσσώσειν ἐμὲ
πάσαις τέχναις, ἤν μοί τι περιπίπτῃ κακόν.

ΕΥΡΙΠΙΔΗΣ

ὄμνυμι τοίνυν αἰθέρ', οἴκησιν Διός.

ΚΗΔΕΣΤΗΣ

τί μᾶλλον ἢ τὴν Ἱπποκράτους ξυνοικίαν;

ΕΥΡΙΠΙΔΗΣ

ὄμνυμι τοίνυν πάντας ἄρδην τοὺς θεούς.

ΚΗΔΕΣΤΗΣ

μέμνησο τοίνυν ταῦθ', ὅτι ἡ φρὴν ὤμοσεν,
ἡ γλῶττα δ' οὐκ ὀμώμοκ', οὐδ' ὥρκωσ' ἐγώ.

ΕΥΡΙΠΙΔΗΣ

ἔα σπεῦδε ταχέως· ὡς τὸ τῆς ἐκκλησίας
σημεῖον ἐν τῷ Θεσμοφορείῳ φαίνεται.
ἐγὼ δ' ἄπειμι.

---

22 From Euripides' *Wise Melanippe*, fr. 487.

23 Perhaps (with schol.) the general and nephew of Pericles, though he had been killed in 424 (Thucydides 4.101).

EURIPIDES

Off with you now!

KINSMAN

Apollo, no! First you've got to promise me—

EURIPIDES

Promise what?

KINSMAN

that you'll use any and all means to help save me if anything bad befalls me.

EURIPIDES

I swear then by Aether, Abode of Zeus.[22]

KINSMAN

You might as well swear by Hippocrates'[23] Apartment House!

EURIPIDES

I swear then by all the gods bar none.

KINSMAN

Well then, remember that your heart has sworn and not merely your tongue, and I didn't get the promise only from your tongue![24]

EURIPIDES

Will you please get going! Look, there's the signal for the assembly at the Thesmophorium. As for me, I'm off.

[24] Paraphrasing a notorious line from Euripides' *Hippolytus* 612, "My tongue has sworn, but my heart remains unsworn," spoken by Hippolytus of the oath of silence that Phaedra's nurse had made him swear before revealing Phaedra's secret passion.

ΚΗΔΕΣΤΗΣ

δεῦρό νυν, ὦ Θρᾷτθ᾽, ἕπου.
ὦ Θρᾷττα, θέασαι, καομένων τῶν λαμπάδων
ὅσον τὸ χρῆμ᾽ ἀνέρχεθ᾽ ὑπὸ τῆς λιγνύος.
ἀλλ᾽, ὦ περικαλλεῖ Θεσμοφόρω, δέξασθέ με
ἀγαθῇ τύχῃ καὶ δεῦρο <καὶ> πάλιν οἴκαδε.
ὦ Θρᾷττα, τὴν κίστην κάθελε, κᾆτ᾽ ἔξελε
τὸ πόπανον, ὅπως λαβοῦσα θύσω ταῖν θεαῖν.
δέσποινα πολυτίμητε Δήμητερ φίλη
καὶ Φερρέφαττα, πολλὰ πολλάκις μέ σοι
θύειν ἔχουσαν, εἰ δὲ μἀλλὰ νῦν λαθεῖν.
καὶ τὴν θυγατέρα Χοιρίον ἀνδρός μοι τυχεῖν
πλουτοῦντος, ἄλλως δ᾽ ἠλιθίου κἀβελτέρου,
καὶ Ποσθαλίσκον νοῦν ἔχειν μοι καὶ φρένας.
ποῦ ποῦ καθίζωμ᾽ ἐν καλῷ, τῶν ῥητόρων
ἵν᾽ ἐξακούω; σὺ δ᾽ ἄπιθ᾽, ὦ Θρᾷττ᾽, ἐκποδών·
δούλοις γὰρ οὐκ ἔξεστ᾽ ἀκούειν τῶν λόγων.

ΚΡΙΤΥΛΛΑ

εὐφημία ἔστω, εὐφημία ἔστω. εὔχεσθε ταῖν
Θεσμοφόροιν,
καὶ τῷ Πλούτῳ, καὶ τῇ Καλλιγενείᾳ, καὶ τῇ
Κουροτρόφῳ,
καὶ τῷ Ἑρμῇ, καὶ <ταῖς> Χάρισιν, ἐκκλησίαν τήνδε
καὶ σύνοδον τὴν νῦν

287 Φερρ- Π1: Φερ- R
289 Χοιρίον Fritzsche cl. Σ^{R}: χοῖρον R
291 Ποσθαλίσκον Dindorf cl. Σ^{R}: πρὸς θάληκον R

EURIPIDES exits by a side passage. Stage hands set up a dais and chairs in front of the stage building. Meanwhile, CRITYLLA, MICA, GARLAND SELLER, Mania, and other Women enter from a side passage and move toward the chairs. KINSMAN also heads for center stage.

KINSMAN

(*to an imaginary maid*) Come along this way, Thratta. Oh Thratta, look! The torches are burning, and such a crowd is moving up to the sanctuary through the smoke! O Twain Thesmophoroi, surpassingly lovely, grant that good luck attend me both coming here and going home again! Thratta, put down the box and take out the cake, so I can make an offering to the Twain Goddesses. Demeter, reverend Mistress mine, and Pherrephatta,[25] grant me plenty for plenty of sacrifices to you, and if not, grant at least that I get away with this! And may my daughter Pussy meet a man who's rich but also childishly stupid, and may little Dick have brains and sense! Now where, where do I find a good seat for hearing everything the speakers say? You go away from here, Thratta; slaves aren't allowed to listen to the speeches.

The CHORUS enters the orchestra with torches, as CRITYLLA mounts the dais.

CRITYLLA

Observe ritual silence; ritual silence please! Offer your prayers to the Twain Thesmophorian Goddesses, to Wealth, to Calligeneia, to the Nurse of the Young, to Hermes and to the Graces, that this assembly and today's

[25] See 83 n.

κάλλιστα καὶ ἄριστα ποιῆσαι, πολυωφελῶς μὲν
<τῇ> πόλει τῇ Ἀθηναίων,
τυχηρῶς δ᾽ ὑμῖν αὐταῖς. καὶ τὴν δρῶσαν καὶ
ἀγορεύουσαν τὰ βέλτιστα
περὶ τὸν δῆμον τὸν Ἀθηναίων καὶ τὸν τῶν
γυναικῶν, ταύτην νικᾶν. ταῦτ᾽
εὔχεσθε, καὶ ὑμῖν αὐταῖς τἀγαθά. ἰὴ παιών, ἰὴ
παιών, ἰὴ παιών. χαίρωμεν.

ΧΟΡΟΣ

δεχόμεθα καὶ θεῶν γένος
λιτόμεθα ταῖσδ᾽ ἐπ᾽ εὐχαῖς
φανέντας ἐπιχαρῆναι.
Ζεῦ μεγαλώνυμε χρυσολύρα
τε Δῆλον ὃς ἔχεις ἱεράν,
καὶ σύ, παγκρατὲς κόρα
γλαυκῶπι χρυσόλογχε πόλιν
οἰκοῦσα περιμάχητον, ἐλθὲ δεῦρο·
καὶ πολυώνυμε θηροφόνη,
Λατοῦς χρυσώπιδος ἔρνος,
σύ τε, πόντιε σεμνὲ Πόσειδον
ἁλιμέδον, προλιπὼν
μυχὸν ἰχθυόεντα
οἰστροδόνητον,
Νηρέος εἰναλίου τε κόραι
Νύμφαι τ᾽ ὀρίπλαγκτοι.
χρυσέα δὲ φόρμιγξ
ἰαχήσειεν ἐπ᾽ εὐχαῖς

convocation be conducted in the finest and most excellent manner, to the great benefit to the city of Athens and with good fortune for you yourselves. And may she have the victory whose actions and whose counsel best serve the Athenian Commonwealth and the Women's Commonwealth. Be this your prayer, and for yourselves all good things. Ié Paion, ié Paion, ié Paion! Cheers to us!

CHORUS

We say amen to that, and ask
the race of gods to signal
their pleasure at our prayers.
Zeus of the grand name, and you with the golden lyre
who live on holy Delos;[26]
and you, almighty Maiden
with the gleaming eyes and golden spearpoint,[27]
who dwell in a city you fought for,[28] come this way!
And you of the many names, slayer of beasts,
seed of Leto of the golden eyes;[29]
and you, august master Poseidon,
who rule the brine, quit now
the fishy deep
so lashable to frenzy;
and you, daughters of marine Nereus;
and you nymphs who range the mountains.
May Apollo's golden lyre
resound in harmony with our prayers,

26 Apollo.

27 Athena.

28 In a contest with Poseidon for Attica, Athena prevailed by her gift of the olive tree, cf. Herodotus 8.55.

29 Artemis.

ἡμετέραις· τελέως δ᾽ ἐκκλησιάσαιμεν Ἀθηνῶν
εὐγενεῖς γυναῖκες.

ΚΡΙΤΥΛΛΑ

εὔχεσθε τοῖς θεοῖσι τοῖς Ὀλυμπίοις
καὶ ταῖς Ὀλυμπίαισι, καὶ τοῖς Πυθίοις
καὶ ταῖσι Πυθίαισι, καὶ τοῖς Δηλίοις
καὶ ταῖσι Δηλίαισι, τοῖς τ᾽ ἄλλοις θεοῖς.
εἴ τις ἐπιβουλεύει τι τῷ δήμῳ κακὸν
τῷ τῶν γυναικῶν, ἢ ᾽πικηρυκεύεται
Εὐριπίδῃ Μήδοις <τ᾽> ἐπὶ βλάβῃ τινὶ
τῇ τῶν γυναικῶν, ἢ τυραννεῖν ἐπινοεῖ,
ἢ τὸν τύραννον συγκατάγειν, ἢ παιδίον
ὑποβαλλομένης κατεῖπεν, ἢ δούλη τινὸς
προαγωγὸς οὖσ᾽ ἐνετρύλισεν τῷ δεσπότῃ,
ἢ πεμπομένη τις ἀγγελίας ψευδεῖς φέρει,
ἢ μοιχὸς εἴ τις ἐξαπατᾷ ψευδῆ λέγων
καὶ μὴ δίδωσιν ἃν ὑπόσχηταί ποτε,
ἢ δῶρά τις δίδωσι μοιχῷ γραῦς γυνή,
ἢ καὶ δέχεται προδιδοῦσ᾽ ἑταίρα τὸν φίλον,
κεἴ τις κάπηλος ἢ καπηλὶς τοῦ χοῶς
ἢ τῶν κοτυλῶν τὸ νόμισμα διαλυμαίνεται,
κακῶς ἀπολέσθαι τοῦτον αὐτὸν κᾠκίαν
ἀρᾶσθε, ταῖς δ᾽ ἄλλαισιν ὑμῖν τοὺς θεοὺς
εὔχεσθε πάσαις πολλὰ δοῦναι κἀγαθά.

ΧΟΡΟΣ

ξυνευχόμεσθα τέλεα μὲν
πόλει, τέλεα δὲ δήμῳ

and may we well born women of Athens
hold a faultless meeting!

CRITYLLA

Pray to the Olympian gods and to the Olympian goddesses, to the Pythian gods and Pythian goddesses, to the Delian gods and Delian goddesses, and to the other gods as well. If anyone conspires in any way to harm the Women's Commonwealth; or negotiates secretly with Euripides and the Medes in any way to the women's harm; or contemplates either becoming a tyrant or abetting a tyrant's installation; or denounces a woman who has passed off another's child as her own; or is a mistress' go-between slave who spills the beans to the master, or when sent on a mission brings back false messages; or is a lover who deceives a woman with lies or reneges on promised gifts; or is an old woman who gives gifts to a young lover; or is a courtesan who takes gifts from her boyfriend while cheating on him; or is a barman or barmaid who sells short pints or liters: put a curse on every such person, that they perish wretchedly and their families along with them! As for the rest of you, ask the gods to give you every blessing!

CHORUS

We join you in praying that these wishes
will fully come true for the people

τάδ᾽ εὔγματ᾽ ἀποτελεῖσθαι,
τὰ δ᾽ ἄρισθ᾽ ὅσαις προσήκει
νικᾶν λεγούσαις. ὁπόσαι δ᾽
ἐξαπατῶσιν παραβαίνουσί τε τοὺς
ὅρκους τοὺς νενομισμένους,
ἢ ψηφίσματα καὶ νόμους
ζητοῦσ᾽ ἀντιμεθιστάναι,
τἀπόρρητά τε τοῖσιν ἐ-
χθροῖς τοῖς ἡμετέροις λέγουσ᾽,
ἢ Μήδους ἐπάγουσι τῶν
κερδῶν οὕνεκ᾽ ἐπὶ βλάβῃ,
ἀσεβοῦσ᾽ ἀδικοῦσί τε τὴν πόλιν.
ἀλλ᾽, ὦ παγκρατὲς
Ζεῦ, ταῦτα κυρώσειας, ὥσθ᾽
ἡμῖν θεοὺς παραστατεῖν,
καίπερ γυναιξὶν οὔσαις.

ΚΡΙΤΥΛΛΑ

ἄκουε πᾶσ᾽. ἔδοξε τῇ βουλῇ τάδε
τῇ τῶν γυναικῶν· Τιμόκλει᾽ ἐπεστάτει,
Λύσιλλ᾽ ἐγραμμάτευεν, εἶπε Σωστράτη·
ἐκκλησίαν ποιεῖν ἕωθεν τῇ μέσῃ
τῶν Θεσμοφορίων, ᾗ μάλισθ᾽ ἡμῖν σχολή,
καὶ χρηματίζειν πρῶτα περὶ Εὐριπίδου,
ὅ τι χρὴ παθεῖν ἐκεῖνον· ἀδικεῖν γὰρ δοκεῖ
ἡμῖν ἁπάσαις. τίς ἀγορεύειν βούλεται;

354 εὔγματ᾽ ἀποτελεῖσθαι Willems: εὔγματα γενέσθαι R: εὔγματ᾽ ἐπιγενέσθαι Burges

and for the polis as well;
and that the women who counsel best
will prevail as they deserve to. But those
who deceive us and break
their solemn oaths;
or try to substitute
decrees for laws;
or reveal our secrets
to our enemies;
or invite the Medes in to our harm
for the sake of gain:
they all commit sacrilege and wrong the city.
O Zeus all-powerful,
ratify these prayers, so that
the gods are arrayed on our side,
although we are but women!

CRITYLLA

Attention everyone! The Women's Assembly—Timocleia presiding, Lysilla being secretary, Sostrate[30] proposing—has passed the following motion: an Assembly will be held at dawn of the middle day of the Thesmophoria, when we have the most free time, its principal agendum being deliberation about the punishment of Euripides, who in the view of us all is a criminal. Now who wishes to speak to this question?

30 Typical women's names.

---

360 *κερδῶν οὕνεκ' ἐπὶ βλάβῃ* R: del. Reisig 361 *νόμους* Blaydes: *νόμον* R 365-6 *τῶν κερδῶν* Austin, cf. 360: *τῆς χώρας* R 373 Τιμόκλει' R Σ S: Ἀρ[χίκλ]ει' Π2

MIKA

ἐγώ.

ΚΡΙΤΥΛΛΑ

περίθου νυν τόνδε πρῶτον πρὶν λέγειν.

ΚΟΡΥΦΑΙΑ

σίγα, σιώπα, πρόσεχε τὸν νοῦν· χρέμπτεται γὰρ ἤδη,
ὅπερ ποιοῦσ᾽ οἱ ῥήτορες. μακρὰν ἔοικε λέξειν.

ΜΙΚΑ

φιλοτιμίᾳ μὲν οὐδεμιᾷ μὰ τὼ θεὼ
λέξουσ᾽ ἀνέστην, ὦ γυναῖκες· ἀλλὰ γὰρ
βαρέως φέρω τάλαινα πολὺν ἤδη χρόνον,
προπηλακιζομένας ὁρῶσ᾽ ὑμᾶς ὑπὸ
Εὐριπίδου τοῦ τῆς λαχανοπωλητρίας
καὶ πολλὰ καὶ παντοῖ᾽ ἀκουούσας κακά.
τί γὰρ οὗτος ἡμᾶς οὐκ ἐπισμῇ τῶν κακῶν;
ποῦ δ᾽ οὐχὶ διαβέβληχ᾽, ὅπουπερ ἔμβραχὺ
εἰσὶν θεαταὶ καὶ τραγῳδοὶ καὶ χοροί,
τὰς μοιχοτρόφους, τὰς ἀνδρεραστρίας καλῶν,
τὰς οἰνοπότιδας, τὰς προδότιδας, τὰς λάλους,
τὰς οὐδὲν ὑγιές, τὰς μέγ᾽ ἀνδράσιν κακόν;
ὥστ᾽ εὐθὺς εἰσιόντες ἀπὸ τῶν ἰκρίων
ὑποβλέπουσ᾽ ἡμᾶς σκοποῦνταί τ᾽ εὐθέως
μὴ μοιχὸς ἔνδον ᾖ τις ἀποκεκρυμμένος.
δρᾶσαι δ᾽ ἔθ᾽ ἡμῖν οὐδὲν ὧνπερ καὶ πρὸ τοῦ
ἔξεστι· τοιαῦθ᾽ οὗτος ἐδίδαξεν κακὰ
τοὺς ἄνδρας ἡμῶν. ὥστ᾽ ἐάν τίς <καὶ> πλέκῃ

MICA

I do.

CRITYLLA

(*handing her a garland*) Put this on first, then speak.

CHORUS LEADER

Quiet! Silence! Pay attention, because she's clearing her throat just like the politicians. She'll probably be making a long speech.

MICA

By the Twain, I have not risen to speak, fellow women, out of any personal ambition; no, but because I have long unhappily endured seeing you get dragged through the mire by Euripides, son of that herb-selling woman,[31] and subjected to the whole gamut of slurs. With what abuse has this fellow not besmirched us? Where, on any occasion where there are spectators, tragic actors, and choruses, has he spared us his disparagement, calling us lover-keepers, man-chasers, wine-oglers, traitors, chatterboxes, utter sickies, the bane of men's lives? That's why, as soon as our men get home from the grandstand, they start right in giving us suspicious looks and searching the house for a hidden lover. We can no longer do anything the way we used to do before, so terrible are the things this man has taught our husbands about us. If a wife so much as weaves a gar-

[31] A perennial Aristophanic jibe, though Euripides' mother was well born; perhaps the jibe refers to an otherwise unknown stepmother.

---

392 *μοιχοτρόφους* (*μοιχο-* S *οι* 128) Daubuz: *μυχοτρόπους* R
400 suppl. Dobree

γυνὴ στέφανον, ἐρᾶν δοκεῖ· κἂν ἐκβάλῃ
σκεῦός τι κατὰ τὴν οἰκίαν πλανωμένη,
ἀνὴρ ἐρωτᾷ· "τῷ κατέαγεν ἡ χύτρα;
οὐκ ἔσθ' ὅπως οὐ τῷ Κορινθίῳ ξένῳ."
κάμνει κόρη τις; εὐθὺς ἀδελφὸς λέγει·
"τὸ χρῶμα τοῦτό μ' οὐκ ἀρέσκει τῆς κόρης."
εἶέν. γυνή τις ὑποβαλέσθαι βούλεται
ἀποροῦσα παίδων, οὐδὲ τοῦτ' ἔστιν λαθεῖν.
ἄνδρες γὰρ ἤδη παρακάθηνται πλησίον·
πρὸς τοὺς γέροντάς θ' οἳ πρὸ τοῦ τὰς μείρακας
ἤγοντο, διαβέβληκεν, ὥστ' οὐδεὶς γέρων
γαμεῖν ἐθέλει γυναῖκα διὰ τοὔπος τοδί·
"δέσποινα γὰρ γέροντι νυμφίῳ γυνή."
εἶτα διὰ τοῦτον ταῖς γυναικωνίτισιν
σφραγῖδας ἐπιβάλλουσιν ἤδη καὶ μοχλοὺς
τηροῦντες ἡμᾶς, καὶ προσέτι Μολοττικοὺς
τρέφουσι μορμολυκεῖα τοῖς μοιχοῖς κύνας.
καὶ ταῦτα μὲν ξυγγνώσθ'· ἃ δ' ἦν ἡμῖν πρὸ τοῦ
αὐταῖς ταμιεῦσαι καὶ προαιρούσαις λαβεῖν,
ἄλφιτον, ἔλαιον, οἶνον, οὐδὲ τοῦτ' ἔτι
ἔξεστιν. οἱ γὰρ ἄνδρες ἤδη κληδία
αὐτοὶ φοροῦσι κρυπτά, κακοηθέστατα,
Λακωνίκ' ἄττα, τρεῖς ἔχοντα γομφίους.
πρὸ τοῦ μὲν οὖν ἦν ἀλλ' ὑποῖξαι τὴν θύραν
ποιησαμέναισι δακτύλιον τριωβόλου·
νῦν δ' οὗτος αὐτοὺς ᾠκότριψ Εὐριπίδης
ἐδίδαξε θριπήδεστ' ἔχειν σφραγίδια
ἐξαψαμένους. νῦν οὖν ἐμοὶ τούτῳ δοκεῖ

land, she's suspected of being in love, and if she drops some utensil as she moves around the house, her husband asks, "Who's the pot being broken for? 'Tis sure in honor of your Corinthian guest!"[32] Say a girl gets sick; right away her brother says, "This maiden's hue does please me not at all!"[33] There's more. A childless wife wants to pass off another's baby as her own and can't even get away with that, because now our husbands plant themselves nearby. He's slandered us to the old men too, who used to marry young girls; now no old man wants to get married because of the line, "The elderly bridegroom takes himself a boss."[34] Then, because of this man, they install locks and bolts on the women's doors to guard them, and not only that, they raise Molossic hounds to spook lovers. All that is forgivable. But now we're not even allowed to do what used to be our own jobs: keeping household inventory and removing supplies on our own, like flour, oil, and wine, because our husbands now carry the house keys with them, complicated nasty things with triple teeth, imported from Sparta. Before, we had no trouble opening the door with just a signet ring ordered up for three obols. But now their household spy, Euripides, has taught them to use little seals etched with complex wormholes, which they carry around fastened to their clothes. I therefore propose that one way

32 Alluding to Euripides' *Stheneboea*, whose adulterous heroine constantly pines for her husband's young "Corinthian guest," Bellerophon; cf. Euripides fr. 664, Cratinus fr. 299.

33 The (Euripidean) source is unknown.

34 From Euripides' *Phoenix*, fr. 804.3.

ὄλεθρόν τιν᾽ ἡμᾶς κυρκανᾶν ἁμωσγέπως,
ἢ φαρμάκοισιν ἢ μιᾷ γέ τῳ τέχνῃ,
ὅπως ἀπολεῖται. ταῦτ᾽ ἐγὼ φανερῶς λέγω·
τὰ δ᾽ ἄλλα μετὰ τῆς γραμματέως συγγράψομαι.

ΧΟΡΟΣ

(στρ) οὔπω ταύτης ἤκουσα
πολυπλοκωτέρας γυναικὸς
οὐδὲ δεινότερον λεγούσης.
πάντα γὰρ λέγει δίκαια.
πᾶσαν ἰδέαν ἐξετάζει,
πᾶν δ᾽ ἐβάστασε φρενὶ πυκνῶς τε
ποικίλους λόγους ἀνηῦρεν
εὖ διεζητημένους.
ὥστ᾽ ἂν εἰ λέγοι παρ᾽ αὐτὴν
Ξενοκλέης ὁ Καρκίνου, δοκεῖν ἂν αὐτόν,
ὡς ἐγᾦμαι, πᾶσιν ὑμῖν
ἄντικρυς μηδὲν λέγειν.

ΣΤΕΦΑΝΟΠΩΛΙΣ

ὀλίγων ἕνεκα καὐτὴ παρῆλθον ῥημάτων.
τὰ μὲν γὰρ ἄλλ᾽ αὕτη κατηγόρηκεν εὖ·
ἃ δ᾽ ἐγὼ πέπονθα, ταῦτα λέξαι βούλομαι.
ἐμοὶ γὰρ ἁνὴρ ἀπέθανεν μὲν ἐν Κύπρῳ
παιδάρια πέντε καταλιπών, ἁγὼ μόλις
στεφανηπλοκοῦσ᾽ ἔβοσκον ἐν ταῖς μυρρίναις.
τέως μὲν οὖν ἀλλ᾽ ἡμικάκως ἐβοσκόμην·

437 πᾶσαν ἰδέαν ἐξετάζει Hermann: πάσας δ᾽ εἰδέας (ἰδ- S) ἐξήτασε(ν) R S

or another we brew up some kind of destruction for this man, either poisons or some other technique whereby he gets destroyed. This then is the argument of my speech; the rest I will draft with the Secretary's assistance.

CHORUS

I've never heard a woman
more intricate of mind
or more impressive as a speaker.
Everything she says is right.
She's reviewed every aspect,
she's weighed each detail in her mind, and
  sagaciously
devised a whole spectrum
of well-chosen arguments.
So if Xenokles, Carcinus' son,
should vie with her at speaking,
I think that all of you would find him
utterly unconvincing.

Garland Seller stands, takes the garland from the Herald, and mounts the platform.

GARLAND SELLER

I have come forward too, to make but a few remarks. This lady has cogently presented most of the charges; but I want to speak out about my own personal sufferings. My husband died in Cyprus, leaving me with five small children that I've had a struggle to feed by weaving garlands in the myrtle market. So until recently I managed to feed them

---

438 πᾶν von Velsen: πάντα R S

νῦν δ᾽ οὗτος ἐν ταῖσιν τραγῳδίαις ποιῶν
τοὺς ἄνδρας ἀναπέπεικεν οὐκ εἶναι θεούς·
ὥστ᾽ οὐκέτ᾽ ἐμπολῶμεν οὐδ᾽ εἰς ἥμισυ.
νῦν οὖν ἁπάσαισιν παραινῶ καὶ λέγω
τοῦτον κολάσαι τὸν ἄνδρα πολλῶν οὕνεκα·
ἄγρια γὰρ ἡμᾶς, ὦ γυναῖκες, δρᾷ κακά,
ἅτ᾽ ἐν ἀγρίοισι τοῖς λαχάνοις αὐτὸς τραφείς.
ἀλλ᾽ εἰς ἀγορὰν ἄπειμι· δεῖ γὰρ ἀνδράσιν
πλέξαι στεφάνους ξυνθηματιαίους εἴκοσιν.

ΧΟΡΟΣ

ἕτερον αὖ τι λῆμα τοῦτο
κομψότερον ἔτ᾽ ἢ τὸ πρότερον ἀναπέφηνεν.
οἷα κατεστωμύλατο
οὐκ ἄκαιρα, φρένας ἔχουσα
καὶ πολύπλοκον νόημ᾽, οὐδ᾽
ἀσύνετ᾽, ἀλλὰ πιθανὰ πάντα.
δεῖ δὲ ταύτης τῆς ὕβρεως ἡμῖν τὸν ἄνδρα
περιφανῶς δοῦναι δίκην.

ΚΗΔΕΣΤΗΣ

τὸ μέν, ὦ γυναῖκες, ὀξυθυμεῖσθαι σφόδρα
Εὐριπίδῃ, τοιαῦτ᾽ ἀκουούσας κακά,
οὐ θαυμάσιόν ἐστ᾽, οὐδ᾽ ἐπιζεῖν τὴν χολήν.
καὐτὴ γὰρ ἔγωγ᾽,—οὕτως ὀναίμην τῶν τέκνων—
μισῶ τὸν ἄνδρ᾽ ἐκεῖνον, εἰ μὴ μαίνομαι.

---

35 Implying commercialization of the tragic art.

36 This speech, like Dicaeopolis' in *Acharnians* (497–566), is modelled on a speech by the hero of Euripides' *Telephus*, the

only half badly. But now this guy who composes in the tragedy market[35] has persuaded the men that gods don't exist, so my sales aren't even half what they were. I therefore urge and advise all women to punish this man for his many crimes, for wild are his attacks upon us, since he himself was raised among wild herbs. But I'm off to the market: I've got an order to plait garlands for a group of twenty men.

CHORUS

This second courageous testimony
turns out to be even classier than the first!
The stuff she ranted on about
wasn't irrelevant, owned good sense
and close-woven thought,
and wasn't silly but altogether convincing.
For this outrage the man must pay us the penalty
in no uncertain terms!

Kinsman mounts the platform.

KINSMAN[36]

It is not surprising, ladies, that you are very keenly enraged at Euripides when he slanders you this way, indeed that your bile is aboil. Why, let me have no profit in my children if I myself don't hate the man; I'd have to be crazy not to!

Greek king of Mysia whose land the Greeks mistakenly attacked on their way to Troy. Telephus disguises himself as a beggar, enters Agamemnon's palace, and pleads his case. Exposed and threatened with death, he seizes Agamemnon's son, the baby Orestes, and takes refuge at an altar; this scene is also parodied in *Acharnians* (325–51) and later in this play (688 ff.).

ὅμως δ᾽ ἐν ἀλλήλαισι χρὴ δοῦναι λόγον·
αὐταὶ γάρ ἐσμεν, κοὐδεμί᾽ ἐκφορὰ λόγου.
τί ταῦτ᾽ ἔχουσαι ᾽κεῖνον αἰτιώμεθα
βαρέως τε φέρομεν, εἰ δύ᾽ ἡμῶν ἢ τρία
κακὰ ξυνειδὼς εἶπε δρώσας μυρία;
ἐγὼ γὰρ αὐτὴ πρῶτον, ἵνα μἄλλην λέγω,
ξύνοιδ᾽ ἐμαυτῇ πολλὰ <δείν᾽·> ἐκεῖνο δ᾽ οὖν
δεινότατον, ὅτε νύμφη μὲν ἦν τρεῖς ἡμέρας,
ὁ δ᾽ ἀνὴρ παρ᾽ ἐμοὶ καθηῦδεν. ἦν δέ μοι φίλος,
ὅσπερ με διεκόρησεν οὖσαν ἑπτέτιν.
οὗτος πόθῳ μου ᾽κνυεν ἐλθὼν τὴν θύραν·
κᾆτ᾽ εὐθὺς ἔγνων· εἶτα καταβαίνω λάθρᾳ.
ὁ δ᾽ ἀνὴρ ἐρωτᾷ· "ποῖ σὺ καταβαίνεις;" "ὅποι;
στρόφος μ᾽ ἔχει τὴν γαστέρ᾽, ὦνερ, κὠδύνη·
εἰς τὸν κοπρῶν᾽ οὖν ἔρχομαι." "βάδιζέ νυν."
κᾆθ᾽ ὁ μὲν ἔτριβε κεδρίδας, ἄννηθον, σφάκον·
ἐγὼ δὲ καταχέασα τοῦ στροφέως ὕδωρ
ἐξῆλθον ὡς τὸν μοιχόν· εἶτ᾽ ἠρειδόμαι
παρὰ τὸν Ἀγυιᾶ κῦβδ᾽, ἐχομένη τῆς δάφνης.
ταῦτ᾽ οὐδεπώποτ᾽ εἶφ᾽, ὁρᾶτ᾽, Εὐριπίδης·
οὐδ᾽ ὡς ὑπὸ τῶν δούλων τε κὠρεωκόμων
σποδούμεθ᾽, ἢν μὴ ᾽χωμεν ἕτερον, οὐ λέγει·
οὐδ᾽ ὡς, ὅταν μάλισθ᾽ ὑπό του ληκώμεθα
τὴν νύχθ᾽, ἕωθεν σκόροδα διαμασώμεθα,
ἵν᾽ ὀσφρόμενος ἁνὴρ ἀπὸ τείχους εἰσιὼν
μηδὲν κακὸν δρᾶν ὑποτοπῆται. ταῦθ᾽, ὁρᾷς,

477 suppl. Dawes

Still, we should permit open discussion among ourselves: we're on our own and there will be no leaking of what we say. Why are we bringing that man up on these charges, and getting so angry with him just for mentioning two or three of our misdeeds, out of the thousands of others he knows we've committed? I myself to begin with, not to mention anyone else, have a lot of awful things on my conscience. I'll tell you maybe the worst. I'd been married only three days, and my husband was sleeping beside me. But I had a boyfriend who'd deflowered me when I was seven and still had the hots for me. He came scratching at the door and I knew right away who it was. I start to steal downstairs, and my husband asks, "Where are you going downstairs?" "Where? I've got colic and achiness in my stomach, husband, so I'm going to the can." "Go on then." And he starts grinding up juniper berries, dillweed, and sage, while I pour water into the door socket and go out to meet my lover. Then I bend over, holding onto the laurel tree by Apollo's Pillar,[37] and get my humping. Euripides has never said anything about that, see what I mean? Nor how we get banged by the slaves and mule grooms if we haven't got anyone else, he doesn't talk about that. Nor how whenever we spend the night getting thoroughly balled by somebody, we chew garlic in the morning so when the husband gets home from the city walls he'll smell it and won't suspect that we've been doing anything nasty. He's never said anything about that, see what I mean? And

[37] A pillar and statue of Apollo Agyieus stood in the street before many houses, and was also part of the permanent decor of the theatrical stage building.

οὐπώποτ᾽ εἶπεν. εἰ δὲ Φαίδραν λοιδορεῖ,
ἡμῖν τί τοῦτ᾽ ἔστ᾽; οὐδ᾽ ἐκεῖν᾽ εἴρηκέ πω,
ὡς ἡ γυνὴ δεικνῦσα τἀνδρὶ τοὔγκυκλον
ὑπαυγάσ᾽ οἷόν ἐστιν, ἐγκεκαλυμμένον
τὸν μοιχὸν ἐξέπεμψεν, οὐκ εἴρηκέ πω.
ἑτέραν δ᾽ ἐγᾦδ᾽ ἣ ᾽φασκεν ὠδίνειν γυνὴ
δέχ᾽ ἡμέρας, ἕως ἐπρίατο παιδίον.
ὁ δ᾽ ἀνὴρ περιήρχετ᾽ ὠκυτόκι᾽ ὠνούμενος·
τὸ δ᾽ εἰσέφερε γραῦς ἐν χύτρᾳ, τὸ παιδίον,
ἵνα μὴ βοῴη, κηρίῳ βεβυσμένον.
εἶθ᾽ ὡς ἔνευσεν ἡ φέρουσ᾽, εὐθὺς βοᾷ·
"ἄπελθ᾽ ἄπελθ᾽, ἤδη γάρ, ὦνέρ, μοι δοκῶ
τέξειν." τὸ γὰρ ἦτρον τῆς χύτρας ἐλάκτισεν.
χὠ μὲν γεγηθὼς ἔτρεχεν, ἡ δ᾽ ἐξέσπασεν
ἐκ τοῦ στόματος τοῦ παιδίου, τὸ δ᾽ ἀνέκραγεν.
εἶθ᾽ ἡ μιαρὰ γραῦς, ἣ ᾽φερεν τὸ παιδίον,
θεῖ μειδιῶσα πρὸς τὸν ἄνδρα καὶ λέγει·
"λέων λέων σοι γέγονεν, αὐτέκμαγμα σόν,
τά τ᾽ ἄλλ᾽ ἁπαξάπαντα καὶ τὸ πόσθιον
τῷ σῷ προσόμοιον, στρεβλὸν ὥσπερ κύτταρον."
ταῦτ᾽ οὐ ποιοῦμεν τὰ κακά; νὴ τὴν Ἄρτεμιν
ἡμεῖς γε. κᾆτ᾽ Εὐριπίδῃ θυμούμεθα,
οὐδὲν παθοῦσαι μεῖζον ἢ δεδράκαμεν;

ΧΟΡΟΣ

(ἀντ) τουτὶ μέντοι θαυμαστόν,
ὁπόθεν ηὑρέθη τὸ χρῆμα,
χἤτις ἐξέθρεψε χώρα

if he abuses Phaedra, what's that to us? Nor has he ever told the one about how the wife showed her husband her robe to admire how it looked against the light, and thus got her lover out of the house all muffled up, he's never told about that. And I know another wife who pretended to be in labor for ten days, until she could buy a baby, while her husband was running all over town buying medicine to quicken birth. An old woman brought it in a pot, the baby I mean, its mouth stuffed with a honeycomb so it wouldn't cry. Then the old woman gave the signal and the wife yells, "Out you go, husband, out you go; this time I think I'm giving birth!" Yes, the baby had kicked the pot's belly! He ran out joyous, she unplugged the child's mouth, and it raised a shout. Then the dirty old lady who'd brought the baby runs out to the husband smiling and says, "You've got a lion, sir, a lion, the very image of yourself, sir, with everything a perfect match, its little weenie too, curled over like an acorn!" Don't we commit these misdeeds? By Artemis, we do too! And then do we get mad at Euripides, though he's done nothing worse to us than what we've done ourselves?[38]

CHORUS

This is really astonishing!
Where was she dug up,
and what land brought forth

[38] Lines 518–19 are adapted from Euripides' *Telephus*, fr. 711.

τήνδε τὴν θρασεῖαν οὕτω.
τάδε γὰρ εἰπεῖν τὴν πανοῦργον
κατὰ τὸ φανερὸν ὧδ' ἀναιδῶς
οὐκ ἂν ᾠόμην ἐν ἡμῖν
οὐδὲ τολμῆσαί ποτ' ἄν.
ἀλλὰ πᾶν γένοιτ' ἂν ἤδη.
τὴν παροιμίαν δ' ἐπαινῶ τὴν παλαιάν·
ὑπὸ λίθῳ γὰρ παντί που χρὴ
μὴ δάκῃ ῥήτωρ ἀθρεῖν.

ΚΟΡΥΦΑΙΑ

ἀλλ' οὐ γάρ ἐστι τῶν ἀναισχύντων φύσει γυναικῶν
οὐδὲν κάκιον εἰς ἅπαντα πλὴν ἄρ' εἰ γυναῖκες.

ΜΙΚΑ

οὔ τοι μὰ τὴν Ἄγλαυρον, ὦ γυναῖκες, εὖ φρονεῖτε,
ἀλλ' ἢ πεφάρμαχθ' ἢ κακόν τι μέγα πεπόνθατ' ἄλλο,
ταύτην ἐῶσαι τὴν φθόρον τοιαῦτα περιυβρίζειν
ἡμᾶς ἁπάσας. εἰ μὲν οὖν τις ἔστιν—, εἰ δὲ μή, ἡμεῖς
αὐταί τε καὶ τὰ δουλάρια τέφραν ποθὲν λαβοῦσαι
ταύτης ἀποψιλώσομεν τὸν χοῖρον, ἵνα διδαχθῇ
γυνὴ γυναῖκας οὖσα μὴ κακῶς λέγειν τὸ λοιπόν.

ΚΗΔΕΣΤΗΣ

μὴ δῆτα τόν γε χοῖρον, ὦ γυναῖκες. εἰ γὰρ οὔσης
παρρησίας κἀξὸν λέγειν ὅσαι πάρεσμεν ἀσταί,
εἶτ' εἶπον ἁγίγνωσκον ὑπὲρ Εὐριπίδου δίκαια,
διὰ τοῦτο τιλλομένην με δεῖ δοῦναι δίκην ὑφ' ὑμῶν;

a woman so audacious?
I wouldn't have thought the hussy
would ever have had the nerve
to say these things so brazenly
right before our eyes!
Now I guess anything is possible,
and I endorse the old saying:
you've got to look under every rock,
or a politician may bite you.[39]

CHORUS LEADER

No, there's nothing worse in every way than women born shameless—except for the rest of women!

MICA

By Aglaurus,[40] ladies, you're not thinking straight! No, you're bewitched, or something else is badly wrong with you, to let this scum get away with slandering all of us so outrageously! Is there anyone out there who'll . . . well, if there isn't, we ourselves, along with our slave girls, will get a hot coal somewhere and singe the hair off this woman's pussy; that'll teach her never again to badmouth her fellow women!

KINSMAN

Please no, ladies, not my pussy! There *is* freedom of speech here, and all of us who are citizens *are* entitled to speak, so if I merely said on Euripides' behalf what I know to be fair, am I to be punished by depilation at your hands?

[39] Substituting "politician" for the proverb's "scorpion."

[40] Aglaurus and Pandrosus, daughters of the mythical Attic King Cecrops, had ancient women's sanctuaries on the Acropolis.

ΜΙΚΑ

οὐ γάρ σε δεῖ δοῦναι δίκην; ἥτις μόνη τέτληκας
ὑπὲρ ἀνδρὸς ἀντειπεῖν, ὃς ἡμᾶς πολλὰ κακὰ δέδρακεν
ἐπίτηδες εὑρίσκων λόγους, ὅπου γυνὴ πονηρὰ
ἐγένετο, Μελανίππας ποιῶν Φαίδρας τε· Πηνελόπην δὲ
οὐπώποτ᾿ ἐποίησ᾿, ὅτι γυνὴ σώφρων ἔδοξεν εἶναι.

ΚΗΔΕΣΤΗΣ

ἐγὼ γὰρ οἶδα ταἴτιον· μίαν γὰρ οὐκ ἂν εἴποις
τῶν νῦν γυναικῶν Πηνελόπην, Φαίδρας ἁπαξαπάσας.

ΜΙΚΑ

ἀκούετ᾿, ὦ γυναῖκες, οἷ᾿ εἴρηκεν ἡ πανοῦργος
ἡμᾶς ἁπάσας αὖθις αὖ.

ΚΗΔΕΣΤΗΣ

καὶ νὴ Δί᾿ οὐδέπω γε
εἴρηχ᾿ ὅσα ξύνοιδ᾿· ἐπεὶ βούλεσθε πλείον᾿ εἴπω;

ΜΙΚΑ

ἀλλ᾿ οὐκ ἂν ἔτ᾿ ἔχοις· ὅσα γὰρ ᾔδησθ᾿ ἐξέχεας ἅπαντα.

ΚΗΔΕΣΤΗΣ

μὰ Δί᾿ οὐδέπω τὴν μυριοστὴν μοῖραν ὧν ποιοῦμεν.
ἐπεὶ τάδ᾿ οὐκ εἴρηχ᾿, ὁρᾷς, ὡς στλεγγίδας λαβοῦσαι
ἔπειτα σιφωνίζομεν τὸν σῖτον—

557 *οἶνον* Küster, cf. Arist. *Top*. 145a23, Poll. 6.19

MICA

What, you shouldn't be punished? You, the only woman with the effrontery to contradict us about a man who's abundantly wronged us by purposely finding stories where a woman turns out bad, by creating Melanippes[41] and Phaedras. But never has he created a Penelope,[42] because she was a woman noted for her virtue.

KINSMAN

Well, I can tell you why: you can't cite me a single Penelope among all the women now alive; absolutely all of us are Phaedras!

MICA

Women, hear how the hussy insults us all, again and again!

KINSMAN

By god, I haven't yet told everything I know: you want to hear more?

MICA

You can't have anything else to say: you've poured out every drop of what you know.

KINSMAN

Not even the ten-thousandth part of what we do. For example, I haven't mentioned, you know, how we take bath-scrapers and then siphon off the grain—

[41] The subject of two plays by Euripides, Melanippe was raped by Poseidon and bore twin sons, then was accused by her father of unchastity.

[42] Odysseus' virtuous wife in Homer's *Odyssey*.

ΜΙΚΑ

ἐπιτριβείης.

ΚΗΔΕΣΤΗΣ

ὥς τ᾽ αὖ τὰ κρέ᾽ ἐξ Ἀπατουρίων ταῖς μαστροποῖς διδοῦσαι
ἔπειτα τὴν γαλῆν φαμεν—

ΜΙΚΑ

τάλαιν᾽ ἐγώ· φλυαρεῖς.

ΚΗΔΕΣΤΗΣ

οὐδ᾽ ὡς ἑτέρα τὸν ἄνδρα τῷ πελέκει κατεσπόδησεν,
οὐκ εἶπον· οὐδ᾽ ὡς φαρμάκοις ἑτέρα τὸν ἄνδρ᾽ ἔμηνεν,
οὐδ᾽ ὡς ὑπὸ τῇ πυέλῳ κατώρυξέν ποτ᾽—

ΜΙΚΑ

ἐξόλοιο.

ΚΗΔΕΣΤΗΣ

Ἀχαρνικὴ τὸν πατέρα.

ΜΙΚΑ

ταῦτα δῆτ᾽ ἀνέκτ᾽ ἀκούειν;

ΚΗΔΕΣΤΗΣ

οὐδ᾽ ὡς σὺ τῆς δούλης τεκούσης ἄρρεν εἶτα σαυτῇ
τοῦθ᾽ ὑπεβάλου, τὸ σὸν δὲ θυγάτριον παρῆκας αὐτῇ.

ΜΙΚΑ

οὔ τοι μὰ τὼ θεὼ σὺ καταπροίξει λέγουσα ταυτί,
ἀλλ᾽ ἐκποκιῶ σου τὰς ποκάδας.

MICA

You should be whipped!

KINSMAN

or how we give cutlets from the Apaturia Feast[43] to our go-betweens and then say the cat took them—

MICA

Mercy me, what nonsense!

KINSMAN

or how another woman bashed her husband with an axe, I haven't mentioned that; or how another made her husband insane with drugs; or how one time an Acharnian woman buried under the tub—

MICA

I hope you die!

KINSMAN

her own father—

MICA

Must we listen to this?

KINSMAN

or how your slave girl had a baby boy and you passed it off as your own, and gave your own baby girl to the slave.

MICA

By the Twain, you won't get away with saying this: I'll pluck out your short and curlies with my own hands!

[43] A kinship festival for men and boys which excluded women.

ΚΗΔΕΣΤΗΣ

οὔ τοι μὰ Δία σύ γ᾽ ἅψει.

ΜΙΚΑ

καὶ μὴν ἰδού.

ΚΗΔΕΣΤΗΣ

καὶ μὴν ἰδού.

ΜΙΚΑ

λαβὲ θοἰμάτιον, Φιλίστη.

ΚΗΔΕΣΤΗΣ

πρόσθιγε μόνον, κἀγώ σε νὴ τὴν Ἄρτεμιν—

ΜΙΚΑ

τί δράσεις;

ΚΗΔΕΣΤΗΣ

τὸν σησαμοῦνθ᾽ ὃν κατέφαγες, τοῦτον χεσεῖν ποιήσω.

ΚΡΙΤΥΛΛΑ

παύσασθε λοιδορούμεναι· καὶ γὰρ γυνή τις ἡμῖν
ἐσπουδακυῖα προστρέχει. πρὶν οὖν ὁμοῦ γενέσθαι,
σιγᾶθ᾽, ἵν᾽ αὐτῆς κοσμίως πυθώμεθ᾽ ἅττα λέξει.

ΚΛΕΙΣΘΕΝΗΣ

φίλαι γυναῖκες, ξυγγενεῖς τοὐμοῦ τρόπου,
ὅτι μὲν φίλος εἴμ᾽ ὑμῖν, ἐπίδηλος ταῖς γνάθοις.
γυναικομανῶ γὰρ προξενῶ θ᾽ ὑμῶν ἀεί.
καὶ νῦν ἀκούσας πρᾶγμα περὶ ὑμῶν μέγα
ὀλίγῳ τι πρότερον κατ᾽ ἀγορὰν λαλούμενον,
ἥκω φράσων τοῦτ᾽ ἀγγελῶν θ᾽ ὑμῖν, ἵνα

KINSMAN

Don't you dare lay a hand on me!

MICA

Just watch me!

KINSMAN

Just watch *me*!

MICA

Hold my jacket, Philiste.

KINSMAN

Just touch me, and by Artemis I'll—

MICA

You'll what?

KINSMAN

That sesame cake you gulped down, I'll make you shit it out!

CRITYLLA

Stop abusing each other! A woman is heading for our meeting in a hurry. Before this gets to be a brawl I want you quiet, so we can hear what she has to say in an orderly fashion.

Enter CLEISTHENES, *beardless and effeminately dressed.*

CLEISTHENES

Dear ladies, my kindred in lifestyle, my devotion to you is evident from my clean jowls. Yes, I am crazy about women and represent your interests always. This time, just a little while ago, I heard a grave business concerning you being bandied about in the marketplace, and I am here to apprise you of it and inform you, so that you may consider it

σκοπῆτε καὶ τηρῆτε μὴ καὶ προσπέσῃ
ὑμῖν ἀφάρκτοις πρᾶγμα δεινὸν καὶ μέγα.

ΚΡΙΤΥΛΛΑ

τί δ' ἐστίν, ὦ παῖ; παῖδα γάρ σ' εἰκὸς καλεῖν,
ἕως ἂν οὕτως τὰς γνάθους ψιλὰς ἔχῃς.

ΚΛΕΙΣΘΕΝΗΣ

Εὐριπίδην φάσ' ἄνδρα κηδεστήν τινα
αὑτοῦ γέροντα δεῦρ' ἀναπέμψαι τήμερον.

ΚΡΙΤΥΛΛΑ

πρὸς ποῖον ἔργον ἢ τίνος γνώμης χάριν;

ΚΛΕΙΣΘΕΝΗΣ

ἵν' ἅττα βουλεύοισθε καὶ μέλλοιτε δρᾶν,
ἐκεῖνος εἴη τῶν λόγων κατάσκοπος.

ΚΡΙΤΥΛΛΑ

καὶ πῶς λέληθεν ἐν γυναιξὶν ὢν ἀνήρ;

ΚΛΕΙΣΘΕΝΗΣ

ἀφηῦσεν αὐτὸν κἀπέτιλ' Εὐριπίδης
καὶ τἄλλ' ἅπανθ' ὥσπερ γυναῖκ' ἐσκεύασεν.

ΚΗΔΕΣΤΗΣ

πείθεσθε τούτῳ ταῦτα; τίς δ' οὕτως ἀνὴρ
ἠλίθιος ὅστις τιλλόμενος ἠνείχετο;
οὐκ οἴομαι 'γωγ', ὦ πολυτιμήτω θεώ.

ΚΛΕΙΣΘΕΝΗΣ

ληρεῖς. ἐγὼ γὰρ οὐκ ἂν ἦλθον ἀγγελῶν,
εἰ μὴ 'πεπύσμην ταῦτα τῶν σάφ' εἰδότων.

and take steps to forestall a great and terrible trouble from befalling you while your guard is down.

CRITYLLA

What is it, my boy? Yes, it's only natural to call you boy, as long as you keep your jowls so smooth.

CLEISTHENES

They're saying Euripides has sent some kinsman of his, an old man, up here this very day.

CRITYLLA

On what sort of mission, or as part of what strategy?

CLEISTHENES

To be a spy, eavesdropping on whatever you women are discussing and planning to do.

CRITYLLA

But how could a man have gone unnoticed among women?

CLEISTHENES

Euripides singed and plucked him, and otherwise decked him out exactly like a woman.

KINSMAN

Do you believe what he says? What man would be fool enough to stand still for a plucking? I for one doubt it, you most reverend Twain Goddesses!

CLEISTHENES

Rubbish! I wouldn't have come here with this news if I hadn't heard it from reliably informed sources.

ΚΡΙΤΥΛΛΑ

τὸ πρᾶγμα τουτὶ δεινὸν εἰσαγγέλλεται.
ἀλλ', ὦ γυναῖκες, οὐκ ἐλινύειν ἐχρῆν,
ἀλλὰ σκοπεῖν τὸν ἄνδρα καὶ ζητεῖν ὅπου
λέληθεν ἡμᾶς κρυπτὸς ἐγκαθήμενος.
καὶ σὺ ξυνέξευρ' αὐτόν, ὡς ἂν τὴν χάριν
ταύτην τε κἀκείνην ἔχῃς, ὦ πρόξενε.

ΚΛΕΙΣΘΕΝΗΣ

ζητητέαι τἄρ' ἐστέ.

ΚΗΔΕΣΤΗΣ

κακοδαίμων ἐγώ.

ΚΛΕΙΣΘΕΝΗΣ

φέρ' ἴδω, τίς εἶ πρώτη σύ;

ΚΗΔΕΣΤΗΣ

ποῖ τις τρέψεται;

ΜΙΚΑ

ἔμ' ἥτις εἴμ' ἤρου; Κλεωνύμου γυνή.

ΚΛΕΙΣΘΕΝΗΣ

γιγνώσκεθ' ὑμεῖς ἥτις ἔσθ' ἡδὶ γυνή;

ΚΡΙΤΥΛΛΑ

γιγνώσκομεν δῆτ'· ἀλλὰ τὰς ἄλλας ἄθρει.

ΚΛΕΙΣΘΕΝΗΣ

ἡδὶ δὲ δὴ τίς ἐστιν, ἡ τὸ παιδίον
ἔχουσα;

603-4 transp. Maas

CRITYLLA

It's a terrible business that's been reported. Well, women, we mustn't sit around doing nothing! We've got to look for this man and find out where he's been sitting unnoticed in his disguise. And you, Mr. Representative, help us in the search, and so add this to our debt of gratitude to you!

CLEISTHENES

Then you've all got to be questioned.

KINSMAN

What terrible luck!

CLEISTHENES

Let's see, you first: who are you?

KINSMAN

How do I get out of here?

MICA

You want to know who I am? I'm Cleonymus' wife.

CLEISTHENES

Do all of you recognize this woman?

CRITYLLA

Yes, we know her; now question the others.

CLEISTHENES

This one, who is she? The one with the baby?

ΜΙΚΑ

τίτθη νὴ Δί᾽ ἐμή.

ΚΗΔΕΣΤΗΣ

διοίχομαι.

ΚΛΕΙΣΘΕΝΗΣ

αὕτη σύ, ποῖ στρέφει; μέν᾽ αὐτοῦ. τί τὸ κακόν;

ΚΗΔΕΣΤΗΣ

ἔασον οὐρῆσαί μ᾽· ἀναίσχυντός τις εἶ.

ΚΛΕΙΣΘΕΝΗΣ

σὺ δ᾽ οὖν ποίει τοῦτ᾽. ἀναμενῶ γὰρ ἐνθάδε.

ΚΡΙΤΤΥΛΑ

ἀνάμενε δῆτα καὶ σκόπει γ᾽ αὐτὴν σφόδρα·
μόνην γὰρ αὐτήν, ὦνερ, οὐ γιγνώσκομεν.

ΚΛΕΙΣΘΕΝΗΣ

πολύν γε χρόνον οὐρεῖς σύ.

ΚΗΔΕΣΤΗΣ

νὴ Δί᾽, ὦ μέλε,
στραγγουριῶ γάρ· ἐχθὲς ἔφαγον κάρδαμα.

ΚΛΕΙΣΘΕΝΗΣ

τί καρδαμίζεις; οὐ βαδιεῖ δεῦρ᾽ ὡς ἐμέ;

ΚΗΔΕΣΤΗΣ

τί δῆτά μ᾽ ἕλκεις ἀσθενοῦσαν;

MICA

That's definitely my wetnurse.

KINSMAN

I'm done for!

CLEISTHENES

(*to Kinsman*) You there! Where are you off to? Stay where you are! What's the matter?

KINSMAN

Let me go pee. (*Cleisthenes offers his arm*) You're a rude one!

CLEISTHENES

All right, then, get along; I'll wait for you here.

Kinsman goes aside.

CRITYLLA

Yes, wait for her, and watch her closely. She's the only woman, sir, that we don't recognize.

CLEISTHENES

You're certainly taking a long time to pee.

KINSMAN

Yes, my good man, because I'm retaining water; I ate cress seeds yesterday.

CLEISTHENES

Cress seeds, eh? Come back over here, if you please.

Kinsman hesitates, and Cleisthenes fetches him.

KINSMAN

Why do you manhandle me when I'm not feeling well?

ΚΛΕΙΣΘΕΝΗΣ

εἰπέ μοι,

τίς ἐστ᾿ ἀνήρ σοι;

ΚΗΔΕΣΤΗΣ

τὸν ἐμὸν ἄνδρα πυνθάνει;

τὸν δεῖνα γιγνώσκεις, τὸν ἐκ Κοθωκιδῶν;

ΚΛΕΙΣΘΕΝΗΣ

τὸν δεῖνα; ποῖον;

ΚΗΔΕΣΤΗΣ

ἔσθ᾿ ὁ δεῖν᾿, ὃς καί ποτε

τὸν δεῖνα, τὸν τοῦ δεῖνα—

ΚΛΕΙΣΘΕΝΗΣ

ληρεῖν μοι δοκεῖς.

ἀνῆλθες ἤδη δεῦρο πρότερον;

ΚΗΔΕΣΤΗΣ

νὴ Δία

ὁσέτη γε.

ΚΛΕΙΣΘΕΝΗΣ

καὶ τίς σοὐστὶ συσκηνήτρια;

ΚΗΔΕΣΤΗΣ

ἡ δεῖν᾿ ἔμοιγ᾿.

ΚΛΕΙΣΘΕΝΗΣ

οἴμοι τάλας, οὐδὲν λέγεις.

ΚΡΙΤΥΛΛΑ

ἄπελθ᾿· ἐγὼ γὰρ βασανιῶ ταύτην καλῶς

CLEISTHENES

Tell me, who is your husband?

KINSMAN

You want to know who my husband is? You know the guy, guy from Phalladelphia?[44]

CLEISTHENES

Guy? Which guy?

KINSMAN

He's the guy who once, when the guy, that son of the guy—

CLEISTHENES

I think you're babbling. Have you come up here before?

KINSMAN

Sure, every year.

CLEISTHENES

And who's your roommate here?

KINSMAN

Mine? A gal.

CLEISTHENES

Good grief, you're making no sense!

CRITYLLA

(*to Cleisthenes*): Step aside; I'll give this gal a proper grill-

[44] Cothocidae, an actual deme, but whose first syllable suggests a word meaning "penis."

ἐκ τῶν ἱερῶν τῶν πέρυσι. σὺ δ᾽ ἀπόστηθί μοι,
ἵνα μὴ ᾽πακούσῃς ὢν ἀνήρ. σὺ δ᾽ εἰπέ μοι
ὅ τι πρῶτον ἡμῖν τῶν ἱερῶν ἐδείκνυτο.

ΚΗΔΕΣΤΗΣ

φέρ᾽ ἴδω, τί μέντοι πρῶτον ἦν; ἐπίνομεν.

ΚΡΙΤΥΛΛΑ

τί δὲ μετὰ τοῦτο δεύτερον;

ΚΗΔΕΣΤΗΣ

προὐπίνομεν.

ΚΡΙΤΥΛΛΑ

ταυτὶ μὲν ἤκουσάς τινος. τρίτον δὲ τί;

ΚΗΔΕΣΤΗΣ

σκάφιον Ξένυλλ᾽ ᾔτησεν· οὐ γὰρ ἦν ἁμίς.

ΚΡΙΤΥΛΛΑ

οὐδὲν λέγεις. δεῦρ᾽ ἐλθέ, δεῦρ᾽, ὦ Κλείσθενες.
ὅδ᾽ ἐστὶν ἁνὴρ ὃν λέγεις.

ΚΛΕΙΣΘΕΝΗΣ

τί οὖν ποιῶ;

ΚΡΙΤΥΛΛΑ

ἀπόδυσον αὐτόν· οὐδὲν ὑγιὲς γὰρ λέγει.

ΚΗΔΕΣΤΗΣ

κἄπειτ᾽ ἀποδύσετ᾽ ἐννέα παίδων μητέρα;

ΚΛΕΙΣΘΕΝΗΣ

χάλα ταχέως τὸ στρόφιον.

ing about last year's festivities. Come on, stand away, since you're a man and mustn't overhear. (*To the Kinsman*) Now, you, tell me which of the holy things was revealed to us first.

KINSMAN

Let's see now, what was the first thing? We had a drink.

CRITYLLA

And what was the second?

KINSMAN

We drank a toast.

CRITYLLA

Somebody told you! And what was the third?

KINSMAN

Xenylla asked for a potty because there wasn't a urinal.

CRITYLLA

Wrong! Come here, Cleisthenes; this is the man you're after.

CLEISTHENES

Well, what do I do now?

CRITYLLA

Strip him: his story's fishy.

KINSMAN

So you people really mean to strip a mother of nine?

CLEISTHENES

Hurry up and get that brassiere off.

ΚΗΔΕΣΤΗΣ

ὦναίσχυντε σύ.

ΚΡΙΤΥΛΛΑ

ὡς καὶ στιβαρά τις φαίνεται καὶ καρτερά·
καὶ νὴ Δία τιτθούς γ᾽ ὥσπερ ἡμεῖς οὐκ ἔχει.

ΚΗΔΕΣΤΗΣ

στερίφη γάρ εἰμι κοὐκ ἐκύησα πώποτε.

ΚΡΙΤΥΛΛΑ

νῦν· τότε δὲ μήτηρ ἦσθα παίδων ἐννέα.

ΚΛΕΙΣΘΕΝΗΣ

ἀνίστασ᾽ ὀρθός. ποῖ τὸ πέος ὠθεῖς κάτω;

ΚΡΙΤΥΛΛΑ

τοδὶ διέκυψε καὶ μάλ᾽ εὔχρων, ὦ τάλαν.

ΚΛΕΙΣΘΕΝΗΣ

καὶ ποῦ ᾽στιν;

ΚΡΙΤΥΛΛΑ

αὖθις εἰς τὸ πρόσθεν οἴχεται.

ΚΛΕΙΣΘΕΝΗΣ

οὐκ ἐνγεταυθί.

ΚΡΙΤΥΛΛΑ

μἀλλὰ δεῦρ᾽ ἥκει πάλιν.

ΚΛΕΙΣΘΕΝΗΣ

ἰσθμόν τιν᾽ ἔχεις, ἄνθρωπ᾽· ἄνω τε καὶ κάτω

KINSMAN

(*to Cleisthenes*) How rude of you!

CRITYLLA

My, she's really a stocky one, and strong! And she certainly hasn't got tits like we do.

KINSMAN

That's because I'm sterile, and never did get pregnant.

CRITYLLA

Really! But just now you were the mother of nine.

CLEISTHENES

Stand up straight. Where are you shoving your cock down there?

CRITYLLA

(*running behind Kinsman*) Here it is! Its head is sticking out; nice color, too, deary.

CLEISTHENES

Where?

CRITYLLA

Now it's gone back in front!

CLEISTHENES

It's not up here!

CRITYLLA

No, it's come back here again!

CLEISTHENES

That's some isthmus you've got there, buddy! You shuttle

τὸ πέος διέλκεις πυκνότερον Κορινθίων.

ΚΡΙΤΥΛΛΑ

ὦ μιαρὸς οὗτος. ταῦτ᾽ ἄρ᾽ ὑπὲρ Εὐριπίδου
ἡμῖν ἐλοιδορεῖτο.

ΚΗΔΕΣΤΗΣ

κακοδαίμων ἐγώ,
εἰς οἷ᾽ ἐμαυτὸν εἰσεκύλισα πράγματα.

ΚΡΙΤΥΛΛΑ

ἄγε δή, τί δρῶμεν;

ΚΛΕΙΣΘΕΝΗΣ

τουτονὶ φυλάττετε
καλῶς, ὅπως μὴ διαφυγὼν οἰχήσεται·
ἐγὼ δὲ ταῦτα τοῖς πρυτάνεσιν ἀγγελῶ.

ΚΟΡΥΦΑΙΑ

ἡμᾶς τοίνυν μετὰ τοῦτ᾽ ἤδη τὰς λαμπάδας ἀψαμένας χρὴ
ξυζωσαμένας εὖ κἀνδρείως τῶν θ᾽ ἱματίων ἀποδύσας
ζητεῖν, εἴ που κἄλλος τις ἀνὴρ ἐσελήλυθε, καὶ περιθρέξαι
τὴν πύκνα πᾶσαν καὶ τὰς σκηνὰς καὶ τὰς διόδους διαθρῆσαι.
εἶα δή, πρώτιστα μὲν χρὴ κοῦφον ἐξορμᾶν πόδα
καὶ διασκοπεῖν σιωπῇ πανταχῇ. μόνον δὲ χρὴ
μὴ βραδύνειν, ὡς ὁ καιρός ἐστι μὴ μέλλειν ἔτι.

your cock back and forth more than the Corinthians![45]

CRITYLLA

What a degenerate! That's why he insulted us in defense of Euripides.

KINSMAN

I'm in a bad spot. What a mess I've tumbled myself into!

CRITYLLA

(*to Cleisthenes*) All right, what now?

CLEISTHENES

Put him under close guard, and see that he doesn't escape. I'll go and report this to the authorities.

Exit CLEISTHENES. CRITYLLA *and the other Women enter the stage house.* MICA *and Mania, holding the baby, stand guard over* KINSMAN.

CHORUS LEADER

Well, our next job now is to light these torches, hitch up our clothes right manfully, take off our jackets, and find out if any other man has come against us, and scour the entire Pnyx,[46] and search the tents and the alleyways. So forward march! First of all we should launch a quick foot and inspect everything thoroughly and silently. Just so we don't take too long, since this is the moment to stop hesitating,

[45] Playing on a slang meaning of isthmus = "crotch," and referring to the causeway built across the Isthmus of Corinth, which linked the Corinthian and Saronic Gulfs.

[46] The hill on which Athenian assemblies and (probably) the Thesmophoria were held.

ἀλλὰ τὴν πρώτην τρέχειν χρή μ᾽ ὡς τάχιστ᾽ ἤδη
κύκλῳ.

ΧΟΡΟΣ

εἶά νυν ἴχνευε καὶ μά-
τευε ταχὺ πάντ᾽, εἴ τις ἐν τό-
ποις ἑδραῖος
ἄλλος αὖ λέληθεν ὤν.
πανταχῇ δὲ ῥῖψον ὄμμα,
καὶ τὰ τῇδε <καὶ τὰ κεῖσε>
καὶ τὰ δεῦρο
πάντ᾽ ἀνασκόπει καλῶς.

ἢν γὰρ ληφθῇ δράσας ἀνόσια,
δώσει τε δίκην καὶ πρὸς τούτῳ
τοῖς ἄλλοις ἀνδράσιν ἔσται
παράδειγμ᾽ ὕβρεως ἀδίκων τ᾽ ἔργων
ἀθέων τε τρόπων·
φήσει δ᾽ εἶναί τε θεοὺς φανερῶς,
δείξει τ᾽ ἤδη
πᾶσιν ἀνθρώποις σεβίζειν δαίμονας
δικαίως τ᾽ ἐφέπειν ὅσια καὶ νόμιμα
μηδομένους ποιεῖν ὅ τι καλῶς ἔχει.
κἂν μὴ ποιῶσι ταῦτα, τοιάδ᾽ ἔσται·
αὐτῶν ὅταν ληφθῇ τις ὅσια <μὴ> δρῶν,
μανίαις φλέγων, λύσσῃ παράκο-
πος, πᾶσιν ἐμφανὴς ὁρᾶν

662 χρή μ᾽ Austin: χρῆν R
666 suppl. Kaibel cl. *Av.* 424-25

and for me to lead the foray on the run, as quick as I can, all around!

CHORUS[47]

Move out then quickly! Get on the track
and trail of any other man
who may be in the area,
entrenched behind our backs.
Cast your eyes in all directions,
over this way, over that way,
and over here;
give everything a good examination!

If he's caught as a doer of sacrilege,
he'll be punished, and more than that:
to other men he'll be an example
of outrageousness, of wrongdoing,
of godless ways!
He'll profess that the gods do clearly exist,
and then he'll be a lesson
to all men that it's well to revere the gods
and righteously follow divine and human laws,
taking care to do what's good.
And here's what happens if they don't:
any man caught in an impious act
will burn and rage in rabid insanity,
his every act a manifest proof

[47] Tragic pastiche, perhaps including material from a chorus in Euripides' *Telephus*, cf. fr. 727a.

---

667 ληφθῇ Reisig: μὴ λάθῃ R 679 suppl. Burges
681/2 παράκοπος Bothe: παράκοπος εἴ τι δρῴη R

ἔσται γυναιξὶ καὶ βροτοῖς
ὅτι τὰ παράνομα τά τ᾿ ἀνόσια
παραχρῆμ᾿ ἀποτίνεται θεός.

ΚΟΡΥΦΑΙΑ

ἀλλ᾿ ἔοιχ᾿ ἡμῖν ἅπαντά πως διεσκέφθαι καλῶς.
οὐχ ὁρῶμεν γοῦν ἔτ᾿ ἄλλον οὐδέν᾿ ἐγκαθήμενον.

ΜΙΚΑ

ἆ ἆ.
ποῖ ποῖ σὺ φεύγεις; οὗτος οὗτος, οὐ μενεῖς;
τάλαιν᾿ ἐγώ, τάλαινα, καὶ τὸ παιδίον
ἐξαρπάσας μοι φροῦδος ἀπὸ τοῦ τιτθίου.

ΚΗΔΕΣΤΗΣ

κέκραχθι. τοῦτο δ᾿ οὐδέποτε σὺ ψωμιεῖς,
ἢν μή μ᾿ ἀφῆτ᾿· ἀλλ᾿ ἐνθάδ᾿ ἐπὶ τῶν μηρίων
πληγὲν μαχαίρᾳ τῇδε φοινίας φλέβας
καθαιματώσει βωμόν.

ΜΙΚΑ

ὦ τάλαιν᾿ ἐγώ.
γυναῖκες, οὐκ ἀρήξετ᾿; οὐ πολλὴν βοὴν
στήσεσθε καὶ τροπαῖον, ἀλλὰ τοῦ μόνου
τέκνου με περιόψεσθ᾿ ἀποστερουμένην;

ΧΟΡΟΣ

ἔα ἔα.
ὦ πότνιαι Μοῖραι, τί τόδε δέρκομαι
νεοχμὸν αὖ τέρας;

for all women and mortals to see
that lawlessness and sacrilege
are punished on the spot by god!

CHORUS LEADER

Well, we seem to have given everything a thorough inspection, and we don't see any other man lurking hereabouts.

Kinsman seizes Mica's baby and runs to the altar in the orchestra.[48]

MICA

Hey! Hey! Where do you think you're going? Stop, you! Stop, won't you? Good grief, oh my, he's even gone and snatched my baby right from the tit!

KINSMAN

Scream away! You'll never feed it again if you don't let me go! Nay, here and now, smitten to his crimson veins by this bodkin atop the thigh bones, shall he begore the altar!

MICA

Good grief! Women, please help! Please raise a great war cry and a victory trophy, and not look aside as I am bereft of my only child!

CHORUS

Ah! Ah!
August Fates, what novel horror is this
that I behold?

[48] See 466 n.

---

685 παραχρῆμ' ἀποτίνεται θεός Henderson: θεὸς ἀποτίνεται· παραχρῆμά τε τίνεται R

ΚΟΡΥΦΑΙΑ

ὡς ἅπαντ᾽ ἄρ᾽ ἐστὶ τόλμης ἔργα κἀναισχυντίας.
οἷον αὖ δέδρακεν ἔργον, οἷον αὖ, φίλαι, τόδε.

ΚΗΔΕΣΤΗΣ

οἷον ὑμῶν ἐξαράξω τὴν ἄγαν αὐθαδίαν.

ΚΟΡΥΦΑΙΑ

ταῦτα δῆτ᾽ οὐ δεινὰ πράγματ᾽ ἐστὶ καὶ περαιτέρω;

ΜΙΚΑ

δεινὰ δῆθ᾽, ὁτιή γ᾽ ἔχει μου ᾽ξαρπάσας τὸ παιδίον.

ΧΟΡΟΣ

τί ἂν οὖν εἴποι πρὸς ταῦτά τις, ὅτε
τοιαῦτα ποιῶν ὅδ᾽ ἀναισχυντεῖ;

ΚΗΔΕΣΤΗΣ

κοὔπω μέντοι γε πέπαυμαι.

ΧΟΡΟΣ

ἀλλ᾽ οὖν ἥκεις γ᾽ ὅθεν οὐ φαύλως
ἀποδρὰς λέξεις οἷον δράσας
διέδυς ἔργον, λήψει δὲ κακόν.

ΚΗΔΕΣΤΗΣ

τοῦτο μέντοι μὴ γένοιτο μηδαμῶς, ἀπεύχομαι.

ΧΟΡΟΣ

τίς ἄν σοι, τίς ἂν σύμμαχος ἐκ θεῶν
ἀθανάτων ἔλθοι ξὺν ἀδίκοις ἔργοις;

ΚΗΔΕΣΤΗΣ

μάτην λαλεῖτε· τήνδ᾽ ἐγὼ οὐκ ἀφήσω.

CHORUS LEADER

The whole world is full of impudence and brass! What a deed he's done this time, fellow women, what a deed this is!

KINSMAN

A deed that'll knock the stuffing out of your arrogance!

CHORUS LEADER

Isn't this an awful business, and worse than awful?

MICA

Awful indeed! He's gone and snatched away my baby!

CHORUS

What can we say to this,
when he is unashamed of such deeds?

KINSMAN

And I'm not finished yet, either!

CHORUS

Still, here you are where you won't easily escape
to boast that you did such a deed,
then gave us the slip. No, you'll get yours!

KINSMAN

I pray that that may never ever come to pass!

CHORUS

Who, I say, who of the immortal gods
would come to your aid in wrongdoing?

KINSMAN

Your point is moot anyway. I'll never give up this girl!

ΧΟΡΟΣ

ἀλλʼ οὐ μὰ τὼ θεὼ τάχʼ οὐ
χαίρων ἴσως ἐνυβριεῖς
λόγους τε λέξεις ἀνοσίους.
ἀθέοις γὰρ ἔργοις ἀνταμει-
ψόμεσθά σʼ, ὥσπερ εἰκός, ἀντὶ τῶνδε.
τάχα δὲ μεταβαλοῦσʼ ἐπὶ κακὸν ἑτερότρο-
πος ἐπέχει τύχη.

ΚΟΡΥΦΑΙΑ

ἀλλὰ τάσδε μὲν λαβεῖν χρῆν ἐκφέρειν τε τῶν ξύλων,
καὶ καταίθειν τὸν πανοῦργον πυρπολεῖν θʼ ὅσον τάχος.

ΜΙΚΑ

ἴωμεν ἐπὶ τὰς κληματίδας, ὦ Μανία.
κἀγώ σʼ ἀποδείξω θυμάλωπα τήμερον.

ΚΗΔΕΣΤΗΣ

ὕφαπτε καὶ κάταιθε· σὺ δὲ τὸ Κρητικὸν
ἀπόδυθι ταχέως. τοῦ θανάτου δʼ, ὦ παιδίον,
μόνην γυναικῶν αἰτιῶ τὴν μητέρα.
τουτὶ τί ἐστιν; ἀσκὸς ἐγένεθʼ ἡ κόρη
οἴνου πλέως καὶ ταῦτα Περσικὰς ἔχων.
ὦ θερμόταται γυναῖκες, ὦ ποτίσταται
κἀκ παντὸς ὑμεῖς μηχανώμεναι πιεῖν,
ὦ μέγα καπήλοις ἀγαθόν, ἡμῖν δʼ αὖ κακόν,
κακὸν δὲ καὶ τοῖς σκευαρίοις καὶ τῇ κρόκῃ.

CHORUS

But maybe soon, by the Twain Goddesses,
your outrageous behavior will prove joyless,
as will your unholy speech!
For we will repay you, as is fitting,
with godless deeds in answer to your own.
Your luck has quickly changed to the bad,
and heads in another direction!

CHORUS LEADER

Here, you should have grabbed these torches and fetched some wood, to burn up the criminal and incinerate him as quickly as possible.

MICA

Let's go for the firewood, Mania! (*To Kinsman*) And I'll personally turn you into a shower of sparks this very day!

Mica and Mania go inside.

KINSMAN

Light me up and burn me down! (*unwrapping the baby*) As for you, off with this Cretan swaddling, quickly. And for your death, my child, blame but a single woman, your mother! What is this? The baby girl's become a skin full of wine, and wearing Persian booties to boot! Women, you overheated dipsomaniacs, never passing up a chance to wangle a drink, a great boon to bartenders but a bane to us—not to mention our crockery and our woolens!

Mica and Mania reenter with firewood.

ΜΙΚΑ

παράβαλλε πολλὰς κληματίδας, ὦ Μανία.

ΚΗΔΕΣΤΗΣ

παράβαλλε δῆτα. σὺ δ᾽ ἀπόκριναί μοι τοδί·
τουτὶ τεκεῖν φῄς;

ΜΙΚΑ

καὶ δέκα μῆνας αὔτ᾽ ἐγὼ
ἤνεγκον.

ΚΗΔΕΣΤΗΣ

ἤνεγκας σύ;

ΜΙΚΑ

νὴ τὴν Ἄρτεμιν.

ΚΗΔΕΣΤΗΣ

τρικότυλον ἢ πῶς; εἰπέ μοι.

ΜΙΚΑ

τί μ᾽ ἠργάσω;
ἀπέδυσας, ὦναίσχυντέ, μου τὸ παιδίον
τυννοῦτον ὄν.

ΚΗΔΕΣΤΗΣ

τυννοῦτο; μικρὸν νὴ Δία.
πόσ᾽ ἔτη δὲ γέγονε; τρεῖς Χοᾶς ἢ τέτταρας;

ΜΙΚΑ

σχεδὸν τοσοῦτον χὤσον ἐκ Διονυσίων.
ἀλλ᾽ ἀπόδος αὐτό.

ΚΗΔΕΣΤΗΣ

μὰ τὸν Ἀπόλλω τουτονί.

MICA

Pile them on nice and thick, Mania.

KINSMAN

Go ahead, pile them on. But tell me one thing: do you claim to have given birth to this?

MICA

Carried it all ten months myself.[49]

KINSMAN

You carried it?

MICA

By Artemis, I did.

KINSMAN

What's the proof—seventy-five, was it?

MICA

How dare you? You've undressed my child—disgusting!—a tiny baby!

KINSMAN

Tiny? It is pretty small at that. How many years old? Three Wine-Jug Festivals or four?[50]

MICA

That's about right, plus a Dionysia. But give it back!

KINSMAN

No, by Apollo there![51]

[49] Lunar months counted inclusively.

[50] During the festival of Anthesteria, three-year-olds were specially recognized, and men competed for a wineskin in a drinking contest.

[51] The image of Apollo Agyieus in front of the stage house.

ΜΙΚΑ

ἐμπρήσομεν τοίνυν σε.

ΚΗΔΕΣΤΗΣ

πάνυ γ᾽· ἐμπίμπρατε.
αὕτη δ᾽ ἀποσφαγήσεται μάλ᾽ αὐτίκα.

ΜΙΚΑ

μὴ δῆθ᾽, ἱκετεύω σ᾽· ἀλλ᾽ ἔμ᾽ ὅ τι χρῄζεις ποίει
ὑπέρ γε τούτου.

ΚΗΔΕΣΤΗΣ

φιλότεκνός τις εἶ φύσει.
ἀλλ᾽ οὐδὲν ἧττον ἥδ᾽ ἀποσφαγήσεται.

ΜΙΚΑ

οἴμοι, τέκνον. δὸς τὸ σφαγεῖον, Μανία,
ἵν᾽ οὖν τό γ᾽ αἷμα τοῦ τέκνου τοὐμοῦ λάβω.

ΚΗΔΕΣΤΗΣ

ὕπεχ᾽ αὐτό· χαριοῦμαι γὰρ ἕν γε τοῦτό σοι.

ΜΙΚΑ

κακῶς ἀπόλοι᾽. ὡς φθονερὸς εἶ καὶ δυσμενής.

ΚΗΔΕΣΤΗΣ

τουτὶ τὸ δέρμα τῆς ἱερείας γίγνεται.

ΚΡΙΤΥΛΛΑ

τί τῆς ἱερείας γίγνεται;

ΚΗΔΕΣΤΗΣ

τουτί. λαβέ.

MICA

Then we'll incinerate you.

KINSMAN

By all means, incinerate away. (*producing a knife*) But this little girl will get sacrificed on the spot.

MICA

Don't do it, I beseech you! Do what you want with me, for this one's sake.

KINSMAN

You've a good mother's instincts. But nonetheless this girl's going to get her throat cut.

MICA

Ah my baby! Give me the slaughter bowl, Mania, so I can at least catch my own child's blood.

KINSMAN

Hold it under there; I'll do you this one favor. (*Kinsman slashes the wineskin*)

MICA

Damn you to hell! You're hateful and cruel!

KINSMAN

The hide here goes to the priestess.

CRITYLLA comes out of the stage house.

CRITYLLA

What goes to the priestess?

KINSMAN

This; catch!

ΚΡΙΤΤΥΛΛΑ

ταλαντάτη Μίκα, τίς ἐξεκόρησέ σε;
τίς τὴν ἀγαπητὴν παῖδά σου 'ξηράσατο;

ΜΙΚΑ

ὁ πανοῦργος οὗτος. ἀλλ' ἐπειδήπερ πάρει,
φύλαξον αὐτόν, ἵνα λαβοῦσα Κλεισθένη
τοῖσιν πρυτάνεσιν ἃ πεποίηχ' οὗτος φράσω.

ΚΗΔΕΣΤΗΣ

ἄγε δή, τίς ἔσται μηχανὴ σωτηρίας;
τίς πεῖρα, τίς ἐπίνοι'; ὁ μὲν γὰρ αἴτιος
κἄμ' εἰσκυλίσας εἰς τοιαυτὶ πράγματα
οὐ φαίνετ', οὔπω. φέρε, τίν' οὖν ἂν ἄγγελον
πέμψαιμ' ἐπ' αὐτόν; οἶδ' ἐγὼ καὶ δὴ πόρον
ἐκ τοῦ Παλαμήδους. ὡς ἐκεῖνος, τὰς πλάτας
ῥίψω γράφων. ἀλλ' οὐ πάρεισιν αἱ πλάται.
πόθεν οὖν γένοιντ' ἄν μοι πλάται; πόθεν; <φέρε,>
τί δ' ἄν, εἰ ταδὶ τἀγάλματ' ἀντὶ τῶν πλατῶν
γράφων διαρρίπτοιμι; βέλτιον πολύ.
ξύλον γέ τοι καὶ ταῦτα, κἀκεῖν' ἦν ξύλον.

ὦ χεῖρες ἐμαί,
  ἐγχειρεῖν ἔργῳ χρὴ πορίμῳ.
ἄγε δή, πινάκων ξεστῶν δέλτοι,
  δέξασθε σμίλης ὁλκούς,
κήρυκας ἐμῶν μόχθων. οἴμοι,

772 suppl. Austin

CRITYLLA

Poor, poor Mica! Who's ungirled you? Who's drained your only lass?

MICA

This criminal here! But since you're here, stand guard over him, so I can get hold of Cleisthenes and tell the marshals what this man has done.

Exit MICA *and Mania.*

KINSMAN

What's my plan for saving myself now? What move? What idea? The man who tumbled me into this mess in the first place is nowhere to be seen; not yet. Well then, what messenger might I send to him? In fact I do know a method, from his *Palamedes*:[52] like that fellow, I'll inscribe the oar blades, and deep-six them. But those oar blades aren't here. Now where could I get oar blades? Where, where? Say, what if instead of oar blades I wrote on these votive tablets and then tossed them in all directions? That's much better! They're wooden too, just like oar blades.

Hands of mine,
you must put your hand to an effective job.
Tablets of planed board,
accept the knife's scratchings,
harbingers of my troubles! Damn,

[52] In Euripides' lost play *Palamedes* (produced in 415) the hero, the inventor of writing and a Greek who fought at Troy, was falsely accused of treason and executed; his brother Oeax sent a message to their father by writing it on oar blades and floating them back to Greece.

τουτὶ τὸ ῥῶ μοχθηρόν.
χωρεῖ, χωρεῖ. ποίαν αὔλακα;
βάσκετ', ἐπείγετε πάσας καθ' ὁδούς,
κείνᾳ, ταύτᾳ· ταχέως χρή.

ΚΟΡΥΦΑΙΑ

ἡμεῖς τοίνυν ἡμᾶς αὐτὰς εὖ λέξωμεν παραβᾶσαι.
καίτοι πᾶς τις τὸ γυναικεῖον φῦλον κακὰ πόλλ' ἀγορεύει,
ὡς πᾶν ἐσμὲν κακὸν ἀνθρώποις κἀξ ἡμῶν ἐστιν ἅπαντα,
ἔριδες, νείκη, στάσις ἀργαλέα, λύπη, πόλεμος. φέρε δή νυν,
εἰ κακόν ἐσμεν, τί γαμεῖθ' ἡμᾶς, εἴπερ ἀληθῶς κακόν ἐσμεν,
κἀπαγορεύετε μήτ' ἐξελθεῖν μήτ' ἐκκύψασαν ἁλῶναι,
ἀλλ' οὑτωσὶ πολλῇ σπουδῇ τὸ κακὸν βούλεσθε φυλάττειν;
κἂν ἐξέλθῃ τὸ γύναιόν ποι, κᾆθ' εὕρητ' αὐτὸ θύρασιν,
μανίας μαίνεσθ', οὓς χρῆν σπένδειν καὶ χαίρειν, εἴπερ ἀληθῶς
ἔνδοθεν ηὕρετε φροῦδον τὸ κακὸν καὶ μὴ κατελαμβάνετ' ἔνδον.
κἂν καταδάρθωμεν ἐν ἀλλοτρίων παίζουσαι καὶ κοπιῶσαι,
πᾶς τις τὸ κακὸν τοῦτο ζητεῖ περὶ τὰς κλίνας περινοστῶν.

this R is a troublemaker!
There we go, there we go! What a scratch!
Be off then, travel every road,
this way, that way, and better hurry!

CHORUS LEADER

Well, let's step forward and sing our own praises! We'd better, because each and every man has a host of bad things to say about the female race, claiming that we're an utter bane to humanity and the source of all ills: disputes, quarrels, bitter factionalism, distress, war. Come on now, if we're a bane, why do you marry us? If we're truly a bane, why do you forbid us to leave the house or even get caught peeking out the window? Why do you want to keep such a careful guard on your bane? If the little woman goes out somewhere and you find her outdoors, you rage like lunatics instead of toasting the gods and giving thanks, as you would do if you'd truly found the bane of your household missing and couldn't find it in the house. If we fall asleep at someone else's house, worn out from enjoying ourselves, every husband makes the rounds of the couches looking

κἂν ἐκ θυρίδος παρακύπτωμεν, ζητεῖ τὸ κακὸν τεθεᾶσθαι·
κἂν αἰσχυνθεῖσ᾽ ἀναχωρήσῃ, πολὺ μᾶλλον πᾶς ἐπιθυμεῖ
αὖθις τὸ κακὸν παρακύψαν ἰδεῖν. οὕτως ἡμεῖς ἐπιδήλως
ὑμῶν ἐσμεν πολὺ βελτίους. βάσανός τε πάρεστιν ἰδέσθαι.
βάσανον δῶμεν, πότεροι χείρους. ἡμεῖς μὲν γάρ φαμεν ὑμᾶς,
ὑμεῖς δ᾽ ἡμᾶς. σκεψώμεθα δὴ κἀντιτιθῶμεν πρὸς ἕκαστον,
παραβάλλουσαι τῆς τε γυναικὸς καὶ τἀνδρὸς τοὔνομ᾽ ἑκάστου.
Ναυσιμάχης μέν γ᾽ ἥττων ἐστὶν Χαρμῖνος· δῆλα δὲ τἄργα.
καὶ μὲν δὴ καὶ Κλεοφῶν χείρων πάντως δήπου Σαλαβακχοῦς.
πρὸς Ἀριστομάχην δὲ χρόνου πολλοῦ, πρὸς ἐκείνην τὴν Μαραθῶνι,
καὶ Στρατονίκην ὑμῶν οὐδεὶς οὐδ᾽ ἐγχειρεῖ πολεμίζειν.
ἀλλ᾽ Εὐβούλης τῶν πέρυσίν τις βουλευτής ἐστιν ἀμείνων
παραδοὺς ἑτέρῳ τὴν βουλείαν; οὐδ᾽ αὐτὸς τοῦτό γε φήσεις.
οὕτως ἡμεῖς πολὺ βελτίους τῶν ἀνδρῶν εὐχόμεθ᾽ εἶναι.

for his bane. If we peek out of our bedroom windows, everyone tries to catch a glimpse of the bane; and if we duck back in from embarrassment, everyone's all the more eager to catch a glimpse of the bane when it peeks out again. Thus it's pretty clear that we're far superior to you, and I've got a way to prove it. Let's take a test to see which sex is worse. We say it's you and you say it's us. Let's examine the issue by pairing the names of each man and each woman one on one. Take Charminus: he's worse than Nausimache,[53] as the record makes clear. And then Cleophon is of course worse in every way than Salabaccho.[54] And it's been a long time since any of you has even tried to measure up to Aristomache—I mean the one at Marathon—and Stratonice.[55] What about a certain one of last year's Councillors, who handed over his powers to someone else: is he better than Eubule?[56] (*pointing him out*) You wouldn't say so yourself! And so we claim to be much better than men.

53 Charminus was an Athenian naval commander defeated the previous winter; the woman's name (a typical name, like the others to follow, except Salabaccho) means "victory at sea."

54 Cleophon was a popular politician, Salabaccho a courtesan (cf. *Knights* 765).

55 The names mean "outstanding in battle" and "military victory."

56 The name means "good counsel."

οὐδ᾽ ἂν κλέψασα γυνὴ ζεύγει κατὰ πεντήκοντα τάλαντα
εἰς πόλιν ἔλθοι τῶν δημοσίων· ἀλλ᾽ ἢν τὰ μέγισθ᾽ ὑφέληται,
φορμὸν πυρῶν τἀνδρὸς κλέψασ᾽, αὐθημερὸν ἀνταπέδωκεν.
ἀλλ᾽ ἡμεῖς ἂν πολλοὺς τούτων
ἀποδείξαιμεν ταῦτα ποιοῦντας,
καὶ πρὸς τούτοις γάστριδας ἡμῶν
ὄντας μᾶλλον καὶ λωποδύτας
καὶ βωμολόχους κἀνδραποδιστάς.
καὶ μὲν δήπου καὶ τὰ πατρῷά γε
χείρους ἡμῶν εἰσιν σῴζειν.
ἡμῖν μὲν γὰρ σῶν ἔτι καὶ νῦν
τἀντίον, ὁ κανών, οἱ καλαθίσκοι,
τὸ σκιάδειον·
τοῖς δ᾽ ἡμετέροις ἀνδράσι τούτοις
ἀπόλωλεν μὲν πολλοῖς ὁ κανὼν
ἐκ τῶν οἴκων αὐτῇ λόγχῃ,
πολλοῖς δ᾽ ἑτέροις ἀπὸ τῶν ὤμων
ἐν ταῖς στρατιαῖς
ἔρριπται τὸ σκιάδειον.
πόλλ᾽ ἂν αἱ γυναῖκες ἡμεῖς ἐν δίκῃ μεμψαίμεθ᾽ ἂν
τοῖσιν ἀνδράσιν δικαίως, ἓν δ᾽ ὑπερφυέστατον.
χρῆν γάρ, ἡμῶν εἰ τέκοι τις ἄνδρα χρηστὸν τῇ πόλει,
ταξίαρχον ἢ στρατηγόν, λαμβάνειν τιμήν τινα,
προεδρίαν τ᾽ αὐτῇ δίδοσθαι Στηνίοισι καὶ Σκίροις

And a woman would never steal about fifty talents a pop from the public treasury and then drive up to the Acropolis in a chariot and pair. The most a woman will filch is a cup of flour from her husband, and then she'll pay him back the same day.

We could show that many of the men here do these things, and are also more likely than us to be potbellies, muggers, spongers, and slave drivers. And when it comes to their patrimony, they're less able to preserve it than we are. We've still got our looms and weaving rods, our wool baskets and parasols. Contrast these husbands of ours: many have let their spear shaft disappear from the household, point and all, and many others have cast from their shoulders, in the heat of battle, their parasols!

Yes, we women have plenty of justified complaints to lodge against our husbands, one of which is very monstrous. If a woman bears a son who's useful to the polis—a taxiarch or a commander—she should receive some honor, and be given front-row seating at the Stenia and the Scira

ἔν τε ταῖς ἄλλαις ἑορταῖς αἷσιν ἡμεῖς ἤγομεν·
εἰ δὲ δειλὸν καὶ πονηρὸν ἄνδρα τις τέκοι γυνή,
ἢ τριήραρχον πονηρὸν ἢ κυβερνήτην κακόν,
ὑστέραν αὐτὴν καθῆσθαι σκάφιον ἀποκεκαρμένην
τῆς τὸν ἀνδρεῖον τεκούσης. τῷ γὰρ εἰκός, ὦ πόλις,
τὴν Ὑπερβόλου καθῆσθαι μητέρ᾽ ἠμφιεσμένην
λευκὰ καὶ κόμας καθεῖσαν πλησίον τῆς Λαμάχου,
καὶ δανείζειν χρήμαθ᾽, ᾗ χρῆν, εἰ δανείσειέν τινι
καὶ τόκον πράττοιτο, διδόναι μηδέν᾽ ἀνθρώπων τόκον,
ἀλλ᾽ ἀφαιρεῖσθαι βίᾳ τὰ χρήματ᾽ εἰπόντας τοδί·
"ἀξία γοῦν εἶ τόκου τεκοῦσα τοιοῦτον τόκον."

ΚΗΔΕΣΤΗΣ

ἰλλὸς γεγένημαι προσδοκῶν· ὁ δ᾽ οὐδέπω.
τί δῆτ᾽ ἂν εἴη τοὐμποδών; οὐκ ἔσθ᾽ ὅπως
οὐ τὸν Παλαμήδη ψυχρὸν ὄντ᾽ αἰσχύνεται.
τῷ δῆτ᾽ ἂν αὐτὸν προσαγαγοίμην δράματι;
ἐγᾦδα· τὴν καινὴν Ἑλένην μιμήσομαι.
πάντως ὑπάρχει μοι γυναικεία στολή.

ΚΡΙΤΥΛΛΑ

τί αὖ σὺ κυρκανᾷς; τί κοικύλλεις ἔχων;
πικρὰν Ἑλένην ὄψει τάχ᾽, εἰ μὴ κοσμίως
ἕξεις, ἕως ἂν τῶν πρυτάνεών τις φανῇ.

---

[57] Like the Thesmophoria, these festivals honored Demeter and were celebrated only by women.

[58] Hyperbolus, a leading popular politician and frequent object of comic ridicule before his ostracism in 417 or 416, was assassinated by oligarchs shortly after the production of this play; his

and the other festivals that we women celebrate.[57] But if a woman bears a son who's a coward and a rascal—a bad trierarch or an incompetent pilot—she should sit behind the hero's mother with her hair cropped in a bowl cut. By what logic, you citizens, should Hyperbolus' mother,[58] dressed in white and wearing her hair down, get to sit near Lamachus'[59] mother and make loans? If she lends money at interest, no borrower should have to pay the interest, but should grab her money by force and tell her, "You're a fine one to be charging points after bearing such a disappointing son!"

KINSMAN

I've gone cross-eyed looking for him, but so far no good. What could be keeping him? No doubt he's ashamed that his *Palamedes* was a flop. So which of his plays *can* I use to entice him? I've got it! I'll do a take-off on his recent *Helen*;[60] after all, I'm already wearing a woman's costume.

CRITYLLA

What are you cooking up now? Why are you rubbernecking around? You'll see one hell of a Helen if you don't behave yourself until one of the marshals gets here.

mother (now in her fifties) had been caricatured in at least two plays as an alien, whore, and drunk.

59 This Athenian commander, ridiculed in *Acharnians* and *Peace*, had died a hero's death in the Sicilian expedition; his mother would now be in her seventies.

60 In this play, produced in 412, the abducted Helen turns out to have been a phantom, while the real Helen spent the war in Egypt in the palace of Proteus, whose son Theoclymenus now wants to marry her. After the war Menelaus discovers the truth and with the help of an Egyptian prophetess, Theonoe, escapes with Helen.

ΚΗΔΕΣΤΗΣ

Νείλου μὲν αἵδε καλλιπάρθενοι ῥοαί,
ὃς ἀντὶ δίας ψακάδος Αἰγύπτου πέδον
λευκῆς νοτίζει μελανοσυρμαῖον λεών.

ΚΡΙΤΥΛΛΑ

πανοῦργος εἶ νὴ τὴν Ἑκάτην τὴν φωσφόρον.

ΚΗΔΕΣΤΗΣ

ἐμοὶ δὲ γῆ μὲν πατρὶς οὐκ ἀνώνυμος,
Σπάρτη, πατὴρ δὲ Τυνδάρεως.

ΚΡΙΤΥΛΛΑ

σοί γ', ὤλεθρε,
πατὴρ ἐκεῖνός ἐστι; Φρυνώνδας μὲν οὖν.

ΚΗΔΕΣΤΗΣ

Ἑλένη δ' ἐκλήθην.

ΚΡΙΤΥΛΛΑ

αὖθις αὖ γίγνει γυνή,
πρὶν τῆς ἑτέρας δοῦναι γυναικίσεως δίκην;

ΚΗΔΕΣΤΗΣ

ψυχαὶ δὲ πολλαὶ δι' ἔμ' ἐπὶ Σκαμανδρίοις
ῥοαῖσιν ἔθανον.

ΚΡΙΤΥΛΛΑ

ὤφελες δὲ καὶ σύ γε.

ΚΗΔΕΣΤΗΣ

κἀγὼ μὲν ἐνθάδ' εἴμ'· ὁ δ' ἄθλιος πόσις
οὑμὸς Μενέλεως οὐδέπω προσέρχεται.
τί οὖν ἔτι ζῶ;

KINSMAN

(*as Helen*):

These are the fair-maidened currents of the Nile,
who in lieu of heavenly distillment floods the flats
of bright Egypt for a people much given to laxatives.

CRITYLLA

By Hecate the Torch-Bearer, you're a villain!

KINSMAN

The land of my fathers is not without a name:
'tis Sparta, and my sire is Tyndareus.

CRITYLLA

He's *your* father, you disaster? More likely it was Phrynondas.[61]

KINSMAN

And Helen was I named.

CRITYLLA

You're turning into a woman again, before you've been punished for your first drag-show?

KINSMAN

Many a soul on my account by Scamander's
streams has perished.

CRITYLLA

You should have been among them!

KINSMAN

And I am here, but my own ill-starred husband,
Menelaus, has never come for me.
So why do I still live?

[61] A proverbial villain.

ΚΡΙΤΥΛΛΑ

τῶν κοράκων πονηρίᾳ.

ΚΗΔΕΣΤΗΣ

ἀλλ᾽ ὥσπερ αἰκάλλει τι καρδίαν ἐμήν·
μὴ ψεῦσον, ὦ Ζεῦ, τῆς ἐπιούσης ἐλπίδος.

ΕΥΡΙΠΙΔΗΣ

τίς τῶνδ᾽ ἐρυμνῶν δωμάτων ἔχει κράτος,
ὅστις ξένους δέξαιτο ποντίῳ σάλῳ
καμόντας ἐν χειμῶνι καὶ ναυαγίαις;

ΚΗΔΕΣΤΗΣ

Πρωτέως τάδ᾽ ἐστὶ μέλαθρα.

ΚΡΙΤΥΛΛΑ

ποίου Πρωτέως,
ὦ τρισκακόδαιμον; ψεύδεται νὴ τὼ θεώ,
ἐπεὶ τέθνηκε Πρωτέας ἔτη δέκα.

ΕΥΡΙΠΙΔΗΣ

ποίαν δὲ χώραν εἰσεκέλσαμεν σκάφει;

ΚΗΔΕΣΤΗΣ

Αἴγυπτον.

ΕΥΡΙΠΙΔΗΣ

ὦ δύστηνος, οἷ πεπλώκαμεν.

ΚΡΙΤΥΛΛΑ

πείθει τι τῷ <κακῷ> κακῶς ἀπολουμένῳ
ληροῦντι λῆρον; Θεσμοφόριον τουτογί.

879 suppl. Scaliger

CRITYLLA

Because the vultures are shiftless!

KINSMAN

Yet something, as it were, tickles at my heart:
deceive me not, o Zeus, in my nascent hope!

Enter EURIPIDES, disguised as the shipwrecked Menelaus.

EURIPIDES

Who, wielding power in this doughty manse,
would welcome strangers sore beset in the briny
deep midst tempest and shipwreck?

KINSMAN

These are the halls of Proteus.

CRITYLLA

Proteus, you sorry wretch? (*to Euripides*) By the Twain Goddesses, he's lying: Proteas has been dead for ten years![62]

EURIPIDES

What land have we put into with our bark?

KINSMAN

Egypt.

EURIPIDES

Ah wretched luck, to have made for such a port!

CRITYLLA

Do you believe the ravings of this awful man, condemned to an awful death? This is the Thesmophorium!

62 An Athenian commander active during the Periclean era.

ΕΥΡΙΠΙΔΗΣ

αὐτὸς δὲ Πρωτεὺς ἔνδον ἔστ’ ἢ ’ξώπιος;

ΚΡΙΤΥΛΛΑ

οὐκ ἔσθ’ ὅπως οὐ ναυτιᾷς ἔτ’, ὦ ξένε,
ὅστις <γ’> ἀκούσας ὅτι τέθνηκε Πρωτέας
ἔπειτ’ ἐρωτᾷς· “ἔνδον ἔστ’ ἢ ’ξώπιος;”

ΕΥΡΙΠΙΔΗΣ

αἰαῖ, τέθνηκε. ποῦ δ’ ἐτυμβεύθη τάφῳ;

ΚΗΔΕΣΤΗΣ

τόδ’ ἐστὶν αὐτοῦ σῆμ’, ἐφ’ ᾧ καθήμεθα.

ΚΡΙΤΥΛΛΑ

κακῶς ἄρ’ ἐξόλοιο,—κἀξολεῖ γέ τοι,—
ὅστις γε τολμᾷς σῆμα τὸν βωμὸν καλεῖν.

ΕΥΡΙΠΙΔΗΣ

τί δαὶ σὺ θάσσεις τάσδε τυμβήρεις ἕδρας
φάρει καλυπτός, ὦ ξένη;

ΚΗΔΕΣΤΗΣ

βιάζομαι
γάμοισι Πρωτέως παιδὶ συμμεῖξαι λέχος.

ΚΡΙΤΥΛΛΑ

τί, ὦ κακόδαιμον, ἐξαπατᾷς αὖ τὸν ξένον;
οὗτος πανουργῶν δεῦρ’ ἀνῆλθεν, ὦ ξένε,
ὡς τὰς γυναῖκας ἐπὶ κλοπῇ τοῦ χρυσίου.

ΚΗΔΕΣΤΗΣ

βαύζε τοὐμὸν σῶμα βάλλουσα ψόγῳ.

EURIPIDES

Is lord Proteus within, or out of doors?

CRITYLLA

You must still be seasick, stranger, if you ask if Proteas is within or out of doors, when you've just heard that he's dead.

EURIPIDES

Alas, he is dead! Where was he duly entombed?

KINSMAN

This is his very tomb whereon I sit.

CRITYLLA

Well, die and go to hell—and you will die for daring to call this altar a tomb!

EURIPIDES

Why do you sit upon this sepulchral seat,
veiled in a shroud, strange lady?

KINSMAN

Against my will am I to serve the bed
of Proteus' son in marriage.

CRITYLLA

You loser, why do you keep hoaxing the stranger? Stranger, this man is a criminal come up here to the women's meeting to snatch their baubles.

KINSMAN

Bark at my person, pelt me with abuse!

ΕΥΡΙΠΙΔΗΣ

ξένη, τίς ἡ γραῦς ἡ κακορροθοῦσά σε;

ΚΗΔΕΣΤΗΣ

αὕτη Θεονόη Πρωτέως.

ΚΡΙΤΥΛΛΑ

μὰ τὼ θεώ,
εἰ μὴ Κρίτυλλά γ' Ἀντιθέου Γαργηττόθεν.
σὺ δ' εἶ πανοῦργος.

ΚΗΔΕΣΤΗΣ

ὁπόσα τοι βούλει λέγε·
οὐ γὰρ γαμοῦμαι σῷ κασιγνήτῳ ποτὲ
προδοῦσα Μενέλεων τὸν ἐμὸν ἐν Τροίᾳ πόσιν.

ΕΥΡΙΠΙΔΗΣ

γύναι, τί εἶπας; στρέψον ἀνταυγεῖς κόρας.

ΚΗΔΕΣΤΗΣ

αἰσχύνομαί σε τὰς γνάθους ὑβρισμένη.

ΕΥΡΙΠΙΔΗΣ

τουτὶ τί ἐστιν; ἀφασία τίς τοί μ' ἔχει.
ὦ θεοί, τίν' ὄψιν εἰσορῶ; τίς εἶ, γύναι;

ΚΗΔΕΣΤΗΣ

σὺ δ' εἶ τίς; αὑτὸς γὰρ σὲ κἄμ' ἔχει λόγος.

ΕΥΡΙΠΙΔΗΣ

Ἑλληνὶς εἶ τις ἢ 'πιχωρία γυνή;

EURIPIDES

Strange lady, who is the crone that vilifies you?

KINSMAN

'Tis Proteus' daughter, Theonoe.

CRITYLLA

No, by the Twain Goddesses, I'm Critylla, daughter of Antitheus, from Gargettos![63] (*to Kinsman*) And you're a criminal!

KINSMAN

Say what you will, for never shall I wed
your brother and so betray Menelaus, my husband
at Troy.

Euripides approaches Kinsman.

EURIPIDES

What said'st thou, lady? Return my pupils' gaze!

KINSMAN

I feel shame—for the violation of my jowls.

EURIPIDES

What can this be? A speechlessness holds me fast!

He removes Kinsman's veil.

O gods, what sight do I see? Who *are* you, lady?

KINSMAN

And who are you? The same thought strikes us both.

EURIPIDES

Are you Greek, or a native woman?

[63] An ordinary-sounding name, patronymic, and deme.

ΚΗΔΕΣΤΗΣ

Ἑλληνίς. ἀλλὰ καὶ τὸ σὸν θέλω μαθεῖν.

ΕΥΡΙΠΙΔΗΣ

Ἑλένῃ σ᾽ ὁμοίαν δὴ μάλιστ᾽ εἶδον, γύναι.

ΚΗΔΕΣΤΗΣ

ἐγὼ δὲ Μενελέῳ σ᾽, ὅσα γ᾽ ἐκ τῶν ἰφύων.

ΕΥΡΙΠΙΔΗΣ

ἔγνως ἄρ᾽ ὀρθῶς ἄνδρα δυστυχέστατον.

ΚΗΔΕΣΤΗΣ

ὦ χρόνιος ἐλθὼν σῆς δάμαρτος ἐσχάρας,
λαβέ με, λαβέ με, πόσι, περίβαλε δὲ χέρας.
φέρε, σὲ κύσω. ἄπαγέ μ᾽ ἄπαγ᾽ ἄπαγ᾽ ἄπαγέ με
λαβὼν ταχὺ πάνυ.

ΚΡΙΤΥΛΛΑ

κλαύσετ᾽ ἄρα νὴ τὼ θεὼ
ὅστις σ᾽ ἀπάξει τυπτόμενος τῇ λαμπάδι.

ΕΥΡΙΠΙΔΗΣ

σὺ τὴν ἐμὴν γυναῖκα κωλύεις ἐμέ,
τὴν Τυνδάρειον παῖδ᾽, ἐπὶ Σπάρτην ἄγειν;

ΚΡΙΤΥΛΛΑ

οἴμ᾽ ὡς πανοῦργος καὐτὸς εἶναί μοι δοκεῖς
καὶ τοῦδέ τις ξύμβουλος. οὐκ ἐτὸς πάλαι

---

64 For the original *es cheras* (into my arms) is substituted *escharas* ("brazier," slang for vulva).

KINSMAN

Greek. But I now would learn *your* story.

EURIPIDES

I cannot help but see Helen in you, lady!

KINSMAN

And I Menelaus in you—to judge from your rags!

EURIPIDES

You have recognized aright the unluckiest of men!

Euripides embraces Kinsman.

KINSMAN

O timely come into your own wife's charms![64]
O hold me, hold me, husband, in your arms!
Come, let me kiss you! Take, oh take, oh take
me away posthaste!

Euripides takes Kinsman by the hand and begins to lead him from the altar.

CRITYLLA

(*blocking their path*) By the Twain Goddesses, whoever tries to take you away is going to be sorry, after he gets pummeled with this torch!

EURIPIDES

Wouldst you prevent me my very own wife, the daughter
of Tyndareus, to take to Sparta?

CRITYLLA

Oh my, you strike me as being a villain yourself, and some kind of ally of this other one. No wonder you kept acting

ἠγυπτιάζετ᾽. ἀλλ᾽ ὅδε μὲν δώσει δίκην·
προσέρχεται γὰρ ὁ πρύτανις χὠ τοξότης.

ΕΥΡΙΠΙΔΗΣ

τουτὶ πονηρόν. ἀλλ᾽ ὑπαποκινητέον.

ΚΗΔΕΣΤΗΣ

ἐγὼ δ᾽ ὁ κακοδαίμων τί δρῶ;

ΕΥΡΙΠΙΔΗΣ

μέν᾽ ἥσυχος.
οὐ γὰρ προδώσω σ᾽ οὐδέποτ᾽, ἥνπερ ἐμπνέω,
ἢν μὴ προλίπωσ᾽ αἱ μυρίαι με μηχαναί.

ΚΗΔΕΣΤΗΣ

αὕτη μὲν ἡ μήρινθος οὐδὲν ἔσπασεν.

ΠΡΥΤΑΝΙΣ

ὅδ᾽ ἔσθ᾽ ὁ πανοῦργος ὃν ἔλεγ᾽ ἡμῖν Κλεισθένης;
οὗτος, τί κύπτεις; δῆσον αὐτὸν εἰσάγων,
ὦ τοξότ᾽, ἐν τῇ σανίδι, κἄπειτ᾽ ἐνθαδὶ
στήσας φύλαττε καὶ προσιέναι μηδένα
ἔα πρὸς αὐτόν, ἀλλὰ τὴν μάστιγ᾽ ἔχων
παῖ᾽, ἢν προσίῃ τις.

ΚΡΙΤΥΛΛΑ

νὴ Δί᾽ ὡς νυνδή γ᾽ ἀνὴρ
ὀλίγου μ᾽ ἀφείλετ᾽ αὐτὸν ἱστιορράφος.

---

65 Dishonest people, according to the Greeks.

66 A length of planking on which criminals were executed by suspension, as on a cross.

like Egyptians![65] But this man is going to pay the price: here comes the Marshal and an Archer.

EURIPIDES

This is bad. I've got to mosey on out of here.

He moves to the wings.

KINSMAN

But what about me? What am *I* going to do?

EURIPIDES

Stay calm. I'll never desert you, as long as I draw breath, or until I exhaust my vast supply of stratagems!

Exit EURIPIDES.

KINSMAN

Well, *this* particular fishing line didn't catch much!

Enter MARSHAL *and* ARCHER, *armed with a whip, bow, and quiver.*

MARSHAL

So this is the villain that Cleisthenes told us about! (*to the Kinsman*) You! What are you skulking for? (*to Archer*) Archer, take him inside and bind him on the plank,[66] then set him up right here and keep an eye on him. Don't let anybody get near him. If anybody tries to, take your whip and hit him!

CRITYLLA

Do that, by god, because just a minute ago a man *did* try to make off with him—a sail-stitcher!

ΚΗΔΕΣΤΗΣ

ὦ πρύτανι, πρὸς τῆς δεξιᾶς, ἥνπερ φιλεῖς
κοίλην προτείνειν ἀργύριον ἤν τις διδῷ,
χάρισαι βραχύ τί μοι καίπερ ἀποθανουμένῳ.

ΠΡΥΤΑΝΙΣ

τί σοι χαρίσωμαι;

ΚΗΔΕΣΤΗΣ

γυμνὸν ἀποδύσαντά με
κέλευε πρὸς τῇ σανίδι δεῖν τὸν τοξότην,
ἵνα μὴ ʼν κροκωτοῖς καὶ μίτραις γέρων ἀνὴρ
γέλωτα παρέχω τοῖς κόραξιν ἑστιῶν.

ΠΡΥΤΑΝΙΣ

ἔχοντα ταῦτʼ ἔδοξε τῇ βουλῇ σε δεῖν,
ἵνα τοῖς παριοῦσι δῆλος ᾖς πανοῦργος ὤν.

ΚΗΔΕΣΤΗΣ

ἰατταταιάξ. ὦ κροκώθʼ, οἷʼ εἴργασαι.
κοὐκ ἔστʼ ἔτʼ ἐλπὶς οὐδεμία σωτηρίας.

ΚΟΡΥΦΑΙΑ

ἄγε νυν ἡμεῖς παίσωμεν ἅπερ νόμος ἐνθάδε ταῖσι γυναιξίν,
ὅταν ὄργια σεμνὰ θεαῖν ἱεραῖς ὥραις ἀνέχωμεν, ἅπερ καὶ
Παύσων σέβεται καὶ νηστεύει,
πολλάκις αὐταῖν ἐκ τῶν ὡρῶν

---

67 In reality, no citizen could be summarily punished without a hearing.

KINSMAN

(*kneeling before the Marshal*) Marshal, by this right hand of yours—which you're so fond of cupping in the direction of anyone who might put silver in it—do me a small favor even though I'm condemned to death!

MARSHAL

What favor?

KINSMAN

Tell the archer he's got to strip me naked before he ties me to the plank: I'm an old man and I don't want to be left dressed in scarves and petticoats when the crows eat me—they'd laugh!

MARSHAL

The Council has decreed that you must die wearing these,[67] so that everyone who sees you will know what kind of criminal you are!

KINSMAN

Aieee! O dresses, what ye have wrought! There's no chance I'll be saved now!

ARCHER takes KINSMAN inside; CRITYLLA and MARSHAL exit.

CHORUS LEADER

All right, now, let's do a cheerful dance, as is the women's custom here, when in the holy season we celebrate our solemn mysteries for the Twain Goddesses—the very ones Pauson,[68] too, honors by fasting, as he joins in our prayer to

[68] Pauson, a painter, jokester, and caricaturist, is elsewhere mocked for being poor.

εἰς τὰς ὥρας ξυνεπευχόμενος
τοιαῦτα μέλειν θάμ᾽ ἑαυτῷ.

ΧΟΡΟΣ

ὅρμα χώρει,
κοῦφα ποσίν, ἄγ᾽ εἰς κύκλον,
χειρὶ σύναπτε χεῖρα
ῥυθμὸν χορείας πᾶσ᾽ ὕπαγε,
βαῖνε καρπαλίμοιν ποδοῖν.
ἐπισκοπεῖν δὲ πανταχῇ
   κυκλοῦσαν ὄμμα χρὴ χοροῦ κατάστασιν.

(στρ) ἅμα δὲ καὶ
   γένος Ὀλυμπίων θεῶν
μέλπε καὶ γέραιρε φωνῇ
πᾶσα χορομανεῖ τρόπῳ.

(ἀντ) εἰ δέ τις
   προσδοκᾷ κακῶς ἐρεῖν
ἐν ἱερῷ γυναῖκά μ᾽ οὖσαν
ἄνδρας, οὐκ ὀρθῶς φρονεῖ.

ἀλλὰ χρῆν,
ὡς πρὸς ἔργον αὖ τί καινόν,
   πρῶτον εὐκύκλου χορείας
εὐφυᾶ στῆσαι βάσιν.

(στρ) πρόβαινε ποσὶ τὸν Ε<ὐ>λύραν

them that from season to season such celebrations be often in his thoughts!

CHORUS

Let's start our number:
go light on your feet, form up a circle
and all join hands;
everyone mark the beat of the dance;
step out with an agile foot!
Our choreography should allow us
to turn an eye in every direction.

And all the while, everyone,
for the race of Olympian gods
lift your voice in reverend song
as the dance turns crazily.

Anyone who
expects that we, being women,
will in this sanctuary utter abuse
against men is mistaken.

Now we should rather
approach another novel task
by first halting the graceful
steps of our circle dance.

Step out singing for the God with the Lyre[69]

[69] Apollo.

---

952 μέλλειν R, corr. Zanetti
956 πᾶσ᾽ ὕπαγε Austin: ὕπαγε πᾶσα R
969 suppl. Zanetti

μέλπουσα καὶ τὴν τοξοφόρον
Ἄρτεμιν, ἄνασσαν ἁγνήν.
χαῖρ', ὦ Ἑκάεργε,
ὄπαζε δὲ νίκην.
Ἥραν τε τὴν τελείαν
μέλψωμεν ὥσπερ εἰκός,
ἣ πᾶσι τοῖς χοροῖσιν ἐμπαίζει τε καὶ
κλῇδας γάμου φυλάττει.

(ἀντ) Ἑρμῆν τε νόμιον ἄντομαι
καὶ Πᾶνα καὶ Νύμφας φίλας
ἐπιγελάσαι προθύμως
ταῖς ἡμετέραισι
χαρέντα χορείαις.
ἔξαιρε δὴ προθύμως
διπλῆν, χάριν χορείας.
παίσωμεν, ὦ γυναῖκες, οἷάπερ νόμος·
νηστεύομεν δὲ πάντως.

ἀλλ' εἶα, πάλλ', ἀνάστρεφ' εὐρύθμῳ ποδί·
τόρευε πᾶσαν ᾠδήν.
ἡγοῦ δέ γ' ὧδ' αὐτὸς σύ,
κισσοφόρε Βακχεῖε
δέσποτ'· ἐγὼ δὲ κώμοις
σε φιλοχόροισι μέλψω.

(στρ) Εὔιε, ὦ Διὸς σὺ
Βρόμιε, καὶ Σεμέλας παῖ,

and for the Archeress,
Artemis the Chaste Lady;
hail, You who Work from Afar,[70]
and grant us victory![71]
It's right that we also sing for Hera,
fulfiller of marriages,
who partners us in all our dances
and holds the passkeys of wedlock.

And I ask Hermes the Shepherd
and Pan and his dear Nymphs
to enjoy these dances of ours
and smile generously upon them!
So begin the double-time
with spirit, for the dance's sake.
Let's get into it, ladies, as custom commands:
we're fasting anyway!

Hey now, jump, swing around with a solid beat,
let all your song peal out!
This way, Lord Bacchus crowned with ivy,
do personally be our leader:
and with revels I will hymn you,
who love the dance!

Euius, you Noisemaker,
son of Zeus and Semele,

[70] Usually indicating Apollo, here apparently Artemis.

[71] That is, in the dramatic competition, and also perhaps in the war.

---

990 Εὔιε, ὦ Διὸς σὺ Enger: *εὔιον ὦ Διόνυσε* R

χοροῖς τερπόμενος
κατ᾽ ὄρεα Νυμ-
  φᾶν ἐρατοῖς ἐν ὕμνοις,
ὦ Εὔι᾽ Εὔι᾽, εὐοῖ,
<παννύχιος> ἀναχορεύων.

(ἀντ) ἀμφὶ δέ σοὶ κτυπεῖται
Κιθαιρώνιος ἠχώ,
μελάμφυλλά τ᾽ ὄρη
δάσκια πετρώ-
  δεις τε νάπαι βρέμονται·
κύκλῳ δὲ περί σε κισσὸς
εὐπέταλος ἕλικι θάλλει.

ΤΟΞΟΤΗΣ

ἐνταῦτά νυν οἰμῶξι πρὸς τὴν αἰτρίαν.

ΚΗΔΕΣΤΗΣ

ὦ τοξόθ᾽, ἱκετεύω σε—

ΤΟΞΟΤΗΣ

μή μ᾽ ἰκετεῦσι σύ.

ΚΗΔΕΣΤΗΣ

χάλασον τὸν ἧλον.

ΤΟΞΟΤΗΣ

ἀλλὰ ταῦτα δρᾶσ᾽ ἐγώ.

994 suppl. Coulon

who enjoy the dances
of Nymphs at their charming songs
as you ramble over the mountains—
Euius, Euius, euoi!—
striking up the dances all night long;

and all around you their cries
echo on Cithaeron,
and the mountains shady
with dark leaves and the rocky
valleys reverberate.
And all around you ivy tendrils
twine in lovely bloom.

ARCHER[72] *enters with* KINSMAN, *now clamped to a plank, and props him up against the altar.*

ARCHER

There, now: you can do your bellyachin' to the open air!

KINSMAN

Archer, I beseech you—

ARCHER

Don' you be seechin' me!

KINSMAN

Loosen the clamp!

ARCHER

No, but I'll do *this.*

[72] This Archer, being a Scythian and a public slave, speaks broken Greek.

ΚΗΔΕΣΤΗΣ

οἴμοι κακοδαίμων, μᾶλλον ἐπικρούεις σύ γε.

ΤΟΞΟΤΗΣ

ἔτι μᾶλλο βοῦλις;

ΚΗΔΕΣΤΗΣ

ἀτταταῖ ἰατταταῖ·
κακῶς ἀπόλοιο.

ΤΟΞΟΤΗΣ

σῖγα, κακόδαιμον γέρον.
πέρ᾽, ἐγὼ ᾽ξενέγκι πορμός, ἵνα πυλάξι σοι.

ΚΗΔΕΣΤΗΣ

ταυτὶ τὰ βέλτιστ᾽ ἀπολέλαυκ᾽ Εὐριπίδου.
ἔα· θεοί, Ζεῦ σῶτερ, εἰσὶν ἐλπίδες.
ἁνὴρ ἔοικεν οὐ προδώσειν, ἀλλά μοι
σημεῖον ὑπεδήλωσε Περσεὺς ἐκδραμών,
ὅτι δεῖ με γίγνεσθ᾽ Ἀνδρομέδαν. πάντως δέ μοι
τὰ δέσμ᾽ ὑπάρχει. δῆλον οὖν <τοῦτ᾽> ἔσθ᾽ ὅτι
ἥξει με σώσων· οὐ γὰρ ἂν παρέπτετο.
φίλαι παρθένοι, φίλαι,
πῶς ἂν ἀπέλθοιμι καὶ
τὸν Σκύθην λάθοιμι;

1013 suppl. Dobree
1017 λάθοιμι Ellebodius: λάβοιμι R

KINSMAN

Good grief, you're *tightening* it!

ARCHER

Wan' it even tighter?

KINSMAN

Owww! Ahhh! God damn you!

ARCHER

Shut up, you damn geezer! Well, I'm gonna go get a mat for while I'm guardin' you.

ARCHER goes inside.

KINSMAN

This is the reward I get for befriending Euripides! (*peering into the distance*) Ah! Ye gods and Savior Zeus, there's still hope! It seems the man won't give up on me: he just popped up as Perseus, meaning I'm supposed to be Andromeda.[73] I've certainly got the requisite chains, and he's obviously on his way to rescue me; otherwise he wouldn't have zipped by!

Dear maidens dear,
how might I get away
and escape the Scythian?

[73] In Euripides' *Andromeda*, produced together with *Helen* in 412, the flying hero Perseus, equipped by Hermes with winged cap and sandals, rescues the maiden Andromeda, whose father Cepheus, the king of Ethiopia, had chained her to a rock to be eaten by a sea monster, hoping thus to appease Poseidon. As the play opens, the desolate Andromeda speaks with the echo of her own voice from the caves on the shore, then is joined by a chorus of sympathetic maidens.

κλύεις, ὦ προσᾴδουσ'
αὐταῖς ἐν ἄντροις;
κατάνευσον, ἔασον ὡς
τὴν γυναῖκά μ' ἐλθεῖν.
ἄνοικτος ὅς μ' ἔδησε, τὸν
πολυπονώτατον βροτῶν.
μόλις δὲ γραῖαν ἀποφυγὼν
σαπρὰν ἀπωλόμην ὅμως.
ὅδε γὰρ ὁ Σκύθης φύλαξ
πάλαι ἐφεστὼς ὀλοὸν ἄφιλον
ἐκρέμασέ <με> κόραξι δεῖπνον.
ὁρᾷς, οὐ χοροῖσιν οὐδ'
ὑφ' ἡλίκων νεανίδων
κημὸν ἕστηκ' ἔχουσ',
ἀλλ' ἐν πυκνοῖς δεσμοῖσιν ἐμπεπλεγμένη
κήτει βορὰ Γλαυκέτῃ πρόκειμαι.
Γαμηλίῳ μὲν οὐ ξὺν
παιῶνι, δεσμίῳ δὲ
γοᾶσθέ μ', ὦ γυναῖκες, ὡς
μέλεα μὲν πέπονθα μέλε-
ος—ὦ τάλας ἐγώ, τάλας,—
ἀπὸ δὲ συγγόνων ἄνομ' ἄνομα πάθεα,
φῶτα λιτομένα,
πολυδάκρυτον Ἀίδα γόον φλέγουσα,
—αἰαῖ αἰαῖ, ἒ ἕ—

1018-19 προσᾴδουσ' αὐταῖς Sommerstein: προσαιδοῦσσαι τὰς R: προσαυδῶ σε τὰν Bothe, cf. E. frr. 118-19
1028 suppl. Mehler 1031 κημὸν Hermann: ψῆφον κημὸν R

Do you hear me, you in the caverns,
who reply in song to my cries?
Permit me, do let me
go home to my wife!
Pitiless he who enchained me,
most sorely tested of mortal men!
I got free of a rotten old hag
only to die anyway!
For this Scythian guard,
long posted over me, has hung me up,
doomed and friendless, as supper for vultures!
Behold, not now in dances
nor with girls my own age do I stand
wielding a voting-funnel;
nay rather enchained in tight bondage
am I set out as fodder for the monster Glaucetes![74]
Mourn me, ladies,
with a hymn
not of marriage but of jail,
for wretched do I suffer wretchedly
—alas alack, woe is me!—
and from kin lawless sufferings, lawless,
tho I implored the man, igniting tearfullest Stygian
groans
—ai ai! oh oh!—

[74] An Athenian elsewhere mocked for his passion for gourmet seafood.

1039 ἄνομ᾽ Blaydes: ἀλλὰν R 1040 λιτομένα Enger cl. ΣR δεομένη: λιτομέναν R: ἀντομένα(ν) γρΣR 1041 φλέγουσα Enger: φεύγουσαν R

ὃς ἔμ᾽ ἀπεξύρησε πρῶτον,
ὃς ἐμὲ κροκόεντ᾽ ἀμφέδυσεν·
ἐπὶ δὲ τοῖσδε τόδ᾽ ἀνέπεμψεν
ἱερόν, ἔνθα γυναῖκες.
ἰώ μοι μοίρας
ἂν ἔτικτε δαίμων.
ὢ κατάρατος ἐγώ·
τίς ἐμὸν οὐκ ἐπόψεται
πάθος ἀμέγαρτον ἐπὶ κακῶν παρουσίᾳ;
εἴθε με πυρφόρος αἰθέρος ἀστὴρ
τὸν βάρβαρον ἐξολέσειεν.
οὐ γὰρ ἔτ᾽ ἀθανάταν φλόγα λεύσσειν
ἐστὶν ἐμοὶ φίλον, ὡς ἐκρεμάσθην,
λαιμότμητ᾽ ἄχη δαιμόνι᾽, αἰόλαν
νέκυσιν ἐπὶ πορείαν.

ΗΧΩ

χαῖρ᾽, ὦ φίλη παῖ· τὸν δὲ πατέρα Κηφέα
ὅς σ᾽ ἐξέθηκεν ἀπολέσειαν οἱ θεοί.

ΚΗΔΕΣΤΗΣ

σὺ δ᾽ εἶ τίς ἥτις τοὐμὸν ᾤκτιρας πάθος;

ΗΧΩ

Ἠχώ, λόγων ἀντῳδὸς ἐπικοκκάστρια,
ἥπερ πέρυσιν ἐν τῷδε ταὐτῷ χωρίῳ

1044 ἀμφέδυσεν Σ^R: ἐνέδυσεν R
1051 βάρβαρον R: ἄθλιον γρΣ^R: δύσμορον Brunck

the one who first shaved me,
who put on me these saffron things
and to top it off sent me up
to this sanctuary where the women are.
O force of my destiny
that a god engendered!
O me accursed!
Who will not behold my suffering,
with its drastic evils, as unenviable?
Ah, would that a fiery bolt from heaven above
would obliterate that barbarian!
No more is it agreeable to look upon
the sun's deathless flame, when I am hung up,
damned by the gods to cut-throat grief, bound for
a quicksilver trip to the grave.

Enter ECHO.[75]

ECHO

Greetings, dear girl; but may the gods obliterate your father Cepheus for exposing you out here.

KINSMAN

And who are you that take pity on my plight?

ECHO

Echo, a comedienne who sings back what she hears, who just last year, in this very place, personally assisted Euripi-

[75] The nymph Echo had foiled Hera's attempt to punish other nymphs with whom Zeus had been having affairs; in revenge Hera made her able to say only what she had just heard. In Euripides' play Echo lived in the cave where Andromeda was chained.

Εὐριπίδῃ καὐτὴ ξυνηγωνιζόμην.
ἀλλ', ὦ τέκνον, σὲ μὲν τὸ σαυτῆς χρὴ ποιεῖν,
κλάειν ἐλεινῶς.

ΚΗΔΕΣΤΗΣ

σὲ δ' ἐπικλάειν ὕστερον.

ΗΧΩ

ἐμοὶ μελήσει ταῦτά γ'. ἀλλ' ἄρχου λόγων.

ΚΗΔΕΣΤΗΣ

ὦ Νὺξ ἱερά,
ὡς μακρὸν ἵππευμα διώκεις
ἀστεροειδέα νῶτα διφρεύουσ'
αἰθέρος ἱερᾶς
τοῦ σεμνοτάτου δι' Ὀλύμπου.

ΗΧΩ

δι' Ὀλύμπου.

ΚΗΔΕΣΤΗΣ

τί ποτ' Ἀνδρομέδα περίαλλα κακῶν
μέρος ἐξέλαχον—

ΗΧΩ

μέρος ἐξέλαχον—

ΚΗΔΕΣΤΗΣ

θανάτου τλήμων—

ΗΧΩ

θανάτου τλήμων.

des in the contest. But now you must play your part: start wailing piteously.

KINSMAN

And you'll wail in response!

ECHO

Leave that to me. Now begin your part.

KINSMAN

O holy night,
how long is your chariot's course
as you drive o'er the starry expanse
of holy Aether
through Olympus!

ECHO

Through Olympus!

KINSMAN

Why o why has Andromeda had
so much more than her share of ills?

ECHO

Share of ills!

KINSMAN

Unhappy in my death!

ECHO

Unhappy in my death!

ΚΗΔΕΣΤΗΣ

ἀπολεῖς μ', ὦ γραῦ, στωμυλλομένη.

ΗΧΩ

στωμυλλομένη.

ΚΗΔΕΣΤΗΣ

νὴ Δί' ὀχληρά γ' εἰσήρρηκας
λίαν.

ΗΧΩ

λίαν.

ΚΗΔΕΣΤΗΣ

ὦγάθ', ἔασόν με μονῳδῆσαι,
καὶ χαριεῖ μοι. παῦσαι.

ΗΧΩ

παῦσαι.

ΚΗΔΕΣΤΗΣ

βάλλ' ἐς κόρακας.

ΗΧΩ

βάλλ' ἐς κόρακας.

ΚΗΔΕΣΤΗΣ

τί κακόν;

ΗΧΩ

τί κακόν;

ΚΗΔΕΣΤΗΣ

ληρεῖς.

KINSMAN

You're killing me, old bag, with your jabbering!

ECHO

Jabbering!

KINSMAN

God, your interruptions are annoying
in the extreme!

ECHO

Extreme!

KINSMAN

Dear fellow, please let me finish my song,
thank you very much. Do stop!

ECHO

Do stop!

KINSMAN

Go to hell!

ECHO

Go to hell!

KINSMAN

What's wrong with you?

ECHO

What's wrong with you?

KINSMAN

You're babbling!

ΗΧΩ

ληρεῖς.

ΚΗΔΕΣΤΗΣ

οἴμωζ᾽.

ΗΧΩ

οἴμωζ᾽.

ΚΗΔΕΣΤΗΣ

ὀτότυζ᾽.

ΗΧΩ

ὀτότυζ᾽.

ΤΟΞΟΤΗΣ

οὗτος, τί λαλεῖς;

ΗΧΩ

οὗτος, τί λαλεῖς;

ΤΟΞΟΤΗΣ

πρυτάνεις καλέσω.

ΗΧΩ

πρυτάνεις καλέσω.

ΤΟΞΟΤΗΣ

σὶ κακόν;

ΗΧΩ

σὶ κακόν;

ΤΟΞΟΤΗΣ

πῶτε τὸ πωνή;

ECHO

You're babbling!

KINSMAN

Damn you!

ECHO

Damn you!

KINSMAN

Drop dead!

ECHO

Drop dead!

ARCHER returns with a mat.

ARCHER

Hey, you, what's all this talkin'?

ECHO

Hey, you, what's all this talkin'?

ARCHER

I'll call the Marshals!

ECHO

I'll call the Marshals!

ARCHER

Damn you!

ECHO

Damn you!

ARCHER

Where's that voice?

ΗΧΩ

πῶτε τὸ πωνή;

ΤΟΞΟΤΗΣ

σὺ λαλεῖς;

ΗΧΩ

σὺ λαλεῖς;

ΤΟΞΟΤΗΣ

κλαύσαι.

ΗΧΩ

κλαύσαι.

ΤΟΞΟΤΗΣ

κακκάσκι<ς> μοι;

ΗΧΩ

κακκάσκι<ς> μοι;

ΚΗΔΕΣΤΗΣ

μὰ Δί᾽, ἀλλὰ γυνὴ πλησίον αὕτη.

ΗΧΩ

πλησίον αὕτη.

ΤΟΞΟΤΗΣ

ποῦ 'στ' ἡ μιαρά;

<ΗΧΩ

ποῦ 'στ' ἡ μιαρά;>

ΚΗΔΕΣΤΗΣ

καὶ δὴ φεύγει.

ECHO

Where's that voice?

ARCHER

(*to Kinsman*) Are you babblin'?

ECHO

Are you babblin'?

ARCHER

You're gonna be sorry!

ECHO

You're gonna be sorry!

ARCHER

You laughin' at me?

ECHO

You laughin' at me?

KINSMAN

God no, it's that woman right there!

ECHO

Right there!

ARCHER

Where is the slut?

ECHO

Where is the slut?

KINSMAN

She's getting away!

1088 *κλαύσαι* Rogers: *κλαύσαιμι* R
1089 suppl. Fritzsche
1092-94 sic supplevi et disposui, alii aliter

ΤΟΞΟΤΗΣ

ποῖ ποῖ πεύγεις;

<ΗΧΩ

ποῖ ποῖ πεύγεις;>

ΤΟΞΟΤΗΣ

οὐ καιρήσεις.

<ΗΧΩ

οὐ καιρήσεις.>

ΤΟΞΟΤΗΣ

ἔτι γὰρ γρύζεις;

ΗΧΩ

ἔτι γὰρ γρύζεις;

ΤΟΞΟΤΗΣ

λαβὲ τὴ μιαρά.

ΗΧΩ

λαβὲ τὴ μιαρά.

ΤΟΞΟΤΗΣ

λάλο καὶ κατάρατο γυναῖκο.

ΕΥΡΙΠΙΔΗΣ

ὦ θεοί, τίν᾽ ἐς γῆν βαρβάρων ἀφίγμεθα
ταχεῖ πεδίλῳ; διὰ μέσου γὰρ αἰθέρος
τέμνων κέλευθον πόδα τίθημ᾽ ὑπόπτερον
Περσεὺς πρὸς Ἄργος ναυστολῶν, τὸ Γοργόνος
κάρα κομίζων.

ARCHER

Where, where ya goin'?

ECHO

Where, where ya goin'?

ARCHER

You won' get away with it!

ECHO

You won' get away with it!

ARCHER

You still yappin'?

ECHO

You still yappin?

ARCHER

Grab the slut!

ECHO

Grab the slut!

ARCHER

Yackety, confounded woman!

EURIPIDES appears on the stage crane as Perseus.

EURIPIDES

Ye gods, to what barbaric land am I come
on sandal swift? For through the empyrean
cutting a swath I aim my wingéd foot
to Argos, and the cargo that I carry
is the Gorgon's head![76]

[76] Perseus kept the head of Medusa in a leather bag and used it to petrify his own enemies before finally turning it over to Athena.

ΤΟΞΟΤΗΣ

τί λέγι; τὴ Γόργος πέρι
τὸ γραμματέο σὺ τὴ κεπαλή;

ΕΥΡΙΠΙΔΗΣ

τὴν Γοργόνος
ἔγωγέ φημι.

ΤΟΞΟΤΗΣ

Γόργο τοι κἀγὼ λέγι.

ΕΥΡΙΠΙΔΗΣ

ἔα, τίν᾽ ὄχθον τόνδ᾽ ὁρῶ καὶ παρθένον
θεαῖς ὁμοίαν ναῦν ὅπως ὡρμισμένην;

ΚΗΔΕΣΤΗΣ

ὦ ξένε, κατοίκτιρόν με, τὴν παναθλίαν·
λῦσόν με δεσμῶν.

ΤΟΞΟΤΗΣ

οὐκὶ μὴ λαλῆσι σύ.
κατάρατο, τολμᾷς ἀποτανουμένη λαλεῖς;

ΕΥΡΙΠΙΔΗΣ

ὦ παρθέν᾽, οἰκτίρω σε κρεμαμένην ὁρῶν.

ΤΟΞΟΤΗΣ

οὐ παρτέν᾽ ἐστίν, ἀλλ᾽ ἁμαρτωλὴ γέρων
καὶ κλέπτο καὶ πανοῦργο.

ΕΥΡΙΠΙΔΗΣ

ληρεῖς, ὦ Σκύθα.
αὕτη γάρ ἐστιν Ἀνδρομέδα, παῖς Κηφέως.

ARCHER

Say what? You got the head of Gorgos, the secretary?[77]

EURIPIDES

'Tis the Gorgon's, I say once more.

ARCHER

Gorgos, yeah, that's what I said.

Euripides alights from the crane.

EURIPIDES

Oho, what crag is this I see? What maiden,
fair as a goddess, moored like a boat thereto?

KINSMAN

O stranger, pity me in my misfortune cruel!
O free me from my bonds!

ARCHER

You, button your lip! You scum, you got the nerve to blab when you're about to be a *dead* maiden?

EURIPIDES

O maiden, 'tis with pity I see you hang there!

ARCHER

That's no maiden! That's a dirty old man, a crook and a creep!

EURIPIDES

Rubbish, my Scythian! This is Cepheus' child, Andromeda.

[77] An otherwise unknown public official.

1102 Γόργος Bothe: Γοργόνος R

ΤΟΞΟΤΗΣ

σκέψαι τὸ σῦκο· μή τι μικκὸν παίνεται;

ΕΥΡΙΠΙΔΗΣ

φέρε δεῦρό μοι τὴν χεῖρ', ἵν' ἅψωμαι κόρης.
φέρε, Σκύθ'· ἀνθρώποισι γὰρ νοσήματα
ἅπασίν ἐστιν· ἐμὲ δὲ καὐτὸν τῆς κόρης
ταύτης ἔρως εἴληφεν.

ΤΟΞΟΤΗΣ

οὐ ζηλῶσί σε.
ἀτὰρ εἰ τὸ πρωκτὸ δεῦρο περιεστραμμένον,
οὐκ ἐπτόνησά σ' αὐτὸ πυγίζεις ἄγων.

ΕΥΡΙΠΙΔΗΣ

τί δ' οὐκ ἐᾷς λύσαντά μ' αὐτήν, ὦ Σκύθα,
πεσεῖν ἐς εὐνὴν καὶ γαμήλιον λέχος;

ΤΟΞΟΤΗΣ

εἰ σπόδρ' ἐπιτυμεῖς τὴ γέροντο πυγίσο,
τὴ σανίδο τρήσας ἐξόπιστο πρώκτισον.

ΕΥΡΙΠΙΔΗΣ

μὰ Δί', ἀλλὰ λύσω δεσμά.

ΤΟΞΟΤΗΣ

μαστιγῶσ' ἄρα.

ΕΥΡΙΠΙΔΗΣ

καὶ μὴν ποιήσω τοῦτο.

1114 σῦκο Sommerstein: σκυτο R: κύστο Scaliger

ARCHER

Lookit that figgie:[78] it don't look little, do it now?

EURIPIDES

Give me her hand, that I might clasp the lass!
Please, Scythian; all human flesh is weak. In my own case, love for this girl has me in its grip.

ARCHER

I don' envy you. But I tell you, if his arsehole was turned around this way, I wouldn't say nothin' if you was to go an' screw it.

EURIPIDES

Why don't you let me untie her, Scythian, that I may couch her in the nuptial bower?

ARCHER

If you're so hot to bugger the old guy, why don' you drill a hole in the backside of that there plank and buttfuck him that way?

EURIPIDES

God no, I'd rather untie the chains.

ARCHER

Try it—if you wanna get whipped.

EURIPIDES

I shall do it anyway!

[78] "Fig" (*sukon*) was slang for the female genitals, "fig tree" (*suke*) for the male; the Archer uses the former sarcastically.

ΤΟΞΟΤΗΣ

τὸ κεπαλή σ᾽ ἄρα
τὸ ξιπομάκαιραν ἀποκεκόψι τουτοΐ.

ΕΥΡΙΠΙΔΗΣ

αἰαῖ· τί δράσω; πρὸς τίνας στρεφθῶ λόγους;
ἀλλ᾽ οὐκ ἂν ἐνδέξαιτο βάρβαρος φύσις.
σκαιοῖσι γάρ τοι καινὰ προσφέρων σοφὰ
μάτην ἀναλίσκοις ἄν. ἀλλ᾽ ἄλλην τινὰ
τούτῳ πρέπουσαν μηχανὴν προσοιστέον.

ΤΟΞΟΤΗΣ

μιαρὸς ἀλώπηξ, οἷον ἐπιτήκιζί μοι.

ΚΗΔΕΣΤΗΣ

μέμνησο, Περσεῦ, μ᾽ ὡς καταλείπεις ἀθλίαν.

ΤΟΞΟΤΗΣ

ἔτι γὰρ σὺ τὴ μάστιγαν ἐπιτυμεῖς λαβεῖν;

ΧΟΡΟΣ

Παλλάδα τὴν φιλόχορον ἐμοὶ
δεῦρο καλεῖν νόμος εἰς χορόν,
παρθένον ἄζυγα κούρην,
ἣ πόλιν ἡμετέραν ἔχει
καὶ κράτος φανερὸν μόνη
κληδοῦχός τε καλεῖται.
φάνηθ᾽, ὦ τυράννους
στυγοῦσ᾽, ὥσπερ εἰκός.
δῆμός τοί σε καλεῖ γυναι-
κῶν· ἔχουσα δέ μοι μόλοις

ARCHER

I'd have to chop off yer head with this here scimitar.

EURIPIDES

(*aside*)

Ah me, what action, what clever logic now?
All wit is lost upon this savage lout.
For work a novel ruse upon a clod
and you have worked in vain. I must apply
a different stratagem, one suitable for *him*.

Exit EURIPIDES.

ARCHER

The lousy fox, what monkey-tricks he tried to pull on me!

KINSMAN

Remember, Perseus, what a wretched state you're leaving me in!

ARCHER

So you're still hungry for a taste of the whip, are ya?

CHORUS

Pallas Athena, the dancers' friend, it is my
custom to invite here to our dance.
Maiden girl unwedlocked,
who alone safeguards our city
and holds manifest power
and is called Keeper of the Keys,
show yourself, you who loathe
tyrants, as is fitting.
The country's female people
summon you: please come,

εἰρήνην φιλέορτον.
ἥκετ<έ τ'> εὔφρονες, ἵλαοι,
πότνιαι, ἄλσος ἐς ὑμέτερον,
ἄνδρας ἵν' οὐ θεμίτ' εἰσορᾶν
ὄργια σέμν', ἵνα λαμπάσιν
φαίνετον, ἄμβροτον ὄψιν.
μόλετον, ἔλθετον, ἀντόμεθ', ὦ
Θεσμοφόρω πολυποτνία.
εἰ καὶ πρότερόν ποτ' ἐπηκόω ἤλθετον
<καὶ> νῦν ἀφίκεσθ', ἱκετεύομεν
ἐνθάδ' ἡμῖν.

ΕΥΡΙΠΙΔΗΣ

γυναῖκες, εἰ βούλεσθε τὸν λοιπὸν χρόνον
σπονδὰς ποιήσασθαι πρὸς ἐμέ, νυνὶ πάρα,
ἐφ' ᾧτ' ἀκοῦσαι μηδὲν ὑπ' ἐμοῦ μηδαμὰ
κακὸν τὸ λοιπόν. ταῦτ' ἐπικηρυκεύομαι.

ΚΟΡΥΦΑΙΑ

χρείᾳ δὲ ποίᾳ τόνδ' ἐπεισφέρεις λόγον;

ΕΥΡΙΠΙΔΗΣ

ὅδ' ἐστὶν οὑν τῇ σανίδι κηδεστὴς ἐμός.
ἢν οὖν κομίσωμαι τοῦτον, οὐδὲν μή ποτε
κακῶς ἀκούσητ'· ἢν δὲ μὴ πίθησθέ μοι,
ἃ νῦν ὑποικουρεῖτε, τοῖσιν ἀνδράσιν
ἀπὸ τῆς στρατιᾶς παροῦσιν ὑμῶν διαβαλῶ.

1148 suppl. Enger 1150 ἄνδρας ἵν' Hermann: οὗ δὴ ἀνδράσιν R 1151 σέμν' Hermann: σεμνὰ θεαῖν R
1158 suppl. Wilamowitz

bringing peace, comrade of festivity.
Come too, gracious happy
sovereigns,[79] to your own precinct,
where men are forbidden to behold
the divine rites that by torchlight
you illumine, an immortal sight.
Approach, come, we pray,
o most puissent Thesmophoroi!
If ever before you answered our call,
now too, we beseech you,
come here to us!

Enter EURIPIDES, *dressed like a bawd and carrying a small harp and a travel bag, with Elaphium, a dancing girl, and Teredon, a boy piper.*

EURIPIDES

(*to the Chorus*) Ladies, if you want to make a permanent peace treaty with me, now is the time. I'll stipulate that in the future none of you woman will ever again be slandered in any way by me. This is my official proposal.

CHORUS LEADER

And what is your purpose in offering this proposal?

EURIPIDES

This man on the plank here is my kinsman. If I can take him away with me, you'll never hear another insult. But if you refuse, whatever you've been doing behind your husbands' backs while they're away at the front, I'll denounce to them when they return.

[79] Demeter and Persephone.

ΚΟΡΥΦΑΙΑ

τὰ μὲν παρ' ἡμῖν ἴσθι σοι πεπεισμένα·
τὸν βάρβαρον δὲ τοῦτον αὐτὸς πεῖθε σύ.

ΕΥΡΙΠΙΔΗΣ

ἐμὸν ἔργον ἐστίν· καὶ σόν, ὠλάφιον, ἅ σοι
καθ' ὁδὸν ἔφραζον, ταῦτα μεμνῆσθαι ποιεῖν.
πρῶτον μὲν οὖν δίελθε κἀνακάλπασον.
σὺ δ', ὦ Τερηδών, ἐπαναφύσα Περσικόν.

ΤΟΞΟΤΗΣ

τί τὸ βόμβο τοῦτο; κῶμό τις ἀνεγεῖρί μοι;

ΕΥΡΙΠΙΔΗΣ

ἡ παῖς ἔμελλε προμελετᾶν, ὦ τοξότα.
ὀρχησομένη γὰρ ἔρχεθ' ὡς ἄνδρας τινάς.

ΤΟΞΟΤΗΣ

ὀρκῆσι καὶ μελετῆσι, οὐ κωλῦσ' ἐγώ.
ὡς ἐλαπρός, ὥσπερ ψύλλο κατὰ τὸ κῴδιο.

ΕΥΡΙΠΙΔΗΣ

φέρε θοἰμάτιον ἄνωθεν, ὦ τέκνον, τοδί·
καθιζομένη δ' ἐπὶ τοῖσι γόνασι τοῦ Σκύθου
τὼ πόδε πρότεινον, ἵν' ὑπολύσω.

ΤΟΞΟΤΗΣ

ναίκι, ναὶ
κάτησο, κάτησο, ναίκι, ναίκι, τυγάτριον.
οἴμ' ὡς στέριπο τὸ τιττί', ὥσπερ γογγυλί.

ΕΥΡΙΠΙΔΗΣ

αὔλει σὺ θᾶττον· ἔτι δέδοικας τὸν Σκύθην;

CHORUS LEADER

Count on us for our part of the bargain; but as for this barbarian, you've got to make your own deal.

EURIPIDES

I'm ready for that job. (*veiling his face*) And your job, Elaphium, is to remember to do what I told you on the way over here. All right, the first thing is to walk back and forth swinging your haunches. And you, Teredon, accompany her on your pipes with a Persian dance tune.

ARCHER

What's all the noise? A bunch of revellers is wakin' me up.

EURIPIDES

This girl was all set to rehearse, officer; you see, she's on her way to dance for some gentlemen.

ARCHER

Let her dance and rehearse; I won't stop her. She's pretty nimble, like a bug on a rug.

EURIPIDES

All right, girl, off with your dress, and sit on the Scythian's lap. Now stick out your feet so I can take off your shoes.

ARCHER

Yeah, sit down, sit down, yeah, yeah, sweetie! Wow, what firm titties—like turnips!

EURIPIDES

Piper, play faster. (*to Elaphium*) Still afraid of the Scythian?

ΤΟΞΟΤΗΣ

καλό γε τὸ πυγή. κλαῦσί γ', ἢν μὴ 'νδον μένῃς.
εἶεν· καλὴ τὸ σκῆμα περὶ τὸ πόστιον.

ΕΥΡΙΠΙΔΗΣ

καλῶς ἔχει. λαβὲ θοἰμάτιον· ὥρα 'στὶ νῷν
ἤδη βαδίζειν.

ΤΟΞΟΤΗΣ

οὐκὶ πιλῆσι πρῶτά με;

ΕΥΡΙΠΙΔΗΣ

πάνυ γε· φίλησον αὐτόν.

ΤΟΞΟΤΗΣ

ὂ ὂ ὄ, παπαπαπαῖ,
ὡς γλυκερὸ τὸ γλῶσσ', ὥσπερ Ἀττικὸς μέλις.
τί οὐ κατεύδει παρ' ἐμέ;

ΕΥΡΙΠΙΔΗΣ

χαῖρε, τοξότα·
οὐ γὰρ γένοιτ' ἂν τοῦτο.

ΤΟΞΟΤΗΣ

ναὶ ναί, γρᾴδιον,
ἐμοὶ κάρισο σὺ τοῦτο.

ΕΥΡΙΠΙΔΗΣ

δώσεις οὖν δραχμήν;

ΤΟΞΟΤΗΣ

ναί, ναίκι, δῶσι.

ARCHER

What a fine butt! (*looking down*) You'll be sorry if you don' stay inside my pants! (*opening his trousers*) There, that's better for my prick.

EURIPIDES

(*to Elaphium*). Well done. Grab your dress, it's time for us to be going.

ARCHER

Won' she give me a kiss first?

EURIPIDES

Sure. Kiss him.

ARCHER

Woo woo woo! Boyoboy! What a sweet tongue, like Attic honey! Why don' you sleep with me?

EURIPIDES

Goodbye, officer; that's not going to happen.

ARCHER

No, wait, my dear old lady, please do me this favor.

EURIPIDES

You'll pay a drachma, then?[80]

ARCHER

Sure I will.

80 A very high price.

ΕΥΡΙΠΙΔΗΣ

τἀργύριον τοίνυν φέρε.

ΤΟΞΟΤΗΣ

ἀλλ᾽ οὐκ ἔκῳδέν. ἀλλὰ τὸ συβήνην λαβέ.
ἔπειτα κομίσις αὖτις. ἀκολούτει, τέκνον.
σὺ δὲ τοῦτο τήρει τὴ γέροντο, γρᾴδιο.
ὄνομα δέ σοι τί ἐστιν;

ΕΥΡΙΠΙΔΗΣ

Ἀρτεμισία.

ΤΟΞΟΤΗΣ

μεμνῆσι τοίνυν τοὔνομ᾽· Ἀρταμουξία.

ΕΥΡΙΠΙΔΗΣ

Ἑρμῆ δόλιε, ταυτὶ μὲν ἔτι καλῶς ποιεῖς.
σὺ μὲν οὖν ἀπότρεχε, παιδάριον, ταυτὶ λαβών·
ἐγὼ δὲ λύσω τόνδε. σὺ δ᾽ ὅπως ἀνδρικῶς
ὅταν λυθῇς τάχιστα φεύξει καὶ τενεῖς
ὡς τὴν γυναῖκα καὶ τὰ παιδί᾽ οἴκαδε.

ΚΗΔΕΣΤΗΣ

ἐμοὶ μελήσει ταῦτά γ᾽, ἢν ἅπαξ λυθῶ.

ΕΥΡΙΠΙΔΗΣ

λέλυσο. σὸν ἔργον, φεῦγε πρὶν τὸν τοξότην
ἥκοντα καταλαβεῖν.

ΚΗΔΕΣΤΗΣ

ἐγὼ δὴ τοῦτο δρῶ.

1198 κομίσις Sommerstein: κομίζεις R

EURIPIDES

Well, let's have it.

ARCHER

But I've got nothing on me! (*offering his quiver*) Wait, take my shaft case; and give it back after! (*to Elaphium*) You come with me! (*to Euripides*) Now you watch the old man, granny! And what's your name?

EURIPIDES

Artemisia.

ARCHER

Remember that name: Artamuxia.

EURIPIDES

Trickster Hermes, just keep on giving me this good luck! (*to Teredon*) You can run along now, kid; and take this stuff with you. And I'll release this one. (*to Kinsman*) As soon as you get loose you'd better run like a man away from here and head back home to your wife and kids.

KINSMAN

I'll do that, as soon as I'm loose.

EURIPIDES

Go free! It's up to you to escape before the archer comes back and arrests you.

KINSMAN

That's just what I'm going to do!

EURIPIDES and KINSMAN run off; ARCHER returns with Elaphium.

1203 ταυτὶ Dobree, cf. Σ[R]: τουτί R
1208 λέλυσαι Bentley

ΤΟΞΟΤΗΣ

ὦ γρᾴδι', ὡς καρίεντό σοι τὸ τυγάτριον
κοὐ δύσκολ', ἀλλὰ πρᾶο. ποῦ τὸ γρᾴδιο;
οἴμ' ὡς ἀπόλωλο. ποῦ τὸ γέροντ' ἐντευτενί;
ὦ γρᾴδι', ὦ γρᾶ'. οὐκ ἐπαινῶ, γρᾴδιο.
Ἀρταμουξία.
διέβαλέ μοὐ γραῦς. ἐπίτρεκ' ὡς τάκιστα σύ.
ὀρτῶς δὲ <σὺ> συβήνη 'στί· καταβήνησι γάρ.
οἴμοι,
τί δρᾶσι; ποῖ τὸ γρᾴδι'; Ἀρταμουξία.

ΚΟΡΥΦΑΙΑ

τὴν γραῦν ἐρωτᾷς ἣ 'φερεν τὰς πηκτίδας;

ΤΟΞΟΤΗΣ

ναί, ναίκι. εἶδες αὐτό;

ΚΟΡΥΦΑΙΑ

ταύτῃ γ' οἴχεται
αὐτή τ' ἐκείνη καὶ γέρων τις εἵπετο.

ΤΟΞΟΤΗΣ

κροκῶτ' ἔκοντο τὴ γέροντο;

ΚΟΡΥΦΑΙΑ

φήμ' ἐγώ·
ἔτ' ἂν καταλάβοις, εἰ διώκοις ταυτῃί.

ΤΟΞΟΤΗΣ

ὦ μιαρὸ γρᾶο. πότερο τρέξι τὴν ὀδό;
Ἀρταμουξία.

1214 ἐπίτρεκ' Gannon: ἀπότρεκ' R

ARCHER

Old lady, your girl is nice and easygoing, no trouble at all! (*looking around*) Where's the old lady? Oh no, now I'm done for! Where'd the old man get to? Old lady! Lady! I don' like this at all, old lady! Artamuxia! The old bag's tricked me! (*to Elaphium*) You, run after her as quick as you can!

Elaphium runs off.

(*realizing his quiver is gone*) Justly is it called a shaft case: I fucked mine away and got shafted! Oh my, what am I gonna do? Where'd that old lady get to? Artamuxia!

CHORUS LEADER

Are you asking for the lady with the harp?

ARCHER

Yeah, yeah! Seen her?

CHORUS LEADER

She went that way (*pointing left*), and there was an old man with her.

ARCHER

Was the old man wearing a yellow dress?

CHORUS LEADER

That's right. You might still catch them if you go that way (*pointing right*).

ARCHER

The dirty old bag! Which way should I go again? Artamuxia!

ΚΟΡΥΦΑΙΑ

ὀρθὴν ἄνω δίωκε. ποῖ θεῖς; οὐ πάλιν
τῃδὶ διώξει; τοὔμπαλιν τρέχεις σύ γε.

ΤΟΞΟΤΗΣ

κακόδαιμον. ἀλλὰ τρέξι. Ἀρταμουξία.

ΚΟΡΥΦΑΙΑ

τρέχε νυν κατ᾽ αὐτοὺς ἐς κόρακας ἐπουρίσας.

ἀλλὰ πέπαισται μετρίως ἡμῖν·
  ὥσθ᾽ ὥρα δή ᾽στι βαδίζειν
οἴκαδ᾽ ἑκάστῃ. τὼ Θεσμοφόρω δ᾽
  ἡμῖν ἀγαθήν
  τούτων χάριν ἀνταποδοῖτον.

1226 κατ᾽ αὐτοὺς ἐς Jackson: κατὰ τοὺς R

CHORUS LEADER

Right! Straight up that hill! Where are you going? No, run the other way! No, you're going the wrong way!

ARCHER

Damn! I've gotta run! Artamuxia!

Exit ARCHER

CHORUS LEADER

Now run off after them—straight to hell, and bon voyage!

Well, we've had our share of fun.
Now it's time for each woman
to go on home. May the two Thesmophoroi
reward you with fine
thanks for this performance!

INDEX OF PERSONAL NAMES

Reference is to play and line number. Italicized references are footnoted in the text.

Aesop: *B 471, 651–53*
Aeschines: *B 823*
Aeschylus: *L 188, T 134–35*
Agamemnon: B 509
Agathon: *T 29–35*, 49–57, 65–69, 88, 95–265
Alcaeus: *T 162–63*
Alcmene: *B 558*
Alexander: *B 1102–04*
Alope: *B 559*
Amphion: B 1247
Anacreon: *T 161–63*
Andromeda: *T 1011–1134*
Antitheus: *T 898*
Archicleia: T 373 (var.)
Aristocrates (s. of Scellias): *B 126*
Aristogiton: *L 633*
Aristomache: *T 806*
Artemisia: *L 675*, T 1200–25

Bacis: *B 962*

Callias: *B 282–86*
Calonice: *L 6–253*
Calyce: L 322
Carcinus: T 440–42
Cebriones: *B 553*
Cepheus: T 1057, 1113
Chaerephon: *B 1296*, 1564
Chaeris: *B 858*
Charminus: *T 804*
Cimon: *L 1144*
Cinesias (1): *B 1372–1409*
Cinesias (2): L 838, 845–1012
Cleisthenes: *B 831*, L 621, 1092, T 235, 574–654, 763
Cleocritus: *B 876*
Cleomenes: *L 274–80*
Cleonymus: *B 289–90*, 1470–81, T 605
Cleophon: *T 805*
Cranaus: *B 123*
Critylla: L 322, T 759–935
Cynalopex: see Philostratus
Cyrene: *T 98*

Darius: *B 484*
Demostratus : *L 391–97*
Diagoras: *B 1072–74*
Dieitrephes: *B 798*, 1442
Diopeithes: *B 988*
Draces: L 254

Echo: *T 1056–97*
Elaphion: 1172

Eubule: *T 808*
Eucrates: *L 103*
Euelpides: B 1–850
Euripides: *L 283*, T 4 and *passim*
Execestides: *B 11*, 764, 1526–27

Glaucetes: *T 1033*
Gorgias: *B 1700–01*
Gorgos: *T 1102–04*

Helen: *L 155*, *T 850–928*
Heracles: B 567, B 1565–1693, L 928
Hippias: *L 619*, *L 1153*
Hippocrates: *T 273*
Hipponicus: *B 283*
Homer: *B 575*
Hyperbolus: *T 839–45*

Ibycus: *T 161–63*
Iris: B 575, *B 1199–1261*
Itys: B 212

Laches: L 304
Laespodias: *B 1569*
Lamachus: *T 839–42*
Lampito: *L 81–254*
Lampon: *B 521*, 988
Leonidas: *L 1254*
Leotrophides: *B 1406*
Lycon, wife of: *L 270*
Lycurgus: *B 1296*
Lysicrates: *B 513*
Lysilla: *T 374*
Lysimache ?*L 554*
Lysistrata: *L 6* and *passim*
Lysistratus: *L 1105*

Megabazus: *B 484*
Manes: L 845–908, 1212
Mania: T 728–64
Manodorus: B 656
Meidias: *B 1297*
Melanion: *L 785–96*
Melanippe: *T 547*
Melanthius: *B 151*
Menelaus: B 509, *L 155*, T 866–928
Menippus: B 1293
Meton: *B 992–1020*
Mica: *T 380–764*
Micon: *L 679*
Myronides: *L 801*
Myrrhine: L 69–254, 829–951

Nicias: *B 363, 639*
Nicodice: L 321

Odysseus: B 1561
Opuntius: *B 153*, 1294
Orestes: *B 712*, 1482–93

Palamedes: *T 770–71*
Paris: *see* Alexander
Patrocleides: *B 790*
Pauson: *T 949*
Peisetaerus: B *passim*
Peisias: ?B 1292; son of: *B 766*
Penelope: *T 547–50*
Pericleidas: *L 1138*
Perseus: *T 1011–13*, 1098–1134
Phaedra: *T 153*, 497, 547–50
Phaedrias: L 356
Pharnaces: *B 1028–30*
Pherecrates: *L 158*
Philemon: *B 763*
Philippus: *B 1700–01*
Philiste: T 568
Philocles: *B 281–83, 476*, 1295, T 168–70

Philocrates: B *14*, 1077–83
Philostratus (Cynalopex): *L 957*
Philurgus: L 266
Phormion: *L 804*
Phrynichus: *B 749*, T 164–66
Phrynondas: *T 861*
Pisander: *B 1556–64*, L 490–91
Porphyrion: *B 553*, 1252
Poseidon: B 1565–1693
Priam: B 512
Procne: *B 15*, 667–800
Prodicus: *B 692*
Prometheus: *B 1494–1552*
Proteus: T 897
Proxenides: *B 1126*

Sacas: *B 31*
Salabaccho: *T 805*
Sardanapallus: *B 1021*
Scellias: *see* Aristocrates
Semele: *B 559*
Simonides: *B 919*
Socrates: B 1282, 1555
Solon: *B 1660–66*
Sostrate: *T 374*
Spintharus: *B 762*
Sporgilus: *B 300*
Stratonice: *T 807*
Stratyllis: L 365
Strymodorus: L 259
Syracosius: *B 1297*

Teleas: *B 168*, 1025
Teredon: T 1175
Tereus: P 1008, *B 15*, 91–675, L 563
Thales: *B 1009*
Tharreleides: *B 17*
Theogenes: *B 822*, 1127, 1295, *L 63*
Theognis: *T 170*
Theonoe: T 897
Thratta: T 280–94
Timocleia: *T 373*
Timon: *B 1549*, *L 808–20*

Tyndareus: T 860

Xanthias: B 657
Xenocles: *T 169–70*, 440–42
Xenylla: T 633

Composed in ZephGreek and ZephText by
Technologies 'N Typography, Merrimac, Massachusetts.
Printed in Great Britain by St Edmundsbury Press Ltd,
Bury St Edmunds, Suffolk, on acid-free paper.
Bound by Hunter & Foulis Ltd, Edinburgh, Scotland.